HOPE CROSSING

THE COMPLETE ADA'S HOUSE TRILOGY

BOOKS BY CINDY WOODSMALL

A Love Undone

SISTERS OF THE QUILT SERIES
When the Heart Cries
When the Morning Comes
When the Soul Mends

ADA'S HOUSE SERIES
The Hope of Refuge
The Bridge of Peace
The Harvest of Grace

AMISH VINES AND ORCHARDS SERIES
A Season for Tending
The Winnowing Season
For Every Season
Seasons of Tomorrow

NOVELLAS
The Sound of Sleigh Bells
The Christmas Singing
The Dawn of Christmas
The Scent of Cherry Blossoms

NONFICTION
*Plain Wisdom: An Invitation into an Amish Home
and the Hearts of Two Women*

HOPE
CROSSING

THE COMPLETE ADA'S HOUSE TRILOGY

INCLUDES THREE FULL LENGTH NOVELS:
The Hope of Refuge, The Bridge of Peace,
and *The Harvest of Grace*

CINDY
WOODSMALL

New York Times Best-Selling Author

WATERBROOK
PRESS

Hope Crossing
Published by WaterBrook Press
12265 Oracle Boulevard, Suite 200
Colorado Springs, Colorado 80921

Scripture quotations are taken from the King James Version or the Holy Bible: International Standard Version® Release 2.0. Copyright © 1996-2009 by the ISV Foundation of Paramount, California USA. Used by permission of Davidson Press, LLC. All rights reserved internationally.

The characters and events in this book are fictional, and any resemblance to actual persons or events is coincidental.

Trade Paperback ISBN 978-1-60142-767-0
eBook ISBN 978-1-60142-768-7

Cover design by Kelly L. Howard; photography by Doyle Yoder

Published in the United States by WaterBrook Multnomah, an imprint of the Crown Publishing Group, a division of Random House LLC, New York, a Penguin Random House Company.

WATERBROOK and its deer colophon are registered trademarks of Random House LLC.

Library of Congress Cataloging-in-Publication Data
Woodsmall, Cindy.
    The hope of refuge : an Ada's house novel / Cindy Woodsmall. — 1st ed.
        p. cm.
    ISBN 978-1-4000-7396-2 — ISBN 978-0-307-45834-6 (electronic)
    1. Amish—Fiction. I. Title.
    PS3623.O678H67 2009
    813'.6—dc22   2009015969

Woodsmall, Cindy.
    The bridge of peace : an Ada's house novel / Cindy Woodsmall. — 1st ed.
        p. cm.
    ISBN 978-1-4000-7397-9 — ISBN 978-0-307-45946-6 (electronic)
    1. Amish women—Fiction. 2. Women teachers—Fiction. 3. Amish—Pennsylvania—Fiction. I. Title.
    PS3623.O678B75 2010
    813'.6—dc22   2010024570

Woodsmall, Cindy.
    The harvest of grace : a novel / Cindy Woodsmall. — 1st ed.
        p. cm.
    ISBN 978-1-4000-7398-6 (alk. paper) — ISBN 978-0-307-72962-0 (electronic)
    1. Amish—Fiction. I. Title.
    PS3623.O678H37 2011
    813'.6—dc22   2011016848

Printed in the United States of America
2014—First Edition

10 9 8 7 6 5 4 3 2 1

Contents

The
HOPE *of*
REFUGE

An Ada's House Novel

CINDY WOODSMALL

To Justin, Adam, and Tyler

The Hope of Refuge *shares the story of several moms—their strengths, weaknesses, joys, and sorrows. I dedicate this book to you because each of you woke a different part of me before I even felt you move inside me. When I held you in my arms, it seemed my very DNA shifted. Without conscious effort, you stirred me with a challenge to be your mom—to become more than I ever was before. I found strength where weakness had once been. As you grew, you stumbled on weaknesses I hadn't known existed. But because of you, I discovered that life had a euphoric side. And I learned that where I ended— where my strength, wisdom, and determination failed—God did not. For Him and for each of you, I am eternally grateful...*

Prologue

"Mama, can you tell me yet?" Cara held her favorite toy, stroking the small plastic horse as if it might respond to her tender touch. The brown ridges, designed to look like fur, had long ago faded to tan.

Mama held the well-worn steering wheel in silence while she drove dirt roads Cara had never seen before. Dust flew in through the open windows and clung to Cara's sweaty face, and the vinyl seat was hot to the touch when she laid her hand against it. Mama pressed the brake pedal, slowing the car to a near stop as they crossed another bridge with a roof over it. A covered bridge, Mama called it. The bumpiness of the wooden planks jarred Cara, making her bounce like she was riding a cardboard box down a set of stairs.

Mama reached across the seat and ran her hand down the back of Cara's head, probably trying to smooth out one of her cowlicks. No matter how short Mama cut her hair, she said the unruly mop always won the battle. "We're going to visit a…a friend of mine. She's Amish." She placed her index finger on her lips. "I need you to do as the mother of Jesus did when it came to precious events. She treasured them in her heart and pondered them. I know you love our diary, and since you turned eight, you've been determined to write entries about everything, but you can't— not this time. No drawing pictures or writing about any part of this trip. And you can't ever tell your father, okay?"

Sunlight bore down on them again as they drove out of the covered bridge. Cara searched the fields for horses. "Are we going to your hiding place?"

Cara had a hiding place, one her mother had built for her inside the wall of the attic. They had tea parties in there sometimes when there was money for tea bags and sugar. And when Daddy needed quiet, her mother would silently whisk her to that secret room. If her mama didn't return for her by nightfall, she'd sleep in there, only sneaking out for a minute if she needed to go to the bathroom.

Mama nodded. "I told you every girl needs a fun place she can get away to for a while, right?"

Cara nodded.

"Well, this is mine. We'll stay for a couple of days, and if you like it, maybe we'll move here one day—just us girls."

Cara wondered if Mama was so tired of the bill collectors hounding her and Daddy that she was thinking of sneaking away and not even telling him where she was going. The familiar feeling returned—that feeling of her insides being Jell-O on a whirlybird ride. She clutched her toy horse even tighter and looked out the window, imagining herself on a stallion galloping into a world where food was free and her parents were happy.

After they topped another hill, her mother slowed the vehicle and pulled into a driveway. Mama turned off the car. "Look at this place, Cara. That old white clapboard house has looked the same since I was a child."

The shutters hung crooked and didn't have much paint left on them. "It's really small, and it looks like ghosts live here."

Her mama laughed. "It's called a *Daadi Haus,* which means it's just for grandparents once their children are grown. It only has a small kitchen, two bedrooms, and a bathroom. This one has been here for many years. You're right—it does look dilapidated. Come on."

Seconds after Cara shut the passenger door, an old woman stepped out from between tall rows of corn. She stared at them as if they were aliens, and Cara wondered if her mama really did know these people.

The woman wore a long burgundy dress and no shoes. The wrinkles covering her face looked like a road map, with the lines taking on new twists as she frowned. Though it was July and too hot for a toboggan cap, she wore a white one.

"Grossmammi Levina, ich bin kumme bsuche. Ich hab aa die Cara mitgebrocht."

Startled, Cara looked up at her mama. What was she saying? Was it code? Mama wasn't even good at pig Latin.

The old woman released her apron, and several ears of corn fell to the ground. She hurried up to Mama. "Malinda?"

Tears brimmed in Mama's eyes, and she nodded. The older woman squealed, long and loud, before she hugged Mama.

A lanky boy came running from the rows. "Levina, *was iss letz?*" He stopped short, watching the two women for a moment before looking at Cara.

As he studied her, she wondered if she looked as odd to him as he did to her. She hadn't seen a boy in long black pants since winter ended, and she'd never seen one wear suspenders and a straw hat. Why would he work in a garden in a Sunday dress shirt?

He snatched up several ears of corn the woman had dropped, walked to a wooden wheelbarrow, and dumped them.

Cara picked up the rest of the ears and followed him. "You got a name?"

"Ephraim."

"I can be lots of help if you'll let me."

"Ya ever picked corn before?"

Cara shook her head. "No, but I can learn."

He just stood there, watching her.

She held out her horse to him. "Isn't she a beauty?"

He shrugged. "Looks a little worn to me."

Cara slid the horse into her pocket.

Ephraim frowned. "Can I ask you a question?"

She nodded.

"Are you a boy or a girl?"

The question didn't bother her. She got it all the time at school from new teachers or ones who didn't have her in their classes. They referred to her as a young man until they realized she wasn't a boy. Lots of times it worked for her, like when she slipped right past the teacher who was the lavatory monitor and went into the boys' bathroom to teach Jake Merrow a lesson about stealing her milk money. She got her money back, and he never told a soul that a girl gave him a fat lip. "If I say I'm a boy, will you let me help pick corn?"

Ephraim laughed in a friendly way. "You know, I used to have a worn horse like the one you showed me. I kept him in my pocket too, until I lost him."

Cara shoved the horse deeper into her pocket. "You lost him?"

He nodded. "Probably down by the creek where I was fishing. Do you fish?"

She shook her head. "I've never seen a creek."

"Never seen one? Where are you from?"

"New York City. My mama had to borrow a car for us to get beyond where the subway ends."

"Well, if you're here when the workday is done, I'll show you the creek. We got a rope swing, and if your mama will let you, you can swing out and drop into the deep part. How long are you here for?"

She looked around the place. Her mama and the old woman were sitting under a shade tree, holding hands and talking. Across the road was a barn, and she could see a horse inside it. Green fields went clear to the horizon. She took a deep breath. The air smelled delicious, like dirt, but not city dirt. Like growing-food dirt. Maybe this was where her horse took her when she dreamed. The cornstalks reached for the sky, and her chest felt like little shoes were tap-dancing inside it. She should have known that if her mama liked something, it was worth liking.

"Until it's not a secret anymore, I think."

One

Twenty years later

Sunlight streamed through the bar's dirty windows as the lunch crowd filled the place. Cara set two bottles of beer on the table in front of the familiar faces.

The regulars knew the rules: all alcoholic drinks were paid for upon delivery. One of the men held a five-dollar bill toward her but kept his eyes on the television. The other took a long drink while he slid a hundred-dollar bill across the table.

She stared at the bill, her heart pounding with desire. If earning money as a waitress wasn't hard enough, Mac kept most of their tips. The money the customer slid across the table wasn't just cash but power. It held the ability for her to fix Lori something besides boiled potatoes next week and to buy her a pair of shoes that didn't pinch her feet.

Would the customer even notice if I shortchanged him from such a large amount?

Lines of honesty were often blurred by desperation. Cara loathed that she couldn't apply for government help and that she had to uproot every few months to stay a few steps ahead of a maniac. Moving always cost money. Fresh security deposits on ever-increasing rents. Working time lost as she searched for another job—each one more pathetic than the one before it. Mike had managed to steal everything from her but mere existence. And her daughter.

"I'll get your change." *All of it.* She took the money.

"Cara." Mac's gruff voice sailed across the room. From behind the bar he motioned for her. "Phone!" He shook the receiver at her. "Kendal says it's an emergency."

Every sound echoing inside the wooden-and-glass room ceased. She hurried toward him, snaking around tables filled with people.

"Keep it short." Mac passed the phone to her and returned to serving customers.

"Kendal, what's wrong?"

"He found us." Her friend's usually icy voice shook, and Cara knew she was more frightened than she'd been the other times.

How could he after all we've done to hide? "We got a letter at our new place?"

"No. Worse." Kendal's words quaked. "He was here. Broke the lock and came inside looking for you. He ransacked the place."

"He what?"

"He's getting meaner, Cara. He ripped open all the cushions, turned mattresses, emptied drawers and boxes. He found your leather book and… and insisted I stay while he made himself at home and read through it."

"We've got to call the police."

"You know we can't…" Kendal dropped the sentence, and Cara heard her crying.

They both knew that going to the police would be a mistake neither of them would survive.

One of the waitresses plunked a tray of dirty dishes onto the counter. "Get off the phone, princess."

Cara plugged her index finger into her ear, trying desperately to think. "Where's Lori?"

"I'm sure they moved her to after-school care." Through the phone line Cara heard a car door slam. They didn't own a car.

A male voice asked, "Where to?"

Cara gripped the phone tighter. "What's going on?"

Kendal sobbed. "I'm sorry. I can't take this anymore. All we do is live in fear and move from one part of New York to another. He's…he's not after me."

"You know he's trying to isolate me from everyone. Please, Kendal."

"I…I'm sorry. I can't help you anymore," Kendal whispered. "The cab's waiting."

Disbelief settled over her. "How long ago did he break in?"

From behind Cara a shadow fell across the bar, engulfing her. "Hi, Care Bear."

She froze. Watching the silhouette, she noted how tiny she was in comparison.

Mike's thick hand thudded a book onto the bar beside her. He removed his hand, revealing her diary. "I didn't want to do it this way, Care Bear. You know that about me. But I had to get inside your place to try to find answers for why you keep running off."

She swallowed a wave of fear and faced him but couldn't find her voice.

"Johnny's been dead for a while. Now you're here…with me. " His massive body loomed over her. "I'd be willing to forget that you ever picked that loser. We could start fresh. Come on, beautiful, I can help you."

Help me? The only person Mike wanted to help was himself—right into her bed.

"Please…leave me alone."

His steely grin unnerved her, and silence fell in the midst of the bar's noise. Thoughts of how to escape him exploded in her mind like fireworks shooting out in all directions. But before she could focus, they disappeared into the darkness, leaving only trails of smoke. Fear seemed to take on its own life form, one threatening to stalk her forever.

He tapped her diary. "I know it all now, even where you'd hide if you ran again, which is *not* happening, right?" The threatening tone in his voice was undeniable, and panic stole her next breath. "I know your daughter just as well as you do now. What happens if I show up one day after school with a puppy named Shamu?"

Cara's legs gave way. Without any effort he held her up by her elbow.

After she'd spent years of hide-and-seek in hopes of protecting Lori, now he knew Lori's name, her school, her likes and dislikes. Shaking, she looked around for help. Bottles of various sizes and shapes filled the bar's shelves. The television blared. Blank faces stared at it. The man who had given her the hundred-dollar bill glanced at her before turning to another waitress.

Apathy hung in the air, like smog in summer, reminding her that there was no help for people like her and Lori. On a good day there were distractions that made them forget for a few hours. Even as her mind whirled, life seemed to move in slow motion. She had no one.

"You know how I feel about you." His voice softened to a possessive whisper, making her skin crawl. "Why do you gotta make this so tough?" Mike ran his finger down the side of her neck. "My patience is gone, Care Bear."

Where could she hide now? Somewhere she could afford that he wouldn't know about and couldn't track her to. A piece of a memory—washed in colorless fog—wavered before her like a sheet on a clothesline.

An apron. A head covering. An old woman. Rows of tall corn.

He dug his fingers into her biceps. Pain shot through her, and the disjointed thoughts disappeared. "Don't you dare leave again. I'll find you. You know I can…every time." His eyes reflected that familiar mixture of spitefulness and uncertainty as he willed her to do his bidding. "I call the shots. Not you. Not dear old Johnny. Me."

But maybe he didn't. A tender sprig of hope took root. If she could latch on to that memory—if it was even real—she might have a place to go. Somewhere Mike couldn't find her and she wouldn't owe anyone her life in exchange for food and shelter. Doubts rippled through her, trying to dislodge her newfound hope. It was probably a movie she'd watched. Remembering any part of her life, anything true, before her mama died seemed as impossible as getting free of Mike. She'd been only eight when her mother was killed by a hit-and-run driver as she crossed a street. Things became so hard after that, anything before seemed like shadows and blurs.

As she begged for answers, faint scenes appeared before her. A kitchen table spread with fresh food. A warm breeze streaming through an unfamiliar window. Sheets flapping on a clothesline. Muffled laughter as a boy jumped into a creek.

Was it just a daydream? Or was it somewhere she'd once been, a place she couldn't reach because she couldn't remember?

Her heart raced. She had to find the answer.

Mike pulled the phone from her hand, a sneer overriding the insecurity he tried hard to cover. "You're more afraid of one thing than anything else. And I know what that is." He eased the receiver into its cradle and flipped the diary open. "If you don't want nothing to cause the social workers to take her..." He tapped his huge finger on a photo of Lori. "Think about it, Care Bear. And I'll see you at your place when your shift is over." He strode out the door.

Cara slumped against the counter. No matter how hard she tried, she landed in the same place over and over again—in the clutches of a crazy man.

In spite of the absurdity of it, she longed for a cigarette. It would help her think and calm her nerves.

Clasped in her fist was the cash the two men had given for their drinks. She rubbed it between her fingers. If she slipped out the back door, no one at Mac's would have a clue where she went. She could pick up Lori and disappear.

Two

Ephraim and Anna Mary gently swayed back and forth in his yard. Chains ran from the large oak tree overhead and attached to the porch swing. The metal chain felt cool inside his palm, and the new spring leaves rustled overhead. He held out his free hand to Anna Mary. Without a word she smiled and slid her soft hand into his.

This small sanctuary where they sat was surrounded by tall hedges on three sides. The fourth side was open and had a view of a pasture, livestock, and a large pond. The hiddy—as he called it—afforded privacy that was hard to come by on Mast property. Ephraim had created the concealed area when he returned to the farm nine years ago, appreciating that his family wouldn't enter unless invited.

Storm clouds moved across the night sky, threatening to block his view of the stars and the clear definition of the crescent moon. Even without his telescope, he could pick out the Sea of Crisis and to its left the Sea of Fertility.

Anna Mary squeezed his hand. "What are you thinking about?"

"The gathering thunderhead." He gestured toward the southwest. "See it? In a few minutes it'll ruin my stargazing, but the spring showers will be just what the corn seed needs."

She angled her head, watching him. "I don't understand what you see night after night of looking at the same sky."

During the few evenings she joined him out here, she paid little attention to the awesome display spread out across the heavens. Her interest in an evening like this was to try to get inside his head. She wasn't one to say plain out what she thought or wanted, but she prodded him to talk. It tended to grate on his nerves, but he understood.

"Vastness. Expanse beyond the darkness. Each star is a sun, and its light shines like day where it is. I see our God, who has more to Him than we can begin to understand."

She squeezed his hand. "You know what I see? A man who is growing restless with the life he's chosen."

Inside the Amish ways that had called him home years ago, he'd found peace. But at twenty-four she wanted promises. He'd been four years younger than she was now when he began moving about the country, free of all Amish restraints. But when he was twenty-three, his stepmother had called, telling him his *Daed* was ill and the family needed him.

He had to come home. His Daed had caught a virus that moved into his heart and severely damaged it. Ephraim needed to take over his father's cabinetry business and provide for his Daed, pregnant stepmother, and a houseful of younger siblings. It didn't matter that part of the reason he had left was because he disagreed with his father remarrying so soon after his mother died. And here he was, nine years later, still not quite fitting into the role forced upon him.

The sound of a horse and buggy pulling onto the gravel driveway caused him to stand and head that way. Anna Mary followed closely behind. As they crossed through the small opening of hedges, he saw his sister and Mahlon pulling the rig to a stop.

Deborah held up a plate covered in aluminum foil. "Birthday cake." She showed him a knife, clearly hopeful of celebrating this long-awaited day. Mahlon stepped out of the carriage and helped Deborah down.

Ephraim had known today was on its way, but it was hard to believe the time had come to give her what she wanted.

Two years ago, at nineteen, she'd come to him, wanting to talk about marrying Mahlon. Since it wasn't Amish tradition for a girl to ask for her father's blessing, let alone a brother's, it'd surprised him. But he'd found himself unwilling to lie to her and yet unable to tell her his concerns, so he had simply told her she needed to wait. Then he'd grabbed his coat and headed for the door…and away from Deborah's mounting frustrations.

But she'd followed him. "Ephraim, we aren't finished talking about this."

He'd slid into his jacket. "Actually, I think we are."

The disappointment in her face had been hard for him to ignore.

"Until when?" she'd asked.

Convinced a couple of years would be enough, he'd said, "When you turn twenty-one."

If she'd decided to ignore him on the matter, he couldn't have stopped her. But she'd thought his only reason for telling her to wait was that the family needed her, so she'd done as he'd wanted without question. Today she turned twenty-one, and she'd just spent most of the day celebrating her good fortune with Mahlon and his mother, Ada. Sometimes Ephraim wasn't sure who Deborah loved the most—Mahlon or Ada.

But his sister stood in front of him now, hoping he'd say she was free to marry during the next wedding season. He glanced to Anna Mary, who waited quietly. Her eyes radiated trust in him and hope for Deborah and Mahlon.

Ephraim had two sisters between his and Deborah's age, but they'd married a few years back and moved to Amish communities in other states. When it came to marriage, no one had interfered with their desires.

In spite of his remaining reservations, Ephraim motioned. "*Kumm* then, and I'll light a fire and brew us some coffee. Then we'll talk."

Deborah passed the cake to Mahlon and mumbled something about the dessert that made Anna Mary laugh softly.

A horn tooted, causing all of them to pause. A car pulled into the driveway behind Mahlon's carriage, and Robbie rolled down the window. "Hey, I took my truck in like we talked about, but the mechanic has to keep it for a few days. Do I need to rent one to drive you to a job tomorrow?"

Ephraim shook his head. "No. Mahlon and I'll load a wagon and hitch horses to it. We're putting in cabinets at the Wyatt place about three miles from here. I have work lined up at the shop for you and Grey."

"Ah, you must've known."

"*Ya.* When you mentioned the mechanic, I rearranged the schedule. It seems every time you get work done to make your truck run better, it doesn't run at all for a while. If it's not ready by Tuesday afternoon, we'll have to rent one. We've got a job in Carlisle on Wednesday. You know, I never have mechanical problems like this when I take my horse in to the smithy."

A toothy grin covered Robbie's face. "The truck should be ready before then. I gave the mechanic the shop's phone number and told him to call us as soon as it's ready." Robbie motioned toward Mahlon. "So you'll go with the big boss, and I'm working with the foreman. They don't intend for us to have any horsing-around time, do they?"

"They never do," Mahlon scoffed.

Robbie laughed and started backing out of the driveway. "I'll see you guys in the morning."

"Sure thing." Ephraim turned his attention back to the group. "Anyone besides me ready for some cake?"

Deborah smoothed the folds of her apron. "Well…I'm more interested in talking to you about what we came here for."

Ephraim nodded. Mahlon had set his cabinetry work aside and left the shop hours earlier than usual today. Unfortunately, it seemed that Mahlon found it too easy to leave work behind and go do whatever pleased him on any given day, regardless of how much Ephraim needed him. But his sister's love for Mahlon never wavered, and it was time Ephraim trusted her instinct.

Mahlon looked a bit unsure of himself. "She's twenty-one today."

"So she is." Ephraim shook his hand, silently assuring him he'd ask for no further delays. "Then it's time plans were made."

Deborah threw her arms around Ephraim's neck. *"Denki."*

Her thank-you was unnecessary, but he returned the hug. *"Gern gschehne."*

She released him and hugged Anna Mary, both of them smiling and whispering excitedly.

"Ephraim?" His stepmother's voice called to him.

He looked back toward his Daed's house and saw Becca crossing the field that separated their home from his. Between business and family, some days he didn't get a break. But he'd put boundaries around parts of his life, and that helped. Of his family members, only Deborah was allowed to enter his home at will, because she tended to ask for very little and always did something helpful—like cook supper or wash dishes.

"Is Simeon with you?" Becca hollered.

"I haven't seen him since before suppertime." But he knew he wasn't far. His brother had a secret—an innocent kind that eight-year-old boys liked to keep.

She continued toward them, and they moved to meet her halfway.

"He's been missing since then." Her hands shook with nervousness as she wiped them on her apron. "This is the third time in two weeks he's disappeared like this. You have to put a stop to this, Ephraim, before he lands your father in the hospital again. He just doesn't seem to understand how frail his Daed is."

"Does Daed know he's missing?"

Becca shook her head. "Not yet. I hope to keep it from him. And when Simeon gets home, I'm tempted to send him to bed without supper."

"Don't say anything to Daed. Simeon's not far. When I find him, I'll see to it he doesn't do this again."

"Denki." Without another word she left.

Mahlon looked across the property. "You want help, Ephraim?"

"No sense in that. Just stay here and help Deborah get a fire going in the cookstove and a pot of coffee on to percolate." He looked to Anna Mary. "I'll be back shortly."

"If you don't take too long, we'll save you some cake." Anna Mary cocked an eyebrow, mocking a threat. He suppressed a smile and mirrored her raised eyebrow.

He started to leave when he thought of something. He pulled a large handkerchief from his pocket. "Can I take a piece of that with me?"

"Does this mean you're planning on being gone too long?" Anna Mary removed the aluminum foil.

His eyes met hers, and he chuckled.

Deborah cut a slice of cake and laid it in the handkerchief. "Here you go."

"Denki."

Mahlon chuckled. "You gonna bribe the boy to come home?"

"Something like that." Ephraim slid the squishy stuff into his baggy pocket. "Be back soon." He strode off toward the back fields.

He walked between the rows of freshly planted corn and onto what he still referred to as Levina's land. Although she'd not been related to his family, Levina had always been like a grandmother to him. When she passed away, he bought the old place, mostly because it connected to the property where he'd built his home.

Under the gentle winds of the night, thoughts of his life before his father's illness nagged at him. When he'd been called to come home, it gave him a reason to leave a world that offered as many different types of imprisonment as it did freedoms. But what bothered him was that each year since he'd returned, his family seemed to need him more, not less.

When he walked down Levina's old driveway, his attention lingered on the conjoined trees that stood nearby—full of majesty and recollections. Habit dictated that he run his hand across the bark as he passed by. Just one touch caused a dozen memories.

Flickers of dim light shone through the slits in the abandoned barn, and he was confident he'd found his brother—half brother, actually. After he crossed the road, he pushed against the barn door, causing it to creak as he opened it.

With a lap full of puppies, Simeon glanced up. "Ephraim, look. I've been working with 'em today, and I've spotted a really good one for ya."

"And I spotted a *Mamm* who's ready to send you to bed without your supper. It's after dark, Sim. What are ya thinking? If she finds out what's causing you to run off, she'll haul these dogs out of here. And the pound is just as likely to kill them as find them a home."

"The mama dog is missing." Simeon picked up the smallest puppy and hugged it. "I saw somebody outside the barn while I was walking this way. He took off when he spotted me. You think he stole the mama?"

"Makes no sense to take an old mama dog and leave the pups." Ephraim placed the puppy in the haystack where Simeon had made a little bed for the mutts. "Look, don't pull another stunt like this—staying out past dark and making your Mamm worry—or I'll put these pups in the auction myself. Got it?" Even though he was twenty-four years older than Simeon, he hated it when he had to sound like a parent. He should be a brother and a friend, but his role was more than just a provider.

Simeon's eyes filled with tears, and he nodded.

Ephraim picked up the lantern. "Now, let's go."

His brother's shoulders drooped as they left the barn. Without another word Simeon headed for the edge of the road to cross it. Ephraim went toward the back pasture.

"Ephraim?"

He paused. "Well, come on. We can't find the mama dog going that way. I just came from there."

Simeon wiped his eyes with the back of his hands.

Ephraim pulled the handkerchief out of his pocket. "I brought cake. If we get anywhere near her, I'll bet she'll get a whiff of this and come running."

Three

The noise and busyness of the Port Authority Bus Terminal raked a feeling of déjà vu over Cara. She'd been in the building plenty of times before, but this time she sensed…something odd.

With her diary clutched in one arm and her other hand holding her daughter's hand, she walked past shops, restaurants, and ticket counters. The strange feeling grew stronger as she stepped on the escalator and began the descent to the subway level.

Suddenly it was her father holding her hand, not Lori. Memories unrolled inside her. A set of escalators taking her and her dad deeper into the belly of the city. A brown paper bag, the top of it scrunched like a rope inside her hand. They kept going and going—hundreds, maybe thousands, of people all around her not caring one bit that her mom had died last week. Her father went into a café and set her on a chair. *"Dry your tears, Cara. You'll be fine. I promise."*

He pulled the map out of his jacket pocket, the one he had drawn for her the night before and had gotten her to help him color. He spread it out on the table. *"See, this is right where you are, New York City's bus station. A woman is coming for you. Her name is Emma Riehl. The bus will take you and her southwest. You'll probably change buses in Harrisburg and keep heading west for another hour or so. Right here."* His huge finger tapped the paper.

She must have said something odd because he gaped at her, and then he ordered a drink. He drank until his words slurred, then he walked her to a bench and demanded she stay put, promising Emma was coming.

And he left.

The terror of watching him walk away faded as the hours passed. Afraid Emma might show up and leave without her if she didn't stay put, she left the spot where her father had set her only long enough to go to the bathroom when she absolutely had to.

Later she fell asleep, and a man in a uniform woke her. He had a woman beside him, and she hoped it was Emma. But it wasn't, and they took her to a place where rows of metal bunk beds were half-filled with mean kids who'd never had anybody show up for them either.

Feeling Lori tug at her hand, she looked down into her innocent brown eyes.

"Are we looking for Kendal, Mom?"

She shook her head. Her days of meeting up with her friend were over. Kendal's complete abandonment earlier today had been a long time in coming. They'd been close once, starting when they'd shared the same foster-care home for a while, but over the last few years, Kendal had stolen from, lied to, and argued with her a lot. Since they were all each other had in the way of family, Cara had refused to give up. But—

Lori pointed to a picture. "Are we going somewhere on a bus?"

"Yes."

"What about Kendal?"

"It's just the two of us this time."

"But…"

"Shh." Cara gently placed one arm around Lori's shoulders as they continued walking. Memories of Kendal mocked her, and she felt like an idiot for trying to keep them together as long as she had. She'd always figured life with Kendal was as much like family as she'd ever have. One doesn't get to pick their family or choose who rescues them. But Kendal had done just that. At nineteen years old she'd opened the grubby door to her tiny, shabby apartment and dared to give a fifteen-year-old runaway food and shelter. The gesture had filled Cara with hope. Without her, she had little chance of making it on her own and no chance of escaping Mike's grip. But it'd been easier back then to ignore Kendal's weaknesses—men and drugs. It'd always seemed that she and Kendal were like a lot of siblings in a real family—extreme opposites.

Her attention shifted to the diary resting on her arm. Maybe the faded words her mother had written to her more than twenty years ago had kept her from seeking men or drugs to help numb the ache inside her—maybe not. But she'd read the beautiful entries ten thousand times over the years and couldn't separate herself from the woman her mother hoped she'd become.

A middle-school teacher once said that Cara's mother's diary sparked her love of dissecting books for understanding. It probably had, and she was a good student, but then life changed, and books and schooling faded in comparison to survival knowledge. That's where Kendal came in.

As one thought strung to another, Cara realized somewhere inside her, beyond her fear and jumbled thoughts, it hurt for Kendal to give up the way she had. No last-minute message of encouragement for either her or Lori. No whisper of wanting to meet up once Cara worked free of Mike again. Just a final good-bye. And *after* she'd packed and hailed a taxi.

The numbness gave way to grief, and in some odd way that Cara couldn't understand, it seemed right to be inside this place—the building where her father had abandoned her.

"Mom," Lori elongated the word, half whining and half demanding, "I want to know where we're going."

Cara thought for a moment. They needed to get out of the city, but their traveling funds were limited. "Jersey, I think. We're fine and safe, so no worrying, okay?" The words didn't leave her mouth easily.

She had no real answers. But she knew one thing—any life she could give Lori would be immeasurably better than foster care, where she'd have to live with strangers who were paid to pretend they cared.

It seemed unfair that Cara had spent all her life trying to be good, always aiming to live in a way her dead mother would be proud of, just to fall victim to Mike's power to find her time and again. Maybe that's what had made her and Lori an easy target for him.

Regardless of whatever she needed to do—lie, cheat, or steal—no one was separating her from her daughter.

Needing a few moments to think, she moved to an empty table outside Au Bon Pain. She opened her diary and thumbed through it, looking for signs of a life she wasn't sure ever existed. The frayed leather binding and bulging pages were hints to how much she loved this book. She didn't write everyday stuff in it. This book was used mostly for sharing things between mom and daughter—first her and her mother and now her and Lori. It made her sick to think of Mike reading her mother's thoughts and hopes for her, the special things they'd done, and Cara's most treasured memories with Lori.

Standing in front of him less than an hour ago, she'd envisioned rows of tall corn, heard a boy's laughter, and remembered feeling welcomed by an old woman in a black apron and white head covering. But her treasured journal revealed none of it. Why?

Lori pulled a baggie of stale cookies from her backpack—the kind that had ingredients dogs shouldn't eat, but they were tasty enough and were always able to remove the worst of the hunger. With Mike probably watching and waiting outside her apartment—maybe inside it—she and Lori would leave New York with the clothes they were wearing, whatever that schoolbag held, and the diary.

Cara flipped page after page, skimming the entries written by her mother. She'd had this book since she was younger than Lori. With one exception every available spot had been written on. Each line had two rows of writing squeezed in. The margins were filled with tiny words and drawings. Even the insides of the book's covers were written on. There were places where she'd taped and stapled clean paper onto existing pages before filling them with words too. Only one spot, about three inches high and four inches long, remained blank.

Her mother's instructions written above that space told her never to write in that spot but to remember. A sadness she'd grown to hate moved into her chest as she read her mother's words.

Don't write inside the area I've marked. When the time is right, my beloved one, I'll fill in the blank.

Beloved one. The phrase twisted her insides as it'd done for what seemed like forever. Had her mother ever loved her like it sounded?

Obviously her mother couldn't fulfill her plan, and Cara had no recollection of what she might have been talking about. According to the date on the entry, her mother wrote those words when Cara was five. She raised her head and skimmed her index finger over the spot.

Demanding the emotional nonsense to cease, she buried her head in her hands, trying to gain control of her feelings.

Lori smacked her palm on the blank spot of the diary. "What's that?"

Cara brushed off the specks of cookie that'd fallen from her daughter's hand onto the page. "An empty place my mother said not to write in."

"Why?"

Cara shrugged. "I don't know."

"Can I sign my name there?"

She hesitated for a moment before sliding the book toward Lori. "Sure, why not?"

Lori dug into her book bag and came up with a pencil. She began trying to write in cursive. At seven, Lori's marks were more swirls than real letters. Cara eyed the few leftover cookies, but she refused to eat one. Money was limited, and Lori might need those before Cara found another job.

The good thing about waitressing was it came with immediate money. She'd have to wait for her paycheck, but she'd make tips the very day she started. Time and again the need for immediate food money after they moved kept her waitressing—that and the fact that being a tenth-grade dropout didn't qualify her for much. But she was capable of more. She knew that. Her school years had proved it. Got great grades, skipped the third grade, and always landed at the top of her classes. But she'd probably never get a chance to prove she wasn't who others thought—a poor quitter with no potential.

"Mom, look!"

Cara glanced while closing the baggie of cookies. Her daughter had given up on cursive and made a thick, double-edged L. Then she'd filled the middle part with light sketching. "Very pretty, Lori."

"No, Mom, look."

She moved the book closer, seeing that letters had shown up under the shading.

"Oh, that's from words written on the opposite page." She slid the book to Lori.

The time is long past, my beloved... Like a whisper, her mother's voice floated into her mind from nowhere.

"Wait, Lori. Stop writing." Cara pulled the book in front of her. Through the light gray coloring of pencil, she saw part of a word. "Let me see your pencil for a minute."

"No." Lori jerked the book away from her. "It's my spot. You said so."

Cara resisted the desire to overreact. "Okay. You're right. I gave it to you." She placed the cookies into the backpack and zipped it up. "If you look at the date on that entry, you can see that I was a couple of years younger than you are now when your grandma wrote that." She pointed to the words her mother had written above the blank space. "Maybe it's nothing. Or maybe your grandma hid a secret in the diary. But…if you'd rather write your name…"

Lori pulled the book closer, inspecting the blank space. "You think she wanted to tell me something?"

"No, kiddo. How could she? She didn't know you. But we should still figure out what she wrote."

Lori's brows furrowed. "Let's do it together."

Cara nodded. "Good idea. We need to run the pencil over the whole area very, very lightly, or we might scratch out the message rather than make it visible."

Lori passed her the pencil. "I already went first. It's your turn."

Relieved, Cara took the pencil and began lightly rubbing the lead over the page. Words that had been there since before her mother died suddenly appeared on the page. It looked like an address. The street numbers were hidden under the heavy-handedness of her daughter's artwork, but the road, town, and state were clear.

Mast Road, Dry Lake, Pennsylvania

"What's it say, Mom?"

Hope trickled in, and tears stung her eyes. Lori had no one but her, a single mom who'd been an orphan. She had no support system. She wanted...no, she ached to give Lori some sort of life connections, a relative or friend of Cara's mother, something that spoke of the things life was supposed to be made of—worthy relationships. Maybe this was the answer. It had to be better than Jersey. "It says where we're going."

"Where's that?"

Cara closed the book. "As close to Dry Lake, Pennsylvania, as a bus route goes." She put the backpack over one shoulder and held her hand out for Lori. "You discovered a secret I didn't know was there. Come on. We've got bus tickets to buy."

In a blur of confusion and fears, Cara bought tickets to Shippensburg, Pennsylvania. The man at the ticket counter said they were heading for the heart of Amish country. When she shrugged, he told her they were easy to spot—wore clothing that looked like something from the eighteen hundreds and traveled by horse and buggy.

With the tickets in hand, they boarded one bus, rode for hours, had a long delay at another station, and then boarded another bus. Now it was night again. Between purchasing bus tickets and food, she had little money left. The uncertainty scared her, and it stole all sense of victory for getting free of Mike and discovering the long-held secret in her diary.

While Lori slept, Cara studied each passing town, hoping something would look familiar.

Hours of light mist turned into pelting rain, making it difficult to see the landmarks. Her eyelids ached with heaviness. She blinked hard and sat up straighter, concentrating on each thing they passed.

Spattering drops smacked the window endlessly. She wiped the fog from the glass, studying the water-colored world. As the bus pulled into a Kmart parking lot, the bus driver said, "Shippensburg. Shippensburg, Pennsylvania."

A peculiar feeling crawled over her. An elderly woman stood and made her way to the front of the bus.

The idea of waking Lori from a safe, dry sleep to enter a rainy, unknown world was ridiculous. She had a few dollars left. Maybe she could pay to ride farther.

"Shippensburg?" The driver looked in the rearview mirror, giving each passenger a chance to get off.

She clutched the armrests, assuring herself any good mother would stay put. When the doors to the bus began to close, Cara jumped to her feet, signaling her intention to get off here.

She stuffed her diary into Lori's backpack and lifted her sleeping child into her arms. She stopped next to the bus driver. "Any idea how to get to Dry Lake?"

"Follow this road for a few blocks." He pointed in front of the bus. "When you get to Earl Street, go right. It'll be about six miles."

"Thanks."

"There's a nice motel straight ahead, Shippen Place Hotel. Only hotel I know of near here."

"Thanks." Cold rain stung her face as she stepped off the bus. Since she didn't have enough money for a fancy hotel, she'd have to find somewhere free to stay for the night.

Lori lifted her head off Cara's shoulder, instantly whining. "No, Mom. I want to go home."

"Shh." Cara eased Lori's head against her shoulder and placed the backpack against her little girl's cheek, trying to shield her from the rain. "Listen, kid, you've got to trust me. Remember?"

Lori wrapped her little hands around the back of Cara's neck, whimpering. Within seconds her daughter fell asleep again, deaf to the sound of the rain beating a pattern against her backpack like a tapping on a door.

Four

Through the window behind the kitchen sink, Deborah watched as broad streaks of sunlight broke through the remaining thick clouds. She continued slicing large hunks of stew meat into bite-size pieces—all the while her mind on Mahlon.

Since her birthday the day before yesterday, she and Mahlon had made the rounds throughout the district, telling their family and friends about their plans to marry in the fall. She didn't think she'd ever had so much fun as they'd had Thursday night, popping into homes to share good news. Nothing would be announced officially until October when the bishop "published" all the couples who were to be married. He'd make a declaration of everyone who would marry that wedding season, but they had to make plans long before then. And she'd ordered an engagement present for Mahlon—one she'd spent a year saving for. She'd give it to him just as soon as her order arrived at the dry goods store.

Her heart raced with anticipation of the coming months. She tossed the freshly cut stew meat into a skillet to brown before she began washing the breakfast dishes. The desire to get done with her morning chores and go to Mahlon's pushed her to hurry. Beds were made, laundry washed and hung out to dry, and she and Becca had cooked breakfast for the family. The items left on her to-do list grew smaller by the hour. Mahlon had taken off work until after lunchtime today so they could start on their plans, and she didn't want to waste a minute of it.

Becca walked into the kitchen, carrying a twin on each hip. Her round, rosy cheeks gave her an appearance of sturdy health. As her brown hair gave way to more and more gray and she picked up a few extra pounds with each pregnancy, she no longer looked like the much-younger second wife of twelve years ago. She looked like and felt like a mom to a large, ever-growing family.

"How many houses do you and Mahlon have lined up to look at today?" Becca placed Sadie and Sally behind the safety gate of their playroom before moving to the stove.

"There are only two inside Dry Lake. Maybe three, because there's one that belongs to *Englischers* that might fall inside our district lines."

She lifted the lid off the meat and stirred it with a spatula. "Ya? Where's that one?"

"About half a mile from Mahlon's place."

"On the right or left?"

"Left. Their last name is Everson."

She shrugged. "That might be Yoder's district. If it is, they have their church Sundays on our between Sundays. It'll make finding time to visit with your family harder. Your Daed won't like that."

"Ya, I know. Mahlon's determined to find a place in Dry Lake, but he said we may have to settle for something in Yoder's district."

"Do you like that home more than the others?"

Deborah dried her hands. "It doesn't matter to me where we live." She went to the refrigerator and pulled out carrots, onions, and potatoes. "I'd be perfectly content to move into the home where he and Ada live now."

"It's small, but it seems like that'd be a great place to start out." Becca turned the eye to the stove to low, poured a quart of water over the meat, and replaced the lid on the skillet.

Deborah rinsed the carrots and potatoes before placing them on the chopping block. "Ya, but Mahlon says the landlord wants his daughter to live there. He has for nearly a year."

"Oh, that's right. I remember now. They rent their place. It was a shame the way Ada had to sell their house after Mahlon's Daed died."

Becca grabbed a dry dishtowel and began emptying the dish drainer. "The community wanted to keep that from happening, but too many of us were dealing with our own losses. Besides, Ada was determined not to burden anyone."

While peeling potatoes, Deborah felt old grief wash over her. It didn't hurt like it used to, but it always stung. Thirteen years ago she lost her mother in the same accident in which Mahlon lost his father. Becca's husband died too and six others from their community. All in one fatal van accident. The Amish of Dry Lake had hired three Englischer drivers to take them to a wedding in Ohio. They were caravaning when one of the vehicles crashed. No one made it to the wedding. At the time there had been thirty families in their district, and nine of them lost a loved one. It'd taken Deborah years to push past feeling that they were cursed.

Becca placed the last plate in the cabinet. "So, will Ada live with you and Mahlon?"

"Ya. It's not Mahlon's favorite plan, but he can't afford two places, one for us and one for her. I don't know why the idea bothers him. Ada will be nothing but a blessing all her days."

"Which will be a lot of days, because she's young. What, forty-three?"

Deborah nodded.

Becca laid the dishtowel on her shoulder. "It seems odd to me that she's never remarried, but as long as you don't mind sharing a home with her, there will be peace in the house."

"The hardest part of living with Ada will be that both of us love to cook. I'm hoping one of the places has a huge kitchen. And then we can both have a workspace, and we could have some cookoffs, and may the youngest cook win."

Becca giggled. "Ada better watch out. It seems to me she's spent years teaching all her best cooking secrets to an ambitious young woman."

For the first time in quite a while, Deborah recalled her one-time dream of owning an Amish restaurant. But they lived too far away from the flow of tourists for it to be practical. Although Hope Crossing had a more touristy Amish community, her family always needed her to live at home to help out. Besides, she'd been in love with Mahlon since she was ten, and she couldn't imagine living elsewhere. But his mother gave her a way to do the next best thing—bake desserts for profit. Ada had taught her how to make all sorts of sweets, and together they made baked goods for a bakery that sent a driver to fetch the items three days a week.

"Anytime you need a kitchen to bake in, you're more than welcome to come here." One side of Becca's mouth curved into a smile. "Of course, what's cooked here stays here."

Deborah chuckled. "But not for long…before it's eaten."

Becca laughed. "Go fetch your horse. Maybe Ephraim will leave the shop long enough to help you hitch it to the carriage."

"You sure?"

One of the twins started wailing as if she'd pinched a finger or the other one had taken a toy.

Becca glanced into the room before she wagged her finger at Deborah. "You better go while the going is good. Your sister Annie has a good bit to learn to be the kind of help you are, but at fourteen and with you marrying this fall, it's time she gets more practice, no?"

Deborah nodded. "Mahlon said if the grounds aren't too wet today, we'll lay plow to the garden again late this afternoon when he and Ephraim get back from a job."

"He's right. What we've planted isn't enough to help provide food for a wedding feast come fall. So while you're out, go by the dry goods store and pick up more seeds, especially packages of celery and carrots. And buy the crates so we can get seedlings started first. We'll need a lot more veggies than usual come fall."

Deborah's cheeks ached from smiling. "This is simply too exciting."

Becca's eyes filled with tears. "Ya, it is. I can't even begin to tell you how excited I am for you. You'll be missed something fierce, but your Daed and I are really happy for you. I'm surprised you've waited this long."

Deborah wouldn't tell her that Ephraim had quietly but firmly said they had to wait. At the time, Becca and Daed had six children under the age of thirteen, and the twins were just a couple of months old. With Daed's health issues, he wasn't much help.

But Annie would graduate in just a few weeks, so she'd be able to help Becca full-time.

With exhilaration pulsing through her, she headed for the pasture to chase down her horse. Mahlon would be surprised when she arrived more than an hour ahead of schedule.

Before she got to the cattle gate, a wagonload of her girlfriends called to her as they pulled into her driveway: Rachel, Linda, Nancy, Lydia, Frieda, Esther. And Lena. They were talking and laughing softly among themselves while waving to her. Lena's smile was enough on its own to stir happiness. But her cousin never left anything at just a grin. She loved laughing and making people laugh. The birthmark across her cheek never dampened her spirits, and Deborah thought she was the most beautiful of any of them, but at twenty-three Lena had never had a man ask to take her home from a singing.

Lena brought the rig to a stop. "We came to help you get your chores done."

"Ya," Nancy said. "That way there's no chance of you having to cancel looking at houses with Mahlon."

"Becca said I'm through for today."

Raised eyebrows soon gave way to broad smiles.

"Then come on." Lena motioned. "We'll take a spin around the block…and play a trick on Anna Mary before we drop you off at Mahlon's."

When Deborah climbed into the wagon, Lydia patted a store-bought sack of pebbles. "We've got a good plan. And Lena just happens to have some inside information, like the fact that Anna Mary hasn't had time to repot her indoor plants, but she's purchased a bag of soil."

The girls began reminiscing about past pranks they'd pulled on each other. When they arrived near Anna Mary's, Lena brought the rig to a stop. Two girls stayed with the wagon while the rest of them snuck past the house and to the shed. They took Anna Mary's bag of potting soil and replaced it with the sack of rocks. Soon they were on their way to Mahlon's, everyone guessing how long it would be before Anna Mary discovered the switch.

Deborah sat up front with Lena. "If she thinks she bought the wrong stuff, Lena and I should try to go with her to return it. Then one of us can pull another switch while she's loading other things."

The girls broke into fresh laughter.

"And yet you look so innocent," Lena quipped.

Deborah pushed the tie to her prayer *Kapp* behind her shoulder. "Not just me, dear cousin. You do too. It's how we get away with such antics, ya?"

As Lena turned onto the road that led to Mahlon's home, Deborah spotted a car coming from the opposite direction. She thought little of it until it pulled onto the side of the road twenty yards from Mahlon's place. A car door opened, and an Amish man got out. It wasn't until the man closed the car door and walked around to the driver's side that she recognized Mahlon. Even at this distance she could tell who it was by the way he carried himself—his slow, easy pace. With all the silly banter and laughter in the wagon, not one of her friends seemed to notice the vehicle or Mahlon. He stood outside the driver's window talking to whoever was inside. Then he stepped away, waved, and started walking through the field toward his home.

Like watching children performing a play at school, memories of their friendship ran through her mind—years of shared lunches, games at recess, and walks to and from school together. It all began when she'd been in fourth grade and he in sixth.

They'd borne each other's grief since the day they'd both lost a parent. They had learned to accept their loss together, learned to laugh afresh, and figured out how to trust in life again. Together they'd weathered change after change as they'd gone through their teen years. He'd been in

New York City on September 11, 2001, and she'd been the one he shared his trauma with, his confusion and sense of helplessness, his hidden desire for revenge, and his recurring nightmares.

Quiet.

Deep.

And…secretive?

The car he'd gotten out of passed the wagon, revealing a man about Mahlon's age, wearing a military uniform of some type. When she looked to where she'd last seen Mahlon, he was nowhere in sight. As Rachel pulled into his driveway, Deborah realized he'd probably gone up the wooden steps that ran along the outside of his home and led straight to his bedroom—the private entrance she thought he never used.

She climbed down, waved to her friends, and headed for the front door.

What was going on? His quietness worked against them sometimes. It wasn't always easy to know his thoughts. But through the years she'd carried his secrets. Few others, if any, knew that the weight of becoming the provider for himself and his mother before he graduated at thirteen had silently panicked him or that after 9/11 he'd struggled to accept the Old Ways.

She tapped on the screen door and then went inside.

Ada placed the flatiron on the stove, stepped around the ironing board, and hugged her. "*Gut* morning."

"Gut morning, Ada. Where's Mahlon?"

"Still asleep. I don't know when the last time was that he needed me to wake him, so I refuse to start now. Besides, with all the work to set up for the auction tomorrow and all he hopes to get done today, I figure he needs every minute of rest he can squeeze in."

Hoping her face didn't reveal how much was going through her mind, Deborah drew a shaky breath. "Do you mind if I go up and wake him?"

"Not a bit."

As she began climbing the narrow steps, she heard water start running overhead. His home consisted of a small kitchen and sitting area downstairs and two small bedrooms and a bath upstairs. A hint of steam escaped under the bathroom door.

She tapped on the door. "Mahlon?"

"Hey, Deb. I'm in the shower. You're here early. I'll be out in a few."

He didn't sound any different. She heard no hint of guilt.

"Okay." Rather than go downstairs, she went into his room. It looked like a single man's room and not much different from the last time she'd seen it, when he was a teen. Clean clothes were stacked on his dresser, dirty ones piled in a corner. Parts of a newspaper lay beside his chair— each folded in a way that let her know which sections he'd read and which he'd chosen to ignore. A wad of cash on his nightstand caught her eye, and she went to it.

He came into the room, buttoning his shirt. His face and what she could see of his chest were still wet, reminding her of the boy he'd once been. "You're just full of surprises today. First you're here early, and then you're in my room." The smile on his face didn't hide the circles under his eyes. He pulled his suspenders over his shoulders and tucked his shirt into his pants. "Something wrong?"

Weighing her emotions against what she knew of him, she refused to sound stressed or harsh. "I'm not sure."

"Well, tell me, and if there is, I'll see what I can do to fix it." His eyes radiated something she couldn't define, but she knew that tone in his voice. The one that hinted of forced patience, usually when life doled out responsibilities he resented.

"You don't have to fix anything. I'm not part of what you consider your lot in life." When he didn't smile or chuckle or assure her she was the best part of his life, she felt suddenly unsure. "Am I?"

He shook his head. "You know better than that. I'm hungry. Are you?"

Hurt that he'd evaded the question, she tried to catch his eye but couldn't. She'd seen him dodge questions from his mother a hundred times, but she'd always thought he confided everything in her.

She went to the nightstand and pointed at the money. "Are you working a second job?"

"No. I wouldn't have time even if I had the desire. Your brother has me logging too much overtime. I'd wanted us to have all day together, but I could only get off until after lunch."

Without saying a word about the money, he turned his back to her and went to his dresser.

"If you're just working one job, then where were you coming from when I saw you get out of that man's car?"

He kept his back to her for several moments. "Oh, is that what this is about?" After pulling a pair of socks out of a drawer, he sat on his bed with his back still to her. "Eric Shriver is home on leave, so we spent some time together. That's all."

"I didn't realize he was back in the States." Nor did she know that Mahlon still considered Eric a friend to spend time with. They'd become friends about six years ago when he and Ephraim installed a set of kitchen cabinets for Eric's parents. But Mahlon had chosen to lay that friendship aside when he joined the faith. Or had he? Was he friends with a soldier?

After he put on his shoes, he stood. "He came home last week. So, you looking forward to house hunting this morning?"

Realizing he didn't want to talk about his time with Eric, she chose not to push, but the hurt from earlier spread through her.

He studied her before moving in closer. "It was nothing, Deb. He came up here last night and wanted to talk, so I went with him."

"You've been out all night…just talking?"

"Hey, you two," Ada called. "The Realtor just pulled up."

"Be down in a minute." He placed his hands on her shoulders. "Is my Deb showing a bit of insecurity? Because if she is, I want to ignore our beliefs, get a camera, and take a photo during this rare event."

She rolled her eyes. "I don't doubt your love or faithfulness—only your good sense, which has been in question on occasion."

He brushed his lips against her cheek. "I have you, which means my good sense is amazing."

"Well…now, that's true."

Laughing, he released her. "You've never been short on friends, so you can't really understand how Eric feels. But I've never made friends easily either, so the two of us are a little alike. Should I cut him out simply because while he's been serving in Iraq, I joined a church that believes in nonresistance?" He grabbed a comb off his dresser and ran it through his brown hair, yanking at the curls with annoyance.

In his first few years of knowing Eric, she wondered at times if Mahlon would join the faith. Sometimes their bond seemed to defy more than the religious and political boundaries that separated them. It ignored reason. But she knew if she pushed Mahlon on the topic, he'd grow quieter than quiet. And that didn't help either of them.

She moved in front of him. "If I don't have you, I'll always be short on friends. So I guess I can understand how Eric feels. But it seems odd for two people who look at life so differently to want to spend time together."

"In certain areas it surprises me how much we see things alike. Besides, isn't being different part of friendship? I certainly don't feel like you do about cooking or kitchens or new dresses."

Choosing to trust his judgment, she put her arms around his waist. "But I think you'd look so good in one of my newly sewn dresses."

He dropped the comb and pulled her close. "You could get away with about any insult as you stand in my bedroom wrapped in my arms…" He bent and kissed her. "But we'd better go." He took her by the hand and led her down the steps.

Five

Doubting herself, Cara kept walking, searching for Mast Road, hoping something would look familiar. It'd be dark again soon, and they were no better off now than when they left New York more than forty hours ago. Time seemed lost inside a fog of stress and lack of food and sleep, but the days were clearly marked in her mind. She'd left the city Wednesday around midnight, got off the second bus late on Thursday, and currently the Friday afternoon sun was beginning to dip behind the treetops.

Last night's rain had soaked her clothing, and now the insides of her thighs were raw. Her legs were so weak she kept tripping. She longed for a hot bath and a bed. But it didn't look like that would happen anytime soon.

Her thin, snug-around-the-waist sweater-shirt was still damp against her skin, but she'd managed to buy a couple of items that her daughter could change in to. After getting off the bus, she'd carried Lori for nearly a mile before spotting a run-down gas station that sold liquor and groceries and even had a rack with overpriced T-shirts, sweatshirts, and hoodies.

The place didn't have the feel of country life, as she'd imagined. It had a roughness about it that felt very familiar, one that matched New York City. A group of six men, all drunk, based on the number of beer cans and whiskey bottles strewn around them, sat on a porch across the road from the store, playing beat-up guitars and watching her every move.

As she stepped into the store, the bell on the door jingled loudly and woke Lori. She wriggled to get down. When Cara released her, Lori scowled, stomping her feet. "I'm all wet! How'd I get all wet?" Her shrieks pierced the air as she threw herself onto the floor—hunger and exhaustion controlling her.

The man behind the register looked from Lori to Cara, disgust written on his face. He appeared ready to throw them out. When Cara left the store with a small-adult hoodie and socks for Lori, along with bagels, milk, and toiletries, the men across the street had whistled, howled, and made rude comments. Thankfully not one of them budged from their spot on the porch. They were probably too smashed to stand up, which was good, because their mannerisms didn't suggest good-natured catcalls. They were capable of malice. She saw the truth carved in their features, and she wasted no time getting herself and Lori out of sight. About a mile down the road, she found an old shed, and they stayed there last night.

After a day of walking through Dry Lake, Lori's feet had blisters. Cara didn't know anything to do but take off her shoes and let her walk in her socks.

Feeling lost and overwhelmed, Cara studied her surroundings. This was just like her—doing something with absolute hope, only to find that reality trumped it every single time. Like the blood flowing through her veins, anger circled round and round her insides. If having to uproot and travel like this wasn't enough to make her lash out, the nicotine withdrawal made her a hundred times more irritable. But so far she'd kept her grumpiness tucked deep inside.

The craving for a cigarette tormented her. Her addiction to smokes had started at fifteen, and unlike the rest of life, it came easy. The fact that she rarely paid to indulge in the habit had made getting hooked even easier. At work some of her regulars offered her a cigarette as she waited their tables. She'd slide it into her waitress pouch for later use. Almost nightly other customers left a half-empty pack by accident or as a tip. If she had four to five bucks to spend on a pack right now, she would. Of course the money for the cigarettes was only one of the issues. The other?

Lori was with her, and she didn't know her mother smoked. When Lori was young and asked about the smoky smell clinging to her mom, Cara had shrugged it off as the fault of waitressing in a place that allowed smoking. Her daughter hadn't asked about the smell in years.

"My feet still hurt," Lori whined. "And look, I got blood on my socks."

"It's from the blisters. Do you need me to carry you?"

She shook her head. "But the pebbles on the road are hurting me, Mom."

"I know, sweetie. I'll figure something out soon."

Lori held her hand and fell into silence again as they kept walking. At the bottom of the hill, another road intersected with this one. Should she go down it in search of Mast Road or keep going straight?

She didn't know. Whenever she spotted someone or passed a home, she didn't dare stop to ask. People would think nothing of a mother and child going for a walk on a beautiful spring day in mid-May. But their curiosity would turn against her once she asked where a certain road was. It'd begin a peppering of questions. Are you lost? Who are you looking for? Did your car break down? Where do you live? What are you doing on foot?

No, she couldn't ask.

Lori tugged at her hand. "That road starts with an M, Mom."

"Does it?" Cara blinked, trying to focus in spite of a pounding headache.

Mast Road.

Her weariness dampened almost all the relief she felt at finding the road. The search for this sign had begun before dawn. Most of the roads in Dry Lake were long and hilly, but they'd at least found the one they'd been searching for—although she had no idea what the place had in store for them, if anything.

They'd barely gone a hundred feet on Mast Road when she noticed a man on foot, leading a horse-drawn carriage to the front of a home.

He went inside for a moment and came back out with a woman and five children. They all got into the rig. To travel like that, they probably were Amish. As they drove past her, she noticed a little girl inside the buggy who was a year or so older than Lori.

Her shoes would fit Lori—without pinching her feet.

As Cara approached the house, she saw only a screen door between her and the inside of the home. "Let's knock on that door."

"What for?"

"Just to see if someone's home."

"Mom, look." Lori pointed at a beer bottle lying in the ditch.

"That's nasty, babe. Let's keep moving."

Lori pulled her hand free and grabbed it. "It looks like brown topaz, like our teacher at school showed us."

"Come on, kid, give me a break. It's an empty beer bottle." Cara took it from her.

"Don't throw it."

Unwilling to provoke her daughter's taxed emotions, she nodded and held on to it.

As they went up the porch stairs, Cara set the bottle on a step. She knocked and waited. When no one answered, she banged on it really hard. "Hello?" She heard no sounds. "Let's go in for a minute."

"But, Mom—"

"It's okay. No one's home, but if they were here, they'd give us some Band-Aids and some shoes that fit you, right?"

"Yeah, I think so. But I don't want to go in."

Leaving Lori near the front door, she hurried through the house, scavenging for clean socks, bandages, ointment, and shoes. With two pairs of shoes, a bottle of peroxide, a box of bandages, fresh socks, and a tube of ointment for her daughter's blisters in hand, Cara hurried out the door, tripping as she went. The items scattered across the porch.

Lori had the beer bottle in her hand, and Cara snatched it from her and set it back down on the porch. "I think one of these pairs will fit. Try this set on, and let's get out of here. Can you wait until later for us to clean the blisters and wrap them?"

"I think so."

"That's my girl."

While helping Lori slip into the shoes, Cara looked around the yard. A man stood at an opened cattle gate, watching them. Her heart raced. How long had he been standing there? But he didn't seem interested in confronting her. Based on the description from the man at the ticket counter, this guy might be Amish. He appeared to be past middle age and had on a dress shirt and pants, straw hat, and suspenders.

Keeping an eye on him, she left one pair of shoes on the porch and gathered up the rest of the items and shoved them into the backpack. "Will those do?"

"Yeah, but my feet still hurt."

She glanced at the man, who remained stock-still, watching her. "I'll put medicine and Band-Aids on later. We need to go."

Cara tripped as she stood, knocking the beer bottle down the steps. Without meaning to, she cursed.

Wordlessly, the man continued to stare at them.

Cara took Lori's hand and hurried down the steps and toward the road.

"Mom, wait. You forgot the beer bottle."

"Lori, shh. Come on." She elongated the last word, and Lori obeyed.

The man seemed unable to move other than rubbing his left shoulder. "Malinda?"

Her heart stopped as her mother's name rode on the wind.

He blinked and opened his mouth to speak, but he said nothing.

"Daed?" A young woman called to him.

He turned to glance behind him. Cara couldn't see who called to him, but based on her voice, she was close. The man looked back to Cara. "It makes no difference who you are, we don't need thieves, drunks, or addicts around here."

"But I'm not—"

He wasted no time getting inside the pasture and shutting the noisy metal gate, ending Cara's attempt to defend herself.

Part of Cara wanted another chance to explain herself and ask questions or at least follow them as they turned their backs to her and headed through the field. Why had he called her by her mother's name? But she feared he might lash out and scare Lori if she dared to ask questions. It would do no one any good if her search for answers began badly. Awash in emotions, she took Lori by the hand and continued down the road. Did she look like her mother had? Did that man know her mom?

"Mom, what'd that man say to you?"

Unwilling to tell her the truth, Cara improvised. "Something about monks and leaves being in the attic...maybe?"

She giggled. "I think he's confused."

"I think you're right. I'm feeling a little confused myself. How do the shoes feel?"

"Pretty good. Thanks. I might not need those Band-Aids."

"You're one tough little girl, you know that?" Cara bent and kissed the top of Lori's head.

She'd thought it could mean a sense of connection for herself and Lori to meet people who knew her mother...but now it felt like a mistake. Her mother's past was hidden to her, and the man looked horrified to think she might be Malinda.

They walked on and on, putting more than a mile between them and that man. While trying to sort through his reaction, she studied the land. Another barn in need of paint stood a few hundred feet ahead of them, but not one thing felt familiar. Her arms and shoulders ached from the miles she'd toted Lori. Surely they'd covered nearly every mile of Dry Lake—every road, paved and dirt. As they walked Mast Road, she had no hint of what to do now.

She tripped again, and it seemed that stumbling got easier as the day wore on. Whatever they were going to do for shelter, Cara had to find an answer soon. There wasn't a house in sight, but perhaps they could sleep in that slightly lopsided barn.

As they approached the old building, Cara spotted something of interest on the other side of the road. Holding on to Lori's hand, she crossed over. Walking up a short gravel driveway, she noticed a huge garden planted beside it. Ahead of her lay a bare foundation with only a rock chimney still standing. She stepped onto the concrete floor and walked to the fireplace. The stone hearth had a rusted crane and black kettle.

"That pot looks like a witch's cauldron, huh, Mom? Like in *Harry Potter*."

Cara ran her fingers along the metal. "It's for cooking over an open fire. The house that used to be here must've been hundreds of years old."

Something niggled at her but nothing she could make sense of.

Lori tugged at her mother's hand. "Look at that tree. I've always wanted to climb a tree, Mom. Remember?"

She remembered.

"I think I can climb that one."

"Maybe so." With reality pressing in on her, Cara tried to hold on to the positive. They were free of Mike. She had Lori. Still, she had no idea how she'd start over and pull together a life for them with no help, no money, and no belongings.

After interlacing her fingers, she gave Lori a boost up to the lowest branch. If nothing else, she'd finally given Lori one of her lifelong hopes— a tree to climb. This one did seem perfect for climbing—large but with a thick branch within five feet of the ground.

Cara looked across the land, wondering if she'd used what little money they had on absolute foolishness. She should be somewhere looking for work, not chasing after shadows of things that once were.

She knew the reality—all children raised in foster care harbor the belief that they have a relative somewhere out there who loves them. She was no exception. Each night after her mother had died, she'd gone to bed hoping a loved one would stumble upon the truth of her existence and come for her. At first she'd been foolish enough to hope her father would come. But as the years passed, she realized that he'd never wanted her. So the fantasy changed into the dream that a relative she'd never met would show up for her one day. By the time she turned fourteen, she refused to give in to that longing. Life hurt less that way. But the desire to have one relative who cared never truly went away. She wished it would. Maybe then the ache inside would ease.

"Look, Mom. It has a spot to ride it like a horse. And that knot thing looks sorta like a horse's head."

Cara glanced. A dip in the branch where Lori sat made a perfect spot for straddling it and pretending she was riding a horse. "It does, doesn't it? All you need is a set of reins."

"How'd you know, Mom?"

Cara turned from looking at the field. "How'd I know what?"

Lori held up a set of rusted chains. They were small, probably from a swing set.

"How'd ya know there were reins here?" Lori tugged at the chains that were wrapped around the part of the branch that looked like a horse's head. "Parts of them have grown into the tree, but they work."

Cara returned to the tree, running her hands over the mossy bark. She recalled the pieces of memory that came to her when Mike had showed up at her workplace—an old woman, rows of tall corn, a kitchen table filled with food, sheets flapping in the wind. As she studied the tree and the land around her, she began to sense that maybe her fragmented thoughts weren't her imagination or parts of an old movie she'd once seen.

Six

Deborah held her father's arm, guiding him up the gentle slope. Their home sat just beyond the ridge of the field, but maybe this wasn't the easiest route to take. "You're pale and shaking. What possessed you to go for such a long walk today?" He didn't answer, and she tried again. "Kumm, let's go home."

He pulled back, stopping both of them. "Did you see that woman and child coming out of the Swareys' home?"

"No." Deborah slid her arm through his, trying to encourage him to keep moving toward home. "Do you know her?"

Her father's feet were planted firm, and it seemed she couldn't coax him into budging.

He looked to the heavens before closing his eyes. "But it can't be her. She'd be much older by now, and her daughter is seven or eight years older than you."

"Who, Daed?"

He massaged his shoulder as if it ached from deep within. "Your mother loved her so. Never once believed the ban against her was fair—not even when she came back eight years later with a child. When she returned with her daughter, I'd been a preacher only a short time." He gave a half shrug, rubbing the area below his collarbone.

"Daed, what are you talking about?"

He turned and headed for the cattle gate. "It can't be her. A ghost…a mirage—that's all it could be. Or"—he quickened his pace—"another one sent in her place to finish destroying what little she left intact."

"Daed." Deborah took him by the arm again, gently tugging on him to go the other way. "You're scaring me, talking such nonsense. Let's go home."

He pointed a finger at her. "I may suffer under a chronic illness, but I'm not a child."

Feeling the sting of his correction, she nodded and released his arm. They came to the gate, and he waited as Deborah opened it. They went through it, and then she locked it back, her heart racing with fear.

She held her tongue, trying to piece together what he might be talking about.

"Even as a newly appointed preacher, I…still don't think I was wrong." He walked a bit faster as he mumbled. "But Pontius Pilate never thought he was either. Rueben swears she has a way about her—a deceiving, sultry, manipulative way. Who should know better than the man who'd been engaged to her? What else could I do? What else should I have done?"

"What are you talking about?"

"And that woman I just saw was stealing from the Swareys and drunk. She wasn't Malinda. Couldn't be."

"Who's Malinda, Daed?"

"You keep the children close to home. I have to warn our people."

He wasn't making any sense. And even though the temperature was barely sixty and a breeze blew, he had beads of sweat across his brow. When he stumbled a bit, she tucked her arm through his, helping him keep his balance.

"*Liewi* Deborah." He patted her arm, calling her "dear." "It's not easy being the daughter of a preacher, is it?"

Concerned that he still wasn't making much sense, she tried to encourage him to turn around and head toward home. There weren't many phones in the district, but the bishop had approved one for the cabinetry business.

He took a few steps and then paused. "Whether I'm right or wrong in a thing, only God knows. But decisions, tough ones that have the power to help or ruin, have to be made to protect our beliefs."

"I understand. You're just and caring and do your best. I've always believed that."

He nodded. "I hope you always do."

He staggered, and she did what she could to keep him from falling. "Daed?"

His legs buckled, and he fell to his knees.

"Daed!"

Cara tried to think of a plan while Lori played in the tree. That man calling her Malinda haunted her, and she knew the memory wouldn't fade anytime soon. The sound of horses' hoofs striking the pavement made her jump. "Come on, sweetie. We'd better get off this property." *Or at least not look like we're trespassing.*

"Not yet, Mom, please." Lori wrapped her legs firmly around the branch and held on tight to the chains.

"Lori, we need to move. Now."

"I am moving. Watch me." She spurred the tree and mimicked all the motions of riding a horse.

The sound of the real horses' clopping grew louder. She couldn't see a rig just yet, but it'd top that hill soon.

"Lori." Cara narrowed her eyes, giving another sharp look. "Now."

Lori huffed, but she hung on to the tree with her arms, lowering her legs as close to the ground as she could. Cara wrapped her hands around her daughter's tiny waist. "Okay, drop."

Lori did.

"Come on. We need to keep walking, like we're just out for a stroll, okay?" They hurried to the far side of the road near the old barn.

Her daughter tugged on her hand, stopping her. "Did you hear that?"

What, the sound of me failing you?

Lori's brown eyes grew large. "I hear puppies." She pulled at her mom's hand, trying to hurry her. "It's coming from that building."

The whole plot looked abandoned, from the empty foundation to the dilapidated barn, and Cara thought maybe it was a better idea to get off the road and totally out of sight. The two ran to the barn door. As they ducked inside, Cara spotted two horses heading their way, pulling a buckboard. That meant she and Lori might have been seen too. She closed the door and peeked through the slats, hoping the rig passed on by.

"Mom, look!"

Her daughter was sitting in the middle of a litter of six puppies, all excited to have her attention.

"Shh." Cara peered out the slit of the slightly open barn door, trying to see where the horses and rig had gone. She didn't hear any clopping sounds.

"Excuse me." A male voice called out to her.

She jolted and looked in the other direction. Two men sat in the horse-drawn wagon, staring at the barn.

"Stay here," Cara whispered firmly before stepping outside.

Ephraim held the girl's stare, feeling as if he'd seen her somewhere before. She certainly wasn't someone he'd met while doing cabinetry work. With her short crop of blond hair, tattered jeans, a tight sweater-shirt that didn't quite cover her belly, he'd remember if he'd been in her house.

But those brown eyes... Where had he ever seen eyes that shade of golden bronze...or ones filled with that much attitude? On one hand, she gave off an aura of a bit of uncertainty, perhaps an awareness that she wasn't on her own property. But there was something else, something... cynical and cold.

She stepped away from the barn. "Is there a problem?"

"I was wondering the same thing. You're on private property."

"Yeah, I didn't figure this was a national park or anything. I'm just looking around. The old place has character."

"Thanks, but it being old is a cause for potential danger. I'd prefer you kept moving."

"I bet you would. I'm sure you're real concerned about my safety."

The sensation of remembering her made his chest tingle. Maybe she was one of the fresh-air teens from New York the Millers sponsored each summer. They usually didn't arrive until mid-June, but... "Are you from around here?"

A bit of surprise overtook the hardness in her eyes for a moment. "Is that the Amish version of 'Haven't we met before?' "

Ephraim's face burned at the hint that he was coming on to her. He removed his hat, propped his elbow on his leg, and leaned forward. "It was the polite version of 'I want you off my property.' But if you're a newcomer to the area who's out for a walk, I was willing to be nice about it."

She raised an eyebrow, and he got the feeling she was holding back from telling him what she really thought. He'd had enough experience with her kind of Englischer women from his days of living and working among them to know that her restraint wasn't out of respect as much as self-serving interest.

She dipped her fingertips into the front pockets of her jeans. "Like I said, we just stopped in for a minute. I didn't think a brief look around would cause such a fuss."

Slipping his hat back on his head, he considered his words. Dry Lake had plenty of teen troubles sometimes, and in his caution he was probably coming across more harsh than he should. "I...I—"

Deborah screamed. Ephraim scanned the area and spotted her running toward them and motioning. "It's Daed. Hurry!"

Ready to dismiss the unusual stranger, he slapped the reins against the horse's back and the rig took off.

Seven

Cara slid through the barely open barn door while keeping her eye on the horse and wagon as it headed down the road. The man who did the talking was every bit as cold and personable as winter with a tattered coat. She'd seen it too many times before—good-looking, strong men as unfeeling and heartless as the dead. "Come on, sweetie. We've got to go."

"No, Mom. Come look."

One glance at Lori erased a bit of stress and fatigue. It felt odd to grin, but the furry black pups, already weighing about five pounds, were sprawled across her daughter's lap, sleeping soundly while she petted them.

Lori gazed up at her. "We can't leave. They like me."

Was that a trace of awe and excitement in her daughter's eyes and voice?

Cara knelt beside her and stroked a puppy. "They're real nice, Lorabean, but we can't stay here. Heartless Man might come back."

"Please, Mom." Lori's brown eyes reflected a desire so strong, so hopeful, as if every empty promise the Santas of the world offered at Christmas could be salvaged by granting her this one request.

Cara sat cross-leggedly, wondering what it could possibly hurt to give Lori a few hours with the puppies. Besides, they had to sleep somewhere tonight. Glancing around the place, she noticed rusted pitchforks, ten-gallon tubs, and moldy bales of hay. A decaying wagon sat in a corner with painter's tarps, ropes, and a watering can. The tin roof had sections missing.

The barn side of a silo caught her attention. She went over to it and tugged on the door, almost falling when it finally opened. Clearly the door had been closed for a long time. If the man came back, she and Lori could hide inside. He'd never think to look in there. When they were on the road, they'd crossed a small bridge not far from here, so the creek had to run nearby. That meant water to drink, wash up in, and brush their teeth with. If she could get the two days' worth of traveling grime washed off of her and Lori, she might be able to sleep—even if she was in a dirty barn.

A piece of tin standing against the wall rattled and shifted. An older dog walked out from behind it. After one glimpse at Cara, the mama dog lowered her head and tucked her tail between her legs.

Cara knelt, motioning for her. "I know just how you feel. But you can't go around acting like it." The old dog came to her and stood still while Cara rubbed her short black hair. "If you act all sad and dumped on, people get meaner. Don't you know that by now?"

The dog wagged her tail. As if sensing their mom's presence, the puppies woke and started whining and going to her. She licked Cara's hand and then moved to a corner and lay down, letting the pups nurse.

"What're they doing, Mom?"

Cara pulled the sack of bagels out of Lori's backpack. "They're nursing. That means they're getting milk from their mother."

"Did I nurse?"

Cara passed her a bagel. "It was free food. What do you think?"

Lori wiped her hands on her dress. "If I only eat half of my bagel, can I share it with the mama dog?"

"Your part *is* half of a bagel, so, no, you can't share any of it. She'll be fine. We should be so lucky as to scavenge like a dog and not get sick."

"You know what?"

Cara shrugged. "I don't want to play guessing games, okay?"

"If I ever had more food than I needed, I'd give it to other hungry boys and girls."

Cara rolled her eyes. "As if." The sarcasm in her tone ran deep within her; Cara knew that all too well.

Remembering how she used to dream of jumping on a horse and riding into a world that had people who loved her and flowed with tables of food, Cara stared at her half of the bagel. "Never be afraid to hope, Lorabean. Never."

Deborah continued to shake as Ephraim pulled into the driveway. Daed sat beside her, with Mahlon on the other side of him, as they rode on the back of the wagon with their legs dangling. She and Mahlon held on to her Daed so he wouldn't fall out as the wagon bumped along. His ashen face tortured her.

Dear God, don't take him! Please. The phrase screamed inside her. The loss of her mother had nearly destroyed her whole family. She couldn't stand losing someone else. Not after Daed and Becca had spent years building a new family while giving strength to the one they each already had.

Mahlon jumped off the back of the wagon before it came to a complete stop. His eyes locked on hers, saying he cared and he understood. She knew he did. He always had, and she relied on his quiet strength.

Becca ran out the door. "Abner?"

"He's had a spell." Deborah choked on tears she refused to shed.

"Call the doctor, and call for a driver." Becca spoke in a whisper that didn't hide her panic.

Ephraim was already halfway to the shop.

"I'm fine now." Daed waved his arm for everyone to let go of him. "Stop fussing over me."

They released him.

"But you will be seen by the doctor, Abner. You must," Becca pleaded. "I said I'm fine."

Deborah stood in front of him. "You were talking nonsense, Daed. And you had sharp chest pains." She wiped her fingers across his forehead. "You're still sweating."

He held her gaze. "I'll be okay. I just need to rest."

"Please." Deborah gently squeezed his arm. "I need you to go to the hospital to be sure of what's going on. Not tomorrow or later in the week. Right now."

He slowly reached for her face and cradled her cheeks in the palms of his rough hands. "Okay. But don't let the young ones slip off while we're gone. You keep them close to home. Away from that drunken thief. And lock the doors." His raspy breathing came in shallow spurts, and his hands trembled. "Once I get to the hospital, those doctors'll want to keep me at least one night. They always do."

Deborah placed her hands over his. "Mahlon will stay and help Ephraim get ready for the auction. And Ada will fill in for Becca. The community can do the auction on schedule even without you giving out instructions left and right."

Daed gave a nod.

Becca stepped forward. "Kumm." She took Daed's arm and helped him into the house.

"He'll be okay." Mahlon came up behind her and placed his hands on her shoulders. "It's probably another incident that's easily fixed. You remember last year when he'd taken in too much salt and had a fluid overload."

"He never had any pain with that."

"No, but anyone with his kind of heart condition has times when his medication needs to be adjusted. We know that from past experiences. I'm sure it's something the doctors can solve."

"He kept saying that he saw a woman coming out of the Swarey home and that she'd stolen things from them and was drunk. I didn't see anyone. Then he started mumbling about a ghost and Mamm having loved her and maybe he'd been wrong, like Pontius Pilate." She swallowed, trying to hold in her emotions. "I couldn't do anything to help him."

"He'll be fine, Deb." He moved in front of her. "You did everything right." Mahlon's deep, soft voice strengthened her. "You used the power of his love for you to get him to do what's needed."

She moved to a lawn chair and sat. "I…I just don't know if I can handle losing him."

"Deb." His back stiffened, and frustration flickered in his eyes. "Don't do this. He'll be fine. And of course you can deal with whatever happens. What other choice do you have—to fall apart? That only makes everyone else need to carry you."

Fear for her Daed took a step back as offense lurched forward. But she knew where he was coming from and why, so she took a breath and gained control of herself. "You're right. I didn't mean… It's just that sometimes life is so scary, and about the time you can deal with one thing, something else happens."

He dipped his head for a moment before he looked her in the eye. "I know. But there's a difference between being concerned for someone and taking on all the anxiety of their what-ifs. You pull so hard for everyone to win, for everyone to be healthy and safe. Just…don't…"

He sounded as if he had more to say. It seemed to her that she deserved an apology, not a lecture, so she waited. A car horn blasted, and she knew the driver had arrived to take Daed to the hospital.

Eight

Thunder rumbled, waking Cara. Her head spun with pain, and she wished she had a smoke and a cup of coffee to ease the effects of her lack of both. Darkness surrounded her, but what little sky she could see through the missing parts of the roof indicated the sun's rays were just below the horizon. The ragged canvas she'd placed over her and Lori didn't keep the chill out. Puppies covered a good bit of Lori, so in spite of the dirt and grime, she was at least warm.

Odors from the hay, the dirt floor, and the aging barn drifted through the air. She saw herself as a young girl swinging on a rope from a loft and dropping into a mound of hay. Could she have been in this barn before?

The mama dog raised her head and laid it on Cara's leg. She patted her, wondering what the day would bring and where they'd sleep tonight. Longing for basic human comforts, she missed having a toilet, shower, and clean clothes.

As she stood and knocked musty hay and dirt off herself, her tiny, pathetic apartment in the South Bronx took on a luster it'd never had before. It had hot water. A kitchen. A bathroom. A front door with keys that said she had the right to be there. She pulled a black beetle from her shirt. And the bugs stayed mostly on the floor during the night, not in her bed.

Trying to think how best to handle today, she slipped out the back of the barn through a narrow hole where a couple of vertical slats used to be. The cool May air smelled of rain. Her eyes burned from lack of sleep or maybe from the layer of moldy dust that covered her. A desire to go to the creek and wash up pulled at her, but she stayed put. The sun slowly climbed over the horizon. Birds sang. Dew covered the field. She'd never seen a sunrise like this. Rays of light danced on the droplets of water that covered the fields.

When she heard a noise, she squeezed through the opening again and saw a young boy standing next to Lori and holding a pup.

"I got to hide 'em," he whispered. "My brother's gonna sell 'em at the auction today."

Cara moved forward. "He's on his way here?"

The boy turned. "Not yet. He'll probably wait till they start selling livestock to come get 'em."

"We gotta hide them, Mom. Simeon said they're too young to leave their mama."

In spite of her inclination to get out of there quickly, something about this scenario felt familiar—the boy's straw hat, collared shirt, suspenders, dress pants.

Simeon pulled a handkerchief out of his pocket and laid it on the ground before unfolding it. The mama dog wasted no time gobbling up the tidbits of food.

"What's an auction?" Lori asked.

"It's where you can buy all sorts of things. We always have it at our place because we're the only ones with enough parking space and a huge building to keep the rain out. We got whopper tents with just roofs and no sides set up, too, so some of the selling can go on there while some's going on inside the shop. And there's enough food to feed everybody." Simeon told where he lived and where his brother's house was, and he rambled about a meeting that would take place at his house tomorrow night and how his brother lived alone. He went on and on as if he'd forgotten what he'd come here to do.

"Simeon!" a male voice hollered.

The little boy's eyes widened. "That's my brother."

Cara grabbed Lori's arm, scooped up the backpack, and hurried into the silo. While closing the door to it, she placed her index finger over her lips, hoping Simeon wouldn't tell.

The boy jerked the door open. "What about hiding the puppies?"

"They'll make too much noise." She closed the door, but the scowl on his face made her wonder if he'd give them away.

"Simeon Mast."

She recognized the man's voice. Simeon's brother and Heartless Man were one and the same. Cara held her breath. Trespassing and loitering were punishable by law. It wouldn't be much of a crime, but it'd be enough that the officials would start digging into her life and soon discover she had no money, no place to live, and a daughter in tow.

"Mom," Lori whispered, "there's food at the auction, and I'm hungry."

Cara gently placed her hand over Lori's mouth. "Shh." How could she explain that lack of money, not lack of supply, stood between them and the goods? After buying food and clothes at that store in Shippensburg, they had thirty-two cents left. If she dug through Lori's backpack, she might find enough change to buy her a little something.

The dark, dank hole crawled with creepy things. What was she doing living like this?

The question made her long to get back at Mike. He'd dogged her moves off and on for more than a decade. He should be in a dark hole with creepy things, not her.

The man's voice grew louder, as if he was heading straight for the silo. "Of course I'm not taking the pups to the auction." He sounded as if he were leaning against the silo. "We'll find homes for them in a few weeks when they're old enough. But with Daed in the hospital and all your sisters busy with the auction work, you need to be my shadow. Now, come on before I lose my patience."

Silence reigned for a bit, and then the barn door slammed shut. She waited a couple of moments, then eased the silo's hatch open and helped

Lori get out. Simeon's brother must've brought a pan of food with him, and the mama dog's tail wagged as she ate.

The sounds of many horses' hoofs grabbed Cara's attention, and she peeked through the barn door. A long row of horse-drawn buggies lined the road, all heading east. Cars moved around them, driving in the same direction.

"Simeon said over a thousand people will be at the auction," Lori said. "Can we go too? Please?"

If they went and if she found a little more money, she might be able to buy a hot dog or something to help ease Lori's hunger. Besides, if this place had any answers for her foggy memories or why that man had called her by her mother's name, she was more likely to learn of them by going to a communitywide event than by traveling down quiet roads with her daughter. Since the auction was open to everyone, it couldn't hurt for them to show up.

Cara grabbed the backpack. "Let's slip out the back and freshen up in the creek first. We can't go looking like we slept in a barn."

The special-event tent over Deborah's head promised to keep out the threatening rain as she spread frosting on a tray of cinnamon buns. She and Ada had been baking since two a.m., and now they were almost ready for the hundreds of customers to begin arriving. Six warming trays were lined up, filled with breakfast food—scrambled eggs, sausage, bacon, biscuits, scrapple, and breakfast breads.

Lists of what else needed doing filled her thoughts, but she wanted a chance to talk to Mahlon. Between her baking hundreds of biscuits and cinnamon rolls for today's auction and her younger siblings needing her, she hadn't caught more than a glimpse of him since the driver had arrived last night.

"Hey, Little Debbie." Jonathan's familiar voice made her turn.

She laughed at the sight of Mahlon's cousin standing before her in the usual Amish attire but with the add-on of a white chef's apron and knee-high waders covered in mud.

He rolled his eyes. "Hey, be nice. My makeshift cooking area is a muddy mess."

"You be nice. Anything I make should be better than a store-bought snack cake. So knock off the nickname thing."

He stuck out his hand, offering to shake hers. "Deal."

She peered at his palm, checking for a buzzer.

He smiled and showed her his empty hand before lowering it. Jonathan usually made some gentle but humorous remark about her name. Maybe some Amish somewhere used the name Deborah, but no one in her life knew of them. She'd been named after her mother's Englischer midwife.

She lifted her leg slightly, glancing at the hem of her dress. It already had spatters of mud. "I know at the end of today, I'll be doing my best to scrub mud out of all our clothing."

"Ya, you will. You should have worn a dark-colored dress. Did you get the change drawer?"

"Not yet. I'd forgotten, actually."

"Nothing like an annoying friend to remind you of things you haven't done." He chuckled. "I can't go get it. I've got sausages cooking. But if you need anything cooked, give me a holler."

"Denki."

It seemed odd that Jonathan and Mahlon were first cousins when the only similarity was the color of their eyes. Jonathan's lighthearted openness was quite a contrast to Mahlon's silent depth. Figuring Mahlon out didn't come easily. But he drew her—as if she were a parched land and he were a deep well of cool water.

Something so faint it almost didn't exist brushed her awareness, and she turned to find Mahlon at the edge of the tent, watching her. How she wished she could fully know what was behind those hazel eyes. A river most likely, a wide and deep one, teeming with thoughts and emotions that went deeper than most people experienced on their most reflective day.

He nodded a quiet hello, and she went to him. The apology she'd wanted from him last night reflected in his eyes.

"Morning." His deep, caring voice caused her skin to tingle. He slid his hand into hers and squeezed it. "Any more updates on your Daed?"

"Becca called the shop around ten o'clock last night. The doctors are pretty sure it wasn't a heart attack. That's the good news." She shrugged, not sure she understood the rest well enough to explain it decently. "It appears he had a spasm in the rib cage muscle. Fluid has built up throughout his body again, including around his heart and lungs. The doctor said that caused the shortness of breath and some of the chest discomfort. They're giving him meds that'll reduce the swelling. But none of that explains his odd behavior and mumbling about seeing a ghost."

"When will he get to come home?"

"Right now they're saying Tuesday. Becca asked me to have the driver come get me that day. She needs some things picked up at the pharmacy and grocery store, and she's too worn out and scattered to think it all through by herself."

Mahlon studied something behind her, and she turned.

Israel Kauffman walked beside Mahlon's mother, carrying a twenty-pound package of raw sausage. He was quite a looker for a man in his midforties—thin yet robust, with lots of shiny brown hair and a smile that never ended. Whatever he said to Ada made her laugh. Ada was only slightly younger, and both were widowed, so it seemed to Deborah they'd make a nice couple, but as far as she knew, they never saw each other outside of districtwide or communitywide events.

Israel took the meat around back of the temporary wall they'd installed, where Jonathan manned the sausage skillets in the makeshift kitchen. Deborah took Mahlon by the hand and moved back to her work station. She handed him a cinnamon roll to eat, and then she began making egg-and-bacon biscuits.

Ada went to the washbowl and scrubbed her hands. "I told Israel we've been at your house baking biscuits and cinnamon buns since two a.m. You know what he had the nerve to say?"

Deborah shook her head.

"That we'd better make more because he could eat all of that by himself before noon."

Deborah chuckled. "He won't have a hole in his stomach after all that, but he sure will in his pocket."

Jonathan rounded the corner with a tray of cooked sausages. He set them next to the warming tray and began moving them into it. "I know we have all the fixings for different kinds of sausage biscuits, but do you know how to make a sausage roll?"

Deborah shrugged. "Not sure that I do."

"You push it."

Laughing, she glanced to Mahlon, who didn't react at all. He had seemed so unsettled the last few days. Then again, their week had been packed with ups and downs since Ephraim gave his blessing on their wedding plans three days ago. He could just be tired.

She placed a sausage-and-egg biscuit in a wrapper and then tore off another piece of plastic wrap. "We need to assemble and wrap as many different kinds of meat-and-egg biscuits as we can. They sell the fastest."

Jonathan lifted the now-empty container. "You want the fresh vat of scrambled eggs?"

"Please."

"I'll bring it quicklike, but I'm not turning it over to you until I get some of your best brewed coffee." He tipped his hat and bowed, a broad smile saying he was teasing.

Deborah grabbed the coffee grinder, added fresh beans, and turned the crank. "You bring me the eggs, and I'll make the exchange."

"Yes ma'am." He disappeared.

Mahlon touched her shoulder. "I'll check on you in a few hours. I need to go."

The few seconds that passed between them as she looked in his eyes assured her that, despite whatever weighed on him, he adored her. "Maybe tomorrow we can go for a long, quiet ride—just the two of us."

"Doubtful with Becca gone and you running the household, but I sure will love it if we can."

She continued getting the place ready for the first customers—unloading paper plates and napkins into their bins, filling the salt and pepper shakers and condiment bottles.

"It's about to get wild, Deborah." Jonathan came around the corner with the huge container of steaming scrambled eggs. He nodded at the crowds parking their vehicles in the mowed fields. They'd soon form a line for Deborah and Ada's breakfast food, one that wouldn't end until nearly lunchtime.

Nine

Cara and Lori followed the horse-and-buggy line heading for the auction. Thankfully they weren't the only ones walking, so they didn't stick out…too much. None of the women had on jeans. She seemed to be in the land of dresses and skirts and hair long enough to be pulled back. There didn't seem to be much point in that. If they were going to pull their hair back all the time, why not just cut it off?

After walking half a mile, she saw cars parked in a field on one side of the road. Buggies sat in a different field with a fenced pasture holding the unharnessed horses. Several portable potties and sinks were set up, clearly brought in for the occasion. Up ahead she spotted a huge farmhouse near the road. Half a block away sat what appeared to be an industrial-size warehouse.

"Smell that food, Mom?"

The aroma filled the air, making her mouth water. Even more appealing than the delectable smell of food was the aroma of coffee—a heavenly scent. But unless she found a bit of money buried inside Lori's book bag, they'd have to be content with the stale half bagel and creek water they'd had for breakfast. "Maybe we can get something later. We just ate. We're fine for now."

The sky began to release some of its threatening downpour. She and Lori hurried to the nearest tent, huddling under it with a lot of others aiming to keep dry. She studied the lay of the land. At the back of the property, some two or three city blocks away and almost hidden behind rows of bushes and trees, sat another building—perhaps someone's home, but she couldn't tell. If it was a house, it was probably the one Simeon had told them belonged to his brother. It looked like there was a shortcut back to the barn if she went through the field and past the building behind the trees. When she left here, she'd try going that way.

From inside the warehouse came the sound of a man's quick words as he auctioned an item. With a gentle tug she led Lori into the oversize structure. It seemed to be divided into stations. A man selling potted plants stood in the first section. Next was another makeshift kitchen area with benches and tables near it. Cara guessed lunch would be sold there later.

A huge wagon full of miscellaneous stuff sat in the middle of the building with people surrounding it. Two men dressed exactly like Simeon and his brother—navy blue pants; a solid-color, collared shirt; suspenders; and a straw hat—stood on the wagon. The auctioneer bent down and grabbed something beside him. "Who'll bid on this?" Frowning, he held up an old cardboard box of items. "What is this, anyway?"

Those around the wagon tittered with laughter. The auctioneer's helper shrugged, took it from him, and passed him a large hand-painted watering pot. "Ah, something I can sell. It's Mother's Day tomorrow. This would go great with some of the potted plants being sold in station one."

Lori's eyes grew wide. "It's Mother's Day tomorrow?"

Cara nodded.

Lori's eyes filled with tears. "But…but I was making something for you at school."

She knelt beside her daughter. "I have you. If all mothers had a daughter like you, there wouldn't be a need for such a thing as Mother's Day."

The hurt in Lori's eyes faded. "Really?"

Cara swiped her finger over her heart, making a crisscross. "I promise."

"I painted you a picture."

"I bet it's so gorgeous it'd brighten up the saddest mom's heart. I think the teacher will give it to Sherry's mom. If anybody deserves a gift because their kid isn't one, it'd be her." Cara didn't know the woman, but she'd seen how her daughter behaved at school and sassed the teacher over every little thing.

Lori smiled and wrapped her arms around her neck and held on. Cara lifted her as she snuggled against her shoulder.

"Mom, I want to go home."

"I know, kiddo." Cara walked past the crowds to the back of the building. Rows of various types of lawn chairs were lined up facing a wall of racks filled with quilts. A table near the racks had a sign that read "Quilt Sale Starts at Noon."

She moved to an empty chair and rocked her daughter. There'd been too many quick changes this week, along with too much walking and too little food. She stroked her daughter's wavy hair, soothing her until she completely relaxed. Lori's back rested against Cara's chest, and she quietly watched people.

The rain fell harder, but under the roof of the building, the auctioneers kept calling for bids. No one seemed to notice Cara. Amish women with clipboards and pens looked at tags on the quilts and made notes. They moved a few quilts from one area to another, speaking in a language Cara didn't understand. She closed her eyes and dozed, odd images floating in and out of her mind. A kitchen table spread with fresh food. A warm embrace from a woman her mother called Levina. Two trees side by side. She climbed one, and some boy climbed the other. He called to her as she straddled a thick branch as if it were a horse and pretended to ride far, far away.

Her mother's laughter filled her. *"Levina, ich bin kumme…"*

Cara jerked awake. An Amish woman stood near her, speaking to another Amish woman. The language… Wasn't it the same her mother had spoken to…to… What was the woman's name, the one she'd just dreamed of?

She couldn't remember, but she needed to know some things about her childhood. It shouldn't matter—not at twenty-eight years old. But it did. And she didn't intend to leave Dry Lake until she had some explanations. When she worked out a few things and was able to answer where she and her daughter lived, if anyone asked her, she'd begin searching for information.

Simeon's brother stood near the front of the room. Thankfully he hadn't spotted her. The desire to leave nudged her, but outside the rain poured. She and Lori would be soaked by the time they returned to the barn or found fresh shelter. Then they'd be stuck in wet clothes all through the day and night.

An auctioneer moved to the desk near the quilts. "We're waiting on the runners to get back with fresh pages, and then we'll begin."

She decided it'd be best to let Lori remain on her lap and hope Simeon's brother didn't notice her. Even if he did, it was a community auction. She had as much right to be here as any other non-Amish person.

The aroma of grilled chicken filled the air. Her stomach rumbled. She'd never seen so much home-cooked food in one place. She searched through Lori's backpack and came up with a dime.

Great. Now we have forty-two cents. Not enough to buy Lori anything.

Women attached one end of a quilt to a long dowel that was connected to ropes and a pulley. Simeon's brother hoisted the quilt up high so everyone could see what they were bidding on. When that quilt sold, he lowered it and moved to the other side, where several women had another quilt attached to a second dowel and pulley.

He helped the women regardless of their age, looks, or weight, smiling as he shared a few words with each of them. He hurried from raising one quilt to the next so they never had to hoist the heavy blankets themselves. She'd never seen a man act so protective over something as nonthreatening as a little heavy work.

The selling of quilts went on for hours. Lori moved to a chair beside Cara and sang softly and flipped through a children's magazine from her backpack, wiling away time the way tired children did. The rain slowed. Cara hoped the storm would be gone before much longer.

The auctioneer told bits of history about some of the quilts, his voice coming through the battery-operated mike clipped to his shirt. "Emma Riehl began this next quilt twenty years ago."

Emma Riehl?

The man's voice turned to garbled nonsense as the name Emma Riehl echoed throughout Cara.

Suddenly she was in the bus station again, walking through the long passageways, her father holding her hand.

"Where are we going?"

"Not we, just you."

"You're gonna leave me here?"

"No. I'll stay until Emma Riehl arrives. She'll be here soon."

Lori tapped her on the arm. "Mom, I'm hungry."

Cara's thoughts didn't slow, but she came to herself to realize afresh the delicious smells that permeated every breath they took. "I know, Lorabean. But all we have left is forty-two cents. That's not enough to buy anything. I'm sorry."

When Lori nodded and wiped unspilled tears from her eyes, Cara thought her heart might break.

"I gotta go to the bathroom."

Cara eyed the Amish women, wondering if one of them was Emma. "Can you wait?"

"No."

"You sure? I just need a few more—"

"I gotta go now."

"Okay. Okay." Cara weaved through the crowd, holding Lori's hand. She looked for the nearest Porta Potti, then they stood in line, waiting.

Emma Riehl? The oddity of this coincidence combined with that man calling her by her mother's name convinced her that, whatever it took, she'd not leave this area until she had some answers.

After their turn in a rest room, they washed their hands at the portable sinks and headed back to the quilt sale.

As they passed a tent with food, Lori tugged on Cara's hand. "Mom, please. Can we buy half of something with that money?"

An Amish woman behind a register looked at them.

"I still have a bagel in the backpack."

Lori stared up at her. "I'm hungry for real food, Mom."

Cara bent over and whispered, "I told you. We don't have enough money."

Lori nodded.

"Wait," a voice called.

Cara turned to see a young Amish woman holding a plate out to her.

"Deborah?" A man called.

"Ya?" the woman answered.

"Where's the aluminum foil?"

"In the box under the register." Deborah extended the plate closer to them. "The rain is keeping our numbers for the auction a little low this year. Is there any chance you could help me out by eating some of the left-over food?"

Lori squealed. "Please, Mom? Please?"

The plate held two huge biscuits loaded with steaming scrambled eggs and sausage. "The eggs and meat are hot off the grill." She smiled, leaving Cara no doubt that she knew Lori had been asking for food.

"Thank you."

"Yes!" Lori did a little jig.

The young woman chuckled. "I think she likes the idea. Come. You can choose a drink to go with it. We have white milk, chocolate milk, orange juice—"

"Orange juice? I love orange juice!" Lori's whole face glowed.

Cara's eyes misted. "Thank you."

Deborah nodded. "Come this way." She poured Lori a glass of juice. She held a foam cup out to Cara. "Coffee?"

Cara pulled out what little change she had in her pocket and handed it to Deborah. "Yes, please." She elongated the last word, making the woman laugh.

Deborah hesitated. Then she took the money.

Cara carefully balanced the plate of food and cup of coffee. "Can you carry your drink without spilling it?"

Lori nodded, thanking the woman half a dozen times.

Cara chuckled. "Thanks again."

"No problem."

They made their way back to Cara's chair in the auction building. Unlike when they'd left, several chairs were empty now, as were the quilt racks.

"We got hot, delicious food, so this is a pretty good day, huh, Mom?"

Wishing she could promise tomorrow would also be like this, Cara nodded. "Yes, it is." But Emma Riehl's quilt had been purchased, and any chance she had to spot which Amish woman might be Emma was gone with it.

While they ate and drank, the auctioneer unfolded a letter-size piece of paper. "This is a contract from a woman who is willing to clean someone's house one day a week for three months. Who'll start the bidding?"

When there was no response, a burly man held up a business card and hollered, "I'm willing to bid for an Amish woman to clean house, cook, and help take care of my wife five days a week until she's on her feet again. Any takers?"

There was a lot of murmuring and jokes, but no one volunteered.

When the burly man stood, it was clear he wasn't Amish. "We could probably get by on someone coming only four hours a day. We'd pay forty dollars each time. Surely there's someone."

Two women behind Cara agreed the pay wasn't bad but said they couldn't find that kind of time to take on another job. She desperately wanted to raise her hand, but if she stood, the auctioneer would ask for her name and where she lived. Every employer wanted an address, and the closeness of this community meant they'd know if she lied. Just from spending the afternoon watching, she had decided that everyone here knew each other. If she could talk to this man alone, she might get away with a lie.

"Okay, I'll raise my offer. Four hours a day at fifty dollars. I'll pay in cash at the end of each workday." The man searched the room. "Come on. I'm like the rest of you, barely eking out a living, and that's good money."

No one raised a hand. Cara began to wonder if there were hidden reasons no one volunteered.

He tossed his business card on a nearby table. "If anyone changes their mind, that has my phone number and address."

Cara stared at the card, longing to snatch it up. All she needed was one break. If she could get on her feet without going outside the law, she could apply to the government for help—if she still needed it. And stop living in fear of losing Lori.

She felt someone watching her. Turning, she saw Simeon's brother staring at her. Her nerves shot pinpricks of heat through her. She'd bet he wanted to question her, and she knew without being told that he had the power to ruin her fresh start. Clearly she had to get out of here.

"Let's go." Cara slid the strap to Lori's backpack over her shoulder and gathered their trash.

"I still got half a cup of juice left. Isn't that cool?"

"Yeah, now come on." But Cara was the one who didn't budge. The man's card lay on the table, begging for her to grab it.

An image floated through her mind again.

Her father tapped the hand-drawn map. *"See where I've drawn this horse and buggy? That's where you're going. It's where your mother never should have left. It did things to her…to us."*

"I'm going to Levina's?"

Her father stared hard at her before he emptied the glass of its golden drink. *"You know about her?"*

"I met her."

He ordered another drink and then another before he stood and led her to a bench seat elsewhere in the station. *"Stay put, Cara Atwater, right here, and don't you budge. Emma will come get you."*

Cara closed her eyes, trying to ward off the pain of being abandoned. Twice. Her father had left. And Emma Riehl never showed.

"You okay, Mom?"

She opened her eyes and forced another smile. "Sure, Lorabean." When she looked up, she met Simeon's brother's eyes. Defiance welled, and she held his gaze. She wasn't leaving, not yet. The man could just choke on his stinginess over his moldy hay and half-fallen barn, but she wasn't running.

Hiding? Yes. Running? Not yet. Not until she had answers.

Simeon hurried up to him, talking and stealing his attention.

The crowds pressed in around the table where the card lay. "Stay close and keep quiet." Cara eased from her chair and melted into the crowd. She reached through the gaps between people and grabbed the card. No one seemed to feel her arms moving past theirs. "Let's go."

On her way out of the huge shop, she saw a counter where a makeshift kitchen had been set up. She paused, watching as a woman slid two hamburgers onto buns and added the fixings before she placed them in a white lunch bag and set them on the counter. Cara sidled up to the spot and snatched the bag. She slid it into the book bag without even Lori noticing what she was doing. But when she glanced up, she saw Simeon's brother on the other side of the room, watching her. Resisting the urge to make a rude gesture, she ducked out the side entrance.

Ten

Cara tossed a pebble into the water. Lori sat on the creek bank, drawing in the mud with a stick. A piece of tarp from the barn lay on the ground under her, keeping her clothes dry after yesterday's earth-soaking rain.

Homeless on Mother's Day. What a joke. Since Simeon's brother had walked into the barn yesterday, she couldn't even let Lori play with the puppies today like she wanted. From now until they found a place to live, she'd have to stay away from the barn until late at night. She'd looked for other outbuildings to sleep in, but they were too close to homes where people lived.

Year in and year out the longing to give Lori a sense of self-worth, to let her know she had someone who adored her, kept Cara trying. She'd come here wanting to find ties to her past, friends or family of her mother's, but even if she did, would it make a difference for Lori?

Maybe getting out of New York only meant a chance for a clean break and a fresh start.

She played with the card the burly man had thrown on the table—Richard Howard on Runkles Road. Even though today was Sunday, she and Lori had gone to his place earlier. Lori would have to go to work with her, so she took her to the interview. After walking through most of Dry Lake while looking for Mast Road, she easily remembered how to get to that road. Once there, the man had led her into his wife's bedroom for an interview. Ginny Howard had broken her femur and was in a hip cast. Her husband had used up all his sick leave at work to stay home with her. He was desperate for help, even if Cara wasn't Amish, and wanted her to come work for him, but Ginny felt differently. She said if Cara put on some decent clothes, she might consider hiring her. Cara figured Mr. Howard must be more anxious for her to work out than his wife knew, or he wouldn't have told her to come back tonight before bedtime if she got the right clothes.

He'd reminded her that he would pay fifty dollars in cash at the end of each workday. With a bit of luck and that money in her pocket, she might find a room to rent in someone's home within a few days. Although she'd only be paid for four hours, she told him that if he hired her, she'd stay until he returned home from work each day. He was excited about that idea, but she hadn't offered out of the kindness of her heart. She knew it'd be easier to work at his home all day than to get off near lunchtime and try to stay out of sight until it was safe to return to the barn.

On her way back from the Howards, Cara had scoped out some "decent" clothes hanging to dry in Simeon's yard. She'd seen that woman who had given them food during the auction hanging the clothes on the line, and Cara would rather not take anything from her. If she snatched a few things and returned them later, would that be stealing? She'd have to wait until after dark.

Something in her ached to understand the connection between her mother and Emma Riehl. If this Emma was the same Emma who'd failed to come for her, why did she leave her at a bus station? What kind of person did that?

The longing to know was as deep and controlling as the desire to talk to her mom had been during those lonely nights in foster care.

As dusk settled over the place, she knew it was time to carry out her plan. "Come on, Lorabean."

Lori stood, dusting off the backside of her dress. "If we had a fishing pole, I could catch us a fish, and we could cook it."

Cara tucked the last bagel into the backpack. Like the two previous ones, it'd have to be soaked in water before being eaten, or they'd break a tooth. But those hamburgers she'd taken from the auction were delicious. She would have saved hers for Lori to eat today, but she was afraid it might spoil and make her daughter sick. "Do you really think so?"

"Yep."

"Then I'll have to get us a fishing pole." She held out her hand for Lori, and they began following the creek bed. Going this way would keep them out of sight until dark. Then they could use the road. "So, what are we going to cook your catch in?"

"Maybe one of those grills the men in hats were cooking chicken on yesterday."

Cara chuckled. "Those things must've held a hundred pounds of chicken."

"Then I'll have to catch a hundred pounds of fish."

"I like the way you think, kiddo."

"Mom? What are we gonna do now?"

"Borrow a few things, I think." Leading Lori across the back field, she spotted Simeon's brother's house. She studied the dark, quiet place. After she snatched a dress, she'd get a few things from his house.

Disappointed in how much time it'd taken them to get here, she hoped the single line of laundry hadn't been taken inside for the day. She continued on. Past the privacy bushes and trees, she saw Simeon's house and the workshop. Gauging distance like she did in New York, she guessed the houses sat about two north-south city blocks apart—about five hundred feet. Inside New York thousands of people would live between these two houses, yet here no other houses were in sight.

Near a tree grove a rock jutted from the ground. She led Lori in that direction. "I need you to stay on this rock until I get back, okay?"

"I guess so."

"There's no guessing. You wait right here, and don't budge until I come back for you."

"Okay."

"Promise?"

As she placed her daughter on the rock, Lori crossed her heart with her finger.

Cara eased around the perimeter of the property until she could see the clothesline. The same outfits still hung on the line. It seemed none had been added or removed. She focused on the row of dresses, two of which looked like they might fit. She moved across the yard slowly, hiding in the shadows and noticing everything she could. A child's red wagon lay in the gutter near the street. A reel mower sat under a nearby tree. The house buzzed with the voices of what had to be dozens of people. The driveway had six buggies, all attached to horses. She suspected busyness worked better for thievery. When people were distracted, they often didn't see right where they looked.

She snatched a dress and moved back into the shadows. No one seemed to notice.

Her next plan made her more nervous. Simeon had said that his brother lived alone and that he'd be at his Daed's house tonight. Simeon had also said this place was never locked. As long as Simeon's brother didn't return unexpectedly, she should be home free.

After snaking her way across the field and through his privacy bushes, she stood on the man's porch. The front door was open, leaving only the screen door. She tiptoed inside, looking for the refrigerator. It took just a few seconds to spot it.

When she opened it, she couldn't believe her eyes. The thing was absolutely packed with food. She grabbed the first container she could, set it on the counter, and opened the lid just to make sure it wasn't filled with raw meat. The aroma of grilled chicken filled her nostrils. Perfect. She took a can of soda and a few napkins. Stuffing them inside the dress, she scanned the dark room—a bathroom, a living room, and a bedroom. Once inside the bedroom, she looked through a chest of drawers and discovered several flashlights. She took one and went to the closet. At the bottom of a stack of quilts, she grabbed what looked like an old store-bought blanket.

"Hey, Ephraim," a man yelled, startling her. "You're not leaving for the night, are you?"

With her arms full, she hurried out the back door. Two men stood in the middle of the field between the two houses, talking. She scurried back to the rock, thrilled at the treasures in her arms, her heart pounding with adrenaline.

"Hey, Lorabean, guess what I have?" She held up the clear container.

"Food." She clapped her hands.

Cara opened it. "All the grilled chicken a girl can eat. We need to walk and eat at the same time, though, or it'll get too late for me to go on that interview." Cara pulled the dress on over her head and peeled out of her jeans. "I saw a little red wagon in a ditch. I'll spread this blanket in the bottom of it, and you can ride while you eat. Deal?"

"We're gonna steal?"

"No, honey. We'll bring it back before anyone even knows we borrowed it."

Lori licked her fingers. "This is delicious. Want some?"

"Just a bite." Her stomach ached with hunger, and she could've eaten the whole container by herself, but she'd settle for the bit of meat on a chicken wing. "You can have four legs, but after that, we'll seal the container tight and anchor it in the creek. That'll keep the rest cool enough so it won't spoil." She tucked her jeans in the backpack. "Come on."

With Monday's workday behind him, Ephraim set up his telescope in the hiddy. He tried to focus on the stars glistening in the dark sky, but frustration at that girl's brazenness to walk into his house last night and steal from him had his attention much more than the heavens. She fit his

Daed's description of the drunken thief he'd seen—the one his Daed had warned the community to watch out for. Ephraim had yet to figure out what she'd stolen from him. But he'd seen her arms filled with something.

Mars had come into view high in the western sky. Around midnight it'd set in the northwest. Since he wasn't taking an eye off his home tonight, he'd probably be here for that too, if he could concentrate long enough to see it.

Because he'd witnessed her leaving his house with an armload of things last night, he'd gone to the barn half a dozen times today, thinking she might be there. He'd ridden through various parts of Dry Lake, but he'd not seen her. He would have a few choice words for her when she did show up. And she would. Thieves returned to easy prey, and he knew his place must look like easy prey.

If his uncle hadn't called to him while coming across the field that separated his place from his Daed's, he would have confronted her right then. But he didn't want any disturbing news getting back to his Daed and Becca.

A faint sound drifted through the air, and he eased to the entryway of the hiddy. He saw nothing, so he started walking around the property, searching the place. Near the edge of the cornfield closest to his home, he saw what appeared to be a little girl sitting on a rock. The thief had to be here somewhere too. Realizing her target might be his father's house, he hurried through the trees and across the field. He saw her at the clothesline, but she had on a dress this time. An Amish one.

He eased up behind her and cleared his throat. Without hesitation she took off running. "Stop." He tore after her and grabbed her arm.

She yanked, trying to free herself. He twisted her arm behind her. "I'm not going to hurt you."

"Don't bank on me promising you the same." She ground out the words as she lowered her body, taking him with her, and then threw back her head, smacking him in the mouth.

"Ow!" He dug his fingers into both her arms and pinned them, wrestling her to the ground. Blood dripped from his lip onto her back. "I'm trying to be easy. Would you just stop?"

She squirmed, cursing at him and trying to throw him off. "Let me go!"

"When you calm down, then we'll negotiate."

For her size her strength astounded him. Her salty language—exactly what he expected from a thief.

Ephraim's mouth ached all the way across his face. "Either you stop fighting and talk to me, or I'll call the police, and you can talk to them."

To his shock she became perfectly still. He released one arm and held on to the other as he stood, helping her stand with him. She was probably five foot three and couldn't weigh much over a hundred pounds. "You've been stealing from us."

"I suppose that was your dress I took?"

"Cute. But it wasn't yours."

"I didn't steal it."

He wiped blood from his mouth. "It wasn't yours, and you took it. Is there a new definition for the word *steal* that I'm not familiar with?"

"I brought money back."

"Sure you did."

"You can argue with me about it or go look for yourself. It's on the clothesline."

Still holding on to her arm, he walked to the spot. A ten-dollar bill hung from the line, pinned securely.

Moonlight shone across her face, revealing her beauty. He saw something else too—the confidence of a woman, and suddenly she didn't look as young to him. With her size and defiant stance and the jeans and a shirt that showed her stomach, he'd assumed she was a teen. But the way she held her own, staring at him with a certain assurance, he truly looked at her for the first time. "So giving money after taking things that weren't for sale is okay?"

"Lofty words coming from someone whose mommy and daddy gave him everything he needed his whole life."

"And what else has your little sister seen you steal?"

She stilled, but she didn't answer him.

"Speak up. What else did you take?"

She studied him, looking rather awed by his question. "You've got so much you don't even know what's missing?"

Somehow he was losing this argument. How was that possible? "Tell me what you took."

"Just some food and a blanket."

"You planning on paying me back too?"

She didn't respond, but he knew the answer. So why did she return to leave money only for Deborah?

"Where do your folks…do you live?"

She opened her mouth but then seemed to change her mind.

"Well?"

"I won't borrow anything else, and I'll never set foot on this place again. I promise. Just let me go."

He figured that answer was the best he'd get from her. Whatever was going on, he didn't have it in him to call the police. After all, she had brought money to replace the missing dress and taken items from him he'd never miss.

He released her. "Go."

She paused, staring at him as if he'd done something she didn't expect. Then she took off running.

Ephraim turned to look at his Daed's house. The dim shine of kerosene lamps barely left a glow on the lawn. Daed and Becca would be home tomorrow, and he intended to keep things calm around here.

She stole food and a blanket? He tumbled that thought around.

Was it possible this young woman and her sister were using Levina's, or rather *his,* barn as a hangout…or maybe even as a place to sleep?

Wondering if his brother knew either of the girls' names, he headed for the house. Once inside he went to the sink, grabbed a clean rag, and ran cool water over it. Placing it on his bleeding lip, he sighed. Why did

she have to show up now? Her presence would only make it more difficult to keep things peaceful and quiet for his Daed.

She knew how to hit a bull's-eye when arguing. But that didn't make her right. Stealing was stealing. Ephraim went into the living room. Annie and Simeon were in the middle of a game of checkers.

"Simeon, do you know the names of those girls you said were in the barn looking at the puppies?"

"The girl's name is Lori. I don't know the mom's."

"The mom's?" Ephraim plunked into a chair. So his second opinion of her was right. She wasn't a defiant teen. "The older one is her mother?"

"Yep. Nice too. Although she's pretty good at hiding from you."

"Hiding where?"

"In the silo."

"Are they living in the barn?"

He shrugged. "Didn't ask. But ain't no one gonna bother those pups with Lori and her mom there."

Ephraim ran his finger over his swollen lip. *"That,* I believe."

"Lori wants the solid black male if her mama will let her keep it. Her mom's really nice. When I complained about Mamm treating me like a baby, she said I should be glad I got people who keep me on a short leash, and if I want to live a long, happy life, I better listen to them."

He really didn't want to hear about any of the thief's alleged qualities. "When did you talk about all this?"

"The first time I saw her."

"When was that?"

"Saturday morning."

His head hurt, making concentrating hard. Maybe she was new to the area. Then why did she look so familiar?

None of her actions made sense. She'd stolen the dress last night, and tonight she'd hung money on the clothesline to pay for it. Why would she need a dress yesterday and then have money for it tonight? Had she stolen the cash from somewhere? That didn't make sense. No one used stolen money to pay for something they'd gotten away with stealing in the first place.

Deciding to pay another visit to the barn, he stood.

As he walked toward the barn, he noticed that his cornfield had been damaged by someone walking right over the sprouts. Before crossing Levina's driveway, he saw a thin beam of light. If he went into the barn right now, the woman would make excuses, lie, and disappear. He'd be better off making himself comfortable somewhere and watching. To his left, near the cornfield, lay a fallen tree. He took a seat and waited. A few minutes later someone turned off the flashlight.

Had they slipped out the back or gone to sleep? He kept watch. About thirty minutes later the woman came out of the barn, wearing her jeans and too-tight top. She leaned against the side of the building for a while, looking rather peaceful under the moonlight. Barefoot, she crossed the road and went to the tree. As she ran her hands across the bark of it, Ephraim felt chills cover him.

It couldn't be.

He leaned forward, watching as she climbed onto the lowest branch, caressed the dip in it, and then rocked back against the trunk. Was it possible?

She ran her fingers through her short crop of hair and then down the side of her neck.

"Cara," he whispered. Part of him wanted to yell her name and run over to see her. It was a foolish thought born from a childhood experience.

Cara Atwater.

Twenty years ago they'd spent the better part of a week building a friendship unlike any other he'd ever had. Her tomboy ways had made her more fun than most of the boys his age. Her eagerness to try everything, mixed with her excitement about life, had been permanently etched into his memory.

When he'd left Dry Lake during his *rumschpringe*—his time to decide whether to become Amish or not—he'd gone to New York, hoping to find her. He'd lived and worked there for two years. He called the number for every Trevor Atwater, her father's name, in the book. He watched for her in every park, restaurant, and store. Finally he gave up and moved to South Carolina.

It might have been fun to reconnect with her back then, but now she'd become her mother's child—returning with a daughter and obviously with a past that could bring nothing but heartache to Dry Lake.

Malinda had caused a lot of division in the community. He couldn't give Cara that same opportunity. Malinda left a legacy of grief—twice. Even Levina, Malinda's grandmother, died waiting to hear from her again. Now Cara had returned to what had once been her great-grandmother's place. Unsure what to think or feel, he watched her. What a mess her life must be in. No car, no house, no husband, no money.

He'd been so sure her mother was turning her life around when she'd left here twenty years ago. She had an Englischer husband, so the community couldn't make a way for her to leave him by giving her a place to live. Because she was desperate for a safe place for Cara, the community was willing to take in Cara. But Malinda had left here with her and never returned.

The young woman in the tree drew a deep breath and folded her arms, looking as peaceful as she was beautiful. But looks were deceiving. Peacefulness did not describe her, and her beauty masked the troubled waters just below the surface.

In spite of longing to talk with her, he wouldn't go to her. The community, especially his father, had to be protected. First thing tomorrow he'd go into Shippensburg and buy her a bus ticket. Then he'd fix her a box of things that would make life a little easier on her and her daughter.

Eleven

As dawn eased the night away, Deborah stood in the laundry room, threading freshly rinsed dresses through the wringer before dropping them into the clean laundry basket.

A driver would arrive for her soon, and she had a lot of clothes to hang out before then. She usually did most of the wash on Mondays, but there had been so much work left over from Saturday's auction, she hadn't managed to get to it yesterday. Late Saturday afternoon she'd washed the clothes she and her family had worn during the auction to keep the mud from staining them. She'd meant to remove the items a few hours later, but she'd forgotten. So that'd caused her to do something she'd never done before—leave laundry on the line on a Sunday. It wasn't acceptable to have the appearance of having done laundry on a Sunday. Early Monday morning realization of what she'd done smacked her, and she hurried out to remove them, but her newly sewn teal dress was missing.

One of her friends was certainly playing a trick on her. When she found out who had masterminded this, that person had better watch her back, because paybacks were…fun. She'd begin by watching which of her friends blushed and who giggled the most the next time she saw them. That was a sure giveaway. Then she'd come up with a plan and get the rest of the girls to help her.

After wringing out the last item, she tossed it in the basket. Carrying the clean, wet load, she went through the kitchen on her way to the front door. One glimpse of the room made her stop. Kitchen drawers were open, and utensils were strewn across the countertops. Obviously while she'd been in the laundry room with the wringer washer running, someone had come in search of something. As she headed for the clothesline, she saw Ephraim loading a crate into his buggy. Without seeing her, he climbed in and left.

She grabbed a shirt and shook it. He must be trying to get a head start on the day too. She wondered what he'd been looking for in the kitchen. It had to be him. Almost everyone else in the household was still asleep.

Her stepmother's sister had arrived last night to help take care of the younger ones so Deborah could go to the hospital this morning. As she reached for a clothespin, she stopped cold. A ten-dollar bill dangled from the line. She laughed at the silliness of it before shoving the cash into her pocket. Money didn't grow on trees, but it appeared to grow on clotheslines. Whichever friend had come up with this prank had planned rounds for it—one day taking the item, the next day leaving money for it. Maybe she should *borrow* ten dresses from the instigator and leave one dollar.

Sunlight warmed her back, making the day feel as if it might be a good one. While she hung a pair of pants on the line, a horse and carriage pulled into her driveway. She'd hoped Mahlon would arrive for his workday in the cabinetry shop before her driver came to get her, but Ada was driving the rig. She stopped the buggy near Deborah, studying her but saying nothing.

Deborah dropped a pair of wet pants into the basket and walked closer to Ada. "Gut morning. What brings you out this early?"

"I thought maybe I left my roasting pan here on Saturday."

"I don't remember seeing it. You know that every year I have a box of lost-and-found items people have left at the auction. But the last time I added something to it, there weren't any pots or pans. We can go look, though."

She shook her head. "If you haven't seen it, I'm sure it's in one of the boxes of stuff I took home Saturday." Studying the barn and pastures, she seemed to be searching for something. "I guess while I'm here, I'll stop in at the shop and speak with Mahlon."

"Mahlon?" Deborah's heart jolted.

Ada wasn't looking for missing pans. She wanted to find her son, which meant he'd been out all night again, and this time she'd realized it. But Deborah hadn't seen him since yesterday when he came by the house after work. If he were already at the shop, his buggy would be parked along the fence nearest her house, and his horse would be grazing in the closest pasture.

She looked but saw no sign of either. "I saw Ephraim leaving a little while ago. Maybe they're meeting at a job site." Or maybe Mahlon had been out with Eric again.

"Oh, ya, you're probably right."

She hoped she was. She hated the concern on Ada's face. If Mahlon was going off with Eric behind Ada's back, Deborah would be tempted to tell him his mother deserved more respect than that. But Mahlon would say he wasn't a kid and he footed most of the bills. She hoped Mahlon didn't put her in this kind of spot once they married. She considered Ada a friend and hated not sharing what she knew to be true.

Mahlon was the kind of man who needed time and space to work through the things that bothered him. Deborah worked through her issues with the help of her friends and church fellowship. Over the years they each had allowed for what the other one needed. When he was ready, he'd tell her everything.

Her driver pulled into the driveway, and she didn't have the laundry hung out yet. Ada wrapped the reins around the bar on the dashboard of her carriage. "I'll finish that for you. Is there more to be washed?"

"Ya, but you don't have to—"

"I know. But I'm here, and you need to go, so shoo."

"Denki, Ada."

"Gern gschehne. Now go."

Deborah gave her a quick hug and climbed into the passenger seat. Unrest concerning Mahlon rode with her for the hourlong drive to the hospital, and she silently prayed for him.

Three hours later and with Becca's errands behind them, she was in the car on her way home with her Daed and Becca. Distant rain clouds moved across the sky, and she hoped someone had taken the laundry inside.

From the front passenger seat, Daed watched the scenery, making occasional remarks to the driver. He looked surprisingly well, and except for admitting to being very tired, he said he felt fine.

As they came closer to Levina's old barn, Daed pointed. "What's that box?"

Deborah peered through the front window, unable to spot it.

Daed tapped the glass. "Pull over and let me take a look."

She saw the wooden box with a piece of a blue tarp covering the top sitting outside the barn door. It looked like the one Ephraim had this morning.

Daed climbed out of the car, lifted the tarp, pulled a folded paper out of the side of the crate, read it, and returned it to the box. He replaced the covering and got back in the vehicle.

"What were you reading, Abner?" Becca asked.

He shrugged. "A note written by whoever left the box. Looked like Ephraim's handwriting."

Becca frowned. "Well, who was the note to?"

"It didn't say. Just boiled down to instructions to keep what they'd taken but telling them they couldn't live in his barn and they needed to leave Dry Lake."

Twelve

Cara pulled Lori in the wagon her employers had loaned her. Scattered drops of rain caused her to head straight for the barn. Without a change of clothes for Lori, she wouldn't chance that the cloud would pass on by. Her muscles ached from her second day of deep cleaning the Howards' house. It was only Tuesday, and after leaving money on the line for the dress, she had ninety dollars in cash. It made her dream of having the comforts of her own place, one with books to read to Lori and beds with sheets and a pillow and a refrigerator with food and—

"Look, Mom, someone left us something."

Cara blinked, snapping out of her daydream. A hundred feet ahead, right at the barn door, sat a box. An uncomfortable feeling stole through her.

While on her lunch break today, she'd called half a dozen places, looking to rent something. The cost of living here didn't compare to the expense of New York, but it was still several hundred dollars. It would take two weeks of working for the Howards to earn that.

She didn't dare hint to them that she had no place to live. They seemed like nice enough people, but that didn't make them trustworthy. Still, they let Lori play in their backyard and didn't begrudge Cara fixing herself and Lori a little to eat when she prepared meals for Mrs. Howard. While Mrs. Howard slept, Cara showered and washed her and Lori's clothes. Hot water, soap, and shampoo had never felt so good.

She went to the crate and lifted the plastic covering. At a glance she saw blankets, cans of food, and a can opener. Someone had figured out they were staying here, which meant they had to get out. Quick.

A note caught her attention. While Lori knelt beside the box, looking through the stuff, Cara read the note.

Whoever had written it had instructed her to leave Dry Lake and pick up two bus tickets that were already paid for. Destination: New York City.

Alarm pricked her skin. Someone knew they were from New York?

"Look, Mom, a cloth doll. She doesn't have a face. You ever seen a doll without eyes?"

"No, but I've seen men without hearts."

She laughed. "You what?"

"Never mind. Look, sweetie, we can't stay here. Whoever left this box of stuff said we have to move on."

"Why? We didn't hurt the puppies or break nothing."

"I know. But we have to go anyway."

"But my puppy!"

"Go tell him good-bye."

"No. He's mine! Simeon said I could have him."

"Lori, we don't even have enough food for us." She bit her tongue to keep from cursing.

Lori ran into the barn, crying.

She followed. "We don't have a choice, honey."

"Why? It's a stupid old barn, and we're not hurting nothing!"

Cara sat down next to her daughter and waited. When the tantrum eased up, Cara would tell her again that they had to go, and then they'd leave without hysterics. The one thing that had made all this bearable for Lori was the puppy she'd claimed as hers, and now...

The barn door creaked open, startling her. A police officer stepped inside. Her knees went weak.

"Ma'am, can you come out of the barn?"

She swallowed her fear and headed for the barn door.

"You, too, little girl."

Panic rose in Cara. "Is there a problem, Officer?"

"Just follow me, please."

Two police cars sat waiting outside. A female officer motioned to Lori. "Can I talk with you, honey?"

Cara's breathing came in short, quick spurts. The rain clouds skirted eastward, and she wished the threat of them hadn't caused her to carelessly hurry to the barn. If only she'd waited...

"You're on private property, ma'am." The man stood in front of her while the woman talked to Lori a few feet away.

"There are puppies in the barn, and my daughter's picked one out."

The woman kept trying to engage Lori in a conversation, and her daughter answered a few questions, but mostly her attention seemed fully on her mother.

"The owner asked you to leave, both verbally and in a written note."

"Yes, but...there's been a misunderstanding. I work not far from here."

"It's our understanding that you've been stealing from the residents around here."

"My mom doesn't steal!" Lori screamed at the man.

No matter what answer Cara gave him, he'd check it out, so lying would only add to her problems. "I did take a few things." She spoke softly, hoping Lori wouldn't hear.

"Where do you live, ma'am?"

Tears filled her eyes. It was over. They'd take Lori. "Please, you don't understand."

"Just stay calm, ma'am. Do you have an address?"

Tears threatened as she shook her head.

"Several homes in the area have been broken into lately." He pointed to her dress. "Amish clothing and quilts are among the missing items."

Cara looked at Lori. Her little girl deserved better than a mom who failed her all the time.

The man took a step back, and the woman moved forward and frisked her while he looked through her backpack. He pulled out the cash that Mr. Howard had paid for her work yesterday and today—nearly a hundred dollars.

He held it up. "All tens, just like the missing cash on the report."

"But I…I earned that. You have to believe me."

"You've entered people's unlocked homes and taken items."

"I said that already, but I didn't steal that money."

The man pulled handcuffs from his belt. "You've been breaking and entering as well as stealing. Before we go any further, I need to tell you that you have the right to remain silent…" The officer rattled off things Cara had heard on television a hundred times.

She tried to think of something that might get her out of this mess. "You can have the money. Please don't do this, please."

The woman placed her hand on Lori's head. "Unless you have a relative or someone who can keep your daughter, she'll have to be placed in protective custody."

Broken, she looked at her daughter. "I'm sorry, baby. I'm so, so sorry."

Lori tried to run to her, but the woman held her.

"Please turn around and place your hands on your head," the man said.

"Leave my mom alone!" Lori screamed and flailed against the woman's hold, but she didn't release her. In a minute Lori would be taken in one car and Cara in the other.

All her years of holding on in the face of hopelessness drained from her. "Lori, honey, listen to me, okay?" Trying to keep from crying, she blinked. "This feels scary, I know, but they'll take good care of you. You'll be okay, and I'll come for you soon. I promise."

"No!" Lori screamed. "Don't let them take me!"

When Ephraim topped the hill, he spotted two police cars in front of his barn. He slapped the reins hard against the horse's back, spurring her to quicken the pace.

As he pulled to a stop, he saw a policeman holding Cara by the arm—or at least the woman he believed to be Cara. Handcuffs held Cara's arms behind her back as her small body shook with sobs. The officer opened the door to the backseat of the patrol car.

"Don't take my mom!" The little girl kept screaming the same thing over and over as a woman officer held on to her arm.

"Lori, you have to calm down," the woman spoke firmly. Lori kicked at her, but the officer avoided being hit.

Ephraim jumped down from the carriage. "What's going on here?"

The male officer turned to him. "Are this barn and land your property?"

"Ya."

Lori couldn't catch a solid breath, but her wails were haunting.

"Then you're the one who called the police about a thief and trespasser?"

"No. Just let her go."

"We can't do that, sir. We need to investigate her for suspicion of child endangerment and neglect."

Cara turned to him. "Please…" Tears brimmed. "Please help us."

What a mess. If he did any more for her than just speak to the police, it was sure to open old wounds. People didn't trust Malinda when she last visited, and they'd be angry that he'd stepped in to help Malinda's daughter—someone they might have heard had been roaming the community, drunk and stealing from them.

She gazed into his eyes, silently pleading for him to help. He moved closer to her, wanting to ask so many questions. As he looked into her eyes, a moment passed between them. He knew she was not who she appeared to be—a worldly, troublemaking thief. He looked at the policeman. "This is all a mistake. The police never should have been called." A flicker of recognition came to him. "You're Roy McEver, right?"

The man nodded.

"Your father used to patrol this area before he retired. You rode with him some even as a kid. I'm Ephraim Mast. My Daed's Abner."

"Oh yeah, he's one of the preachers. And I remember you. While I was here with Dad one time, you invited me to play ball."

He'd taken quite a harassing from the other guys for inviting an Englischer to play. Ephraim nodded, feeling like he might get Cara out of this fix yet. "She's not done anything to deserve handcuffs."

"She confessed to stealing."

Her honesty needed better timing.

Cara shook her head. "Only that dress, which I paid for, and a few items I borrowed from you. I swear it. Anything else that's missing—especially money—wasn't taken by me. You've got to believe me."

"Nothing was taken that I wasn't glad to give," he assured the officer.

"She had cash on her. Nearly a hundred dollars. In tens."

"I work for Mr. Howard, on Runkles Road. Ask him."

"You could check her story out and let her go, right?" Ephraim asked. "I think you'll find that someone else must have stolen whatever money or other stuff is missing from elsewhere."

The man sighed. "It's not that simple. I could let her go, but the girl has to come with us. This woman is homeless. We have to file a report and turn the case over to social services."

A sinking feeling of just how deeply Ephraim was getting involved nagged at him. He couldn't ask anyone in Dry Lake to let a stranger he couldn't vouch for stay in their home. If he told them he needed their help to keep her from being arrested, they'd never take her in. Still…he couldn't ignore her need for help—not and live with himself.

"She can stay at my place until she gets on her feet."

"Are you saying you'll take responsibility for the child's care?"

Ephraim nodded.

Roy hesitated, but then he unlocked the cuffs and released Cara. "Ephraim, I'll need your information. What's your address?"

Lori pulled free from the policewoman's grip and ran to her mother. She jumped into her arms. While Ephraim told Roy what he needed to know, Lori sobbed, clinging to her mother.

"Shh. It's okay, Lorabean. Everything's going to be okay." Cara held her tight, looking pale and shaken while stroking her daughter's hair.

But Ephraim knew everything wasn't going to be okay. What would his father's reaction be? He could only assume he was the one who called the police. His Daed wanted this drunken thief, as he called her, away from their community.

Thirteen

As the police cars pulled away, stress and strength drained from Cara. But even before she took in a breath of relief, suspicion about the man's reasons for helping crashed in on her. Sure, she'd begged him, but why was he really doing this?

She'd split his lip last night, the evidence of it still clear on his face. Did he intend to pay her back? Whatever his motives, she couldn't afford to defy the police. That would be a mistake Lori would have to pay for. Weighing her options, she tried to stop trembling.

He turned to face her. "You got things inside?"

His things, actually, and if he wanted them back so badly, she'd give them to him. She nodded, wondering if her legs would actually carry her. With Lori's arms wrapped firmly around her neck, she walked inside and jerked on the door to the silo. It didn't open. She tried to set Lori down, but her little girl started screaming, clearly afraid to be released.

Cara held her close, stroking her hair. "Shh. We're fine now."

He stepped forward, opened the silo door without any trouble, and grabbed a flashlight, an empty food container, and a blanket. "This it?"

He made no remark about it being his stuff. Everything they owned, including her change of clothes, was stuffed inside the backpack the policeman had left near the barn door. "And the little wagon that's outside with the backpack." Her words came out barely audible.

He motioned to the door. She went to the buggy, awkwardly climbing the high step with Lori in her arms. He placed the items in back, including the box of blankets and food, and then he went to the other side and got in. One slap of the reins against the horse's back, and they were off.

She'd been in this spot before, needing serious help from a man, only that was long before Lori. Anger churned. She'd been running from Mike then too. If she hadn't been in a similar predicament—desperate for help—there would have been no marriage and no Lori.

Feeling too many things at once, Cara rode quietly. Lori's breathing caught and jerked uncontrollably every few seconds. Her tiny hands clung desperately to her mother.

When they came to the street the man lived on, he kept going. She glanced at him, wanting to know his plan, but she kept her mouth shut. He had too much power for her to question him, to chance getting into an argument.

A few minutes later he pulled into a narrow lane. Unease wrapped around her throat. The path seemed to go on forever, with pastures on both sides and no other homes nearby. When his house came into sight, she realized that he'd brought her in a back way.

He pulled into a small barn. After he jumped down, he came around to her side. If climbing in while holding Lori had been difficult, getting out was worse.

"Can I help you?"

Lori clung to her tighter, locking her feet around her.

"No, thank you."

He backed away. Cara struggled to get out without falling as she toted Lori. Then she waited. Silently he unfastened the horse, hung the leather straps on a peg, opened a gate at the back of the building, and put the horse out to pasture.

"Let's go in and get you settled." He led the way to the door and opened it for them.

Still carrying Lori, Cara stepped into his home. The beige walls of the kitchen stood bleak and empty except for a lone clock. A small oak kitchen table looked sturdy and expensive, yet something about it made it seem hundreds of years old. Stacks of thick books sat here and there. Late-afternoon rays stretched across the wooden floors.

Weak and shaky, Cara pried Lori free of her and set her feet on the floor.

The man removed his straw hat and walked toward them. Lori screamed. Cara moved in front of her daughter, shielding her from the unknown.

He leaned in and hung his hat on a peg. "I was just putting my hat up."

Feeling embarrassed and just as skittish as her daughter, Cara took a step back.

Bewilderment played across his face. "I won't hurt you. Surely you know that."

Cara didn't know that, and she kept Lori behind her.

Looking uncomfortable in his own home, he stepped away from them. "Are you hungry?"

Cara shook her head. "You wrote the note telling us to leave?"

"Ya."

"That means yes?"

He nodded.

"You bought us bus tickets to New York City. Why there?"

"Isn't that your home?"

Her heart turned a flip. "Why would you say that?"

He stared at her as if asking a hundred questions. "My name's Ephraim."

"Yeah, I heard you tell the policeman." She shifted Lori. "I'm Cara. This is my daughter, Lori."

He tilted his head, his eyes narrowing for a moment. "There's plenty of food in the refrigerator. Clean sheets and towels are in the bathroom closet." He grabbed a set of matches off the counter. "When the sun goes down, you can light a kerosene lamp if you wish. Since you've been staying in a barn, I guess the lack of electricity won't bother you much. I'd like us to talk, but that can wait until Lori is asleep. Or tomorrow if you're too tired. In the meantime if you and your daughter can stay out of sight, I'd appreciate it."

"Sure, I guess so."

"I just don't need my family to know about you, not yet."

She wondered who he was trying to kid. Himself maybe. He wouldn't want *anyone* to know she was there. She'd read it in his eyes as the police left. She was trash, and he was an upstanding member of his community.

He drew a deep breath, looking unsure. Not at all like a heartless man. "Lori, do you like books? I've got a few children's books in the storage room."

Lori looked at her mom before nodding.

He disappeared into a room and returned within a minute carrying a small stack of books. "They're quite worn but still just as good as the first time they were read. Books are funny that way."

Lori eyed the stack and eased closer to him until he could place them in her hands.

"Thanks," she whispered.

"You're welcome. Well, I guess that about covers it. I'll sleep in the shop." He started toward his hat but then headed for the door instead.

Lori flew toward the door and spread her arms out. "Don't leave us!"

Looking baffled, he stared at the little girl. "You're safe here." He glanced to Cara as if it was his turn to beg for help. "She's both afraid of me *and* afraid of me leaving?"

Cara shrugged, unwilling to try to voice all that her daughter must be feeling. Besides, it should be obvious that her emotions were irrational right now.

He eased into a chair, rubbing his forehead. "I can't stay. I could be excommunicated."

"What?" Cara asked.

He shook his head. "Nothing. I shouldn't have said my thoughts out loud."

Lori moved to her mother's side. "Please, mister. Those policemen could come again."

Cara knew it wouldn't do either of them any good to try to explain why the police wouldn't return, not to a panicked kid and not when social services would show up again soon.

He sighed. "Okay. I won't go anywhere for now. Maybe Lori won't feel so strongly about me leaving after she has time to calm down, because I have some chores I need to do a little later. But for now I'll just be in the storage room. It's right there." He pointed to a door.

Clinging to Cara's dress, Lori nodded. Ephraim left the room and shut the door. Cara melted onto the floor and snuggled with her daughter. What an embarrassing, unpredictable mess.

Fourteen

Disbelief rippled through Ada as she stared into her son's eyes. "You want time away? From what? Why?"

Mahlon shrugged before turning his attention to the bowl of potato soup in front of him.

Ada passed him a glass of milk. "You've talked to Deborah about this?"

"Not yet."

"We only have thirty-three days before we have to be out of here."

"That's more than a month, and it'll only take one day to move."

"Move to where? You haven't even decided on a place. We need solid plans. Not procrastination."

He looked up at her. "I think the Eversons' home is best. But they're asking too much for rent, so I'm waiting them out."

"We don't need a place nearly that big or expensive."

"It'll give all of us elbow room."

Elbow room? She'd worried for quite a while that he considered her a burden. It didn't matter that he'd been the one who hadn't wanted her to remarry because he hated watching all the adjustments Deborah had to make when her Daed remarried. Ada had thought she was doing the right thing when she agreed to remain single, so she had come up with a plan to support them. But to make her plan work, she needed to move to Hope Crossing. She could have made a decent living off her pies and cakes if they'd moved there. But he'd been stressed over that plan. To make up for his strong opinions, he'd come up with plans of his own. Maybe she'd been wrong to go along with them so easily. When she lost her husband, all she could see and feel was her love for the one child they'd had together. During all the years since his Daed had died, maybe what Mahlon thought he needed and what he really needed were two different things.

Regardless of all that, nowadays he seemed frustrated that she needed his financial support. She hated to even think it, but maybe he'd be happier if she found a rental she could afford on her own. If it was in a touristy spot, she could sell her baked goods to local restaurants. He and Deborah could live alone.

"Why do you have to get away now?"

"Because it's now or never." He pushed the bowl back and stared at the table. "You know it is, Mamm." He gazed at her through those earnest hazel eyes. "I'm twenty-three, and I've worked full-time for nine years. *Nine years,* Mamm—eight of them for Ephraim. Come November I'll be married, and by next fall you'll have your first grandchild. And probably one every couple of years after that until I can no longer remember being young. I just need a few days away on my own. Is that so wrong?"

"Are you…unsure about getting married?"

He scoffed. "The only thing I know for sure in this whole stinking mess of life is that Deborah Mast means everything to me." Taking his bowl with him, he stood and went to the sink. "Little else makes any sense. Things I don't want to think about wake me at night. In the space between asleep and awake, I hear whispers about wars and homeland security, and I see the Twin Towers falling all around me again. When I'm asleep, every object in my hand turns into a weapon of some sort. And when I wake, I'm filled with a desire for…vengeance, I think."

Unable to bear the grief he'd just heaped on her, she sat. And in ways others wouldn't see, she wasn't sure when she'd ever get up again. "But a few years back you said the strength and number of the dreams had faded into nearly nothing."

"I know, Mamm. But they started back."

"Why?"

He shrugged. "It doesn't matter. But I think I can make peace between me and God if I have some time by myself."

She studied him, hoping words of help and comfort would come to her.

He turned his half-empty glass of milk round and round. "Eric's home for a while."

The pieces began to fit, and she had a few concerns as to what the image would be when the puzzle was complete. "Maybe the dreams returning has to do with your renewed friendship with him. I'm sure he came home with war stories."

"He came home to bury a mutual friend."

"Who?"

"Stewart Fielding."

Her heart ached with things she couldn't say. "He's one of the boys you and Eric used to hang out with, one that wrote you letters regularly from Iraq."

"Ya."

"Did you go to his funeral?"

He nodded.

"Does Deborah know you went?"

"No."

They'd been down this road many times before. He wanted to follow the Amish way of life, but then he mingled with friends who pulled him in the opposite direction. Ada knew Amish folk who had Englischer friends and it wasn't an issue, but the way Mahlon's friends lived challenged the core beliefs of the Amish. That had to stir conflict in her sensitive son.

"Mahlon, I think seeds were scattered over you without your permission, and others you've planted without realizing it. But you have to know when to pull away from certain friends before—"

"Mamm, please. Just back off. I'll find us a new place. I'll do whatever it takes to keep the bills paid. Just trust me and help Deborah to do the same. I don't want her getting hurt. Not ever."

The sounds of a horse and buggy caused Ada to look out the window. "I saw Deborah this morning."

Concern etched across his face. "When you were looking for me?"

"Ya. I didn't tell her you went out last night and never came home, but she's bound to be wondering." Seeing Deborah driving the buggy down the road toward their house, Ada pointed out the window.

Mahlon glanced. "She'll think I was with Eric, which I wasn't. I was just walking, alone. Must have gone eight to ten miles. It helped, but not enough. I kept thinking someone I knew would see me, and Deborah would be embarrassed by my odd behavior. I need a couple of days someplace where no one knows me. Where no one expects work or help or answers. Can you understand that?"

Hoping he knew what he was doing, she hugged him. "Ya, a little."

"Denki, Mamm. I'll go for a ride with Deborah and talk to her."

Ada watched as her son left the house and climbed into the carriage next to his betrothed. If anyone had the power to help Mahlon navigate the muddy rivers within him, Deborah Mast did.

It pained her to watch him struggle. If he could just let go of trying to make life fit inside his understanding, his hands would be free to grasp the richness around him. She shouldn't worry. She knew that.

Maybe all he needed was a week to think things through and for her to find a home of her own. But she couldn't do that on the meager amount of money she could make inside Dry Lake. She'd have to move elsewhere if she hoped to make a living.

Deborah passed the reins to Mahlon when he climbed into the rig beside her. He guided the horse onto the road before shifting the reins into one hand.

"How's your Daed?"

"Adjusting to new medicines and feeling decent."

"Good." A slight smile radiated from his lips, and his hazel eyes bore into her as he patted the seat beside him. When she slid closer, he put his arm around her shoulder. They rode in silence, but the warmth of who he was filled her. Most of their evenings started out quiet unless she did all the talking, but soon enough he'd open up. And when he did, they grew even closer.

Finally he cleared his throat. "Mamm said she came by this morning."

"Ya. Looking for you, I think."

"I went out last night but not with Eric."

"All night?"

He nodded. "It was foggy and quiet, so I walked until the sun began to rise. I found a few answers, a bit of peace, but…mostly it seemed to only confuse things."

"I don't understand, Mahlon. I try. You know I do."

He fidgeted with the reins. "Remember when I went away for nearly a week about four years ago?"

"Ya."

It'd been one of their secrets. Ephraim had a week-long job out of town. So Mahlon told his mother he was going with Ephraim, and he told Ephraim he needed to stay at home with his mother. No one but Deborah knew the truth.

"I came back with my mind clear and all sorts of things worked out, ya?"

She shifted, staring at him. "You're going away again?"

"Just for a few days. I need a little time. That's all."

"I don't understand. What is it you want time to do?"

"Easy, Deb."

"Don't try to calm me, Mahlon. I have as much right to feel things as you do, and I don't like how you're acting. Less than a week ago we began telling our friends and family of our plans to marry, and now you need to get away?"

"This has nothing to do with you."

Mahlon told her about his nightmares and insomnia, but she also heard what he wasn't saying—that the responsibility of finding a home, getting married, and starting his own family had triggered old feelings of panic. When he lost his father at ten years old and took on the responsibility for his widowed mother, it seemed to dig a channel inside his soul, like the wheel of a buggy caught in a deep, muddy rut. Being in New York on September 11 during the terrorist attacks made it a thousand times worse, and now Eric's return seemed to have triggered questions inside him that he had no answers for.

He pulled onto Jonathan's long dirt driveway and came to a stop. "If this was happening to you, you'd need a lot of time among your friends and family. You'd spend hours and hours with your many friends, me included, talking until you unearthed the answers that put things in perspective and brought you peace. But that's not me, Deb."

Her heart twisted, and her eyes brimmed with tears. "You need time completely alone." She cupped his face with her hands. "I'm sorry I got aggravated."

He pulled her closer and placed his lips over hers. After the gentle kiss he studied her. "Sometimes I get mad at me too, but I'm still the same anyway."

"I love you for who you are. You go talk to yourself and God. And find peace."

He wrapped his arms around her, and she felt him tremble. Whatever had been unleashed inside him was making him more miserable than he could bear. Silently she prayed for him, as she had every day for as long as she could remember.

"When will you go?"

"Saturday most likely. Ephraim has a lot of work scheduled for the rest of this week, and I can't leave yet. I'd like you and me to go out Friday night, and then I'll leave the next morning. I'll tell Ephraim tomorrow that I'm taking off a few days next week."

Fifteen

The edge of darkness began to take over as Ephraim left the barn with a full and sleepy pup in hand—the one Simeon said Lori wanted. He'd taken clean clothes from the clothesline back to Cara and Lori over an hour ago before going to visit his Daed.

Cara had said nothing when he'd set the items on the table. He'd added a little more wood to the oven in case she wanted to scramble some eggs or fix a grilled cheese sandwich. Without experience on a wood stove, she wouldn't be able to cook much, but he assured her she could use any of the food in the house to fix her and Lori something to eat. He had no idea why, but an accusing look had returned to her eyes when he said the words.

It made him miss Anna Mary. Her friendly, easily understood ways were much more welcome than this mess…except he wasn't sure how well she'd take the news of Cara when the time came.

He stepped onto his porch with the full intention of tapping before walking in, but Lori sat in a ladder back chair in the kitchen, staring through the screen door. In that brief moment he saw a very worried little girl. She seemed to think if he didn't keep his word and come back, the police would show up again. Her wet hair hung about her shoulders, and her shiny-clean face eased into a slight smile at the sight of him.

Ephraim came inside and held out the pup.

"Mom, look!" She jumped up from her chair and scooped the dog from his hand.

Cara walked out of the bathroom, towel drying her hair and wearing one of his shirts over her jeans. Her eyes questioned him.

Ephraim removed his hat and hung it on the peg. "He's full right now, but I'll take him back to his mother in the morning."

Lori cuddled the puppy. "Whatcha gonna name him?"

"Name him?" He had no plans to keep the mutt.

"Mom said we don't have enough food for us, let alone a dog. But if you want him…"

Ephraim chuckled. "Well, I've been thinking maybe I need a dog around here." He noticed dozens of bug bites on Lori's arms and legs. He went to the kitchen cabinet where he kept some over-the-counter stuff, grabbed a tube of anti-itch cream, and passed it to Cara.

"Thanks." Cara read the side of the package and removed the lid.

"Not a problem." He patted the dog's head. "How about Better Days?"

A faint look of cynicism crossed Cara's face, but she said nothing.

Lori set the dog on the floor and walked across the room. "Here, Better Days." The puppy ran to her. "Look, he likes it."

Ephraim closed the front door. "Actually, he likes you, and he would have come no matter what you called him. But he'll get used to the name."

"Can he sleep on the bed with me?"

"I suppose for tonight. If it's okay with your mom."

She looked to her mom, who gave a silent nod. Contentment seemed to erase the last of Lori's stress, and she smiled.

Cara sat on the floor near Lori and dabbed spots of medicine onto bug bites. Ephraim grabbed yesterday's newspaper off a counter, took a seat at the kitchen table, and opened it. Half reading and half listening to the banter between mother and daughter, he felt the depth of the bond between them.

He'd been nineteen when his mother died, and although he hadn't realized how much he loved her until after she died, the pain of losing her wore on him night and day, slowly easing with time. Even now he had nights when he dreamed of her and heard her voice in his sleep.

The room grew quiet as Cara and Lori moved into the bedroom. Cara's soft voice rode through the silence of his home as she read from one of the children's books, not sounding anything like the woman who'd split his lip last night.

Hoping she'd come back into the kitchen when Lori was settled, he added a bit of wood to the cookstove and put on a pot of coffee to brew. After returning to the kitchen table, he read through a different newspaper. She came out of the bedroom, closed the door behind her, but remained near the doorframe.

Her eyes seemed glued to the table. Taut lines across her face had replaced the tenderness he'd seen there when she was with Lori. "I appreciate your kindness to my daughter." She lifted her eyes, staring straight at him. "I don't suppose you're ready to tell me the bottom line in all this."

Ephraim went to the stove and poured her a cup of coffee. He set it on the table. "That's percolated coffee, meaning it's boiling hot." He placed cream and sugar in front of her before pouring himself a cup and taking a seat. He motioned to a chair. "Sit." She slowly moved forward and took a seat.

Without touching her cup, she stared at the black liquid in front of her.

He dumped a bit of cream and sugar into his cup. The clock ticked off the minutes. "Is it too late in the day for you to drink coffee?"

She shook her head.

"Do you take your coffee black?"

"I'll keep close tabs on what I use while we're here. You'll get what I'll owe you. I'll even pay for your kindness to Lori. But I won't use anything I don't really need, like coffee or cream or sugar."

Not liking her tone, Ephraim wondered if they would get along only when Lori was around. "So you're figuring on paying me for each thing, are you?"

"Are you saying I won't?"

Ephraim tried to steady his growing frustration. "I'm saying you couldn't possibly pay me for the trouble your presence is going to cause. I don't need your money anyway. But an attitude overhaul on your part might make this situation bearable."

She ran her hands across the edge of the table, and he noticed a slight trembling of her fingers. It dawned on him what she thought he might want.

His offense at her faded. Hidden inside her was a steely determination. He wouldn't be surprised if she'd fed her daughter dinner tonight but not herself.

He reached into his pocket, feeling the toy horse he'd dug out of the storage room. When he knew her as a child, she'd treasured it above all else, and then she'd given it to him.

She drew a shaky breath. "Did the policeman say how social services will contact me?"

"They could just drop in, but he thinks they'll call first because Dry Lake is a long way to drive just to find out no one is home."

"You drive by horse and buggy, but you have a phone?" She looked around, searching for it.

"Not in the house. The few Old Order Amish people who own a phone never have it inside their home. The church leaders gave me permission to have one because of my business. It's in the cabinetry shop. It has a loud speaker directed this way, so I can usually hear from this distance—except in winter when my windows are shut."

He went to the refrigerator and pulled out a coconut pie his sister had made for him. He slid it onto the table and grabbed two plates from the cabinet. "This is the best pie you'll ever have. And it has no strings."

She stared at the pie as he cut a piece and put it onto a plate. "I appreciate everything you've done for us. Unfortunately, I know how situations like this work…even if you don't."

He held the plate out to her. When she didn't take it, he set it on the table. He put some cream and sugar into her coffee and pushed it toward her. "Relax, Cara."

She stared at him with those bronze eyes he remembered so well—only back then they carried hope instead of cynicism. The only dare those eyes had carried as a child was the fun kind that lacked fear. She'd trusted him when he said she'd be safe to jump from a loft or drop from a rope into the creek. He motioned to the slice of pie. "It's free. I promise."

She didn't look like she believed him, but she didn't argue. "I've been looking for a place. I want to be gone within a few days at most."

"The sooner the better for me too."

She studied him without a trace of trust in her eyes.

"I want nothing from you except respect. I'm sure there are plenty of men who'd like more from you. I'm not one of them. It's angering that you can't believe that." He took a sip of his coffee. "But I understand it."

"It's angering?" She blinked several times. "You certainly don't look or sound angry."

Suddenly he remembered why her mother had come back—to find a place of safety from a man who'd grown too violent to control. She'd made arrangements with Levina to take Cara in. Even received permission from the bishop for her to give Cara up and for Levina to take care of her.

At the time he'd really liked Cara. Not as a girlfriend or anything, but as a pal who wasn't afraid to try things she'd never done before. He'd been glad the church leaders were going to allow her to live with Levina.

But her mother had never brought her to Levina as she'd arranged. What had her life been like because of that?

"Saying something directly is all it should take to get a point across. Don't you think?"

She gave a half shrug. "Most talk is a waste of time. Actions mean a lot more."

He nudged the mug of coffee and the plate of pie closer to her. "Then let my actions say I'm on your side in this."

After a few moments a half smile created a faint but familiar dimple in her cheek. She slowly took the cup in hand. Breathing in the aroma, she lifted it to her lips. Her eyes closed, and she took a sip. "Oh, man. If I had a cigarette, I might believe in heaven." She ate the pie slowly, as if savoring every crumb.

He had dozens of questions to ask and a hundred things he wanted to tell her, but he doubted if either held any wisdom. She needed time to get past the trauma of being kicked out of a run-down barn, of almost losing Lori, of begging for help. "So you've been walking to the Howards for work every day?"

"I've been thinking of firing the chauffeur. He never shows up on time."

He chuckled. At least she still had a sense of humor, even though it had turned rather bitter. "Cara, no one can see you leaving this house. My father's sick. He just came home from the hospital today. I need time before I can tell him you're staying here."

"I'll take Lori with me, and we'll go out the back way, through the fields. We'll leave before daylight and not come back till after dark. I need the money if I'm going to get out of here in a few days, and I just can't leave Mr. Howard hanging. If he loses more work hours, he'll be fired."

Her personality was an odd mix of sarcasm, humor, honesty, and courage. In some ways she seemed a lot like the girl he knew twenty years ago. If she wasn't such a danger to him, he could enjoy getting reacquainted.

"Fine. Use the same route I brought you in by, and try not to be seen." She angled her head, questions etched on her face.

"You're not a prisoner. We're in this together."

He pulled the toy horse out of his pocket and laid it on the table. He thought he saw a shadow of recognition cross her face, but then she stared into the bottom of her empty cup. Either she didn't recognize it, or she didn't trust him enough to want to discuss any part of her past.

Leaving the toy on the table, he rose. "Good night, Cara."

Sixteen

Consciousness tapped against the numbness of sleep. Waking, Cara snuggled on the softness beneath her, enjoying the luxury. Unlike when she'd slept in the barn, she didn't wish to hurry daylight along. The pleasure of a mattress beneath her and covers surrounding her caused a sense of dignity to return, even if she and Lori never had much.

She reached across the bed until she felt the warmth of her daughter's back. Her eyes misted. Waking could have been so miserably different for both of them if Ephraim hadn't come along.

Lori's breathing came in slow, rhythmic sounds, renewing Cara's strength for the battles ahead. Through all the haze of panic and shame yesterday, she'd not given much thought to Ephraim's actions. She'd only fixed on her unease about his hidden motives.

She put her feet on the clean wooden floors, grateful not to be in that cold, smelly barn. She eased into her jeans. The toy horse Ephraim had pulled from his pocket and left on the kitchen table now sat on the nightstand. She'd taken it with her when she went to bed last night. He'd acted like it should mean something to her, but she'd been too leery of him to ask and too drained to think straight.

She didn't mean to be so callous toward Ephraim. But she'd lost herself once. Her sense of self-respect had died a painful death. Buried the year she turned nineteen. Of all the things in life she grieved for, giving up her own self in exchange for food and shelter and safety was the worst.

American tradition lied. Black was not the color worn during loss and grief. White was. White lace. Tulle. Chiffon. Silk. But in spite of marrying Johnny when she wasn't in love with him, the life they built became one she cherished.

She took the toy horse in hand, studying it. Ephraim was not Johnny, and he wasn't helping her so she'd owe him a lifetime debt. He wanted her out of his life as much as she wanted out. And he deserved to be treated with respect, not jaded bitterness. As she clutched the horse in her hand, a vague memory moved through her like a shadow.

Standing barefoot on a creek bank, she watched a boy as he stared at the horse in the palm of her hand. Words were coming out of her mouth, but she couldn't make them out. Closing her eyes, she concentrated. *"You keep it,"* she heard herself say. Goose bumps ran over her whole body. *"Keep it until I return."*

Cara's heart raced at the memory. She wanted to remember more, but the scene ended right there. "Until I return," she whispered.

From the foot of the bed, the puppy responded to Cara's movements and waddled up to her. He licked her hands while she tried to keep him calm. Figuring he'd pee if she didn't get him outside quickly, she picked him up. She tiptoed through the dark bedroom and tripped over a stack of books. They fell like dominoes. With her free hand she put them back in place. Wondering if Ephraim collected books or if he actually read them, she walked through the dark kitchen, heading for the front door.

A movement flitted before her. She stopped short, her heart pounding.

"Cara?" Ephraim sounded startled.

"Yeah. Did I wake you?"

He drew a sleepy breath. "No. I was on my way to get a drink of water."

"I think the puppy needs to go out."

"Pffft. The whole point of better days is that they are supposed to come in and stay," he mumbled, trying to lift the puppy from her.

"What?" She didn't release the dog.

"It's a joke. We named the dog Better Days. Get it?"

Was it normal to make jokes when so much stress existed between them?

She passed him the dog. "I'm afraid I don't, but you should take the pup out before *you* get it."

He chuckled. "If Better Days starts peeing on us before the day begins, what can we expect next?"

She figured he must be a morning person. "Do you really want an answer to that?"

He went out the kitchen door. His laughter clung to her, and something about his movements made a memory jump into her mind. A cool breeze stirred the tall grass as water rippled over her bare feet. A boy grabbed a rope and swung out over the deep part of the creek, laughing as he let go.

Was Ephraim the boy in her memories?

The screen door banged as he walked in. She jolted, taking several steps back. As if he didn't see her, he went into the kitchen, set the pup on the floor, lit a kerosene lamp, and grabbed some milk out of the refrigerator. He tore off small chunks of homemade bread, tossed them into a bowl, and poured milk over them.

He set the container on the floor. "Another week or so and they'll be ready to be weaned. Guess I better start taking them some soggy food once in a while." He scrunched a few pieces of newspaper and placed them in the wood stove. He added small strips of wood on top, struck a foot-long match, and held it inside the stove. "If anyone from social services shows up here today needing to talk to you, I'll tell them where you're working." He dropped the match inside the stove and put the solid metal eye back in place.

She watched from the shadows. "Ephraim?"

He dumped coffee beans into a hand-crank grinder. "Ya?"

There were many things she wanted to know, but asking questions might start things she couldn't stop. Still, if she remained silent, she might

never know any parts to her past. Having any sort of connection to people her mother knew could give her and Lori ties to family or friends or
something. But could those connections do more harm to Lori than the
lack of them? She wished she knew the safest thing to do.

He added water and coffee into the percolator and set it on the stove.
"There's a lot going on inside that head of yours, isn't there?"

She swallowed. Why was he acting so easygoing? "Do…do you
know me?"

"Ya, I do." He said it calmly, so matter-of-factly. "We met when we
were kids. You were eight. I was twelve. Do you remember?"

Tears stung her eyes. "Some of it started coming back to me about a
week ago. What I remember covers about five minutes of time."

"Is that when Malinda told you how to get here?"

"You knew my mother?"

Ephraim stopped all movement, staring at her. "Knew?" A few moments later he set two mugs on the table. "Only a little. Things I've heard.
A few conversations I had with her that time you visited." The puppy
finished his meal and began whining. Ephraim brought him to Cara.
"When did she…die?"

Cara pulled the mutt against her, wishing Ephraim hadn't asked,
hadn't moved in so close. Of all the things she hated talking about, losing her mother was the worst. "You don't have to say it so careful like. It
doesn't matter when, does it?"

"I was nineteen when my mother died, and, yes, it mattered."

She scoffed. "There's a whole world of hurting people out there—
starving, dying horrific deaths, being mutilated in accidents or by wars or
by violent people."

He stroked the puppy's head. "If we're feeling sorry for ourselves, that
type of thinking can help us get some perspective. But their misery doesn't
stop my pain or yours. Losing a mother is tougher than it sounds."

His insight made it hard for her to respond. "People could lose themselves completely if they let it all start to matter."

"True. But a person can just as easily lose themselves if they don't let it matter."

"Great. Now I understand. No matter what we do, we lose."

He walked to the kitchen table. "There's definitely truth in that. So, if Malinda didn't tell you how to get here, your dad must have."

"Fat, stupid chance of that."

Ephraim watched her, looking as if she'd just cursed or something.

She rolled her eyes and huffed. "He went MIA a long time ago." His brows furrowed in confusion. "MIA," she repeated. "Missing in action."

"I know what it means, but…" He shook his head. "I'm sorry."

"Makes no difference. I'm sure I'd be in a worse jam if he'd hung around."

"How *did* you land here?"

Her heart beat as if a rock band drummer were pounding against it. If Ephraim knew she was running from a stalker, he'd kick her out. Now.

Lori came out of the bedroom, and Cara's nerves calmed. He'd already proved he wouldn't ask awkward questions in front of her.

Lori rubbed her eyes. "Morning, 'From."

"It's Ee-from, honey." Cara set the puppy on the floor. His little legs couldn't carry him to Lori fast enough as he ran across the slick floor, sliding and falling.

" 'From will do." He set the milk on the table. "I want to drop you and your mom off near the Howards', so we need to head out soon. Do either of you want some eggs?"

Lori scooped up the dog, giggling when he licked her. "Me and Better Days like scrambled eggs."

Seventeen

The moment Ephraim stepped out of Robbie's truck after work, he smelled food cooking. He headed straight for his house, hoping Deborah wasn't fixing him a meal at his place today. He'd cut the workday short because he had a plan, one that had nagged at him since it sprang to mind. And he had questions that he hated to ask Cara, but he needed answers.

As he drew closer to his home, he heard female voices. He looked through a window and spotted Anna Mary and Deborah in his kitchen. Since Cara and Lori couldn't come back here until after dark, he'd wanted to get some food to take to them. He'd planned to pick them up near the Howards' and find a suitable spot to stay until dark. But now he couldn't grab food, not without his sister and Anna Mary asking him questions he wasn't ready to answer. Cara had stuffed every piece of belongings she and Lori had into her backpack this morning. At the time he'd thought it a little odd, but right now he was glad she'd left no evidence of staying here last night. He had to tell everyone, but they didn't need to find out yet, and certainly not like this.

He changed course and went to the gate inside his barn that led to the pasture. Trying to spot his horse in the pasture, he wondered again how well Anna Mary would take the news of his dealings with Cara. The concern over his father's health and the need to find Cara a place to live was all he'd thought of since yesterday. He'd scoured the newspapers today and made several calls, but he'd found nothing, not even an empty room in some Englischer's home.

When he didn't see his horse, he whistled. Under a grove of shade trees, she raised her head, angling it as if wondering if she'd truly heard him. He whistled again, and she whinnied before breaking into a gallop.

Ever since dropping off Cara and Lori near the Howards' place that morning, he'd felt their presence. The first rays of dawn had spread their fingers across the land as he'd stopped his carriage just out of sight of the Howards. Cara thanked him, her voice barely audible and her mood invisible. She helped Lori out of his buggy, not glancing up even when Lori blew him a kiss. As he watched them go down the road, he knew he couldn't let them walk back to his place after a long day of work. But they'd need to stay somewhere out of sight until after dark, so he'd come up with a plan. A reasonable one. Except lurking inside was an emotion he didn't want.

His horse trotted toward him, and he opened the gate, letting her inside the barn. He bridled her and began connecting the leads.

"Ephraim." Anna Mary's voice made him pause.

He put the horse collar and hame over the animal's neck. "Ya?"

"Deborah helped me cook a meal for you on that awful wood stove."

One reason he didn't own a gas cookstove was to keep women out of his kitchen. Anna Mary knew that. If he ever grew serious about someone, he'd buy a gas oven. The wood stove was an unspoken line of defense against pushy women who wanted to win his fondness by showing what a great wife they could be. But he'd never considered Anna Mary pushy, and he'd actually been considering buying a gas stove.

He ran the harness traces through the whiffletree. "Sorry, but I have plans tonight. I'm heading out as soon as I hitch the buckboard."

"Won't you come eat something first? I've spent most of the afternoon cooking."

He shook his head as he fastened the leads.

She stepped forward and petted the horse. "I don't suppose I can go along."

"Not this time."

"I made fried chicken. Can I at least pack some to send with you?"

"No, thanks."

She touched his hand. "Are you leaving because I dared to cross one of your not-so-invisible lines?"

"No, but I have to question why you'd do such a thing if you thought I might mind."

She said nothing. He stopped what he was doing. After a year of courting, they knew each other pretty well, and they rarely argued, but he was being difficult, and he half expected her to tell him off and leave. Although he had no idea how he'd feel about that if it happened, he wasn't one to walk lightly.

She shrugged. "I figure the fact that you didn't tell me to never go in your kitchen is a pretty good indication of how you feel about me."

His blood ran hot. She'd been talking to her older sister. He'd courted Susanna years ago and had broken up with her over this issue. A year later she married someone else and now had three children.

Ephraim never regretted letting Susanna go. Or any of the other girls he'd dated. But Anna Mary was different.

"I just wanted to do something nice for you."

"That's not all you wanted. You're trying to figure out where you stand—if I'm the same with you as I was with Susanna. Or whoever. You told me once you don't want to be compared to anyone else, and yet you're testing to see if I'll react to you the same way."

She sighed. "Guilty, but I didn't know that until right now." She wrapped her hand around the buckle he was fastening on the horse and gazed into his eyes. "I promised myself that I wouldn't get this way over you, that'd I'd keep things light and easy. But I can't stand trying to figure out if I'll become just another girl you once courted."

Ephraim realized he'd become somewhat callous over the years; otherwise, he'd have recognized the spot she was in. He placed his hand over hers, seeing afresh that in some ways she was very tender-hearted and was willing to be vulnerable with him.

Taking her hands into his, he chose his words carefully. "You mean more. Only time will tell us what we both want to know."

She closed her eyes, looking both disappointed and relieved. He placed his hand on her shoulder, and she wrapped her arms around him. When they connected really well, like now, he hoped he'd never court anyone else. He longed to have a family of his own. To have the warmth of a woman in his bed. To make the circle of life complete by becoming a husband and father. But...

Anna Mary backed away. "Fried chicken is great for taking with you."

Ephraim couldn't help but smile. "It smells delicious. How much did you burn before figuring out how to regulate the heat?"

"Only a few batches."

He laughed. "You're teasing, right?"

"Ya, but if Deborah hadn't been with me, I'd be in tears, and your freezer would be empty of chicken."

"I guess we could eat a quick bite together before I head out. If it doesn't taste like burned grease," he teased, "I could take some with me too."

"You know, Ephraim, I appreciate honesty, but there are times when a bit less truthfulness would be appreciated."

"I see what you mean." Ephraim placed his hand on her shoulder as they walked across the yard. "I'll gladly take some chicken with me even if it does taste like burned grease."

She laughed and elbowed him in the ribs. "You're awful."

"I know. I'm just making sure you know that."

Eighteen

With her backpack across her shoulders and Lori falling asleep in her arms, Cara walked back toward Ephraim's. Just as she topped one hill, she stared at another one. Her goal was to get a little closer to Ephraim's and then find somewhere out of sight to rest until after his family's bedtime. Since Lori got up before dawn and had been helping Cara clean out closets today, she needed this nap. Unfortunately, her taking one right now was quite painful for Cara. But if she knew her daughter, she'd be up and moving again in twenty or thirty minutes.

A horse and wagon came across the horizon, making her think of Ephraim. She'd spent most of the day wondering if he'd heard from the social worker. The idea unsettled her, making her thoughts as scattered as her emotions were raw.

She kept walking, the rig heading toward her at a steady speed. She'd never expected the man she'd dubbed Heartless to be so even-tempered and…pleasant. He didn't seem unfeeling or conniving, but she wasn't convinced he had no ulterior motive. She'd learned long ago to keep the walls around her firmly braced. People weren't trustworthy. It seemed they often wanted to be. But human weakness won out time and again.

The rig grew closer.

Could that be Ephraim?

Her heart beat an extra time. Was he in the area by coincidence, or had he come to pick them up?

"Whoa." Ephraim brought the horse to a stop, a warm smile hidden beneath a layer of seriousness or maybe caution. "Hi." He watched her, and for the briefest moment she thought she actually remembered those gray blue eyes.

He set the brake and climbed down. Better Days stuck his head out from under the bench seat, wagging his whole body. Ephraim placed his hand on Lori's back. "Let's get you two in the wagon."

Half asleep, Lori raised her head, easily shifting from Cara's arms to Ephraim's. As the pressure of carrying Lori lifted, the aches and pains running through Cara's body eased.

Ephraim took her elbow and helped her onto the wooden bench. A paperback book titled *The Whole Truth* lay on the seat beside her. A bookmark peeked out about midway through the pages. She used to love reading before life took every minute of every day just to survive. Ephraim had to be a reader.

He climbed up easily with Lori and placed her in Cara's arms.

"Thank you." Her words came out hoarse.

"Not a problem."

For reasons that made no sense, tears threatened, and she licked her lips. Trying to gain command over her emotions, Cara rubbed her lower back. "I didn't know you were coming."

"Me either, at least not when I dropped you off this morning. I meant to be here earlier. Since we can't go to my place until after dark, I thought we'd go to a secluded spot near the creek. I brought some food and blankets."

"And a book." She held it up.

"Ya."

The dog nudged her with his nose.

"And Better Days."

"I figured it was about time somebody brought you better days." He chuckled at the joke and slapped the reins against the horse's back.

Cara stroked Lori's head, realizing she'd fallen back to sleep. "Any word from social services?"

"Not yet."

"What if your father sees them when they show up? Or someone else sees them and tells him?"

"I don't know. Like you, I don't have many answers right now."

"No wonder you keep toting the dog all over the place. You want Better Days to stick around."

The lines on his face curved upward, but seriousness made the hint of a smile fade. "We need to talk about a few things. Can I ask you some questions?"

A memory flashed in front of Cara. About two decades ago she'd stood in front of a boy who'd asked her the same basic thing. "The barn Lori and I hid in and the house that used to sit on that now-empty foundation—they belonged to an old woman, didn't they?"

He nodded. "Levina."

"Levina was the one Mama and I stayed with?"

"Ya, that's right."

"And you asked me if I was a boy or a girl."

Under his tanned skin his face flushed a pale pink. "Well, you were a skinny eight-year-old kid who wore jeans, and your hair was cut shorter than most newborns."

She ran her fingers through her hair, tugging at the end of the short crop. She liked her hair like this, regardless of what he might think of it.

"Nobody would mistake you for a boy now."

"No, just a thief, a drunk, and a troublemaker."

He winced. "Sorry."

A small burst of laughter escaped her, catching her by surprise. "Well, I feel so much better now."

"Then my work is done, because I came to make you feel better."

"Don't quit your day job."

He laughed, and she understood why that sound had stayed with her all these years. But why had the memory of Levina's name returned to her but Ephraim's hadn't, even when she stood inside his home and he told her?

"Remember seeing the creek for the first time?"

"No. But I do remember cool water rushing over my feet. And someone..."

"If there's a boy in that memory, it would've been me. I don't think you saw anyone else that week. Other than Levina and the bishop."

"What's a bishop?"

"The head church leader over several districts. He helps us stay strong in our faith and reminds us of the meaning of the vows we've taken."

"Like a guild master in World of Warcraft."

His brows crinkled. "Like what?"

"It's an Internet game. I've never played it, but I worked with people who do."

He chuckled. "The bishop would take exception to using the Internet or playing any type of war game."

His amusement skittered through her. "I remember your laughter. It was one of the first things that came to me last week. You laughing when you jumped into the creek or into a pile of hay in the barn."

"Do you remember our playing for hours in the trees?"

"Not really. Although part of me must, because I knew about the chains on the tree before I saw them."

"That was your favorite tree. We hung those chains there ourselves, wrapping them around and around the branch for you to use as reins. I'd say we did a good job since they're still there."

"I guess so. It just seems like I'd remember your name if we spent so much time together."

"You never called me Ephraim. You called me Boy, said it was something about a Tarzan movie."

She chuckled. "Ah, I probably came up with that because of the trees and rope climbing stuff."

"Makes sense." He pulled to a stop, got out of the wagon, opened a cattle gate to the pasture, and led the horse through it. After closing the gate, he climbed back in. "I'll park at the grove of trees near the creek bank. We can eat and rest there until it's dark. I…I'm sorry about needing to hide and sneak around."

She scoffed. "I've been hiding for as long as I can remember."

The wagon creaked as he drove over uneven ground. "I remember Malinda telling Levina about hiding you from your dad." He drove to the far side of a stand of trees. "She tried her best to get you somewhere safe. I don't really know what stopped her, but I know she wanted you to have a good life."

Embarrassed at all he knew about her, she whispered, "Yeah, well, that didn't happen."

Ephraim drew a long, slow breath. "Cara, I can't afford to get caught off guard. I need to know. Is Lori's father likely to show up looking for her?"

Now she knew why he'd gone out of his way to pick her up. And why he was being so friendly. He wanted answers to personal questions.

"What you're really asking is whether I have a no-good boyfriend or husband somewhere, right?" She snarled the words, not caring how angry she sounded. The insult made her skin burn.

Without saying anything else, he climbed down, took a blanket from the wagon, and placed it in a clearing ahead of the horse before returning to her. As he lifted Lori from her arms, his eyes met hers. "I meant no offense."

She bit back her sarcasm, reminding herself that it didn't matter what he thought of her. Her mistake had been allowing the easy banter between them to make her think he had any sense of who she might be. But attitudes like his got old fast.

He took Lori to the blanket on the ground and gently laid her there. She didn't stir. He returned to the wagon and grabbed a basket from it. He held out his hand, offering to help her down. She turned and climbed out the other side.

When she glanced across the wagon, he was watching her, and she couldn't keep her thoughts silent any longer. "I was married to Lori's father. In spite of what your kind might think, he was a decent man. If he'd lived, I'd never have set foot in this stinking place."

"My kind?"

"Yeah, the ones who were born having it all. You dare judge the rest of us by a standard you claim to be God's. And just to prove your greatness, you create a God who favors you over us."

He stared at her as if sizing her up. She wanted to lash out until his high-and-mighty eyes opened. All humans were equal. Some started out with more because of their parents, but that wasn't through their own skill or worthiness. She'd started with nearly nothing and continually lost more as life went on. He'd been given everything. And yet he thought he was better than her?

"Mom?" Lori called, waking.

Cara hurried to her. "I'm right here, Lorabean."

She rubbed her eyes, searching her surroundings. "Where are we?"

"On a picnic." Ephraim set the dog on the blanket beside her.

"Better Days!" Every trace of fear drained from her, and she scooped the puppy into her arms. "Thanks, 'From." She grinned. "Me and Better Days are hungry. We got any food?"

Ephraim tapped the top of the basket. "Fried chicken, potato chips, lemonade, and cake."

"You do way better picnics than Mom." The puppy licked her face. She giggled and jumped to her feet. "Can we go to the creek? Better Days would love it."

"I thought you were hungry," Ephraim said.

"First I wanna see if he likes the water."

Cara pointed to a sandy area that sloped to a shallow section. "No deeper than your ankles, and don't get out of my sight."

"Come on, Better Days." Lori took off running with the puppy dancing around her feet, half tripping her as they went.

Cara sat on the blanket. "You are better at doing picnics." She peeked into the basket. "All she's going to remember of her childhood is what I couldn't provide."

Ephraim sat beside her. "You're a good mother, Cara. She'll remember how much you loved her."

The gentleness in his voice made guilt run through her. All he'd requested were a few reasonable answers, and she'd been defensive and rude. Tears threatened, reminding her how weary she was. "Sometimes I can barely remember my mother. Other times the memories are so strong I can't break free of them. I think she died not long after we were here. Then life became an endurance test."

"Not long after…" The hurt in his eyes surprised her.

He dropped his sentence and looked out over the fields. While they rested on the blanket, waiting side by side for night to come, an unfamiliar pull to talk openly tugged at her. Her anger at him still rumbled, but she'd finally met someone who'd known her mother, someone who had enough honor to do what it took to keep her and Lori from being separated.

A leaf floated downstream, drifting powerlessly on the creek's current. That's how she felt—caught by a desire as normal and natural as water flowing and a fallen leaf. Rather than treat him like she did everybody else, she decided to ignore her offense and give in to her need. "I…I met Johnny when I was seventeen. He was a huge, burly man, and he became my shelter. Of course that safety came with a price, and we married a year later. He believed in your God too. Said he met him in prison." She shrugged. "Somewhere during the first years of our marriage, I fell in love with him."

Ephraim grabbed a Mason jar out of the basket. "I've never heard of anyone falling in love after they got married. Although I have known a few who fell out of love."

"We got married at the courthouse, but we went to upstate New York for a honeymoon in the Catskill Mountains. The first day we hiked and canoed and had a picnic. It was the most wonderful day I'd ever had...or at least remembered having. That night he said his stomach hurt, so he slept on the couch. Much to my relief."

"He knew how you felt, didn't he?" Ephraim loosened the lid on the jar.

"He knew. I guess he didn't care about the time it took to change my mind about him. By the fifth night of our honeymoon, he was still making up excuses to sleep on the couch, but I invited him to stay with me." In her mind's eye she could see him clearly as he eased into bed next to her. How many times since he'd died had she wished he'd come to her bed again or been there for meals or watching Lori grow?

Ephraim held the jar of lemonade out to her. "Sounds like you found a truly good man."

She took a sip of lemonade and passed the jar back to him. "I did. When I got pregnant a couple of years later, I thought he'd be furious. But when I told him..."

The memory haunted her, and regrets twisted her insides. "I watched all this worry cross his face, and I realized he really did love me. I mean, he'd said he did even before we were married. But I hadn't really believed it." She sighed. "We thought we could give our child more than either of us had growing up. But before her second birthday...he died." She rubbed her forehead. "I never have a cigarette when I need one."

Ephraim leaned back, propping his elbow on the blanket. "I'm so sorry. I...I just needed to know whether to expect someone to show up looking for you and Lori."

She bit back saying, *Whatever.* In spite of how badly his words had stung, her anger wasn't completely justified. As her bitterness shrank back, she realized the obvious. What he'd been asking was, did she have someone looking for her?

" 'From, look," Lori called. "What kind of fish is this?"

He rose from the blanket and went to the creek bank.

Relaxing a little as he left, Cara exhaled slowly. She dug the toy horse out of her backpack, trying to remember owning it. But whether she ever remembered it or not, the past wasn't her goal. She only had today and the opportunity it afforded her to give Lori a better life than she and Johnny had.

Of course, she hadn't told Ephraim about Mike. But hadn't he earned the right to know the reason she fled New York?

Nineteen

A swath of crimson sky touched the horizon, signaling that nightfall was close at hand. Ephraim and Lori sat in the middle of a fallen tree that stretched from one side of the creek to the other. With their feet dangling several feet above the surface of the water, Ephraim passed the last bits of bread to Lori to toss below. Catfish circled, snatching the food as soon as it hit the surface. Better Days sat on the creek bank, watching their every move.

In spite of telling himself to do otherwise, his eyes kept returning to Cara. She sat on the blanket with her legs pulled to her chest, his sister's dress flowing around them like a large sheet. She watched the horizon as daylight drained from the sky. She looked like something out of a movie or a distant dream—a curious mix of delicate softness and unyielding stone.

He should have waited until she'd rested and eaten before he asked her questions. Too little food and sleep, along with the trauma of yesterday and the work today, had overloaded her with stress. He should have known not to insult her dignity. She'd shared some of her life with him, so it didn't seem that he'd done any damage to whatever small amount of trust he'd manage to earn. But it really ate at him that she'd been right.

His kind.

Her bull's-eye remark wasn't a revelation. Even after his time living among the Englischers, he had a tendency to judge people unfairly some-times…too often. After being raised by a very conservative group, he had no clue how to finish breaking the measuring stick. But if he wasn't careful, he'd only strengthen her disbelief in God.

"'From, look," Lori whispered. She pointed to an area of tall grass. A swarm of lightning bugs circled, making quite a show.

He stood on the log and held out his hand. "Ever caught one of those?"

She took his hand, balancing herself as she stood. "No way."

He chuckled. "Your mama was the best bug catcher I've ever seen." They made their way across the log, and he helped her get on solid ground.

"Do they bite?"

"Lightning bugs? No. But if they did, your mom would've bitten them right back."

"Yuck."

Cara cleared her throat. He glanced up, realizing she'd moved from the blanket to the creek side. "Are you saying I eat bugs?"

Holding back a smirk, he hoped a little teasing might ease the tension between them. "Maybe."

The last of the anger faded from her face, and gentleness replaced it.

He stared at her, wondering a hundred things. He wished he could see inside her heart and *really* get to know her beyond the few sentences she shared about her past. Ephraim placed his hands on Lori's shoulders and angled her toward the meadow. "If you hurry, you might get to those fireflies before Better Days, and then you can be the one to scatter them."

She took off running, the pup scurrying after her.

Ephraim turned to Cara, but he had no idea what to say. He would never really understand how it felt to grow up the way she had. To marry for all the wrong reasons yet have it turn out right. And then bury the man she'd grown to love and raise a child alone.

She held out the toy horse to him as if it symbolized a truce. "I'm Cara Moore now, not Atwater."

He placed his hand over it, sandwiching it between their hands. "For years I was sure you'd come back for this. Then I gave up. But I couldn't make myself throw it out."

He removed his hand, and she stared at the horse. "Ephraim, I…I had a guy following me…for years. He's the reason I needed Johnny and the reason I came here. He won't find me now. I'm sure of that. Anyway, while he was camped out in front of my apartment building, I took what cash I had, and Lori and I boarded a bus. When I got to the bus station, I had no idea where I'd go. So he has no way to know where I am. And no way of tracking me—not this time."

She has a stalker?

He could still see the defensive bitterness inside her, but now he felt amazed that she carried as much hope and trust as she did.

She started walking toward the blanket. "I have one desire, Ephraim." Tears brimmed her eyes, and she cleared her throat. "To protect Lori. She's innocent in this mess that started so long before she was born. You asked me this morning when my mother died. I was eight. And my dad disappeared within a few weeks."

"Cara." Ephraim wanted to scream *no* long and loud. "You were raised in foster care?"

"Yeah, one of those homes is where I met Mike, the psycho teen who turned into a stalker."

A desire to understand her outweighed any need to proceed carefully. "When he started threatening you, why not go to the police?"

She sank onto the blanket. "Lots of years, lots of reasons. I tried to go to the authorities once while living as a foster kid under his parents' roof. Long story, but he won and I ran. When he showed up later, turning him in would've been the same as turning myself in. I was a fifteen-year-old runaway who served drinks and danced in skimpy clothes at a bar. I had to stay below the radar."

He sat beside her. "And after that?"

"By the time I was of legal age, I had Johnny to take care of me. He managed a diner, and I worked as one of the waitresses. He never told me what happened between him and Mike, but the other waitresses said he caught Mike skulking around one day and put a gun to his gut, saying he better not see his face again. Mike disappeared. I didn't see him again until a year after Johnny died."

"What happened to Johnny?"

"Brain tumor—an aggressive, high-resolution glioma. There were four months between the time he was diagnosed and the day I was standing by his grave. When Mike heard Johnny was dead, he came after me, and it all started again—changing jobs and moving apartments. I'd shake him for a while but never for more than a year."

"Why didn't you go to the police then?"

"I was afraid for Lori. I knew a lot of girls with terrible boyfriends or husbands, dangerous guys, and they'd end up really hurt sometimes, especially if they talked to the cops. I couldn't afford to provoke a crazy, violent man, and Mike is both. If I killed Mike and went to jail for it or if I made him angry enough to kill me, Lori would suffer either way."

As Ephraim understood, he found it hard to sound casual. "She'd go into foster care."

"Ain't life grand?"

Ephraim felt the sadness inside her, even though her face showed little emotion. "This last time Mike found me, he'd figured out too much—Lori's name, her school, her likes and dislikes. He threatened my roommate. She said he tore up our place. He wants me, and it seems he finally figured out that he'd never have me—unless he had Lori. I got lucky, really, that he didn't nab her at school while I was working."

A landslide of thoughts tumbled through him. While waiting for the right words to come to him, he spotted movement near the fence line. With dusk falling he couldn't make out what was moving. Maybe his father's cows were heading for the barn.

He returned his focus to Cara. "I'm glad you found your way back here."

Cara drew a deep breath. "As soon as we can get social services off my back, I'll be on my way. This place has nothing for me. I thought maybe I'd find some magical connection that would mean something special for us, for Lori. I should have known better. Levina must have been eighty when I was child. And if Emma Riehl, whoever she is, cared so little she never came for me, why did I think she might have some tie or relationship to offer me or Lori now? It was stupid."

Emma Riehl? His stomach twisted. Emma was Cara's aunt. She was married to Malinda's oldest brother, Levi. Why would Cara think Emma was supposed to come for her?

"Where does Emma Riehl fit in, Cara?"

She rolled her eyes, looking more jaded than her years allowed for. "A few weeks after my mom died, my dad took me to a bus station. He promised that Emma Riehl would come for me, and then he left. She never showed up. So the next thing I knew, someone from social services was hauling me off to the land of the lonely."

Why would her father leave her at a bus station if he didn't believe that Emma was coming for her? He couldn't ask Emma, not with Cara living in his house. He couldn't tell Cara either. Not yet. If she handled it wrong, the community would hold him responsible. It hadn't dawned on her that he probably knew Emma, or maybe it had and she just didn't care after the incident with the police.

Ephraim eased his fingers over hers. "You're exhausted. You need a few days of regular meals, rest, and some peace. Maybe I can get one of my sisters to go to the Howards for a few days."

She slid her hand free and ran her fingers through her short blond hair. "I appreciate the offer. But I need to work, to prove to social services I can support Lori and myself. I want out—out of your home, out of Dry Lake. If you didn't turn in that report to the police, someone else did, which means people around here think poorly of me and Lori already. I won't start a new life fighting a battle I've already lost."

Odd as it seemed, he didn't want her to leave Dry Lake altogether. She had family and roots. It wasn't the right time to tell her that, but it would be after she had her own place. Then the community would see her in a different light. Right now they'd only see her through the eyes of the rumors about a drunken thief. "Don't you want to know why your mother came here? Or how Emma Riehl fits into the picture? Or why your dad thought she would come for you? Or why she didn't?"

"I came here thinking that's what I wanted, but now I know none of that matters. I need to build a life for Lori. Her childhood matters. Not mine."

Behind the tough exterior, Cara was still the little girl who'd swum in creeks, jumped from haylofts, and looked at life through eyes of hope. He'd waited years for her to return, longing to see her again. To look into those eyes and rekindle the feelings of friendship that tied them. Cara shifted, glancing behind her. "Hey." She tapped his shoulder and nodded backward.

He turned to see Simeon and Becca walking toward him. Dread climbed onto his heart and clung there. The lay of the land kept this little area unseen, so Ephraim had thought it was a safe spot. He came here often, and no one ever showed up.

He turned back to Cara. "Just sit tight, okay?" He stood.

"Hi, Lori!" Simeon pointed. "Look, Mamm, there's the missing pup we're searching for!" He ran to the spot where Lori and Better Days were chasing fireflies.

Becca came up to Ephraim, concern written across her face. Her hands moved to her plump waist. "What's going on?"

He'd broken many of the written and unwritten rules of his people by being alone with an Englischer woman. He had no defense for it, no excuse or rationalization that would be accepted by her or anyone else. "I know what I'm doing. I don't need a lecture."

Shock drained from her face, and accusation took its place. "News of something like this could kill your father."

Her words squeezed him like a vise. He'd known since yesterday that what she'd just said was true, but as he saw the fear reflected in her eyes, he realized he was caught between what was right for his Daed and what was right for Cara. No matter what he did, one of them could be hurt.

"This isn't about him. And it isn't any of your business."

She looked from Cara to Ephraim. The pain in her face was evident, even under the night sky. He let out a slow stream of air.

"This is wrong." She spoke softly, as if trying to keep Cara from hearing her. "Alone, after dark, sharing a blanket with an outsider. You're in serious violation of everything we hold dear, things you took vows concerning."

"This woman needs a little help for the next few days, maybe a week."

"Is…is she the one your Daed's been telling me about, the one Simeon said was staying in the barn and your Daed called the police about?"

"He shouldn't have done that. She's not the type of person he thinks."

Becca massaged her temples. "I want to trust your judgment, Ephraim. If you think she's a worthy cause, give her money and send her on her way, and I'll say nothing to anyone about tonight."

"She needs more than money. She needs…a friend."

"Ephraim, please, put an end to this tonight, before it's too late."

Stunned at her gentle threat, Ephraim saw that she cared about his choices the way any mother would. He knew she honored his sense of duty toward the family, but he hadn't realized she carried maternal feelings for him. "She stays. At least for a while. I'm sorry."

Becca's eyes narrowed, studying Cara. "If she's just someone who needs help, does Anna Mary know about her?"

"Not yet."

"Where is she staying?"

"I'm trying to help her find her a place. Until then I'm sleeping in the shop."

Becca clutched her throat, wavering as if she might faint. "She's staying in your home?" She drew several breaths. "I'll give you until Saturday to get her out of your place. Then you must go to the church leaders and come clean about what's been going on. After that…" She turned toward the creek. "Simeon," she snapped, "kumm." Without waiting, she stomped off toward the gate.

Ephraim turned to Cara, who stared up at him from the blanket. "None of this changes anything."

"I'm really sorry about all this. I had no idea the Amish had strict rules about such things."

"Being here with you is against what I vowed when I joined the faith. And for good reason. But right now we have no choice." He took a seat beside her and watched Simeon walk toward the gate, waving to Lori as he left.

"Is Anna Mary your girlfriend?"

"Ya. She's the one who made the fried chicken and cake we just ate."

"Then you'd better tell her what's going on."

What could he say to Anna Mary? That he'd allowed a strange woman to stay in his home and sleep in his bed overnight when he wasn't keen on Anna Mary cooking a meal in his kitchen?

Twenty

The shrill of the hydraulic saw in Ephraim's hand didn't keep him from hearing the amplified ring of the office phone. Stopping the wood in front of the rotating blade, he glanced up. His foreman moved toward the corner office to answer it. Grey's lively steps gave no hint to the troubles he kept buried. Despite how long they'd known each other, the two never spoke about what weighed on him.

Tomorrow was Saturday—Becca's deadline day—and Ephraim had no more answers now than when she'd given him the ultimatum day before yesterday. Trying to focus on the piece of wood in front of him, Ephraim couldn't keep from thinking of Cara. She needed help, and he wanted to give it to her, but was Becca right? Was he going about this the wrong way? He'd taken a vow to live according to the Ordnung. Having a young Englischer woman in his home was in direct violation of the Old Ways. It wouldn't be considered wise by any Christian standards.

How could helping her be right if it had the potential to cause division between him and everything he believed in—if it separated him from his family and community? The Amish reached out to those who weren't Amish. But never like this.

The community would have issues with her living at his place, but the real problems would arise when they learned who she was—the daughter of Malinda Riehl Atwater. He didn't want to tell Cara that her mother had left a trail of devastated loved ones. Twice.

When he was twelve, he'd overheard the adults saying Malinda had broken her vows to the church. She left Dry Lake and her fiancé mere weeks before their wedding. All for an outsider. A drifter who'd come through and stolen her good sense. Was her daughter doing the same thing to him, coming to Dry Lake as a drifter and on a course to ruin his life? Even if she wasn't, would the community believe her innocent of that?

Sunlight shifted across the concrete floor, catching his eye. He glanced up to see Grey. Ephraim turned the saw off.

"Call for you. Someone from social services," Grey said softly.

"Thanks." He went to the office and closed the door behind him. The woman on the phone asked a few questions before telling him of her plans to conduct an in-home visit that afternoon. He thanked her and hung up the phone, his heart racing. His time was up for keeping secrets. Once the social worker pulled into his driveway and went into his house, the news would permeate the community like pollen in springtime.

He picked up the newspaper from his desk. A dozen large red *x*'s filled the little boxes on the for-rent page. He'd made calls for two days, searching for an apartment for Cara and Lori. He'd found nothing. His Daed would take the news much better if Ephraim could say she'd be leaving in a day or two.

He studied each square he'd made an *x* in, wondering if there was any way he could get her moved before Sunday. Church was to be held at his place this week. If Cara could be gone by then, his punishment from the church leaders wouldn't be as severe.

By this time tomorrow everyone in the district would probably know he'd shared his home with a woman. He knew Becca hadn't said anything, not yet. She wanted to give Ephraim time to alter the situation. But he had to tell Daed before someone else did. Anna Mary needed to know too. But when he'd gone by her place earlier, her mother said a driver had taken her to her sister's last night.

He tossed the newspaper into the trash. His anxiety rose, as if a firestorm were headed straight for his house.

As Cara placed the clean lunch plates in the cabinet, the doorbell rang.

"Get that, please," Mrs. Howard called from her bed.

Cara glanced through a window into the backyard, checking on Lori.

After three nights of staying in a house instead of a barn, she could feel the effects of regular meals and sound sleep at night. It was midafternoon, and she still had a bit of energy, and her hands were steady.

When she opened the front door, a middle-aged man with red hair and freckles stared back at her. "Cara?"

A nervous chill ran down her spine. "Do I know you?"

He shook his head. "I'm Robbie. I work for Ephraim." He pointed to the front seat of his car, where a young woman sat. "That's Annie, Ephraim's fourteen-year-old stepsister. She's to take your place here, and you're to go back to his house. He said to tell you a Mrs. Forrester called, and she'll be at his home in about an hour."

Feeling as if she were suffocating, she nodded. "Okay, give me a minute."

"I'll be in the car."

Her mind whirled with disjointed thoughts as she went down the hallway to Mrs. Howard's bedroom. Ephraim's willingness to help her was unbelievable. She felt he wasn't the least bit attracted to her, but he did seem as honest and direct now as twenty years ago when he'd asked if she was a boy or a girl.

An image of him popped into her mind, followed by a thought that made her chuckle. Hollywood would love to get hold of him. She didn't know if he could act, but he was definitely a looker with that strawberry blond hair and those gray blue eyes. Six feet of pure drawing power, as Kendal would say.

When Cara entered the bedroom, Mrs. Howard looked up from her book.

"Remember when I told you I might need to leave during the day sometime this week?" Cara waited until she nodded. "Well, I need to go now. There's a driver outside, and he brought Annie, a young Amish woman, to sit with you until your husband gets home."

"No problem, dear. Can she weed the garden?"

"Being fourteen and Amish, she's sure to be better at it than I am."

Twenty-One

With only an hour before social services arrived, Ephraim dialed the number to his Daed's doctor's office. He finally had his Daed's nurse on the line. Because of privacy rules, the nurse couldn't tell him anything specific about his Daed's health. When Ephraim asked for general information concerning cardiomyopathy, she freely shared the information.

Listening intently, Ephraim tried to hear everything—spoken and unspoken. "Do you think his heart can withstand the stress of some difficult news?"

"Stress is a part of life. Patients who have cardiomyopathy can't rid their lives of stress. And bad news can usually be shared in a way that's not jolting or shocking."

"He seems more fragile with each passing year. I don't want to do or say anything that would cause an episode, but his symptoms continually weaken him."

"We often suggest that patients who have cardiomyopathy with symptoms similar to your dad's have a procedure called AICD. A cardiac defibrillator is implanted into the chest wall, and it causes the heart to reset its rhythm as needed."

"Has he been told about this procedure?"

"I'm sorry. I can share about diseases, but your question falls under doctor-patient confidentiality."

Ephraim thanked her and hung up. He needed to tell his Daed about Cara in a way that wouldn't shock him.

He left the office and entered the main part of the workshop. "I'm heading out for the day."

Mahlon set aside the carving tool in hand. "Did you put my time off on the schedule for next week?"

"Can we talk about it later? I have some other things I need to deal with."

"Ya. Don't forget Deb wanted you and Anna Mary to go out with us tonight."

"I won't forget. You and Grey be sure to clear the center of the room and put the paints up high. The bench wagon will be here tomorrow." Church met at his place only once a year, just like it did at everybody else's home in the community, but the timing of it being this Sunday couldn't be worse. Since his home was small, he and his family had to set up the benches in the shop.

Needing a few minutes to think, he went into the field. The pasture was thick with grass, the pond sparkled in the distance, and a breeze stirred around him. He closed his eyes.

An odd feeling nagged at him, as if he'd missed a step in planning the next few hours. What was stirring such unrest in him? *Have I missed something I should do?*

A little unsure if that was a prayer or him questioning himself, he was surprised when peace eased through him. He took a deep breath. Maybe this afternoon wouldn't be so bad after all. Lingering in the quiet moment, he welcomed more of God. Suddenly it seemed as if he were in church during one of those rare and special moments when His spirit seemed to rest all around him.

Be me to her.

The thought made his heart race, and he stumbled back. He couldn't be anything to Cara but a friend—for a very short time. She was fascinating, and under different circumstances they could enjoy being friends. But she was from a different world, an outsider—and the daughter of Malinda Riehl.

"Ephraim?"

He turned to face his Daed. "Good to see you out and about."

He propped his foot on the bottom of the split-rail fence. "I came looking for you. You've not been around much lately. Do you have that much going on with work?"

"Just the usual stuff. How're you feeling?"

"Pretty good. I'm watching my salt intake, hoping I don't get another bout of fluid overload."

"Daed, I need to talk with you about some things that are going on. Do you think you're up to it?"

Half of Daed's face lifted in a smile. "Sure."

"Maybe we should go back to your house and sit."

"You're not going to start mollycoddling me like Becca does, are you?" He laughed. "I don't think I could stand that. I know the woman doesn't want to lose a second husband, but if she doesn't lighten up, I'm going to quit trying to pacify her. She's got every daughter in the house following her lead. Don't you start too."

"Well, let's at least go sit in the side yard."

They moseyed that way, and each took a seat in a lawn chair. The breeze carried the aroma of one of Becca's suppers cooking.

Without telling his father who Cara was, he began explaining about the woman he'd found staying in the barn. "Daed, Becca said you called the police."

"Ya, I did."

Ephraim tried to keep his voice even, but he wanted to snap and growl. "You should have talked to me first."

"You wrote a letter, telling her to leave."

"It's my barn and property, and I was handling it. The police came and were going to separate her and her daughter, so I said she could stay at my place. She's been there for the last three nights."

"An Englischer woman and child, without a husband?" He looked more concerned than angry. "I can't believe you handled it this way. If she is destitute, why not bring her to our home?"

"For a lot of reasons." Not only would no one have wanted them, but Cara and Lori needed a quiet place to ease the harshness of what they'd been through, not the discomfort of being a guest in a houseful of people. "You'd just come home from the hospital. And your home is always bursting at the seams with children."

Lines of disappointment carved into stone around his Daed's eyes. "Better her in a bedroom with children than jeopardizing your soul." He stared at Ephraim as if he no longer understood him. "But years ago you came home when I needed you, and you've been more to this family and to me than I ever had the right to ask. I won't let the bishop forget that when he's talking with us preachers after you go see him."

"Daed." Ephraim paused. "I'm not taking this to the bishop. I'm just telling you what's going on, forewarning you about what's ahead."

"She's not gone?"

"No."

Daed stared, wordlessly lecturing him before saying, "You're not asking for forgiveness, ready to take your discipline from the church and put this behind you?"

"No."

"No?" His voice rang across the land, echoing back to them. "You have to put a stop to this. You need to repent—to the church leaders, to this community, and to God, who you knelt before and vowed to keep the Ordnung and to live according to our ways."

Ephraim had taken that vow. And since returning to Dry Lake nine years ago, he'd always aimed to be a good influence on the younger generation, to help them learn to respect the Old Ways.

Be me to her.

The thought seemed to float on the wind, entering his soul from outside himself. "It's not against our ways to help someone."

"It's not against our ways to be with a woman either, but that doesn't make it right except in one circumstance, does it?"

"Daed, I'm asking you to trust me. Please."

He leaned forward. "I trust in God and in the Old Ways and in the authority of the church. The Word says every way of man is right in his own eyes. We have the Ordnung because man cannot allow emotions and quick decisions to guide him."

He knew his father's words were true, but did one truth negate another? "We're also told not to withhold good when the power is in our hands to do it."

"You really think you're doing any good in this? You need to remain faithful to your oath." Daed rubbed the center of his chest. "Even as a preacher, I doubt I can cut down on the shunning time that's ahead of you."

Ephraim nodded. The night he chose to stay in his home for Lori's sake instead of going to the shop to sleep, he'd known he would be shunned.

Daed drew a long, tired breath. "Who is this woman?"

Ephraim shook his head, wishing he hadn't asked.

A knowing look went through Daed's eyes. "You knew her before she showed up in the barn. She's from your days among the Englischers, isn't she?" He pounded his fists on the arm of the chair, his face turning red. "You absolutely cannot continue this."

Ephraim had no choice. Telling him the truth of who she was would be better than his thinking an Englischer was seeking to renew some imaginary relationship. "She's Malinda Riehl's daughter."

His father's face drained of all color. "Cara?"

Ephraim nodded.

Daed's eyes filled with tears. "I thought I saw Malinda walking down the road with Cara beside her last Friday. I thought I must be imagining things. But it didn't dawn on me it might be Cara. I'll tell you what I did see—a drunken thief, or maybe worse."

"No, Daed. You saw someone who needed help. She's not a drunk. I'm sure of it."

His Daed looked toward heaven. "Oh dear Father." He focused on his son. "Listen to me. Malinda Riehl grew up one of us, was taught the same things you were. But when she ran off the first time, she left betrayal and brokenness behind her. You think her daughter's any better? I tell you, she'll be worse. Shunning will be the easiest of what's in store for you."

Ephraim closed his eyes, searching for peace as he listened to the birds sing and the wind rustle the leaves. "I don't know what happened the first time Malinda left, but the second time around wasn't by choice. I understand that she stirred a lot of negative emotions while trying to find Cara a safe place to live, but—"

"Don't tell me what happened," his Daed interrupted him. "You weren't much more than a child. I remember well the trouble she caused. It was only six months after I'd been chosen as a preacher. Her presence caused a rift between your mother and me, but the church leaders agreed that Cara could come here to live. Levina, Malinda's own grandmother, was willing to raise Cara. But we couldn't give permission for Malinda to stay. For dozens of reasons all three of us church leaders fervently discussed over and over again, we couldn't do anything that would make it easy for Malinda to run from her husband as she'd run from the community that loved her. Malinda said little in response to our decision except that she needed some time with Cara to prepare her. They went back to New York, and she never returned. Never even called."

"Daed...she died. Had an accident not long after she left here with Cara, and it killed her instantly."

His father grew quiet. "If your mother were alive to learn of that..." He closed his eyes. "I'm sorry. I really am." He drew a jerky breath. "You'll never know how much I hate this. But the mess isn't our fault, even though I was the one who called the police. You can't risk your salvation because Malinda chose the world over God. Tell me her daughter isn't of the world too."

He couldn't. The weight of what was ahead settled over him. "I know you can't understand all this. I'm not sure I do. But my mind is made up. I'll do whatever I can to help her."

His father stared at him. "She's already caused you to turn your back on God and family. Don't let this woman stay. If you do, all that will be left for you is ruin and regret."

"My decision isn't out of rebellion. It's the right thing to do, and I'm the right person to do it."

Daed placed his hand on Ephraim's shoulder and gently squeezed it. "You're wrong. But it seems I won't be the one to convince you of it." He stood and walked into the house.

Ephraim closed his eyes. "Be Me to her." He mumbled the words, wondering what they really meant.

Twenty-Two

As they rode in Robbie's vehicle toward Ephraim's place, Cara felt like a voiceless child again. The words she would need jumbled into nonsense inside her brain. Through years of dealing with social workers, she'd always hated the meetings. Those she'd had experience with didn't see things that were clear and saw all sorts of things that weren't even there.

"You known Ephraim long?" Robbie asked.

Cara folded her arms, wondering if she owed it to Ephraim to answer this man agreeably. "Long enough."

He frowned and shrugged. "Where'd you get that dress?"

"Excuse me?" Cara tried to keep the snarl out of her tone.

"It's a Plain dress, but you're not Amish."

"The Howards insisted on extreme modesty, so I wear it when I have to. Can we just ride in silence, please?"

"I reckon so." He straightened his ball cap. "I was just trying to make conversation."

Who was he kidding? He was on a fishing expedition, hoping to reel in answers. But she wouldn't tell him so, in case that'd be disrespectful to Ephraim.

Her mind moved from thought to thought like fire on a wind-swept hill. What if the social worker didn't accept her living arrangement as stable enough? What if she took Lori because Cara had been forced to steal to feed her daughter? She was making enough money to keep them fed now. But Mrs. Howard would be out of her cast within two weeks. Then what would she do? If Ephraim stopped helping her, she'd be homeless again. How was she going to prove to the social worker that she was capable of providing for Lori when everything hinged on one man's generosity? Suddenly it felt as if she'd left one corner only to be backed into a different corner. And wouldn't Mike be pleased to know the misery he'd dished out?

She tapped her fingertips against her thighs, wishing she could relax. "You don't happen to have a cigarette, do you?"

"Sorry. I gave up smoking years ago."

Forcing herself to sit still, she tried to focus on something besides Mrs. Forrester. Ephraim had planned on seeing Anna Mary this morning to tell her what was going on. He didn't seem the least bit nervous, so she figured they must have a really good relationship.

Robbie barely tapped the brakes before pulling into the shop's driveway.

"Did Ephraim say to come in this way?"

He shrugged. "Didn't say."

"Then drive to the road that leads to Ephraim's driveway. Let's not use the shop's. Please."

"You should've said something sooner. It's too late for that now." He passed the main house and pulled up in front of the shop.

Wondering if the man came this way on purpose, she mumbled a sarcastic thanks. She hoped Ephraim's family hadn't seen them pass, but what was done was done.

She turned to her daughter. Haunting images of social services taking Lori sent a nervous chill through her. No one was going to take her daughter. Logic told her that social services wasn't looking for an excuse to separate children from their mothers. Still, her nerves were driving her up the wall. If she had nothing to fear, why were her emotions in overdrive?

When the engine shut off, she found her voice. "Lori, we're going across the field and straight to Ephraim's house. If you see him in the shop, don't call out to him or do anything that might draw attention."

Robbie scowled. "Guess I should've taken you the long way around."

"I guess so." They got out of the car, and she took Lori's hand in hers. Without a word they crossed the parking area and entered Ephraim's yard.

They went inside. The quiet beauty of his home whispered hope. Surely one look at this place would tell the social worker that Lori had a good place to stay now. Sunlight lay across the gorgeous hardwood floors, and for the first time she wondered if they were Ephraim's handiwork. The beige countertops were spotless, and everything except their breakfast dishes was neat and clean.

A breeze stirred the warm air as Cara set the backpack in a chair. "Remember when the police let us come home with Ephraim?"

Lori nodded.

"Well, because we were sleeping in the barn, they needed to turn our names in to someone who looks after little kids. They just want to make sure you're being taken care of. A woman named Mrs. Forrester is coming to see us today. She's going to ask questions, and we're going to be very polite and answer her."

"I liked it better in the barn with the pups than in New York. Can I tell her that?"

Wishing she knew how to instruct Lori to answer, Cara moved to the kitchen sink.

"Can I tell her about Better Days?"

Cara licked her lips, trying to calm her nerves. "Sure, but he's not your dog. You remember that, right?"

"He's just as good as being mine as long as you don't make us leave."

Cara turned on the hot water, trying to drown out the accusation in Lori's tone. To Lori, every move had been her mother's choice. Cara let Lori feel that way rather than have her believe a bogeyman was after them. She deserved to feel safe—even if she came to resent her mother in the process. That decision stood like every other decision she'd made: choosing the lesser of the two evils.

Desire washed over Cara. A longing so deep it seemed to have the power to pull her into another world. She ached to call upon a higher being…to ask some unseen life form to smooth things out, not only with social services, but with Ephraim's family.

Realizing she still had on an Amish dress, she dried her hands and went into the bedroom to change. It wouldn't do for the woman to ask any questions about the dress, like where she got it.

Lori followed her. "Can I go outside?"

"Not today." Cara slid into her jeans and sweater. Somehow she had to keep Lori pinned up inside until Ephraim's family had gone to bed for the night. "You can read a book or draw or play with the toys Ephraim brought you."

"Are we hiding again?"

Cara sank onto the bed. "Lori, I need you to stay inside today and be really, really good. Can you do that for Mom?"

Her daughter studied her. "How come I got butterflies in my belly?"

Placing her hand on Lori's head, she smiled. "Because I do, and you can feel it. But we'll be fine. Ephraim won't let anything bad happen to us."

She hoped that was true, but she hated herself for needing his help. Hated Mike for putting her in this situation. Hated relying on handouts. But she saw no other way. Not right now.

Someone knocked, making Cara jolt to her feet. She motioned for Lori to hop up, and Cara straightened the bed.

"Hello?" A girl's voice rang through the house. "Ephraim?"

Cara hurried out the bedroom door to find a pretty Amish woman with jet-black hair and blue eyes waiting by the door. The woman's eyes moved from the top of Cara's head to her feet and back up again. "What are you doing here?"

A second woman, the one who'd served Cara and Lori food for free at the auction, stepped forward. "Where's Ephraim?"

Unsure what Ephraim did or didn't want her to say, she stayed silent. The blue-eyed one shrugged. "He doesn't seem to be here."

Lori moved in close to her mother. "I saw him in the shop when we came home."

"Home?" the blue-eyed one echoed, her face reflecting shock.

The screen door flopped open, and Ephraim stepped inside. One quick glance around the room, and he turned his focus to the blue-eyed one.

She offered a sweet smile, searching his face for reassurance before lowering her eyes. This girl was in love. She had to be Anna Mary.

"Mamm said you came by this morning to see me."

"Ya, I wanted us to talk." He glanced to Cara and Lori.

The blue-eyed girl kept her focus on Ephraim. "I spent the night with my sister."

He looked at Cara. "You doing okay?"

She forced a nod.

He gave her a half smile, but his eyes carried a look of stress. "Deborah, Anna Mary, this is Cara Moore and her daughter, Lori. They're staying here for a while."

Deborah stared at Ephraim, stunned into silence.

Anna Mary's eyes grew large. She pointed both index fingers at the floor. "Here?"

Ephraim's face became stonelike. "Ya."

"She can't stay *here*."

Lori hid behind her mother as the tension in the room became suffocating. A knock on the screen door made Cara jerk. Ephraim glanced to her, and the undercurrent of understanding that ran between them didn't need words. The social worker had arrived, and she'd overheard Anna Mary's proclamation.

With no hint of nervousness, he turned toward the newcomer. "Mrs. Forrester?"

"Elaine Forrester, yes."

"Come right in."

He let the thirty-something woman inside. She didn't look anything like the social workers Cara remembered. No funny-looking glasses or wild gray hair half pinned up and half falling down, and she wasn't peering down her nose at them. Holding a blue canvas briefcase in one hand, she looked straight at Ephraim. "You must be Ephraim Mast." He nodded and shook her hand.

"I'd like to talk with you too, but first I'm here to see Cara and Lori Moore."

Cara's skin felt like a pincushion as she stepped forward. "I'm Cara, and this is my daughter, Lori."

"Nice to meet you. You're living here now. Is that correct?"

"Yes," Ephraim spoke up. "For as long as they need."

His bold statement shocked Cara. Anna Mary clenched her jaws and said nothing.

"Mrs. Forrester, this is my sister Deborah and a friend, Anna Mary."

"Nice to meet you." She walked to the kitchen table and set her briefcase on it. After pulling out a leather clipboard, she tapped it. "I'm just going to look around the place." She faced Cara. "Then we'll chat."

Feeling almost as vulnerable as if Mike were looming over her, Cara nodded.

Ephraim motioned Deborah and Anna Mary to the back door. They filed out in silence. He turned to Cara. "You'll do fine. I'll be in the hiddy. It's the area inside the hedges. When she's ready to talk with me, just call."

"Thanks."

Ephraim followed Deborah and Anna Mary into his hiddy. He'd barely stepped through the narrow opening in the hedges when they came to a stop and faced him. Obviously Daed or Becca hadn't said anything to his sister about Cara. Deborah's eyes begged for answers, looking more worried than he'd seen her since their mother died. He hadn't expected that, or maybe he hadn't taken the time to really think about it.

Instead of looking jealous, Anna Mary seemed confused. "What's going on?"

He realized the news, all of it, had to come out within the next few minutes, but sharing it as slowly as possible seemed wise. He was on the brink of being shunned, and Anna Mary should hear the truth from him. "Cara needs help, and I'm giving it to her."

"Ephraim, where is she from? Who is she?" Deborah demanded. "How do you know her?"

"She's from New York. Came here about a week ago. She was living in Levina's barn, and I gave her a place to stay."

"In the barn?" Anna Mary shuddered. "So where are you staying?"

"It's complicated. Her daughter, Lori, was afraid the police would come back for them, so I stayed in the storage room the first night. Then I spent the last two nights in the shop."

"The police? Were they after them?"

"No. Not really. It was mostly a misunderstanding, but they did show up."

His sister stared at him. "Why would you do this?"

"Sometimes doing the right thing doesn't look right at all."

Deborah angled her head, looking worried. "If this gets back to the bishop, you'll be excommunicated. And I can't think what this could do to Daed."

"Daed knows. I talked to him earlier. Healthwise, he took it well. I've made my choice."

Anna Mary took a seat on the wooden swing. "Without even talking to me?"

He squelched his desire to say that he didn't need her permission to help someone. Besides, there hadn't been time for a committee meeting, and she wasn't home when he decided it was time to tell her.

"You'd do this, knowing you'd be shunned?" Deborah wiped a stray tear. "This Cara person must be someone more to you than a stranger who hid in your barn. Who *is* she? And who is that Elaine Forrester?"

Ephraim took a seat next to Anna Mary. He wasn't willing to talk to them about Cara's ties to the community until he could first tell Cara that she had relatives here and that her mother had been raised Amish. "Elaine is a social worker. Cara's a friend from long ago, and she needs help in order to hold on to her daughter."

"Has she taken possession of your good sense?" Deborah asked softly.

Anna Mary sighed heavily. "Don't make it sound like he's interested in her. Do you really think he'd allow any girl this much access to his home if he was attracted to her?"

Thankful Anna Mary was thinking about this reasonably, Ephraim eased his hand over hers. "I've looked through ads and made calls, trying to find a place for her. There's just nothing out this way."

"There should be some jobs and apartments in Shippensburg," Anna Mary offered.

Like a stick being flailed into a hornets' nest, her statement struck him, stirring emotions and thoughts that stung. He didn't want Cara in Shippensburg.

Stunned at the feelings surging through him, he turned from Anna Mary's probing eyes and gazed out across the field. Answers to Cara's past were hiding among the Amish of Dry Lake. And whether anyone in his community liked it or not, Cara deserved to be treated as a treasure once stolen and now returned to them by a power not her own.

Twenty-Three

Cara had replied to a hundred questions, including some probing ones about her relationship with Ephraim. Now she waited in the living room while Mrs. Forrester and Lori strolled through the home, chatting. She could hear Lori telling the woman about life in New York, being hungry some days since leaving there, and going on a picnic with Ephraim.

"Lori," the woman said, "what's your mommy like when she gets really mad?"

Without a moment's hesitation, Lori answered, "She gets on her knees in front of me and points her finger right here." Cara couldn't see, but she was sure Lori was pointing to her nose. "She calls me Lori Moore, real quicklike. Then she says, 'You stop.'" Lori mimicked her mother's voice. "Sometimes she says, 'Give me a break, kid. When you're the adult, we'll do it your way.'"

"Does she ever hit you?"

"No. But she hit a man at a bus station once. She wouldn't tell me why, and I didn't ask twice."

"Has she ever left you with anyone who hit you?"

They walked into the storage room, and Cara couldn't make out all their words. It sounded like Mrs. Forrester was going into more personal questions. A few minutes later the two reentered the room. The woman set the leather clipboard beside her and dug into her briefcase. Cara tried to catch a glimpse of her notes.

Mrs. Forrester tapped the legal pad where Cara's full name and Social

Security number were listed. "If I run your info through the New York database, will I get a hit?"

Cara swallowed, not sure she was ready for Lori to know. "I was in foster care from eight years old until I was fifteen."

"Because?"

"My mother had died, and my dad…left."

"But you were only in the system until you turned fifteen? Why?"

"I ran away."

The woman pulled out several pamphlets and set them on the coffee table. "What made you leave New York?"

"Does it matter?"

"I won't know that until you talk to me."

Cara stood firm, not wanting to give an answer in front of Lori. "There are reasons. Good ones."

The woman leaned forward. "I'm not here because of an anonymous tip. This visit was initiated because the police filed a report based on what they had witnessed. Added to that, you removed Lori from school the first part of May. School doesn't end in New York until mid-June or here for another week. Technically, she's truant, and you're the reason." She tapped the pamphlets. "My gut says something's going on that has nothing to do with questions about your parenting ability. Although your decision-making process does seem questionable."

Great. More viewpoints from the clueless. Cara figured the woman might survive two weeks with someone like Mike hounding her, maybe less.

Mrs. Forrester shrugged. "I'm only here to help, but I want answers to every question."

Cara didn't want her kind of help, but she stood. "Come on, Lori. You can wait outside with Ephraim."

Lori took her hand and walked silently until they were outside. "Is she gonna put cuffs on you and take you somewhere?"

"No."

"You sure?"

"Yes." She wasn't sure of much else, but that part didn't worry her. They walked to the six-foot hedges and found the slight entrance. She spotted Ephraim on the swing with Anna Mary. They made a striking couple. "Can she stay with you for a few minutes?"

"Ya."

Lori clutched her hand tighter. "I wanna stay with you."

Ephraim stood. "How about if we walk to the barn and check on Better Days?"

Lori shook her head.

"We'll bring the pup back here." Ephraim held out his hand, but Lori didn't take it.

Cara pulled her hand free. "I'll be here when you get back. I promise."

"No." Lori clutched her mother's leg.

Cara pried Lori's hands free and knelt in front of her. "Come on, kiddo. I'm going nowhere. Can't you trust me on this?"

Lori wrapped her arms around her mother's neck. "I'll be good. Just don't leave me."

"You couldn't get rid of me if you turned into a whole gang of trouble. Never forget that." Cara hugged her tight and then stood. "I'll be here when you get back."

Lori swiped at her tears and took Ephraim's hand.

He moved in closer to Cara. "How's it going in there?"

"Good, I think, except I'm afraid she's going to ask questions about my life that I don't have the answers to."

Ephraim chuckled, but it sounded forced, making her wonder if he actually cared. She knew he had honor to him or he wouldn't be doing all this to help her. But that was different. Honor was what made people do certain things so they could live with themselves. Caring? Well…that meant she and Lori mattered.

When she went back inside, Mrs. Forrester was on the couch waiting for her. Cara went to the rocker and sat, ready to answer the toughest questions yet.

"Cara, what caused you to leave New York that you're not willing to talk about in front of your daughter?"

In spite of wanting to stonewall the woman, Cara described her years of dealing with Mike, and the woman took notes.

Mrs. Forrester tapped her pen on the legal pad. "Logically one would think he'd have given up stalking years ago. But when you were in foster care and told the authorities, somebody blew it, Cara. I might be able to do some investigating, but you need to contact the police."

"No."

"He could be doing this to others."

She cursed. "That's not my problem. When I tried to turn him in years ago, everyone ignored me. The only thing that matters to me is staying alive so I can keep Lori safe."

"Okay, okay." She took the pamphlets off the table. "There are programs that offer assistance. Lori's past the age to be eligible for WIC, but there are other policies in place to help provide food and shelter."

Cara held her hand up. "I don't understand. Am I in a battle to keep Lori or not?"

"Did you know your daughter saw Kendal doing drugs?"

Cara swallowed. "Yes…Lori told me. Kendal and I had a big fight about it. It didn't happen twice."

"Having no friends can be better than having bad ones."

"Oh yeah? When you have some maniac running everyone out of your life, let's see how you feel."

The woman sighed. "Cara, you have a new start now, and I see no reason to consider removing your daughter from you."

Hope hung frozen in the air. Afraid it might turn to vapor and fade into nothing, Cara didn't move.

The woman stood. "I'll do a follow-up or two. You need to get her enrolled in school before the next year begins."

"Is…is that it?"

"We're done for now."

Cara's heart danced inside her chest, some weird, excited tap she'd never felt before.

"I've seen and heard a lot in my years as a social worker, and overall you've handled a bad situation pretty well." She passed the pamphlets to Cara and explained how to get government help.

"I don't want assistance. I just want to be left alone."

"Your decision. If you change your mind, let me know."

When they stepped outside, Ephraim walked toward them. Cara's eyes met his, and she wondered if he knew what he'd done for her.

Mrs. Forrester turned to her. "Thank you, Cara. I'd like to speak to Ephraim alone for a few minutes."

Deborah and Anna Mary told Ephraim good-bye and left. Cara took Lori inside, hoping Ephraim would come talk to her as soon as he could.

"How'd I do, Mom?"

She knelt in front of Lori. "You were you." She licked her lips, trying to keep the tears at bay. "And that was absolutely perfect."

"Are the police coming back?"

She tugged on her daughter's dress. A week of wearing mostly the same dress day and night made for a very tattered outfit. It'd been a long journey to get free of Mike, but they finally had a new start. "Nope."

"We don't have to hide anymore?"

Cara gasped, fighting harder against the tears. "No, honey, we don't." She eased her arms around Lori, and the matchless comfort of the gesture swept through her.

She heard footsteps on the porch and looked up, not caring if Ephraim noticed her tears.

"Mrs. Forrester is gone." He opened the screen door and walked inside. "She likes you. She said she wished all moms were as determined to take care of their little ones as you are."

Cara laughed. "Who cares whether she likes me or not?"

His smile warmed her, and she rose to her feet. "You do, trust me."

The puppy whined, and Ephraim let him in. Feeling years of heaviness fall from her body, Cara felt giddy. The desire to dance around the room pulsed through her.

Ephraim leaned against the counter. "Seems to me this deserves a celebration."

Lori ran to the center of the room, Better Days nipping at her heels. "Let's dance! One, two, three." She clapped her hands as she said each number.

Cara laughed and hurried to her side. Better Days ran around them, barking. She and Lori hummed "My Girl" and clapped and danced a jig as they often did when the tiniest bit of good news came their way. They raised their arms and twirled, a tradition that cost them nothing but always made Lori happy. How long had it been since they'd danced and laughed? They twirled around and around, laughing and making their favorite wild moves with their bodies.

When the dance was through, they gave themselves a round of applause. But suddenly Lori darted behind her, causing her to glance up. Two men dressed in black stood beside Ephraim. When had they come in? Lori pressed her body against Cara's leg, holding on tightly.

One man rubbed his chest. *"In dei Heemet?"* The man looked upset, and his voice wavered.

The older man pulled his stare from Cara. "Ephraim," he whispered, shaking his head. *"Kumm raus. Loss uns schwetze."*

Ephraim nodded, and the two men left the house.

He walked to Lori. "This is your home until we find something better suited to you with electricity and your own bedroom. No one is going to change that." He placed his hand on her head. "Trust me?"

Lori released her firm grip on Cara's leg, her body relaxing as she nodded.

The joy of a few minutes ago faded from Cara. "Is everything okay?"

"Ya. But I need to leave. I'll sleep in the shop tonight. I don't have time to start a cook fire. Can you?"

"Sure. Are you in trouble?"

"I'm not in trouble with the One who counts."

"What?"

"For you, the police and Mrs. Forrester counted. We all have someone we don't want to be in trouble with."

She laughed. "Maybe you should take her somewhere extra nice."

A puzzled look covered his face for a moment. "Oh, you think I meant…" He chuckled and tipped his hat. "Good night, ladies."

Twenty-Four

Still fighting tears, Deborah slipped into a clean dress for tonight. She and Mahlon had made plans, but she was in no mood for going out. Part of her wanted to crawl into bed and pull the blankets over her head. But she hoped to get Mahlon to change his mind about leaving tomorrow, and she wouldn't pass up the opportunity to be near Ephraim. Maybe once she had time with him, she'd begin to understand why he'd done such a brazen, foolish thing.

Hearing men's voices outside, she moved to the window. The bishop and her Daed stood in the side yard, talking to Ephraim. She raised the window higher so she could eavesdrop.

"I understand how this looks," Ephraim said, "but I've done nothing wrong. I'm just asking for some time to work with her, to help her get on her feet."

"She's worse than her mother," Daed said. "Malinda would never have dressed like that or stolen from us or dragged her child around, homeless. If you don't put a separation between you and her, you'll put one between you and God."

"It's not like that. She's on a path she didn't choose. It was chosen for her, and I want to help her get off it. And she's not a bad influence." Deborah heard the ire in her brother's voice as he defended himself. She couldn't imagine him giving in to any temptations with a girl, but she never would've believed he'd invite an Englischer woman, this Cara, to stay with him either.

"Did we not see her dancing in your home? In that tight clothing, with too much skin showing, even her belly." The bishop's voice remained calm as he tried to reason with Ephraim.

"She doesn't see things like we do. You see her ways as sinful. She sees them as normal."

"It doesn't matter how she sees them. Get her out of your life and away from this community," Daed added.

Deborah wondered why they wanted to get rid of the girl. She understood getting her out of her brother's house and away from him, whether he was sleeping in the shop or not. But why would they want her out of Dry Lake?

"I can't do that."

A knot formed in Deborah's stomach.

"Please don't do this," the bishop said. "If you refuse to submit, we'll have no choice but to be very strict on you until you're willing to follow wisdom. A shunning is always painful, but will I be forced to draw lines even more severe than is normal?"

Someone knocked on Deborah's door. "Kumm."

Anna Mary held out Deborah's black apron. "All pressed and ready to go."

"Denki."

The bishop stood near Ephraim, talking softly, and she could no longer hear him.

"What are you looking at?" Anna Mary moved to the window.

Deborah felt like a dress being run through the wringer. Why was Ephraim being so stubborn?

Anna Mary's face turned ashen. "The bishop knows?"

Deborah slid into her apron. There wasn't anything she could say that would make this better. The damage had been done.

Anna Mary slowly turned from the window and sat on the bed. "Don't worry so much about Ephraim. He wanted to help this girl, but I also think he wants to test me."

Deborah pinned the apron in place around her waist. "What do you mean?"

"He's been single all these years, goes for long spells without courting. He's been seeing me longer than anyone. We've been getting really close. I can feel his voice inside me even when he's working out of town." She pulled a pillow into her lap. "And now he does this? You can't tell me it's not odd."

Mulling over her friend's conclusions, Deborah placed her Kapp on her head. "If he's shunned, will you wait for him?"

"Of course. We'll be allowed to visit him, and we can take him special dinners. Singings and outings will be forbidden, but we can work around that."

Deborah sat beside her friend. "I heard what the bishop said. I don't think the normal restrictions will apply."

"Why?"

"Because Ephraim's refusing to remove Cara from his home or separate his life from hers. He intends to do as he sees fit."

Hurt filled Anna Mary's eyes. "For me there is no one else. But the waiting won't be the hardest part. The damage to his reputation won't fade for years."

Deborah grabbed straight pins from the nightstand and weaved one through the Kapp and strands of her hair. "It makes me feel sick thinking about it."

"Cara is nothing more than a troublemaking nobody...a...a tramp." Anna Mary tossed the pillow onto the bed. "He felt sorry for her and was willing to help. The idea of people thinking otherwise just makes me mad."

Taken aback by her friend's harsh view of Cara, Deborah moved to the window. The yard was empty now, the conversation over. Ephraim and Mahlon were probably downstairs, waiting for them. "Excommunicated." She hated the feel of the word in her mouth. "Ephraim's doing this. Mahlon is getting away because he feels like it. Why do men have to be so hardheaded sometimes?"

Anna Mary opened the bedroom door. "I have no idea. And they say women are difficult to understand." She shrugged. "Maybe the bishop won't be so tough on him after all."

"Maybe." But Deborah didn't think so, not after hearing what the bishop had said to Ephraim.

As they walked into the living room looking for Mahlon and Ephraim, she caught a glimpse of movement in her parents' bedroom. "I'll be back."

She went to the doorway. Her Daed was sitting on the side of the bed, his elbows propped on his knees and his head in his hands.

Becca stood near him with her back to the doorway. "He won't be allowed to work at his shop? That's never been part of a shunning before. Will the business survive without Ephraim?"

"I can't think of that right now."

"That shop puts food in our babies' mouths."

Deborah tapped on the door. "Daed?"

"Deborah." He stood, wiping his eyes. "You look nice, like a young woman ready for her beau."

She nodded. "Are you okay?"

"Ya. A bit rattled, that's all."

"Your brother…" Becca burst into tears. "All these children left to raise, and the oldest, who's been a man of faith for many years, now begins to waver?"

"He's not wavering." Deborah choked back the tears. "He's not. He stepped outside the Ordnung, but he'll take the discipline and go through the steps to become a member in good standing again. I know he will."

Her Daed brushed her cheek with his hand. "Of course he will. Now, what did you need to see me about?"

"I was looking for Ephraim and Mahlon."

"They've gone to the shop. Your brother needs to teach Mahlon a lot between now and Sunday."

She couldn't believe the procedure for a shunning was moving so quickly. "Sunday?"

Daed nodded. "The announcement will happen at church."

Her heart thudded against her chest. "Why so soon?"

"This situation with Cara is worse than Ephraim said."

The ache that settled inside her chest was familiar, like she was losing a family member all over again. "Oh, Daed."

"It'll be fine, Deborah. Just a little storm. We'll get through it."

But she knew he didn't really believe that. She could see it in his eyes and hear it in his voice. "I'll be with Ephraim, Mahlon, and Anna Mary tonight. I'll talk with him. Okay, Daed?"

He smiled, his eyes misting. "Sure. Do what you can." He rubbed his chest. "I…I think I'll lie down for a bit."

Deborah helped him get comfortable and kissed his cheek. "Please don't take this too hard. He's doing this because he's a good man, not because of sin."

Her Daed patted her hand. "I hope you're right."

She left, eager to try to talk some sense into her brother.

Standing at his desk, Ephraim tried explaining unfamiliar things about the business to Mahlon: bookkeeping and ordering hardware, lumber, and various items from the paint store. Open in front of them was a color-coded calendar that mapped out daily goals as well as long-term goals. It all had to do with the business of cabinetmaking, including customer service.

Mahlon shoved his hands into his pockets. "I thought your roots and your respect for the Old Ways went deeper than doing something like this."

Ephraim tossed his pen onto the work-load chart. "Are you hearing anything I'm saying about the shop operations?"

"I can't get all this by Sunday. You're the owner. Grey's the foreman. I just build cabinets and do what I'm told."

As the reality of the impending ban began to press in tighter, Ephraim couldn't stop wondering how his family and business would fare without him. He moved to a file cabinet and began searching for any records that might help Grey and Mahlon during his absence. He'd expected to be excommunicated, but he'd never imagined the kind of strictness the bishop had just imposed on him.

A shunning was a rare thing. When the bishop did see it as necessary, the disciplinary time usually included a few painful restrictions. People couldn't take anything from his hand, but they could give things to him and were encouraged to do so to show love. He wouldn't be allowed to sit at a table with others during mealtime. He knew his family; they'd simply choose not to eat at a table. Instead they'd share meals while sitting in the living room or outside in lawn chairs, and Ephraim could join them in those settings. Being under the ban would cause conversations to be awkward at first, but he and his family and friends would work their way through that discomfort, and inside a normal shunning he would have been allowed to do his job, even if he couldn't hand things to anyone Amish or tote one end of a set of cabinets.

Typically, the hardest parts about a shunning were the embarrassment and the fact that the person couldn't stay for any of the after-church meals and couldn't attend any kind of fellowships or singings.

But this kind of shunning?

Be me to her. The phrase returned, jarring him out of his self-centered thoughts.

With several files in hand, he turned to Mahlon. "Bills have to be paid for Daed's household and the shop." He tossed the information onto the desk. "Grey's going to need your help, and you have to try. You said you would stay next week instead of going on your trip. But will you stick around until I'm no longer being shunned?"

"Why are you letting this happen over an outsider? I could understand if your own heart pulled you to step outside the Ordnung, but some stranger coming through?"

Ephraim didn't miss that Mahlon hadn't answered his question. "She showed up and needed help. I couldn't exactly say, 'Could you come back next year when my Daed is better and when Mahlon gets his head on straight?'"

"Get my head on straight?" Mahlon mumbled. "Try being more direct next time." He leaned in. "Who is she?"

"Someone who's paying the price for her parents' choices—just like the church leaders always warned us about when we were growing up."

"She has Amish roots?"

Ephraim nodded. "She doesn't know. She thinks her mother had Amish friends."

"If her life is an example of what happens when relatives from the past have left the church, I'll hold on with a death grip."

"One would hope you'd hold on to the Old Ways because you believe in them."

"You're in no position to lecture me."

Ephraim changed the subject. "I hate to bother Grey at home, but I think we should go by his place tonight and prepare him for what's going to happen next week. It'll help Monday go smoother. If you need to know something, ask Grey. But he's going to need you to do your part plus some."

The shop door opened, and Deborah and Anna Mary walked in.

Anna Mary's eyes reflected worry. "Is it true? Starting Sunday?"

He moved to her and wrapped her in his arms. She'd handled hearing about Cara staying in his home pretty well. But learning that the shunning had been confirmed and that it'd begin so soon seemed too much for her. He hated it, but he had to warn her about the enforcement of his shunning, beginning Sunday, and she would barely be allowed to acknowledge his existence until the ban was over.

Mahlon went to Deborah and whispered something, causing her to nod. So much rested in Mahlon's hands over the next few weeks or months. Ephraim hoped he was up to it.

Twenty-Five

The sound of rain against the tin roof pattered its way into Ephraim's dream, stirring him. The cement under his pallet and the aches running through his body assured him he was too old to sleep on the floor. The dream of God calling to Cara through thick clouds and strong winds slowly faded. How many times during the night had he dreamed of God calling to her? And how many times had she spit at Him and walked off?

He sighed. Right now Cara didn't even believe in God, so she wasn't spitting at Him. Maybe it was just a dream—more about his own fears than a hazy premonition.

He sat upright, waiting on energy to start flowing. After today he'd have no job and no fellowship with friends and family. He missed his life already. Running the shop, baseball and volleyball games, church, community meals, singings, family—all of it was a part of who he was.

During the service the preachers would contrast his actions with the wisdom of the Word. The bishop would explain his decision and then share his edict, and Ephraim's life would become immediately and intensely silent.

A cup of coffee and a shower would feel really good about now. Instead he went to the half bath in his office and washed up in the mud sink. He wouldn't chance seeing Cara this morning. He didn't want her to catch a hint of what was going on. She had more than enough to handle without his adding guilt to it.

She deserved to know who she was and that she had relatives here in Dry Lake. And he intended to tell her when the time was right, but first the community needed to become more open and more tender toward her. They would, given time. But right now they were reeling from the news that the drunken thief Ephraim's father had warned them about had shared a night with Ephraim in his home. They would assume she was her mother's daughter and want to get rid of her. He'd tried to explain to both his Daed and the bishop about Cara's good points and why she needed a second chance, but they didn't feel they could trust his judgment. A few believed him—Deborah, Mahlon, Anna Mary, and a couple of friends—but no one else. Not yet. But they would. They were good people. Even the shunning was out of love and a desire to redirect Ephraim, not out of spite or anger. But they were letting fear help make their decision. The events with Malinda leaving Dry Lake the first time took place when he was a toddler, so he knew only some of the baggage through hearsay. What he had heard was hefty enough.

The scariest thing of all was that even if Cara had the means to leave Dry Lake right away, he didn't want her to. There was something about her, something as strong and fascinating as it was vulnerable and frozen. He'd never seen anything like it in another human. No wonder God called to her. Even He didn't like being shut out from such a rare being.

Since Ephraim wouldn't give the bishop a set date for Cara to be out of his home, the bishop refused to set a date for the shunning to be over. So today began a blurred journey with no definite end. He could still come to church, and he would.

He drew a slow breath, trying to dispel the weight of his reality.

After shaving and practically bathing in the mud sink, he put on his Sunday clothes and walked into the shop area. All woodworking equipment had been moved to the sides, and benches were lined up for the church meeting—the men's side to the right and the women's to the left—facing one another with the "preachers' stand" in the middle. In an hour people would begin arriving. Even though the bishop had been scheduled to be at a different church today, he'd come here instead. Just to carefully and gently declare Ephraim shunned.

Hating the hours that lay ahead, he felt more alone and nervous than ever. He sat on a bench. "God?" He whispered the word, wishing he knew what to ask. A thousand memories of growing up within this community flooded him. Even though he'd left for a while before officially joining the faith, he'd never hurt anyone—not like he was doing now. He'd been barely twenty and a nonmember when he headed for New York. Now he was a man, and he'd made his choice to join the faith long ago. So what was he doing in this mess?

The aroma of coffee rode on the air, and he looked up.

His father sat down on the bench beside him and held out a mug of coffee. "Did you sleep here again?"

Ephraim took the cup. "Ya."

"Son, what are you doing?"

He sipped the coffee, enjoying that his father knew the exact amount of sugar and cream to put in it. "I don't know, Daed. The right thing, I hope."

No one wanted him shunned, not the bishop or preachers or friends or family, but without discipline and holding one another responsible for following the Ordnung, their faith would have scattered in the wind long ago.

For Ephraim's refusal to adhere to correction, as the bishop called it, he wouldn't be allowed to work or have visitors come to his home, and he couldn't be spoken to until the bishop changed the boundaries of his discipline.

In spite of wanting to always submit to the Ordnung, he found himself at odds with it. But if that's what it took to offer at least a tattered, faded image of who God is to Cara and Lori, so be it.

"You said she doesn't see things like we do. But is she at least a believer?"

He shook his head.

"Whatever she does believe could have the power to draw you away from the one true God."

Ephraim stared at the caramel-colored liquid in his mug, wishing he had the right words. If he took days to explain everything to his Daed, he still wouldn't understand. He'd only warn his son with Scripture and fret over Ephraim's difference of opinion. There was plenty written in the Word to support both sides—avoiding those in and of the world and reaching out to them. Wrangling about it would solve nothing and only put more distance between them.

Ephraim wrapped his hands around the mug. "Why did Cara's mom leave?"

"Malinda was engaged to one of our own. He'd gone to Ohio to work for his uncle for the summer. Her father hired Englischers each summer to help with crops. That summer before the wedding season, she fell for one of them. The Amish man she was engaged to had no hint she was falling for someone else. A few weeks before the wedding, she took off with the Englischer. Malinda's fiancé said she was pregnant with the Englischer's child and had no choice. Your mother never believed it. I figured she must've been, though, because she never came back here—not until years later when she feared she couldn't keep Cara safe from her drunken husband."

They sat in silence, watching the rain. When the sounds of horses and buggies and muted voices filtered into the place, Ephraim knew his time to share anything with his Daed was drawing to a close. "I don't know what all happened with Malinda, but Cara was raised in foster care, and her life's been a nightmare. I feel God calling to her. Maybe I'm wrong, but I think He's asked me to show Him to her. That's all I want to do."

His father gazed into his eyes. "I believe most of what you said is truth."

"Most?"

He raised a brow. "That's *all* you want?"

Unable to continue looking his Daed in the eyes, Ephraim turned to stare out the open double-wide doors.

"I've seen the way you look at her, Son. She calls to you in ways you're not owning up to. And she'll break you in ways no one will be able to fix." His voice wavered.

Anna Mary stepped into the shop, looking pale. The skin around her eyes was puffy, as if she'd been crying for hours.

Daed shook his head. "Even she won't be able to repair what Cara will do to you."

Fear shivered through Ephraim. Was he tricking himself into thinking God wanted this of him? Were his own hidden motives pulling him?

Unsure whether to go to Anna Mary or not, he stayed put. She took a seat on the women's side. One by one families arrived, taking seats according to gender and age group without speaking. By sunset last night, news of what today held had spread throughout the community.

The service began as any other. Soon the songs were over, and the first preacher stood to share his message. Ephraim's father followed. The aroma of food cooking wafted through the air, and he knew Cara had started a fire and was baking something. Anna Mary's eyes moved to his. She knew it too. In spite of their reality, she offered an understanding smile. He could only hope she'd hold on to that accepting spirit throughout this ordeal.

With the women's benches set to face the men's, his and Anna Mary's eyes kept finding each other. The three preachers, including his father, took turns speaking, each for nearly an hour. Children went to the bathroom and came back. Mothers who needed to nurse their infants went into a large storage room at the back of the shop, where chairs were provided, returning later with sleeping babes.

The bishop stood before the congregation, speaking in their own language about how the Amish couldn't afford to let the children of those who'd chosen to leave the church waltz right into the community and cause the baptized ones to disregard the Ordnung.

He held up a German Bible. "Scripture says to suffer not a man to touch a woman and to refrain from the appearance of all evil. How then can a man share a home—a one-bedroom home—with a woman, even for a night and be considered in submission to the Ordnung? Where the heart is, the flesh will follow."

He set the Bible down. "Ephraim is telling us that his heart isn't with this woman and that his flesh won't follow anything but God. But I think he's lying to himself. I don't believe he's committed the sin of fornication, not yet. But even so, can we allow such rebellion? Unless boundaries are set up and those under the submission of the church stay within those boundaries, our standards of accountability are no better than the world's. We have no choice but to offer discipline in love in hope"—he looked at Ephraim for the first time—"in great hope that he will choose to stop going his own way and instead follow the ways of his people. The ways of the Ordnung."

"Better Days, come back here." Lori's voice came through the open door and echoed within the tin building. The bishop continued as if he'd not heard her, but every eye started scanning outside.

"Better Days!"

The puppy ran into the shop, quickly followed by Lori.

"Lori Moore." Cara rounded the corner, wearing her jeans and tight sweater that showed an inch or so of her belly. She came to an abrupt halt, her eyes showing obvious alarm. "Lori," she whispered and motioned for her daughter to come back out of the building.

Every eye moved to Cara. Whatever relatives she had inside Dry Lake, those who knew or would soon know who she was, would not easily let go of their shock and offense at such inappropriate dress. Especially on Amish property during a church service.

Lori pointed at Ephraim. Cara shook her head, but the little girl walked straight to him and sat beside him. "Mom told me not to leave the yard. She's gonna be so mad at me. Can I stay here?" She whispered the words, glancing to her mother as she spoke.

He saw bits of Cara in her. Smart. Strong willed. Defiant. And alarmingly shrewd.

Cara studied him for a moment, and he gave a nod. Lori probably thought she'd won, but the look in Cara's eyes said her daughter was in plenty of trouble. The least disruptive course right now was for Lori to stay. Besides, how wrong could it be for a fatherless child to want to sit with a man—to feel the comfort of his presence, the way he had as a child with his own Daed?

Thankfully, whatever the bishop had to say about the shunning would all be spoken in High German or Pennsylvania Dutch. Lori wouldn't understand a word of it.

Cara left, and Lori crawled into his lap. Her cool skin reminded him that she didn't own a sweater for the warmer weather of springtime— only an adult-size hoodie that dragged the ground. The dampness from the earlier rain clung to her, and he wrapped the sides of his black coat around her. The shivering soon stopped.

By the time the bishop stepped forward to give his summation of Ephraim's wrongdoings, Lori was relaxed and peaceful in his arms and the dog at his feet. It was not an image anyone in the room approved of. But as the bishop explained everything to the congregation, Ephraim found Lori's presence comforting. His district would have to turn their backs on him, but he would not turn his on Cara and Lori.

The bishop asked Ephraim to stand. He shifted Lori to his left arm and stood. She watched, wide-eyed, but she didn't wiggle to get down. If she'd never been in church before, she might not think that much about what was going on.

The bishop gestured toward him, and from their seats the congregation faced him, each one seeming to stare at him with sadness and confusion.

"Until further notice you will not speak to him or do business with him. I want to encourage you to write him letters, reminding Ephraim of who he is to you and the calling God has placed on his life. Tell him how much you miss him, and share God's wisdom as you see fit, but there will be no visitations until he removes the woman from his home. Does everyone understand and bear witness to this act?"

"We do."

The echo of their agreement rang in his ears. He glanced to his father, who had tears in his eyes. The stricken look on Anna Mary's face bothered him, and he hoped she had the strength to endure the rumors that were sure to circulate after today.

"Then as an act of obedience that we may cause him to submit to the teachings of our forefathers, we begin this journey with great grief, and we will pray for him daily."

Ephraim remained standing as the bishop prayed. When he said "amen," the muffled sound of loved ones leaving without a word spoken rocked him to his soul. Anna Mary wept softly, and she didn't budge until her mother placed her hands on her shoulders and guided her out of the building.

Lori watched the people filing out in stony silence. "What are they doing?"

"The service is over," Ephraim whispered.

When the place was empty, he sat. Lori leaned her back against his chest, asking nothing.

It was over.

And yet it was the beginning.

His head pounded worse than his heart, but he collected himself as best he could before heading for his house.

As he stepped inside, he heard Cara in the storage room. "Lori Moore, is that you?"

The little girl's eyes grew large.

Cara came to the doorway, wagging her finger at her daughter. "What did I tell you—"

Ephraim raised his hand. He'd had all the controversy he could stand for one day. "Don't. Not now."

Cara raised her eyes to his, clearly ready to challenge him. Understanding flickered through her eyes. "You okay?"

"Ya." He set Lori's feet on the floor. "And you obey your mother when she tells you something."

He'd spoken softly, but Lori's eyes filled with tears. He'd never been so weary of emotions battering like a tempestuous sea. He wondered how Cara had managed to cope all these years. She'd moved from one loss to another—always fighting to survive, always having people turn their backs on her or worse—and yet she did what needed to be done without giving up.

The puppy yelped, wanting inside.

A half smile of understanding tugged at Cara's lips. "Better Days is yapping to get in. I think you should be the one to open the door."

She couldn't know what was going on between him and his people, but she'd picked up on his stress. He drew a relaxing breath. If she could lose everything over and over again, surely he could stand the trial of being shunned for a season without carrying it on his sleeve.

He let the dog in. Then he stepped to the doorway of the storage room. She'd cleaned the whole thing. "Amazing."

"Yep, that's me," she teased, then pointed to rows of boxes along one wall. "You'll need to go through those, because most of it looks like junk. I've sorted the rest and labeled each box."

He looked through some of the possible rubbish bins. Old shoes, rusted lamps, and broken stuff. "Hey, this is definitely not trash."

She shrugged. "You still milk cows?"

He laughed, and for the first time in days, stress drained from him. "This has nothing to do with storing fresh milk. Although I guess I can see why you might think so." He lifted a silver cylinder. "This is an ice-cream maker, a hand-crank one."

"Yeah? When's the last time you used it?"

"Oh no. We're not cleaning out this room based on a woman's point of view. It's my stuff, and it stays if I say so."

"I'm beginning to see why you're still single. Women don't take too kindly to the 'my way or the highway' approach, you know." She shoved a sealed box onto the shelf. "Do people actually make ice cream at home? Or is that one of those things you bought 'As Seen on TV,' and it doesn't really work?"

"Ice-cream makers work. And how do you suppose an Amish man would buy something 'As Seen on TV'?"

She shrugged. "I don't know. Do they make a gas-, fire-, or kerosene-run television?"

Amusement stirred in him. "I'll get all the right ingredients together and make some. Then you'll see."

"Ice cream, hand cranked by a man whose idea of an oven is fire in a hole? As long as I can just see it and not have to taste it, you have a deal." Her golden brown eyes met his, calling him to enjoy the day and forget whatever weight demanded to be carried.

He longed to search the hidden regions of her heart and take his discovery into his own. Emotions pulled at him, causing feelings they shouldn't. He hoped his motivations for helping her were as pure as he'd thought. They'd started out that way. And he needed his drive to help her to be based on godliness and that alone. Otherwise everyone's greatest concern was rock solid.

And he was a fool.

Twenty-Six

Cara slid most of her breakfast into a bowl and set it aside. She'd take it to the mama dog later. Lori was sprawled on the living room floor, reading and playing with Better Days.

Ephraim was nowhere to be seen. He came each morning in time to drive them to work, showed up at the Howards' each evening to bring them home, and stayed hidden in between. It'd been four days since that fateful church service, and except for eating a late dinner with Lori last night, he hadn't joined them for a single meal.

He had a nice home with plenty of food, but in spite of his words, she knew they weren't welcome here any longer. Since Sunday, when she'd accidentally interrupted the church service, she'd felt him pulling away.

As Ephraim took her to and from work, she'd seen people in their buggies, and they'd seen her. But the friendliest gesture she or Ephraim received was a nod. Like the smell of the musty barn clinging to her clothes, she carried the scent of their dislike throughout each day.

If that was how the rest of them felt, she could easily ignore it. But the opinions of his family and friends seemed to have affected Ephraim. Clearly her friendship with him was dying. She wished she could find a place of her own before he started resenting her.

Knowing they could have been good friends if things were different grieved her. Friendships were like food—each had its own taste, texture, and nutrients. She and Kendal were like a cheap dessert that shouldn't be eaten often and at its best was only so-so.

But she'd valued Ephraim's friendship like she'd valued food when starving.

After wiping off the kitchen table and drying her hands, she went into the bedroom. She peeled out of her jeans and sweater top and slid into the teal-colored dress, hating it more each time she had to wear it. She stuffed her dirty clothes into the book bag, planning to wash them at the Howards' today. The constant use of the clothes they'd left New York in was causing them to fray quickly, but that only made the jeans more comfortable. This weekend she'd walk into town and buy Lori a couple of outfits.

Ephraim knocked, making Better Days start yapping. "You ladies ready?"

Cara slung the backpack on her shoulder and hurried out of the bedroom. "Yeah." She grabbed the bowl of food. "Can we stop by the barn?"

Ephraim looked from the bowl in her hands to her.

Cara motioned for Lori to go on out to the buggy. Ephraim's eyes didn't budge from her as she headed out in front of him. "What?"

"Did you eat anything, or are you giving it all to the mutt?" He picked up Better Days and closed the door behind him.

"I had plenty."

They climbed into the buggy, and he and Lori began talking about the book she was reading. When he slowed the horse near the barn, he turned to Cara. "I'll feed the dog from now on. If you cook it, you eat it."

Ire ran through her, and she jerked her backpack off, took money out of it, and threw it in his lap. "Here. Does that cover it?" Without glancing at him again, she climbed down and went into the barn. The mama dog wagged her tail. Cara knelt, calling to her while taking the foil off the bowl. "I brought you some scrambled eggs."

About the time the dog was finished, the barn door squeaked open.

Ephraim loomed over her. "I don't want your money. I want you to eat."

She stood, realizing how short her five-foot-three stature must look to him. "Have some control issues, do you?"

"I have concern issues." He took her hand and wrapped his thumb and index finger around her wrist. "You're losing weight."

She jerked away. "You have no idea what size I was before."

"How did your jeans fit when you left New York?"

"What?"

"Going by Englischer style, I'd say they fit snug. Now they must be nearly a size too big. Eat, Cara. Okay? I'll feed the stupid dog."

Wondering if the words he said and the words she heard were anywhere near the same, she nodded. When she first met him, he seemed bossy and haughty, so maybe the way she listened was the issue.

"She's not stupid." The sentence made her sound like a spoiled child, and she regretted not staying silent.

"Fine." He rolled his eyes. "I'll feed the highly intelligent dog."

"I'm not incapable, you know. I can take care of Lori and myself and even feed a stray dog here and there. I know it doesn't look that way."

"Mom, help!" Lori's scream pierced the air, and they both took off running.

Ephraim's horse, hitched to the rig, trotted into the street, following another horse and buggy. Lori sat on the driver's bench, staring back at them, wide-eyed with fear. The two people in the first rig looked behind them. Their buggy seemed to slow, causing Ephraim's horse to do the same.

Lori tried to make her way to the side of the buggy.

"No. Stay there," Ephraim commanded as he ran toward the runaway horse and buggy. Cara tried to keep up with him, but she fell farther behind every second.

"Lori, grab the reins and pull back on them," Ephraim instructed as he picked up speed. Cara couldn't tell if her daughter was following his instructions. The rig in front of Ephraim's slowed more, causing Ephraim's horse to follow suit.

Ephraim passed his buggy. He lunged across the base of the horse's neck and grabbed the reins. Within a few seconds he stopped the horse.

The people in the other buggy slowed, almost stopping as they watched for a moment. When Ephraim gave a nod, they nodded in return and went on their way. Cara kept running for Ephraim's rig. She could see Lori crying and Ephraim talking to her. She finally caught up and climbed into the buggy. She drew her daughter into her lap. "Why would the horse do that?"

Still breathing hard, Ephraim took a seat on the bench. "That was Mahlon's rig. Just for fun my horse was trained to follow it. I guess I didn't set the brake."

"Why didn't your friend stop?"

"He slowed his rig in a way that kept my horse from running into the back of his buggy."

"Yeah?" She motioned toward the moving buggy. "And then he and your sister barely acknowledged us before they kept going."

"Let it go, Cara."

Frustrated but unwilling to argue, she rode in silence the rest of the way to the Howards' place. When she climbed out of the buggy, she muttered a thank-you. He nodded and left.

Something weird was happening between her and Ephraim, but she had no idea what.

The hours passed quickly as she cooked and cleaned and washed clothes, but she still had no answers to her questions as her workday drew to a close.

"Cara," Mr. Howard said when he came home, "we need to talk." He pulled his billfold from his pocket. She studied each bill as he placed it in her hand. "You've been great. Wish we'd had you before I used up all my leave time during those first weeks of Ginny's injury. You've gotten here earlier and stayed later than I dared ask of you. But we learned during her last appointment that her bone healed quicker than expected. I just spoke to her doctor's office, and rather than a regular checkup visit tomorrow, she'll have her hip cast removed. We'd love to keep you, but our budget says we can't. As much as we hate it, we'll have to make do on our own."

It was odd the way disappointment stung every single time it happened. "You don't know anybody else who needs help, do you? I can do almost anything with a little practice."

"No, not that I know of." He shoved his wallet into his pants pocket. "Okay."

Lori was in the side yard, playing with dolls under a shade tree. When Cara went to get her so they could give Mrs. Howard a proper good-bye, she spotted something she'd noticed twice already this week—a horse and wagon a few hundred feet away with one of the middle-aged men she'd seen at Ephraim's. He sat on the open tailgate of the wagon, selling what looked like some type of vegetables. Probably asparagus and rhubarb since that was all that was ripe in the Howards' garden. But this road seemed like an odd place to try to sell anything. It had almost no traffic. And the man in the wagon appeared more interested in watching her as she worked the garden or hung clothes on the line than in selling.

She'd wanted to ask Ephraim about him, but he seemed in no mood to answer any questions about his people. Deciding it was time she asked the man directly, she headed that way. When he spotted her, he jumped off the tailgate, shoved the crates farther into the wagon, and hurried to the seat. He slapped the reins and took off.

Was it time for him to go, or did he not want to speak with her?

She and Lori went inside and told Mr. and Mrs. Howard good-bye. The Howards apologized again for needing to let her go so abruptly, and she knew their decision was based on something they couldn't control. She assured them it didn't matter and gathered all of her and Lori's clean laundry before leaving. Going down the front walk, she wondered if Ephraim would still pick them up after their tiff this morning.

"Wait," Mr. Howard called.

Cara stopped. "Yeah?"

"Ginny just reminded me of something. My sister lives up the road a piece. She bought paint a few months back. Started painting a room but never finished it, let alone the rest of the house. Don't know how good your painting skills are, but I could put in a good word for you."

"Thanks."

He pointed. "Straight that way about two miles. It's 2201. Two-story brick house, black shutters, pale yellow trim."

"Think she'll mind if I go by there now?"

He shook his head, chuckling. "You do that, missy. She should be there this time of day. I'll go in and give her a call."

Lori tugged on her hand, and they started walking again. In the distance a horse and buggy topped the hill, heading for them.

Ephraim.

Her heart beat a little harder. She'd never met anyone like him. In spite of their having a bit of trouble getting along and him being a believer in things that didn't exist, she liked who he was—determined, honest, and giving. The man had a lot going for him. And he was so attractive. If he wasn't Amish, she might even be tempted to fall for him. For her, that'd really be saying something.

"Look, Mom. 'From is coming."

"Yep, I saw him top the hill a few minutes ago."

"Think he brought Better Days?"

"He's brought him every day this week."

"It's Saturday tomorrow. Maybe he'll make ice cream for us."

"Tomorrow is Friday, honey."

Lori cursed.

"Lori Moore, watch your mouth."

"You swear."

"Yeah, well, when you're almost an adult, we'll discuss this again. Until then you talk like a little girl. Got it?"

She shrugged. "Why?"

"I don't know, kid. It's just the way it is."

" 'From doesn't curse."

"Good. Then take after him."

Ephraim pulled to a stop beside them. He had a bit of a smile on his face. That'd been a rarity since she'd interrupted their Sunday service.

"Afternoon, ladies."

Lori put her foot on the step and hoisted herself up. "Hey, 'From."

Ephraim looked beyond Lori, studying Cara with a serious expression. She smiled. "Hi."

"Afternoon."

Better Days danced all over the seat, welcoming them.

"Mom said I need to take after you."

Ephraim rubbed his chin. "You need to start shaving? I can lend you my razor."

Lori slid closer to him. "She said I'm supposed to talk like you."

Cara sat down. "Hey, Lori, zip it."

Ephraim said something in Pennsylvania Dutch. The sincerity in his voice and reflected on his face added to her puzzlement. Was he annoyed with her intrusion in his life or not?

That aside, his words sounded like something he'd said earlier in the week. He gave Lori a half smile. "Is that what she meant?"

"Nope," Lori chirped. "She meant I'm not to curse."

Ephraim tilted his head at Cara. "We wouldn't want your mother to watch her mouth too, would we?"

Cara harrumphed. "Shut up, both of you."

"Be nice, Mom."

Ephraim laughed and slapped the reins against the horse's back.

"I'm careful what I say most of the time."

"Can you go a week without cursing?" Ephraim asked.

Cara raised her chin. "Shut up, 'From, before I'm tempted to say so much more than a few harmless curse words."

He chuckled.

She pulled her pay out of the pocket she'd sewn on the dress. "Today was my last day with the Howards."

"Did you know that?"

"No. Mrs. Howard is getting out of her cast earlier than they'd figured. Even so I'd thought they'd keep me working until she did a week or so of physical therapy and was able to get around better on her own again. Something must have come up with their finances."

He slowed the buggy to turn it toward his place.

"I got a lead on another job a couple miles straight ahead. Would you mind taking me by there?"

"What kind of job?"

"Painting."

"You ever painted before?"

"No. But before a few days ago, I never cooked on a wood stove either, and you weren't complaining about the meal I fixed last night."

He looked at Lori and rubbed his belly.

He'd come in late last night to get his telescope. That had been his mode of operation all week. When every trace of daylight was gone, he'd slip into the house long enough to get his telescope out of the storage room, tell them good night, and leave. But last night Lori had talked him into eating a second dinner with her.

"When your mom was about the same age you are now," he said, loosely holding the reins, "I asked her if she'd ever picked corn before, and she said, 'No, but I can learn.' And then she started helping me."

Confused by his sudden trip down memory lane, Cara stared at him. Maybe she should relax and enjoy the friendly mood he was in, but she couldn't shake the feeling that he was setting her up for something. "What's with all the nice banter?"

He sighed. "I can't win. If I'm concerned and say so, you tell me I'm being bossy. If I give too much, I must want something. If I give too little, I'm mean and can't possibly understand your situation."

His words bit, but she knew they were true. "You get stung every day of your life, and we'll see how you feel about bees."

"I'm not a bee."

Even as guilt washed over her, she knew he'd never understand. Life had trained her to regard every action with suspicion. And that a swarm of bees could attack at any moment.

Twenty-Seven

Inside his hiddy Ephraim stared through the telescopic lens, seeing nothing except his own thoughts. He'd been a sky watcher since he turned twelve, but he'd taken up stargazing through a telescope over a decade ago.

Now the vast expanse of the night sky and the brilliance of the stars and planets were hidden behind Cara's face. Those golden brown eyes and soft features seemed to linger with him like his favorite nighttime view of the heavens in the fall—the harvest moon. In the right season the soft orange luminance of a true harvest moon outlined the terrain of bright highlands and darker plains, making them easily visible to the naked eye. And its beauty was a part of him. Too amazing to look away from, it seemed as if he could reach out and touch it. But regardless of how close a harvest moon appeared, it was more than two hundred thousand miles away.

A lot like Cara.

The couple she'd gone to see about painting for them—the Garretts according to the mailbox—walked outside with her as they said goodbye, and he'd overheard what they'd said to her. If she could find someone to help her move furniture and have the painting done by the end of next weekend, they'd hire her.

She hadn't declined the job, nor had she accepted. He'd expected her to ask him for help during their long ride home, but she hadn't. He refused to volunteer. Asking for help was one of the oldest biblical principles and one of the ways people showed each other respect.

Trying to focus on the sky, he adjusted the telescope. He didn't hear or feel anything, but he knew the answer. *Be me to her.*

When God loved people, He didn't count what something cost Him. He only counted what it'd do for the ones He helped. His Son's life proved that. But Ephraim wasn't God. And Cara irritated him as much as she fascinated him.

The Pennsylvania Dutch phrase he'd spoken to her last week circled through his mind. *Die Sache, as uns zammebinne, duhne sich nie net losmache, awwer die Sache as uns ausenannermache schtehne immer fescht.* He hadn't intended to say it out loud, and he could never tell her what it meant. But one evening he was next to the buggy as she climbed out of it. She'd stumbled a little, and he'd helped steady her. As she stood so close to him, he'd spoken the truth, and some of the tension of the moment broke.

It wasn't like he was interested in her romantically. Certainly not. His attentions belonged to Anna Mary. She was cut from the same broadcloth fabric he was. But Cara—

A terrified scream came from the house. He bolted across the yard. As he entered the house, he heard Cara shriek, "No, Ephraim!" The fear in her voice swirled feelings inside him like dust caught in a windstorm.

As he hurried through the kitchen, a shadow moved across the room. Cara ran into him, bouncing off his chest like a rubber ball. She staggered back.

Ephraim grabbed her arms to keep her from falling. "What's going on?"

Her labored breathing didn't slow as she gently splayed her hands across his face, touching him as if he might not be real.

"It's okay, Cara. You're awake now."

She backed away. The image of her in his shirt, swallowed in it like a teenager, burned into his mind. She slumped into a kitchen chair. His Bible lay open on the table in front of her. Had she been reading it?

Her hands covered her mouth, and the silvery moonlight reflected a lone tear. She lowered her arms to her side. "What are you doing here?"

"I was watching the stars when I heard you scream."

She glanced at the clock but said nothing about it being after two in the morning.

Cara drew a shaky breath. Against his better judgment he sat down across from her. The moon's glow lay across parts of her body, shadows filling in the rest. Pages of the Bible rustled as a breeze crossed the kitchen. Tree frogs and crickets played summer's tune. She swiped the tear from her cheek and wrapped her arms around herself.

Ephraim waited for her to speak. But within moments her vulnerable side retreated, and she regained control of her breathing. The woman in front of him squared her body and became as unyielding as the day he'd met her.

Be me to her.

How was he supposed to do that? She didn't trust him, and he wanted to be trusted—at least in some distant, "I won't do any more damage to your life" sort of way. He angled his head, trying to make eye contact.

She pushed the Bible to the side, slid the chair back, and stood. "Good night."

"Wait."

Trying to think of something she'd talk to him about, he settled on her job situation. "What did the Garretts say?"

"Not much."

Wondering if anything short of the threat of losing her daughter would make her ask for help, he stifled a sigh. "Will you take the job?"

"I could make really good money. The kind that would help me get out of here."

Was his place that bad? He motioned for her to sit, but she didn't. He went to the kitchen cabinet. "So what's the holdup?" He grabbed a glass.

"I have to work a few things out."

"For Pete's sake, Cara. If you need help, just ask."

She stared at him. "You heard what they wanted?"

He drew water from the tap and set the glass on the table near her. "Ya."

"You have a full-time job. It's already a huge cut into your time to chauffeur us back and forth. How could I ask you for more?"

"You could ask me to help you find someone." His curt tone didn't seem to faze her.

She took a sip and leaned against the counter, seeming neither angry nor stressed. At this moment he'd give her his house if she'd open up and help him understand her. She wanted to make that money. He knew she did. It'd mean the start of independence for her and Lori. Why was she still afraid of him?

Frustrated with her, he couldn't keep his silence any longer. "Fine. I'll help. Thank you for asking."

"You?"

"You don't have to sound so confident in my abilities."

"But you already have a job."

"Actually, I'm off for a while."

"Off?" Lines of uncertainty creased her brows. "And you're willing to paint a house while you're on vacation?" The confusion on her face faded. "Oh."

"What *oh*?"

"If you help me do this, I can get out of here sooner. That's worth painting during your vacation." She looked pleased with herself, and he wasn't going to correct her.

"Here's the deal. I'll be your employee for a week, do everything you need. But you have to answer one question."

"Depends on the question."

"Words like *stubborn* and *mulelike* aren't strong enough to describe you."

She laughed softly. "Hey, your beliefs can't be turned off and on at will. When you have to be stubborn to survive, it becomes a part of you. And then you're its slave."

He wondered if she had any clue how much some of her thinking followed the teachings of God. "You were screaming at me in your sleep. What'd I do in the dream?"

Her fingers moved over her lips, across her cheek, and back again.

"I just want to know so I can help."

She opened her mouth three times before words squeaked out. "I was blindfolded, and you were leading me somewhere. When we got there, you told me to take off the blindfold because you had something special waiting." She placed the glass on the table. "This is silly. I'm going to bed."

He shrugged. "Fine. Go to bed." He wouldn't be out-stubborned by a woman—a featherweight at that.

She huffed. "There was a hot-air balloon with a basket. You talked me into getting in it. It went up and up. Everything below was gorgeous, and I felt free. Then I noticed a rope attached to the bottom of the basket. The end of it dangled inside a black hole that kept expanding, but with every inch of growth, it made the basket shudder and begin to unravel. I screamed for you to help me." She sighed. "The bottom fell out of the basket, and I woke right before I hit the ground."

Ephraim's heart thudded.

"Happy now?"

He shook his head. "I won't lead you to a place where the weight of the world can be defied only to watch you fall."

"It was a stupid dream."

"Or maybe it's your greatest fears surfacing while you sleep—fear of trusting a man, fear that when troubles come, no one can help you."

She lifted the glass, took a sip, and set it down. Then she shifted from one foot to the other, but she didn't respond to what he'd said. She pointed to the Bible. "That says some really odd stuff."

His mother had bought him an English version of the Bible when he was a teen. Reading a German Bible had been difficult, and she'd wanted to make it easier for him to turn to God's Word if he ever had a mind to. At the time he hadn't considered it much of a gift, but it'd grown to mean a lot to him.

"Ya, it does."

"You think so too?"

"Sure. Everyone does. Parts of it are thousands of years old. If you and I have trouble understanding each other because of cultural differences, imagine if we weren't from the same generation and country or if we didn't speak the same language."

"Do you honestly believe there's a God?"

"Ya. And I believe He sent His Son Jesus and that He left His Spirit to help guide us."

"My mother believed in God. In his own way Johnny did too."

"His own way?"

She shrugged. "The diner he managed was open seven days a week, so going to church was out. I never saw him read a Bible, but sometimes I'd see him praying—not just at mealtime, but walking the floors, talking out loud to God. A lot of it seemed to be for me and Lori." She moved to the Bible and smoothed her fingers across the page. "I can see why people would want to believe in something stronger than themselves."

In spite of wanting to open a discussion on this topic, he decided to say nothing rather than the wrong thing. She didn't know it, but God was having a conversation with her.

She closed the Bible and pushed it away. "If you can be there for me for another week, maybe two, that's all I need." She ran her fingertips across her lips. "Can you?"

It was as if she'd calculated how much inner strength he had to continue helping her, and all she could come up with was a week's worth, possibly two. "Yes. I promise you that much."

She nodded, but he didn't think she believed him.

Twenty-Eight

Ephraim ran the paint roller up and down the Garretts' bedroom wall, listening to Cara and Lori in the next room.

Cara had begun to open up a little, even dared to ask a few questions about his beliefs. He'd started to tell her about her roots half a dozen times, but it seemed that sharing eternal truths was more important than factual ones, especially since the ones based on her mother were sure to cause pain and provide no answers. She thought her mother had been in Dry Lake to visit friends. And for whatever reason, her family's *friend* never came for her at the bus station. He hated how betrayed she'd feel when she learned the truth and realized he'd known everything all along. But to tell her too soon would take so many things from her, especially if she reacted like he figured and bolted—never to be seen or heard from again. But holding on to the secret sometimes made him feel as if the smithy was shoeing his insides.

He dipped the roller into the oversize bucket and carefully loaded it with paint before applying it to the wall. He had no doubts that the news of who she was had reached the Riehls. They knew she was staying at Ephraim's, but not one of them had come by to see her.

The thought of Cara finding that out hurt, and he longed to protect her from it. But if she stayed around long enough, he hoped the community would choose to do the right thing and stop ignoring her. They were trained to shut out the world and all its trappings, but sometimes, in trying to avoid ungodliness, they shut out the wrong things. Warming up to the idea of Malinda's daughter returning would take time, especially since she'd been seen wearing unacceptable clothing and short hair, living in a barn, and dancing inside his home.

But if they'd ever give her a chance, they'd see a remarkable person.

Cara's soft voice caught his attention as she chuckled about something. Five days of working twelve to fourteen hours, and he wanted more. More laughter, more sharing of lunches under the shade tree, more working until midnight, and more times of talking softly while drinking their first cup of coffee each morning.

Carrying the roller with him, he moved through the hallway. The Garretts had fully accepted the Howards' recommendation of Cara. Before they left for vacation, they'd given her a key to the house and permission to empty their belongings out of the closets so she could paint them. He stopped outside the family room. Cara propped her hands on her hips. The new overalls she'd bought in town last Saturday and washed umpteen times in his wringer washer before wearing them once were now covered in paint. She took long strides through the room.

"Walking," Lori said.

"You tried that one already. Come on, kid, use your imagination." She moved her hips slowly. "Give me a good synonym for what I'm doing."

"Tripping."

"Tripping?" Cara laughed. "Remember the words in the book we read last night? How about swaggering or sashaying."

Ephraim cleared his throat. "Or shuffling like an old lady?"

She wheeled around, a look of surprise in her eyes before she shook the paintbrush at him. "Is that bedroom finished?"

"No ma'am."

"Then I suggest you shuffle back in there before I sashay over and whack you upside your Peeping Tom head."

He stood his ground. "I think the title of boss has gone to your swaggering head."

Lori giggled. "Earlier she tried to make me learn about idioms."

"Oh, I agree. Everyone needs to be warned about idiots."

" 'From,' " Cara fussed, threatening him again with the loaded paintbrush, "idioms, not idiots."

"Where'd you learn about idioms?"

"Ninth-grade grammar. Clearly it wasn't your favorite subject like it was mine. An idiom is a type of phrase, as in 'I walk all over you.' "

"I'll say it again; this boss thing has gone to your head."

She raised her eyebrows. "Get back to work."

He shook his head. "It's Friday afternoon. We've done enough. We'll be finished tomorrow and have everything back in place before the Garretts get home."

"I don't know."

During the nights, while he slept at his house, she'd stayed here at the Garretts, sleeping a little before getting up to prepare the next room to be painted. She'd emptied closets, applied painter's tape, and edged paint along the ceilings, baseboards, and corners. When he arrived, the room was ready to be rolled. "You've stayed here all week. You need to spend tonight at my place, where you'll actually sleep. And I'm making ice cream again."

Lori started dancing around the room. "Yes! Yes! Yes!"

"If you can get your mother to leave work, that is."

"You're using my child's love of ice cream to manipulate me." Cara held the paintbrush under his chin like a sword. "You cheat."

"Yep, and I win too."

She laughed. "Fine. After we rinse out the brushes and rollers, we'll leave."

"Nope, we'll put them in a bucket of water and take them with us. I'll rinse them out later."

She frowned and huffed and then left the room, mumbling under her breath. After being around her all week, he knew her venting and teasing were rolled into one. He found it amusing. He'd caught glimpses this week of the woman she was when life offered a bit of security and dignity. Now he understood why he'd waited for her to return to Dry Lake. Why he'd gone to New York in hopes of seeing her. He'd never had a friendship like hers. He couldn't define it, but it seemed she carried magical powers to remove the calluses from his heart and cause him to see life in a refreshing way.

Lori tugged on his pants. " 'From?"

He ruffled her hair. "Is that ice cream calling your name?"

She nodded. "And the puppy's name too."

"Guess you better go get him from the backyard and put him in the wagon."

He went to the bedroom and placed the roller in the paint tray beside the bucket. He'd never considered it important for a woman to be able to earn money, to have that same sense of power he got from running the cabinetry shop. He'd been a fool in that, and he wondered what else he'd been wrong about all his life.

He heard her moving about in the kitchen and went to join her.

She glanced up while rubbing her lower back. "Grilled cheese tonight okay?"

He nodded, wishing he had a better stove. Aside from breakfast food, there weren't many dishes he could prepare on the stove either. It worked decently enough, and he had other reasons for owning it, but cooking on it hadn't been important. Before the shunning he ate half his lunch and supper meals at his Daed's place, and Deborah provided him with the other half.

His Daed needed him to share a meal at his table as often as he could. It gave them time to talk business and relieved his Daed from the guilt of requiring so much help. Concern flickered through him as thoughts of his Daed, family, and the business pushed to the forefront again. He missed sitting around the supper table with his family, but it hadn't left a hole inside him like he thought it would.

Cara snapped her fingers, a lopsided smile on her face. "Do I have to lug the buckets of water with rollers and brushes out to the wagon myself?"

"Sorry."

It didn't take long before he was loading the last of the items into the wagon. Cara locked the house and then placed her backpack on the floorboard. She stretched her back several times, clearly achy and stiff.

"Ephraim, who's that?" She nodded at the buggy stopped on the side of the road ahead of them.

He glanced that way and saw Rueben Lantz. "Anna Mary's Daed."

"Oh. I guess that explains why he's been watching me."

"You think he's been keeping an eye on you?"

"I'm sure of it."

"Maybe it isn't you he's watching. Maybe he doesn't trust me." Unfortunately, right now Ephraim didn't blame him. He never thought he'd feel such a bond to any woman he'd known for only a couple of weeks. Still, it wasn't romantic feelings. Cara was a friend, and that word had taken on new meaning lately.

Ephraim hoped Rueben would move on before they passed him, but he didn't.

"Aren't you going to stop and speak to him?" Cara asked.

"No."

"At least wave?" She studied him as if waiting for some piece of information to make sense.

"He wasn't looking our way."

It did seem a little odd that Rueben hadn't made eye contact or acknowledged them, but in a way Ephraim couldn't blame Rueben for being angry with him.

Thankfully, she dropped the matter. Soon they were entering his driveway.

He slowed the horse as he pulled into the barn. "I haven't been home before dark all week."

She rubbed her thumb and index finger together, mimicking what she'd told him represented the world's smallest violin.

"Slave driver."

"Rich boy."

She slid the strap of the backpack onto one arm and climbed down. He unhitched the horse and put it in the field. Better Days ran after the horse, and Lori took off.

She gazed beyond the gate that led to the pasture. "Look at that pond."

He'd seen it a million times, but today the golden amber shades reflecting the almost-setting sun reminded him of the harvest moon. "Want to walk that way?"

"Yeah, I do."

As they strolled, Cara seemed to soak in her surroundings, studying the trees and wildflowers as they drew close to the pond.

" 'From, look." Lori ran up to them, holding a stick. "Watch this." She tossed it, and Better Days raced to it. He stared at it before running back to Lori.

"Here, boy." Ephraim whistled. The puppy ignored him, but the mama dog came running from nowhere. Lori giggled and grabbed another stick. While Cara gazed at the pond, Lori tossed the stick, and, surprisingly, the mama dog fetched it each time.

Cara tucked her arms around herself. "It's gorgeous."

"A night sky is better."

She went to the water's edge, and he wondered what she was thinking. And feeling.

The leaves on the trees that lined the upper banks whispered in the breeze. A group of mallards landed on the water in front of her, causing ripples.

Lori ran toward her mother but couldn't stop in time to keep from pushing her forward. Lori fell back on the bank, but Cara almost landed in the pond. While regaining her balance, the mama dog crashed into the back of her legs, making her knees buckle. Cara fell headfirst into the shallow water.

Ephraim ran in, grabbed her by the arm, and helped her to her feet. Mud dripped from her arms and chest. Her white sneakers were hidden under the soft, gooey mud.

"You okay? The dog—"

She slung filth from her hands. "I'm well aware of what happened."

"Come on, let's get you out of here." He held on to her arm as he took a step toward dry land.

Cara tried to move forward, but she seemed stuck. She yanked on one leg. Her bare foot suddenly jerked free, and she jolted against Ephraim, and they both began to topple. As he reached for her other arm to steady her, the dog jumped on him, sending both of them into the water.

He got to his feet, feeling the slimy muck seeping through his clothes. He grappled for better footing and then took her by the arm, trying to help her stand. As she pulled against him to get upright, he slipped and took her down with him.

Cara sat in the shallow water, looking at him as if he'd planned all this. "We can do this, right?"

He laughed. "We haven't been successful so far. But I don't think we can give up." He stood and reached for her.

She put both hands in the air like a stop sign. "Oh no. Not a chance. You've helped me enough, thanks."

Every moment he spent with her seemed to make him crave more. Suddenly he realized they were in far murkier waters than the pond.

She pulled herself to her feet and dug in the mud until she found her shoe. Tossing it to the bank, she almost fell again.

With her feet and hands in the shallow water, she half walked, half crawled onto dry land and sat on the grass. "I smell like fish and sludge. Yuck." She glanced up to see tears in Lori's eyes. "If you cry, kid, so help me I'll push 'From back in the water."

"What'd I do?" He took two giant steps out of the water and flopped onto the ground next to her. "Let's throw the dog into the water. This was all her fault."

The tension in Lori's face eased. "You're not mad, are you, Mom?"

"Yes, yes I am."

Lori laughed. "Seriously?"

"I'm also wet and muddy." She stood. "One bathroom for two adults to get cleaned up. Now, how's that supposed to…"

She let her sentence trail, and Ephraim looked to see why. On the hill above them stood Mahlon, Deborah, and Anna Mary. They stared. His sister looked as if the scene in front of her made no sense. She turned away. Mahlon waved and then followed her. He knew what was happening. They'd heard the ruckus and had come to see if someone needed help, but now they had to leave without talking to him. Anna Mary didn't budge.

"Tough crowd," Cara mumbled. "What's going on?"

He shrugged, watching as Anna Mary came toward him. Was she going to sidestep the ban and talk to him?

Cara got to her feet and started up the hill. "Anna Mary, hi."

Anna Mary didn't respond. She focused only on him. "This is wrong, Ephraim. Are you trying to make her think you could actually be interested in someone like her?"

"Someone like me?" Cara's voice took on an edge.

She faced Cara. "I'm not blaming you. He should think. But men don't, you know."

"Someone like me?" Cara repeated.

He wasn't surprised at Cara's seething tone. But he didn't understand why Anna Mary wasn't sounding at least a bit jealous. Since they began seeing each other, she'd had times of flaring with jealousy over girls he'd spoken to or taken home from a singing umpteen years ago. And none of them meant anything. Never had. Yet his feelings for Cara were multiplying faster than made any logical sense.

"While he's been *helping* you, his business didn't meet its scheduled work load."

"That's enough, Anna Mary." But it was too late. He saw in Cara's eyes that she understood more than he wanted her to.

Anna Mary clenched her jaw. "Then we need to talk. Privately." Cara snatched the backpack off the ground and held her hand out for Lori. When they were out of hearing range, Anna Mary turned back to him. "The bishop gave me permission to be here."

Ephraim's heart rate increased. "What's going on?"

"The shop is already getting behind on orders, and you've only been gone a week. Grey and Mahlon tried to keep up, but your Daed had to step in. It's too much stress for him. His arrhythmia went wild, and now he's in the hospital."

As if the past week had been a fling and now reality had closed in around him, he couldn't catch his breath. "I want to see him."

"The bishop said he's willing to lift the ban concerning your Daed."

"Good. And I want to talk to his cardiologist."

"Becca's been trying to see the doctor too. Last I talked to her, she said he's supposed to be making hospital rounds tomorrow morning."

Ephraim's heart twisted. Cara couldn't finish that painting job by herself, not before the Garretts came home. But he couldn't let himself be sidetracked any longer. The last time he spoke to Daed's nurse, she hinted there might be an option concerning his heart problems. He needed to check into that before his father's heart failed altogether.

Trying to plan a dozen things at once, he felt as if he were trapped inside the old dark silo where Cara once hid. "I need you to do several things for me. One, ask Mahlon and Grey to help Cara tomorrow. She's wrapping up a painting job. If either of them will go in my stead, I'll head straight to the hospital."

"They'll do it. You know they will. But I have more that I need to tell you."

He wasn't sure he could handle more.

"My Daed, the bishop, and a few members of the community have found a place for Cara to move to—in Carlisle."

"Your Daed got involved?"

"He's more upset than I am about that woman being here."

With his mind lingering on Cara day and night, Ephraim could see why Rueben felt concern. The emotions churning inside him alarmed him at times. Maybe he should let the wisdom of the men in the community prevail over his current choices.

"The twenty-mile distance will more than satisfy the bishop's desires that she move on, but it's not so far you can't keep up with how she's doing. Daed and some others pitched in to cover three months of rent plus the deposit. The bishop also has a list of potential jobs within walking distance of the place."

Duty to his family and community and desire to be with Cara warred within him.

"Let her go, Ephraim. Stop trying to be her answer to everything, and do what's best for your family. For the business and community. For us."

He knew she was right. With his Daed sick and the shop struggling, he had no choice. Besides, finding Cara a place and making sure she and Lori weren't separated was his goal—that and getting the community to accept who she was and treat her right. If the bishop, Rueben Lantz, and some others had gone through all the steps to find her a place, they must be willing to accept her—at least somewhat—in spite of the rumors concerning her and her mother.

Ephraim made himself respond. "Ya. It does seem to be time."

Cara's friendship seemed to fade, like a dream he couldn't hold on to once he awoke, leaving only longing in its stead.

Twenty-Nine

"How could he do this?" Deborah fought against tears. "It's like he's enjoying being shunned. Did you see him laughing and horsing around?" She stopped at the clothesline and yanked a towel from its clips.

Mahlon slid his hand into hers. "It was a funny situation. That's all. They'd both fallen into the water."

"What was he doing at the pond with her anyway? Having a stroll has nothing to do with giving her a place to live." Deborah half folded the towel and dropped it into the basket. "And what if Daed had seen that? Does Ephraim understand what it could do to him?"

Mahlon picked up the laundry basket and held it for her. "Your Daed wasn't there. Don't borrow trouble."

She took a dress off the line and folded it halfheartedly before tossing it in the basket. "I wanted to be the one to talk to him."

"I know. But the bishop was right. If Ephraim was going to feel drawn back into the fold, it'd be Anna Mary doing the pulling. If a woman in love can't make a man see and hear what he needs to, no one can."

"Mamm could've gotten through to him. If she were around, he'd not have done any of this."

"You can't know that. Come on, Deb. Ephraim deserves a little room. He's stepping out to do something he feels is right. Do you really think he's that wrong?"

Without answering him Deborah pulled more clothes from the line and wiped at tears. This past week had been miserable. And knowing Mahlon wanted to get away by himself only added to the hurt she carried.

Seeing Anna Mary coming toward them, Deborah stopped messing with laundry. "How'd it go?"

She gave a nervous shudder. "I've never been so bold with Ephraim. But I told him what he needed to do, and he agreed."

"He's going to do it?"

Anna Mary nodded.

"Did Cara agree?"

"I didn't talk in front of her." Anna Mary crossed her arms. "But I told Ephraim it's not right to act so friendly around her. She's gonna get the wrong idea about how he feels toward her."

Deborah sighed. "I just hope Daed doesn't find out that Ephraim's not keeping his distance from her as he should."

Ephraim knocked on his own front door, waited a few moments, and entered. How would he explain to Cara that his family and business needs dictated his life? They had for years.

She was standing beside the double kitchen sinks, still wearing the wet, muddy clothes. Her face and arms dripped with clean water as she grabbed a hand towel. The backpack sat in one of the sinks. She turned to face him. "You've been lying to me."

"I have not."

She ran the rag over her face and bare arms, keeping her eyes fixed on him. The hurt she tried to hide sliced into him. "Fine. Don't be honest with me."

With no clue what to say, he wrestled with everything that had to be said.

"I can't believe this." She slung the towel into the sink.

"Look, it's complicated, and I can explain it."

"You lasted a little over a week. It's more than I should have expected. And I appreciate it."

Her calm, matter-of-fact tone belied the betrayal reflected in her eyes. The walls between them that had been removed now reappeared like a magic trick gone bad.

"You need to work at your shop tomorrow. I'll finish at the Garretts' on my own and bring your share of the money once I get paid. Then Lori and I will move on."

"You caught wind that something's not right, and that's it? You're done?"

"I may not dress appropriately or wear my hair just so or know anything from inside that Bible you read every night, but I don't play people."

"I wasn't playing you." He walked toward her, feeling his shoes and socks squish with mud and water. "I've kept a few things from you but not to trick or deceive you. I was trying to protect you until the time was right."

"What things?"

"Why don't you get a shower, and we'll talk after we eat."

She shook her head. "It doesn't matter anyway. I'm not about to trust anything you have to say now."

He'd done a horrible job of trying to be God to her, but he had to make her understand. "For a dozen reasons I can't make you see, I was trying to do the right thing. There are more people involved in this than just you, Cara. People I care about."

She made a face. "What are you talking about?"

He pulled a chair out for her. "I think you should sit."

"No." She gazed into his eyes, once again looking as defiant as the day he saw her at the barn. "I have things to do." She went into the bathroom, closed the door, and turned on the shower.

He couldn't help but wonder if some sliver of this was how God felt sometimes. God gave up things He didn't have to. He cared so much it hurt, and at the first sign of a perceived wrong, His people stopped trusting Him or even trying to hear Him. But as the thought came and went, he knew this wasn't about who God was to her. It was about who she was to God. Wondering if that's how relationships with God always started out, he prayed for her.

The door to the bedroom creaked as Lori opened it. "Can me and Better Days come out now?"

"Sure. Are you hungry?"

Lori moved to a chair, her brown eyes reflecting concern. "Mom's mad, huh?"

"A little."

"Does this mean we gotta leave?"

He hoped not. He wanted to give her a promise, but he had no control over Cara. She could pack her things and walk out at any minute. Maybe he should have talked to Cara earlier in the week while they painted and Lori slept on the couch, but it'd been easier to put the ugliness of the truth to the side and let Cara enjoy the progress she had made. Now he needed to talk to her without Lori nearby. "I have an idea. Would you like to meet my sister?"

"You got a sister?"

He laughed. "Lots of them, but the one I want you to introduce yourself to is Deborah."

"Can Better Days come too?"

"Ya. Kumm."

They walked across the yard, through the parking lot of the shop, to his Daed's place. Deborah stood in the yard, talking with Mahlon and Anna Mary. None of them noticed him.

"Go to the girl in the blue dress and tell her you want to show her your puppy and stay with her for a bit."

"I gotta stay?"

He knelt in front of her. "Just for a while. I want to talk to your mom, okay?"

"That's all you guys have been doing all week."

"I know, but this is different. If you do this, I'll make ice cream later tonight, even if it's midnight."

She studied him, looking unsure. "Mom won't like me staying here without her."

He had a feeling Lori was the one who didn't like the idea. "She won't mind. I'll make sure of it."

Lori hugged his neck. In spite of having so many younger sisters, Ephraim was surprised by the tenderness that washed over him for this little girl. He placed his hand on her back, hoping he could make a significant difference in her life. But it wasn't all up to him. Cara's will and choices could override everything.

Lori walked toward the group, a muddy Better Days running alongside her. All three of them glanced to Lori when she said something. His sister immediately responded to the young girl with kindness. Deborah bent, petting the dog in spite of his wet fur. While kneeling on the ground and chatting with Lori, she noticed Ephraim and held his gaze, her warm smile assuring him of her loyalty before she lowered her eyes.

Anna Mary gave him a cold look, as if warning him to follow through on his agreement. He turned for home but decided to wash up and put on something clean. Since he'd been staying at the shop at night, he had several sets of fresh clothes there. And the workers had left for the day.

After a quick cleanup, he hurried back to his house. It wouldn't do for Cara to think Lori had slipped outside and off the property while she was in the shower. As he entered the house, she came out of the bathroom, barefoot and in Deborah's dress, towel drying her hair. Whether she was covered in mucky pond water, paint-covered jeans, or Amish clothes, her beauty was evident. Her hair was as short as his, and it grated against everything he'd been taught about a woman never cutting her hair, yet he liked it.

She barely looked at him as she headed for the bedroom. "Where's Lori?"

"She's with my sister."

"You had no right—"

He held up his hand, stopping her short. "I need to tell you some things, and you aren't going to want her to overhear them."

She went to the sink, where the grubby, wet backpack sat. "I told you, forget it." After opening it, she pulled out its contents. The soggy clothes she tossed in the sink, but when she pulled out a thick leather book, her movements became slow and gentle. She flipped the pages, checking the water damage.

"After you and your mother left, I climbed our tree every day, waiting for you to come back."

She tossed the book onto the table as if it didn't matter, but he'd already seen that it did. "So what's your point?"

"You were supposed to come back. Malinda intended for you to be raised by Levina. That's what she was doing here that week—getting permission."

The taut lines on Cara's face melted as every trace of emotion drained. "She wouldn't send me away."

"She didn't want to. I was finishing up some chores for Levina really late one night, and I overheard your mother through an open window, sobbing like her heart was breaking. The plan was to take you back with her and prepare you for what needed to be done."

"That's ridiculous." She snatched up the book. "I've heard enough."

He stood and blocked her exit. "Cara, listen to me. The church leaders decided they couldn't provide a place for your mother. She'd joined the church, but then she left here with a man who wasn't Amish. When she came back with you, she was married to that man. They wouldn't support her leaving him, but they were willing to take you in because you were a child, and she was willing to give you up."

"My mother wouldn't have passed me to some friend to raise. She used to hide me from Dad sometimes, but—"

"Levina and Emma Riehl weren't friends. They were relatives. Riehl was your mother's maiden name. And Levina was your great-grandmother."

She froze, seemingly unable to catch her breath.

He touched her arm, and she jerked.

"The old woman?"

"She was your mother's grandmother. She died a number of years ago."

"But I…I have relatives here?"

He nodded.

"Why didn't you tell me?"

"Whatever bad feelings your mother caused in Dry Lake still cling to most."

"Meaning they know who I am and don't want anything to do with me?" Pain and utter disbelief reflected in her eyes.

"At first no one knew you were here. When they found out a woman was staying at my place, most didn't know who. Now, among other reasons, they need some time to adjust."

"Adjust?" She tried to bury the hurt from his sight. "They need time? After leaving *me* in a bus depot?"

"I don't know why that happened. Maybe your dad just thought Emma was coming."

She rolled her eyes, looking disgusted. "Yeah, right. It had to be him. We can tell that by how welcoming those same people are now." She stared at him. "Why are they being like this? You know something you're not saying."

"They've heard things about you. Rumors."

"Enlighten me."

"They believe you're a thief and a drunk. I never said a word about you taking anything from me, but—"

Her brown eyes bore into him, and he could almost see the puzzle pieces fitting together. "The man who saw me coming out of that home must've started people talking." She slammed her palms on the counter. "I only took what I had to. And I wasn't drunk. Exhausted and clumsy, but—"

"I know, Cara. I get it. And they will too if given time."

"So now they think I'm worse than my dad, who ruined the life of an Amish girl."

He nodded.

She sidestepped him and left the house, letting the screen door slam behind her.

He went after her, surprised she wasn't going to his Daed's house to get Lori. Instead she went the back way toward the cornfield.

"Cara, wait."

She turned to him. "All this time I've shared parts of my life with you, and you knew more than I did. Go away, Ephraim. Go back to your tight-knit community and leave me alone."

He followed after her. She didn't stop until she stood on the empty foundation of Levina's place.

He moved onto the platform with her. "I'm sorry. If I could have prevented this, I would've."

Her eyes brimmed with tears. "All those years of having no one was easier than this."

"I know it's hard to understand, but it takes rules, restrictions, and avoiding the ways of the world to live as we do. Our boundary lines don't change because someone wants more freedom. A person either agrees to live by the rules of being Amish and joins the faith, or they leave. Your mother joined the faith and then left. She didn't return until she was trying to protect you."

"So it didn't really matter what I did. They would've been set against me anyway because of what she did."

"Not exactly. Whatever trouble your mother caused is only part of the wall. The half-truths going around about you have done a lot of damage. And you carry an aura of the world, and that makes you suspect. We slept in the same house together. When the church leaders stopped by, you and Lori were dancing. Still, if you'll give the community a little time, they'll come around. Their attitudes toward you are already changing."

"What makes you say that?"

"The bishop found a place for you to live. It's not too far from Dry Lake. And the rent is already covered for three months."

"They're paying me to leave?"

He hadn't thought of it like that. "Cara, I'm sure that's not how they meant it."

"So is that what your girlfriend came to tell you—that the community has a plan for getting me out of Dry Lake?"

"No, the real news is that my Daed's in the hospital, and I need to go see him."

"What? I'm sorry. I'll get Lori right now, and we'll stay at the Garretts for the night."

"No, I didn't mean that. He's stabilized, so it's not an emergency."

"Why didn't they tell you sooner?"

He rubbed the back of his neck, realizing he'd just stepped into another pile of horse manure. "I made the choice, Cara."

"What are you talking about?"

"I'm under the ban."

"In English, please."

"I'm being shunned. I can't talk to or be talked to or work with any Amish person around here—not even family."

"On vacation, huh?" she mumbled as she walked to the far end of the foundation. A few moments later she squared her shoulders slightly. "Do I need to do something to help set all this straight for you, or is just getting out of here enough?"

"I don't want you to go, especially not like this."

"Yeah, and I didn't want to grow up in foster care. But life happens, 'From."

Her use of his nickname told him her anger was gone. Resignation had seeped into her, and she was ready to make amends and leave.

He moved to the edge of the foundation and sat. "I went to New York about a year after my mother died. I went looking for you. I actually thought I had a chance of finding you."

She sat beside him. "I'm sorry I called you a liar. You've been nicer to me than anyone could expect."

"I'm glad we *had* to get to know each other. I'll never see life the same since seeing it through your eyes. But being Amish is who I am, and my family needs me. Especially with my Daed's health as it is. I provide for the family."

"And your God wouldn't want it any other way, right?"

His heart felt as if it might plummet to his feet. "Die Sache, as uns zammebinne, duhne sich nie net losmache, awwer die Sache as uns ausenannermache schtehne immer fescht."

"Back atcha." A half smile tugged at her lips as it had half a dozen times this week when he'd said that to her. "You ever gonna tell me what that means?"

Gazing into her eyes, he longed for more time. "The things that bind us will never loosen, but the things that separate us will always stand firm."

She eased her hand over his, sending warmth and loneliness through him. "And what doesn't separate us allows us to be friends…at least for now."

He held on to her hand. "We'll pace what needs to be done. Take the time to get Lori used to the new place and to find yourself a job."

Cara gazed at the horizon, looking peaceful in spite of the storm. He didn't push for her to respond. Plenty had been covered for now. They waited as daylight faded into dark and a few stars became visible.

Thirty

Before getting out of bed, Cara pulled Lori's warm body closer and kissed the back of her head.

She slid into her jeans, leaving Ephraim's shirt on. It hurt to know she had relatives in Dry Lake who didn't want to talk to her. But she couldn't dismiss what Ephraim had done to improve their situation. Lori's life was better and would always be better because of the path he'd cleared for them. That alone was enough to soothe the Grand Canyon–size ache in her chest.

She tiptoed out of the bedroom as daylight loomed. The idea of seeing Emma Riehl ran through her mind. Maybe if she understood why her dad had left her at the bus station and told her that Emma was coming, and why she hadn't, Cara could lay it to rest.

Heat radiated from the cookstove. A percolator prepped with coffee and water sat next to the sink, ready to be placed on the stove. Ephraim must've slipped inside at some point and started the fire and fixed the percolator for her. On his own, without his community pulling at him, Ephraim was quite a man. He had integrity.

And something beyond that.

He'd captured a piece of her heart. She wasn't sure why it had happened. Maybe because he was a truly nice guy or maybe because she felt connected to him since he'd known her mother. Whatever the reason, her heart had really poor judgment and timing. But he'd taken only a sliver. She'd move on and get it back.

Moving as quietly as she could, she placed the percolator on the stove. She'd had a lot harder wallops in her life than learning her relatives wanted nothing to do with her—losing her mother, growing up in foster care, dealing with a stalker, and marrying a man she didn't love. This latest hit had her staggering, but not for long. She'd start new and find something she was really good at. Maybe she should start her own painting business.

The Bible lay open on the table. The two men she'd been closest to had beliefs founded in that book. A shred of hope that strength could be found inside those pages drew her to it.

She sat down and pulled it in front of her. The words were barely visible in the dim glow of dawn. She lit the kerosene lamp and flipped pages, pausing here and there as a phrase caught her eye. Its beautiful prose and imagery were fascinating, even without believing in its origin. As she turned the thin, delicate paper, she remembered her mother loving this book. She had scribbled verses inside Cara's diary, along with thoughts of love and short lectures of wisdom from mother to child.

Daughter. The word caught her eye, but she'd already flipped past it. Turning back through the pages, she began scanning each one.

Daughter. The word popped from the book. She placed her finger under it and traced back a few words.

"I will be your Father, and you will be my sons and daughters."

The longing to be a beloved daughter hit so hard she couldn't breathe.

If only it were true.

Ephraim sat on the bench swing in his hiddy. Concern for his Daed's health pushed in on all sides, but that wasn't enough to keep his mind off Cara.

The top of the sun edged over the horizon, bringing stronger rays of daylight with it. The green fields sparkled with dew. Horses and cows grazed on nearby hills. Mist rose from the valley and from the shop's roof. Everything he saw spoke of a promise—the best this earth had to offer. The pursuit of happiness. Peaceful living. And freedom.

But all he could feel was emptiness and duty.

He'd hardly slept last night. His whole body ached for things he never knew existed before Cara. She woke the sleeping parts of his soul, just as she had as a child. Existence before her was shallow and only satisfying because he didn't know anything different.

Now he knew. Part of him wished he didn't. The other part longed for there to be answers.

Was he falling in love with her? It didn't matter. It couldn't. He tried to think about something else.

Since the house was quiet, he wondered if Cara and Lori were still asleep. After Cara had picked up Lori from his sister, he'd made ice cream as promised. Then he'd gone to the shop. Cara probably hadn't slept much either. Or maybe she had. She was certainly more used to upheaval and grief than he was. Did she feel grief over him? Or was he the only one who felt so stirred by their friendship?

He knew she needed to get to the Garretts' this morning to finish the job, but he hesitated to wake her. He went to the clothesline in his Daed's yard, where he'd created a trough of sorts using a sheet strung between two lines. He'd placed the freshly washed paintbrushes and rollers inside. It must've been about midnight when he remembered he needed to finish cleaning the soaking items. He placed the tools into a bucket he'd scrubbed for this very purpose.

The door to his Daed's home swooshed open, and he glanced up.

Anna Mary looked as weary as he felt. With Becca at the hospital with Daed, Anna Mary must've stayed to help Deborah with the younger ones. She headed for him without hesitation, apparently confident in continuing the special privilege granted to her by the bishop.

She came to a halt, her bare feet wet from the dew. "Mahlon and Grey both offered to help Cara today. The bishop gave permission, provided one of the elders can visit at will. I told him that wouldn't be a problem. One of the men will be here in about an hour to drive them over."

"Why the big production? Cara isn't going to try to seduce them, for Pete's sake."

"That's not the point. The bishop is our head, and we submit to his word. Have you forgotten the ways of your people so quickly?"

Chafing at her tone, one she never would have used before the shunning, he put the last two paintbrushes in the bucket.

"Robbie will be here to take you to the hospital about the same time. I want to go with you."

"I'm sure Deborah needs your help around here. Besides, I'd hoped to talk to Daed alone."

She moved in close and laid her hand on his chest. "Look, this is hard on both of us, but I have to know that you care about us—that when this is over, you'll be ready to commit to me the way you have to that woman and her child."

Like a spring rain, drops of realization fell on him, and he understood what his heart had been trying to tell him. He placed his hand over hers and removed it from him. "I'm sorry. But I can't do that."

He doubted if he ever could have, not without settling. But now that he knew what it meant for someone to connect with his soul, for someone's very presence to make a difference in how he perceived a day, he had to let Anna Mary go.

"What are you saying?"

"You can tell people you ended things between us. That you're tired of me. Ashamed of me. They'll sympathize. Probably even think you've done the right thing."

Her face turned red, and she burst into tears. "But why?"

"You don't really want an answer to that. If it helps, I don't want an answer to that either."

Her face scrunched with confusion. "Maybe you're just irritable from all the stress. Or angry at all that's happening and taking it out on me."

"Have I ever taken anything out on you?"

She used her apron to wipe her cheeks. "Then I need you to explain this to me."

She really didn't know? He removed his hat, fidgeting with it. Then he realized. She thought so little of Cara that she couldn't imagine Ephraim might have feelings for her. "I'm not in love with you."

"But…"

"I really am sorry."

She jerked the bucket from the ground and slung it across the yard. "I can't believe this. You should be begging me to stay in your life."

"I agree. But I'm not." He heard Lori chattering and looked that way. Across the field Cara stood basked in sunlight, a complete array of the forbidden. And all he wanted was more of her. She wasn't just an Englischer with her short hair, worldly dress, and permissive ways. She lacked every element inside her soul to become Amish. And still he longed to spend time with her.

Anna Mary squeezed his arm. "Look at me."

When he did, he saw the pain he'd inflicted. He hated it, but he couldn't change it.

"Her?" She sounded incredulous. "She's seduced you, hasn't she?"

"No. She has no idea how I feel. I'm not even sure how I feel. I may die a lonely bachelor. But that doesn't change anything between you and me."

She tightened her hands into fists before bolting across the yard.

As guilty as he felt, relief washed over him. Whatever discoveries within his heart lay ahead, they wouldn't involve betraying Anna Mary on any level.

Thirty-One

Cara stood at the kitchen counter as Joe Garrett wrote out a check. With his hand blocking her view, she couldn't see the amount. She heard Lori in the next room, talking with the Garretts' little girl.

Mr. Garrett paused, holding the payment in his hand. "You did an amazing job. Not a scratch on any of the floors or furniture, closets not only painted but organized. Every room painted beautifully. And no spatters of paint anywhere to be seen. I never expected all this. And in a week? You must've been logging some major overtime."

"I'm glad you're pleased."

He passed her the check. "I think that should say how impressed we are."

She glanced at the amount and nearly choked. Five hundred more dollars than they'd agreed on. All she'd hoped to do was ensure the Garretts were happy to pay her fee.

Heather Garrett motioned around the room. "I love it. Absolutely love it." She took the checkbook from her husband. "I've been threatening to clean and organize forever."

Cara's heart pounded like crazy. She had money, real start-up money. She was so excited she wanted to dance. Instead she folded the paper and slid it into her pocket. "There's a box of stuff in the garage, things that seemed obsolete when I cleaned out the closets."

"I'll go through it later this week."

Cara went upstairs to help Mahlon and Grey finish. They were busy moving pieces of furniture back into place. In spite of her being a stranger and an Englischer to boot, they'd let her manage the day without complaint. She liked both of her co-workers, which surprised her. They weren't at all what she'd thought they'd be—stuffy, judgmental, and difficult.

With a check in her pocket, her portion of it worth more than a month's pay, she felt hope buoy her again. "I really appreciate all you've done today." She peeled a strip of painter's tape off the baseboard.

Grey straightened his shoulders, working the kinks out of his neck. "Glad to help. The brushes, rollers, and most of the drop cloths are clean and loaded in the wagon."

Cara tossed a wad of tape into the trash. "We need to gather up the remaining supplies from the basement and walk through every room together to make sure we covered each item on the checklist, and then we're ready to go."

Mahlon pulled tape from a different section of the room. "Maybe you could help Deborah paint after I find us a place."

"I thought I was taboo."

Looking a bit uncomfortable, Grey set a lamp on the dresser. "I'll tell you plain out. You've made some huge blunders. Surely many Englischers would see it that way too, no?"

As much as she hated to admit it, he was right.

"See, among the Amish certain lines are not crossed. Ever. But if you move out of Ephraim's place and show yourself trustworthy, folks will come around eventually—if you're interested in that."

She peeled off the last bit of tape and reeled it in. There it was, staring her in the face again—the need to move out of Ephraim's place. "Except for Ephraim, I don't care what the rest think."

Grey set another lamp on the nightstand and plugged it in. "Right or wrong, he hid things from the church and community where you're concerned. He joined the faith years ago, and it's against our ways for him to open up his life to a woman who's not Amish, so you'll never be allowed much leeway with Ephraim."

She appreciated Grey's honesty. It stung a bit, but his tone and facial expressions said he wanted to help her understand. She longed to look in the faces of her relatives just once to see what they were like. The desire grew, and thoughts of going to the Riehl place tugged at her.

Mahlon threw a wad of tape into the trash. "Ephraim can do as he pleases if he's willing to turn his back on everyone and live shunned the rest of his life."

What? Feeling the room grow smaller, she leaned against the dresser. That's what had happened to her mother, wasn't it? And not only had her mother paid a price, she'd suffered too. And now Lori was paying a price as well. "Being friends with me will cause continued division? I don't want that." Should she walk away and never look back? "Isn't there some middle ground here?"

Grey slid the curtains back onto the rods. "Maybe. If you dress modest, watch your mouth, and behave in reserved ways so it's clear you're honoring our lines of morality."

"That's a tall order."

"For us too." He snapped the curtain rod in place. "But God gives us strength. And the church leaders set good examples and hold us accountable. Our ways cause bumps, bruises, and misunderstandings that get pretty heated sometimes. But after everything settles back down, we all learn from the mistake."

She couldn't imagine the type of management it took to keep an entire Amish community together for hundreds of years. The understanding Grey had just opened to her eased the pain of the people's stance against her. But like Ephraim said—the things that bound them would never loosen, but the things that separated them would always stand firm. Suddenly, for Ephraim's sake, she wanted to get out of his life so he could begin repairing the damage she'd caused. And she needed to get out as soon as possible.

But first she wanted to look in Emma Riehl's eyes and ask what happened.

Ephraim sat next to the hospital bed. His Daed had slept most of the day. His breathing was fast and shallow, his legs, ankles, and feet were swollen, and his fingernails had a bluish tint. The progression of the cardiomyopathy seemed rapid of late, and in spite of what Scripture said about trusting God, Ephraim worried.

The midafternoon sun reflected off the walls. An emergency had interrupted the doctor's rounds this morning, so he hadn't been by yet. Just as well, Ephraim supposed, because when his Daed was awake, he expressed reluctance to let him talk to the doctor. He kept saying he didn't need his son to treat him like he was a kid. But there was more to his objections than that; Ephraim was sure of it. With Becca finally gone to the cafeteria for lunch, he intended to find out what.

"Daed." He touched his arm, waking him. "We need to talk." He gave him a minute to wake before he passed him a glass of ice chips.

"I'm thirsty, and all they allow are ice chips? This is a lousy hotel."

He hoped his father's bit of humor was a good sign.

"Daed, I need to be here when the doctor comes to talk to you. I want to hear what he has to say."

"We discussed this already. I'm fine. There's nothing to know."

"Then let the doctor explain that to me."

"Did you come to visit or to wear me out?"

"I came to see if there's anything that can be done about these episodes. Your heart condition is worsening, landing you in the hospital time and again. What aren't you telling me? I think you owe me the truth."

"Owe you?" His father stared at him.

"Yes."

"You're the one who owes me. Letting that girl sleep at your place. I'm being dishonored in front of the whole world."

The turmoil inside him eroded every semblance of peace he'd found among his people over the years. If his father had an inkling how Ephraim felt, he might need to be moved to ICU. "I'm sorry for the stress the situation has caused you. But right now I want to discuss your health. Nothing else."

His father set the glass on the tray table. "I don't like being treated like a child."

"Me either. But you're treating me like one. Shouldn't we act more like business partners? We don't have to always agree, but we can love and respect each other as equals."

His father picked at the tape where the IV was stuck into his arm. "The meds that improve my heart's ability to pump aren't working like they used to. We've tried a lot of different things, but the symptoms are just getting worse. There's nothing to be done."

"I talked to a nurse a couple of weeks ago, and she said there's this thing called an AICD."

Daed's eyes misted. "Not acceptable. It requires a blood transfusion. And I refuse to mingle my blood with that of a sinner. I'd rather die."

Weary of rules and constraints and family needs, Ephraim's frustration peaked. "We need to consider all the medical options."

"You're asking me to ignore my convictions. All those years of working by my side, and you still don't understand me? Where is the respect for everything I've done for you? I built that business up and practically gave it to you."

"When you asked me to come home because of your illness, I came and took over supporting the family. So don't even start about *giving* me the shop. I work twice as hard as I should so I can give you and your family more than half of all the profits. Now, I want to discuss your medical options, and we'll decide together."

"I won't be put to sleep and have my chest ripped open. Those doctors aren't God. My life is in His hands."

Grinding his teeth, he tried to temper his answer. "He's not the one you've been relying on to support you. I've been carrying that burden. So if there are ways to ease the symptoms, we need to consider them. Don't let your illness be worse than it has to be."

His father gazed out the window, and Ephraim watched the minute hand above his bed circle the clock twice. "You didn't need to be *draus in da Welt*. If God wanted to use my health to get you home, I'm not arguing."

"Whoa." Ephraim jumped to his feet, a dozen arguments against that nonsense running through his mind. "You were bad off, and I had to come home. But you can't hold my life ransom unless you have no other choice. I won't stand for it—not anymore."

"Not anymore?"

Ephraim looked out the window, seeing miles and miles of a world he didn't belong to. "I gave you my life, Daed. Too freely. Too easily. I'm not sure why, except I loved you and I respected what you wanted more than what I wanted. At the time it made sense to become who you needed me to be. But you've taken it too far. And I've let you."

His father held his gaze, seemingly stunned at the turn of the conversation. "You want your freedom to chase after that woman, don't you?"

Bright sunshine illuminated the earth, but Ephraim's thoughts and feelings suspended inside him like thick fog. "I want you to stop controlling my life. You've made choices, and I carry the weight of them. You chose a wife more than ten years younger than you. You chose to continue sleeping with her even after you were too sick to support the children you already had. She brought two children into the marriage, and you had three more after you became sick. I should have realized this long before now, but doesn't it seem wrong that I have to pay for your choices?"

The muscles in his father's throat constricted. Minutes droned on, and his father's eyes misted. "Are you saying you're leaving the faith?"

"No. I'm saying if there's a possibility of you getting well by trying certain things, then you should try them."

"If I allow a surgery, I'll have to sign papers to accept a blood transfusion if the need arises." Tears moistened his eyes. "Besides, part of me wants to see your mother so badly."

As the layers of Daed's thoughts unfolded, Ephraim saw there wasn't just one issue stopping him from pursuing his medical options. He had a tangled mess of reasons. "Daed, it was more awful to lose Mamm than we could bear for a long time."

"I still miss her."

"Me too. One of the first things I remember after you married Becca is her standing at the kitchen sink, washing dishes. Because she wore her hair the same way and had on the Amish garb, she looked a lot like Mamm. She put good meals on the table for us, just like Mamm had. She packed my lunch like Mamm. She even sat on the couch reading to the little ones, kissed them tenderly, and tucked them in like Mamm. There wasn't one physical act Mamm did that Becca couldn't do. But she wasn't Mamm. And our hearts knew it."

"I'm sure Becca would understand. She ached over losing her husband too."

"I know." He sat next to his father and placed his hand on his arm. "You fill a place in our family that I can't fill. If I have to, I can make the necessary decisions and earn the money to pay the bills. But we all want and need you. You've got to fight. If not for yourself, for your youngest children who won't even remember you if you give up now. For Deborah, who adores you more than you know. And for me. I'm tired of trying to be you but more than ready to be your son again."

Someone tapped on the door while opening it. "How are you feeling today, Abner?" He nodded at Ephraim. "I'm Dr. Kent."

Ephraim stood and introduced himself. "I've been talking with my Daed, and I'd like you to explain his options to both of us."

The man looked to Daed. When he nodded, the doctor took a seat. "Sure. I'll cover a few basics, and we'll go from there. To begin with, your father doesn't have heart disease. Years ago a virus moved into the organ and caused physical damage. He's been on medicines for a long time, and that worked for a while. But this past year their effectiveness has been waning, and he's having more episodes. His thyroid has suffered a lot of damage, which is stealing his energy. Monitoring his diet is no longer enough. His heart rate is becoming more difficult to control, as is the fluid retention in his body. He's not bad enough to be eligible for a heart transplant. And I hope he doesn't get to that point, because the waiting list is longer than most can survive. But we've had good success with AICDs. It will be able to decrease his heart rate when needed, and I believe implanting one is the best treatment plan for Abner, though it's not without problems."

"Will he need a transfusion for that?"

"Unlikely. But I won't operate without blood from the bank already in the OR. His blood doesn't clot well, so I'm particularly cautious." He glanced from Daed to Ephraim and back again. "Is that a problem?"

Ephraim nodded. "It's a pretty big obstacle for my Daed."

"Why?"

Ephraim waited on his Daed to speak up, but he didn't. "He's uncomfortable with the thought of having a stranger's blood going into his body."

"Abner, I had no idea that was part of the holdup. As long as the blood type matches or is compatible, you can have friends and relatives donate blood for you."

His father didn't move for several moments. Then he looked at Ephraim. "I didn't know that."

Irritation pounded inside him. Ephraim had suffered years of unfairness, and it threatened to turn into deep-seated anger. His father should have been slower to stand against the unknown and quicker to ask every possible question.

"Ephraim, are you convinced I should do this?"

Ephraim couldn't be sure his father would fare better after the procedure or even that he'd survive any possible complications. "I won't take on the responsibility of deciding for you."

His father shook his head. "I've been wrong. I can't begin to make it up to you unless I try to gain my strength back." He looked to the doctor. "I'll do it."

Thirty-Two

Standing at Ephraim's stove, Cara stirred the pot of beef stew she'd slow cooked at the Garretts and then brought here.

"Are you sure about this?" Ephraim's eyes held such concern she had to look away.

"I have to know why my dad told me Emma was coming and why she never showed."

"Cara." He whispered her name, but she refused to look into his face. He moved beside her. "Once you start asking questions, you're likely to hear things about your mother that you may not want to know."

"Look, I already figured that out." She waved the wooden spoon at him. "Maybe she wasn't a good person when she left here, but she was a good mom to me. I've got proof of it in my memory and more in the diary. She wrote things about God and Scripture." Her heart raced, feeling the rush of secrets her mother had probably hoped she'd never know.

Ephraim opened the cabinet. "I'd forgotten until just now, but I remember her talking to me during your visit. She said something about trusting God. Oh, and being good to you when you came back."

Her eyes stung with tears. "Pity you didn't remember that before I had to give you a fat lip."

He took three glasses from the shelf. "I'll drive you over there, if you want, and wait near the road."

"I can walk, thanks. News flash. I survived the streets of New York, alone and with a stalker. I'm not weak, Ephraim."

He passed her three bowls. "A blind man could see that. I just don't want to wait here alone, wondering how it went. How will I know if the conversation is over at seven, nine, or twelve o'clock?"

She took a ladle out of a drawer. Clearly he didn't want her facing this alone and then walking back. He cared…maybe more than just as a friend. A tremble went through her. Too much separated them for them to become more involved than they already were. And whatever relationship they did have had to end. Or at least move to more distant ground.

She dipped up a bowl of stew. "I'm leaving tomorrow."

"What? Why?"

"I have some start-up money. And you have to get unshunned from your family, community, and friends as quickly as possible."

"We talked about this."

"It's time, Ephraim. We both know it. And I'm not going to that apartment your people picked out for me."

"But it's already been paid for."

"I won't be paid to leave. And if it wasn't for you, I'd tell them so myself in not-so-nice terms."

"Where will you go?"

"Jiminy Cricket, you ask a lot of questions."

"The social worker, remember her?"

"When I get settled, I'll call her." She swallowed, trying to hide how much she was hurting. "We accomplished our goal. I have money now and can stand on my own two feet."

"A thousand dollars won't go far."

"I'll get another job."

"How?"

She slammed the bowl on the counter. "What do you want from me?"

"Time. You just found out about your relatives, and you're ready to bolt. I'm not ready for you to leave. Besides, Lori needs—"

"Ephraim," she whispered, "the things that separate us will always stand firm."

He clenched his jaw, staring down at her.

"Let's eat. Then you can drive me to Emma Riehl's place."

She couldn't swallow a bite, and she heard none of the chatter between Lori and Ephraim, but soon enough all three of them were in the buggy. The sun slid behind the mountains, and darkness eased over the earth—deep purple faded to a dark blue, and then the very air itself seemed to go black.

Ephraim pointed. "There, to your left."

A bonfire blazed in the side yard. Two or three dozen people sat around in lawn chairs. Children played freeze tag, and teens played volleyball near the barn.

"The American dream lives." The bitterness in her tone surprised her, but Ephraim didn't flinch.

"Half the community is here. We don't have to do this now."

"Yes I do."

He tugged the reins to slow the buggy. "Maybe you should try being stubborn for a change, Cara."

"Sarcasm doesn't suit you, 'From. You should leave that to experts like me."

Before he came to a complete stop, a broad-shouldered man with a beard left the crowd and walked toward them. She couldn't tell in the dark, but he appeared to have gray hair around the edges of his hat.

"That's Levi Riehl. He's Emma's husband and your mother's oldest brother. He might not like that I'm here."

"Good, then I won't be the only one who wishes you'd stayed home. I'll be back." She stepped down from the buggy, wondering if she should have worn Deborah's dress instead of her jeans. But it seemed wrong to put on an Amish dress, as if she were pretending to be part of something she wasn't. Besides, she hated that thing. It made her look heavy, old, and frumpy.

The man looked at Ephraim and waved. He started to turn back toward the house, but then he caught a glimpse of her. He stopped all movement. "You're Cara."

She nodded.

He studied her face. "You favor your Mamm, even under the night skies."

"I don't really remember what she looked like. But I remember other things."

Her hands, her voice…her love.

He stood there without saying anything else, and she thought she'd suffocate under the stiltedness of it. "We didn't have any hint that she might have passed away until ten years after her death. I'm sorry for how hard growing up without her must have been on you."

"You didn't know?" Her mind tried to process that detail. "Emma— she's your wife, right?"

"Ya."

"My dad said she'd come for me."

Levi stared at the ground. "We had no idea where you were." He shook his head. "If we'd known your mama had died and how to get you, we would have."

Children's laughter from the side yard surrounded her like a cyclone. She could have grown up here? Since that never-ending day at the Port Authority so many years ago, each day had carried pain and loneliness. Now all those years of grief stacked on top of her, squeezing her until she couldn't breathe or think.

He glanced behind him. "I need to get back."

Her legs shook, and her head spun.

"Levi?" A woman walked from the bonfire area. When she spotted Cara, she gasped. *"Ach, es iss waahr."*

Levi went to her side and whispered something in her ear.

"Enough." The woman pulled away from him. She stood directly in front of Cara and touched her cheek as if making sure she was real. "Oh, dear child." She burst into tears. "God forgive me."

"You did nothing wrong, Emma." Levi put his arm around his wife, supporting her. "Kumm."

Shaking her head, Emma wiped falling tears from her cheeks. *"Nix meh. Schtobbe."*

Whatever she'd said, she appeared to be waiting on Levi to answer. After a pause that seemed to last forever, Levi nodded. "We've talked about coming to see you, but it's just so complicated with Ephraim being shunned because of…of…your being there." He shrugged. "I could explain a dozen honest reasons, but none of them seems worthy as I stand here."

Emma stepped closer. "Your father called our phone shanty about twenty years ago. His words were slurred. He ranted about Malinda wanting you to be raised Amish. Kept mumbling that I had to come get you. I tried to reason with him, telling him he was asking too much. That Levina was going to raise you. The agreement was that Malinda would bring you back to Dry Lake, not insist we come get you. Levina was too old and unfamiliar with traveling to go by bus. I was pregnant with twins and mostly on bed rest. Levi was working overtime to make ends meet. And your Daed's words were that of…of a…"

"A drunk." Cara finished the sentence for her.

"He never said Malinda had died. He only said he'd found our number in her personal phone book and we needed to come get you. Finally I agreed and wrote down the details about where you'd be and when. As I thought about it over the next few days, I discounted the conversation. He was drunk, and I figured if Malinda wanted you here, she'd have brought you."

"So you just dropped it?"

Tears choked Emma when she tried to speak, and she looked at Levi. He rubbed her back. "A few days later we tried reaching him by phone, but the line had been disconnected. I called information, trying to find another number for Trevor or Malinda Atwater."

Teary-eyed, Emma drew a breath. "We decided Malinda must have changed her mind about giving you up but that your dad wanted you gone from there." She rubbed her hands together, looking as nervous as Cara felt. "We thought she was still alive. I knew she didn't want to give you up."

"We didn't hear from him again until a decade later when he sent a package here, addressed to you," Levi said. "That's when we realized Malinda might be dead, and he thought you were living here."

"But…Ephraim had no idea my mom had died."

"We shared what we suspected with just a few people—mostly your uncles. There was no way to be sure she'd died, and…and the news would only have stirred guilt and conflict in our district again."

Emma moved in closer. "When your dad called here, if we'd thought for a moment Malinda had died…"

Cara's knees gave way, but she didn't sink to the ground. Someone seemed to be holding her up. Ephraim? When did he get down from the wagon? Would he be in more trouble for this? Her thoughts jumped as if her mind were a Polaroid, registering isolated scenes here and there.

Children held marshmallows on skewers over leaping flames. Moms passed out graham crackers and chocolate bars while guarding the children so they didn't get too close to the fire.

The next thing Cara knew she was in the buggy. Warmth from Ephraim's hand seemed to be her only anchor to reality. The clip-clop of the horse's hoofs echoed against the night. Lori's faint voice spoke to her, but she couldn't make out the words.

Slowly a few solid thoughts formed. "My father didn't follow through long enough to put me into safe hands. What kind of man does that?"

Ephraim said nothing.

"Why would my mother marry someone like that?"

He pulled into his driveway. A buggy stood nearby with a man in it, staring at them.

She waited for Ephraim to guide the horse around back, but he sat still, watching the man. She recognized him. Rueben Lantz, the one who'd seemed to watch her for more than a week. She sat up straight. "What? You got something to say to me?"

He didn't respond, not even a shake of his head.

She jerked the reins from Ephraim and slapped the horse's back. He lunged forward, coming dangerously close to the man's rig. Both horses whinnied and pranced skittishly. Ephraim pried the reins from her hands and guided the animal away from the other one. Rueben drove off, and Ephraim didn't stop the horse until they were in the barn.

Feeling like her heart had been trampled under a dozen horses, she got out and went to the gate.

Ephraim helped Lori down.

"I want to be alone," she growled at him.

"Not yet."

She moved in close, whispering, "Please. Take Lori inside before her mother turns into a lunatic in front of her."

He nodded and took her daughter into the house.

The silhouette of the rolling hills and massive trees, the silvery glow of the pond, the calls of night—all of it mocked her. These would have been her childhood memories. Instead her life was filled with concrete and asphalt, as unyielding as the people she'd grown up with—people whose names she didn't even know anymore, except for Mike Snell's family.

The ache that rolled over her threatened to steal her good sense, and she started walking. She went through the cornfield and soon stood next to the trees. Memories washed over her freely. She wished she could stop them. Wished she'd never come here.

A horse and buggy stopped on the road. "Hello." The warm, friendly voice reminded her of her mother's. Tears began to flow. The woman drove the carriage beside the trees. "I was at the Riehls' place. I saw you leave. I was hoping I'd find you."

Cara wiped her tears. "Whatever you want to say, don't. I can't stand hearing one more thing."

The woman stepped down from the buggy. "I'm Ada. I've been praying for you since before you were born."

"And what a great job your mighty God has done."

She placed her hand under Cara's chin. "You made it back here against all odds. You have a few stout supporters in this community who want to set things right. I'd say He's been quite busy. He's had a few obstacles to work around, ya?"

Cara wanted to lash out about the community's "support." She also wanted to turn and walk away. But the softness in Ada's voice, the tenderness in her touch called to her, and she fell against the woman, sobbing.

Thirty-Three

Cara woke with rough fabric against her skin, a sheet over her, and a hard pillow under her head. The aroma of coffee filled the air, and she remembered walking back to Ephraim's last night with Ada.

Streams of sunlight made it difficult to open her eyes. She splayed her fingers across the cloth and sat upright, realizing she was on Ephraim's couch. The warm stuffiness of the room said it was at least midmorning. Soft voices floated from the kitchen. She headed that way.

Ada sat in a chair at the table, and Ephraim was leaning against the counter near the sink. A shoebox-sized package wrapped in brown paper and yellowed packing tape sat on the kitchen table.

He glanced out the window. "She's dead set against moving into the place some of the men have paid for."

"Do you blame her?"

"No, but that little bit of money in her pocket isn't enough."

"I'll talk to her. Maybe she'll agree to—"

"Cara." Ephraim pulled a chair out for her.

She rubbed her temples, desperately wanting a pain reliever. "Where's Lori?"

He pointed out the window. "She and Better Days and her dolls are having a picnic."

"Did I miss something? I thought you were shunned."

"He is," Ada offered. "I spoke to the bishop, told him I wanted a chance to talk some sense into Ephraim." She smiled. "Made for a good excuse. Besides, I didn't want you staying alone last night, and I didn't want Ephraim to get in even deeper trouble with the church leaders, so I slept over."

Cara took a seat. "I feel horrible."

Ephraim placed a mug of coffee in front of her. "This will help."

"Do you have any pain reliever?"

He pulled a bottle of ibuprofen out of the cupboard. "Cara, Ada has something she'd like to talk to you about."

She shook her head. "I'm not staying in Dry Lake, no matter what she says. I'm leaving today. I'm going to get a shower and soak my aching head. If I'd known crying gave a person such a headache, I'd not have done it. Great lotta good it did. Everything's the same, except now my head hurts."

Ada slowly pushed the package toward Cara. "Levi and Emma brought this by earlier."

The box looked well kept, yet the yellowed tape that sealed it made it appear quite old. It had no return address, only a name. Trevor Atwater—her father. She angled the box so she could see the faded date stamp. It'd been sent a few days before her birthday ten years ago. She would have been eighteen.

Pushing it away from her, she rose. "Idiot. He leaves me at a bus station and assumes I'm living here ten years later. I'm getting a shower." She walked off.

"You have family," Ephraim called out to her.

She turned to face him. "I've had family here my whole life. Big fat stinking deal. It made no difference when it could have. And none of them want me here now. Open your eyes, Ephraim. I meant so little to these people that Emma Riehl never called anyone to check on me. Not the police or social services or even the place where my mother worked. They didn't want to know the truth about where I was, how I was. And I'm sorry for what I know about them. I wish I'd never come here."

Cara stormed into the bathroom and slammed the door. She flicked on the shower. In spite of her exhaustion, tears trailed down her face. Emma and Levi had cared less about her than Simeon did for those stray pups. It seemed impossible right now to accept that fact, but the pain would fade eventually. She stayed in the shower until the water turned cold. She dried off and slid into the only piece of clean clothing she had— Deborah's dress. When she came out, Ada was at the stove, loading pancakes onto a plate.

The sight only made her hurt worse. If her father had made contact with Ada instead of Emma, everything would have been different.

Cara walked to the table.

"Ephraim and Lori have gone for a walk by the creek. Lori said they're going to teach Better Days to be a better dog than his mama and not to knock people into the water." Ada chuckled. "Wonder who the guinea pig for that will be." She set the plate of pancakes on the table, clearly offering them to her.

"I'm not hungry. Thanks, anyway." She picked up the package, walked to the trash can, and threw it in.

"I'm a few years younger than your mother would be. One summer we were hired to work the cornfields, detasseling. You know what that is?"

Cara shook her head.

"The pollen-producing tassel on top of the cornstalk is removed by hand and placed on the ground. It's really hard work, but the pay is great. We began before sunup, took a short lunch break, and worked until suppertime. Mr. Bierd handled his workers differently than most farmers. He gave each worker a section to get done according to age and height. If you didn't finish your section by the end of the week, you were given half pay and never hired again. I needed the money bad, but each day I got further behind. The day before time to get paid, your mother realized I was behind. She asked a few others to stay and help, but they were too tired. She stayed with me, and we worked until nearly dawn. That's the kind of person your mother was, Cara. Over and over again." Ada went to the trash and pulled out the package. "Don't be afraid to look."

The desire to run had never been stronger than at this moment, but Cara took the package from her and forced herself to open it. On top was an envelope. She pulled out the card. In jagged heavy cursive, it wished her a happy eighteenth birthday.

My beautiful daughter, you deserved to grow up with someone as great as your mom. I figured sending you to live with her brother would be the next best thing. I wasn't much of a dad, or a hus-band, or a human for that matter. For that, everyone I loved has suffered. I'm winning over the addiction for now. I'm ashamed to even think about how hard and how often your mother tried to help me overcome my dependency.

I've sent you a few items, along with a letter explaining the story between your mother and me. I didn't sweeten it. At times you'll probably wish it was more gentle, more like how parents should be. But we didn't start out as parents. We started as two reckless nineteen-year-olds.

If you can find it in your heart to see me, I'll be staying at the Rustic Inn on West King Street in Shippensburg for a week, beginning on your birthday.

Happy Birthday,
Dad

She searched through the box, finding photos of her and her mother at various stages of Cara's infancy and childhood. Until Cara was eight.

Deeper in the box she found a few stuffed animals, a Bible, her birth certificate, and her parents' marriage license. At the bottom was a stack of letters with Cara's name written on the envelope of each one. She set them on the table next to her.

The last item was a green spiral-bound notebook with the words "The Book of Cara" scrawled on the outside. The bottom right corner of the cover had her father's name on it.

Unsure she wanted to know the *unsweetened* story, she laid the book on the table.

"May I?" Ada tapped the birth certificate.

Cara shrugged. "Sure."

Ada unfolded the document. "This doesn't make sense." She pointed to the date of her birth.

"Why not?"

Ada shook her head and opened the marriage certificate. "Something's wrong. This says your parents were married fifteen months before you were born."

"I don't see the problem."

"That means she wasn't pregnant when she left here. Or if she was, you aren't that child."

"So? She wasn't pregnant when she married my dad. If you'd ever read the entries my mother wrote in my diary, things about honoring God and always trying to do right, that wouldn't surprise you."

"Your mother was engaged to an Amish man. He told us she ran off with an Englischer because she was expecting his baby."

"With the reception I've received here, I figured something along those lines. They must've had it wrong…or maybe Mama changed after they knew her."

"The rumors don't fit the time line. That's for sure." She read the dates again, as if triple-checking her facts. "She left so quickly. As far as I know, she didn't return or write or call or anything until about ten years later when she showed up with you." Ada waved the papers at her.

"Maybe I'm not the child she was pregnant with when she left here."

She tapped the book. "I bet the answers are in there."

Cara laid it to the side. "Later."

Ada slid her hand under Cara's, holding it palm to palm. "You know what I think?"

Cara didn't answer.

"I think you need some mulling-over time. You want out of Dry

Lake. Ephraim thinks you should stay. I think we need to find a solution."
She rubbed her neck. "My son, Mahlon, is supposed to be finding me and
him a place to live. But he hasn't really tried. I think he'd like it if I wasn't
living with him. So, instead of hitting him upside the head, I started looking for a place on my own."

"I didn't think the Amish believed in violence."

"Oh, honey, nobody *believes* in violence. Some think the outcome
justifies it. Amish don't. I was only joking. Even Amish people joke about
things."

"I guess I don't really know the Amish, do I?"

"No, and they don't know you." She placed a hand on Cara's back.
"Maybe that will change with time. I've got an appointment to look at a
certain place tomorrow afternoon. I've been told it needs a lot of painting and fixing up, but it has plenty of bedrooms, bathrooms, and a huge
kitchen. The Realtor says it's a bit rough, but the owner is interested in
exchanging work for rent, which is where you could come in. Mahlon
says you're quite good at painting. Maybe you can live and work there
with me."

"I…I…" Searching for the most respectful way to refuse, Cara fid-
dled with the edges of the letters.

Ada looked at her as if reading her thoughts. "Just think about it.
Okay?"

"You're very generous. But wouldn't you get in trouble for that? I
mean, Ephraim's been shunned over his dealings with me. What'd happen if I moved in with you?"

Ada drew a deep breath. "I won't lie. It might be an issue even though
I'm not a single Amish man. You've got quite a reputation of being worldly,
and the bishop's going to have lots of reservations. But I can work it out.
I think."

"I have money now. And I really think I should leave. I've caused
enough trouble in everyone's life."

She tapped the notebook. "You should read that. Your dad took the time to write it, and it's been sitting here in Dry Lake for ten years. Seems to me it's begging to be read." She stood. "I need to go, and you need to think." She headed for the door and then paused. "Could I take your birth certificate and your parents' marriage license with me?"

"Why?"

"I have an idea." She looked unsure about saying more.

Cara held them out to her. "Sure. Why not?"

The screen door banged shut as Ada left. Cara lifted the spiral-bound notebook and stared at it. She didn't really want to read it. Not anytime soon. The desire to pack her things and get out of Dry Lake was so strong she thought it might lift her straight off the chair.

But more than any other feeling was the desire to see her parents, if only through the eyes of a man who admitted he struggled with addiction. Torn between curiosity and resentment, she opened the thin cardboard cover.

I met your mother when she was nineteen years old. She was the most striking woman I'd ever seen, with brown eyes and blond hair that she parted down the middle and wore in a bun with the white prayer Kapp. I was an Englischer by her standards, and she was in love with another man. She was more loyal and honest than anyone I've ever known, but she wasn't perfect. Neither of us was. She'd had her heart broken and was desperate to leave Dry Lake, so I took her away from there. She regretted that decision, and I understood, but by then we were married, and neither of us could undo the choices we'd made. I hope—and at times dare to pray—that you found Dry Lake to be as wonderful a place to grow up as she remembered from her childhood.

The words released a lifetime of bottled sentiments, and she closed the book. When she'd longed to feel something besides cold and emptiness during her teen years, this overload wasn't what she had in mind.

Confusion swirled in a dozen directions, pulling at her to believe different things. Desperate to escape before she suffocated under the swell of emotions, she went into the bedroom and stuffed her and Lori's things into the backpack. Ada's mothering voice washed over her, making some tiny fragment of Cara wish she could stay.

When she went outside, she heard Ephraim and Lori talking in the hiddy. She walked to the entryway. "I'm ready." His eyes met hers, causing a fresh surge of tormenting feelings. He'd been a good friend in spite of the trouble her presence had caused him. "Will you take me, or do I need to hire a driver?"

He slowly rose, looking disappointed in her decision. "I'll take you."

"Where are we going, Mom?"

As Ephraim headed toward the barn, Cara moved to the bench swing and patted the empty place beside her. Lori snuggled against her.

"Are we going to the Garretts' again?"

"Tell me about your walk."

Lori shared her excitement over what Ephraim was teaching Better Days. " 'From and me are going to find a home for all the pups next week."

"Lori, sweetie, it's been great staying here, but Ephraim needs his home back, and we need to find a place of our own. We have money now, so we'll find a good place, okay?"

Lori jumped to her feet, fists tight, hurt and anger etched across her tiny body. "No."

With the backpack on her shoulder, Cara lifted her daughter's rigid body and toted her out of the hedged area. Ephraim brought the carriage to a stop. Lori arched her back and screamed, causing Cara to nearly drop her as she eased her feet onto the ground.

"Get in the buggy, Lori."

She ran to Ephraim and grabbed his hand. "No!"

Cara refused to look in Ephraim's eyes. They said the same thing Lori's did—that Cara was wrong. "Don't say no to me again."

"I won't go. So there. And I didn't say the word *no*."

Cara had forgotten how sassy her daughter could be. Lori clung tighter to Ephraim's hand. "I got 'From and a dog, and I'm not leaving!"

"One...two..."

Lori began a panicked cry, afraid her mother would reach the number ten. Cara had no idea what was supposed to happen if she reached it. Lori had never disobeyed past the number four.

"Stop." She held up one hand, still clinging to Ephraim with the other. "There ain't nobody after us, and I'm not going."

Cara's world tilted. Her daughter knew they'd been running from Mike? She looked to Ephraim before sinking to her knees. "All right. I hear you." She looped her daughter's hair behind her ears. "Who do you think would be after us, Lorabean?"

"The police. That lady that came here, Ms. Forrester, said they wouldn't come looking for us."

Cara's heart skipped several beats. Lori didn't know about the stalker after all.

Cara looked to Ephraim, searching for answers he didn't have.

He placed his hand on Lori's head. "Take Better Days inside and get him a bowl of water, okay? I need to talk with your mother."

"You better listen to him." Lori shook her finger at her mother. "Or I'm never talking to you again."

The screen door banged shut, and Ephraim helped Cara to her feet. "She's not ready to leave."

"She'll be fine. And we can't stay here. I'll only make things worse for you. Your people aren't talking to you. You can't work. You can't even see your family or Anna Mary. You should be shoving me into that buggy and promising Lori it's the right thing to do. She'd believe you."

"I won't lie to her to make you feel better."

"Then lie to her for her sake!"

"You're being stubborn."

"You're being just as bad, insisting I stay when we both know I should go."

"I've plowed the fields with mules more cooperative than you."

Chafing with frustration and hurt, Cara glanced to Ephraim. If he had an inkling how betrayed she felt by her relatives, he'd help her get out of here before she lashed out at them and caused him more trouble in the process.

Images of Ephraim climbing the tree with her as a child floated across her mind. "I can't stand the churning emotions inside me. It's like someone opened a dam and I'm stuck in the pool at the bottom of the falls."

"I don't have to imagine it. I feel it." He took her hand and placed it on his chest. "It's enough to rip an ox apart, and I don't want you facing it alone."

Her eyes burned with the threat of tears, but she willed them away. She pulled her hand free. "Whatever it is you want from me, I can't give it."

"We're not talking about what anyone wants here. That passed by so long ago nothing can repair it. You need help getting your feet under you, emotionally and financially. I give you my word, I'll ask for no more than that."

She closed her eyes and listened to the sounds of spring: wind, birds, the distant mooing of cows. Wishing she could pray, she took a deep breath.

Ephraim placed his hand on her shoulder. "Think of the difference this could make for Lori."

Unable to reject his reasoning, she nodded. "Okay. For a little while. But not here in your house."

"Ada's determined to find a place to rent. She really likes the idea of you staying with her."

"I'll help her get settled and paint whatever rooms she wants. But when the painting job is done, it'll be time for me to find a place away from here."

"In the meantime I'll do my best to help Lori accept that and adjust." His eyes said he meant it. "I'm sure she won't be mad at you if we do it right."

The need to cry seemed to vanish, and she couldn't help but smile at him. "Using Lori to get your way? You cheat."

"Yep, and I win too."

But she couldn't hold on to the faint smile. It wouldn't be long before she'd regret going with this plan; she was sure of it.

Thirty-Four

Ada opened the oven and removed a pie. Haunting questions kept looping through her mind, but she had no answers. Not yet.

She set the pie on a cooling plate and turned off the gas stove. Her baking was done for today, and, like always, every bit of space on her kitchen table, chairs, and countertops was covered in baked goods. The bakery's courier would come by soon, but Ada had too much to get done to wait. She scribbled a note and taped it to her front door, telling the courier to let herself in. They'd handled it this way a few times over the years.

With Monday's orders filled, she changed into a fresh dress and apron and headed out the door. It was three thirty by the time she had her horse hitched and was on her way. But she didn't want to hire a driver. She needed time to think, and for her the gentle speed and rhythmic sounds of a horse-drawn carriage always helped.

She'd let Mahlon make decisions for her for so long that her desire to put a stop to it had her thoughts running in circles. If she could just understand herself and why she'd made the kinds of decisions she had in the past, maybe she could find a few answers for her future. Baffled or not, she had to keep moving toward helping Cara. And she knew if she wanted to ease Cara's pain and make a difference for her and Lori, it'd begin with the church leaders and Cara's uncles. So when she left Cara yesterday, she'd gone to see the bishop. She'd talked to him about finding a place of her own and having Cara move in with her. He listened patiently, but then he told her that her plan wasn't a good idea, which meant no.

It would be impossible for Ada to become a church member of the Hope Crossing district without being a member in good standing in the Dry Lake district, so she couldn't ignore his stance. After talking with him for nearly an hour, explaining that people's reactions to Cara were based more on rumors than facts, she showed him the documents Cara had loaned her. He said little, but he decided to have a districtwide meeting tonight. In a little over four hours, everyone would gather at Levi Riehl's farm.

But Cara was only one issue weighing on her.

Ada gently pulled on the reins, bringing the rig to a stop as she stared at a fork in the road. To her left the road headed straight out of Dry Lake. By steering right, she could stop by Israel Kauffman's before heading to Hope Crossing.

She couldn't keep living based on what Mahlon thought he wanted from her, but if she wasn't that woman, who was she?

The Realtor would meet her at the rental place in an hour and a half. And here she sat, feeling almost as confused as the day her husband was killed. Israel's wife died that day too. Did he ever have times of feeling as lost now as he did then?

He probably didn't. Grown children and even a few grandchildren surrounded him on all sides. He'd freely admit he had strong support that kept a smile on his face most days. His middle daughter, Lena, was his biggest help, not just because she handled the chores and was so good to her younger siblings, but because she radiated happiness and humor all the time.

Lena and Deborah were cousins, and aside from Amish traditions they'd been raised very differently, but both took pleasure in trying to bring joy to others. Deborah's sense of humor was subtle compared to Lena's more boisterous approach where she tried to make people roar with laughter. Ada remembered one night at her home when Deborah, Mahlon, and Lena were playing board games. As out of character as it was for Mahlon, Lena's wit kept him chuckling for the entire evening.

Worry for Mahlon nagged her. He continued to search, for…something. Peace? Stability? Something that would stop him from wavering like wheat in a field. Whatever it was, Ada had begun a search of her own.

She'd never considered herself a strong woman, one who knew what she wanted and went after it. Whatever her husband had wanted, that's what she wanted—even down to the flavor of ice cream she chose at the local creamery. After he died, her personality type had made it easy for Mahlon to lead her in whatever direction he wanted.

What had made her be someone who never trusted her own thoughts or desires or dreams? Why had she feared being wrong so much that she let others be wrong for her?

She didn't know, but she had a fresh chance to follow her heart, especially where Cara was concerned. It was time to trust her gut and find a way to follow her heart.

If she went to every Amish home in Dry Lake and asked their opinion of what she should do next, some would think one way and some the other.

But what did *she* think?

Finally ready to trust her own desires, she slapped the reins against the horse's back.

It was time to talk to Israel. As a former homebuilder, he knew housing structure and probably some of what it'd take to expand her business. He had a way of giving sound advice when asked without trying to sway the person one way or the other. That was Israel—state the facts and let the person decide.

When she pulled onto his driveway, she saw him and several of his children sitting on the porch, casually visiting on this warm Monday before suppertime. She knew his family tended to have an early meal and then he'd return to his work of building furniture.

He rose from his chair and walked to her, studying her face intently. "Ada." He nodded. "This is a first."

"You may wish for it to be the last too."

He cocked an eyebrow, looking rather amused. "Doubtful. What's up?"

"I know this is awfully bold of me, but I got some things on my mind, and I need a man's… No, I need *your* opinion."

"Of course. I thought maybe you'd come by to make sure I'd heard about tonight's meeting. Care to come inside?"

She shook her head. "I'm going to Hope Crossing to look at a place. I was wondering if you might go with me."

"You're thinking of moving to Hope Crossing? That's quite a piece from here."

"About an hour by carriage."

"You want to find a home that far away?"

"I'm aiming to do what I should have done ten or more years ago— find a place where I can expand my baking business. Better to get started at forty-three than not at all."

He smiled and took a step away from the buggy. "Lena, I'm going with Ada. I'll be back in about three hours."

"Supper will be ready in twenty minutes." Lena stood. "Do you and Ada want to eat with us first?"

Ada fidgeted with the reins. "The Realtor is meeting me there in about ninety minutes."

He looked back toward his house. "We need to go on, Lena."

"Can I fix you some sandwiches to take with you?"

He looked up at Ada. "Are you the least bit hungry?"

Although she'd spent her day baking, she'd eaten almost nothing. As she began to make her own decisions, she already felt stronger. "Ya, I think I am."

"Good. Wait right here." Ada stayed in the buggy while Israel went inside. It wasn't but a few minutes before he came back out with a basket in one hand and a toolbox in the other. As he set the items inside the wagon and climbed in, she noticed he'd changed from his more casual clothes into pressed ones.

Tempted to pass him the reins, she clutched them tighter. She needed to steer her own buggy, even if she made mistakes and didn't handle it as smoothly as the person next to her would. Then again, maybe she'd handle it better. When she thought of all Cara had gone through—fighting to hold on to Lori and not caring if people misjudged her and yet seemingly remaining tender-hearted in so many ways—it did something inside Ada.

Israel propped his arm on the back of the bench seat. "So Mahlon's up for moving to Hope Crossing?"

Ada tapped the reins against the horse's back, trying to gain some speed for the upcoming hill. "I didn't ask him. I'm doing this on my own. And even though I'm not sure what *this* is, I want Cara Moore, Malinda Riehl's daughter, to be a part of it. When I have a set plan, I'll talk to the bishop again about allowing Cara to live with me."

As he asked a few questions about Cara and she answered, he pulled a couple of sandwiches out of the basket and passed one to her. The conversation flowed easily although Israel acted a bit nervous. He'd never seemed that way before. Maybe she should have let him guide the rig.

Once they were in Hope Crossing, Israel read the directions to her until they stopped in front of the saddest-looking house she'd ever seen. It sat on a large corner lot, with roads and sidewalks on two sides and a cornfield on another side. She couldn't see what was behind the home. It was huge; she'd give it that much. Two stories of unpainted clapboard with crooked black shutters and one half-fallen column holding up a wraparound porch.

"You say that girl paints?"

Ada nodded. "With a brush and roller, not a magic wand." They stepped out of the rig. Israel grabbed his toolbox, and they headed for the front porch. It only took her a moment to find the hidden key the Realtor had told her about. "The windows and doors have been redone recently, don't you think?"

Israel nodded. "Ya, I do."

When she pushed the door open, she saw newspapers and boxes scattered everywhere. A ladder stood near a half-painted wall. "Somebody began renovating the place."

"Ya. And left it worse off for it, I think."

They slowly climbed the wooden stairs, which had a swatch of old carpet running down the center. At the top of the landing, they found four bedrooms and two baths—all with the most hideous wallpaper she'd ever seen.

Ada ran her fingers along a broken strip of wainscot. "Look, somebody tried painting over the wallpaper."

"I can't say as I blame them."

Ada laughed. "The Realtor said it was bad, but I hadn't expected this."

Israel got out a flashlight and some odd-looking tools before he stepped inside one of the bathrooms. "The tub is filled with junk." He went to the faucet. "And there's no running water."

After he'd poked around under the sink of each bathroom, he grabbed his toolbox, and they walked downstairs. When she opened the swinging wooden door to the kitchen, chills ran over her skin. "I…I had a dream about this kitchen years ago." She looked inside the sink and saw the pipes were missing.

"You sure it wasn't a nightmare?"

Ada opened a door to discover a huge walk-in pantry. "That's bigger than my whole kitchen."

"Ada." He pointed to the glass on the back door.

She walked over to him and stared at what appeared to be a trash pit. "The barn at the far end of the yard and the pasture behind it come with the house."

"I'd bet this place belonged to an Amish family at one point."

"That's what the Realtor said. But that was a long time ago." She moved to the center of the kitchen, feeling hope run through her in spite of the reality surrounding her.

Israel opened the back door. "I want to take a look under the house. I'll be back in a few."

As she ambled through the house, a sense of expectancy grew, defying all logical reasoning. Israel came back inside. "It's in bad shape as far as how it looks, but it's structurally sound.

"I want to do this."

"It's a lot to take on. You'll need plumbers first. I got an Englischer neighbor who does plumbing."

"The Realtor said the owners will pay to get the plumbing working. And she said they are willing to subtract from the rent all the cost of supplies and most of the cost of work done. All we have to do is submit the receipts and let them verify every so often that the work is being done. And we have the opportunity to buy the house at a set cost, regardless of the amount of fix-ups we do."

He set the toolbox on the deeply scratched wooden floor. "Whether you know it or not, I've seen you make success out of more difficult situations than this, Ada Stoltzfus."

"Me?" She watched to see if he was trying to be funny, but he looked serious. "You really think so?"

"I know so. You work in a closet of a kitchen with an apartment-sized stove and sink, and yet you've supplied desserts to that Shippensburg bakery for a decade. Just imagine what you could do with a kitchen this big and a full-size stove and double sink."

"Hello? Ada, are you in here?" the Realtor sang out.

"In the kitchen." She stepped closer to Israel. "You can't believe how much I want to do this for both me and Cara. But even if I sign a contract, I can't begin to make the kind of difference I want to for her without getting her uncles to see her another way."

"And since she's the reason Ephraim is shunned, I'm sure she can't move in with you without the bishop's approval. We'd better get you home so you're not late for tonight's meeting."

"I'd like to put a deposit down first."

He looked fully entertained by her as he gave a nod. "Then do it."

Inside Levi Riehl's home, Ada's palms sweated as she set up another folding chair. The warmth of the early-June air had nothing to do with the perspiration trickling down her back or the palpitations of her heart. Through the open windows and doors, she could hear carriages as they arrived and people chatting with one another.

A quick glance out the window let her know that most people were leaving their horses hitched to their buggies, which meant no one expected to be here long. When she'd arrived, her horse had seemed as worn out as she was, so she'd put him in the Riehl pasture.

She'd stopped by her house on the way here, thinking she might catch Mahlon and tell him of her plans, but he wasn't there. Despite feeling antsy and exhausted, she kept praying. She needed tonight to end with Cara's uncles—Levi, David, and Leroy Riehl—seeing the situation as she did. Levi seemed uneasy as he moved to the far side of the room and set up the last chair. He glanced at her several times as if he wanted to ask her something, but instead he just straightened the rows of chairs.

The bishop intended to separate rumors from truth tonight, and then he'd make a decision. But he told her that whatever he decided, it had to settle the issue. No more appeals. No more trying to change his mind. Ada agreed. And now she was miserably nervous.

Levi strolled over to her, looking as uncomfortable as he might with a stranger. "How's Cara?"

"I gave her the box you and Emma brought by. Mostly she's shaken, angry, and hurt."

He nodded. "Emma is pretty shaken too. Having to face Cara was heartbreaking for her."

"I think—"

"Mamm," Mahlon interrupted, hurrying toward her through the growing crowd. "What are you doing?" he whispered.

"What do you mean?"

He held up the papers she'd signed on the house in Hope Crossing. "I found these on the kitchen table."

"Can we talk about this later?"

"Are you picking out a house for us?" His tone was stern, but his words were barely audible.

"No, of course not. You know I wouldn't do that."

She saw in his eyes some undefined emotion that looked a bit like… hope.

"Then what are you doing?"

"You and Deborah should go on with your own plans. That's what I need to do. I'm going to move to a place where I can sell baked goods to local restaurants and maybe to another bakery or two."

While Mahlon stared at her, David and Leroy, two more of Cara's uncles, strolled through the door, chatting with Rueben Lantz. She'd hoped Rueben, Malinda's former fiancé, wouldn't be here for this. It'd be so much harder for her to say what she needed to with him in the room. She wasn't interested in stirring up conflict, but if that's what had to happen…she prayed for courage.

"Why would you do this without talking to me?"

"I intended to tell you, but things are happening fast. Look, all it means is that you and Deborah make plans that don't include me living with you. Do you really mind?"

Mahlon studied her, looking unsure and pleased and terrified all at once. She'd seen these emotions in her only child many times over the years but never mingled into one confusing array.

"I guess I didn't realize you had that much independence in you…not to be disrespectful or anything. You really think you can make a go of this?"

"I do. It's what I wanted years ago, but you wanted to stay in Dry Lake. You're a man now, about to take on a wife, and I'd like to do this with your blessing."

He smiled. "My blessing?"

She nodded.

He looked past her, and she turned to see Deborah standing across the room. "I only wish you'd told me how important this was to you years ago, Mamm. If you'd done it then, things could be different."

"What things?"

He lowered his eyes, staring at the floor. "It doesn't matter."

But she had a feeling it mattered a lot. "Mahlon?"

Looking to Deborah again, he shook his head. "How can I be so in love and at the same time so restless for what might be or could have been?"

"Ada." David spoke from several feet away, interrupting her and Mahlon. "You came without your famous coconut pie." He shook the bishop's hand while he teased her.

His broad grin and easy ways didn't indicate the temper that tried to get the best of him at times. Leroy stood near him and gave Ada a nod. He was the quietest of the Riehls and probably the one who'd grieved the most when Malinda took off.

"What I've come for is a bit more serious than that."

A few nearby conversations stopped.

"Is this about Cara?" David asked.

Ada nodded, and Mahlon touched her arm, letting her know he was going to where Deborah stood.

Three of the men's wives—Anne, Susie, and Rueben's wife, Leah— entered, talking comfortably and keeping Ada from needing to say anything else right now. She moved to a chair and reached into the hidden pocket of her apron, assuring herself that the documents were still there. She wanted to get them back to Cara tonight.

Mahlon's eyes focused on her, as if he was trying to figure something out.

His reaction to her news confused her. Then again, his responses to daily events were often difficult to understand, and she hoped Deborah was better at figuring him out than she'd ever been.

As more people entered, Levi clapped his hands once. "Okay, whoever would like a drink of water or lemonade, help yourself and take a seat. It'll make it easier for those coming in behind you."

The volume of friendly banter decreased as people made their way to a chair. Most perceived Cara as a troublemaker who needed to be avoided. Rumors about her unacceptable behavior were fresh in their thoughts. Few knew why Ephraim had shared his home with Cara. They didn't know much about her, except that she was Malinda's daughter and was a homeless thief with a daughter and no husband. Oh, and that she caused Ephraim to be shunned. But none of that really told them who Cara was. If Ada could convince them to give her a chance, maybe healing could begin for all of them. The Howards would probably put in a good word for Cara, but Englischers were never a part of Amish meetings—not this kind.

Emma hurried inside, wiping her wet hands against her apron. "Levi, those grandbabes of ours had the hose out, watering each other to see if they could make themselves grow." She wiped her brow. "I passed them to their mothers."

Everyone chuckled as Emma took a seat.

Ada said a silent prayer that the Riehls would set aside every obstacle that separated them from Cara.

The bishop moved to the front of the room. "Rueben and I found Cara a place in Carlisle. Thanks to the donations of everyone here, we paid the rent for three months. Cara chose to turn it down."

Murmurs floated throughout the room.

"What happens to the money?" one man asked.

"We made sure beforehand that we could get the money back, so no problem there. More important is why Cara turned it down. Ada said that Cara feels we were trying to pay her to leave. At first that sounded ridiculous, but after thinking about it, I realized there's some truth in that. It's possible we've reacted to Cara out of misunderstandings and unfair judgment. And a lot of that is because of rumors and who her mother was."

Levi stood. "Ephraim's had the most contact with her. Maybe he should be here."

The bishop took a seat. "What he did crossed the line, and he'll remain under the ban. Ada, will you tell everyone a little about Cara and what brought her to Dry Lake?"

Ada stood. Her voice shook as she explained how Cara grew up, why she came to their town, and her plans to leave. "She has no family outside of Dry Lake. Do we not bear some of the responsibility for what's happened to her? With only a few scattered memories from her childhood, she found her way back here. Will we let her slip through our hands a second time?"

The bishop stood. "In order to separate rumor from fact, I'd like to hear from those of you who've talked to Cara or seen her do anything firsthand. That means we set aside what you heard Abner say he saw."

Various people took turns sharing information about Cara. They told of her using drugs, smoking with Amish teens, and letting cows and horses out of pastures. The bishop took the time to look for an eyewitness for each rumor, and everyone soon discovered that no one had actually seen Cara doing any of those things.

When Anna Mary entered the room and took a seat at the back, Ada feared the damage she could do.

"Deborah had a dress go missing," one young man said. "I know 'cause she asked if I took it."

"I sure did," Deborah said. "If you'd taken it, I wanted to see you wear it."

Ada chuckled along with everyone else. If anyone knew how to bring humor and peace into a room, her future daughter-in-law did.

Deborah folded her arms. "Whoever took it left money for it the next night."

Ada figured Deborah knew at this point that Cara had taken her dress, but true to her nature, she wasn't going to make matters worse by adding that kind of information to the meeting.

Levi explained the conversation he'd had with Cara the night before. Then he added, "She didn't seem at all like the rumors have said. I'd like to help her, but I won't go against the bishop's wishes."

A man stood. "We offered her help, and she turned us down."

When he sat, a woman spoke up. "I wasn't living in Dry Lake when her mother was here, but I saw Cara at the auction. I don't like the way she dresses, and it's easy to believe the rumors about her. We can't afford to welcome someone like her."

Trying not to look as angry as she felt, Ada measured her words and tone carefully. "Have you once looked her in the eye and talked with her? I have. She's not to be feared. We might even learn a few things from her."

"Ephraim looked in her eyes," a man from the back of the room said, "and now he's shunned."

The group started murmuring, and Ada knew she was losing.

"I've wondered if maybe it was God's will that she didn't make it here as a child," David Riehl said over the crowd.

"David." Emma gasped. "She's your niece, and the mix-up that left her alone wasn't her fault. It was mine and Levi's and even yours. All of us talked about what to do, and we made careless mistakes and didn't try to find out what was going on."

"That's because she's Malinda's daughter," another man said, "and everyone in this room over the age of forty knows what that means."

The room vibrated with disagreements, and Ada feared the night would end without anything being settled. Cara would leave Dry Lake, and it'd be over.

Anna Mary stood, and silence soon fell. "I have more reasons to distrust her than any of you. And she's caused me to ask myself a thousand questions. But I have only one question for all of you." She cleared her throat. "Will Ephraim be the only man to stand up for her?"

Ada watched people's faces, witnessing many attitudes begin to change. Rueben's face went ashen as he watched his daughter.

Shaking and teary-eyed, Anna Mary took a seat.

Ada gave a nod. "Thank you, Anna Mary. Last night Levi and Emma brought a box for Cara. It was one her father mailed to her here for her eighteenth birthday."

Rueben started coughing as if he'd choked. "But…I…I thought you'd tossed it without looking at what was inside."

"We didn't open it, but we saw no reason to throw it out," Levi said. "Ada, what was in it?"

"Letters, journals, Malinda's Bible, and documents—her marriage license, Cara's birth certifi—"

"Wait." Rueben stood, interrupting her. He fidgeted with the hat in his hand. Leah, his wife, tugged on his arm, gesturing for him to sit down. He shook his head. "Before this goes on, I need to speak with Malinda's family and the bishop…alone."

The bishop cleared his throat. "I think Rueben's right. We've cleared up all we can as a large group. Thank you for coming. May we all be reminded that rumors cause trouble and are usually based on lies. Along with Malinda's brothers and their wives, I'd like Rueben, Leah, and Ada to stay, please."

Within minutes everyone had left the room except the folks the bishop had named.

The bishop took a seat at the kitchen table. The rest of them followed suit.

He drew a deep breath and bowed his head in silent prayer. He opened his eyes. "Before I begin, is there something you wanted to say, Rueben?"

He stared at the table. Children's voices from outside filled the room, but not one adult uttered a word.

Rueben wiped his brow several times and finally spoke. "Malinda's leaving didn't go exactly as the rumors have it."

"Just how did it go?" Levi's voice had an edge to it.

Rueben struggled to speak. "Your sister didn't break up with me. And she wasn't pregnant when she left here."

Levi jumped up. "What? You told us she'd been seeing Trevor while the two of you were engaged and that she ran off with him after breaking up with you."

Breathing deep, Rueben stared at the floor. "I never actually said that. You just believed it."

Emma looked at Rueben's wife. "Did you know this?"

The stricken look on Leah's face said that she did, although all she managed was a shrug and half nod.

David glared at Rueben. "You make this make sense—now." He shoved his index finger against the kitchen table with each word.

"Well…I was working about an hour from here. That's where I met Leah. I'd been there most of that summer. When I didn't return home for a few weekends, Malinda hired Trevor to bring her to me. She…saw me kissing Leah. We argued, and she left with Trevor. She begged me not to say anything."

"How convenient for you." David smacked the table.

"It sounds like she wanted to leave with some shred of pride intact," Leroy said.

Emma scrunched a fistful of her apron and then released it, over and over again. "She was nineteen with a thousand broken dreams. She always felt abandoned by her Daed because he gave her to Levina to raise. She must have been devastated to be rejected by another man."

David shrugged. "I still say that Daed did his best when Mamm died giving birth to her. He couldn't take care of a newborn and the rest of us while holding a job."

The pain in Levi's eyes went deep as he put his head in his hands. "We shouldn't have left her in our Grossmammi Levina's care all those years. But our house never seemed like a good place for a girl to grow up—all boys and no mother?"

"Malinda made her own choices," David said.

Several started talking loudly at the same time.

The bishop raised his hands, silencing everyone. "Let's not forget that Malinda joined the faith, and then she ran off. She broke her vows, regardless of the reason. Still, it sounds as if shock and hurt were the reasons for her decisions, not rebellion."

Levi stood and began pacing. "For nearly thirty years we've believed she lost faith, that she ran around like a tramp. I questioned you, Rueben, because I'd never seen any signs of her being wild, even during her rumschpringe. And you led me to believe we simply never knew her."

"You decided that on your own. You told me she called not long after leaving and said that she was too ashamed to come home but that Trevor wanted to marry her. According to you, the next and last time you heard from her, she'd written to say she had a little girl."

Levi pointed at him. "By words or silence, sounds to me like you've been lying to us for years."

"I wasn't trying to lie."

"You weren't trying to tell the truth either," Leroy said.

Rueben gestured with his hands. "Look, I met Leah that summer, and we…we fell for each other. We were going to tell her, but she found out first. Those of you who knew Malinda know how high-strung she was."

"High-strung?" one of her aunts rang out. "I remember Malinda getting permission for one of her Daed's hired helpers to drive her to Ohio to see you. The wedding was only three weeks away. Trevor was the driver, and he brought her to you, didn't he?"

Rueben nodded.

Emma sobbed. "She never returned home after that trip. We assumed she'd planned to run off with Trevor and used visiting you as the excuse to get away. And you helped us believe that. You know you did."

"You were mean not to tell her how you felt *before* you kissed someone else." Leroy shot an accusing look at Rueben. "You and Leah didn't get married for a year after that. Was that just to make yourself look good? Now that we see who you are, we all know the answer to that. And don't you tell us our sister was high-strung after nearly three decades of letting us think she left here pregnant."

"She didn't have to leave the way she did," Rueben said. "And she didn't have to stay gone or marry Trevor. Even when she came back years later, looking for a safe place for Cara, I tried to get her to tell everyone what happened. I wanted to clear it up."

"You talked to her by yourself when she came back to Dry Lake with Cara? Without me or anyone?" Leah's tone said it all. She didn't trust her husband's heart when it came to Malinda. Ada wondered if Rueben had really been in love with Leah, or if once Malinda discovered him and Leah kissing and left, he felt compelled to marry her. Maybe waiting the year to get married had been more of a grieving time for Rueben than anything else.

Rueben didn't answer his wife, but Ada figured he would…for a long time to come.

"When Malinda returned with Cara, she didn't want it set straight. She said it wouldn't change that her father and brothers didn't want her returning to Dry Lake and that anything I said would only cause trouble for me and Leah."

Levi turned to his wife. "She thought we didn't want her even if we knew the truth?"

David slammed his hand down on the table. "We can't believe what Rueben is saying about Malinda not wanting to set things straight. He talked to her privately, and we'll never know what was or wasn't said, will we?"

Leah stood and folded her arms, her face taut with embarrassment and guilt. "When she came to Dry Lake with Cara, you had just as much opportunity to go talk to her as Rueben did. But you chose not to. All of you. So don't lay this mess fully on him."

Ada pulled the documents from the hidden pocket of her dress. "Finding all the right people to blame will not solve even one of the problems facing Cara." She unfolded the papers. "Trevor and Malinda married several months after they left here. Cara was born fifteen months later. If it's true that Malinda always felt rejected and you wish you could change that, I'm asking you to start with her grown daughter. And don't hold what Ephraim's done against him."

The bishop looked over the documents again, as if verifying what he'd read earlier. "The ban will not be lifted from Ephraim. We cannot ignore a single man allowing a woman to stay in his home overnight. But we need to do what we can to set things right with Cara, try to heal some of the hurt we've caused."

Ada interlaced her fingers. "I don't think trying to speak to her face to face is the answer right now. She's not one to trust people's motives. She'll want to know why you're coming to see her now and not a few days ago. When she figures out that we've met to decide what to do and she was the topic of a district meeting, we'll never get past her defenses."

"Sounds like she's as stubborn as her mother," Leroy said.

The brothers chuckled, breaking some of the tension in the room.

"Ada, you know her better than anyone here," Emma said. "If she won't trust us and doesn't want to speak with us, how do we break through that?"

"Letters, for now. But more than anything, I'd like permission for her to move in with me. I've found a place in Hope Crossing."

Questions came from several of them all at once.

The bishop held up his hand. "You have my approval, Ada."

Thirty-Five

The sounds of night—mostly crickets and tree frogs—echoed hour after hour. The kerosene lamp sputtered beside the bed, and Cara's eyes grew heavy as she read the letters her mother had written to her father. Other correspondence was stacked on the nightstands—ones from her mother to her, from her dad to Cara, from her dad to her mom. She studied them again and again, trying to piece together the missing parts of her life. Through the open window, a summer breeze carried a sweet scent of flowers. Silvery moonbeams lay across the bedspread.

The differences between here and the Bronx were vast, and she could understand why her visit as a child had been chiseled into the recesses of her memory. Compared to the continual sirens, loud neighbors, and locked windows of her place in New York City, this was a vacation spot—except, just like New York, the people had issues. Not the same ones she'd been used to seeing, but problems nonetheless. She had them too. Clearly both her mom and dad did as well. But she'd expected more from a people who avoided worldly goods.

She skimmed a letter she'd read several times before. It seemed her mother had married her father without knowing he was an alcoholic. A lot of the letters were from her mother to her dad while he was in rehab. But her father's problems weren't the only ones her mother carried. She wrote about a horrible pain from childhood, but Cara hadn't yet discovered what it was. Trevor's father had been bad news, and Trevor came by his addiction honestly. Her parents were two hurting people who united in hopes of easing their pain. In some ways their relationship seemed to work…part of the time.

But reading these notes, letters, and journal entries was like catching the tail end of a conversation—confusing—and she wished she understood more. But right now she was tired of trying to sort out her parents' past.

Ready to get out of Dry Lake, she tried to temper her restlessness. It'd been three days since she'd agreed to move to Ada's house in Hope Crossing. Between Ada needing to square the rental agreement with the owners and Ephraim's dad's surgery, Cara was still stuck here. Ephraim hadn't been around much since Sunday, and Lori constantly asked for him.

A slow cooing sound eased across the night air. Whatever bird made that noise, it was her favorite sound—soft and gentle as nightfall in the country. She placed the letters inside the box and slid into her jeans. From the foot of the bed, Better Days jumped up, wagging his tail. She picked him up and headed outside. It seemed the puppy would be fairly easy to housebreak, which would be important to Ephraim since the dog wouldn't be under Lori's watchful eye once they moved. After setting the dog on the grass, she studied the landscape.

The quiet beauty of Dry Lake contradicted her inner turmoil. She wondered if all Amish communities were this closed or if it simply seemed closed to her because of who her mother had been and who they thought Cara was. A whisper carrying her name floated through the night air, and she turned to see Ephraim in the entry of his hedged sanctuary.

She walked toward him. "How's your dad?"

"Doing well. He'll be released tomorrow. Actually, that'll be today. What are you doing up?"

"I've been reading letters my mom wrote to my dad when he was in rehab." She looked across the fields and to the pond. "I want out of here so badly, and yet there is something about this place. I can see why my mother missed it so much. Where did she live as a kid?"

"With Levina, but the rest of the family lived in the house next to

Levi and Emma Riehl. Leroy Riehl and his wife live there now. Your grandmother died giving birth to your mother, and Levina, her grandmother, raised your mom. Fifty years ago we didn't have a midwife in or near Dry Lake, and hospitals were a long way away. I heard your grandfather talking to some other men one time. He said your grandmother was a tiny woman and had a lot of difficulty with each birth, and she didn't survive the night Malinda was born. Levina's children were all grown, and she welcomed Malinda into her home. I've always heard there was bad blood between your mom and her dad—as if she resented him for giving her to someone else and never asking her to come home after she was no longer a baby. She didn't move into her father's home until Levina had some health issues and couldn't take care of her. By that time your mother was sixteen or seventeen years old."

"And my mom's dad?"

"Your granddad died in the same car accident as my mother, and Mahlon's dad, and Becca's husband, and several others from the community. Three vanloads of Amish had hired drivers to take them to a wedding in Ohio. The driver of their van was going too fast and not paying attention to the road, and they slammed into a concrete highway divider."

"Ephraim, I'm sorry."

He stared at the night sky. "It was a huge loss, and I think it's part of the reason the community is so defensive about outsiders. None of the adults in the community trusted the driver of the van that crashed, but everyone ignored their gut feeling and paid a really high price. Now they're overly cautious about anything to do with outsiders."

She could understand some of that. Breaking trust only took a moment, and regaining it could take a lifetime or more. "Maybe my mom felt abandoned by her dad and that had a lot to do with why she took up with an Englischer and left."

"Maybe."

Cara moved to the bench swing. "It all seems like such a lie."

"All what?"

"How picturesque life can look. You get this quick view of something, and it looks appealing and wonderful—like the quaint appearance of being Amish. But it's all a lie."

He took a seat beside her. "Sunday evening you and Lori were near the huge trees by the pond as the sun was setting, and if someone had taken a snapshot of that, it'd warm the heart of every person who saw it. But the struggle for food, shelter, and safety is huge. That fight doesn't discount the truth seen in that flash of time. Love is real, and it's worth the battle. That's not a lie, Cara."

"Maybe you're right." She rubbed the back of her neck. "I'm so tired of thinking about all of it."

He reached into his pants pocket and pulled something out. Dangling a key in front of her, he smiled. "Maybe this will help. Paint and tools have been delivered. One bathroom is now in working order. The kitchen sink will be fixed tomorrow. A gas stove and refrigerator will be delivered early next week at the latest."

She placed her palm under the key, and he dropped it. Clutching the key in her fist, she relaxed against the back of the swing. "You were right, you know."

"Well, as my *Daadi* used to say—"

"Your who?"

"My grandfather."

"Okay."

"He used to say that even a blind squirrel finds a nut every once in a while."

She laughed. "You're weird, Ephraim. Who cracks jokes before sunup?"

He suppressed a smile, making slight lines around the edges of his mouth. "You were saying I was right about something?"

"I needed this transition, a place to live while coping with all I've learned. But what does my leaving mean for you?"

"That I get my bed back."

She elbowed him. "How long before you're not shunned anymore?"

"The bishop hasn't put a set time on it."

"But I'll be gone."

"It's a discipline for past actions, similar to grounding a teen or taking away certain privileges. Only unlike getting in trouble with your parents, none of your friends thinks it's cool."

"You know what I think?"

"Do I want to know?"

She huffed and pointed at him. "I think if God were real, he'd make that bishop apologize."

Ephraim started laughing and seemed unable to stop.

"What?"

"You're only going to believe He's real if He makes the bishop own up to something he's not really wrong in?"

"Not wrong? We didn't do anything close to going against that Bible of yours." As soon as she said it, she lost her confidence. "Did we?"

"Well, ya, sort of. Godliness asks us to abstain from the appearance of evil, and you staying in my home overnight…well, you know. There's nothing wrong in being held accountable, Cara."

"It's ridiculous. With all the bad in the world, you're shunned because you did something that *appeared* wrong? Where's the proof of your God's love in that?"

"You love your daughter, but you can't hold something in your hand as proof of that. Love is action on her behalf all the time. God's love is action on our behalf all the time. But we're in the middle of a battle. Part of life is 'fighting the good fight' to keep the faith. If there were no evil coming against us, we wouldn't have to fight to keep the faith, right?"

A feeling of being offended jabbed needles at her, yet chills and confusion washed over her. "I like you. And I think you like me. So let's do our friendship a favor and not discuss this God issue again, okay?"

He stood. "Do you believe in nature?"

"Well, of course."

"Then come look at its glory through the telescope."

When she shook her head, he held out his hand. "I'm not going to chance messing up our friendship by trying to convince you about God. That's His job. I only want to show you some spectacular things in the sky."

Cara placed her hand in his. They walked the few steps to his telescope.

She looked through the lens. "I don't see anything but my own eyelashes."

Ephraim made a few adjustments. "Here, try again. But don't blink right before you place your eye against the eyeglass frame."

Cara tried again. He stood right behind her, showing her how to adjust the finder scope and focuser. She wondered how many times he'd done this with Anna Mary. Had she felt like Cara did at this moment?

"Cara?"

She blinked. "Sorry. What'd you say?"

"Place your eye near the rim, and then adjust this until you can see."

"Okay."

She could barely think with him so close—the softness of his tone as he spoke, the warmth radiating from his skin, the gentleness in every move. But then she saw a view so breathtaking she couldn't believe her eyes. A strip of stars hung in the sky on a backdrop of gold and silver dust. She'd always heard there were way more stars in the sky than were visible to the naked eye. Suddenly every problem she'd ever faced took on a different perspective—as if it were a fleck inside earth's time line.

Thirty-Six

Deborah studied Mahlon as he guided the horse and buggy toward Hope Crossing. It'd take them the better part of an hour to get there, so he'd slipped away from the shop before closing, hoping they could ride there and back before dark. They both wanted to see the place Ada would move into this Saturday.

The only noise was that of the horse's hoofbeats and the creaking of the buggy. Deborah felt that Mahlon had grown quieter with each day that had passed since Ephraim's shunning, and he seemed to be sharing less and less with her. He hadn't even noticed when she came out of her house with something behind her back or when she tucked a package under the seat of the carriage. Maybe he just needed to find something to laugh about. She certainly did, especially after going by Anna Mary's last night and finding out she and Ephraim had broken up.

A night out together before the weekend arrived would probably do both her and Mahlon some good. It had to be upsetting him that his mother had made a decision about a house without his approval. Now that her father was home from the hospital, the hardest thing for her to accept was that Ephraim and Anna Mary were no longer seeing each other. The shunning would end in time, but Ephraim had never changed his mind once he stopped seeing a girl. She held on to the hope that he would this time.

Ada had told her a little about what took place at the meeting last Monday after the bishop dismissed most of them. She wouldn't say too much about that, but she told Deborah all about the house in Hope Crossing and that Cara was moving in with her. Knowing all the odds Cara had beaten to find Dry Lake, Deborah couldn't wish she hadn't come, but she was glad that in two days she'd be moving away from her brother.

Drawing a deep breath, she tried to relax. She touched Mahlon's cheek, hoping to pull him from his thoughts too. "Where are you?"

"Thinking about all the changes happening in Dry Lake. It's like everyone's suddenly chosen to follow their own heart."

"Everyone's trying to do what's best. Even your mother."

"Maybe."

"So what's bothering you the most?"

"I stayed because I didn't feel she could make it on her own. And now…"

"Stayed?"

He said nothing.

"As in stayed in her house or stayed Amish?"

He shook his head and sighed. "Stayed with her."

"It didn't hurt anything for you to live at home these extra few years, did it?"

"No." He shrugged. "Do you ever wonder if after all this Ephraim will stay Amish?"

"Too often and too much. I think that's the main reason I'm not more upset that your mother has decided to move to Hope Crossing. She's getting Cara out of his place and out of his sight. I'm really sorry Ada's moving so far away from our community, but maybe he and Anna Mary can work things out once Cara's gone."

"I had no idea Mamm had that kind of independence in her. I only wish I'd known it years ago." He lightly slapped the reins against the horse's back.

"Well, you're free now. And you can find a place just for us. I'm so excited, but I'm nervous about all of it. Can you find us a place in ten days?"

"Just trust me. I'll handle it." Mahlon looked at the directions in his hand and brought the buggy to a stop in front of an old house.

"This is it?" Deborah asked.

He looked at the address on the paper in his hand and then to the mailbox. "Ya."

They sat in silence, staring at the place. It looked like a haunted mansion. The absolute worst home in Hope Crossing. Mahlon pulled around back and into the driveway.

Deborah scanned the surrounding area. The place sat on a corner lot, with a cornfield to one side of it and houses nearby but not too close. "It has a nice little barn, pasture for her horse, and a huge backyard."

"Ya, and a backyard so full of junk and fallen limbs she can't use it for anything."

"That can be changed with a bit of work."

They both got out, and Deborah held his hand as they followed the sidewalk around the side of the home, up the front walk, and onto the wraparound porch.

The gray paint on the six-foot-wide porch needed stripping and redoing. The white clapboard sides held so little paint it wouldn't require much cleaning, just fresh coats.

"No wonder your mother could afford this place."

"She says she gets money taken off the rent for every bit of work done to the place."

"I guess with Cara here to paint, your mother will be living free of charge for a while."

"One would think."

Deborah slid the key into the lock and turned it. "I love the door. The old-fashioned mail slot, beveled glass, and tarnished brass knobs. They're perfect."

"Perfect for what?"

"For fulfilling your mother's dreams. The old place looks full of potential."

·They crossed the black-lacquer floors. Wallpaper peeled from the ceiling, musty boxes of junk sat everywhere, and newspapers were strewn all about. They walked into the kitchen.

Deborah studied the room. "It's certainly big enough for her to do her baking."

Mahlon looked down the sink. "This place is just a hull; even the pipes are missing."

"Ada said the plumber will return tomorrow, and the owners are covering the cost of that."

They walked through the rest of the house.

Mahlon shook his head. "I can't believe she wants this. It needs so much work."

"Don't all dreams need lots of work?"

He gave a half shrug. "Most dreams need to be ignored."

An uneasy feeling came over her. "Ignored?"

"Forget it." He motioned toward the front door. "I've seen enough. You ready to go?"

"I love this place, Mahlon. Can't you see that it's something she's always longed for? You wanted to stay in Dry Lake while growing up, and she did so. But now she's ready to try some things on her own."

"Great. She's making her dreams come true while I'm stuck doing Ephraim's job."

"Mahlon." Deborah stopped. "Are you angry with your mother over this?"

He shook his head. "I'm just tired of it all. Aren't you?"

"Tired of what?"

He closed the front door behind her. "I wanted to take one week to get away, and Ephraim needs me, and Mamm goes out and gets a run-down place, and...I..."

"You what?"

After locking the door, he shoved the key into his pocket. "Never mind."

"Never mind? It's like you're trying to tell me something without having to actually say it." As they walked down the porch steps, Deborah tugged on his hands. "I don't want to get into an argument just because you're in a foul mood, but if you keep dropping hints and saying they don't mean—"

"Okay," he interrupted and then slid his arms around her. "You're right." He kissed her forehead. "I just need a few days away, but I shouldn't take that out on you." He kissed her again. "Sorry, Deb."

She climbed into the buggy, hoping her present would help him feel better. She pulled it out from under the seat. "I special-ordered a gift for you from the dry goods store. It came in today."

He smiled. "And how did you manage to hide it from me?"

"You're not with me all the time. I've barely seen you the last few weeks."

He lifted it from her hands. "You shouldn't have done this."

"You're going to provide me a home soon. I think I can buy you one thing to go in it."

He tore the paper, saying nothing as the clock came into view. It was the most gorgeous clock she'd ever seen and exactly like the one he'd pointed out to her a year ago, saying he hoped to own one like it someday.

"It plays music on the hour."

"It's beautiful, Deb," he whispered as he removed the cardboard from around it.

"Flip that button, and we can hear every tune. There are twelve of them."

He notched the button to On. The tinny music seemed to grab him, and he didn't move. "That tune…"

"I don't know it, do you?"

He nodded. "It's everywhere I go lately. Every store. Every client's home. In my sleep."

"What do the words to the song say?"

"It's based on a scripture: to everything, there is a season. Only the song says 'turn, turn, turn' a lot."

"It's a good tune, ya?"

He shrugged. "Except sometimes it feels like God is trying to tell me something. How do we get it to play another tune?"

"Press that little gadget."

He did. The same tune started over again.

"That's odd." She pushed the button again. "The clock was working when I wrapped it."

The same tune played every time she pressed the button. Chills ran up Deborah's arms and down her back.

Mahlon passed her the clock. "Let's just turn it off for now, okay?"

"Sure." She flipped the knob to Off, but the music didn't stop.

He retried the same switch, but the song played faster. "Try removing the batteries."

She turned the clock over, removed the plate for the batteries, and paused. "What happens if it keeps playing?" Forcing a smile, she couldn't ignore that her heart was thumping wildly. When she removed a battery, the music stopped.

"We just won't turn the musical part on, okay?"

"But that is the special part. We can pick songs to mean certain things over the years, and then no matter where we are in the house, when we hear it, we'll remember our love."

Mahlon's hands trembled as he removed his hat. "Wherever I go, whatever I do in life, I'll never forget your love. Ever."

The oddest sensation ran through her.

He took her hand into his and kissed her fingers. "I love you more than you'll ever know." He stared into her eyes as if trying to tell her things he couldn't find the words for. "Let's go on home. I have work tomorrow, and you need rest so you can help Mamm pack."

Feeling more anxious than ever, she jolted when Mahlon put his arm around her.

"I think I'll take a few days off. Will you be okay if I do that?"

"But the shop needs you. It'll get even further behind. And you've got to find a place and get moved."

He rubbed her back. "I have relatives in Dry Lake I can live with for a week or two."

"You always hated that idea before."

"Things have changed. And the shop's going to be behind no matter what I do. I can't go from being the provider for Mamm to doing so for your Daed and all his children. That responsibility shouldn't have been laid in my lap."

"But that's how things work with family. You know that. What about your mother? Have you told her?"

"No. I'll write to her and explain. She'll be so busy settling into that place, having work done, and building this dream business of hers, she won't even think twice about it."

"Where will you go?"

He shrugged. "Somewhere quiet where no one knows who I am." He pulled her closer and kissed her head. "Your Daed is mending, and you'll be busy helping Mamm and Becca. You won't even have time to miss me."

"Well, I've been missing you for a while now. And I'd love to see you return with…you. Okay?"

"You are the most amazing girl any guy could have."

"Now see, that's the man I agreed to marry. So when will you leave?"

"Saturday."

"When will you be back?"

"Wednesday, probably. That next weekend we'll finish packing up my belongings that are still at the house."

"Okay. But someday, when you're ready, let's talk. I want to know what you've been thinking about."

"When I figure it out, you'll be the first to know."

She chuckled. "Fair enough."

Thirty-Seven

Ephraim bowed his head in silence, trying to block out thoughts of Cara during the meal prayer.

When he opened his eyes, Lori smiled at him. "I got done praying first."

Ephraim chuckled. "I don't think that's the point."

At a table several feet away, Ada took a piece of fresh-baked bread and passed the basket to Cara. She rose from her table, walked over to his, and set the container near him.

Ephraim took a roll. "Denki."

"Gan gern?" Cara asked.

He laughed. "Gern gschehne."

"Yeah, Mom, gern gschehne." Cara made a funny face at her daughter and returned to the other table. Lori giggled.

He studied Ada for a moment. Something weighed on her, something written in that letter he'd seen her read a hundred times. He didn't know who it was from, but she kept it tucked inside her apron, and he'd seen her shed a few tears when she thought no one was looking.

From the moment Ada had left his home after spending the night helping Cara nearly two weeks ago, she hadn't been allowed to talk to him. Between her writing to him and them sharing a conversation with each other through Cara, they talked fairly easily. He understood why the bishop had added unusual restrictions to his shunning, but the hardest part was a normal restriction—not being allowed to sit at a table with her. Cara came up with a plan that made the rules easier to live with. She and Lori took turns sitting at either his or Ada's table during mealtimes.

Ada's place in Hope Crossing was an hour from Dry Lake by horse and buggy, because the rigs couldn't use the highway, but it was only ten to fifteen minutes by car. So Robbie drove him here each morning and picked him up around ten or eleven each night.

In between those hours he and Cara worked to restore the home, then talked and kidded until the exhausting efforts felt like a game. Every morning they sat on the steps of the front porch and drank coffee. Each evening when it was too dark to work by kerosene or gas lamps and Lori was asleep, Ada stayed here, and he and Cara went for a long stroll. It's what he'd longed for when they finished painting the Garretts' place— more time with Cara.

He watched her as she ate, enjoying how quickly she'd begun to heal. The shock and grief of learning about her roots had quieted, but her heart hadn't changed toward her family. Several had written letters to her, but she'd not opened even one of them. She'd accepted their past indifference, not forgiven it.

When she caught him staring at her, she frowned. "You got a problem, mister?"

He had one all right. And he was looking straight at it. Everything about her fascinated him. The way she ate bread by tearing off a small piece at a time. The way she tried to tuck her hair behind her ear now that it was growing a bit, but it was still too short to stay. The way she whispered in early mornings and spoke deep and soft in late evenings. And the thousand other movements she made throughout a day. All of it had captured his thoughts.

When she didn't answer her, she stuck out her tongue and made a face. He didn't allow the smile he felt to show on his face. Even though he wasn't sure what he wanted from life anymore, he kept that confusion to himself. The shunning hadn't convinced him of the things the church leaders had hoped.

Without going to any Amish person's place, he and Lori had found homes for every puppy. After he paid to have the mama dog fixed, they even found a great family for her.

Even though living without modern conveniences seemed silly to Cara, she was clearly interested in trying to understand the whys of their religion. Each day she asked questions about living Amish. And despite her arguing against those ways, she grew to understand their culture a little more. Her insights were remarkable, but it was head knowledge to her. She seemed to accept none of it as a reasonable way of life.

Still, he was convinced she needed to see the good parts of the Amish way of life before she'd find peace and acceptance of her heritage. So he guarded his words and never spoke of his frustration with being shunned. According to the restrictions of the shunning, he probably shouldn't be doing anything that helped Ada build her new business, but it seemed to him he could get away with doing things that helped Cara, who happened to share the same home.

He was four weeks into a shunning that the bishop hadn't set an ending date to. It might last five more months or longer. Ada's dilapidated place seemed like the perfect solution to his problem of having too much time on his hands. It wasn't the painful situation the bishop had intended—not for him or Cara—and Ephraim figured he'd get a visit from the church leaders when they realized it.

"Hey, 'From." Lori took a drink of milk and set the glass on the table. "Does Better Days miss me when you take him home at night?"

"Ya, he does. Just last night he was telling me all about it while I was trying to sleep."

"Can he stay here tonight?"

"Lori—"

"Actually," Ephraim interrupted Cara, hoping to stop her from issuing a firm no, "I've been wanting to talk to your mom about that."

"Really?" Lori's eyes grew big.

"Yeah, 'From, really?" Cara raised an eyebrow. "Before or after you cause trouble for a busy single mom?"

He knew that each day took a lot of strength. Between painting and helping Ada bake, she worked long hours, and as the summer temps climbed, the lack of air conditioning and fans seemed to wear on her more than it did on him and Ada.

"I have a plan."

"One that works? Or one where we work, but it doesn't?" Cara teased.

His eyes defied his will and stayed focused on her as he soaked in who they'd become since meeting. Love was weird—and he no longer doubted that he loved her. No matter how much he gave or helped, he wanted to do more. He didn't know how she felt about him other than seeing him as a good friend whose company she enjoyed. But he did know she was happier now that she was out of Dry Lake, had a stable place to live, and had lots of work to do.

"What's the plan?" Lori asked around a mouthful of fresh-baked wheat bread.

I wish I knew.

He cleared his throat and looked to Lori. "I'm going to clean up the backyard so an adult doesn't have to put a leash on Better Days and take him to a side yard every time he needs to go out."

Lori looked pleased as she took another bite of her sandwich. Cara's face was not readable.

Yesterday afternoon when she corrected Lori for nearly knocking over a can of paint, he heard it in Cara's voice: she needed a safe place for her daughter to play *outside*.

With town shops close by and traffic as busy as it was, Cara didn't let Lori go outdoors alone. Part of the reason was because Better Days had to be kept on a leash, and if he pulled free of Lori's hand, she'd take off after him. But when Cara wouldn't trust Lori to play on the wraparound porch, it dawned on him that her caution was magnified because her mother had died from being struck by a car. That's when he decided to stop his repair work on the inside of the house and clean up the junkyard out back.

"Can I help?" Lori asked.

"Maybe later, after I've shoveled the broken glass into trash bags and mended the fence so little girls and puppies can't walk right through it, okay?"

"Okay. Me and Better Days will be in my room playing when you're ready."

Cara rose and began stacking plates. "She thinks you'll get that done before supper."

He scuffed Lori's hair. "I will, just not before today's supper."

He stood. "Guess I better get started."

Ephraim put on work gloves and began loading lawn bags with broken bottles and trash. The mid-June heat bore down as he lifted a half-rotted log and carried it to the wagon. He'd picked up all the large pieces of glass he could, but he knew there were hidden shards. The worst of it was in two corners that'd been used as trash piles. He wasn't yet sure what he could do about that.

While lifting another oversize log, he saw two men in a horse and buggy coming toward him. When the rig stopped near the carriage house, he recognized them. Two church leaders, the bishop and a preacher. He'd known this speech was coming, was surprised it'd taken a full week for them to make this visit. What he didn't know was if his father realized how much time he was spending here. Normally, as a preacher, his Daed would be with the other two church leaders during this type of visit. But the bishop's wisdom probably caused him to shield his Daed from the news.

Hoping to keep Cara or Lori from hearing what Sol and Alvin would have to say, he weaved around the trash and junk until only a wire fence separated them at the back part of the yard.

"Ephraim." Sol shook his hand, effectively reminding Ephraim that brotherly fellowship was heartily waiting for him as soon as he took the right steps to bring an end to the shunning.

Alvin moved to stand next to the bishop. "We regret the need for this visit and that we had to travel so far in order to connect with one of our own."

Robbie took him home each night, but that wouldn't count for much.

The bishop studied him. "Because of the vows you've taken, this is like flirting with betrayal. You've promised to marry within our sect, and Cara is not a part of us."

"She might be if everything had been handled right."

"If she'd come to us at the age of eight, she *might* have joined the faith. Big difference. And is that why you're spending so much time here, to set right a wrong? I think not. You are here because you let desire take root, and now it controls you."

Alvin opened the gate and came inside the messy yard. He placed his hand on Ephraim's shoulder. "You can't get free of the ban living like this, and you have a duty to your family."

"If that's your argument, it's a weak one. I've fulfilled more than my share of family obligations. I've worked for eight years to provide for my father's family."

The bishop came inside the fence too. "We've tried to give you a bit of flexibility, thinking you'd help Ada and then return to safer ground for your soul. But you haven't. One is not Amish because their parents are or once were Amish. Cara's an Englischer. Will you forsake God, family, and your business to follow this…this lustful path?"

"My being here has nothing to do with lust." It had plenty to do with desire, but Ephraim knew himself well enough to recognize when lust tempted him.

The bishop placed a hand on his shoulder. "Anything that pulls you away from your walk with God, from the principles you believe in, or believed in before, is lust. If this was happening to someone else in our community, you'd be able to see it for what it is. Trust us, Ephraim. And come away." He spoke softly. "Let us do our job in correcting you. Please, for the love of all God has done for you, don't turn your back on Him."

"I haven't turned my back on God."

"No, you haven't," the bishop said. "But one who's been raised as you have doesn't turn his back on God overnight. It will happen slowly, until one day you realize you've lost all faith and you don't know when or how it happened. But I can tell you this: it began the day you took that woman into your home unsupervised. And it will continue as long as you come to Hope Crossing each day to work beside her."

"She needs someone to tell her of our faith, to show her all the good parts of being Amish. Her mother wanted her raised with us. That opportunity was stolen from her. She's been asking questions about our ways. Will you prevent me from sharing that with her?"

"Most Englischers will ask questions about our beliefs, given a chance. It doesn't mean they're remotely interested in doing what it takes to live as we do. And what happens if, after all her questions are answered, she's uninterested in living Old Order? What then?"

Ephraim stared at the lush green hill, wishing he had answers. Cara had a few favorite spots she liked to walk to in the evenings. He was looking at one of them. They'd go through the pasture behind Ada's house, across the footbridge, and up that steep hill to a dilapidated barn and outbuildings. He had no idea why she found the half-ruined structures so interesting, but that's where they walked. They'd sit on a fallen tree or jutted rock or sometimes a blanket and watch the night sky. He could talk to Cara there, tell her about parts of himself that were hidden from everyone else. She shared things with him, and that only served to make him want her more. The only secret he kept from her was that he was no longer seeing Anna Mary. Surely, if she thought about it, she'd know that. But telling her would shift the relationship and add to all the confusion going on inside her.

"Ephraim," the bishop called to him, "what if she's uninterested in becoming Amish?"

"I don't know."

The bishop stared at him, looking deeply concerned. "Will you leave the faith? Will you make the same mistake Malinda Riehl made? You've lived a solid Old Order Amish life since your father needed you nine years ago. You did that out of love, but love is not always enough to accomplish what we want it to."

Ephraim held the man's gaze, unashamed of what was happening within him. His heart belonged to Cara. At thirty-two he'd finally experienced the connection he'd always longed for. "And there are times when it is."

The bishop drew a deep breath. "Ephraim, listen to me. Even if she chooses to join the faith and goes through all the right steps, if her decision isn't based on the right reasons, she is likely to leave after some time."

"She wouldn't do that."

"You care for her. That's clear. Does she return those feelings?"

He shrugged. "I don't know."

"If she gets so caught up in her feelings that she goes through all the steps to marry you, then she might only stay because she's married. But if you back off, she'll have a chance to choose for herself, not based on a life with you, but based on our faith."

Ephraim shoved his hands into his pockets and gazed at the sky. "You may be right about that."

"Ya." The bishop smiled. "I am right. I learned much of my wisdom from you over the years before you became all *verhuddelt*."

Was the bishop right? Had he become confused?

Alvin shifted. "We don't want to lose you or add any more punishment. But as much as it grieves us to say it, this is your final warning. You have until Monday to decide. You must keep away from Cara at all times until we see progress in her. If she makes a decision to accept our ways and become Amish, that will change everything."

The bishop removed his hat, looking peaceful and confident. "You can't be the one to help her, not without jeopardizing your own soul. Let Ada do as she has permission to. Cara is out of your home now. If you'll return as we ask, I'll repeal the extreme restrictions of your shunning within a week. If you'll show some willingness to follow our wisdom, it won't be long before I'll end the shunning altogether. Then you will be a member in good standing before you know it."

Each man placed a hand on Ephraim's shoulder and bowed for silent prayer. "Be wise, Ephraim. There is much more than just your soul at stake. Many within the younger generations of Dry Lake are now questioning the ways of our people."

Feeling the weight of responsibility smothering him, he looked to Ada's house. Inside was a woman who possessed more of him than he did.

"Did you know Mahlon has been gone all week?" the bishop asked.

"What? He said he'd wait until I returned to work before he took time off."

"He left last Saturday and told Deborah he'd probably be back by Wednesday. Today is Saturday again, and she's not heard a word from him. She doesn't even know where he went. He's supposed to be out of his place by tomorrow at midnight, and from what we can tell, he made no plans for where to live."

The news quaked through him. His sister's heart would break if Mahlon didn't return. Was the letter Ada had been reading over and over again from Mahlon? He could think of a few reasons she wouldn't say anything yet and felt fairly confident she'd only speak up if she was positive what her son was up to.

"Can I talk to my sister?"

The bishop shook his head. "I'm sorry. I've made enough exceptions already. I let you talk to your Daed when he was in the hospital and to Ada several times when Cara found out she had relatives in Dry Lake."

Ephraim looked to the clear blue sky with its streaks of white clouds and golden sun, knowing that right where he looked there were the stars he couldn't see—not until darkness fell. "What you'd really like to tell me is that if I keep seeing Cara, I'll live under the weight of my choice for the rest of my life." He took a step back and began putting on a work glove. "Well, that's a price I just might be willing to pay."

Thirty-Eight

Cara blew out the flame to the kerosene lamp on the kitchen table, gathered several letters that her mother had written, and walked to the back door of Ada's home. Ephraim moved through the darkness, repairing the gaps in the fence as if fixing it tomorrow would be too late. She'd seen two men in black suits arrive in a buggy and talk with him hours ago. He hadn't come inside since—not even for supper. She'd left him alone, knowing there were times when work did for a man what talking did for a woman.

Robbie had arrived an hour ago, spoken to Ephraim, and then left by himself. Whatever was going on, she'd bet the roof over her head that her presence was still making his life harder. She stepped onto the small back porch. Ephraim stopped cold and watched as she walked to him.

"I knew they'd come for you—those men in black. And yet you're still here."

"Faith in God is required. Remaining Amish is not."

She wanted to ask if he meant that he was willing to leave the Amish faith. If he said yes, part of her wanted to throw herself into his arms. But with the weight of her mother's past resting inside the letters she carried, she steadied her emotions. "Faith." She made a small gesture toward the sky. "I have faith that night will come and day will follow, again and again." She looked back at the house. "I have faith that either a need will be met or I'll have the strength to survive if it's not. Of late, I even have faith in you. But, Ephraim, I have no faith in your God, and I never will."

His eyes moved over her face, but he said nothing.

She held out the letters. "In my mother's own handwriting, in letters meant for me when I came of age, she confesses that she was never the same after leaving Dry Lake. She latched on to a different life for all the wrong reasons—out of hurt, betrayal, even out of my dad's need of her. So she stayed and married him. When she realized who she truly was and what she'd given up to marry him, her loyalty would not let her leave."

She stared at the letters. "Go home, Ephraim. Live as you need to, repair whatever damage has taken place. You've seen Lori and me safely through the storm, and we're fine now. My guess is you and Anna Mary are not so fine." She slid the letters into her back pocket. "She loves you, Ephraim. Don't throw that away because of a few crazy weeks with an outsider. I'm sure she's not happy that you spend so much time here with me. But given a chance, she'll forgive you. Go, make the right choice— not just for you, but for your children and grandchildren and all generations to come."

Crickets chirped, and the beauty of night seemed to move around them, but he said nothing. After long minutes of silence, he motioned for them to walk. They went through the back gate, across the wooden foot-bridge, and up to the top of the hill.

The darkened landscape surrounded them—the silhouette of rolling hills, trees, and valleys. A few stars shone through the hazy summer sky. They moved to the fallen tree and sat.

"Mahlon took a few days off starting last Saturday and hasn't returned." He pointed to the edge of the wood nearby, and she spotted three deer slowly entering the open field. "Since he was a teen, I've known he has a deep restlessness inside him—the kind that makes a man either leave or always wish he had."

"What will the community do?"

He sighed. "Grieve. And wait to hear from him."

"You need to be there for Deborah."

"I can't even talk to her." He rose. "It's all so frustrating. My sister's

probably sick over Mahlon's absence. If any woman around is worth coming back for, it's her."

"Is there anything I can do to help?"

He removed his hat and ran his hands through his hair. "It's possible.
I don't know if it'll work, but maybe Deborah could talk to you while
I'm nearby."

"And you could talk to her through me, like we do with Ada."

"I need to see if she's okay. And I know she'll draw strength from
you."

"From me?" Cara scoffed.

He smiled and put his hat on. "Yes, you. If anyone knows how to take
what a man has dished out and become stronger, you do."

"You're strange, you know that? Who else would see a homeless
woman with a child and call that strong?"

"Possessions don't make a person strong—decisions do. Although I
never thought about that before knowing you. While you were in the
midst of the battle, you decided what you were and were not willing to
give up, and you never let go. Deborah needs to see that."

"I don't think she'll see what you see in me, but I'll go. When?"

"Ada's hired Robbie to come by around eleven in the morning and
take her to Dry Lake for a Sunday visit since there's no service. You could
ride with her. Go to my Daed's house and ask to talk to Deborah in the
hiddy. I'll meet you there."

"It won't cause you problems for me to be there again?"

He shook his head. "It shouldn't, but I don't care if it does."

It seemed Ephraim had changed inwardly even more than her life
had outwardly. He wasn't the same man who'd asked her to get off his
property the first time he saw her, or the one who'd paid for two bus tickets to New York, or the one who'd tried to hide her from everyone he
knew. But like he always said, the things that separated them would always
stand firm. That's why she had no choice but to send him home to Anna
Mary.

She cleared her throat, wishing she could undo the damage she'd caused him. "Does Ada know about Mahlon?"

"She hasn't said so, but I think she does."

"I got the mail from the box a few days ago. I think he'd written to her, but I don't know what the letter said. It didn't seem to be good news, though. Why wouldn't she tell anyone about it?"

"Whatever he wrote, I'm sure she doesn't want to alarm anyone."

"I came here and totally disrupted your life. You chose to ignore the Amish rules and are being shunned. Mahlon's mother decided to move out of Dry Lake and take me with her. Is it possible Mahlon's absence has something to do with me?"

"No. Although I see why it could look that way. Mahlon's been odd since the day we lost so many members in the car wreck, his Daed among them. He got worse after being in New York the day the Twin Towers fell. Deborah says he felt the earth shake, saw the smoke rise, and heard the screams of those trapped inside. His mother had been in the towers the day before. The experience did something to him."

"That would affect anyone."

"Deborah has loved him since she was a child." He sighed. "I have no idea what this might do to her."

Cara stood. "You need to go home tonight, 'From, and start acting like the Amish man you are."

He stayed on the log, looking up at her. "Ya. I know."

When he rose, mere inches separated them. Regardless of the Amish stance against electrical energy, it ran unrestricted between them.

Afraid to keep lingering, she turned away and started walking. But she wasn't ready to go back to Ada's. Tonight was all they had, and so they'd walk.

Ephraim stayed beside her, saying nothing for a long time. Finally he cleared his throat. "Since I didn't leave with Robbie, I'll use Ada's horse to get back to Dry Lake. I'll put the mare in the pasture, and to-morrow Israel Kauffman or Grey or someone will recognize her, realize

I borrowed her, and see to it she's returned to Ada by tomorrow night."

She appreciated his effort to make small talk. "How can you know all that?"

"Too many years of experience among my people." His half smile looked more sad than happy, but she knew he was right—the Amish were *his* people.

Deborah sat on the floor of Mahlon's bedroom, too weary to cry anymore. She held his shirt to her face, breathing in his aroma. Except for the occasional headlights of passing cars, darkness surrounded her. She kept telling herself to light a kerosene lamp or walk back home, but she continued to sit here hour after hour, trying to make sense of it all and figure out a way to fix it.

She longed to hear from him, to know he was safe. But if something hadn't kept him, if he hadn't been in an accident of some sort…if he'd chosen to leave like this…she wasn't sure she wanted to know that. And yet, not to know the truth meant living in limbo every second of every day. She couldn't stand that either. So she'd prayed until she was sick of it, but she kept praying anyway.

Israel Kauffman and Mahlon's cousin Jonathan had come here with her long before dark. She'd emptied his dresser, footlocker, and nightstands. They'd dismantled his bed and moved all the heavy furniture. She'd asked them to go on home and let her pack his huge, messy closet on her own. They'd taken the grandfather clock with them, so she didn't know what time it was. But it didn't matter. It was somewhere between yesterday and tomorrow.

The closet was empty, and boxes were scattered throughout the room. Her prayers had changed shape and purpose since four days ago, when he should have come home and didn't. But her feelings had not altered. She was scared, and more than that she felt like a fool. Who lets a loved one go off without knowing where or how to reach him? Who lets someone talk in jumbled circles without insisting he make sense?

Car lights shone on the wall, but rather than moving around the room as they did when a vehicle passed the house, they stayed in one spot. Then they disappeared. She got up from the floor and moved to the window. Through the blackness of night, she saw a car parked on the shoulder of the road a hundred feet or so from the house. A light came on inside the car, and the door opened.

Mahlon!

She wanted to scream his name and run to see him, but neither her voice nor her body would obey her. He moved to the side of the car and leaned against it. Staring out at the field, he lit a match, and soon she saw smoke circle around him. A man got out of the driver's side and sat on the hood of the vehicle. They just stayed there, smoking and talking as if nothing mattered—not her pain or worry or anything.

Another vehicle headed toward them. Mahlon glanced at it before tossing his cigarette to the ground. He walked to the cattle gate, opened it, and called for his horse. A truck with a trailer attached to it pulled up beside the car. While Mahlon harnessed his horse, his friend opened the tailgate of the trailer. After the horse was loaded, the driver of the truck held something out the window. Mahlon went to the man, took whatever it was, and stepped away before the man left.

He stayed in the middle of the road, looking at the place where he'd grown up. As she stood there too bewildered to move, realization bore down on her like a merciless drought. She longed for a man she clearly didn't know. No matter how she tried, she couldn't put together the pieces of her childhood love and the lonely stranger she was now watching.

He was safe. But her heart broke anyway.

The man she'd willingly give herself to had no intentions of returning to her. Somehow she was seeing what he couldn't tell her—as if she was meant to be here, meant to see the truth for herself.

When he got into the car, she ran down the steps, out the back door, and toward the road.

As the car came toward her, she waved her arms. "Mahlon, wait!"

Mahlon looked straight at her, but the car kept going.

"Mahlon!" she screamed as loud as she could.

The brake lights glowed bright red, and then small white lights shined as the car backed up. It stopped. When Mahlon opened the door, she saw Eric in his military uniform. Mahlon got out and closed the door, but Eric didn't drive off.

"Why?" She choked on her tears.

He studied her as he'd done a thousand times before, but his face was a mixture of uncertainty and hardness. "I'm sorry."

"Sorry?" she yelled. "I didn't ask for an apology. I asked for an explanation."

He shook his head and held out an envelope. "I was going to leave this in your mailbox. It's for you and Mamm."

Wondering what could possibly end the twisting confusion inside her, she snatched it from him and looked inside.

"Money?" She gasped. "You're leaving me, and you're going to fix it by giving me money?"

He stepped toward her, his hands reaching for her shoulders, but she took a step back. "I can't do this, Deb."

"Can't do what?"

He said nothing, but she saw a tear trail down his face.

"You have someone else?"

"Never, not in a million years. I swear that to you."

"Then why?"

"I joined the faith, but not all of me did. Parts did, slivers too small to find most days. You were all that held me here, and finally I know that I can't live like this."

His words were short, and she should understand them, but her mind couldn't grab on to any of it. "I…I believed you. All this time I thought you really loved me. But you don't, do you? Why? Why can't you love me like I do you?"

"Don't do this to yourself, Deb."

"You're the one doing this! And what about your mother? You're her only child. She gave up everything to raise you."

"That's what parents do."

"You promised to always be here for her, and now you do this?"

"She'll be fine. She's already proved that. And eventually you will too. But I never will—not if I stay."

Deborah's legs shook, and she feared she might fall over. "This can't be. It just can't."

"Take the money. I'll send more when I can."

She thrust the money toward him. "I don't need anything from you, Mahlon Stoltzfus. Absolutely nothing ever again!"

He closed his eyes, and fresh tears fell onto his cheeks. When he turned to get into the car, she threw the envelope at him, and money scattered everywhere. She left it there and hurried down the road, glad her home was in the opposite direction from the way his vehicle was headed.

"Deb, I'm sorry!" Mahlon yelled, but she refused to turn back.

Unable to see for the tears, she kept running until her legs and lungs were burning. She thought she might pass out, but she refused to stop.

The sound of hoofbeats came from in front of her. Dizzy and confused, she couldn't make out who got off the horse that stopped somewhere ahead of her. Then Ephraim filled her view.

When he tried to reach for her, she shoved him away. "He was here, and he…he left." She sobbed. "Why, Ephraim? He doesn't love me. Why doesn't he love me?"

Her brother stepped forward. When he placed his arms around her, she was too weak to lash out. She melted into his arms and wept.

Thirty-Nine

Cara looked at herself in the mirror, wondering if wearing the Amish dress and apron was a matter of respect or hypocrisy. Although she hated the style, she loved the teal color. It seemed a shame to cover most of it with a black apron, but Ada thought she should wear both to Dry Lake today. The purpose of the apron was to hide a woman's curves. Thing was, she had no problem showing her figure. She was petite but well built. It was part of who she was, so why hide it?

People were so odd—not just the Amish, but people in general.

Some men paid big chunks of their salary to see half-naked women or prostitutes, while others lived in celibacy, hoping God would bring them the right woman. Some women did anything for fun or money, while others denied all temptations to remain loyal to men they didn't even like. Most people fell between those two points. Right now she'd like to know where she landed on that imaginary line. Had she become more of a teal-dress girl than a short-top, bare-belly one?

If there was a God, was he ever confused by the choices people made? Or disappointed? It seemed to her that even among the most religious, there was error that caused division and hurt as much as any sin did.

Ada came to the doorway. "You look nice."

"I feel like a bag lady."

Ada's eyes reflected a deep sadness, but she smiled anyway. "Would you rather stand out for men and women who only want to please their eyes or for those who see beyond this life into the next?"

Cara shrugged. "Jeans are comfortable."

"I'd guess men's flannel pajamas and clown suits are comfortable too. When you're willing to wear those in public day in and day out, I'll believe your rationalization about those tight-fitting clothes you wear."

By an act of determination, Cara didn't roll her eyes. "I'd rather live free and make my own choices than be told what to wear."

Ada stepped inside the room and motioned for Cara to turn around. She adjusted the apron ties. "We all submit to something. Athletes submit to the rules of their game. Lawyers and judges submit to the laws. The highest court in the land submits to the Constitution. Even the most rebellious person is submitting to something, usually the darkest part of their sin nature. The Amish choose to submit to the Ordnung in order to be strong against desires that want no boundaries. The preachers, deacons, and bishops help us keep those written and unwritten rules. If you don't want to submit to that, you don't have to, but don't believe that you're free." Ada's voice cracked, and when Cara turned to face her, she saw tears in her eyes. "No one is, Cara. And those who think they are just haven't thought about it long enough."

Cara constantly balked at Ada's explanations about anything Amish. Maybe she'd gone too far. "Is something wrong?"

Ada pulled an envelope out of the bib of her apron. "This had been pushed through the mail slot of the front door when I woke this morning." Ada passed it to her, then went to the window and stared out.

Cara read the writing scrawled on the front. *Mamm, this is the hardest thing I've ever done. I'm not coming back. I'm sorry. Take care of yourself, and help Deborah to forgive me. Love, Mahlon*

The words twisted inside her. At times the endless rules seemed enough to run anyone off. And yet, for most, their way of life came with an undeniable strength against all that the world sought to steal—a person's soul, family, and faith.

She didn't have to believe in God to know that her soul could be trampled on and that right and wrong existed. So why would someone like Mahlon give up the power of the good parts to get free of the weakness of the bad parts? It was a little like what Ada said about everyone submitting to something. Every way of life had frustrations and error.

Ada sat on the bed, looking hurt beyond description. "He sent a letter earlier this week that made me think this might be coming, but I kept praying it wouldn't. I did my best raising Mahlon. There wasn't a day when I didn't put real effort into being a good Mamm and a positive influence."

Her words reminded Cara of something her own mother had written to her dad. She went to her dresser and flipped through the letters. When she found the right one, she took it to Ada and sat beside her. "Mama once wrote that the reason she gave her all to help my dad get free of his addiction was because she had to know she'd done her best, and then she could accept whatever came of it. But she writes it much better than I can say it." Cara passed her the letter.

"Denki." Ada ran her fingers over the folded pages. "I can remember from our school days that Malinda had a special way of saying things."

Cara went to the dresser and gathered a large stack of letters. "Then read these as it suits you."

A horn tooted, which meant Robbie had arrived.

Ada held on to the letters as if embracing a delicate teacup. "I can't go visiting, not today."

"Those men in black—"

"The church leaders aren't men with guns from an Englischer film. They are servants of God who are doing their best, whatever may come of it."

For the first time Cara understood who the men were and why. "You're right. I'm sorry. The church leaders told Ephraim that Mahlon might have left, and he's concerned for his sister. He wants me to come to Dry Lake today and be a go-between for him and Deborah so they can sort of talk."

Ada nodded. "Go. I'll keep Lori here."

"Better Days is still here. The backyard needs more work, but it's safe enough for them to play in. Ephraim roped off two corners that have a lot of glass shards down in the grass. Tell her not to go inside those areas."

"I'll take good care of her." Ada wiped a stray tear. "I don't think Deborah will ever want to see me, so it's just as well I live so far from Dry Lake now. But will you tell her I'm sorry?"

"I will."

The horn tooted again. Cara hurried down the steps and out the front door. The awkwardness between her and Robbie wasn't as miserable as their first ride together, but returning to Dry Lake was difficult enough without trying to hold a conversation with him. After they shared a polite hello, she settled back in her seat, glad he was staying quiet.

"The Masts are good people." Robbie startled her when he spoke. "Abner, Ephraim's dad, just doesn't know who you are. One day you're in jeans, stumbling around like you're drunk, and the next you're wearing a dress you stole off his clothesline. You lived in a barn his son asked you to leave, and then you moved into his son's home. I think that's enough to stretch anyone's trust."

"You know too much."

"I shoot the breeze with Abner pretty regularly. Unlike Ephraim, he's a talker. So, were you stealing from the Swareys and drunk the day he saw you on the road?"

"Good grief." She rolled her eyes. "Yes. I stole a pair of shoes and some stuff for Lori's blisters. And I'd do it again if need be. But I wasn't drunk."

He shrugged and said nothing for a few minutes. "I know that most of the Amish in Dry Lake are sorry for how they treated you. The rest don't know what they think, not yet. So you just say very little and nod a lot when you're around a group of them. Almost all of them know Englischers they like. The Amish are extremely careful who they let have an influence on their children. You seem to have a lot of influence on Abner's child—a grown man, but still Abner's child."

"You know, you actually make sense when you're not being obnoxiously nosy."

Robbie laughed. "At first I didn't trust you being in Ephraim's life either."

"And now?"

"He doesn't care whether I like it or not. And I can't stop you from being in his life. Since I can't get rid of you, I'm trying to keep you from making things worse between him and his family."

"Denki."

Robbie smiled and held up a small plastic bag. "This is for you."

Cara took it and looked inside. He'd bought her a pack of cigarettes. "You know these things kill a person slowly. So if your goal is to get rid of me, that's a poor plan."

He chuckled. "No. I had to stop to get gas on the way here, and I remembered you wanted a smoke last time we rode together."

She held the bag out to him. "That was thoughtful, and I'm impressed. But I'm fully detoxed, by no choice of my own, and I don't intend to re-tox."

"Smart woman." He pulled into the Masts' long driveway. There had to be twenty people under the shade trees, and most of them were looking right at her as the car passed by.

"What was Ephraim thinking?"

"He wanted you to come?"

"Yeah."

"That's interesting. They're here to support Deborah, but I don't see her. She's probably in no mood to be seen, but they want to make a statement to her by their presence." He clicked his tongue in disgust. "I worked beside Mahlon for a lot of years, and I never saw this coming. Leaving is one thing. But to go after joining the faith and asking someone to marry you is just not done—and never like this."

"I need to keep my mouth shut and nod a lot, you say?"

"Yep."

"I don't think I'll be more than a few minutes. I'm going to see if Deborah will come to the hiddy and talk to me. Will you wait?"

He stopped the car. "Abner's under one of the trees behind us. I'll go talk to him for a bit."

"You're welcome to come and go among the Amish as you please?"

"It took a few years of being a good neighbor and a good employee to have this type of ease. But I'm still an outsider, so the rules of play are different. Mahlon could repent and return tomorrow, and it'd take him a decade to be truly welcome in many of the homes."

"And Ephraim?"

"I don't really know. It's different with him. He crossed a line, to be sure. Now that they know who you are, some admire what he did. Others think the two of you probably, well, you know."

"Slept together."

"Yep. And they're offended that he let you stay the night. After the shunning is over, it'll take years to regain most people's respect. He'll never have everyone's."

"You know, there are perks to not having a family or community."

"Yeah? Is it worth it?" He opened the car door.

As soon as they got out, several men and women headed their way. She recognized Emma and Levi Riehl.

"Cara." Levi stepped forward. "You remember my wife, Emma."

Looking unsure of herself, Emma held out her hand. "Welcome."

Welcome? Who was the woman trying to kid?

But she remembered Robbie's advice, so she shook the woman's hand and nodded without saying anything.

"I have some people I'd like you to meet," Levi said.

The names flew at her as Levi introduced aunts, uncles, and cousins. She only nodded and smiled as each person shook her hand, either apologizing to her or welcoming her. Looking past the small crowd, she saw Ephraim leaning against the side of the house, a gentle smile revealing his thoughts. He'd paid the price for this day, and he continued to pay. Had he known this would happen when he asked her to come to Dry Lake today?

To her left, Robbie stood talking to the man she'd seen in the pasture her first day in Dry Lake and who'd come to Ephraim's the night she and Lori were dancing. He slowly walked toward her.

Levi didn't introduce them as he had with everyone else.

"I'm Abner, Ephraim's father. I...I was wrong to tell everyone to beware of you—that you were drunk or on drugs when I'd only caught a glimpse of you."

Cara swallowed, wishing a simple nod would do as an answer. "I'm sure I looked as odd to you that day as you did to me. Besides, soon after you called me a drunk, I called your son heartless." She stole a glimpse of Ephraim. "It seems we were both wrong."

Abner held out his hand, but when she placed hers in his, he didn't shake it; he patted it. "Denki."

"How's Ada?" A woman's voice came from somewhere above her.

Abner looked to a spot at the side of the house, and Cara followed his gaze. Deborah stood at a second-story window, looking out.

Cara stepped closer. "She said to tell you she's sorry."

Without saying anything else, Deborah moved away from the window.

Levi motioned to a chair.

Cara took a seat. Women were whispering. Some were crying.

"We don't understand why he left." Emma sat in a chair beside her. "It just doesn't make sense."

In her mind's eye Cara could see how much sadness they must've felt when her mother left. It struck her that when she left a place, no one cared—except Mike. Maybe living under a set of rules that helped hold families together was worth it.

"When your mother left, we thought we understood. It wasn't until recently that we found out her real reason."

Cara wanted to ask what Emma meant, but she kept nodding. Besides, she didn't want to get all friendly and comfortable with these people.

They felt remorse and pity. That wasn't good enough. She'd outgrown taking scraps of affection from a family's table a long time ago.

Deborah came around the side of the house, barefoot and no apron. Wisps of hair dangled around her face and neck, and her white cap sat a bit off center on her head, but no one seemed to mind. Her face held little of the gentle beauty Cara had seen at the auction. Right now her complexion reminded Cara of a puffy gray storm cloud. "I want to go to Ada, Daed."

Her father studied her. "Of course you can go to her. She needs a visit from you."

"I want to be her Ruth."

Abner shook his head. "Child, listen to me."

"No." Deborah broke into tears. "You listen. Please, Daed."

Confused, Cara turned to Emma. "Who's Ruth?" she whispered.

Emma leaned closer to her. "She's talking of Naomi and Ruth. From the Bible."

Cara was tempted to tell her she wasn't into fairy tales, but she simply raised her eyebrows like she understood. Vapory thoughts floated to her, ones that doubted her doubts rather than God. It did seem that sometimes that book spoke clear and honest truth about who people are—not that she'd read it very much.

Abner looked to Cara, studying her. If she knew about the story of Naomi and Ruth, she might be able to piece together what he was thinking.

"This is your home, Deborah. We need you. But if you want to spend a night or two away, you should."

"Ada needs me. Her only child has left. Your health is much improved since the surgery. And even if I leave, you have six children still living at home—five of them daughters. Can't you spare one for a woman who has spent her life being a good Mamm but now has no children at all?"

Cara realized that Deborah was asking to live with Ada. Forever.

Abner looked to Cara again, and she almost read his thoughts. He was afraid of losing Deborah altogether if she lived in the same house as Cara. She couldn't blame the man. Cara had little allegiance to this faith of theirs, and she'd done damage to Ephraim's life without even knowing it.

Anxiety crept over her as she realized that for Deborah to move in with Ada, Cara probably needed to move out. They wouldn't want her to have that much time or possible influence with Deborah. Cara looked to Ephraim. He'd done so much to see that she had a roof over her head and could sit among her mother's people and talk with them like this.

"I can move out." She said it softly, but enough people heard her that they began to pass the word along to those who hadn't.

Deborah stepped closer to her father. "That's not what I want. Ada's rental agreement is based on the work Cara is doing." She turned to Cara. "And she believes you're meant to be beside her. I don't want to take anything from Ada. I want to make up for what's missing now."

Abner sighed—a deep and weary one—as he took a seat beside Cara. "My first wife, Ephraim and Deborah's mother, loved your mother as much as Ada did. Were you aware of that?"

Cara shook her head.

"It's the reason Ephraim was allowed to spend so much time with you that summer your mother brought you here. My wife took one look into your eyes and trusted who you were. But I was so wrapped up in my fears of what Malinda would do to this district that I believed all the wrong things. It was easier to believe Malinda got what she deserved than to take a chance on reaching out. So we told her you could return but she couldn't."

Deborah moved a chair beside her father and sat.

He took Deborah's hand in his. "I've spent years too afraid of losing what's mine to see who anyone else really is. As a preacher I encouraged people to build an invisible fortress around themselves and their families. But that caused us to start carrying so much suspicion toward outsiders that there was no way for a stranger not to look guilty over the slightest thing. Then it became easy to turn to each other and say, 'I knew they couldn't be trusted,' or 'I knew they'd cause trouble.'"

He looked to Ephraim, who stood at the far edge of the house, an outcast inside his family's yard. "Ephraim and Deborah take after their mother." He turned to his daughter. "And Ada has a good heart like your Mamm. If you want to reach out to her like this, you do it, child. I won't stop you."

Deborah broke into tears and hugged him. "Denki." She stood, and several women surrounded her and walked with her back into the house.

Forty

In spite of the open windows, the humid late-August air didn't stir. The aroma of Ada's baking filled the house as Deborah steadied the ladder for Cara while she rolled the wallpaper-piercing tool over another section of the wall.

Ada's telephone rang loud and long. The bishop had approved the installation of the phone for business purposes. Soon the screen door slammed, and Cara knew Ada was scurrying across the backyard and to the barn in hopes of catching the call.

It'd been two long months since Mahlon had left. Deborah's grief and confusion seemed to have no bounds most days, but Cara tried to keep her moving. Ada's grief was quieter and maybe deeper, but Deborah's presence seemed to help by giving Ada someone to tend to. Cara struggled with a sadness that had nothing to do with their loss, but she wouldn't tell them. Mahlon was gone and not coming back. Ephraim was in Dry Lake, with Anna Mary, she guessed, but she tried not to think about it.

Lifting the hem of her dress, Cara moved up a rung. With Amish coming in and out of Ada's home, Cara decided to stick to wearing dresses. Deborah had lots of clothes to share, and Cara hoped that her choices might reflect well on Ephraim. It couldn't hurt, and if it made any difference in how the church leaders looked at him, she'd wear the not-so-quaint garb without argument.

She passed the piercing tool to Deborah. "This area of scoring is done."

Every move Deborah made was slow, like that of a woman bearing thick, heavy chains. She lifted a bucket of warm water and vinegar to Cara. "Here you go."

Cara dipped a thick sponge into the solution and began soaking the walls with it while Deborah continued to hold tight to the wobbling ladder.

Many a night after Deborah first moved in, Cara lay atop the covers beside her and held her while she cried. Those first few weeks Cara had to prod both women to keep moving toward an unknown future. Now, with the help of the Amish communities in Dry Lake and Hope Crossing, Ada and Deborah even had times of laughter. And they'd expanded their business by selling baked goods to a local hotel for its restaurant and continental breakfast bar.

Cara stepped off the ladder. "Let's move to that segment. It should be ready to peel."

They slid the ladder to the right spot, and she climbed it again.

After one of Deborah's rare visits to Dry Lake, she came back saying that Ephraim's ban was over. Once he'd proved his intention to live as the church leaders wanted, the bishop reconsidered his shunning. Since the first part of July, Ephraim had been considered a member in good standing, and he'd returned to work.

She'd seen him just three times since June, when he'd cleaned up the backyard. Even then he came in with others from Dry Lake, and she only saw him in a room full of people. Their quiet mornings over coffee, humorous banter during the workday, and long walks at night were gone, but she'd remember them forever.

Would he?

Even though she still wished things were different for her and Ephraim, she'd found a bit of peace with her past and had chosen to stop blaming those who may or may not have been guilty of anything. And now she tolerated, maybe even enjoyed, getting letters and visits from her aunts, uncles, and cousins.

"You might want to hold the ladder from behind me, Deb."

Deborah gasped. "Oh my, you're right. That Amish dress does nothing for modesty when a girl is on a ladder."

"Red silk bikini—is that the view, Deborah?" Cara grabbed the top edge of the wallpaper and slowly pulled it toward her. "Cross your fingers."

"And let go of the ladder?"

"Which is more important, this wallpaper coming off in one piece or me not falling?"

The rare sound of Deborah chuckling warmed Cara's heart. "Do I have to choose right now?"

A thick splat of wallpaper remover hit the floor. "Sorry. Nothing's harder to get off than ancient wallpaper. What'd they use on this stuff?" Cara stepped down a rung on the ladder.

"I've decided it's elephant glue."

Peeling the wallpaper slowly, Cara came down another notch. "What's elephant glue?"

"You know, the kind of stuff that would make an elephant stick to the walls."

Cara peered down at her.

Deborah made a face. "It made sense to me when I thought of it."

Cara pursed her lips, suppressing laughter. "Was that one of those thoughts you have when you're half asleep, half awake?"

"Why, yes it was."

"I like those. They're amusing. Not much help, but always worth a good chuckle. My favorites are the ones you mumble right before falling asleep."

"So, are you going to the Hope Crossing church meeting with me and Ada this Sunday?"

"Once was enough for me, thanks."

"Girls," Ada called, "lunch is ready. The deliveryman called, and he can't do his pickups today, so I've got my pies all loaded up in the buggy to take to the bakery, hotel, and diner. I'll be back in a couple of hours. Lori's going with me."

"Okay, Ada. Thank you."

"Denki." Deborah shifted to the side. "Was it the backless bench or the length of the service?"

"Neither." Cara tugged on the last part of the attached paper and stepped down to the floor. "In spite of your great efforts over the last month to teach me your language, I have no clue what's being said. Why sit through it when I need you to do a summation afterward?" Cara took the wallpaper to the tarp in the corner and dropped it, then wiped her hands on the black apron. She slid her arm around Deborah and guided her out of the room. "So, what does *geziemt* mean?"

"Depends. It can mean suitable, as in a suitable mate. Or it could mean becoming, as in beautiful to God in dress and behavior." They walked down the stairs. "Where did you hear it? Maybe I can figure out which meaning was intended."

"I heard it at church."

"The pastor was talking about living true to who God made you to be and not seeking to be who the world wants to make you into."

"Why is it so important to you to go to church? It's an off day. Why ruin it?"

"Because—"

Cara held up her hand, interrupting Deborah. "I meant that as a rhetorical question."

"Meaning you didn't really intend for me to answer?"

"Exactly." Cara pushed against the swinging door to the kitchen. Heat smacked her in the face. "Living Amish gives new meaning to the phrase 'If you can't stand the heat, get out of the kitchen.'"

"Let's sit under the shade tree out back."

"I vote let's buy an air conditioner."

"An air conditioner wouldn't be much use without electricity, my dear Englischer. But a battery-operated fan is an idea I could go for, not that our bishop would."

They grabbed the plates with their sandwiches, chips, and fruit. "How does Ada stand it during summer months?"

"I'll take that as a rhetorical question. It'll save me trying to explain it." After they sat at the table, Deborah bowed her head for a silent prayer, and Cara waited.

Deborah lifted her head. "A couple of girls from this district asked if I'd go with them to the singing this Saturday. I'm not sure I'm ready. Just thinking about going makes me start crying all over again."

"Why?"

"Because Mahlon leaving me like he did was equal to a public flogging. Everybody knows he not only broke my heart, but he humiliated me."

"Pffft." Cara rolled her eyes. "If they have any sense, they're thinking of how insane he is for leaving you. What he did was about him, Deb. If I were you, I'd lift my head and dare them to think less of me because of someone else's stupidity."

"If you're right, why am I the one who feels like a total idiot for loving him?"

"Because he sucker-punched you."

"He didn't do it on purpose."

"And he didn't do it by accident either."

Deb shrugged. "Maybe you're right. If I go to a singing, do you want to come with me?"

"No way. It's for singles, not widows, right?"

"Ya. To me singings are for so much more than finding someone. It's a time for making friends who'll still be friends fifty years from now. The walls vibrate from the songs and laughter. I think I'm ready to make some real friends in Hope Crossing."

"Then you better start inviting people over more often."

Deborah sat back in her chair, smiling. "So you're saying you're not a friend?"

Cara blinked. "I…I…me?"

"I like your humility, Cara. It'd serve you well as an Amish woman."

"It's hard to be Amish if you don't believe in God, don't you think?" Deborah opened her mouth to speak, but Cara held up her hand. "Just take it as a rhetorical question, Deb."

Thunder rumbled, and the smell of rain hung in the air as Cara snuggled with Lori on the bed, reading to her. When Ada found this children's book in a box of things while moving here, she gave it to Lori. At first *Shoo-Fly Girl* seemed harmless enough. But it was all about a little girl growing up Amish, and Lori loved it.

"She loved going to church, huh, Mom?"

"Yes. Now nestle down and go to sleep." Cara got off the bed and laid the sheet loosely over her daughter, wondering how anyone slept in this August heat.

"I want to go to church with Ephraim again."

A dozen emotions washed over her at the mention of his name, and the ache of missing him stirred again. "I'm not sure sneaking in to sit in his lap that one time could be considered *going* with him." She kissed her daughter's forehead. "Besides, you can't even understand what's being said."

"I know some of the words now. Deborah's been teaching me. I don't have to know all the words. But I can feel what they're saying, can't you?"

She brushed strands of hair away from Lori's face. "Yeah, sometimes, I guess."

Hearing the thunder grow louder, Cara hoped Deborah's night out with her new friends in Hope Crossing didn't get rained out.

The longing to believe in something other than what she could see had wrapped around her heart lately. Sometimes it seemed God was everywhere. And yet, at the same time, she didn't know if she could really believe that. Santa Claus and the Easter Bunny seemed real too when she was little.

"Shoo-Fly Girl loves being Amish."

"It's ridiculously hard, living as they do. There are more rules than bugs in a barn."

She giggled. "But there's rules to everything. You told me that lots of times before we even met the Amish."

"Yeah, I guess I did. Go to sleep. Do you want me to leave a low-burning kerosene lamp on the dresser tonight?"

"Nope. I'm trusting God like Shoo-Fly Girl. Do you wanna pray?"

No, she didn't. Not now. Not ever. She had prayed when her mother died, begging him to give her back. She had prayed when in foster homes, crying out for someone to care. But one day she realized no one was listening to her prayers.

"I'll close my eyes, and you say the words, okay?"

Lori shut her eyes tight. "Dear God, forgive me for doing wrong, and help me do right. Amen."

"Amen."

Cara picked up the kerosene lamp. "Good night, Lorabean."

"Mom?"

"Yes?"

"Do you trust God?"

"You need to go on to sleep now, okay?"

"Okay. Night, Mom."

"Good night." Cara patted Better Days and then pulled the door shut behind her.

She stood at the top of the stairs, tempted to read the same diaries and letters from her mother that she read every night. But it seemed she should use this time to do something else. There was nothing new inside that box her dad had sent her, but she made her way down the steps and to the hall closet anyway. After setting the lamp on a side table, she reached to the top shelf and grabbed her gateway to the past. With the box in hand, she picked up the lantern and went into the kitchen. Once seated at the table, she opened the box.

She set her mother's Bible to the side before opening all the letters and spreading them out on the table. She'd read every one and all of the journals a dozen times.

The stairs creaked, and Ada walked into the kitchen, carrying a lantern. She ran her hand across Cara's back as she passed her. "Can I fix you a glass of ice water?"

"No thanks." Cara leaned back in her chair. "Ada, if your district had never learned the truth about why my mother left Dry Lake, would they be writing to me or visiting?"

"I think so, but it's hard to know." With a glass of water in hand, Ada took a seat.

"It had to break my mom's heart to discover her fiancé's secret just weeks before the wedding."

"Rueben's been in a lot of trouble for the secret he kept."

"But not shunned?"

Ada shook her head. "He might be later on, but the bishop hasn't decided what to do yet. He's in a bad spot—needing to issue discipline to a man who did something wrong more than thirty years ago. If he's not careful, a lot of the youth will look at another shunning, along with Ephraim's and Mahlon's troubles, and not want to join the faith."

"It still makes me mad. It'd be okay with me if they shunned both Rueben and his wife forever."

"And it's harder to take since it's Anna Mary's parents, no?"

Cara nodded. "Too hard sometimes."

"You remind me so much of your mother. You've helped me and Deborah survive the worst thing imaginable. I couldn't have handled the last couple of months of bearing what Mahlon's done without looking at what God brought out of your heartache. And that awful imaginary whip you keep cracking to make me and Deborah stay focused on building a business. I'm actually glad you've been a jaded little taskmaster."

Cara's eyes stung with tears as she looked at one of her mother's letters. "Sometimes I almost feel whole again, like I've found answers that make sense out of some of my crazy life. At other times I feel so confused, bitter, and lost I can't stand myself." She dropped the letter onto the table. "I keep going over every piece of writing as if trying to verify that life's worth it."

She looked at her mother's closed Bible. Of all the items her dad had sent that she'd read and reread, she hadn't yet opened that book. She'd stolen a few minutes with Ephraim's or Ada's but not her mom's. It always gave her an eerie feeling, as if it contained more of her mother's heart than her letters.

Ada slid her hand over Cara's. "Only God can redeem life and make it worthwhile. Without His worth covering us and being in us, man's history carries only faded hopes and broken dreams." She picked up the Bible from the table and handed it to Cara. "He can redeem your past and all the pain that awaits in the future."

Cara held the Bible between her two hands and let it fall open. The pages fluttered, and a yellow piece of paper caught her attention. She laid the book on the table and looked through it. After a few moments she found the paper and pulled it out. Unfolding it, she immediately recognized her mother's handwriting.

I will be your Father, and you will be my sons and daughters.

The words flooded her heart.

Choking back tears, she stood. Her heart pumped against her chest as thoughts and understanding pounded against her. "He's real." The room seemed to be shrinking, and she felt desperate for time alone. "I need to go for a walk. You'll stay with Lori?"

"Sure I will."

She hurried out the back door. Mist fell from the sky as she walked as fast as she could. Pain flooded her heart as if she were reliving every loss she'd ever sustained. Fragments of her past ripped at her, begging for answers. But there were none. There was only a dark hole in her soul, draining her of strength. The rain fell harder as she followed the narrow trail to the top of the mountain.

Looking out over the valley below, she clenched her fists. "Why?" she screamed into the rain. "I want to know why!" Her tears mingled with the rain, but no answer returned to her.

Thoughts of being inside Ephraim's barn, hungry and miserable as she sought refuge, filled her view more than the rain-drenched sky. She'd landed there out of desperation. The long journey began because she had pieces of memories and her mother had hidden a message inside her diary. But most of all, she'd landed there because something inside her, something beyond herself, had led her.

As if watching a movie in her mind's eye, she saw Ephraim standing at the door of the barn, holding out his hand. He didn't offer answers to all she wanted to know, but he gave her a way to a better life. He offered help and strength and himself, as a shield of sorts—but not the kind of protection she tried to give Lori, where the sharpness of reality was hidden until she was older. The shield didn't hide reality or pain; it simply absorbed the impact of each blow before it made its way to her.

Suddenly he changed, and a man she didn't recognize held his hand out to her. He was dressed even more oddly than the Amish, with darker skin, hair, and eyes. But most of all he had compassion for her and a love so deep she couldn't begin to understand it.

It had to be Jesus. As He looked at her, it seemed she was no longer the woman she thought herself to be. It was as if she was part of something bigger, and yet she knew she was nothing. She felt fully accepted, like a member of the family, but only because He'd opened the door— similar to the way Ephraim had.

Her earlier question of why didn't matter. The only question that mattered now was what she would choose from this point forward.

She sank to her knees.

Forty-One

With a book open and a mug of coffee in hand, Ephraim sat on his couch, listening to the rain.

He'd spent thousands of quiet evenings by himself since building this house nine years ago. Before Cara none of those times had been lonely. Well…maybe a little. But he'd never been lonely for someone in particular.

Then Cara showed up, and without her knowledge she passed on to him a long and healthy life of true loneliness.

The lonesomeness tempted him to…

He stopped himself cold, growled softly, and went to the kitchen. Lightning flashed across the sky, immediately followed by a loud boom of thunder. He thought he heard a phone ring. Setting his mug on the table, he cocked his head, listening. He did hear a phone ring. Three. Four. Five rings. Then silence.

Inside his dark home he waited. The phone rang again. He grabbed his black felt hat and flew out the door. Five rings, a pause, and then more rings meant it wasn't a business call or a wrong number. It was someone trying to reach him. He bolted across the soaked field and driveway. Fumbling through the dark, he grabbed the phone.

"Hello."

"Ephraim." Ada's voice held concern. "I'm in a little fix."

"What's up?"

"Cara went for a walk, but then the skies opened up. She's been gone over two hours. The creek's flooded. I'm watching Lori, and Deborah's not here, so I'm not sure what to do."

"I'll hire a driver and be there as soon as I can. Whatever you do, don't leave Lori, and don't try to cross that creek with her in tow."

Ephraim called half a dozen drivers before finding Bill at home. He arrived within ten minutes. In another fifteen Ephraim was climbing out of the car at Ada's house. She opened the door for him.

"Has she returned?" Ephraim had to yell to be heard over the pouring rain.

Ada motioned him in, leaving the door open for Bill to follow. "No. She was pretty upset when she left here."

"Why?"

"We were talking, and she had her mother's Bible in hand, the one her dad mailed to her. She found a note in it. I think she was shaking when she looked at me and said, 'He's real.' Then she bolted."

Excitement poured into him, making his head spin for a moment. But if learning she had relatives in Dry Lake was stressful, realizing God was real had to be hundreds of times more emotional. "Where was she headed?"

"I don't know, but she went through the pasture where that winding creek is sure to catch her. As a city girl, will she understand how danger-ous the currents get in weather like this?"

Ephraim knew where she'd gone, but Ada's question worried him. "I'll take your horse."

"You want help?" Bill asked.

"No. We only have one horse, and it's too dangerous on foot. I'll find her." He hurried down the steps.

"Ephraim," Ada hollered through the pouring rain. He stopped. She motioned to him and then disappeared back inside. When he reached her door, she passed him a quilt and a two-way radio. "Let me know the minute you find her. If I don't hear from you within an hour, I'll call the police."

Ephraim spoke what he prayed would be true. "You'll hear from me."

Riding bareback, he spurred the horse along the muddy trail. Thunder rumbled in the distance as the rain slowed. When he came to the creek, he found it had flooded its banks and spanned into the lowlands of the pasture. As he carefully guided the horse through the shallowest area, he tried to block thoughts of Cara struggling to cross and being swept downstream. Soon the horse was on the other side. "Cara!" He cupped his hands around his mouth and called to her.

He wondered how she felt about her discovery. The problem with believing was it changed everything inside a person without altering the past. And sometimes it didn't change the present either—only the person's heart.

Even under the canopy of trees, large scattered drops pelted him. He pulled his felt hat down tighter and kept the horse moving forward along the slippery trail. "Cara!" he called against the rain, but his voice didn't carry far.

Through a clearing he spotted the old barn she loved so much. Hoping he'd find her safe, he felt peace warm him. When he came within a hundred feet of the barn, a flash of lightning illuminated the fields briefly, but he didn't see any sign of her. He spurred the horse onward. "Cara!"

The barn door opened. She stood in the entryway with dripping wet hair and clothes. He urged the horse toward the barn. She stepped back, giving the animal room to enter the rugged structure. He tugged on the reins and came to a halt.

When she looked up at him, hope and longing tempted him to say things he knew he shouldn't.

"He's real." Her tone sounded both certain and surprised.

Too emotional to speak, he pointed to a wooden cattle gate behind her, and then he held out his hand. With the rain pouring and the creek rising, they needed to get to the valley and cross over before the currents grew too strong, or they could end up stranded on this side for the next day or two. She climbed up several rungs of craggy gate and took his hand. He pulled her onto the horse behind him.

He passed her the blanket and waited while she draped it around her. He shifted so he could look into her eyes.

Using the blanket she wiped rain off her face. "Just for a second I saw a man. He...He died so that no one would be separated from Him the way I was from my family." In spite of her proclamation, confusion was reflected in her eyes.

Ephraim placed his hat on her head and brushed one finger down her cheek, feeling more connected to her than to his own self. He squared himself on the horse. She wrapped her arms around him and laid her cheek on his back. He pulled the two-way radio out of his pocket. "Ada."

"I'm here. Have you found her?"

"Yes. We're heading back."

He slid the two-way into his pocket. With one hand he guided the horse, and with the other he kept his hand on hers, glad the darkness and rain hid the tears that stung his eyes.

She was safe.

And she believed.

The creek water swirled higher and faster when he crossed the second time, but soon they were in Ada's barn, and he was helping Cara off the horse. She passed his hat back to him. The place smelled of fresh hay. Bundled in the wet quilt, Cara leaned against a stall, watching him wipe the horse down with an old towel.

He tossed extra oats into the horse's trough. "I...just want you to know you shouldn't feel the need to be Amish." He tossed hay into the stall and closed the gate. "You're free to go wherever. Join wherever."

"Thank you, 'From. For everything."

He wrapped her in his arms, feeling her tremble even through the blanket. "You scared me." He propped his cheek against her head, and they stood, watching the rain.

Forty-Two

Deborah put the finishing touches of frosting on the last cake, hoping she and Ada had enough goodies for tonight. It seemed the perfect way to spend Labor Day—baking and preparing for company. Ada was out front, tending to her flower garden, and Cara had gone for a long walk with Lori. All of them giving Deborah a few minutes alone before she had to greet a houseful of people—friends, family, and near strangers who knew about Mahlon running out on her.

Even though longing for him still held her prisoner some days, she'd grown weary of being embarrassed over what he'd done to her. She talked to Ada about the shame they both carried, and they admitted to only going out when necessary. So they decided to have an open house, welcoming Amish from both districts—Dry Lake and Hope Crossing.

Cara was right; it wasn't Deborah's or Ada's fault that Mahlon hadn't cherished them or the Old Order lifestyle.

The word *cherished* made her thoughts turn to Ephraim. Since the church leaders had lifted the ban from him, he'd probably come tonight too—if for no other reason than to catch a glimpse of Cara. It wasn't always easy, but Deborah said nothing to either of them about the other. They'd asked that of her, and she'd stuck to it. But she didn't need a conversation with Ephraim to know he was in love, and Cara didn't seem to know it.

The church leaders had insisted Ephraim return to Dry Lake in mid-June, and it was now early September, yet he'd already returned to the status of being a member in good standing. Deborah agreed with the bishop's point on the matter—it'd be hypocrisy to continue punishing Ephraim for handling Cara's situation wrong when all of them had been wrong concerning her in one way or another. Even though Ephraim had permission to see Cara, he'd yet to do so. He didn't want to influence her decision of whether to choose the Old Ways or not, so he kept his distance. But he'd told Deborah it drove him crazy.

Thankfully, Daed's health was still improving, so he had been some real help to Ephraim after Mahlon left without notice. That took some weight off Ephraim and gave Daed some of his self-respect back. With business booming like it was, Ephraim was looking to hire Amish men outside of Dry Lake.

When Deborah heard a horse and buggy stop near the house, she glanced at the clock. Whoever had just arrived had come much earlier than expected. She looked through the window and saw Lena heading for the house. Her beautiful cousin never seemed bothered by the blue birthmark across her cheek. Deborah was slowly and painfully adjusting to the idea of being alone, but she couldn't imagine what Lena felt—twenty-three years old and had never been asked out. Warmth wrapped around Deborah as she finally grasped what Lena always said—it's not about what's on her face that makes people whisper or the men avoid her. It's about what's in their own hearts.

Mahlon left because of his heart, and Deborah was ready to admit she'd never really known him. But now, nearly three months later, she knew a time would come when she'd be grateful to be free of him. But her love for Ada grew with each passing week.

The back door opened, and Lena stepped inside. "Oh my, it smells good in here." She held the door open, and Jonathan soon appeared, carrying a keg on his shoulder.

He set the barrel on the floor. "Hey, Little Debbie. I made a batch of the good stuff. Thought you might want a strong drink to get you through the next few hours."

It seemed odd that he understood tonight wouldn't be easy for her. "How strong?"

"Extra lemons, less sugar."

She puckered her lips and made a smacking sound. "Jonathan's famous lemonade gone sourer just for me."

He dipped his finger in the almost empty bowl of frosting and placed it in his mouth. "Man, I miss you and Ada being right up the street from me."

"Ya, but we make a profit now."

Lena laughed. "You say he kept eating the profits?"

"Hello?" Anna Mary's voice echoed from the back steps.

"In here." Deborah stepped to the doorway and saw Rachel, Linda, Nancy, Lydia, Frieda, and Esther. They were all together again, and it'd never felt this good.

"Hi." Anna Mary hugged her. "We rode with Jonathan, but we got off the wagon out front and talked with Ada for a bit."

"We all came early to help you and Ada get ready," Rachel said.

Anna Mary looked around the room conspiratorially. "And to make sure we're in place early to scope out any single men who come from Hope Crossing."

The girls laughed, but Deborah knew it couldn't have been easy for Anna Mary to come tonight either. Cara lived here, and if Ephraim showed up, which he was likely to do, it'd be tough on Anna Mary. Yet here she stood.

Strength seeped into every part of Deborah, and she passed a ladle to Jonathan. He opened the lid to the keg while Deborah grabbed a stack of plastic cups and passed one to each girl.

Deborah set a bowl of ice on the table. "So, Jonathan, you brought eight girls with you, four of which are totally single, and it sounds like not a one of them is interested in someone from Dry Lake."

"That's okay." Jonathan dipped a ladle into citrusy liquid. "I'm not interested in anyone living in Dry Lake either."

Lena chuckled as he filled her cup with the shimmering yellow juice.

Ada walked into the kitchen from the front hallway. "So where are Cara and Lori?"

Deborah passed a cup of lemonade to Ada. "They went for a long walk. Cara wanted to be sure Better Days was tired so he'd stay settled as people come in and out."

When everyone held a cup of lemonade in hand, Jonathan raised his. "To Ada's house—"

"Ada's House!" Deborah interrupted him. She turned to Ada. "That's what this place needs—a good name, ya?"

"Ada's House?" Ada looked a little unsure, and then she broke into a huge smile. "Ada's House." She lifted her cup toward Jonathan.

He smiled. "To Ada's House. May God bless it beyond all they can ask or imagine."

Deborah knew well Jonathan's favorite Bible passage, the one he'd just spoken a few words from—Ephesians 3:20. She'd never been touched by those words like he always had, but this time they took on new meaning. She took a sip of the lemonade as the words filled her with hope and dreams of what lay ahead.

Ada placed her arm around Deborah's back. "He already has blessed me above what I'd asked or dreamed, because of you," Ada whispered.

Deborah raised her eyebrows, playfully. "But I'm open to even more. Ya?"

Ada laughed and nodded. "If you are, I am."

Ephraim ran his hand across the wood in front of him, removing the dusting of sawdust. Thoughts of Cara lingered continually. And rumors about her swirled like mad. Some said the church leaders intended to welcome her into the Amish community. Others said that there were two single Amish men in Hope Crossing eager to court her and that the Riehls were trying to build a relationship with her.

He'd love to be first in line to court her. Actually, he'd like to be the only one in line. But he wouldn't pursue her.

When she first entered his home, she'd made it clear she didn't want to owe him anything. He understood what had happened with Johnny— Cara marrying him for protection and a roof over her head without being in love with him. But even as he reminded himself of his stance, every part of him longed to see her, to tell her how he felt.

She wasn't the same person she would have been if she'd been raised Old Order. Innocence and trust had been stripped from her, one bad experience after another. Still, he found even her less-than-trusting attitude fascinating. She beckoned him so much it scared him.

He drew a deep breath and set the tools in their place. Maybe he should go to Deborah's gathering and at least get a few minutes with Cara. She should know he wasn't seeing Anna Mary anymore, shouldn't she?

Was that too self-serving?

Still unsure what he should or shouldn't say to her, he went into his office and dialed Robbie. No sense in taking an hour to get to Hope Crossing when Robbie could have him there in ten minutes.

In her caped dress, black apron, and bare feet, Cara spoke to Deborah's visitors before she walked past them and to the front porch. They seemed like a nice group, even Anna Mary, who was clearly uncomfortable around Cara—not that she blamed her. A lot had taken place between Cara and Ephraim, and whether he'd told Anna Mary about it or not, she had to sense it.

The sun danced through the leaves as the late-afternoon shadows of September fell across the yard. It didn't matter how hard she tried not to, she missed Ephraim just as much now as when the church leaders came here to reason with him and he returned to Dry Lake in mid-June.

She'd talked to him briefly and only a couple of times since the night she was caught in that rainstorm. Had anything ever felt as powerful and right as being in his arms while they watched the rain? But if he came tonight, he'd spend his time with Anna Mary.

Regardless of Ephraim or anything or anyone else, Cara was close to joining the faith. A few things nagged at her. She'd talked to Deborah and Ada about putting down roots of her own in Hope Crossing after she finished working on the house. Ada said that'd be quite a while, but then she said if Cara wanted to stay near them and yet live as an Englischer, the storage rooms above the carriage house could be refinished for her, and electricity and a phone could be added.

They were of the same mind-set as Ephraim—joining the Amish faith wasn't necessary to being a part of their lives. She leaned back against a porch column and closed her eyes. With each passing week more of her wanted to join the faith. It had aspects she wouldn't find easy—like never cutting her hair, wearing black stockings even in summer, answering to a church leader as her authority, and trying to understand the language. But she'd grown accustomed to most of their ways.

A man cleared his throat, and she jolted. Two men in black suits stood in front of her. Since the hitching posts and space for the carriages were around back, she hadn't expected anyone to come in or out the front door. She recognized one of them and realized she should greet them more properly, so she jumped to her feet.

The familiar man held out his hand. "My name's Sol Fisher. I'm Ephraim's bishop."

She wondered how odd she must look to them with short hair and no Kapp but in an Amish dress. She shook his hand. "I'm Cara Moore. Malinda Riehl's daughter."

"Yes, we know." He gestured to the man next to him. "This is Jacob King. He's a deacon in Hope Crossing."

She shook his hand too. "Ada's inside, as well as Deborah. Others too. Did you want me to call one of them?"

"We'll visit with them in a bit. First we'd like to talk to you." Sol ran his hand down his gray beard. "Ephraim was wrong to have you in his home unsupervised. Do you understand that?"

More than ever. She nodded.

The man drew a deep breath. "That's a serious matter. But I ask you to forgive me for being so upset with him that I didn't see you—the one who needed our help. I didn't look beyond your outward appearance or the rumors. If he hadn't reached out to you, none of us would have. I apologize for that."

Remembering her words to Ephraim—that she'd believe there was a God if the bishop apologized—she had to suppress her amusement. "Thank you."

Jacob stepped forward. "You need to say, 'I forgive you.' It's the Amish way."

Trying to say the words, she realized how humbling some of the Amish ways were. "I forgive you."

He held out his hand again. "I stand before Him forgiven. Thank you."

"Is it that easy?"

"No, but it's the first step. I'll wrestle with regret and you with feelings of resentment at times. But we've begun the journey by an act of our will and faith. If you need to talk about it more, my door will always be open to you."

Jacob nodded. "A fine first step you've taken, Cara."

Feeling awkward and out of place, she couldn't think of anything to say.

"We've been keeping an eye on you since you moved in with Ada," Jacob said. "You've come to a few services with her and Deborah."

"Yes."

"Since your mother was Amish and she wanted you raised in our faith," Jacob continued, "we feel you should know that we have no reservations if you want to consider becoming one of us. I brought you a schedule and a map to each home where services will be held."

Sol nodded. "It's not easy to live as we do, and it should not be considered lightly, but we're here to answer any of your questions."

"Thank you."

"And you're welcome to visit and move about either community. Of course we will come see you if an issue of improper behavior arises."

She had come to accept that rules were a part of every society and that if they accomplished a lofty goal, they were worth it. And it was clear that living Amish had more promise than it did restrictions.

A desire to see Ephraim swept over her. She wanted to tell him the bishop had apologized. Far, far more than that, she was tired of missing him. The men went inside, and Cara sat on the porch again, thinking everything through.

Lori would love joining the faith. It was all she ever talked about. She already wore Amish dresses to public school and didn't care what the other kids thought. She'd never liked wearing pants, which used to frustrate Cara. Once Cara went through all she needed to in order to join, Lori could go to the one-room Amish schoolhouse not far from here. She'd love that too. But none of those things were why Cara wanted to join the faith.

It was an odd way to live, but she understood the value of it.

Robbie's car pulled to the curb, and Ephraim got out.

The hardest thing in becoming Amish would be knowing it'd make no difference between her and Ephraim. But if Deborah could see her future without Mahlon, Cara could find a way to see hers without Ephraim. Even so, she wanted to tell him about her decision to join the faith before she told anyone else, and she wanted to tell him about some of the Amish skills Deborah and Ada had been teaching her.

Anna Mary would just have to deal with her talking to Ephraim.

He ambled up the sidewalk, a half grin across his handsome face. "Hey."

"Hi."

He stopped at the foot of the steps. "What are you doing out here by yourself?"

"Wishing you were here to talk to. Got a minute?"

His gray blue eyes mesmerized her, and she tried to slow her heart. He took a seat beside her. "I have all evening."

"I don't think Anna Mary will appreciate that sentiment."

He propped his forearms on his knees. "Well, that's sort of what I came to tell you. Anna Mary and I have stopped seeing each other."

Her heart went crazy. "What? Why didn't Deborah tell me?"

"Because I asked her not to."

"Why?"

"Reasons we should probably talk about in a few months, okay?"

"Yeah. I knew Anna Mary would be hurt and angry, but I didn't think she'd dump you for being friendly to me."

"She didn't, and can we change the subject?"

"Not yet. When did you two break up?"

"Before you moved out of my place."

"Three months ago?"

He nodded. "So what did you want to talk to me about?"

She blinked, trying to gain control of her emotions. Could he read in her expression the hope she felt? "Oh yeah. Uh. The bishop came by. Not only did he welcome me to attend the church meetings and to consider joining the faith, he apologized."

Ephraim chuckled. "So does this mean you believe in God now?"

She laughed. "Can we go for a walk?"

"Sure."

"Give me a minute to check on Lori and make sure Ada will watch her for me. Last I checked, Lori was in the kitchen sitting in Deborah's lap." Cara hurried into the house, made arrangements with Ada, grabbed her sweater, and bounded out the door.

Without a word spoken she and Ephraim headed for their favorite spot. "If Anna Mary's not the issue and I'm not taboo anymore, why are you staying away?"

Laughing, he tilted his head heavenward. Then he mocked a sigh. "Why don't you just say what's on your mind?"

"Obviously one of us has to."

"You know why. I don't want to pressure or influence you in the choices that lie ahead."

"That was good thinking, but I've already made my choices."

Ephraim stepped in front of her and stopped. "Well?"

"Ah, so you left me hanging for months, thinking you still had a girl-friend, but you want my answer right now?"

"I'd have preferred an answer long before you even knew you needed to give one. And I've been unbelievably patient."

"You word things in a way that's very hard to argue with."

"And yet it never stops you, does it?"

"Shut up, 'From. I'm trying to tell you something." She pinned a lock of hair behind one ear. "I intend to join the faith."

He didn't smile or move or anything.

"The world has nothing to offer that could ever mean anything to me like being a part of a community that holds the same values."

His eyes moved over her face. "How sure are you?"

"Completely."

He studied her, and slowly a lopsided smile hinted at what she wanted to know—hope for who they might be was the reason he'd stopped seeing Anna Mary.

"I've missed you so much, Ephraim."

He took her hands into his, looking oddly shy. "Everything is empty without you. I'd like to start coming here more, and maybe one day you'll feel comfortable coming to Dry Lake."

Cara finally had one untarnished moment of complete happiness. "Like dating?"

He nodded. "What's the English word for when you're not seeing but one person?"

"Exclusive."

"Ya, that's it."

"Worried about me becoming interested in other Amish guys, are you, 'From?"

He released one of her hands and brushed her cheek with his fingers. "Maybe a little."

Forty-Three

Cara washed the supper dishes while Lori dried them and passed each item to Deborah to put away. Ada stood inside the walk-in pantry, going over the list of tomorrow's baked goods and matching that against the ingredients.

The bishop had come to see her last night, and she was bursting with news to tell Ephraim. It'd only been three weeks since the bishop had visited on Labor Day, and yet he'd been back to tell her good things.

Deborah placed a dish in the cabinet. "I miss Ephraim being here tonight. He hasn't skipped a day of coming since Labor Day."

"I know. All of us going to the top of the mountain and stargazing every night has been so great I feel spoiled." Cara barely wiped her wet hand against her black apron before she tucked a wisp of hair behind her ear. Even with a hair net, pins, and a prayer Kapp, her short hair found its way free.

"Don't think I'm climbing that mountain again tonight." From inside the pantry, Ada half griped and half laughed the words. "Where is he, anyway?"

Cara rinsed a glass. "He's working late, something about hardware for a set of cabinets didn't come in on time. I'm a bit tempted to just show up and help him. Anyone up for the drive to Dry Lake?"

Deborah took a plate from Lori. "I need to visit Daed. Ada, you want to ride with us?"

She stepped out of the pantry. "I told Lori I'd teach her how to sew some doll clothes tonight."

"We're gonna make my doll an Amish dress just like mine."

Deborah put the last item in the cabinet. "Ephraim will be surprised to see you in Dry Lake. I was beginning to think it'd be six months before you crossed that border."

"Ephraim says I'm stubborn. Sometimes I think he's right."

Ada dropped her list and mocked complete shock. "You? He had to be mistaken."

Deborah pulled her lips in, trying not to laugh. "I'll go pack to stay at Daed's for the night. You can share my clothes and my bedroom. You get the horse hitched."

"We're going *and* staying the night?"

"It'll be good for you. You need some time around Daed and Becca."

Cara dried her hands and tossed the towel into the dish drainer. "I guess. I mean, if you say so."

Deborah put her arm around Cara and hugged her. "You and Lori have family and friends in Dry Lake. Get used to it." Deborah smiled, but tears brimmed. "Go get ready. Ephraim will love being surprised. You do know none of us have ever seen Ephraim so…well… I've never seen him even slightly crazy about anyone. I always figured it was just who he was—unable to care passionately about anyone."

Lori grabbed Ada's notepad off the floor. "He loves me and Mom."

Cara's heart startled, and she looked to Deborah and then to Ada. "He said that?"

"Yeah," Lori said. "And he hopes we'll be a family someday. But he doesn't think you're ready to talk about that yet."

Cara chuckled. "I guess I better keep you around, kiddo, so you can keep me posted on things."

Lori helped Cara hitch the horse to the buggy. Her daughter and Ada waved as Cara and Deborah drove out of sight. It was freeing to have people in Lori's life that she fully trusted. She asked Deborah a dozen things about the Amish lifestyle as they spent more than an hour getting to Dry Lake—things like how a preacher, deacon, or bishop was chosen, how the Amish always seemed to find work among their own, why some of the younger girls wore the aprons and some didn't. Soon they were nearing Levina's old place.

"Hey, Deb, why don't you let me off here at the conjoined trees?"

"Okay." Deborah pulled the buggy to a stop. "But whatever you do, don't go to my brother's place and fall asleep."

"Very funny. Just tell him someone's hanging around the barn with a batch of puppies. That'll make him head this way."

"It could make him run for the hills."

"Then I'll be in that tree waiting all night." She jumped down from the buggy and ran to the tree. A dozen memories flooded her as Deborah drove off. Wishing she had on jeans, she managed to climb it, then she rocked back against the trunk and waited.

Ephraim glanced up from the wood in front of him, catching another glimpse of his sister. She looked better every time he saw her. He wasn't naive enough to think the grief was totally behind her, but it didn't own all of her anymore. Cara had been very good for her. A little of her New York, in-your-face toughness could go a long way in helping someone like his sister.

Deborah stood in the doorway of the shop. "You need to go to Levina's barn." She'd said the same thing a few minutes ago. He ran the plane across the flat surface, removing a bit of wood. "I'm busy."

His sister huffed. "If it wasn't important, I wouldn't have mentioned it."

Her tone startled him, and he laughed. "I do believe I just heard Cara in your voice."

"Ya, I think you did. G'night, Ephraim." The screen door to the shop slapped loudly as his sister left.

He drew a deep breath and set the tools in their place. Maybe he should check out what was going on at the barn. Walking through the dried cornfield, he thought of the first time he'd met Cara. If she'd lived in Dry Lake as she should have, they'd have married years ago. He probably wouldn't have courted anyone else. She spoke to his soul like no other. They fit.

The more time they had together, the more time they wanted. And he knew it'd be that way for the rest of their lives.

As he came out of the edge of the cornfield, he saw movement in the tree.

"A girl could spend a lot of time up here waiting for you to come by."

His heart filled with pleasure as he stepped forward. "It's almost too dark to see you, and I started not to come this way at all, but like my Daadi always said, even a blind squirrel can find a nut every once in a while."

"Are you calling me a nut, Ephraim?"

He moved closer. "What are you doing up there?"

"Waiting for you."

He propped the palm of his hand against the trunk. "I'm here. Are you coming down?"

"Nope. I have things I want to know first."

"Like how hard you'll hit the ground if you fall out of that tree?" Wondering if she had any idea what she'd done to his heart, he leaned back against the tree. "Fire away."

"I'll be allowed to go through instructions this spring."

"Really? The bishop said that?"

"Yep. You know what that means, right?"

"Ya. You'll be a member of the Old Order Amish faith come summer."

"That too."

"Too?"

"As in *also*. Meaning not the main thing."

"So what's the main thing, Cara?"

She shifted her body until her stomach was on the branch. As she clung to the thick branch and lowered herself toward the ground, Ephraim wrapped his hands around her waist and helped her make a soft landing.

They stood face to face, but he couldn't find any words.

Sliding her fingertips against the palm of his hand, she leaned against the tree. "That you can marry me next fall, or technically winter if we choose to wait that long."

Ephraim wanted to ignore prudence and kiss her, but he forced himself to think logically. "I know you're aware most Amish have large families, but have we discussed the fact that the Amish allow God to choose how many children they'll have? That's usually a breaking point for those who've been raised as Englischers."

"Are you trying to talk me out of a marriage proposal you haven't even given?"

Soft laughter rose within him. "You're something else, Cara Moore. And I want nothing but more time with you and more of your heart. But you've got to understand some things."

"I understand. You hope to get lucky often enough to have lots of children, and you're trying to make sure I agree to that now."

"You know what I really think?"

"No, but I bet you're going to tell me."

He placed one hand on her waist. "I think you're in love with me."

"You *think*? You mean you don't know?"

Could his heart beat any faster? "I hoped."

"You'll still have to wait like thirteen or so months from now." She pointed a finger at him. "But you will wait for me."

He cupped her face in his hands. "And why would I do that?"

"Because you're in love with me."

He brought his lips to hers, feeling the power of things he'd always hoped for. "I am. You're absolutely right about that. I think maybe I always have been, so waiting until the next wedding season isn't all that bad."

Ada's House Series

Main Characters

Cara Atwater Moore—twenty-eight-year-old waitress from New York City who lost her mother as a child, was abandoned by her father, and grew up in foster care. Cara has been stalked for years by Mike Snell.

Lori Moore—Cara's seven-year-old daughter. Lori's father, Johnny, died before she turned two years old, leaving Cara a widow.

Malinda Riehl Atwater—Cara's mother.

Trevor Atwater—Cara's alcoholic father.

Levina—Malinda's grandmother who raised her from infancy.

Ephraim Mast—thirty-two-year-old single Amish man who works as a cabinetmaker and helps manage his ailing father's business and care for their large family.

Deborah Mast—twenty-one-year-old Amish woman who is in love with Mahlon Stoltzfus. She's Ephraim's sister.

Abner Mast—Ephraim and Deborah's father, Becca's husband.

Becca Mast—Ephraim and Deborah's stepmother, and the mother of two of their stepsiblings and four of their half siblings.

Anna Mary Lantz—Ephraim's girlfriend.

Rueben Lantz—Anna Mary's father.

Leah Lantz—Anna Mary's mother.

Mahlon Stoltzfus—twenty-three-year-old Amish man who works with Ephraim and is Deborah Mast's longtime beau.

Ada Stoltzfus—Forty-three-year-old widow who is Mahlon's mother, and she's a friend and mentor to Deborah Mast.

Better Days —a mixed-breed pup: part Blue Heeler, black Lab, and Chow, resembling the author's dog, Jersey.

Robbie—an Englischer who is a co-worker and driver for Ephraim's cabinetry business.

Israel Kauffman—a forty-five-year-old Amish widower.

Acknowledgments

Each novel is a journey filled with long months of writing alone, but if it weren't for the following people, Cara's story would never have become worthy of publication:

To my husband, who continually opens many more doors for me than the physical ones of a car, home, or business. I'm grateful you've shared over three decades of reality with me—the fulfilling, the satisfying, the difficult, and the yet unseen.

To my dearly beloved Old Order Amish friends who wish to remain anonymous. Your honest answers, insights, and determination have caused me to write Cara's story with great authenticity, which means so very, very much to me. From the most difficult questions during our first sit-down meeting to your review of the finished work, you've been good friends and willing co-workers. Thank you.

To Marci Burke, who always finds time to do critique rounds even in the midst of a continually growing, successful career. As vital as your input is in each story, your friendship means numerous times more.

To Timothy A. Scully, MD, FACC, Northeast Georgia Heart Center, PC, Vice Chief of Staff, Northeast Georgia Medical Center, Gainesville, GA, who shared his knowledge and insight into medical conditions that affect the heart. You wove your expertise in with my story line until I had solid medical advice for every situation. Thank you!

To my editor, Shannon (Hill) Marchese, who works diligently so readers can share in her love of books. I'm continually amazed at you.

To WaterBrook Multnomah Publishing Group—marketing, sales, production, and editorial departments—who used their expertise, talent, and energy to get this novel into readers' hands. It is an honor to work with you!

To my line editor, Carol Bartley, who always helps me see the story through fresh eyes. Your task to help me find a balance between realistic-sounding characters and grammatically correct prose is never an easy one. Denki!

To my agent, Steve Laube, who always understands the heart of a writer, offers perfect solutions to the influx of issues, and who stands sentry at all times. My family sends their gratitude.

The
BRIDGE
of
PEACE

An Ada's House Novel

CINDY
WOODSMALL

*In loving memory of the best, most dedicated
teacher in my life—my mom.*

*You were strong, gentle, wise, and flawed. You taught me to
read, write, and never give up on God. You taught me to
cherish friendships, be stalwart in hardships, and take great
pleasure in the little things life offers. I am grateful for
everything you took time to teach me, and I'm grateful for
everything I learned while you were simply being you.
It was your passing that caused me to begin writing,
for when I lost you, I lost a part of me:
I'll miss you forever.*

One

Quiet hung in the air inside the one-room schoolhouse as the children waited on Lena's next action. The curiosity she loved to stir in her scholars now filled their minds in ways she wished she could erase. The hush wasn't out of respect or desk work or learning.

Staring into defiant eyes, she stood. "Return to your seat, Peter."

With his back to the other students, he leaned across her oak desk. "Make me." The threat in his voice was undeniable. She'd spoken to his parents about his behavior, but they'd believed that their son was only kidding and that she was taking his words and actions all wrong.

Nothing about the conduct of this six-foot man-child hinted at humor. He wasn't teasing, but he was toying with her—like her barn cats did with field mice before killing their prey.

Feeling as unsightly as a wounded rodent was part of daily life for her. It even slipped into her dreams on a regular basis. But Lena was no mouse. When dealing with Peter, her will battled with her emotions. The teacher in her wanted to find a way to reach inside him, to get beyond the prejudices and surliness and find something of value. The rest of her simply wished he'd never moved to Dry Lake.

Still, she believed that most people had hidden wealth, good things within that made them more worthy than they appeared on the outside. For reasons that had nothing to do with Peter, she had to hold on to that belief.

She offered a teacher-friendly smile. "The assignment stands, and it's due tomorrow. Take your seat, please."

He slid her well-organized papers onto the floor and crawled onto her desk and sat. At fifteen he was the oldest student she'd ever taught—or *tried* to teach. He should have graduated sixteen months ago from an Amish school in Ohio, where he'd lived before moving to Dry Lake. Although she had no idea what happened to put him so far behind in his studies, he seemed to think *she* was the problem.

It would be easier to tap into his better self, or at least better behavior, if there was someone to send him to when he got this bad. During her *rumschpringe,* her running-around years, she'd used her freedoms to attend public high school. When her public school teachers faced a difficult student like Peter, they sent him to another teacher, a counselor, or a principal. If there was another adult nearby, Peter probably wouldn't consider it a game to try to take control of her class. Maybe she needed to talk about this situation with her *Englischer* friend Samantha. Surely with her degree in psychology and her working this year as a school counselor, she would know some helpful tips.

"At your desk, Peter."

"I'm not doing the work, and I better not get a zero."

She swallowed and drew a breath, refusing the temptation to scream at him. "You have the right to decide your actions, or maybe a better word is *inactions,* but you do not have the right to insist on what grade I can give." Hoping to continue with class, Lena walked around the desk and settled her attention on the first-grade students.

"Who has their penmanship papers done?" Her three first-grade scholars raised their hands. "Good."

She could feel Peter behind her, seething with anger that had little to do with her. Wondering if she should face him or keep her focus on teaching, she took Marilyn's spiral-bound notebook in hand and began looking over the young girl's work. "To your desk, Peter," she repeated as she made a smiley face at the top of Marilyn's page.

His breath was hot on the back of her neck as he whispered, "You won't win, so don't even try."

The threat unleashed her anger, and suddenly she became its slave. Even while telling herself to ignore him as he was finally making his way toward his desk, she spun around. "You're a bully, Peter. Do you understand that about yourself?"

His face and eyes became like stone. "I'll convince the school board you're the problem. They're already whispering behind your back about how to get rid of you. I bet they only hired you because they felt sorry for you. I mean, what else would someone like you do, marry?"

His personal attack caused a storm of insecurities about her looks to rise within. But that aside, she was sure he was wrong about the school board wanting to get rid of her. She'd made one good-sized error they'd not been pleased with, but surely…

He slapped the side of his face really hard and laughed. "Look, I'm making my face blotchy like Teacher Lena's."

The younger students looked horrified as he mocked her. Some of the older boys laughed, but most were clearly embarrassed for her. Peter kept smacking the side of his face, egging on the class to laugh at his antics.

"Mandy and Rachel,"—Lena looked to the oldest girls in the class— "please take everyone outside for a brief recess."

Peter sat on her desk again, but at least he'd hushed. Smirking, but silent. The room filled with the sounds of desks shifting slightly and the rustle of clothing and soft, padded shoes as her scholars went outside. Willing her irritation to calm, she took several deep breaths and focused her thoughts on what could be accomplished with patience and effort. Good memories of teaching moved into her mind. At twenty-three years old, she'd been teaching for five years, and with only a few exceptions, she'd basked in the fulfillment of it.

Soon her scholars were outside, and the room was quiet.

"I don't want to embarrass you in front of the class, Peter. I only wish you'd show that same respect to me. If you want to color the side of your face to match mine, there are still a few blueberries on the vine out back, but nothing you do to your face will alter the real problem, will it?"

"Not unless you quit."

"How will getting a new teacher solve anything? Why don't you try fighting against the part of you that has no regard for your future."

"I hate this place." He picked up a book and hurled it across the room.

Lena flinched as the text hit the ground, but she forced her voice to remain calm. "I understand that learning doesn't come easy for you, but I can help you overcome—"

"Learning comes plenty easy," Peter interrupted. "I just ain't interested."

She knew he struggled to learn, and maybe Samantha would have some suggestions about this too, but Lena's best chance of reaching him wouldn't be found in trying to make him admit to his difficulties. "Why not?"

"What do you care?"

"If I knew why, maybe I could help change how you feel."

He rolled his eyes. "I don't want your help. *Mamm* says I can't stop coming to school just because of my age, so I just want to pass the eighth grade this time and get out of here."

"Then do your work. If you're struggling, I'll help you."

"You teachers are all alike. You say that, but…"

Piercing screams of young girls vibrated the room, and Lena moved to the window. Aaron Blank's meanspirited bull stood mere feet from the ragged fence that separated the pasture from the playground. Elmer, a third-grade student, seemed to be harassing the animal with two eighth-grade students egging him on. She hurried past desks and ran outside. The older students banged on the metal gate with their hands while cheering for Elmer. The third grader poked a stick against the angry creature's face and nose while the younger girls squealed with fear and excitement.

Enraged, the Holstein tossed his head back and forth, slinging spit and mucus as it stormed at the stick, coming closer to the fence with each move.

"Boys, stop that right now." While Lena hurried toward the boys, the older girls left the first and second graders at the swing set and ran toward them as well. Clearly the girls hadn't been watching this group. Aaron had promised her that he'd fix the fence and keep this bull out of the pasture that bordered the school. Moving to a spot between the angry bull and the students, Lena took the stick from Elmer. She gestured for the children to back up. "Everyone return to the classroom. We'll discuss this inside."

As Mandy and Rachel encouraged the others to go inside, Lena turned to look at the bull. The massive creature could easily plow through the pitiful wire fence.

"One would think they'd know better," she mumbled quietly, taking a few moments of serenity to gather herself. "Why would they do such a thing?" She glanced up to see Peter standing in the doorway, watching her. He was probably hoping the bull would come through the fence and destroy her. She sighed. *I think I'm looking at the source of influence over those other boys.* After a quick, silent prayer of thanks for everyone's safety, she tossed the stick onto the woodpile and headed inside. Her students often hit a baseball or sometimes even a volleyball into this field and went after it. What if someone had done so today while others had that bull riled?

It was time for a lesson in using good sense. Surely even Peter couldn't keep them from seeing the wisdom of not provoking the bull. But Peter had many of them viewing her with as much disrespect as he did. How she looked had nothing to do with the job in front of her—arming her scholars with skills that would serve them all their lives and keeping them safe while they were in her care.

After school she'd drop off a few of the children at their homes and then do something refreshing before going to see Aaron about keeping that bull away from the schoolhouse.

As Grey left his barn and crossed the driveway, he smelled supper cooking—probably fried chicken by the aroma of it. Pieces of freshly mowed grass that were almost too small to see were scattered throughout the lawn. The porch and walkways were spotless, and the windows sparkled as the sun moved low on the horizon. A familiar, tainted feeling rose within him as he opened the screen door to his home.

His wife stood beside the oven, scouring a nearby countertop. She glanced at the clock and then to him. "Hey." Her eyes moved over his clothing, and he knew the quick study of his outfit was to assess just how dirty he was today. She returned to the task in front of her.

"Hi." He set his lunchpail in the sink. "Where's Ivan?"

"At your Mamm's."

He nodded. The light in their five-year-old son's eyes strengthened Grey. After he removed the plastic containers from his lunchpail, he rinsed them. "Been there all day?"

"Just since he got up from his nap. Supper will be ready by the time you're showered."

Inside her softly spoken sentence, he'd been dismissed and given respectful instructions to come to the table clean. He needed to bathe and change clothes before the school board meeting anyway, so he went to his bedroom. While working in the cabinetry shop, he'd seen Lena Kauffman drop children off at the Mast house. He'd considered stepping out and speaking to her for a minute to try to get a feel for her side of the complaints the Benders were lodging against her. But if she knew the board was meeting to discuss those criticisms, she'd want to attend. Michael Blank, his father-in-law and the chairman of the school board, had said earlier this week that he intended to discover if the Benders had any real justification for their grumbling before he was willing to share any of the negative talk with Lena. Grey appreciated Michael's reasoning, but he doubted that Lena would. As a kid she'd had a fierce temper when pushed. It'd been many a year since Grey had seen it, so he was confident that hadn't played into Michael's decision.

The memory of Lena's brother provoking her beyond her control probably still stood out in a lot of people's memories. Her temper made her an easy target and caused her brother to declare war, so the harassment of Lennie became a full-time game as she was growing up. One time her brother had brought Grey and a group of friends with him on a romp through the woods. Soon enough they'd taken over an abandoned tree house. They were teens, around sixteen years old, and wanted a private place to get away from their parents, a place to talk freely and smoke a cigarette. But the playhouse was Lennie's, complete with books, papers, and a diary.

She must have heard their voices because she called out to them. When her brother realized she was climbing up the rope ladder, he'd shaken her loose, causing her to fall. Rather than going home, she raged at them while trying to climb the ladder again. Once she'd been dumped again, some of the guys pulled the ladder inside the tree house and dangled her diary and books over the sides. She'd thrown rocks at them, calling out the worst things her ten-year-old mind knew to say—that they all stunk and they looked like old mares. One of the guys began reading from her journal. Lennie's eyes filled with tears as she screamed for him to stop. Feeling sorry for her, Grey had freed her diary from the tormentors. He tossed it to her, but she kept throwing rocks through the oversized window frames until she pinged her brother a good one.

"Rumschpringe teens." Grey sighed. It was amazing the Amish community hadn't imploded from the turmoil they caused.

The dimness of the fading day settled over the quiet space as he entered the bedroom. Beige sheers fluttered gently in the late September breeze. The bedspread was tucked crisp and perfect with the pillows adjusted just so, and not one item sat on the top of his dresser. He moved into the bathroom and turned on the shower. His razors. His toothbrush. His shaving cream. His combs. All lined up perfectly on a rectangular piece of white linen.

Plush, clean towels were stacked neatly on a shelf. He grabbed one, hung it on the peg near the shower stall and peeled out of his clothes. Feeling tempted for a moment to leave his stuff on the floor, he mumbled to himself to grow up. Elsie wouldn't say a word. Conversations didn't pass the threshold of the bedroom. Ever.

As the hot water and soap rinsed the day's grime from his body, he wondered if she ever missed him.

The discomfort of the thought drained his energy. For too long he'd searched his mind and heart for answers. At twenty-eight he no longer had much youthful nonsense in him. He tried to think and act like a considerate man, but whatever was wrong lay outside his grasp to understand. Was it his fault? Was it hers? He didn't know, and sometimes he was so weary he didn't care.

But giving up would only break them worse.

Sing for me, Grey.

The memory haunted him. How long had it been since she'd wanted him to sing for her? He turned off the shower and grabbed his towel. He knew of only one possible answer for their marriage—an avenue that might bring relief—but he'd have to be willing to publicly embarrass her and himself to pursue it. There had to be another way to find answers.

Two

Deborah closed her eyes, trying to block out a reality she could not yet welcome. Heat from the gas-powered stove continued to pour into the kitchen as it had since before daylight. The orders for baked goods were almost done for the day. With her eyelids shut tight, she tried to still the fresh ache.

Not one breath of air came through the open windows or screen door. Still. Dry. Unmoving.

Exactly like her life.

He'd left.

Not only the faith. And his friends. And his mother, Ada.

But her.

Three months ago. Some days she could feel beyond the blackness and laugh again. But now was not one of them, not after receiving a note from him in today's mail. He hadn't actually written to her as much as sent money along with a scribbled apology. His admission of regret only stirred hurt and anger. He wasn't coming back. She wanted to burn the cash he'd sent. But how could she? She and his mother needed money. Badly.

The Amish community would help her and Ada if they knew of their plight. She and Ada had discussed telling their people, but now they couldn't accept anyone's hard-earned money since Mahlon had sent cash. She might not be able to make herself burn it, but she wouldn't use it. And when she told Ada about the *gift*, Ada would agree that they couldn't use it. They were on their own now. Truth was, in ways they'd not realized until after Mahlon left, they'd been on their own for a really long time.

She slid her hand inside her hidden pocket, feeling the envelope thick with twenties. Once again, Mahlon had made life harder for her and his mother.

Drawing a deep breath, she opened her eyes, grabbed the bowl of frosting, and scraped up the last dollop of it and dropped it onto the cake.

The kitchen door swung open, and Cara waltzed into the room, her Amish dress spattered with paint and much of her short hair coming loose from its stubby ponytail and sticking out around her prayer *Kapp*. The young woman carried the confidence of being happy and loved, making Deborah wonder if she'd ever feel that way again. Deborah's brother Ephraim was thirty-two when he found love for the first time in his life. And even though he broke up with Deborah's closest friend in order to pursue the Englischer girl, Deborah had grown to love Cara too.

Cara glanced through the screen door, and Deborah knew she was checking on her daughter. "You about done?" She grabbed an apple out of the refrigerator, walking and talking much like the Bronx-raised Englischer she was. Or rather *was* until recently.

Deborah motioned at the load of dishes in the sink. "No. You?"

"For the day, yes. Though I'll never be done painting as long as the little elves keep building onto this old house each night while we sleep. Do you know how long it takes to paint the inside of a two-foot-wide, nine-foot-deep space? What did they do with a room like that in the eighteen hundreds? Show it to relatives as a guest bedroom? It'd keep down on guests, right?"

Cara's nonsense made Deborah smile, and she longed to be free to enjoy her days again.

Cara took a bite of apple and sat on the countertop. "Is Ada out purchasing ingredients for tomorrow's baking orders?"

"*Ya.*"

"If I help you finish up, will you go to Dry Lake with me?"

Wondering whether to tell Cara she'd received a note from Mahlon, Deborah continued smoothing the frosting over the cake.

Cara finished her apple and then tossed it across the room and into the trash can. "Hellooooo?" She dipped her finger into the bowl and scraped some frosting off the side.

"Hmm?"

Cara licked her finger, hopped off the counter, and fixed herself a glass of water. "You made two of those cakes?"

"Ya. It's a new recipe, and I'm taking one by Select Bakery and one by Sweet Delights as a sample of a new item on our list."

Cara moved next to Deborah and nudged her shoulder against Deborah's. "It's one of those really bad days, huh?"

Deborah's eyes stung with tears, but she didn't respond.

"I expect grief will come and go for a while, but any idea why you're feeling smothered by it today?"

Deborah pulled the envelope from her pocket and held it up. "Mahlon," she whispered.

Cara's eyes grew large with concern. "Oh no." Her words came out slowly. "Deborah, I…I'm sorry." Cara pulled Deborah into a hug. The tone of Cara's voice and the warmth of her understanding surrounded her like no one else's could. Cara knew loss and imprisonment of circumstances a thousand times greater than Deborah did. Cara placed her hands on Deborah's shoulders. "Do you want to share what he said?"

It seemed a little odd how careful Cara was being with her words. Then again, maybe she thought Mahlon wrote to say he was coming back so she was withholding what she'd like to call him. Deborah passed her the envelope.

Cara pulled out the note and cash. She ignored the money and read the message. "Dearest Deborah, I hope you are well. I'm so very, very sorry for the pain I've caused you and Mamm. Please allow me to ease my guilt by helping you financially. Mahlon." Cara rolled her eyes, but she said nothing.

The note sounded just as detached as Mahlon had been in the weeks leading up to his disappearance. Hearing it aloud brought back so many memories, and Deborah felt stupid for not seeing the obvious until he humiliated her in front of everyone.

Cara replaced the money and note in the envelope. She again hugged Deborah and stayed there. The pain didn't ease, but hope trickled in. "Patience, Deb," Cara whispered. "Just keep muddling through. The pain always fades at some point."

Deborah swallowed and tried to pull strength from somewhere inside her. She took a step back. *"Denki."*

The back door swung open, and Lori ran inside with muddy hands and an even muddier dog. "Better Days!" Cara grabbed the dog by the collar. "Out."

"Mom, you'll hurt his feelings."

"He'll survive." She shoved the dog outside and closed the screen door. "Although you may not. What have you been doing?"

"Mississippi mud cakes. Want to try one?"

Cara glanced apologetically to Deborah and shrugged. "It's probably as good as the frosting Deborah just made."

"Really, Mom?" Lori's dark brown eyes reflected excitement.

"Afraid so."

"What?" Deborah scraped frosting off the knife with her finger and tasted the fluffy stuff. "Oh, yuck!" She snatched the cake off the counter and slammed it into the trash can. "What on earth happened?" She grabbed the second cake stand and headed for the can.

Cara took hold of the sides of the stand. "What are you doing?"

"Tossing it out."

"You're going to let a perfectly gorgeous cake go to waste when we could use it to trick someone?"

As if rust had broken from Deborah's face, she smiled freely and released the stand.

Cara set it on the counter. "I vote we give it to Ephraim."

"Maybe. Did you know that my good friend Lena has long been considered the queen of pranks?"

"The schoolteacher in Dry Lake?"

Deborah nodded. "Remember the van wreck Ephraim told you about? The one our mother died in?"

"Yeah."

"Lena's mother was killed too, and Ada's husband, and seven others from the community, including your *Daadi*—your grandfather. It was awful for months. Anyway, Lena—who was about eleven by then, I think—had been looking for some way to make people smile again, especially her *Daed*. While in Philadelphia with an aunt, she found a plastic thing that looked just like a little pat of butter at a gag store. Her Daed never ate his biscuit or peas until the butter he'd put on them had melted. According to Lena, she put two hot *buttered* biscuits on his plate. He opened a biscuit and saw the little pat of butter, closed it, and waited for it to melt. Between getting other foods, sipping on his drink, and chatting, he checked the biscuit several times over the next five or six minutes. Finally he poked the butter, asking why it hadn't melted. When he touched it and realized it was plastic, he broke into an uproar of laughter. She said he laughed until tears rolled down his cheeks. There's been no stopping her since...except she hasn't pulled anything on me since Mahlon left."

"Then Lena it is."

"She hasn't been stumped or tricked in years. I'm not sure she'll fall for it."

"She might this time. It won't be expected." Cara dusted flour from Deborah's black apron. "An unspoken truce was called the day Mahlon left. She wouldn't dream of you pulling this on purpose. If we handle it right and slice a piece for her while we visit, she'll probably eat nearly a whole slice, just to be nice."

"You know, I fear for my brother sometimes." Deborah giggled, feeling sadness loosen its death grip.

Cara's laughter came from a spring of contentment within her, and Deborah enjoyed a refreshing sip. Cara wasn't even close to being someone Deborah would have chosen for her brother. She'd been raised as an Englischer in foster care and often struggled to accept the Plain ways. She behaved like a sharp-tongued heathen sometimes without even realizing it, but as odd as it seemed, Ephraim respected her deeply. The longer Deborah knew her, the more she understood why her brother had finally fallen in love.

Deborah smoothed Cara's hair back and tried to pin the short strands where they'd stay under the prayer Kapp. It was no use.

Cara tucked a strand behind her ear. "Since no one's pulled a prank since Jerk Face left, I say it's time to end the truce."

"Mom, Ephraim won't like that you're calling names. Who's Jerk Face, anyway?"

"It doesn't matter." Cara turned to Deborah. "Does it?"

Deborah took a cleansing breath. "No, it…he doesn't."

They both knew it wasn't true. Not yet. Maybe not ever.

Cara mocked a frown. "What'd you do wrong to make that frosting taste so bad?"

"I don't know. Is the cake itself just as bad?"

They moved to the tossed-out cake. Cara jabbed a fork in the very center of it, where it hadn't touched any part of the trash can. She took a tiny nibble and shuddered. "It's both frosting and cake."

"So what'd I do?"

Cara made a face. "Salt."

"Too much salt?" Deborah glanced to her work station. "How did I manage that?"

Cara shrugged.

Trying to recall what she'd done, Deborah went to the canisters and opened the one that said sugar. If she'd been paying any attention, she'd have realized that it held salt. Lori had filled them for her earlier today, but when? How many items had she made using salt instead of sugar?

"Lori," Deborah spoke softly, "when did you refill these canisters?"

"Today."

"No, honey, I mean when today?"

Cara put her finger into the canister and then licked it. "Yep, that's salt."

Lori shrugged. "Did I do something wrong?"

Cara placed her hand on Lori's head. "Nothing that another lesson with Ada about being a good kitchen helper won't fix. Besides, seven-year-olds are supposed to make cute mistakes. It's part of your job description. Did you fill the canisters before or after school?"

"After. I did it when Deborah left to get the mail."

Deborah sighed. "And then Deborah read her note and sank onto the porch steps in a state of depression before eventually making her way back into the kitchen in a complete cloud of confusion."

"And she began talking about herself in third person too." Cara winked at her. "Lori, honey, why don't you go upstairs and get cleaned up while Deborah and I tackle this kitchen mess and start making a quick supper? Ada will be back soon, and then we'll eat."

Lori headed out of the kitchen, and soon the sound of her tromping up the steps echoed through the quiet home.

Deborah grabbed a few dirty utensils off the cabinet and tossed them into the sink. "Ingredients in the wrong canister or not, I should have recognized the difference between salt and sugar."

"It's not a big deal, Deb."

She rinsed her hands and dried them. "Ya, it is. Money's even tighter than you know. Ada doesn't want to talk about it, but she's making deliveries to all three bakeries because we can't afford to hire a driver. Hitching and unhitching the horse and wagon, along with her making the deliveries every day, cuts into our baking time, so our workday is getting longer and longer, but we've got fewer goods to sell."

"I thought the bakeries paid for the courier."

"They did…sort of. I mean they were taking money out of our profit to pay for them, so Ada's getting that money, and we're making the deliveries ourselves. Lately she has to wait until we make a few bucks off what we sold in order to buy supplies for the next round of baking."

"So"—Cara shrugged—"Jerk Face sent you money today. Use it."

"I'll starve first." Deborah couldn't believe her own tone as she spoke—or the determination she felt.

"Your brother wouldn't like that plan."

"You cannot tell Ephraim." She motioned to the six-foot stainless steel commercial oven. "He's already done too much for us. This place was unlivable until he gave so generously."

"I…I didn't realize he was the one…"

"Well he was. A few others pitched in a little, but in this economy there are too many in our community who are hurting. I can't ask them for help when Mahlon sent us money. Ada and I will have to succeed…or fail…on our own."

Three

Lena climbed the wooden steps of her home and walked inside. Quietness greeted her. As she set her grading book and student papers on the table, a nearby mirror caught her eye. She moved to the wall hatrack with the oval mirror and looked at herself. Tears stung as she studied the bluish-purple stain that began halfway down her right cheek and continued down the side of her neck. She placed her hand over her birthmark. The width of her fingers all pressed together covered it with a little room to spare.

Was the birthmark all people saw?

Vivid memories of overhearing her brother's friends saying they felt sorry for her added to the hurt. In her teen years and before she joined the faith, she'd tried covering up the stain with different shades of concealer and foundation makeup. She'd never found one that could cover the blotch, only ones that streaked or made it look orange rather than blue. She wondered if Peter had seen how deeply he'd cut her today or if her well-rehearsed poker face hid the truth like she hoped.

The back door opened. "Lena, you home?" her Daed called out.

Studying herself, she removed her hand and angled her head a little one way and then the other. "Ya."

She could tell by his footsteps that he'd headed straight for the mud sink near the back door.

The sound of water coming on and his scrubbing up barely registered as she traced the mark. Thoughts of her mother came to her. She'd died a long time ago, but the memory of standing in the flower garden, crying in her Mamm's arms, played out in front of her. Lena hadn't been more than nine years old, and some of the boys at school had taunted her about her looks. They'd said she'd die an *Alt Maedel*—an old maid. Even now Lena could feel the warmth of her mother's love as she'd placed a rose in Lena's hand. *When the time is right, you'll be drawn to the right man. And he'll be drawn to you. He'll see beyond the mark, and he'll love you deeper and higher than most men are capable of. I promise you that.*

It wasn't like Lena wanted just any man, but oh how she dreamed of finding a good man, of having sons and daughters fill their home. The love stored inside her longed for him to show up. But not one man had even looked her way. How would she find the right one if none gave her a chance? She wanted to be under the wisdom and strength and leadership of a good husband, just like her people believed was right. She believed it too, but had God marked her for a different life yet not removed her desire for a husband?

Upstairs, hidden inside her hope chest, she had a very old but still well-loved list of her favorite children's names. The idea of never having a family of her own scared her.

"You didn't come out to the shop to see me when you got home." Her Daed came into the room, drying his face on a guest towel. He scrubbed the towel over his mostly brown beard with a few gray hairs peeping through. It didn't matter that he'd been widowed for thirteen years; once married, a man grew a beard and kept it the rest of his life. "At least greet your poor dog. She is begging for a little attention." He pointed at Nicky, who had managed to come into the room without her noticing. Nicky watched Lena's every move while her whole body wriggled in hopes of being petted.

She patted Nicky's head. Her dog stood and slowly turned in circles as if chasing her tail, making it easy for Lena to stroke her from head to tail without moving her hand.

Daed dried his hands. "I was hoping for a fresh cup of coffee between now and dinner."

Lena tried to shake the sickening feeling in the pit of her stomach. "Sure thing, Daed. Do you need a little something else to hold you until dinner is ready?"

"Nope, just a cup of coffee with you." He tossed her the dishtowel. "Then I need to get back to the shop before and again after dinner. The owners of Bissett's would like the kitchen table and chairs done by tomorrow if possible." He paused. "You look a little pale. You feeling okay?"

"Ya." She wouldn't tell him, or anyone else, what weighed heavy on her. He and others would try to assure her she was beautiful and the mark wasn't all that noticeable. Why bother? She wouldn't feel any better by people saying things they felt obligated to say.

Suddenly ready for time in her flower garden, she tossed the towel back at him. "I have things I'd like to do tonight too, as well as things I must do, so I'll get dinner started now."

With the harness in one hand and a cube of sugar in the other, Cara eased toward Rosie, talking to her as she drew closer. But Rosie kept moving just out of reach. This reminded her of trying to catch a cab in New York on a Saturday night. She could see them, but they wouldn't stop for her. She knew so little about horses. Maybe the old girl didn't want to work on such a beautiful fall day. Cara sang softly while holding out her palm. Finally Rosie grew more interested in getting the sugar than in avoiding Cara. A moment after the horse's soft lips grasped the sugar from Cara's palm, she slid the rope harness on her.

She led her across the field and into the barn. Once inside Cara guided the horse to stand between the shafts of the buggy. "Easy girl." She patted her, but the mare shifted nervously. Cara bent forward to place the bridle on her, but Rosie jerked her head, hitting the side of Cara's face. Struggling to keep her balance, she managed to get the bridle in place. She threw the leather strappy thing over the horse's neck and attached the rigmarole that hooked into the bellybands. Ada had told her the names of this stuff. So had Ephraim, but none of it stuck in her brain. Couldn't one thing about being Amish be easy?

Forcing herself to focus, she continued connecting this thing to that until she was finally ready to stick the shaves into their holders on each side of Rosie. Once she'd threaded the leads through the rings, she was done connecting the horse to the buggy…maybe. She studied her work for a moment, wondering if she'd remembered each step. The gear sat a little odd. Cara angled her head a bit. That seemed to make it look straighter. She shrugged, hoping that everything was connected right or at least that everything *important* was connected.

Once Rosie was hitched to the buggy, Cara went inside. Ada stood beside Lori as they refilled the canisters with the correct ingredients. Better Days sat on the floor, watching Lori and Ada like he was trying to understand their words. What could be seen of Ada's light brown hair from around the head covering shined like she was still a young woman. At forty-three her face had no lines and her skin was vibrant. Cara bet she'd had very oily skin when younger and now she was reaping the benefits. "You be good for Ada." Cara kissed the top of Lori's head.

"Ada's gonna teach me how to wash, dry, and iron a prayer Kapp."

Ada shrugged. "One of you two needs to know how to care for the coverings."

"Yep, you're right." She missed being able to ruffle Lori's hair, so she tugged on one of the strings to her Kapp. "Did you guys want to go to Dry Lake with me and Deb?"

"You girls will be out too late for me." Ada placed the lid on the sugar canister. "I need to be up long before dawn again tomorrow."

Lori took the remaining sugar to the pantry. "Not me, Mom. Takes longer to get there and back than we get to see 'From. I hate that."

"Okay. If that's what you want to do." Cara kissed the top of her head again, feeling the starched prayer covering against her lips.

Deborah came into the kitchen, pinning a clean apron in place.

"There you are." Cara gestured toward the back door. "The horse is ready. Are you?"

She grabbed the cake box. "Ya."

They said their good-byes to Ada and Lori and went to the barn. When Deborah walked into the barn, she stopped and turned to Cara. "Harnessed her by yourself, did you?"

Cara tilted her head to the left. "If you do your head like this, it's not so bad."

Deborah angled her head and then her body. "Ya, you're right." She stepped into the driver's side, but once they were on the road, she held out the reins to Cara.

Cara shook her head. "You're the one in the driver's seat. What are you doing?"

"We're not in a car. And it's time you learn to drive…Amish style."

Cara folded her arms. "You drive. I'll ride."

"Did you rig this thing to separate from the horse while I'm driving it?"

"No. Of course not."

"Then take the reins."

Cara took them. The straps of leather felt totally different in her hands now that the horse was trudging along. She and the horse jolted when a van zoomed around them, but she continued heading toward Dry Lake. The cool fall air begged Cara to open her heart and soak in the very joy of being alive.

The sensation was new and exhilarating, making her wonder how long it would last. She knew that life offered no one a break for very long.

The sounds of town were far behind them now, and as much as she was enjoying the ride, she couldn't stop thinking about seeing Ephraim.

When she came to a fairly steep slope, she tried to gain speed so they could make it up the next hill, but Rosie seemed uninterested in going faster. "I've never driven anything before. But I know that a car or truck can't hear or care when the owners yell at it. Will Rosie?"

"Probably not, given that she never listens, but there are some things you just don't do as an Amish person, and yelling like a maniac in public is one of them. Once you're married, I'm sure Ephraim will appreciate it if you can hold on to that tradition."

Cara chuckled. "Now that's good info to know."

Deborah scrunched her forehead. "Did I miss something?"

"You said the Amish have no problem with me yelling at my horse or my husband as long as it's not in public."

"That's not what I meant."

"I'm pretty sure it's what you said."

"Poor Ephraim."

Cara chuckled. "What about Rosie?"

Deborah looked a bit lost for a moment, and then she laughed. "Knowing Rosie, I'm more inclined to say, 'Poor Cara.' Of course, you'll figure that out as time goes on."

The ride seemed to be pulling Deborah out of that dark hole Mahlon had dug inside her, so Cara did what she could to keep the silly banter going. By the time they'd traveled for nearly an hour, she almost had the hang of driving a rig.

"You need to slow down so you can take the next right turn up ahead."

Cara slapped the reins against the horse's back, making it gain speed. "You've got to be kidding. I didn't drive all this way to see Lena first."

"Fine. But I'm not delivering this cake on my own."

"Why not?"

"There are several rules to pulling a prank, but only two you need to understand right now. One, whoever thought of the prank must be in on delivering it. Two, no one goes alone."

"I'll repeat myself, why not?"

"Because, afterward, telling what took place isn't nearly as fun as reliving it together. Don't you know anything about pranks?"

Cara pulled into the driveway of Ephraim's cabinetry shop. "Nope. Pranks are for rich girls." She set the brake. "And you can trust me, Deb. In every way that matters—faith, family, friends, food, and shelter—you grew up rich." She hopped down and strode to the entryway of the huge warehouse-type shop.

Ephraim. He stood near the center of the vast building, scrubbing sandpaper over a cabinet that was sitting on a pair of sawhorses. Dark blue pants. Light blue shirt. Brown suspenders. Although it was a couple of hours before dark, he had lit several gas pole lamps. Under the glow of them, his hair looked more reddish brown than the usual strawberry blond.

The glimpse of him filled her soul. She'd once been so empty, and now it was as if he'd stolen the awfulness of her past and buried it somewhere. But it'd taken more than his physical strength to help her. He'd given up everything for a season—had been shunned and disgraced, all the while hiding the truth from her of what he was going through. And sacrificing.

He stirred her in ways she didn't figure the Amish were familiar with—physical desire. But she bridled it and tried to behave like an upstanding Amish woman.

Deborah nudged her, whispering, "Is this what you meant by seeing him?"

Cara took a deep breath. "No, but I could stay right here all day and just watch him."

"We have a cake to deliver."

Ephraim looked up, a gorgeous smile instantly erasing the blankness that'd been there moments before. He tossed the sandpaper onto the cabinet and headed for her. Cara moved to him and wrapped her arms around his waist. The warmth and power of his hands made her feel both strong and weak. How was that possible?

He released her. "I wasn't expecting a visit."

"Deborah brought something for Lena. And I said I'd go with her to deliver it."

He looked past Cara and seemed to notice his sister for the first time. "Hi, Deborah."

"Hey. I think I'll go say hello to everyone at Daed's. Meet you at the buggy in ten?"

"You're only here for ten minutes?" Ephraim looked disappointed.

"No, we're coming back after we see Lena for a bit."

"Good. That'll give me a chance to finish up here and catch a shower."

Movement inside the office area of the shop caught her attention. *Anna Mary.*

Ephraim's ex-girlfriend stood in his office with the phone to her ear. Anna Mary knew the language, customs, and all the ways of the Amish. Cara knew almost nothing. If she'd been raised here as her mom had wanted, she would've grown up knowing all the Amish ways too. Anna Mary put the receiver in its cradle, blew out the kerosene lamp, and came out of the office. The moment she saw Deborah, her eyes lit up, and she hurried over to her friend. She engulfed her in a hug the way best friends do. The two whispered something before Anna Mary turned toward Cara and Ephraim. "Hi, Cara. How are you?"

"Hello. I'm good. You?" The words caught in her throat and tumbled out sounding rather frozen. Ephraim traced his fingers along the side and back of her neck until settling his hand there.

"She came to use the community phone."

Embarrassed that he felt the need to reassure her, she forced a smile and turned to Anna Mary. "I…I hope everything is okay."

"Ya, just making plans to visit one of my sisters who doesn't live in Dry Lake."

Cara shifted, trying to think of how to make small talk with her. "That sounds like fun."

"Ya, should be."

"I'll see you at the buggy in ten." Deborah waved, and then she and Anna Mary left the building.

Ephraim squared himself in front of her and placed both his hands on her face. "I'm glad you're here." He kissed her forehead before gazing into her eyes. "I have something I want to show you." He led her to his office. After he lit the kerosene lamp, he passed her a paper with a drawing on it.

"It's a sketch of a floor plan, right?"

"Ya. Plans for our new house."

"Ours? But you already own one."

"*We,*" Ephraim corrected and then waited.

Her throat felt dry, but she made herself say it. "*We* own one."

"Ya, but it has one bedroom, two if we make that storage space into a room for Lori. Plus, I thought we might want to build elsewhere on the property, maybe not so close to my Daed and stepmother."

Her hurt from moments earlier shrank, and feathery-light contentment filled the gap. She didn't have much in the way of good memories from her past, but she had a future. "But I like your..." She cleared her throat. "*Our* house. You built it yourself. Just those hardwood floors you put in from some old barn are too much a part of you to leave behind."

He gave that 'I understand' smile of his. "But it's awfully small."

"If we make the living room into bedrooms, it'll work."

"You're going to be a demanding wife, aren't you?"

She studied him for a moment, wanting to know if he was teasing her. His eyes reflected amusement and love, and she felt his pleasure with her thaw a little more of her heart.

"I could probably build a set of stairs and add a couple of rooms above the main floor if living there is what you really want."

What she ached for more than anything else was for them to marry...

soon. But Amish rules said that she couldn't go through instruction until spring and that they couldn't marry until next year's wedding season. Because she'd been raised an outsider and had only been living as an Amish woman for a short while, the bishop had the power to make them wait several years, if he wanted to.

Ephraim laid the sketch on his desk. "Your plan will cost us a lot less money and keep me close to the shop, so it's great for me. I was thinking it might not be so wonderful for you. You're not used to having a large, somewhat intrusive family living next-door."

She shrugged. "I can hold my own without you having to build us a new house."

"Okay. We'll wait on building a place. In a few years we'll both be ready for a bigger one."

Longing to feel his lips against hers, she settled for giving him a kiss on the cheek. "I'm not interested in where we live or how big and comfy the house is. I just want to be your wife."

Four

Lena knelt and dug her bare hands into the dirt, loosening the ground around her aster plants. Nicky lay near her, stretched out in the warm sun while dozing contentedly. The sight of blossoms and petals renewed and connected her to hope.

She scooped her own concoction of mulch, fertilizer, and potting soil out of a bucket and onto the needed areas. The feel and smell of the earth, along with the beauty of the flowers—the delicate blooms and the rich shades of the purples, blues, and pinks—soothed her frazzled nerves.

While trying to get over the hurt, she looked for some answers for Peter. But even if she did discover a way for him to learn, would he accept her help? He discounted her as a worthy being. Getting past that wouldn't be easy, especially as he constantly made it easier for her to want little to do with him.

If she didn't need to go see Aaron later tonight, she'd visit her friend Samantha. She and Samantha had met while Lena attended public school for a few years. Despite getting together only a couple of times a year and Samantha's Englischer lifestyle, the women had a lot in common. In her work as a school counselor, Samantha always had a trick or two for dealing with difficult schoolchildren. Surely Samantha could help Lena push past Peter's stinging remarks and find a way to reach him.

"Lennie?"

Her brother Allen called to her. His rather craggy voice sounded just like her other brothers, but without a glance she always knew when it was him. Only a handful of people called her Lennie—Allen and two of his best buddies. While still kneeling on the lush grass, she turned to see him walking toward her. "Ya?"

"I guess you didn't hear me calling you. Is it noisy out here today?"

She wiped her forehead with the back of her wrist. "Extremely so inside my head. Did you want something?"

"No. Just checkin' on you."

"I'm good, thanks."

"Wow, are these from your greenhouse?"

She cleared her throat, refusing to laugh at her brother. He always meant well, but the man noticed almost nothing about her flower beds. It'd be her best guess that this was the first time he'd seen her asters, and she'd planted them here as seedlings two springs ago. "At one time they were from my greenhouse, ya."

"I dropped by to visit you and Daed and was surprised you weren't eating supper with him. If I cooked a meal, I'd eat it."

"You sure about that? Because if *you* cooked a meal…"

He chuckled. "Okay, fine, Teacher Lena. If I were you and cooked a meal, I'd eat it."

As sisters went, Lena had cooked a lot of meals for Allen over the years. After their Mamm died when Lena was ten, she began learning from her older sisters how to cook and run the house. Their community was never the same after that day—her brother most of all.

The day after their mother was killed, Lena heard odd noises coming from the attic. When she climbed the stairs, she found her big brother sobbing. He looked up and saw her, and she expected him to usher out threats and throw things at her. But there Allen was, sixteen years old, sitting on the floor of the attic, crying uncontrollably. When he caught his breath, he stammered through an apology for all his years of being mean to her, and then they cried together. Slowly he'd grown into a man worth having around, but like all her siblings, he had a family of his own now.

A rig turned into their driveway and ambled toward the house. Just the sight of Deborah Mast refreshed Lena's spirits. Cara sat beside her. Lena hadn't had much chance to get to know her yet.

Allen grabbed his suspenders. "Mahlon bailed on Deborah, and Ephraim broke up with Anna Mary for an outsider. For a while I feared all your closest friends would marry off, leaving you feeling like an outcast, but with all that heartache going on, maybe never dating isn't such a bad thing."

With soil covering Lena's hands, she stood. "I know you were trying to say something nice, but…" She wiped her hands down the front of Allen's shirt, pressing hard as she did so. "That's all I have to say on the matter."

"Lennie, Emily's going to shake the rafters when she sees this," Allen complained as he brushed off his shirt, taking extra time on the ground-in dirt.

Lena chuckled and walked toward the buggy, Nicky quietly shadowing every step she took. "Now this is a pleasant surprise."

Deborah brought the horse to a halt, got out, and hugged Lena. Cara climbed out, holding on to a cake box.

"Hi, Cara." Lena wasn't sure whether to hug Cara or offer to shake her hand or just speak. No one but Ephraim really knew Cara. Since she now lived in Hope Crossing with Deborah and Ada, they were getting to know her. The rest of the Amish community was still grappling, trying to get past the awkwardness of Ephraim breaking up with one of their own to welcome an Englischer stranger into the fold. People left the Amish faith to join the world, but she'd never seen it work in reverse—although she'd heard of a few Englischers who'd spent months or a couple of years aiming to join, only to change their minds.

"Hey, Lena." Cara passed the box to Deborah.

"We brought you something." Deborah gave it to Lena. "I made two cakes with that recipe you gave me and brought you one."

"Well, that's very sweet and thoughtful. Denki."

"Yep, that's me." Deborah placed her arm around Lena's shoulder. "Let's go in and share a bite. I want your opinion."

"I wouldn't care for any right now, but I'll cut a slice for each of you."

"Not care for any?" Deborah glanced to Cara. "How can you turn down my dessert? Ada is one of the best cooks ever, and she's trained me for years."

"Personally," Allen said, having followed Lena from the garden, "I think she's had a rough day at school." With a glint in his eyes, he continued to brush dirt off his shirt, clearly letting Lena know he was telling Deborah as a payback for rubbing dirt on him. "Lennie, I'm going on home."

"By all means, go home." She kept a straight face as he chuckled.

Deborah guided her toward the house. "You need to try this cake. It'll make me happy if you do."

"I'm really not the least bit hungry. I'll have some later tonight. May I cut a slice for you two?"

Deborah and Cara glanced at each other and shook their heads.

"We've already had plenty of the other one. Some of the scholars giving you trouble at school?" Deborah asked.

"Scholars?" Cara's brows scrunched. "I know you are not talking about a class full of Rhodes scholars, so what is it?"

"That's what you call students," Deborah said. "We call them that too sometimes, but mostly we call them scholars. So are they being difficult, Lena?"

"A few." They walked up the porch steps and into the house. Nicky zipped past them, heading for her doggy bed next to the stove.

Once they were in the kitchen, Cara took a seat at the island. "It's a one-room schoolhouse with Amish kids. How bad can they be?"

Lena set the box on the counter. "Just because we dress plain and live simple doesn't mean some of our youth don't push every boundary there is." She scrubbed her hands, taking note that her Daed had washed the dishes. After grabbing a kitchen towel out of a drawer, she sat on a barstool across from Deborah and Cara. Lena settled in, enjoying the banter.

After they'd talked for a while, Deborah gestured toward the cake. "You sure you don't want to try a bite?"

"I'll use the cake as a treat when the hard parts of the day are over."

"What else needs to be done?" Cara asked.

"I have to see Aaron about his bull. It's getting into the field nearest the school."

Deborah made a face. "Again?"

"Ya."

Deborah splayed her hands against the countertop. "We'd better go. You have things to do, and Cara didn't travel for an hour with me just to spend her evening waiting to see when you're going to eat that cake."

"Again with the cake. What is it with you tonight?" Lena rose.

Cara brushed wisps of hair out of her face as she got up. "Lena, about that ca—"

"Cara." Deborah jumped up. "We need to go." She took Cara by the hand and pulled her toward the door. "We only had a minute to stop by. We went by Ephraim's first, and I gave him my word I'd have Cara back real quicklike."

Lena followed them onto the porch. Deborah shooed Cara to the rig and then gave Lena a quick hug. "Good to see you."

If Lena didn't know better, she'd be convinced Deborah was pulling some sort of prank on her. And it'd be a welcome relief if she felt up to pulling pranks again. "You didn't even let me and Cara say a proper good-bye. Have you been spending too much time in a hot kitchen lately?"

"Maybe. But come see us in Hope Crossing this weekend if you can. Then you can say anything you wish to either of us. Bye."

Perplexed, Lena remained on the porch. Maybe Deborah just realized it was getting late. "Bye."

After watching Deborah and Cara's buggy pull onto the road, Lena knew she couldn't delay going to Aaron's any longer. She went inside and washed her face before putting on a clean apron. After hurrying to the barn, she hitched her horse to the carriage. But before she left, she went back inside and grabbed the box containing the cake. She knew that talking to Aaron for the third time about his bull being in the wrong pasture would be easier if she had a gift in hand. Passing him one of Deborah's desserts was a perfect plan, and surely Deborah wouldn't mind the cake being used as a peace offering.

When she pulled into the Blanks' lane, she noticed three rigs with horses tied to a couple of hitching posts. Clearly the Blanks had company, but all she needed to do was speak to Aaron for a moment. She looped Happy Girl's reins around a small tree, grabbed the box containing the cake, and headed for the house. She knocked on the front door and waited.

Dora Blank opened the door. "Lena." The fifty-something woman glanced behind her as if unsure what to do. "Were we expecting you?"

Lena held up the cake. "I need to see Aaron."

"Oh." She took a step back.

The moment Lena walked inside she understood Dora's cool reception. The members of the school board—Michael Blank, Enos Beiler, Jake Fisher, and Grey Graber—were sitting at the large kitchen table. Three wives, including Dora, were with their husbands. Grey's wife, who was Dora and Michael's daughter, wasn't there. For reasons Lena could only guess at, Elsie always avoided the school board gatherings. Maybe the meetings were too high-spirited for her more gentle nature.

The group appeared to be engaged in a serious conversation with Peter's Mamm and Daed—Crist and Mollie Bender—and with Sylvan and Lillian Detweiler. She wouldn't blame the Detweilers for being set against her. Her brief lapse in judgment last May could have cost them their oldest son's life. Their son John and his three siblings had left their lunches at home. If she'd had enough food from her lunch as well as other scholars' to feed them, as she'd done in the past, she'd have given it to them. But that day she'd only brought an apple, and she'd given it to the youngest Detweiler. No one else had extra in their pails either, so rather than letting them go hungry, she'd hitched her horse to its rig and told John to go back for the lunches. The Detweiler place is only a short distance from the school. But he must have been daydreaming, because her horse took over and automatically headed for home, her home, which meant the rig came to a four-way stop. Once at the four-way stop, John realized he'd gone the wrong way and slapped the reins on the horse's back without realizing that he didn't have the right of way and that a vehicle was coming. The car almost slid sideways trying to stop, and it nipped the back of the buggy, toppling the rig. Her horse came loose from the buggy and ran on home. John had a few bumps and bruises, and the people in the car took him home. It'd been a foolish mistake on her part, and the board had put her on probation for this school year, but surely they weren't still reviewing that incident.

"She's not fit, and every one of you know it," Peter's Mamm said.

"Michael," Dora called, stopping the conversation cold.

In only a brief moment the looks on their faces turned from one of studious consideration to awkward remorse. "Lena." Michael stood. "Would you care to join us?"

Join them? If they'd wanted her here, they would have invited her. Besides, she needed fresh air. She was good at her job, and she loved teaching. That was all she'd ever wanted to do, and no one had ever taken a teaching position at a younger age than she had. Would they take it from her because of Peter's nonsense and her one mistake with John Detweiler? "No…no thank you. I didn't mean to interrupt. I was looking for Aaron."

Michael placed his hands on the table, looking stiff and in pain. "I think he's still at the barn. We almost never see him before bedtime anymore, not since I hurt my back and can't do much farm work."

"He…he's"—Dora stammered— "sleeping there some nights. But you're free to go down and look for him."

"Denki." Shaken, Lena hurried outside, still holding the box with the cake in it. She drew in air, trying to fill her lungs. It wasn't so much that they were having a meeting but that they were having it behind her back. Couldn't they have told her about it and said she didn't need to come? Still determined to do what she'd come here for, she strode toward the barn. It only took a few seconds to figure out Aaron wasn't there. She went back to her horse, removed the reins from the small tree, and climbed into the buggy.

"Lennie?" Grey's smooth voice caused her to stop. He hurried over to the buggy. "You okay?"

She tried to swallow her embarrassment. "I've certainly been better."

"Michael saw no reason to upset you with these complaints. We're just hearing them out. If we have any concerns when tonight's over, we'll talk to you."

"It seems I should get a say in front of my accusers."

"You will, if it comes to that."

"It has come to that, Grey. Don't you think I need someone in there to defend me?"

He studied her, as if waiting for her to answer her own question.

And then she knew. He'd do a better job defending her than she would. Where she might get riled and make matters worse, he wouldn't. He'd never failed to stand up for her since becoming a member of the school board a few years ago. It was possible he defended her out of pity. She'd certainly overheard him saying he felt sorry for her on more than one occasion when they were young. The thought stung. Maybe Peter was more right than she was willing to admit. She took a deep breath, refusing to allow her fears and insecurity to get the best of her. Whatever Grey's motivation, he wouldn't let rumors or nonsense cloud the school board's judgment. She hoped he took her side because he trusted and respected her as a teacher, but she couldn't ask. If that wasn't his reasoning, what answer could he possibly give except denial? She drew a deep breath and decided to tease. "You better do a good job in there, Grey, or I'm tellin' Daed."

He laughed and tipped his hat. "No doubts on that one, Lennie."

She slapped the horse's back, trying to assure herself she wouldn't lose her job.

Before she got to the end of the lane, she spotted an Amish man in a nearby field. She watched as he walked with purpose toward a large patch of woods. She directed the rig off the beaten path and toward where the man was headed. She soon saw what he saw—a cabin, one that used to be for farmhands. He went inside. It was on Blank property, so Aaron might be there. She'd forgotten about the old cabin sitting in the woods, just out of sight. An Englischer family had owned this farm about seven years ago, before the Blanks moved from Ohio. And then Grey met his future wife— Elsie Blank.

Lena's rig groaned as she went down the rough path and stopped in front of the place. Music blared, and electric lights shined through the windows. Four or five horses grazed nearby, but an old, half-rusted car sat in the dirt driveway.

A hangout.

Since there were no electric lines running to the place, she assumed a generator provided the power. Its existence as a hangout was news to her. Probably a secret from all the parents too.

She took the cake with her and knocked on the screen door. "Hello?" She raised her voice over the din of music.

From the door she could see the living room, where young men lounged in chairs and couches or sat on the floor. One guy, with a beer in hand, turned toward the screen door. "No one in Amish costume welcome. Thanks anyway."

"I'm looking for Aaron Blank. Is he here?"

A girl in a tank top and jeans came to the door. Lena didn't recognize her, so she could be a rumschpringe Amish from another community, but more than likely she was an Englischer girl.

"Hi." She unlatched the screen door. "Come on in."

"Is Aaron around?"

"Uh, well." She turned back toward the others. "Come on, guys. Stop goofing off and help the woman."

One of the guys stood and took a long drink of beer before belching. "I'll get him." He went to a door and pounded on it. "Aaron! Somebody's here to see ya."

The group returned to their lounging around as if Lena weren't standing there. Aaron came out, rubbing his eyes like he'd been asleep. She couldn't imagine sleeping with all this noise. He staggered a few times, but he made his way to her. "Lena, hi. What's up?"

"Lena?" a man's voice boomed. "As in Kauffman?" Disbelief and sarcasm marked his voice as he stood up so he could see her better. When he rose, something small and metallic fell from his lap and onto the floor, but he didn't notice. "It is you. Has to be." He wiped his cheek several times as if trying to remove her birthmark from his face. "You fit the description."

Unsure who he was but quite confident he was drunk, Lena ignored the man. "Aaron, we talked about this before, but we still have a problem."

"What?" The drunk scowled at her. "Making my brother miserable during school ain't enough? Now you're gonna come here and pick on my friend Aaron?"

The drunk had to be Peter's brother. She knew all her other scholars' families. She stayed focused on Aaron. "The bull was in the field next to the schoolhouse."

"So?" the drunk barked.

Lena didn't answer him. "Aaron, surely you know how dangerous that is. The Nicols owned this farm for generations and always kept bulls and steers out of the pasture closest to the school." She held the cake out to him. "Please."

Aaron stared at the box.

"It's a cake."

He smelled of stale beer as he took it from her. "Ya, ya, you're right. I'm sure a fence needs mending. I'll see to it that it doesn't happen again."

"What?" Peter's brother took a step, sending the object he'd dropped earlier skidding across the linoleum floor. Lena looked down when it bumped her shoe.

A pocket watch?

He came toward the doorway. "You are kidding me. There's a fence there, right?"

"Of course," Aaron said, "but sometimes the boys hit their baseballs or volleyballs into that field during recess."

"Yeah?" the drunk scoffed. "If she knew how to control a class, inside or outside the schoolhouse, it wouldn't be a problem."

"I'm Lena Kauffman." She held out her hand. "And you are?"

"Not interested." He walked off.

"Sorry, Lena," Aaron mumbled. "Dwayne's had a case too many."

Lena reached for the watch and noticed it looked like the one her Daed had lost. But it couldn't be. It'd been missing for months. She'd never really thought her Daed lost it. For a while she wondered if Cara entered their unlocked home and took it, along with a huge roll of tens. She'd been suspected of a few burglaries when she'd first arrived in Dry Lake, but she had proven the accusations were false.

Lena picked up the watch, opened it, and read the inscription: *To Israel with love.*

She held it out toward Dwayne. "This is my Daed's watch."

"What?" Dwayne gawked at her.

"My Daed lost his watch last spring. It was the last gift my mother gave him before she died."

"Well, that's a real sad story and all, but I found it along the shoulder of a road when walking, and it's mine now." He reached for it, but Lena clutched it tightly and put her hand behind her back.

"I'm glad you found it, and I'll give you a reasonable reward, but it's my Daed's watch."

Dwayne hovered over her, swaying back and forth. What was it with these Bender men, Peter and Dwayne, that they liked to stand so close while peering down at her? Aaron set the cake on an end table. "Clearly it's her Daed's. Just let her have it."

"Oh, I'll be more than glad to let her have it."

His words were as immature and threatening as Peter's, but she wasn't giving up the watch. It meant too much to her Daed, and he'd not stopped searching for it yet.

Aaron stepped between them. *"Kumm."* He motioned Lena to the door. "Keep the watch. But it'd be good if you didn't come back here again. I'll see to it the bull stays out of that field, okay?"

"Denki, Aaron." Clutching her Daed's watch, she went to her carriage.

Five

Grey walked out of his bedroom at the same time Elsie walked out of hers. Startled and a bit curious what had kept her in her room past daylight, he stopped in his tracks. They stood in their small hallway, staring at each other under the soft glow of early morn. His shirt was not yet buttoned, and his suspenders were attached to his pants and dangling near his knees. She stood as erect and graceful as a deer when watching for danger. Each part of her clothing was tended to as perfectly as women did on their wedding day.

Sing for me, Grey. The memory of their earlier years echoed inside the emptiness of who they now were.

She lowered her gaze. "May I fix you breakfast?"

The question came at him most mornings, as if she were giving him a choice. It didn't matter that he hated breakfast. A wife cooked each meal for her family. At one time he'd thought it was her way of showing respect, maybe even love, but he knew better now.

"Ya."

While she moved about the kitchen, he sat at the table, reading the newspaper.

Saturday. Regardless of what he did to use up the day, Saturdays were a reminder of the emptiness between them. The aroma of bacon frying filled the room. Sunlight and cool air streamed in through the open windows. He and Elsie were in the same room, about to sit at the same table.

Those things made it look and smell as if normal life went on inside this house.

The clock ticked louder by the minute, telling him time was moving, and yet he wasn't. He and Elsie were in the same place they'd been for at least three years. With each week and month that passed, he was getting farther and farther from all chance of contentment. He'd let go of wanting happiness quite a while ago. But life was too long to live it like this, wasn't it? He closed his newspaper and set it to the side. "Any plans for today?"

"Usual. You?"

The morning begged to be enjoyed, and he knew what they needed to do. "I'm taking Ivan fishing. Would you like to go?"

"There's work to be done."

"There always is, and it'll still be waitin' after we've caught a few fish."

Cracking another raw egg into a bowl, she shook her head. She beat the eggs mercilessly with the whisk, but one would have to know her well to notice the slight, sharp movements as she dumped them into the pan and set the glass bowl firmly, but not too loudly, into the sink. She didn't let her movements reflect too much emotion. If she did, he could point it out and try to get her to open up.

She'd held her silence for years, never saying what really ailed her. Her complaints ranged from not liking the way he breathed to not understanding how he could get so dirty during a workday. If he dared to hum, she'd walk out. But, contrary to how he'd felt over the last few years, he wasn't a fool. When one person picked apart everything about another, the things being mentioned weren't really the problem. They were the side effects.

He understood the grief that had captured her when she gave birth to a stillborn son. He'd mourned the loss deeply, but it'd been three years since then. Did that painful time still cling to her? Her response to burying their second son hadn't seemed much different than her reaction to Ivan's birth. Perhaps that's how she dealt with pregnancy hormones, or maybe it was just her ways. Without them talking, he had no way of knowing.

When he tried to unravel the binding that held them prisoner, she grew more distant, more quiet. So as she carefully and yet sharply plunked his plate in front of him, he wasn't going to ask what was wrong. It could be that she wanted the work done before he went fishing, or that she resented that both Ivan and Grey would return with dirty clothes smelling of fish, or that he'd leave some fish scales in the yard after cleaning them. Even if he asked or tried to prod her to talk, they'd land in the same place they always did—only with a little more deadness between them each time.

No matter what or where they were right now, he still held on to hope that one day they'd really talk and she'd decide to accept her disappointments in being married to him, own up to her part of where they were and why, and be willing to start from there.

It'd taken him a long time to be willing to forget blame and simply start from where they were, but he'd done it. Could she?

"Daed!" Ivan stood in the doorway to the kitchen, a huge smile on his little face. His feety-pajamas covered all but his neck and head. One sleeve hung empty from his elbow down.

His little boy ran to him, and Grey scooped him up. "Ivan." He ruffled his hair and pulled him close, whispering good morning and his love in the only language the little boy spoke, Pennsylvania Dutch.

Ivan hung on tight. *"Du bischt daheem!"*

"Ya, witt fische geh?" Grey agreed that he was at home today and asked Ivan if he wanted to go fishing.

Ivan turned and slapped the table with his one hand, yelling, "Ya!"

"Ivan," Elsie scolded him. *"Net im Haus. Is sell so hatt zu verschteh?"*

Grey flinched as his wife fussed, *Not in the house. Is it that hard to understand?* "He's just excited." Grey aimed to keep his voice even as he spoke to Elsie in English. Ivan hadn't been taught much English yet, but even a child years younger than Ivan could pick up on tone.

"There are rules, Husband. Even for a little boy without an arm. You're not helping by indulging him. When will you see that?"

Ignoring her, Grey sat Ivan on the table facing him. *"Bischt hungerich?"* He nodded, letting Grey know he was hungry.

"Gut. Mir esse un no gehne mir."

Ivan's eyes lit up when Grey told him they'd eat and then go. Without looking at Grey, Elsie set a plate of food for Ivan on the table and returned to the sink. He studied his wife. "Elsie." He waited until she turned to him. Except for the dullness in her eyes, she looked much like she had the day he'd married her nearly six years ago. "Go with us. You could sit on a blanket and watch. Or pick wildflowers. We could share a lunch and maybe even a laugh."

Instead of her usual shake of the head and mumbling a "no thank you," her eyes welled with tears. "And then what will we share? Lies? Dreams we know can't come true?"

His heart quickened. Had she just shared a hint of what separated them? He stared at her, trying to understand what she might mean. "Lies?"

A cold, hauntingly familiar look covered her face. Silence suffocated his hope, but he held her gaze. "Surely believing in dreams would be better than this reality we're in."

The hurt in her eyes was clear, but he thought he caught a hint of her wanting to say more. From the moment he'd seen her in the hallway, she seemed less distant than usual. Did something in her want to open up? Wouldn't that be as vast and high as the heavens—for them to talk and plant some type of seed that didn't grow discouragement and sorrow?

He put Ivan in his chair and placed his food in front of him. He walked over to her, standing so close he could smell the lilac soap he'd given her for her birthday. "Talk to me," he whispered.

She grabbed a cloth and started wiping the counters. "You two go."

"We will." He took her by the arm, and she gazed up at him. "Why do we live like this, Elsie? Even if you married me for all the wrong reasons, why can't we let that go and embrace life as it is?"

Fresh tears filled her eyes. How long had it been since he'd seen her care?

"Please, talk to me."

Ivan finished the food on his plate, but Elsie remained still, staring out the window. The fact that she wasn't pulling away gave him more hope than he'd had in ages.

"You're wrong." Her words were barely audible. He waited, longing for her to say more, but she didn't.

"Okay," he whispered. "But why and when and how? And how do we fix it?"

"*Loss uns fische geh!*" Ivan declared loudly.

"*Ya, in paar Minudde.*" Although Grey assured Ivan that they'd go fishing in a few minutes, he kept his eyes glued to Elsie.

She shook her head, tears falling gently.

"Can't you just tell me some piece? I can't understand without words."

"I…I know. I…think about saying things." She laid her hand on her heart. "Words move through me like fish in a pond, but my pole has no hook, and I own no nets." She turned the water on, washed her face, and dried it on a kitchen towel.

Those few words were the most insight she'd given him in years, and now it was over. He could see it in her face. "We need help, Elsie."

"No." She stiffened, eyes wide, staring at him in horror. He'd never hinted at bringing in the support group before. She was such a private person that it'd tear her up inside to share with others their awful, ugly truth. He knew that about her, but wasn't the way they were living ripping her apart too? She probably took the idea of the council as his threatening her, but he saw it as the only option left. "Grey, please. Everyone will know everything if you do that."

"You know it's handled as privately as possible. Only the church leaders, the three chosen couples, and a few others would have to know. But even if the whole community learned of it, we need help."

"You have the right to tell on me, and God is your witness that I deserve it, but…please."

He stared out the kitchen window, wondering if being married would always be like this—no way to win, no way to forfeit, only a way to carry on.

Six

Standing beside the sink, Deborah counted out the last of the cash and shoved it into an envelope. The propane tank had to be filled early next week, or the gas stove would stop working. Thoughts of using the money Mahlon had sent tempted her. But how could she allow herself to use his money? He'd left them. Probably considered them a burden. Then he sent money?

Feeling caught in a thorn patch, she placed a stamp on the envelope and headed for the mailbox. She'd taken only a few steps when the back door opened. Ada smiled as she entered, but there was no happiness inside her greeting.

Deborah squared her shoulders, wanting to look strong for Ada. "You're done with deliveries already?"

Ada moved to a kitchen chair and sat. "Afraid not." She wiped perspiration from her forehead. "It was so much easier when the bakery sent a courier to pick up and deliver our goods."

"What happened?"

"Rosie went lame. I knew she was favoring her right front leg when I hitched her this morning. Anyway, I got our first delivery made and was halfway to the second when she refused to go any farther. At first I thought she was just being her usual obstinate self, but when I checked her out, I realized she'd thrown a shoe at some point, and her hoof is split pretty bad. It felt hot to me, so it's probably infected."

Deborah's skin tingled as stress crawled over her. Mahlon always took care of Ada's horses. Deborah hadn't even thought to look at the creature's hoofs, and they'd been taking the poor girl on paved roads to make deliveries and to go to Dry Lake and back. No creature deserved that kind of treatment. "Where is she?"

"Tied to a tree about a mile before Select Bakery. After she refused to go any farther, I made several trips back and forth, carrying as many boxed desserts as I could to the bakery. I took the most expensive and perishable ones, but cakes and pies get really heavy when toting them for a mile. I couldn't keep it up and knew we had to come up with a better plan, so I came on home."

Home. The reality around her didn't match the hopes she'd once had for this place.

Ada wiped another round of sweat from her brow. "Before leaving the bakery, I called Stoltzfus Blacksmith Shop. I know it's an hour away by carriage, but it's the only blacksmith I know. I didn't reach anybody, so I left a message."

"Okay, that's a start." Deborah poured Ada a glass of ice water. "Couldn't someone at the bakery drive to where the carriage is parked to pick up the rest of our goods?"

"That would only solve getting our goods to them. I haven't made the drop at Sweet Delights either. I asked the folks at Select Bakery if they could help me out. But two of their people always walk to work, and the other one's car is on the… She called it something. I didn't recognize the word, but someone dropped her off at work, and clearly her car doesn't work any better than my horse."

"Fritz," Deborah offered. "Cara uses the word." She wouldn't say it aloud, but the truth was, everything about her and Ada's lives was on the fritz. Was that how Mahlon felt? Like he'd never get ahead but was too trapped to do anything about it?

"Where is she?" Ada asked.

"Hmm?" Deborah looked up, wondering how long she'd been lost in her own thoughts. "Who?"

"Cara."

"Oh, ya. She and Lori are doing some yard sales. She called it window-shopping. I'm pretty sure she packed them a picnic lunch too and plans to spend the afternoon at Willow Park." Deborah reached her hand across the table. "I'll find the pushcart and get our goods to both bakeries. At least you made most of the deliveries to the farthest one out."

"I guess it's good they open first and want the items earliest."

"Maybe if I unhitch the mare and walk her slowly, she can make it to the barn without the need of borrowing someone's horse trailer." She slid the envelope with the money to pay the propane bill to Ada. "I better not pay that bill. Looks like we might need that cash today."

Ada took a sip of the water. "We made a few dollars today from what the bakeries sold yesterday but only enough to cover food for the next couple of days and fresh supplies for our next round of baking. I've got that birthday cake order for tonight, and I can't wait any longer to get started on it. If you can get the goods to the bakeries and the horse back home, we'll figure out everything else when you return."

"Ya, you're right. First things first." Deborah went to the barn, found the pushcart, and started walking toward Select Bakery.

The sting of feeling overwhelmed and incapable pricked her like hundreds of bees. Before Mahlon left her, she'd had confidence. She missed soaring on the winds, feeling strong and beautiful and hopeful. Had those feelings been a lie? Lately she messed up everything she touched, from making cakes to tending to their horse.

If this business failed, she hated to think what that would do to Ada. She'd lost her only child to the world.

The now-familiar questions started pounding at her again. *Why? Why didn't I know Mahlon wasn't in love with me? Why did life have to become so hard, so humiliating and lonely?*

She didn't hear anything from God. Maybe He couldn't be heard over the river of her own whining. As much as her bellyaching disgusted her, it didn't begin to express how she really felt. She wanted her life back. The one...the one Mahlon ran from?

It didn't make sense to want that.

She spotted the horse under a tree, waiting patiently to be rescued. Rosie had her right front hoof barely touching the ground. Deborah set the legs to the pushcart on the ground and moved to the horse, caressing her head and nose. The poor thing nuzzled against Deborah's touch. What an awful price Rosie was paying for Deborah and Ada's negligence.

"I can't seem to get anything right, Rosie." Deborah placed her forehead against the horse's, waiting on a peaceful thought or answer to float down and rescue her. It didn't.

She took a step back, longing to hear a whisper within her own soul. Something faint brushed her awareness. She knew this feeling. In the past this sensation swept over her when Mahlon was nearby, usually when he was watching her from a distance. She'd had it many times, but she didn't think she'd felt it since he left.

She stepped out from under the tree and looked up and down Main Street. A couple of women milled about, going nowhere in a hurry, and one man stood at the automated-teller machine outside the bank.

Mahlon wasn't there. Part of her wished he was. As much as he'd done to her, the biggest part of her still loved him. *How is that possible?*

"Hey, Deborah."

She jolted and looked behind her. Jonathan Stoltzfus, Mahlon's cousin, was astride his chestnut stallion, riding it bareback.

She wondered how she hadn't heard his horse coming up the side street behind her. "What are you doing here?"

Jonathan slid off his horse. "Ada left a message at the shop about an hour ago, saying you guys had a lame horse." He grinned and straightened his straw hat. "It took me about two, maybe three, seconds to realize there was a wagonload of desserts that needed rescuing."

The feeling of being caught in a briar patch eased. "I'm glad to know that I can always depend on you—as long as free desserts are involved."

"Never ever forget that, Little Debbie." He passed her the reins and moved to where Rosie stood. Within moments he had the horse's knee bent and part of her leg resting on his thigh while he inspected her hoof. "Ya, it's split and infected. She'll be out of commission for a while. I should've thought to check her shoes when I was at Ada's three weeks ago." He stood straight. "So, we need to connect Rosie's wagon to my horse without making the desserts slide into one another. Up for it?"

She doubted it. She'd do something stupid and mess everything up again.

Jonathan ran his hands down Rosie's shoulder and slowly moved past her fetlock, looking for other signs of injury.

"Ya. I guess."

Jonathan turned to face her. "If Rosie could talk, even she'd sound more confident than that."

She shrugged, trying to keep tears at bay.

He moved closer. "You want to talk about it?"

"There's nothing to say that you don't already know."

He lifted her chin, making her look him in the eyes. "We go way back, Deborah. I'd guess I realized you weren't so bad when I was in eighth grade and put a frog in your dress at school. You must've been in third grade at the time, just a little kid, and you didn't even tell the teacher on me."

"Ya." She remembered feeling the creature wriggle against her back, and she'd run out of the classroom without permission and danced around outside until that frog fell to the ground.

"Of course"—Jonathan folded his arms—"the day before, you'd used the backside of my homework to draw a picture on."

"You're the one who put it on my desk."

"I was busy and just set it down."

"And I made it more beautiful with swirly things and hearts and rainbows."

"Just what I wanted while standing in front of the class reading the report—the part facing them filled with girly stuff." He laughed, but she only shrugged. "Come on, Little Debbie. That image is worth a chuckle."

"How can I laugh about anything? All of me *believed* that Mahlon loved me. I thought he wanted a life with me…and every bit of that was a lie."

He rubbed his fingers across his shaven face, making a light sandpaper noise as he did. "Like you, I've known Mahlon my whole life. He loved you. You've got to know that's true. He was just…too immature and confused to deal with life."

When she didn't answer, he began fastening the rigging to his horse. That odd sensation washed over her again. She went to the sidewalk and studied the old town.

Across the street, more than a block away, a man stood watching her.

Is it possible?

The hair on her arms and neck stood up. *Mahlon?*

Emotions pounded at her like hoofs from a dozen horses. What should she do? What did she want to do? Was it even him?

If it was…

Silence fell inside her, and emotions waited on the edge for an answer. Her own soul wanted to know, if it was him, then what?

When he left her, she quickly moved from beloved fiancée to the "humiliated one," and now she understood something about herself—she'd slipped from shock and mourning into a really bad place. And she had to fight her way free before she gave Mahlon the power to destroy even more of her life than he already had.

Jonathan peered in the direction she was staring. "What are we looking at?"

I have no idea. Even if the man was Mahlon, she still wouldn't know who she was seeing. "A creation of my imagination."

The man took a few steps toward her, and Deborah's heart went crazy. If it was Mahlon, she didn't want to face him. Not today. Not while she was a walking heap of…of…failure. He strode toward her, but his walk didn't look like Mahlon's slow, easy gait. Still, it could be him.

Whether or not the man she was looking at was Mahlon, he would return one day—probably with a wife and children. And he'd eventually walk right onto the porch of Ada's house and wait until they invited him in. When he did, she intended for her and Ada to own a very successful business. Somehow.

Jonathan brought his horse alongside her. The man was still too far away to know if it was Mahlon. A car pulled up in front of him and tooted the horn. The man seemed to be staring at her, but then he got into the vehicle.

"You ready to get moving?" Jonathan asked.

The car drove out of sight before she managed to look up at Jonathan. "Actually…I think I am."

Seven

With Ivan perched on his shoulders and a basket of fish in one hand and poles in the other, Grey walked toward home. He heard a woman saying one-syllable words—"Got ya," "No way," "I win," "I don't think so"—but he couldn't see her. He was on the road beside the Kauffman house, and by the sounds of it, Lennie was somewhere nearby, probably in the side yard or under a shade tree, playing a board game with her Daed. He kept walking, but still he didn't see either of them.

Ivan laughed.

"Was iss es?" Grey waited, expecting his son to point or tell him what he was laughing at, but the boy broke into a long cackle. A little concerned he might fall, Grey dropped the basket of fish and his poles and steadied his son's shaking body. He glanced around the yard and saw what his son was watching.

Lennie and her dog. Nicky was facing her, squatting low. When Lennie made a playful step toward Nicky, the dog ran in huge circles before stopping. Nicky then squatted again, ready to lunge toward or run from. Lennie ran toward her. The dog took off, but not before Lennie touched her side. "Ha, I won."

The dog barked like mad, as if arguing with Lennie's announcement of victory. Nicky ran several circles and squatted low on her front legs, her tail lifted high in the air, wagging. Lennie danced around, her fists taut as she made circles with them in rhythm. "Oh no. I won. Game done."

Nicky ran at her, stopped abruptly, barked, and then took off. While teasing the dog and hopping around, Lennie caught a glimpse of Grey. The victory dance ended midstep. Her eyes grew large, and something between embarrassment and amusement played across her face.

"Teacher Lena." Grey nodded once. "What are you doing?"

She gained control over her surprise. *"Wie bischt du Heit?"* She straightened, asking Ivan how he was today.

"Hund!" Ivan chirped loudly.

"Ya, en verhuddelder Hund."

Ivan laughed at Lennie saying she had a confused dog.

Before he'd married, Grey raised dogs, and one year Lennie's Daed had asked Grey to keep an eye out for a particularly good dog for her, one that matched a whole list of things she would like in a pet. By the time Nicky was eight weeks old, Grey knew she'd make a perfect dog for Lennie. Grey thought Nicky was the best kind of dog—a mixed breed. She had a little Chow, Labrador retriever, and Australian Shepherd in her, and weighed about fifty pounds fully mature.

Lennie dusted off her hands. "Any news from the board I need to know about?"

"No. We got it all settled."

She nodded, crossed the yard, and held out her hand for Ivan's. He placed his inside hers. She talked to him in Pennsylvania Dutch, telling him that he was growing fast and that he'd be in her class, ready to learn how to read and write, by this time next year.

"Haldscht Schul fer die Handikap?" Ivan asked.

Startled, Grey found it hard to catch his breath. *Did she teach at a school for the handicapped?* He was sure his eyes mirrored the same confusion as Lennie's.

She looked at Ivan and told him no.

"Ich geh in die Handikap Schul," Ivan said.

Grey couldn't believe his son's words. What made him think he would go to the handicap school?

Lennie searched Grey's eyes for a moment. Feeling insulted by whoever had told his son that, Grey lifted him off his shoulders and held him. His son was small for his age and missing part of an arm, and if Grey dared to be painfully honest, Ivan was a good bit less mature than most five-year-olds, but none of that qualified him to attend a school for the handicapped. Speaking in Pennsylvania Dutch, Grey asked who'd told him he was going to the handicap school.

"Mamm."

Anger—years of it—swooped through Grey. Their son was missing part of one arm. What would possess his wife to tell him he needed to go to a school for the handicapped?

Silently fighting offense as he never had before, he felt displaced, as if he weren't really there. Yet he noticed every movement and heard every word. Lennie held out her arms for Ivan, asking if he wanted to pet the doggy. Ivan went to her. She gently commanded Nicky to lie down. The dog obeyed, and Lennie knelt beside Ivan while they petted the dog and talked about her fur being soft, like a rabbit's.

When Grey regained his ability to move, he picked up the basket. "He'll go to our local school."

Lennie stood. "I…I'm sure she's only thinking of his best interest."

"Oh, ya, sure." Grey doubted that his effort to conceal his frame of mind hid anything at all.

Lennie shrugged. "It's nearly a year away yet."

"Ya." Grey motioned for Ivan. *"Kumm mol, loss uns geh."* As soon as Grey said, *Come on, let's go,* his little boy hurried to him, telling Lennie bye.

He put Ivan on his shoulders again. Lena grabbed the poles off the ground and passed them to him. He mumbled his thanks and started walking. Hard. Fast. Unforgiving.

The closer he got to his house, the more resentment woke inside him. When he came to the sidewalk that led to his front door, he walked straight past it. He didn't trust what he might say…or how he'd say it.

He and Elsie were fragile. Although he was hard pressed to imagine how they could be more distant than they already were, he didn't doubt it was possible. Ignoring his intense desire to set her straight about their son, he took Ivan with him and kept walking.

"Daed? *Heem geh?*" Ivan asked.

Needing to answer his son's question about where they were going, Grey quickly decided on his destination. He told him they were going to the cabinetry shop. They often went there on Saturday afternoons, and Ivan enjoyed it. With Grey's long strides and his taking shortcuts through several fields, he was soon on Mast property.

As he approached the shop, he heard the air compressor running, followed by bursts of noise as nails were shot into wood. When he crossed the threshold, he saw Ephraim inside a frame of what would eventually be a standing pantry. He'd like to talk to Ephraim, but he wouldn't. His burdens were between him and Elsie.

Ephraim glanced up and gave a nod before continuing with his work.

A few moments later Ephraim walked to the generator and turned off the compressor. "Been to the pond, huh?"

Grey set the fishing tackle on the concrete floor. "Ya." He took Ivan off his shoulders. His son went to the barrel of scraps and pulled out blocks of wood to build with.

"Grab that crown molding for me, will ya?" Ephraim asked.

Grey brought four sections to him.

Ephraim passed him a piece of sandpaper. "The Wertzes want this same molding to run along the wall from the top of the pantry to the floor. It works in spite of the wave that's in the Wertzes' walls, but I could use your help coping these inside corners to fit against the pantry. I was at their place earlier, so I've already measured and marked everything accordingly."

Grey gave a nod, and they began sanding the wood.

"I appreciate you coming in on Saturdays and helping here and there."

Grey didn't want to admit that he was using this time today to avoid going home, so he nodded again.

"If you ever have something you want to tell me…"

He shook his head. "Can't. But thanks."

The two worked in silence for a while.

Then Ephraim laid the wood to the side. "Cara didn't trust me at all at first. Did you know that?"

"No."

The sound of Ivan smacking wood against the concrete floor echoed through the room.

Ephraim rested against the workbench. "All I remember thinking about her at first was that I wanted her out of Dry Lake before anyone else could catch wind of who she was. When I had to step up and speak to the police to keep her and Lori from being separated, I realized she wasn't just an inconvenience who had showed up in my life at the worst time ever. She was a real person who hadn't been given a break in a really long time." Ephraim shrugged. "I think the only reason I recognized that in her is because I'd seen it in you time and again."

The weight around him grew stronger, pressing in like he was caught under deep water. "I…we need help," Grey whispered, releasing years of hidden truth. "I…can't imagine going on like this, and there is no way out. You know that." Grey's eyes burned, and he glanced across the room at his son. Ivan had surrounded himself with blocks of scrap wood and was stacking them as high as he could. "We've been in separate rooms for years. She refuses to talk about anything. How can I make that work?"

"Separate…" The look on Ephraim's face and the tone of his voice held alarm and distress, and Grey found comfort in it. With that one awful word, Ephraim understood Grey's isolation and the impassable cinder-block wall surrounding him and Elsie. "Why?"

"I don't know, at least not the real reason. There are times when I'm not sure I care anymore." Grey clasped his hands around his head. "Maybe I'm pushing her away."

"What makes you say that?"

"It…" He lowered his hands and walked to the doublewide open door. Gazing out over the fields, he tried to find the courage to confess. "The regret began without my permission… I'd wake at night, or maybe it woke me, but I wish we'd never married."

Ephraim moved next to him. "It can't be all that uncommon for people to feel that way sometimes."

He stared off in the distance, wishing he hadn't started this conversation and yet too desperate to keep it all inside any longer. "If she's picking up on how I feel, maybe I carry more blame than I think I do."

"Or maybe she's causing those feelings. Whatever's going on, there have to be answers."

He turned around to check on Ivan before he looked straight at Ephraim. "I'm so stinking mad at her right now that I'm afraid to go home. Just before I came here, Ivan said she plans on sending him to the handicap school." Grey smacked the metal frame of the door with the palm of his hand. "As the head of our home, I have final say about where he goes, but why would she tell him that? Is he not perfect enough for her? Does she want to hide him from our district?" Even though Ivan didn't understand much English and was at the far end of the building, Grey had whispered his words. "The closest school of that kind is nearly two hours away. We'd have to move, and I'd have to find a new job. If I thought he needed it, I'd do it. Is she seeing him wrong, or am I?"

The sound of wooden blocks tumbling made both Ephraim and Grey look at Ivan. He stood in the middle of strewn blocks, kicking them.

"I know he's a little immature, but—"

"Grey," Ephraim interrupted, "if we sent every immature first grader to the handicap school, a lot of us would've gone there. Including me."

"He's smart. I know he is."

"He seems bright to me."

"Then why would his own mother want to send him there?"

"Don't know. He's suppose to start school next year, right?"

"Ya."

"If I were you, I'd refuse to argue about it. You need an outside opin-ion, and I'd bet Lena would be the best help. I could be biased, since she's my cousin, but she's really good at what she does—understanding and helping her scholars. If she spent an afternoon testing him, like she does her first-grade students right before they start school, she could tell you how close he is to lining up with the other children his age. And she could probably let you know how much of a handicap he has because of his missing arm."

"I hadn't thought of that. She'd be honest too. She can always be trusted for that, but I don't know if Elsie will hear her."

Ephraim placed his hand on Grey's shoulder. "I find it hard to believe, but you still care what your wife thinks."

He gave a nod before he turned to study the fields, willing wisdom and direction to come to him. "The one thing I've learned about being married is that how I feel changes nothing. Ever."

"Whatever you do will be tough, but maybe what love you two do have is tougher."

Ephraim's words butted against the constant negative whispers inside Grey—the ones that spoke to him of defeat over and over again.

Love never fails.

He caught a glimpse of understanding, as if seeing inside an unfamil-iar room for a brief moment. Love had a hope all its own.

"Daed?" Ivan tugged at Grey's pant leg. "Heem geh?"

Feeling tears sting his eyes, Grey lifted his son and held him close. *"Ya, loss uns Heemet geh."* He looked to Ephraim. "It's time I go on home now."

Eight

In her jeans and with her short crop of hair down, Cara continued reading the Sunday paper, enjoying the slower pace of between Sundays. Lori sat on a kitchen stool beside her, giggling over the comics. Cara hadn't seen Ada or Deborah yet this morning, although she knew they were up. A fresh pot of coffee and a small fire in the potbelly stove had greeted her and Lori when they'd entered the kitchen about thirty minutes ago.

Deborah walked into the kitchen looking every bit as Amish as she did on the other six days of the week, except she had on a white organdy apron that didn't cover the top half of her dress. Her hair was fixed just so. She made living Amish look easy. *"Guder Marye."* Deborah bid a good morning before grabbing the poker. She opened the lid to the potbelly stove and stirred the embers. "We don't want this burning for long, but we needed a little something to remove the nip in the air. I take it you're not going to Dry Lake with us for services this morning?"

Cara bit her tongue and shook her head. It was an off day, for Pete's sake. Besides, she had yard work to do. While shopping at yard sales yesterday, she'd found an item she wanted but didn't have the money for. An older woman at the sale offered to buy the item for Cara in exchange for some yard work. So the two of them struck a deal, and by tonight Cara would have earned a fantastic gift for Lori. Of course it was used, but Lori wouldn't mind that part—if she even noticed it.

Deborah fixed herself a cup of coffee. "Ada will be down in a minute.

We're leaving extra early so I can visit my family first. You're welcome to join us. We'll stay for the meal afterward and probably visit until midafternoon."

"Nope, we're good. Thanks." Cara liked between Sundays ever so much more than church Sundays. Ephraim had church today in Dry Lake, and he would come to Hope Crossing next Sunday to go to church with her, Lori, Ada, and Deborah. But so far he'd not pressed her to come to Dry Lake on her off Sundays. She appreciated that. It was enough for her that she sat through three hours of unintelligible preaching every other Sunday. Of course Ephraim understood the language spoken during the service, and he'd grown up attending three-hour services.

What possessed the Amish to have such long services anyway? But sometimes, when a few Pennsylvania words that she understood were strung together, she found it exciting. And those rare moments helped move the service from hair-pulling boring to slightly interesting.

Deborah sipped her drink. "Just as well, I suppose. The meeting will be held at the Lantzes' today."

"Lantz?" Cara tried to hide the snarl she felt. "As in Anna Mary Lantz?"

"Ya. It's at her parents' place."

Anna Mary's parents—just the thought of them set her on edge. Their deceit had ruined Cara's mother's life and had opened the flood-gates of bad luck. It'd overflowed into Cara's life and even Lori's, yet the Lantzes were still members in good standing. She'd never understand the Amish ways. Not ever.

"But if you don't go… Well, I just want some backup when Lena returns the favor for our prank on her."

"She won't pull anything on a Sunday during church, will she?"

"No, not during the service but maybe afterward."

"Good luck with that, Deb." Cara patted her on the shoulder.

"You're awful. The plan was yours after all."

Cara shrugged. "Yeah, but Lori and I met an old woman yesterday. She lives a few doors down, and we're going to her house in a little bit."

"To visit?" Deborah asked.

"Sort of. I'll tell you the rest when we get back." She placed her index finger over her lips before pointing at Lori. "It's a surprise."

"But you're not wearing that, are you?"

Cara looked down at her clothes. "Yep. It's my off day. I'm comfortable. And I'm in my rumschpringe."

"Well, now, see, you're a little wrong. It's the Lord's Day. You've already admitted that dresses are just as comfortable as jeans. And the rumschpringe doesn't apply to you since its purpose is for freedom to find a spouse and you've found one."

Cara rolled her eyes. "Hair pinned back and prayer Kapp too?"

"You don't have to, but do you think wearing only part of our Amish apparel is a good idea?"

"I guess not." She sighed. "Great."

Ada walked into the kitchen, wearing what looked like a new burgundy dress under a new apron. Cara whistled.

Ada's cheeks grew pink. "Don't be ridiculous, Cara."

"Oh, so there isn't a man in Dry Lake you're hoping to look good for?" Cara continued to tease.

Deborah's face radiated behind her mostly hidden smile, and Cara knew she hoped the same thing for Ada.

"That's more than enough, girls," Ada said firmly before she took a chair. "I feel too old for such nonsense."

"You're not old. Don't you know forty is the new thirty?" When Ada looked torn between amusement and true embarrassment, Cara decided to change the subject. "How are you getting there if the horse is lame?"

A car horn tooted, and Cara had the answer to her question. A driver was picking them up.

"Ephraim's driver for the cabinetry shop stopped by yesterday and volunteered to come get us and bring us back home today without charge, so we took him up on it." Deborah gave Lori a quick hug. "You be good."

"Gut is was ich bescht duh." Lori beamed at her, saying something along the lines of, "Good is what I do best."

Ada gave Cara a hug. "The way you see me and tease, you do make me feel younger." She took a step back. "I don't know how we'd have gotten through these past few months without you."

"Denki." Cara winked. "Be sure to bring Ephraim back with you, okay?"

"You think we or *anybody* could stop him?"

"I hope not."

After she closed the door behind them, she scurried upstairs and changed her clothes. By this afternoon she'd have helped an elderly woman and bartered for something Lori had only dreamed of. Excitement coursed through her. She couldn't remember when she'd had the ability to give Lori something truly special.

Grey stood at the sink with a cup of coffee in one hand while reading a newspaper he wished he hadn't picked up. The words made his heart thud with longing and…and jealousy? The Amish Mennonite newspaper had been neatly tucked in its rack since last Wednesday. While walking past it, he'd spied his own name—Benjamin Graber. Folks called him Grey, but Benjamin was his given name. So the newspaper had caught his attention, and he'd grabbed it to see what the man who shared his name had been up to. The impulse had seemed innocent enough. But now here he stood, flooded with emotions.

"Reading the paper on a Sunday before church?" Elsie asked.

He heard her complaint, but he continued reading the article. The man who shared his name lived in Ohio with his wife. It was common for the Amish to have the same given name and surnames. That was part of the reason for his nickname. According to the article, this Benjamin had been married for three decades, and he and his wife finished each other's sentences, laughed easily, and shared their heartaches freely. They'd enjoyed blessings and suffered losses by leaning on each other.

Grey set his coffee and paper on the counter and stared out the kitchen window. How did he and Elsie get to such a miserable place? Each of them living in their own world, yet they shared the greatest bond this planet had to offer—marriage vows. And a beautiful child as proof of that unity.

But it was as if they stood on opposite sides of a wide canyon. They could see each other, but even when shouting across the chasm, they couldn't understand much, if anything, of what the other one said, and there seemed to be no way to cross over.

When he'd come home last night, he'd tried to keep to himself what he'd learned of Elsie's intention to send Ivan to a special school. His thoughts were still lingering on the words *love never fails,* but when she'd grumbled about his clothes smelling like fish and about his wasting too much of the day on nonsense, he'd snapped at her, saying that Ivan would go to the local school. She'd stood in front of him speechless, looking frustrated by his anger. They'd muddled through the rest of the evening, offering stilted half sentences when conversation couldn't be avoided. The moment Ivan was in his bed for the night, he'd retired to his bedroom, closing the door behind him without another word being spoken. Never had such a gulf existed between them as the one last night.

When he stopped gazing out the window, he saw Elsie skimming the article he'd just read. Pursing her lips, she slid the paper onto the table. Then she went to the refrigerator and grabbed several large blocks of cheese. It was their contribution to the after-service meal. "It's almost time for us to leave for church. Is the horse hitched?"

Were her hands trembling?

"Is that all you have to say?"

She dumped his coffee in the sink. "It's a church day. And if we don't leave soon, we'll be late."

"Ya." Grey took his hat from the coatrack. "It wouldn't do for anyone to think we're less than perfect." Sunlight and cool air filled his senses when he stepped outside, but as he continued to fight and grumble with his wife, he seemed less able to enjoy the simple things. He went to the barn, got the horse out of the stall, and began harnessing her.

At the start of their marriage, only a few feet had separated them. Normal things—like not knowing or understanding each other's ways in certain areas—but he'd expected love to override those things. Wasn't embracing someone else's faults part of what friends did for each other? And marriage was supposed to be the best friendship of all.

His wife's shadow fell across the dirt floor of the barn. He led the horse and carriage toward her. Ivan stood beside her as she held a basket filled with cheese. "Whatever is going on inside that heart of yours, I can't go on living like this. Something has to change."

She started toward the buggy. "We need to go."

"Does anything I want even matter to you?"

Stopping abruptly, she lowered her gaze. "If you could just accept…"

He took the basket from her and set it inside the carriage. Was she waiting on him to finish her sentence like the other Benjamin Graber could for his wife? He had no clue what she might say. Back when they'd been married only a couple of months, he realized that he didn't understand her at all, because when she'd told him she was pregnant, he was excited. She wasn't.

After Ivan was born, she'd become distant and temperamental. He'd tried to help her by sharing her load of the work, making her breakfasts, and spending extra time with her. He didn't know if those things helped her, but within a year she was doing better. They began sharing a bed again. When their second son was stillborn, the grief had been unbearable.

By the time the intensity of their pain began to lift, he realized the distance between them was vast.

Elsie raised her eyes to his. "I made a vow to never tell you."

"Ivan." Grey pointed to the swing set in their backyard and told him to go play until he called him.

Ivan looked up at his mother. She didn't allow playing outside on Sundays until the afternoon. She said nothing, and he hurried toward the house.

"Whatever your secret, you've done a good job of keeping it. Too good. And if you knew how sick I am of how we live, you'd shout the secret from the rooftop."

She looked steely cold as she shrugged, and Grey wanted to shake her.

Slowly she went toward the buggy. "We'll be late."

"I don't care!"

She jolted, and embarrassment engraved itself on her face. He drew a breath and tried to keep his tone civil. "I may not be much of a husband in your eyes, but answer me this: don't I at least deserve to know what stands between us?"

She rubbed the center of her forehead. "Okay," she whispered. "I…I've always feared that the truth would finish destroying what little love you have for me."

He studied her, seeing raw ache under all her layers of organized perfection. Did the pain come from losing one son? Or from being married to Grey? As her husband, he should know. "What truth?"

"You know it, Grey. You just don't want to admit it."

"For the love of my sanity, Elsie, please stop talking in circles."

"Fine. You want to make me say it aloud? You want to make me take the blame? Then I will. We can't have more children. We *must* not. Not ever."

Alarm rang inside him, warning him not to let this conversation end until he understood. "Why?"

"Don't be absurd. You know why."

As he struggled to grasp what she meant, he took her by the arm. "Tell me why."

She pulled away. "Can't you see it? Ivan is missing part of one arm, and he...he's slow. When our second son was stillborn, the midwife told me something genetic was probably wrong with him. I can't...I won't have a family of children with physical and mental issues because I want to be with you. That's selfish."

Barely able to breathe, Grey leaned against a nearby wall for support. This was what separated them? He'd imagined hundreds of reasons over the years but never once thought of this.

Elsie moved to him. "I know I'm not an easy woman to love. And I'm not sure what I expected to happen to us when I started shutting you out, but I've only wanted to spare you."

He felt sure he should have compassion for her, but he didn't. "I had the right to know what caused you to behave as you do."

"Why? So you could change my mind, only for us to have another child that broke our hearts?"

"Ivan did not break my heart. He's a strong, healthy boy. And I don't think he's slow, not like that. And even if he is, no part of me enjoys him any less. Besides, what do you want from him? To be perfect? Like who? You? Me? May God spare him from our type of perfection, Elsie."

Needing to get away from her, he walked outside. He looked toward the house, making sure the best part of the last six years was still safe inside their yard. His little boy's blond hair shined like a white pillowcase in the sun. His hat lay on the ground, and his belly was on the seat of the swing as he dragged his lone hand lightly across the dirt.

Elsie walked to where he stood.

Grey couldn't even look at her. "You locked me out of your heart and our bedroom because you decided that was the best solution. You didn't ask your husband or the church leaders. Didn't seek out medical advice.

Didn't try to ease my loneliness by being honest. You did exactly as you chose." He turned to look her in the eyes.

"Grey, that's…that's not fair."

He pointed at her. "You do not have the right to talk to me about what's fair!" As he stood in his driveway yelling at his wife, Grey hated himself, hated who he'd become. For years he'd wanted them to talk, and now he couldn't gain control of his rage.

Studying him, their home, and their son, she seemed to waver in her position, as if some small bit of what he'd said might have merit. Part of him wanted to shake her. Part of him wished he could embrace her…and never let go.

He went toward the house. All these years he'd thought she didn't love him. He'd been convinced she regretted marrying him. He stopped and went back to her. "And it's not true. We do not have some defect that caused Ivan to have a deformed arm or caused our other son to be still-born. It's not us. Not you. Not me. Not who we are together. Those things just happen sometimes. That's all." He walked away again.

Elsie grabbed him by the arm. "It *is* true. Do you think I'd pull away from you if I didn't believe it? I'm trapped between a husband I love and a body that bears unsound children. Will you hold what I've done against me?"

"You've made our lives miserable, Elsie. And you had no right."

Tears fell, and she swiped them away. "Tell Ivan it's time for us to go."

Grey stared at her, remembering a hundred church Sundays of riding side by side while engulfed in loneliness and silence. Nothing carried weight like emptiness did. And it had stood between them most of their married years. Would they finally get to this point of her sharing her burden, regardless of how wrong she'd been, only to start over in the same dark, horrid place? "Why would you do this to us based on a guess?"

Her face was taut as she pursed her lips. "I…I…can't."

As he studied her, he saw more than just her failure. He saw his own.

His mind churned with memories, and he knew he'd made it too easy for her to shut him out. And his anger eased.

At twenty-seven, Elsie had lines of weariness creasing her face, and in that moment he felt the depth of her struggle to speak, and the heaviness of the guilt she felt, and the pain of the fears that rested on her day and night.

"We need help, Elsie."

"There's no help. There's only putting one foot in front of the other. You know that."

He used to think her no-nonsense personality would keep him straight. Now he'd give about anything to be able to get past that. "So you've stopped believing in hope altogether?" Ivan's voice carried on the wind as he sang loudly. Elsie's eyes moved to Grey's, and they shared a moment of parenting pleasure. They knew he was singing to God, not as a worship-type song, but as entertainment *for* God.

She watched their son, her eyes filling with tears. "You know that I...I have an aunt in Ohio...who...has five children with birth defects. After Ivan was born, she said that whatever is wrong with her, I must have the same thing." Tears trailed down her face.

Maybe she was right. Maybe they couldn't have completely healthy children. As his confidence waned, he reached out to put his arms around her.

She backed away. "I'm sorry for the way it is."

"We can't live on just a notion of yours. We never should have, and I won't let it continue. We've got to know for sure about Ivan, about our DNA. And then we'll make decisions from there."

She cleared her throat and gave a weak nod. "Don't, Grey. Please. The answers will not give us peace. It'll only bury the rest of what hope you have."

"I won't let fear stop us."

"Then truth will, and you will learn that I'm right."

Nothing they discovered would be any harder than coping with her years of silence.

Ivan hollered to them, asking why they weren't going to church.

They'd be more than thirty minutes late to a three-hour service, but Grey wanted to go. He had hope that it might offer some nugget to help him and Elsie.

Nine

After ringing the doorbell, Cara brushed strands of hair off her forehead. While waiting on the woman to answer the door, she surveyed her work. What had been an overgrown yard hours ago now looked manicured. She'd mowed and weeded. Lori had worked too. While they were hauling clippings and weeds to the mulch pit, Cara finally told her about the item they were working for—a beautiful bicycle.

She wasn't sure which Lori was the most excited about, the bike or the fact that they were working side by side to earn it.

The elderly woman came out of her home, eyes bright with appreciation. "Just look at this place." She turned to Lori. "You're a lucky little girl to have a mama who'd do all this for a bike."

Lori put her arms around Cara's waist and hugged her.

The woman motioned. "Come on. It's right inside the garage." They went down the steps. "I'm sure that's the last the yard will need for the season, but if you're around next spring and are interested in making money, stop on by. I have a yard boy, but by the time he can get here every few weeks, I need someone to bale hay rather than mow grass."

"It might be a good extra job for me, but I don't know right now. We can talk about it next spring, okay?"

"Sounds good." The woman went to a keypad and punched in several numbers, and the garage door opened. Motioning for Lori to follow her, she walked inside. "There it is."

Lori's eyes grew huge as she gaped at her mother. "It's...it's perfect!" She grabbed it by the handlebars and ran outside. The purple and pink metallic swirls glittered under the rays of sunlight. "Oh, Mom, this is just too cool." She straddled it and put her feet on the pedals. The bike fell to one side, and Lori jolted, putting her feet back on the concrete. "Teach me how to ride this thing."

Her daughter's excited voice rang out as she waved at the woman. "Thank you." Lori put her feet on the pedals again, and the wheels started turning.

Cara grabbed the bike's seat and smiled at the woman. "I...I better go."

The woman laughed. "I guess you better. Bye for now."

Cara ran on the sidewalk beside Lori, trying to give helpful instructions for how to find her balance. By the time they'd gone around the block once, Cara could let go of the seat for several seconds at a time. As they made their way around the block a second time, Cara only grabbed it when Lori was about to fall. Finally she released her and clapped as Lori rode about fifty feet before stopping herself.

Cara trotted to where she was. "That's great, honey. You are so good at this." They worked their way around the block for the third time, and as they approached Ada's House, she noticed two Amish men in front of the place, watching her.

Lori came to them first and stopped. Cara couldn't hear what her daughter was saying, but she could tell by her movements she was showing them her bike.

As Cara approached, she recognized them. One was a preacher from right here in Hope Crossing. The other was a bishop for several Amish communities: Dry Lake, Hope Crossing, and some other Amish district Cara wasn't familiar with. But he lived in Hope Crossing.

Cara straightened her prayer Kapp and tried to tuck loose strands of hair back into place before she stopped in front of them. "Hello."

"Hi, Cara."

She looked at the bishop. "I thought you'd be at the service in Dry Lake."

"I often am. Each district has visiting preachers from time to time, and they had plenty of preachers for today, so I stayed home. I went to the door, but it seems Deborah and Ada aren't here."

"They're attending the service in Dry Lake."

The bishop nodded as if that answered all sorts of questions he had. "Can we speak to you alone for a bit?"

Suddenly feeling unsure about what they might want, she turned to Lori. "You can ride up and down the sidewalk that leads to Ada's front porch."

"That's all? How about from here to the end of the block?"

"Not by yourself."

"But you can see me the whole way."

"Nope. You might keep right on going until you're in the middle of the street."

Lori started to argue, but Cara splayed her hand as if she was going to start counting. Lori nodded and began riding up the thirty-foot segment that led to Ada's front porch.

Cara took several breaths, glad not to be chasing that bike around the block. "So what's on your mind?"

"You're new to our ways, Cara. And you've been doing well. That's first and foremost to remember, but do you know what today is?"

"You mean aside from it being a between Sunday for those of us in Hope Crossing?"

The bishop shifted. "It is still a Sunday, and you were mowing some-one's grass."

Her heart raced as she realized they'd come to correct her. "How do you know what I've been doing?"

"Someone saw you over an hour ago and came straight to us."

"Ah, so the Amish system of accountability depends greatly on tattletales."

The bishop scratched his beard, not looking even slightly perturbed at her retort. "Let's keep this friendly, Cara. You've made a couple of mistakes. That's all. If it helps, the person who told isn't Amish."

"Why would anyone do that?"

He shrugged, looking sympathetic. "People and motives are hard to figure, but we came as soon as we heard, in hopes of stopping you from doing anything else that might cause trouble for you."

"But I wasn't making any money, and mowing a yard isn't any more tiring than those boys playing baseball or volleyball on Sunday afternoons. That's allowed, right?"

"Ya, in the afternoon after they've had time to reflect on God," the preacher said.

Unable to accept their stance, Cara put one hand on her hip. Frustration circled round and round. "You're splitting hairs."

"It's our way not to work on Sunday. Surely Ephraim's shared that with you."

She did seem to remember him saying something about that. "Women fix food on Sundays, don't they?"

"We do as much preparation as possible on Saturdays, but fixing meals is allowed." The bishop's tone changed from one of explaining to one of slight frustration.

She squelched her irritation by counting. It was then that she realized what he meant by stopping her "from doing anything else that might cause trouble." If she hoped to be allowed to go through instruction starting late spring, she needed to stay in good standing with the church. They'd come over immediately to keep her from messing up her future plans. "Okay, fine. I won't do anything like this again."

"Good. And I…uh…well, when you talk to Ephraim, mention to him the type of lawn mower you used." He gave a nod as if they were ready to leave.

"Wait. Are you saying part of the reason you're here is because I used the wrong kind of mower?"

"I know how it probably sounds to you, but next time you mow grass, use a reel mower, not a gasoline-powered one."

Tinges of embarrassment began to mix with her anger. "But we use gas stoves."

"Natural gas is allowed to come into our homes through a propane tank. We don't use gasoline-powered anything—not cars, tractors, or lawn mowers."

"Well, Amish certainly ride in gas-powered vehicles."

"Sparingly so is the goal. Another, stricter goal is to avoid hiring a driver on a Sunday. The exceptions to that are situations like the one Ada is in, a widow wanting to return to her home community on church Sundays, or Ephraim, who catches a ride with a friend. Once we allow our people the right to hire a driver for absolute necessities, like medical needs or making a living, we do little to control what else a driver is hired for. We try to leave that up to their good judgment. But to hold on to our ways, we do not operate gas-powered machines ourselves."

As annoyance tried to get the best of her, she thought of Ephraim. Anything she said or did reflected on him. He'd withstood a shunning for her sake, and he deserved better than her arguing with the church leaders. "I'll use a reel mower next time."

A genuine smile began in the bishop's eyes and spread to his mouth. "Good. Very good. I'm pleased to have this kind of talk with you."

The preacher turned to the bishop and made a motion. The bishop shook his head.

She glanced from one bearded man to the other. "There's more, isn't there?"

The preacher turned to the bishop. "The longer you allow it, the more we look like hypocrites."

The bishop shook his head, and she could only guess he didn't want to say whatever the preacher wanted said.

"Well?" Her tone could cause frostbite, but she didn't care.

"Bicycles are forbidden," the preacher said.

The skin on her face burned. Finally, after years of poverty, she'd been able to give Lori something she wanted, something really, really nice. "What?" She crossed her arms. "No way. I'm not asking her to give that up."

"It's the way it is for members and their children. You have no choice."

She stared at the man. "Oh, there's always a choice."

"It's forbidden."

"Yeah? Well, that's just too stinking bad. This conversation is over."

Deborah closed her eyes during the final prayer of the service, willing answers to come about how to make Ada's House a success. She'd sat through three sermons given by different men and the congregational songs she loved so dearly, all the while searching for solutions. The constant hunt had kept her up half the night, but she didn't have one new idea to show for it.

The service ended soon after the last song, and within minutes the home was a buzz of noisy activity as the hosts and many helpers began preparing for the after-service meal. Some of the adults held a quick discussion as to where they'd set up. The heat of summer was gone, and this early-October day seemed to be begging to be enjoyed, so Deborah hoped they'd decide to eat outdoors.

Jonathan held one end of a bench and Ephraim the other, waiting on directions.

"Let's set up outside," Rueben said.

The men quickly moved the wooden benches through the kitchen and out the front door. They would alter the underpinnings on half the benches, making those seats into tables. She helped the women hosts get the tables set and food laid out family style—homemade breads, sliced cheese, ham, cheese spread, peanut butter spread, pickles, red beets, and seasoned pretzels, along with some raw veggies and a few fruits.

Soon Rueben had the ministers seated as well as the oldest men in the district. While they began eating, Deborah helped the Lantz women set a table for the oldest women in the district. As soon as the group who'd been seated first was finished, women swooped in and cleaned off the tables. Deborah and Anna Mary washed rounds of dishes while fresh bread and cheese were sliced and the makings for sandwiches were placed for the next group to eat. Just as the married men and women sat separately during church and the meal, the single men sat separated from the single women, but later tonight the singles would attend a singing. After they'd sung the good-bye song, they would mingle at will while eating.

Deborah and Anna Mary stayed busy helping. Finally it was time for them to stop washing dishes and eat. Deborah dried her hands and passed the towel to her friend. A look passed between them, and she knew that neither of them enjoyed these Sunday mealtimes as they once had. She and Anna Mary used to feel that the after-service meal was a romantic lead-up to the Sunday night singings. They'd steal looks at their beaus, who sat at a nearby table, and share a smile or a nod. But that was over for both of them. Anna Mary had rarely caught Ephraim's attention during these times anyway, but Mahlon had always been attentive to Deborah, or at least he'd pretended to be.

Even after all Mahlon had dragged her through, she still couldn't make herself believe the depth of his deceit. He'd lived a double life, and the most awful thing about it was that Deborah had believed she knew him, understood him. They'd grown up together. Attended the same school. Spent their Sundays—

Jonathan's hazel eyes met hers, bringing her previous thoughts to a full stop. His pale blond hair hung below his straw hat, and his black suit fit snugly across his wide shoulders, making her wonder if he'd accidently worn one of his brother's jackets. What was the man doing watching her—setting her up for a prank? Lena had probably told him about the cake Deborah had given her, and now the two of them were plotting against her. He'd always treated her like a mix between a good friend and a kid sister, both of which made her easy prey for pranks and teasing.

When she and Anna Mary drew closer to the table, Lena waved for them to sit next to her. She sat next to Lena, but while she ate, her thoughts returned to Ada's House. What could she do to make it a success? Preoccupied with her search for answers, she quietly nibbled on her food.

Against the tradition of keeping to the men's table, Jonathan straddled the bench beside her. When she glanced around, she realized people were starting to leave for home. The official church time and its customary ways were over, so he was free to shift into a more relaxed mode. Jonathan and Lena chatted, but Deborah couldn't stop trying to figure out a solution for Ada's House. There had to be one. What was she overlooking?

Lena poked Deborah's side, making her look up. Deborah's Daed stood beside the table, and he must've said something, because he and several other men standing with him were seemingly waiting for an answer.

"He's glad you came," Jonathan mumbled while pouring ice water into her cup.

She nodded at her Daed. "Me too, Daed. You should come visit us in Hope Crossing and go to Sunday meetings with us when you're up to it."

Her father smiled. Those few moments were very important. With other men around him, her Daed had stopped to acknowledge his pleasure with her, even though she was single and had moved out of his home and into another community. He'd given her a seal of approval during a church gathering in front of everyone. For her not to notice when he spoke would have been an insult. When he and the men walked off, she relaxed. Jonathan and Lena laughed softly.

"What are you two laughing at? It's not my fault my mind was elsewhere."

"Nope, it was your Daed's," Jonathan heckled.

On impulse she picked up her cup and tried to dump the contents on him. She leaned back just as he knocked it out of her hand, and they ended up dousing Lena.

Lena wiped her wet face and slung water at them. "Denki."

Deborah pointed at Jonathan, and he pointed at her, each blaming the other. Lena grabbed a napkin and soaked up some of the moisture from her dress.

Grey passed by, holding an empty glass with one hand and Ivan's hand with the other. "Taking showers after you've dressed for the day again, Lennie?"

"I keep forgetting which one comes first," Lena retorted. She raised an eyebrow at Deborah while trying to hide her smile. "Jonathan helps you save face, and you two do this to me? Some friends you guys are."

Deborah watched as Grey stopped near a small group of men and started talking. She'd seen him and Elsie come in really late. Elsie had shed a few tears during the service, and Deborah had said a silent prayer for them. They'd been married six years and had one child. That wasn't the norm for an Amish family, but no one asked them any questions. Since they'd buried a son, she was sure no one ever would ask—not even Grey's or Elsie's friends, siblings, or parents.

Ephraim moved closer. "I'd like to go to Hope Crossing as soon as we can. Robbie's coming by my place in just a little bit."

"Ada and me hoped to stay here longer than that."

Ephraim grabbed several clean napkins that were a few feet away and passed them to Lena. "If Ada wants to stay longer, Robbie can take her home later this afternoon. But I want as much time with Cara as I can get before the workweek starts again."

Deborah was sure he'd rather have skipped service and spent his morning with Cara. Next Sunday was a between one for Dry Lake but not for Hope Crossing. Deborah, Ada, and Cara would need to attend the service in Hope Crossing next week. Courting was always easier when both people lived in the same church district. Then they were free to spend every other Sunday visiting all day. "I'll let Ada know."

Ephraim left.

"Listen, Deborah," Jonathan said, "I have a horse I can loan you. He's young, about two and a half years, and a little too inexperienced to wait for long periods while harnessed and tethered somewhere, but he'll be perfect for what you need until Rosie is ready to return to work."

"You didn't mention anything about having an extra horse yesterday. How do you have one now?"

"Because I'm magical." He splayed his hands, moving them around in circles as if he were a magician. "Or because the man who owns him owes me money he can't pay, so I'm borrowing his horse for a spell."

"You're holding the man's horse hostage?"

"It's called bartering. You need to understand that concept, because if you use that horse, I want desserts. Lots of them."

Deborah looked at Lena and pointed at him. "How does he stay so thin when all he does is devise ways to get desserts?"

"Because his plans never work. How many goodies has he talked you out of so far?"

Deborah chuckled and held out her hand to Jonathan. "We have a deal."

He shook her hand. "I'll get paid this time. You can count on that, Little Debbie." Rather than releasing her hand, he tugged at it. "Come on. We can ride to my place, tie the colt to the back of the carriage, and head for Ada's."

Deborah rose. "You'll go with us too, won't you, Lena?"

Lena's eyes moved to Jonathan for a moment. "No, I...I have things I need to do."

Deborah studied her. Lena and Jonathan were usually inseparable on Sundays.

"Or I could go to my place and get the colt while you spend a little more time with your friends."

"Okay," Deborah agreed.

Deborah went inside and found Ada in the sunroom, talking with two women and two men. Waiting for a break in the conversation, she looked out one of the windows. Jonathan crossed the road to where most of the horses were tethered to the sides of hay wagons. A wagon loaded with fresh hay under a shade tree kept the horses happy until they were needed again.

The discussion paused, and Deborah quickly explained what was going on and asked Ada how she wanted to handle the afternoon. All but Israel excused themselves, saying they'd catch Ada in a minute but they needed to get their containers out of the kitchen first.

"Did you want to ride with me and Jonathan in the buggy or go with Ephraim in Robbie's truck?"

"When are you leaving, Deborah?" Israel asked.

"Pretty quickly. Maybe fifteen minutes?"

Was that a trace of disappointment on Israel's face? Deborah knew that he'd not courted anyone in the thirteen years since Lena's mother and the others had died. Ada hadn't either.

"Ada." Israel spoke softly. "If you want to stay and visit family and friends for a while, I don't mind taking you home later on."

"Oh no, I couldn't..."

Deborah placed her hand on Ada's back, pressing her fingers firmly and hoping Ada took the signal. "Since you're here and it's a visiting day... us girls will be fine for a couple of hours without you."

"But it'll take Israel two hours round trip."

Israel's eyes danced with laughter. "A minute or two more than that if I can beg a cup of coffee."

Ada's hands moved to her hips, and she huffed. "Coffee? Well, I guess there's probably some left in the percolator from this morning. Can I serve it to you cold, or must I warm it up first?"

Was Ada flirting? Deborah wanted to make a quick exit before she interrupted whatever it was these two were doing. She kissed Ada on the cheek. "See you later."

Ten

From Anna Mary's bedroom, Deborah kept watch out the window, waiting for Jonathan to return. Her girlfriends, all eight of them, talked nonstop, but there was no hint about the stunt Cara and Deborah had pulled on Lena. Deborah figured she'd better watch her back. Everyone seemed united in their innocence, as if Deborah and Cara hadn't brought a salty, yucky cake to Lena four days ago. Whatever their game plan, Deborah would try to be ready for it.

When Jonathan pulled into the driveway with the colt tethered to the back of the carriage, she gave everyone a hug and invited them to Hope Crossing when they had time. She hurried outside, and as soon as Jonathan saw her, he got out of the rig. He came around to her side and offered a supportive hand. Getting in and out of these boxes known as carriages, even with the little footstep, wasn't easy, but she'd never had someone help her before—except her Daed when she was a little girl.

"The chestnut colt looks really sturdy and energetic," Deborah commented as she sat.

"Ya, I think he's a good one." He made sure her dress was inside before he closed the door. He went to the driver's side and got in.

"I appreciate you loaning us a horse."

"My pleasure, Deborah."

"Especially when you're eating all those cakes and pies."

A wonderful smile filled his face as he slapped the reins against the horse's back. "Ya."

The horse picked up speed as they left the driveway, and so did Deborah's thoughts. There had to be a way to make Ada's House a success. As they passed the Graber house, she saw Grey just inside the barn, unfettering his horse. Elsie was walking up the sidewalk toward their home, looking every bit as unhappy as when she'd arrived at the service.

Jonathan took a deep breath. "This year the first of October is as beautiful as I've ever seen."

She didn't say anything, and he nudged her. "Do you live in Hope Crossing most of the time or inside your own thoughts?"

Deborah shrugged, trying to snap out of her reclusive mood.

Jonathan matched her shrug with a smile that said he was teasing. "Ever get tired of thinking about him?"

She bristled. "Actually, I wasn't thinking of him at all."

The surprise on Jonathan's face was sincere. "Oh...well...you are now."

She chuckled. "Not really. I want to make a success of Ada's House so badly I can't think of much else, except..."

"Except?"

"Elsie and Grey. I wonder about them."

Jonathan nodded. "There's a story between those two, a sad one seems like. And here I was hoping you were thinking about how to fill a huge order of baked goods for me."

It bothered her for a woman to be as unhappy as Elsie seemed. Grey was harder to read. He always had a little humor or a kind word to add to every conversation. "Do you ever watch married couples and wonder if they're happy?"

He looked from the road to her. "This is odd—I know it is—but I've been watching pairs since I was a kid. From the time they start seeing each other and on through years of being married. It's like a game of sorts. I pick who I think would make a good pair. Or when two people are seeing each other, I think, are they an okay, good, or great couple? Unfortunately, once I grew up, I had to add a group to my list called the fed-up couples."

"Wow, you're deeper and weirder than I thought."

"I agree, but it came natural. I must've been five when I started couple watching."

"So what'd you think of Grey and Elsie before they married?"

He slowed the rig as they came to a yield sign. "My observations are private. I've never told anyone what I think of a couple."

"Not even Lena?"

"Nope."

"Then it'll be our secret."

Jonathan studied her for a moment, as if deciding something. He nodded. "I hate to admit it, hated to feel it, but I thought Grey was making a poor choice. I couldn't quite put my finger on what bothered me about her then, but now I'd say that Elsie's chronically unhappy. Aren't there too many spells of sadness in life for a person to be unhappy before the bad days even arrive?"

"Ephraim and Anna Mary?"

"Both great people. Could have been moderately happy at least half of the time, in my opinion."

"Half of the time?"

"She's a little needy—nothing ridiculous, mind you—but Ephraim is a little leave-me-alone-ish. Not the best union but better than lots."

"Okay, what about Emma and Levi Riehl?"

"They're almost old enough to be my parents, so I wasn't around when they started seeing each other. But I think they fit like most solid couples do. They know how to help each other enjoy the good times and get through the tough ones."

"I can agree with that. What about Ephraim and Cara?"

Jonathan chuckled. "Now there is an odd, odd pair. And I think they'll always have some difficulty fitting in with the community as a couple, but within their home, within the relationship with just each other, I bet they'll be happier than any couple I've ever known."

"Actually, you're very good at this. I've thought similar things to everything you just said. So what did you think of me and Mahlon?"

"Not going there, Little Debbie."

"Why not?"

"Because I think you are really peculiar. You're just not the kind of girl I'd ever talk to or share a buggy with," Jonathan teased. "And if I tell you all that, you'll get out of my buggy, and then you won't be around for me to talk to."

Deborah chuckled and sat back, enjoying the company. She'd always taken pleasure in a few smiles, laughs, and pleasant snippets of conversations whenever Jonathan was around, but she'd never spent any time with just him. Once alone, Mahlon was rarely cheerful. He was deep…or maybe just secretive. But Mahlon aside, she'd never realized how fun Jonathan could be. "So, if I made you a gazillion desserts, what would you do with all of them?"

"Hmm, well, that's a good question. Let me think. Umm. Oh, I got it. I'd sell them. Yep. Well…I'd sell the ones I didn't eat. Or maybe I'd eat half of each one I sold. Whatever. But I'd set up a booth outside Ada's House, reel in Englischer tourists with my adorable Amish clothing, maybe offer a carriage ride or two, and then sell them every dessert you paid me with."

She laughed but stopped when his words caused an idea to pop into her head. "That's it! That's the answer I've been looking for!" Deborah grabbed Jonathan's arm and shook it so hard the whole buggy wobbled. "You are a smart man!"

"Now see, that's what I've been telling everybody for years. No one ever listens to me. You tell them, Little Debbie." He paused, looking amused and gentle and even a little unsure of himself. "So what was my brilliant idea, anyway?"

She took the reins from him and pulled onto the shoulder of the road. "I'm serious."

The everyday gentleness seen so easily on his face deepened. "Then I'm listening."

"I've been trying to figure out how to make Ada's House a success. We're in over our heads. We owe bills we didn't expect and can't pay. You know, new business-owning difficulties."

"I didn't know all that."

"Well, now you do. Just keep it between us. Okay?"

"Sure. But Ada is supposed to live there nearly rent free because of all the painting Cara's doing."

"Cara's done most of what she can, so this month's rent increases. Plus we need to pay for gas to heat the water and stove, food, phone, baking supplies, and water bills. The hay in the pasture will be dried up soon, and we'll need to supplement through buying hay and a lot more horse feed. Oh, and those boxes for putting the desserts in so we can take them to the bakeries get really expensive. Sometimes I see why Mahlon felt so under it all the time."

He shook his head. "Don't believe it. People are under a load, or two or three of them, at times. But running out like he did is—"

Deborah raised her hand. "Change of subject, please."

"Ya, you're right. So what was my brilliant idea?"

"I…I'm not sure."

Jonathan started laughing so hard his tanned face turned a captivating shade of pink. "Wow, I have such a great idea you have no idea what it is. I'm good."

Tears welled in her eyes as she laughed. Every time they looked at each other, they started laughing all over again. Finally they took a deep breath. What was so funny, anyway? Was it her excitement at his idea or his sense of humor or what?

"Jonathan," Deborah said firmly, "pay attention and help me sort this out."

He took the reins from her and pulled back onto the road. "You think better when riding in a buggy."

"I tend to believe you're right." The sounds of the horses' hoofs and the creaking of the carriage did seem to help her think. "Ada's House used to be an Amish home before Englischers bought it a long time ago. Now that we're in it, we're slowly fixing it up to look Amish again. It's near a busy town. Why can't we sell our own goods?"

"Like Ada's Coffee House or something?"

"No, I don't think so, but you're close. What else could we do?"

As they started throwing ideas at each other, Deborah wished she had paper and pen with her. Excitement and hope washed over her, scrubbing away some of the black stain Mahlon had left inside her.

Jonathan turned onto the road where Ada's House sat. Three Amish men, all dressed in their Sunday suits, stood on the sidewalk a few doors down from Ada's House. Ephraim was one of them. They rode past them, and Ephraim flailed his arms while talking, as if he was frustrated. "That doesn't look good, does it?"

"Not particularly."

"Cara was doing something today she wouldn't tell me about. Think she caused a problem?"

"Don't know, but your brother's awfully good at finding a balance between what Cara needs and what the church leaders want. It's pretty impressive."

"He's not that great at it. He was shunned for months and has been a member in good standing again for only a few weeks now."

"Ah, but he's no longer shunned, and he won the girl's heart. Don't sweat it, Little Debbie. No one thinks through issues more carefully before taking a step than your brother."

Realizing Jonathan was right, Deborah chose to stop worrying. Ada's House came into view. It still needed a lot of work, but Cara didn't have the ladders or supplies she needed to paint the eaves or most of the clapboard siding. Using the one ladder they did have, she'd painted the few shutters she could. And she had the porch looking perfect from ceiling to wooden floor.

As he slowed the rig, a faint idea tried to wriggle into Deborah's mind. Touching his hand, she studied the place. "Jon," she whispered, "keep going."

Without questioning her, he did.

Chills ran all over her. "Wait."

He came to a halt.

"Look at that dried-up cornfield."

He studied it and turned back to her, waiting.

"There's got to be something…you know…some…"

"Dried-up ears of corn?"

"No." She climbed down, crossed onto her neighbor's property, and entered the field.

Jonathan followed her. "Some women make dolls out of parts of cornstalks."

"Maybe." Deborah went deeper into the rows. The corn had been harvested, but the stalks remained. That stood out as very odd to her. The field didn't belong to an Amish person either. Suddenly, as clear as if God were passing her a picture book, she saw it. "A maze!" She spun around slowly. "And Amish-made cakes and pies and apple cider. Maybe other goodies too, along with pumpkins and hayrides. I know it's late in the season, being the first of October and all, but is it possible we could turn Ada's House into a pumpkin-patch-type place?"

"Now that is the best idea I've heard in a really, really long time." Jonathan's face radiated such pleasure and confidence in her. "Since it's too late to grow them yourself, you'd need to buy the pumpkins and have them hauled in. But the real problem is that a pumpkin patch is just needed for a month or so once a year."

Her mind spun like the wheels on a carriage. "Maybe we could find a special niche for each season."

His eyes grew large. "That's really good. Focus on the pumpkin patch idea. That's for the here and now."

Insecurity covered her like a blanket. "Ya, but can we lease the field, and even if we could, can me and Ada actually make money from our work? Will we know how to plan and organize for such a thing? Or will we just be taking on more bills?"

He stood inside that cornfield, studying her. "What does your heart say?"

"Part of it says try, and part of it says run." She moved in closer. "I want to try. But I've never felt so scared in all my life."

"Then do it while you're scared," he whispered, and the rustling of the wind carried his words round and round through the dry stalks. "I'll help you...if you want."

Eleven

Cara didn't know how far they'd gone when she finally began to have a reasonable thought or two enter her mind. She trotted along while Lori rode her bike. They kept going farther and farther from Ada's. Lori loved it, and she didn't know her mother was furious…and hurt. Stupid rule. She couldn't take the bike from Lori. Despite that, she'd been gone a long time, and Ephraim might be looking for her. "Lori, honey."

Lori stopped her bike.

"Let's head on back to Ada's now."

"Yeah, my legs are getting wobbly."

"That's my fault. We've gone too far. You want to walk for a bit?"

"No way."

They crossed a dozen streets on their way back, but soon enough they were on their block again.

Ephraim stood on the sidewalk, looking one direction and then the other. When he spotted her, he wasted no time getting to her.

"'From, look!" Lori chirped. "I got a new bike. Mama and me did it. And I'm good at riding, even in this dress. Watch me." Lori passed him and kept going.

Cara cupped her hands around her mouth. "Stop at Ada's, Lori. Don't go any farther."

"Okay." Lori's voice vibrated as she jolted along.

Ephraim studied her. "You okay?"

"I take it the men in black came to see you too."

"I spoke to them, ya."

Cara rolled her eyes and kept walking. Ephraim held out his hand for hers. She tucked her hands inside her folded arms. "What, you're not too embarrassed to hold my hand after I've spattered this horrible stain across the Amish?"

"Not today. Not ever." He tugged on her sleeve.

She unfolded her arms and slid her hand into his. Lori pulled onto the walkway that led to Ada's, dropped her bike, and ran into the house. Ephraim gently squeezed Cara's hand.

"You're not ashamed." Cara stopped. "Why?"

"Because I know you." They started up the walkway. "And I get it— the stumbles and mishaps." He shrugged. "Plain out, I expected a few to crop up."

"Look!" Lori ran back out the door with Deborah and Jonathan following close behind.

When Lori pointed to her bike, Deborah looked to Cara. "The surprise?"

"Yes!" Lori clapped her hands. "Isn't it great?"

"It's quite a...a surprise." Deborah searched her brother's eyes, clearly trying to figure out what to say. "Where did you get it?"

"Me and Mama mowed grass and picked weeds for it!"

Deborah's eyes grew large. "On a Sunday?"

"Yeah." Cara tugged at her dress. "And thanks for the great advice about changing out of my jeans and wearing my Amish clothes, Deb. It seemed to be a dead giveaway that I shouldn't be working on a Sunday, and someone told the church leaders."

"Oh dear." Deborah placed her hand over her mouth, trying to smother her laughter. "This isn't funny. I know it's not, but..." She glanced at Jonathan, who looked a little more sympathetic to Cara's troubles.

Clearly, Lori was too preoccupied with her bike to hear much of what the adults were saying.

Ephraim stepped forward. "You'll have to excuse my sister, Cara. She seems to be regaining her sense of humor…at the *totally* wrong time." He smiled at Deborah, letting her know he wasn't the least bit annoyed. "Lori, how about if we put the bike away for now and take Better Days for a walk?"

"Okay, but first I'm hungry. We've been gone all day. Mama just doesn't get hungry like me."

Deborah held out her hand for Lori's. "Kumm. I'll fix you something to eat."

"Can I take my bike inside with me?"

Ephraim nodded. "Ya."

Jonathan toted the bike inside as Lori jabbered about it the whole way.

Cara pulled her hand from Ephraim's. "I'm not asking her to give that up."

His gray-blue eyes stayed focused on her. "Let's talk about this later. You're tired and hungry and angry."

"Don't treat me like a kid. Even the church leaders didn't do that."

He took a seat on the porch steps. "I didn't mean to."

"The Amish don't ride bicycles?"

"Some do in other states. But you shouldn't see it happening here, not among the members."

"What's so wrong with a bike?"

"It's one of those old rules we've stuck by. They're a bit flashy, and they allow a person to travel a lot longer distances than a foot scooter." He shrugged. "I never said I agree with all the *Ordnung*. I just trust that for the most part the regulations are needed to protect our ways and help us stay close and accountable. Bikes are forbidden for us, and I can't change the rules or stop them from being enforced."

Her heart jumped. "I didn't get you in trouble again, did I?"

"Nope. This one's all yours. But the bishop and preacher's little talk with you is most of the discipline you'll get since you're not a member.

They'll want to talk again when you've had time to think. Did you really invite them to leave?"

Realizing just how snarky she'd been, she took a seat beside him. "I…I might have." She looped her arm inside of his. "Okay, fine. I definitely did. Will I ever get to the end of this list of rules?"

"You mean without breaking each one? Nah, I don't think so."

She sandwiched his hand between hers. "I can't ask her to give up her bike." He didn't respond, and her eyes filled with tears. "This just stinks. And it hurts too, not just a little either. All those years of having nothing— not even on Christmas—and then when I finally get to where I can give her something special…" Cara sighed. "I was so excited about today I couldn't sleep last night."

"I'm really sorry. I never once thought about the bike rule."

"It's a stupid one."

"Maybe. But it's there, and the rule is not open for debate."

"Now what?"

He leaned in and kissed her, his warm lips easing her anger and disap- pointment. With his forehead against hers, he drew a deep breath. "You mean everything to me, Cara." He whispered the words so softly, as if they came from a place deep within him. "That's all I know. You have to decide the rest for yourself."

"Some choice," she mumbled. If she didn't do it their way, she couldn't join the faith, and they couldn't marry. If he left the faith, he'd hurt his family, damage the business, and lose a huge part of himself. Over a bike?

Grey tucked Ivan in for the night, sliding the covers gently over his son's arms as his little boy snuggled under their warmth. When Grey looked up, Elsie stood at the doorway. Surprise at seeing her there jarred him, but he kept his face expressionless.

He'd wrestled with his soul all day. A wave of forgiveness would come to him for a moment, but then realization of what she'd done would explode inside him like a volcano scattering ash so thick he couldn't see or feel anything but the aftereffects of the eruption. And now he fought to gain control of his will. He'd told her they'd find answers, but as the day wore on, all he'd found was hurt and resentment pounding inside him.

When he stood to leave the room, her eyes bore into him as they had all afternoon, willing him to understand. He understood. Her decisions had affected their lives like a cancer, and finally admitting what she'd done had not brought them closer. She seemed to think it should. After years of manipulating him through her silence and actions, she wanted him to understand and accept.

He went to the dresser, picked up the kerosene lantern, and motioned for her to leave the room. They walked into the hallway, and he passed the lantern to her. "Good night, Elsie." He turned to go into his room.

"You're furious with me."

Her words stopped him, and he stayed put as she went into her room and set the lantern on the nightstand. "I did what I thought was right. But even if I was wrong, this is how you forgive?"

She didn't get it, might not ever, and he couldn't make her. Remaining in the hallway with her standing beside her bed, he pulled the door closed. That door was the least of what blocked them from each other. She needed things from him he didn't possess—a way to build a bridge to cross the gulf that separated them. If he'd known how to build one, he'd have done it long, long ago. If one existed for him to cross over to her right now, he might burn it himself.

He walked to his back porch and took a seat on the stoop. The dark October air had a little nip to it. Voices carried from across the back field and beyond the creek bed. Allen's home sat on that piece of property. Like a lot of evenings, his friend's place was a bustle of activity.

"God, help me. I…I'm so angry with her." He put his head in his hands, torn between seeing his own faults and the bitterness he felt toward Elsie.

The back door squeaked as Elsie opened it. She stepped outside and pressed her back against the house, staring off in the distance. "I…I finally opened up, and now you're really angry. It's not fair, Grey."

Bitter thoughts washed over him. The moment Ivan was born missing part of one arm, fear began growing inside her. She should have told him… or at least someone.

She removed her Sunday apron. "What do you plan to do?"

"About us? I'm going to need some time. But I have a plan concerning Ivan and school."

She walked down the few steps and onto the grass before turning to face him. "He'll thrive in the Lancaster school for the handicapped. I know he will. And those children won't make fun of him. Rather than being at the bottom of the rung, he'll be at the top. Don't you want that for your son?"

"I want Lena to work with him."

"Lena?" Elsie scoffed. "She does not know Ivan like I do."

"She's the best teacher this district has ever had and my guess is probably the best Amish teacher in the state."

"Just because she attended a public school for a while doesn't make her a great teacher."

"Her reason for going is what makes the difference. She wanted to learn all she could so she'd be a good teacher. And she was a teacher's assistant of some type in a classroom for special-needs students. I trust that she'll know where Ivan should attend better than either of us does."

"You have that much confidence in her?"

"Ya."

"I worry she'll pick my mothering skills to pieces, given the chance. But if you're wanting an honest opinion, I've never seen her shy from speaking her mind when asked."

"You're afraid *Lena* will judge you? That's not her way. And you can't go on letting fear rule you and our family." Grey shifted. "Until today I didn't realize that's what holds us captive. But you did."

"You say that as though fear is some shadow that can be dispelled at will."

"And you treat it like it's a god to revere and bow down to."

"If Ivan is under her, she'll…know."

"Know?" That eerie feeling ran through him again, as if alerting him that what she was trying to say was important. "Know what?"

"About us…where you sleep."

How had he lived with her all these years and not known she was afraid of everything? "Ivan doesn't even know."

"But he will, given time."

While anger rumbled, he prayed. She had manipulated too much of their lives in order to hide her fears. No wonder she kept her distance emotionally as well as physically. She didn't want him to object to her reasoning.

One of the children at Allen's place let out a horrifying scream. *"Nee! Helf."*

Grey rose and moved closer to the creek bank.

Phoebe. Allen's youngest daughter. Grey stood too far away to see if she was hurt. Lennie flew out of her brother's house, running barefoot and like wildfire toward Phoebe. Lennie grabbed her up, clearly checking her out and talking to her. Phoebe wrapped her arms and legs around Lennie, sobbing. More adults came from around the corners of the house or from inside, hurrying toward the wailing. When Allen arrived, Lennie passed Phoebe to her Daed.

"Should you go?" Elsie asked.

The creek that separated their properties was fairly wide and deep. The only way to cross it was by horse. "I don't think so."

Allen looked up and waved. "Phoebe saw a raccoon coming toward her. We're fine."

"Okay, thanks," Grey hollered.

Phoebe raised her head and looked toward them. She hollered in Pennsylvania Dutch that she wasn't fine and that if Grey saw that thing again, he was to shoot it.

Allen laughed and patted her back. Soon the adults had rounded up all the children and taken them inside.

"You think it could be a rabid raccoon?"

"Doubtful. It obviously ran off when she screamed. It's a nocturnal creature hunting for food."

Elsie stood in the darkness, studying the sky. "Or God trying to tell me something I should have already known."

He didn't know what she meant, but he wouldn't bother to ask.

Tears welled in her eyes. "I didn't want you to know my genes were poor ones. I…I'm sorry."

Beyond her tears, he saw her self-righteousness begin to break, and a dusting of forgiveness settled over his heart.

Under the starless night, Dwayne studied Lena's house. The chilly air seeped through his clothing. A dog perched its paws on a second-story windowsill and barked at him through a closed window. Dwayne set his toolbox next to the tree and stayed put, not caring what fit the dog threw. If they let the mutt outside, he'd slice its throat.

A woman came to the window, but the dark night shrouded his view. It was probably the stupid teacher herself. As far as he knew, only she and her Daed lived here. She opened the glass pane. The girl was an idiot and an ugly thorn in his flesh. He didn't put up with thorns. She seemed to spot him, and he propped against the tree and lit a cigarette.

He intended to get even, and she might as well know it now. Picking on his brother in class. Taking the watch back. That awful cake she brought to the cabin. It had to be poison, and Aaron refused to say a word about it to her. He said he knew Lena and it must be a joke of some type.

Dwayne spat on the ground. She knew exactly what she was doing, and so did he.

As he looked at her, new plans floated to him out of thin air. Deciding that a low profile would profit him more than giving himself away, he grabbed his toolbox and got off their property.

He walked the two miles to the schoolhouse and looked around. The playground was a perfect setting for causing trouble. He set his toolbox down, pulled out a pair of tin snips, and began working away at the chains that held up the swings. It might take a few times of someone swinging before the chain broke, but when it did, somebody would be hurt, and poor Teacher Lena would answer for it. It wasn't much, but it seemed like a perfect opening chapter to what he intended to be a very long book.

A cat meowed, drawing his attention. He tossed the tin snips into the toolbox. "Here kitty, kitty, kitty." The creature slowly came to him. Its soft, warm fur felt good against his cold hands. The cat purred as he rubbed her ears. "What are you doing hanging around an empty school? Maybe you've been out catching field mice. Now that you've seen me, you won't tell, will you?" He laughed and reached for the knife in his pocket. "I think not."

Twelve

Lena brought her horse to a stop near the schoolhouse barn. *"Zerick."*
She repeated the word as the horse backed up until the small cart she'd
ridden in today stood under the lean-to. The brisk ride in an open rig
had done wonders for her. She'd finally shaken that eerie feeling she'd
had since seeing a man staring at her house during the wee hours of the
morning. Probably a drunk. Possibly a Peeping Tom. Usually both were
harmless.

A fresh week lay ahead of her. The air smelled like fall, and leaves had
begun to change color. She put her old mare in its small pasture, the one
designed just for the teacher's horse. After she grabbed her goodies off the
seat of the cart, she hurried into the school, wanting to get a fire started in
the potbelly stove. Her scholars loved putting their lunches near a warm
stove in cool weather. It wouldn't be cold enough to build a roaring fire
and bank embers today—just a little one to knock the chill out of the air.
But she'd brought homemade chocolate chip cookies, and when those got
warm from sitting on the stove, she'd have a treat her scholars would work
hard to earn.

She built the first fire of the year in her faithful old stove. After she set
the cookie tin on top, she went to each student's desk and opened the
spiral-bound notebook left there for her. She read the entries and left
smiley faces, asked humorous questions, and shared a thought or two.
These works didn't get a grade. Her students wrote to her whatever they

wanted to, and she responded. Some wrote the beginning to made-up stories, and she'd finish the tale. Others shared events from their own life, but they didn't tell the whole story. That was her job. Their goal was to stump her so that the real ending was nothing like what she wrote. When they read them aloud, they shared the real ending and then read what she'd written. Their laughter never rang as loudly as when they read her responses. The older ones knew she cloaked her responses under the pretense of telling what probably took place. She spun yarns in hopes of making them love writing, reading, and using their imaginations.

She sat at Peter's desk, bracing herself for what he'd written to her.

I rided down the road on my way home aftr scool when I saw my
teacher in her yard plantin more flowers. I hate flowers. I'd ruther
be tended to than tend to somethin. But the teach must like them.
They don't like her. I know this cuz…

Wow. That wasn't a bad entry at all. Nothing biting or threatening. That improvement alone refreshed her. He'd written several sentences and spelled correctly most of the words she'd been working with him on. Definite improvement.

She tapped her pencil on the paper. *Hmm. I know this cuz…*

"Think, Lena." She put her pencil on the paper, hoping an answer would come that he'd enjoy.

I know this cuz…one day the petunias ran away from her
and chased after me.
Peter, Peter, petunia hater,
Didn't want flowers, but wanted something greater
Teacher Lena chased them down
When she caught them, they wilted to the ground.

"That's not good enough, Lena. *Kumm uff,* think." She tapped her pencil on the paper, looking about the room for inspiration. Surely she could think of a better little ditty than—

She noticed a pool of liquid under her desk. She stood and moved in closer. When she rounded the side of her table, she saw a white cat in her chair, covered in its own blood. The thick red syrup dripped onto the floor, making Lena's skin crawl. Her mouth went dry, and her body shook. Who would do such a thing?

Feeling dizzy and sick, she eased up to it and touched it. She jerked back, appalled at how death felt. Its stiff body sickened her, and she ran outside for fresh air. Teachers had some awfully mean tricks pulled on them at times, usually by the older boys in school or the ones who'd graduated not long ago. Drawing cool air into her lungs, she knew what had to be done—and before her students arrived. Ignoring her desire to sit down and cry, she hurried to the lean-to and grabbed a shovel and old towels that were usually reserved for craft days.

On the verge of being sick to her stomach, she moved the cat's body onto the blade of the shovel and carried it outside. Her body disobeyed her, trembling as she walked across the gravel driveway and to the far side of the lean-to. It seemed like the best burial spot. If anyone passed by while she dug the grave, they weren't likely to spot her between the huge tree and the far side of the lean-to. She eased the cat's body onto the ground and returned to her classroom. The next step was no easier—mopping up its blood. Trying to hurry so she could bury the cat and the bloody towels before anyone arrived, she couldn't keep her tears at bay.

Who would do this and why?

The older boys, and sometimes girls, could be pretty spiteful—seemingly angered by Amish restrictions and spurred into action by wild hormones, pettiness, and immaturity. But of all the nasty things she'd heard of over the years, mutilating someone's pet and leaving it bleeding in a teacher's chair was beyond normal. An occasional squirrel or deer's head might greet an unsuspecting teacher on the steps leading to the school. But someone's pet? She shuddered, trying to reason out who might've done this. The culprit could be from any district around here, not necessarily one of her students or former students. Even though she didn't have grandiose sentiments of how some students felt about her, she found it hard to believe any of her students, past or present, had the type of cruelty to do this. Still, thoughts of Peter's attitude toward her kept tumbling inside her. Surely he hadn't. She saw good inside him. Of course she saw meanness too.

The eerie feeling didn't leave her as she mopped up the blood and scrubbed the chair and floor until they looked clean again. After dumping the kindling out of its crate, she used it to carry the items outside. She grabbed the shovel and jammed it into the ground. Her body jolted, but the rocklike ground barely gave way. She slammed the blade into the edge of the earth again and again, making very little progress. Children's voices filled the air as they walked toward the schoolhouse. Buggies came and went as parents dropped their children off.

Should she run to get one of the Daeds to help her? A man could make quick work of this solid ground, but then her scholars would find out for sure, and it'd cause days of emotional unrest. Doubtful of her best course of action, she kept digging, hoping no one came looking for her. Once past the hardest-packed dirt, she made better progress and managed to carve a decent-sized hole.

"Lena." The door to the schoolhouse slammed as several scholars called to her. They'd begun hunting for her, but she needed only a few more minutes. Using the shovel, she tried to pick up the cat. She couldn't get the blade under it.

"Kumm uff." She tossed the shovel to the side and picked up the cat. As she laid it in the hole, Marilyn screamed. "Snowball! Why are you throwing my Snowball into the ground?"

The shrill sound of her youngest student's voice caused others to come running. Lena knelt in front of her. "She...she died, sweetie."

"No!" Tears streamed down the little girl's face as she reached for her cat. Lena stopped her.

Marilyn pulled away from Lena. "You can't throw my cat in the ground!"

Marilyn's older brother pushed through the crowd. Levi's emotions reflected across his nine-year-old face, and soon he was sobbing too. Lena directed them toward the schoolhouse. "Could one of you older boys please finish what I started?"

"What are we, your slaves?" Peter retorted.

Lena turned to Jacob, who gave a nod.

Lena knelt in front of Marilyn. "You need to go inside, but you can stay with Levi and sit on the reading couch. I'll be inside in just a few minutes, okay?"

Marilyn nodded and clung to her brother, crying as they walked toward the schoolhouse.

Lena lifted her head, ready to give loud instructions. "I want everyone to go inside and take a seat."

The children headed in that direction while Lena went to the hand pump. She lifted the handle and lowered it several times before water gushed out. After grabbing the soap dispenser out of its bucket, she scrubbed her hands and arms with a fury that could not remove the filth of what was taking place.

Mandy came back outside with a towel in hand. "Marilyn can't catch her breath. She seems to think you killed her cat, and she doesn't want to be thrown into a hole with some bloody towels when she dies."

Bracing herself for the long week ahead, Lena took the towel and dried her hands. "Let's go see what can be done to console—"

A piercing yell sliced straight through Lena. Had Jacob hurt himself while burying the cat?

Jacob came from the side of the lean-to. "What's wrong now?"

Too frazzled to even think, she headed for the playground area, followed by Mandy and Jacob. Elmer lay on the ground, crying. What was he doing out here? One glance at the swing set explained everything. The chain had broken, and based on where Elmer had landed, he'd been swinging really high.

"Stay put, and tell me what hurts."

"My arm!"

"Okay, lie still for just a moment, and let's make sure nothing else is hurt." She made a quick assessment just like her Red Cross classes had taught her. After running through her checklist and getting reasonable answers, she helped him to his feet.

"It hurts! Ow. Ow. Ow. Ow." Elmer's whining concerned her, but more than that, his hand had already begun to swell, and it had a slight blue tint to it.

"Can you move your fingers?"

As he wiggled them a little, her mind whirled with conflicting thoughts on what to do next. If she took him with her while going for help, someone else could get hurt, not to mention the emotional state Marilyn, Levi, and most of the class were in. Sending an older student might cause problems with the school board since she was on probation for a similar incident. Regardless of that, she couldn't leave. If she let one of the older children drive Elmer to the closest phone, and they didn't handle it like an adult, Elmer could have permanent damage done to his arm. Buggies hit potholes. Cars spooked horses. And if, in their nervousness, they drove too fast or too carelessly, more than just a child's limb could be in danger. She'd seen far too many incidents of that sort in her lifetime.

Deciding Mandy had the best head on her shoulders, she turned to her. "Can you drive my rig to Ephraim's place by yourself? He's got the closest phone. Tell him Elmer has fallen off a swing and may have broken his arm."

Upon hearing those words, Elmer started crying harder. Lena placed her hand on his head, comforting him. If he'd done as she'd said, he'd be at his desk safe and sound right now.

"Ya, I think so."

Lena moved in front of Mandy. "I need you to drive careful and deliberate. This isn't an emergency, but we need an Englischer driver and Elmer's parents so he can be taken to the doc in Shippensburg. Can you be very, very careful?"

She nodded.

"Jacob, hitch my horse to its rig, and then come directly inside. Is that clear?"

"Ya." Jacob's wide eyes told her he'd do exactly as she'd just demanded.

With her arm around Elmer, she guided him toward the schoolhouse.

No matter how she handled the next couple of hours, she'd hear from upset parents. If not tonight, then at the school board meeting next Tuesday. She'd have to explain these incidents and her actions.

And all she wanted to do was work with her students and teach, not be second-guessed by the parents.

Dwayne laughed so hard he almost choked on his dinner as Peter finished telling about the dead cat and Elmer getting hurt.

"That girl is sorely lacking in what it takes to be a good teacher." His Mamm pointed a finger at him. "But what happened to those children isn't funny, Dwayne." Mamm held a plate out to him, offering him more pot roast.

Dwayne slapped his brother on the back. "Does serve her right, though, don't it?"

Peter shrugged. "It's not like cats matter no way. They fill up the barns like mice and rats, and we shoot 'em, but I did feel a little bad for

Marilyn. She's terrified people are going to throw her in a dark hole if she dies."

No one said a word. Dwayne finished his meal and shoved his chair back from the table. "Don't be such a wuss, Peter. What do you care how anybody feels? Set a goal—like getting even with that teacher—and enjoy hitting the target. It's that easy."

"Dwayne," Mamm corrected, "watch your language, and we don't want to get even with her. I'd like to see her step down and get somebody in there who knows what she's doing. It's just like at our last Amish school. The teacher has no quality to her. That's all."

Daed pushed his empty plate away and propped his forearms on the table. "Now your mother was a great teacher in her day."

"Ya." Dwayne stood, wiping his mouth on his sleeve. "So we've heard." Unwilling to listen to any more stories about when his mother taught some twenty-five years ago, he walked out the back door and straight to the barn. At the back, under stacks of baled hay, he removed a Hot-Shot— his brand-new electric-current cattle prod. If that teacher thought a dead cat and a broken swing were problems, she hadn't driven a horse after it'd been on the receiving end of a Hot-Shot all night.

Thirteen

Deborah turned another page in the magazine, reading a true account of a family using a portion of their farm for a pumpkin patch. The aroma of shoofly pies and Amish bread pudding filled the kitchen as she waited on them to finish baking. Their commercial-sized oven had six shelves, all filled with pies, and their family-sized oven had the bread pudding.

Based on what she'd read, she and Ada could not do this venture alone, not even with Cara's help. "According to this article, we'll need a lookout tower of some sort."

From her position at the sink washing dishes, Ada glanced over her shoulder at Deborah. "A lookout tower?"

"Ya, it's a structure built in the middle of the cornfield maze. One of us can climb it to see the people inside the maze. If someone gets stuck, we can have a visual of them to send someone else in to lead them out, or we can give directions through a bullhorn. If you're selling baked goods and I have to go in to get them, who will come lead me out?"

Thoughts of all it'd take to set up a pumpkin patch kept running through her head. Unfortunately, she hadn't yet managed to secure use of the cornfield. She'd gone to the owner's house on Monday and Tuesday, but no one answered the door or appeared to be home. She'd had the same result this morning and intended to return again this evening, just like the other two days. Maybe they were on vacation.

Ada rinsed her hands and grabbed a dishtowel. "You're saying that like it's a joke, but you're really worried about getting lost in that maze, aren't you?"

It surprised her how well Ada read her sometimes. "A little." But the truth was, parts of her were terrified. Since Mahlon had left, she either felt grief or anxiety wadded up like a bale of hay smack in the middle of her chest most days. And she'd had enough.

When she heard voices and an odd noise, Deborah went to the back door and peered out. Not seeing anyone, she turned back to Ada.

Ada slung the dishtowel over her shoulder. "We'll get the hang of all this. I just know we will."

Jonathan's words ricocheted around inside her like one of those super bouncy balls her little brother bought from a vending machine in town. *Then do it while you're scared.* She'd never heard such perfect words in her life.

The buzzer went off. Deborah took the pies out of the oven and set them on a cooling rack. "There's so much to do, and we're six months behind before we even start. But I think our goal should be to do what we can this year—buy pumpkins to sell. Next year we'll grow them and let people pick them off the vine. We'll build a small maze if we can get use of the field and have a simple hayride—and really be ready for business next year. Do you agree?"

"Absolutely. I just hope the permits I have for operating my home business will cover what we need for a pumpkin patch."

"Ya. Robbie's taking me to the courthouse later this week." She tilted her head, listening to voices that seemed to be getting closer and the rhythmic echo of something being whacked.

Ada looked out a side window. "I think someone's in the cornfield, cutting stalks."

Deborah grabbed her sweater and ran out the front of the house, across the yard, and down the side alley until it opened up into the cornfield. There appeared to be about two Plain Mennonite men and one woman and then ten or so Englischer teens, all either cutting cornstalks or gathering them and hauling them to a nearby truck.

"Excuse me," Deborah called while hurrying toward them.

One of the men stopped cutting stalks. He looked about twenty-something and had dark brown hair. The woman passed an armload of stalks to a teen and then walked closer while dusting off her cape dress. Deborah hoped the right words would come to her by the time she stood directly in front of the man.

When she reached him, she drew a few deep breaths and straightened her apron. "I…I've been trying to reach the owner of this field."

The man jabbed the end of his machete into the ground. "An Englischer gentleman by the name of Carl Gilbert owns the field, but we work with a teen mission out of Harrisburg, and we rent the pasture from him."

"I'm Deborah Mast. My…business partner and I moved into the house that adjoins this property nearly four months ago, and I was hoping to rent this field with the stalks still standing."

"Business partner?" he asked.

"Ada. We bake goods for some local bakeries. But we hope to expand."

"Is she the older woman? And the man we see around here regularly, is he a partner too?"

"You've seen us?"

"I suppose a better question is, you haven't seen us? We harvested a lot of corn throughout the summer."

He would've had to set off dynamite for Deborah to notice anything but her own pain and confusion since moving in. "We…*I*…have been distracted. I apologize if in my state I was rude in any way. The older woman is Ada. The man is my brother. He lives in Dry Lake, and the younger woman is his fiancée."

He pulled a work glove off his right hand and held it out. "Ray Yoder." She shook his hand.

"And this is my mother, Joan." She had a pleasant smile as she nodded.

"Hi." Deborah returned the nod before focusing on Ray. "Any chance we could work something out?"

"We use this plot each year to teach inner-city teens about planting and growing and reaping. We do everything by hand, and right now we need these stalks for various fall festival events."

"There must be two acres here," Deborah defended. "Do you need all the stalks?"

His lips pursed, showing what might be amusement. "What we don't use, we sell to local churches and schools who need some fall festival decorations, and then that money goes for the mission. We do it each year, and it brings in decent money—for dried-up stalks, that is."

"I think I can match that money. I sure was hoping to build a maze— you know, with huge swatches missing all throughout it."

He scratched his head, looking thoughtful. "Yeah, I know what a maze is. You're thinking we could use the stalks from those cutout places to meet our real needs, and then you'd pay us for our losses in sales." He studied her. "How much you figure is reasonable to rent this cornfield?"

"I…I have no clue, and I don't actually have any money to pay you right now. But I will…at least I think I will, if you could…give me time."

"Now how can I turn down such a sure thing?" He suppressed a smile.

"I know how I sound, and I might not sleep tonight for feeling like I made a fool of myself asking to rent this field, but my concept for running a pumpkin patch is solid—a maze, hayrides, pumpkins, and baked goods to sell."

Joan pulled up the sleeves of her sweater past her elbows. "You don't sound foolish. A little inexperienced maybe."

Ray rubbed his chin and lower cheek, staring at the field. "Usually by this time I've arranged to have most of the stalks removed. It just hasn't worked out this year. Even today we only have a few who qualify to use machetes, and we only have a few hours to work." He made a clicking sound with his mouth. "I guess if you harvested the stalks from the swatches you clear and were willing to pay...*after* you've made your money from the pumpkin patch, I can rent this field to you for the difference in sales."

"The difference between what you sell this year and what you sell when you clear the whole field?"

"Yes. My guess is that will be somewhere between a hundred and a hundred and fifty dollars."

She liked his willingness to treat her like a businessperson and not a confused girl. "That sounds great to me, although I don't have anything to base it on. Can I talk to Ada first?"

"Sure."

Deborah's heart beat a little faster. "Would you care to come inside and have a slice of pie and some coffee while I talk with her? Everyone can come in."

"That's an invite we'd never turn down," Ray said.

As they followed her into Ada's, she commanded herself to breathe. She'd just made a step in the right direction, and it'd paid off. Mahlon had broken her, but she'd begun to heal.

The Amish health clinic buzzed with people. Grey rolled up his sleeve and held out his arm to the lab technician. She placed an elastic band around his bicep, swabbed the skin in front of his elbow, and pushed a needle into his arm.

"You've got great veins," the young woman said. "Your wife does too."

Grey looked to Elsie. Her faint smile reflected cautious optimism, and he winked at her. Whether they received good news or bad when the time came, they'd agreed to make changes so their daily lives could move out of the *miserable* stage. Marriage could be a lot of things and people still be able to make it work, but few survived living in gloom.

The lab technician removed a tube full of his blood from the syringe part and placed another tube inside it. They'd taken three vials of blood from Elsie.

Doctor Stone had set up this clinic because some leaders in Grey's community had sought him out before he finished his internship. Most Amish shied away from doctors, tests, and hospitals, but because Dr. Stone had been willing to learn about the Plain community and respected them, the people were becoming more open to seeking medical help. Grey trusted the man's opinion, but the doc had said little about their concerns. He'd asked a lot of questions and then focused on Elsie's side of the family. He uncovered the main reason why her aunt probably had so many children with birth defects. Her aunt was the fourth generation in a row who'd married a relative. But he'd agreed that it'd be best to run tests and then talk. Every word he said seemed to remove some of Elsie's fears and inject hope into her.

After snapping the third vial in place, the lab tech loosened the elastic on Grey's arm. "We'll send this off to the lab. Did the nurse or doctor tell you that it'll take about two months to get the results back for this type of test?"

"Ya."

Two months. He and Elsie had to wait two months before they'd learn the truth—either she'd been wrong all this time, or they had some tough realities to face.

"Okay." The woman placed gauze on his arm and removed the needle before securing the gauze with tape. "You're all done."

Grabbing his jacket off the coatrack, Grey unrolled his sleeve. He and Elsie walked down the hallway and signed out. After he paid cash for the visit, they went out the back entrance to where he'd parked the buggy. So far the most important discovery they'd made over the last four days was the acknowledgement that they...actually, *he* needed a way to get from his plot of ground to hers. That whole concept felt very foggy right now, but it'd given him a clear goal…sort of. She'd admitted she couldn't find it within herself to come to him—in any sense of what that might mean. But as they'd talked this week, she'd lowered a few of her walls and spoken more honestly than in the six previous years. If the blood work proved that she'd been right about their having a genetic issue, they would go to the bishop and ask for the right to use birth control. Grey had no idea what their chances were of getting permission, but what they most needed to happen between them had nothing to do with sex. He untied the reins from the hitching post, tossed them through the front open window of the buggy, and climbed inside. He accepted where they were as a couple, even where they might be years down the road.

Acceptance of what couldn't be changed was what couples did, wasn't it?

He drove down the side alley and waited until he could turn left. They rode through Shippensburg and kept going until they entered Dry Lake. He'd been so absorbed in his own thoughts, he'd not even tried to get her to talk.

Ahead of them, at the Dry Lake Amish School, children were either getting into buggies or leaving on foot. Lennie stood on the steps, waving and speaking to parents as they picked up their children. He'd been told about the trouble happening at the school. A meeting had been called for next Tuesday, but he'd barely given it a thought. Disgruntled parents were the norm some years. Lennie knew that going in. The school board covered three Amish schools. He knew the goings-on in dozens of other Amish districts as well, and Lennie had more stamina for the difficult parts than any other teacher he'd heard of. But he hadn't told Elsie about the scrapes happening under Lennie's watch. He didn't want her to doubt Lennie more than she already did.

As they approached, the schoolyard cleared out, and Lennie went inside. He knew firsthand that the scholars under Lennie left the eighth grade better educated than most. She'd turn flips through a graveyard if she thought it would help those students learn a reading, writing, or math lesson.

He looked to Elsie. "School's out. And Ivan's with Mamm. Do you want to drop by to talk to Lena now?"

Elsie stiffened and then surprised him when she eased her hand over his and nodded.

He pulled onto the graveled circular area and brought the rig to a stop.

She pulled her hand away. "I…I really do want the tests to say I've been wrong."

"I know." Grey got out of the buggy and tied the horse to the hitching post. "And I know you're nervous about this, but I think it'll do us both some good to get Lena's opinion about Ivan."

As he looped the reins onto the post, Elsie climbed out of the carriage. Once on the steps of the schoolhouse, Grey opened the screen door for Elsie and walked in behind her.

From behind her desk, Lennie stood.

"Hey, Lennie. You got a few minutes?"

"Ya. *Kummet rei.*" She stacked the papers up in front of her and slid them to the side.

Grey grabbed a couple of foldout chairs that were resting against the back wall. "We came to talk to you about Ivan."

Lennie shook Elsie's hand, welcoming her. But she and Grey went too far back for them to use any formalities. He leaned back in his chair and raised their questions about Ivan's development. Lennie's blue-green eyes reflected a lot of thoughts, but he knew she'd guard her words carefully.

She folded her hands, looking more like a teacher than his closest friend's kid sister. "When Ivan has been at my brother's, I've spent time with the children, and we've played all sorts of games over the years, and I've never once thought he might be slow." She angled her head, her sincerity shining through. "He's quite introspective."

"What's that mean?" Elsie asked.

"He thinks a lot and talks only a little. He feels deeply, but he's not one to share his thoughts or feelings easily. Basically he's the opposite of me, which will keep him out of a lot of trouble in school, probably in life." Lennie fidgeted with a pencil on her desk. "But don't let his quietness give you the impression he's not bright."

Elsie shifted in her chair. "But what about his arm? The other kids will tease him."

Lennie set the pencil down and smoothed her fingertips across the table. "I was certainly harassed about my birthmark. I still am some days. And I won't lie. It'll hurt him. I'll do what I can to stop the mockery. If the adults make too big a deal out of trying to control the children on the topic, we'll make things worse for him. But the best thing for Ivan is already taking place—his Daed believes in him."

Elsie blinked, looking guilt-ridden. "I…I didn't mean to not believe in—"

"Oh no." Lennie glanced to Grey, looking baffled. "That's not what I meant. Ivan is Grey's shadow on the weekends; that's so good for him. When he sees his Daed able to do stuff, I imagine he sees himself as able to do it."

"Oh, I get what you mean. So can you test him?" Elsie asked.

"Of course. I mean, it's not anything official like the public schools do, but it'll let us know what we'd like to know. Why don't you bring him by the house Saturday around eight and let him stay with me for a couple of hours? Jonathan and I are heading for Hope Crossing around ten."

Grey laced his fingers and popped his knuckles. "I missed working today, and Ephraim's really behind, so after I drop Ivan off with you, I'll go to the cabinetry shop. Can you and Jonathan bring him by there before leaving Dry Lake?"

"Sure."

"We'll be glad to pay you for your time," Elsie offered.

Lennie bit her bottom lip, hiding a smile as she kept her eyes focused on her desk for a moment. "Because your husband is my brother's friend, he pays quite regularly as it is. But now that you mention it, I do have something I'd like at the top of the list this year."

Elsie turned to him, a slight smile in place as she silently looked to understand. She stayed so secluded from his life she had no idea what Lena meant.

"She means the spring rounds Allen and I do at our house, his house, and Lena's house."

"Oh, ya."

Lennie pushed back from her desk, drawing the meeting to a close. "Wooden planters under the windows… I do believe this will be the third year in a row I've requested them."

Grey tipped his hat as he stood. "I'll make sure they get done in time for your spring planting of flowers. And we'll have Ivan at your place around eight. Thanks, Lennie."

"Anytime."

Grey folded the chairs. "Oh, there's a school board meeting Tuesday night, and the board would like you to be there."

Lennie opened a drawer and pulled out a set of keys. "Ya, I figured as much. Dump one dead cat in the ground…"

Her sarcasm caught Grey off guard, and he laughed loudly.

Lennie walked from behind her desk. Grey set the chairs against the wall, and he and Lennie followed Elsie outside.

"I could use a minute to share a school incident privately before that school board meeting begins."

Since wives were encouraged to attend the board meetings, Lennie's request had him curious.

"Now's as good a time as any." Grey turned to his wife. "Would you wait for me for just a few minutes?"

"Denki, Lena."

"*Gern gschehne.*"

When Elsie walked off, Lennie turned to him. "I didn't want to undermine her confidence concerning this school. The cat wasn't just dead, Grey. Its neck had been slashed, and it probably died a slow death as its blood drained onto my floor. Someone had placed it in my chair."

"What?" It seemed wrong that while some parents lodged complaints, she had to deal with difficult scholars and then defend every action to the board—and made hardly any money in the process.

"Ya." She went up the three steps to the door of the school and put a key inside what appeared to be a new lock. The whole mount rattled, and she had to pull and push the door several times to get the bolt to line up with the strike plate.

"Any idea who?"

"I just can't imagine anyone who's that angry with me or with the community—past or current schoolboys included."

"Anyone giving you a hard time in class?"

She finally got the door locked. "Well, ya. Peter Bender has times of being disrespectful and mulish toward assignments, but I don't believe he'd do such a thing."

"Because he's not capable, or because you don't want to believe he's capable?"

"Now how could I possibly know the answer to that question?"

"Fair enough. I'll check with some of the youth and see if they know anything." They walked toward his buggy. "Where's your horse and rig?"

"I walked. My horse is acting up, and, besides, I love walking in fall and spring whenever I can."

He opened the door to his carriage. "Care for a lift? We could drop you off on our way home."

"No, but thanks anyway."

He got in and hung one arm out the open window. "Install that lock yourself, did you, Lennie?"

"Oh, be quiet before I strap that lock to the door of your carriage."

He took the reins in hand. "Yes, Teacher Lena. But I'll bring tools one day next week and see if I can adjust that lock to work a little better." He tapped the reins against the horse's back and tried to keep a straight face. "Of course it may need an entire new door as well as a frame."

"Grey, stop teasing her." Elsie peered around him, checking on Lennie. He knew Lennie didn't mind. If she ever did, she'd definitely let him know.

Lennie put her hands on her hips, mocking offense before breaking into laughter. Grey and Elsie pulled onto the main road.

Elsie shook her head. "I can't believe you tease her as you do, but clearly she has no problem speaking her mind."

He laughed. "We used to aggravate her to no end just to hear her logic on the matter."

"She's an awfully pretty girl. I…I hate to admit it, but before today I only saw that birthmark. Aside from that one thing, she's flawless. I doubt if she's a teacher many more years."

"Maybe not."

"I've never seen eyes that color. I couldn't stop staring." Elsie rubbed just below her neck. "I…I didn't realize she'd spent so much time with Ivan."

Grey always invited Elsie to go with them when they visited Allen. "She's at her brother's place sometimes when Ivan and I visit."

"So when she said she doesn't think he's slow, it's got a real basis to it and not just her being nice."

Elsie saw Ivan so negatively. He didn't understand it, and he certainly didn't appreciate it. "It has a real basis. And you're right; Lena would be nice about Ivan, but she'd also be very straightforward."

"I…I wish we knew already."

It wasn't like Elsie to be so chatty. Going through the steps today to begin to find the truth had her talking and even hopeful, and for the first time in years, Grey began to feel optimistic about their marriage.

Fourteen

Lena rode beside Ivan as Jonathan brought the rig to a halt in front of Ephraim's shop. She didn't think Grey would be worried about his son, but testing him had taken longer than she'd planned on. Jonathan had made it clear he wasn't pleased that they were running late. A few days ago they'd agreed to leave Dry Lake and head for Hope Crossing at ten. Even so, it wasn't much past ten thirty.

Lena opened the door, but before she stepped out, Grey came out the doorway of the shop and walked to them. Ivan jumped down and ran to his Daed. Grey picked him up.

"We had a very productive couple of hours. He's a great kid."

Grey spoke to his son in Pennsylvania Dutch, asking if he wanted to help him work in the shop. Ivan nodded.

"How'd he do?" Grey asked in English so Ivan wouldn't understand.

"Good. Like everyone, he has strengths and weaknesses. I'd like to discuss it privately, but right now Jonathan is in a hurry to get to Hope Crossing. Why don't you and Elsie come by the school next week, and we can talk about my findings in great detail?"

"I…I sort of expected you to just tell me."

"I got the feeling that Elsie is hoping for a somewhat professional opinion, not viewpoints shared over a back fence…or in this case through the open door of a carriage while she's not around."

Grey chuckled. "You're right about that. Denki, Lennie. We'll both come to see you one day next week."

"You're welcome. And since I began this on a Saturday and won't wrap up the report until Monday morning, I should get the best window boxes you can create." She grabbed Ivan's straw hat off the carriage seat and held it out to Grey.

He took it and peered in at Jonathan. "Is she always so picky about how things are handled?"

"Oh, ya. When it comes to her class, she's pickier and more business-like than most men could tolerate."

She scowled playfully at Jonathan. Grey chuckled as he stepped back. She waved as Jonathan tapped the reins, and the horse started down the driveway.

Jonathan clicked his tongue, making the horse gain speed quickly. "I'm so ready to be in Hope Crossing."

"Believe me, I know." Feeling a little too cool, Lena fastened her side of the front window. Jonathan used to be patient and didn't mind plans changing or whiling away the hours on a free Saturday. His new focus on Deborah meant Lena would have to adjust. Clearly in his mind and heart, Lena had been sent to the backseat of the carriage. She and Jonathan were friends. That's all. But over the years they'd helped each other ward off the loneliness for someone special. All these years, even though he'd dated at will, it'd been their secret how much he cared for Deborah.

"Hey." Jonathan nudged her with his elbow. "I didn't mean to be self-ish. I'm sorry."

"It's just happening quicker than I expected."

"What?"

"I went from being someone you hung out with on free weekends to simply an excuse for you to spend time around Deborah without looking like you're interested in her. I can't imagine where we'll be a few months from now. And all that's good. I'm glad for you. I am. It's just…"

Deep concern reflected in his eyes, and he slowed the rig. "You…don't feel…anything special…toward me, do you?"

Lena laughed. "Oh, heavens, no."

He laughed quietly. "Whew. You scared me, because the last thing I'd ever want is to hurt you. And I happen to know firsthand that a person can care about someone without the other one knowing it."

"It's not like that at all. You're supposed to know that. But I'm being demoted, and I thought I was ready, but it's harder than I expected."

"Ya, I can see that. Now that I think about it, it'd be that way for me too if you'd found someone before I did. I'll do better. Just tell me or kick me under the table or something."

Lena chuckled. "That I can do. I might even buy steel-toed shoes."

"Ouch." He clicked his tongue, urging the horse to pick up speed again. "And you know Deborah. It'll probably be another year before she even notices that other men besides Mahlon exist on this planet. We have plenty of time for you to adjust."

"Gut." She reached into the covered basket at her feet. "Care for a piece of peanut brittle?"

"Store bought?" He shrugged and took the canister. "I'm surprised it's not homemade, but sure." He opened the lid. Two five-foot cloth snakes leaped out of the can. He hollered and all but jumped out of his skin. Lena kept her composure and stayed focused looking out the window. "I'll get you for that, Lena Kauffman."

"You can try, Jonathan Stoltzfus." She pulled a felt hat lined with straw out of the basket. "I have a plan to trick Deborah. You in?"

"What all did you bring?"

"After the awful way my week started at school, I needed to self-medicate, so I hired a driver to take me to Philly, and I went to a gag store. I felt so much better afterward. Poorer, but better."

"I've heard self-medication can be dangerous."

"It is…for the other people in my life." Lena gave her best evil laugh.

"What happens if after you find someone, he doesn't approve of the money you've spent on gags?"

"I'll tell him that I'm very careful with money—giving, spending, and saving. I've tended to my Daed's home, laundry, and meals for half of my life. I help family and friends when they need it, and added to that, I began working full-time before I became a teacher. If I can't spend a little money on fun items without it being questioned, he needs to keep moving because I'm not interested. Besides, everyone who's single and works spends a few dollars here and there to enjoy something important to them. If this imaginary fellow doesn't admit to that, he's a hypocrite."

"Wow. Say you have an opinion?"

She laughed. "Always. Did you forget?" Her skin tingled from her overreaction. She longed for a husband and was willing to make sacrifices for the right person, but if any man thought he knew better how she should've handled her life while waiting for him, she wasn't interested. Period.

Jonathan adjusted his hat. "You are something else. If a man ever questions how you've spent your money, I'm leaving the state before you respond, okay?"

She laughed. "You best take him with you."

He chuckled and nodded several times. "So, aside from the various gags you're going to pull, what's the plan for Deborah?"

"She needs a scarecrow as a decoration for the cornfield maze, right?"

"Ya, I guess."

Lena pulled a painted flour sack over her head and flopped the felt hat lined with straw on her head. "Once I'm in my full outfit, you'll get me set up outside and tell Deborah you made a scarecrow for her. I'll do the rest after that."

Jonathan laughed. "Please remain my friend…because it's scary to think of you as an enemy."

Fifteen

Sitting in the cabinetry office, Grey shifted in his chair while on the phone with a potential client. For the first time in years, he didn't feel that work and Ivan were the only hopeful things in his life. Hope. It hung in the fall air itself—light, airy, brisk, colorful, and an indication that something had shifted within the universe.

"Ya," he answered the woman's question for the third time. "I understand you live in Kentucky. If we work out all the details, we'll stay in your area for a week at a time, coming home on the weekends, until the job is complete."

The office door opened, and surprise ran through Grey as his wife stepped inside. "I'll drop a packet of info in the mail to you tomorrow. If you like what you see, just give us a call back, and we'll go from there." As the woman confirmed her address and said good-bye, he stared at his wife. She'd never come to the shop except when church was held here. "Hi."

She removed a cloth from a plate. "I…I made some cookies."

"Denki." He took a cookie. "Is Ivan with you?"

She shook her head.

He took a bite of the cookie. *Pumpkin spice.* "Oh, that's good."

She smiled and ran her fingers along the messy desk, looking at the various sets of plans. Piecing together his wife's actions, he had a suspicion of what was on her mind. She wanted to meet with Lena and get the results concerning Ivan. Grey stole a look at the clock. "School's not out for more than an hour yet."

Elsie didn't respond. She flipped through the calendar.

He took another bite of the cookie. "It's not likely she can step out of the school to talk with us."

Elsie kept her attention focused on the desk, but past her stoic nature, he saw disappointment.

The cookie seemed to lose some of its flavor as he tried to read her. "I guess we could go on and wait there until school is over. It's been quite a while since I saw her teaching methods in action anyway."

The muscles in Elsie's throat constricted as if she were swallowing or at least trying to.

Grey rose. "I…I think she'll have good news for us."

Elsie set the cookies on the desk and pressed her hands down the front of her neatly pressed apron. "I hope you're right."

He motioned for her to leave the office ahead of him. "Excited about being proved wrong?"

"Grey, that's just mean."

The way he breathed and moved no longer grated on her nerves, or at least not all her nerves, and for that he was very grateful. If that's all they had for a long while yet, he'd be satisfied, but in a place inside him where no one would ever know what he thought or how he felt, he longed for her to grow a sense of humor.

He spotted Ephraim. "I'm going out for a bit. I'll be back in a couple of hours and finish my work."

"Sure thing. I'll be here."

He got into the carriage Elsie had driven here, and they headed toward the school. The brilliance of the October sky and the gentle winds refreshed him as he thought about their future. The stiltedness between them still reigned, but his isolation had eased, and he dared to hope where they'd be in a few months or a year from now.

The schoolhouse looked like a photo—a one-room, white clapboard building surrounded by huge oaks with the leaves changing color, a playground with swings to one side, a turnaround driveway on the other, and a rolling pasture behind it. Had it been almost fifteen years since he'd graduated from that school?

He stopped on the far side of the lean-to, leaving room for the parents to pick up their children when school let out. He and Elsie got out and rounded the side of the outbuilding and walked toward the schoolhouse. A man's voice sounded angry, and Grey hurried closer, listening.

"I'm not doing it, and you can't make me. You're just too stupid to accept it."

Grey bounded up the steps and jerked the screen door open. Peter stood in the center of the classroom, inches from Lennie.

"What is going on here?" Grey strode into the room. "You!" He pointed at Peter. "Sit down." Grey stood there, daring Peter to do otherwise.

When Peter balked for a moment before taking his seat, Grey's blood pounded harder against his temples. "This behavior is not acceptable and will not be tolerated. Is that clear?"

"Ya," Peter mumbled.

"Excuse me? I had no problem hearing you earlier."

"Ya," Peter said clearly.

All eyes were on Grey, and he tried to gain control of himself, but this kid did not begin to understand the boundaries he'd crossed. "Elsie, would you take the other children outside for a few minutes? Lena and I need to talk with Peter. Then I want to talk to everyone."

Elsie motioned, and the children exited quietly and quickly.

Grey paced the room before feeling calm enough to grab two folding chairs. He set them next to Peter. "If you don't want to be at school, I can arrange for that."

Lennie took a seat. "I want you here, Peter. I really do think you're more capable of learning than a lot of boys your age. We just haven't figured out *how* you learn best yet."

Grey blinked, trying to accept what Lennie had just said. Was she serious? "Before we do anything else, you give Lena an apology, a sincere one."

Peter looked at Lennie like she disgusted him.

Grey smacked the boy's desk. "You apologize now."

Peter folded his arms and stared at his desk.

Grey wanted to drag him out of the school and refuse him the right to return, but clearly Lennie felt differently. "We'll sit here until you can humble yourself enough to apologize."

Peter slumped in his desk, and Grey used the passing minutes to gain control of himself. Lennie sat there so poised, appearing ready to forgive and start with Peter again. As he considered her belief in others, he found it easier to calm down. Hadn't she had the same determined belief in her own brother?

Grey had been ready to give up on Allen during his wild days, but Lennie had never faltered. She never let him off the hook, always holding him responsible for his behavior, but at the same time she never quit believing he could become even more than she could imagine. And Allen became a good man. It wasn't who Peter was today that made her want to teach him. It was her belief in who he could become if he only wanted to.

Children's voices chanted and laughed from the playground. Lennie rose and went to the window.

She gasped. "Dear Father, no!" She spun around. "Grey! Go. Go." She pointed at the door, and they both ran.

He made it outside first and searched for what had her so upset but saw nothing.

Lennie passed him, pointing. "The pasture. The bull."

One glance and his body halted. His wife stood in the field some two hundred feet out, facing the bull while waving her arms. Two young boys were even farther out in the field.

"Get to the fence!" Elsie screamed at the boys while trying to distract the animal. The bull headed for his wife, and the boys ran for the closest fence, but they had hundreds of feet to cross before they'd get there.

Grey took off running and scaled the barbed-wire barrier with no effort.

Staying outside the fence, Lennie dashed to the area where the boys were heading. "Here!" she screamed while running, motioning for them. "Elsie, run a zigzag…a zigzag!"

"And head for the tree!" Grey clapped his hands. "Hey! Hey! Over here!" he screamed with all his might, trying to get the bull's attention.

The bull remained focused on Elsie, chasing her farther and farther from Grey.

"Elsie! Cut left! Go behind the tree!"

The bull picked up speed. All of Grey's motions seemed awkward and slow. As he continued running toward her, he watched the bull plow full force into his wife's back. Her body was lifted into the air, and then landed with a thud. The bull lowered his head and stomped her.

"No!" Grey rammed his shoulder into the bull's side, trying to get its attention. It didn't seem to even notice what he'd done. He kicked the bull's underbelly, and finally it turned. Grey cut right, hoping the bull would follow but not stomp on Elsie in the process. His idea worked. Sprinting toward the tree, he shifted right, then left, slowing the bull's ability to catch up to him. The bull snorted, slinging its head as it ran. Once behind the tree, he shifted one way and then the other, able to keep the bull from getting to him.

A quick glimpse of his wife made him want to scream out in pain. He'd made the bull follow him, but he couldn't help his wife. She lay sprawled on the ground, and Grey wanted to kill the stupid beast that separated the two of them. Lennie bolted for Elsie. While Lennie hurried across the field, Elsie slowly eased to her hands and knees, trying to get up.

The bull stomped and snorted, kicking up dust as it dodged one way and then the other, trying to get to him. He longed to get a good look at his wife, but every time he tried to see her, the bull came at him. Still he caught glimpses of her.

Elsie only looked addled and weak, but what had the two-thousand-pound, thick-skulled beast done to her insides? By the time Lennie arrived, Elsie had staggered to her feet. She wrapped her arm over Lennie's shoulder, and they made their way toward the fence.

His heart pounded like mad as he kept moving and screaming at the bull to keep its attention. It seemed to take Lennie and Elsie a week to get to the fence. Finally arriving, Elsie got on the ground and rolled under it.

The bull moved one way and then another, clearly wanting to get past the tree between them. Grey had to find a way to get to his wife. She needed medical help. He considered trying to outrun the bull, but the distance from here to the closest fence was too great. A clanging sound echoed again and again, and he realized he'd been hearing that noise since entering the pasture. From the backside of the field, near the broken fence, Grey saw the silhouette of a man coming toward him. The sun's rays hindered his view, but the man hollered and clanged metal objects together as he ran. When he drew close, the bull turned to the new distraction. Concern for whether the man could outrun the bull caused Grey to stay put.

"Go," the voice hollered while banging the objects together. "Get to safety, and take care of my sister."

Aaron.

The moment his brother-in-law had the creature's full attention, Grey ran for his wife.

"Jacob." Lena crawled out of the field on her hands and knees. "Get Grey's horse. Unfasten it from the carriage, and remove everything but the bridle. Bring it here right away."

Elsie swayed, and Lena helped her ease to the ground, wishing Dry Lake didn't sit so far from a hospital. Dozens of thoughts competed for her attention as she tried to prioritize what needed to be done. No blood on Elsie's body. No bones protruding through the skin. Elsie quaked. Her lips had no color. Her eyes seemed unable to focus. Someone had to get to a phone and quick. "Mandy, you and Rachel take the children into the schoolhouse. Someone get me the blankets we use for sitting on during story time."

Mandy and Rachel began doing as they'd been told.

Jacob's voice broke through the commotion. "Get off the horse, Peter! She sent me."

Mounted on Grey's horse, Peter brought the animal to a stop about ten feet from her and Elsie. "I'll get to a phone and call for help. I'm faster on a horse," Peter said.

Torn between distrust and something unknown tugging at her, Lena shook her head. Mandy had taken a good bit of time to get to Ephraim's the other day, but she'd done the job as told. Jacob would too. Should she go herself? As horsemen went, she could outride all her siblings. She rose to her feet and took the horse by one rein.

Peter jerked at the reins, and the horse backed up. "I can do this." His voice cracked. "Please, let me do this."

For a brief moment Lena saw a repentant child who couldn't undo what his actions had set in motion. But did that make him trustworthy? She'd seen him ride bareback, and he could handle a horse better and go faster than she could. "Go. The closest phone is at Ephraim's shop, and tell him we need the parents to come get their children."

Grey leaped over the fence and knelt beside his wife. "Elsie." He drew deep breaths, too winded to speak.

Lena choked back her emotions. "I've sent...one of the boys to call for an ambulance. He's bareback on your horse."

Grey stroked his wife's face. "Can you tell me what hurts the most?"

Elsie tapped the center of her chest. "My heart." Tears rolled down the sides of her head. She licked her lips, giving color to her mouth. "All my married years of scrubbing and cleaning. All trying to make others see how perfect I was." She tugged at Grey's suspender. "In a week no one will ever be able to tell." She licked her lips again. "Except the one who's carried my imperfection with silence and honor."

"I'll scrub and clean every day," Grey murmured. "The cabinets and the walls and anything else while you recuperate."

Was that blood on her mouth? Rachel brought several blankets and held them out.

Lena took them. "Denki. Go on back now, and help the younger ones."

Rachel left. Lena knelt on the other side of Elsie and covered her with the blankets. She ran her finger over Elsie's wet lips. Blood. Hoping Elsie had only split the inside of her mouth when she hit the ground, Lena turned Elsie's head slightly, looking at her ear. Blood. She wiped the fluid from her earlobe and studied it, wishing…

Lena's eyes met Grey's. "No. Do you hear me? I said no."

His desperation broke her heart, and Lena's tears fell onto Elsie's grubby dress. Grey couldn't admit it, but they both knew Elsie was bleeding internally.

And there was nothing they could do but wait, hoping the ambulance would arrive in time.

Elsie shook as if she were in icy water. She closed her eyes, and Lena slapped the back of her hands. "She can't go to sleep. We've got to keep her awake." But Elsie didn't respond.

Grey sat on the ground, cradling her in his arms. "Elsie," he whispered, and she opened her eyes. "Don't you dare leave me now, not after…"

Elsie whispered something. Lena stood and slipped away unnoticed, praying help would arrive soon.

Cold sweat covered Grey. His body shook, and his mind raged against what was happening. "You'll be okay, Elsie. Help's coming. Just…just stay with me. Please."

She closed her eyes.

"No. Stay awake. Listen to me…please." He tucked the blankets around her, feeling desperation like never before. His heart railed at him, despised him for not doing more for their marriage sooner.

Dear God, please. Don't let this happen to us. We've been such idiots. Forgive me.

Pleadings screamed inside him, but nothing changed his reality. He wiped a trickle of blood from the side of her mouth.

Please, God.

"Elsie," he called to her loudly, and she opened her eyes. "I need…us. Can't you feel that? Hang on. Just hang on."

She looped her hand through one suspender and tugged on it. "Tell… me…about the day…we…met."

Grey choked back tears, praying the ambulance would arrive soon. She wanted to talk about the past? He'd just begun having hope for their future. She had to survive this. She had to. "It was on a church Sunday, on a beautiful fall day like today. The windows at my house were open. Mamm and Daed had already gathered all my siblings and were in the buggy waiting for me, but I couldn't find my Sunday pants…or any others that would fit. I went to the window and hollered down at Mamm, 'I can't find my Sunday britches.'

"She shifted, looking a little nervous as she answered, 'Did you check in your dresser?' And I said, 'Ya.' And she said, 'Look in your closet, and maybe in the dirty clothes basket.'

"I searched through everything quickly, grabbed what I could find, and headed out the door. I walked outside, whistling like a man without a care."

She breathed a whispery laugh. "Then what happened?"

"Everyone in the buggy broke into laughter as I came outside wearing my pressed shirt, suspenders, dress shoes, Sunday jacket and hat…but no pants."

Elsie's breaths came in short, rapid spurts, but she smiled at the memory.

Grey wiped the back of his hand across his mouth, taking several deep breaths in hopes he could finish the story. "Then I looked up and saw that you and your family were passing the house, walking to church."

Her breathing came in shallow gasps. "Tell more."

"Then I tipped my hat at you as if nothing unusual was going on. You screamed and covered your eyes."

"Later…your Mamm s…s…said."

He pulled Elsie closer, trying to warm her. "Well my Mamm looked you up before the service to try to reassure you that wasn't a normal event in Dry Lake. She thought you and your family were visitors, but then we learned your Daed was trying to buy the old Englischer farmstead up the road a piece and was thinking about moving here from Ohio. She told you that I was keeping things light so no one would be mad at her about me not having pants and that I didn't usually run around in my boxers."

"M…m…more."

"Your eyes met mine, and you told me later that's when you knew you wanted to marry me. You wanted a man who…who…" Heaviness settled into his chest as he realized how badly he'd let her down all these years. "Had two good senses—ya, that's what you said—the sense to be himself and the sense to laugh instead of get mad. And I told you that when a person has chicken legs like I do, they have to have a sense of humor. And because you'd seen those scrappy legs and still weren't running away, I said you must be the right girl."

She swallowed. "You…find your good senses…again, Grey. You find them and don't let go."

"I will. You'll help me, right?" He placed his hand on her cheek, staring into her eyes. But as he held her, light faded from them, making her look… "Elsie!" He placed his hand on her neck, looking for a pulse. She had one, barely. "Elsie, listen to me."

Her body became heavier against him, but she didn't respond to his voice. Without looking at him again and without even a gasp or twitch, she exhaled. And never took another breath.

Sixteen

Inside the barn, Cara painted a strip of wainscot lying across sawhorses. She swayed to the music coming from her battery-operated radio.

"'From!" Lori squealed as she ran out of the barn, Better Days yapping at her heels.

In Hope Crossing on a Monday afternoon? Cara turned. Ephraim was on foot, which meant Robbie must have dropped him off out front. Lori ran to him and jumped into his arms. Rather than his usual quick swing of her body into the air as he shared a bit of banter, he pulled her close, one hand embracing her head as all movement halted. He kissed her head and set her feet on the ground.

When he stopped in the doorway of the barn, his focus didn't budge from Cara. Realizing the radio was not acceptable, she went to the bale of hay where it sat and turned it off. He said nothing.

Cara shrugged. "I…I just wanted to hear some familiar tunes."

"Mama's been dancin'."

"Just a little," Cara added quickly. "There's good news, though. I didn't set up my work station in the yard like I'd wanted to on this gorgeous day, so no one but Lori heard the music or saw me."

"I tried tellin' her not to, 'From. She never listens to me."

Cara found Lori's exasperation with her cute, but Ephraim's face held emotions she'd not seen before. Had she taxed his patience too much?

"I…I'm not a member, so music is okay until I begin my instruction, right?"

Without answering, he walked to her and pulled her into a hug. He held her in a way he never had before. His warm embrace renewed her spirits even more than the beautiful October day.

"I had to see you, had to feel you in my arms." His deep voice sounded different today.

Lori squeezed between them. "Yuck." She put a hand on each of them and pushed them away from each other.

Ephraim playfully nudged her back before kissing Cara gently on the cheek.

"I'll say it again. Yuck." Lori hurried out of the barn.

"Hey," Ephraim called to her. "Run inside and tell Ada we're going for a long walk."

"Yes!" Lori whispered loudly. "You want me to grab our picnic blanket?"

"Ya."

"And make some sandwiches?"

"Ya." Ephraim's eyes never moved from Cara, and she knew he'd come to tell her something.

"What kind?"

Cara snapped her fingers. "Lori, just go."

Lori put her hands on her hips. "I was just asking 'From, Mom."

"Mind your tone, Lori," Ephraim corrected her.

Lori lowered her hands, looking hurt. She walked into the barn and wrapped her arms around Cara's waist. "Sorry."

Cara bent and kissed the top of her head. "Forgiven. Now take off."

Without asking anything else, Lori and Better Days ran through the backyard and into the house.

Ephraim moved to the radio and picked it up. He turned it around as if inspecting it. "You're finding it harder to give up the Englischer ways rather than easier."

It wasn't a question, so she decided not to respond. Of course it was hard. She missed having electricity and her choice of clothing, but of late those preferences seemed a lot easier to give up than music and television. The new fall season of shows had been going for a couple of weeks now, and she didn't even know if *Survivor* was still in the lineup. She'd never owned a television, but the restaurant where she'd worked had them hanging from the ceilings. And today while listening to a rock station, she'd heard half a dozen new songs—good ones.

He set the radio back down on the bale of hay. "I don't care about bikes or music or you dancing. When I lived among Englischers those few years, I could see how tough it'd be to live Amish if one hadn't been raised that way." He moved to her. "But the longer it takes you to accept our ways, the more likely it is that church leaders won't think you're ready to join the faith, and then it'll be even longer before we can marry." Ephraim slowly brought his face to hers, as if letting all of her—her mind, will, heart, and body—awaken to what he was trying to tell her. He kissed her long and slow. "And I want to marry you...as soon as possible."

When he released her, she could barely think. "I...I didn't think Amish...had feelings like that. I thought they...you were too practical."

Ephraim backed away, drawing a deep breath. "What you don't understand about people of faith is sort of baffling." He took her hand into his. "I've got some bad news. Grey's wife died this afternoon. Attacked by a bull. She had massive internal injuries."

"Ephraim, I'm so sorry. Do I know her?"

He shook his head. "Elsie was a quiet woman who avoided gatherings as much as possible and kept to herself even when she attended church. But Grey is...bad right now." Ephraim reflected a sadness that made Cara hurt for him. "The whole community is. The schoolchildren saw the incident."

"What? That's horrible. I...I..." She wrapped her arms around him, aching for the children and their parents.

"The bull belonged to Elsie's brother Aaron. Aaron got his hunting rifle and shot the bull—again and again and again. Elsie died before the ambulance arrived, but Grey rode with her to the hospital. Friends and family hired a driver so they could meet him there. He and Elsie have one child, a five-year-old son, who doesn't know yet. Grey will tell him when he returns to Dry Lake, but I imagine Grey has forms and reports to fill out, so that will be hours from now. It's bad, Cara."

They tightened their hold on each other.

"I know you're not at ease in Dry Lake, running into your estranged relatives and all, but I'd like for you to come stay for a few days. You and Lori and Ada can stay at my place, and I'll stay at the shop."

"Ada and Deborah have a business to run."

"They'll close their doors for a few days, as will most Amish businesses in and around Dry Lake."

"Stop all business?" The idea sounded bizarre. People took time off from work, as little time as possible, but life never slowed. When her husband died, one of the most painful realities was that life never paused. New York didn't care. The restaurant he'd once managed had replaced him when he could no longer work, and on the day he died, she received a two-week notice to move out of the apartment that belonged to the owners of the restaurant. "Okay, I'll come…and try my best not to embarrass you."

"I'm going to keep saying it until you believe me. I will never feel that way. Not ever." He took her by the hand, and they began walking toward the house. He hollered for Lori.

She stuck her head out the back door. "Be there in a minute. Jonathan's helping me make sandwiches."

Cara shielded her eyes from the sunlight. "Jonathan's here?"

"Ya."

They walked back into the barn. Ephraim sat on a bale of hay and picked up the radio. "He came with me to tell Deborah and Ada. The driver will take them on to Dry Lake as soon as Deborah and Ada are packed. I imagine Lena needs Deborah about now."

"Why's Lena taking it so hard? Oh, you said the schoolchildren saw, and she's their teacher." Grief settled over Cara, and she began to understand how interwoven the Amish were.

"When one of the schoolboys arrived at the shop to use the phone and told me what had happened, I'd hoped it wasn't as bad as it sounded. I went to the school and learned that Elsie had died, and I felt sick for Grey and Ivan. But something else happened inside me. Something I'd never experienced before."

"What?"

He drew her hand to his lips and kissed it. "Over the years if someone died and I was seeing a girl, the news sobered my thinking. Every time. Beyond the sadness I'd think about the girl and know she wasn't who I wanted to spend the rest of my life with. Even if that day was my last day on earth, I was ready to walk away. Something about death made it clear. I…I always felt so shallow when that happened. Those types of events cause people to want to hold on to who they have. Today when the news hit, I felt vulnerable, and I needed you, longed to hold you and talk to you." He squeezed her hand. "I had to see you, to make sure you and Lori were safe, to reassure myself we will become a family." He stared at the radio.

"Then you arrived, and I'm…sneaking around and hanging on to some of my former ways."

"You're you, Cara. I don't want you to be anyone else, and we can be imperfect together, but it seems as if you own more of me than I do, and… yet other things possess your heart. I understand it, but it scares me. I need *you,* but what do you need?"

Wishing she could snap her fingers and change for him, she tugged on his hand, leading him out of the barn. "I'll adjust to living the Old Ways… I will."

Seventeen

Lena woke, startled from her nightmare. More exhausted than when she went to bed, she longed for her thoughts to settle. All she could do was doze and jerk awake after another dreadful dream. She kept reliving the trauma she'd witnessed less than sixteen hours ago.

What must the children be going through?

She pushed off the covers and sat upright. Grief weighed heavy, making her head spin.

And what about Grey?

He'd begun yesterday with a wife, his family intact, and a good road ahead of him. Today he was missing half of himself.

All night she'd dreamed of Elsie teetering on the edge of a rocky cliff and of Grey running to grab her. Instead they both plummeted. Elsie died instantly. Grey lay at the bottom of the gorge—broken, bloody, but unable to pass from this life to the next.

Nausea returned. She went to the window and opened it. Cold air rushed in. Nicky stretched and moaned, wagging her tail a few times before going back to sleep. Lena glanced through the open doorway, seeing Deborah in the adjoining bedroom, motionless under the quilts. A hired driver had brought two Amish families here from Ohio late last night, families Lena had never met before. They were friends of Elsie's family from Ohio, but Elsie's parents' home couldn't house any more people.

Lena breathed deeply, trying to rid herself of queasiness. It didn't matter how poorly she felt. There was much that needed doing. Foods of all sorts had to be prepared for Elsie's visiting relatives as well as for the day of the funeral. She closed the window, gathered clean clothes, and went into her bathroom. Maybe a warm shower would make her feel better. It usually helped, but after drying off and slipping into her dress, she still felt nauseated and weak. She pinned up her wet hair and secured her prayer Kapp in place.

It was just as well school was closed for the next few days. She knew nothing to say or do that would ease the shock and pain her pupils were going through. Urie and Tobias, the boys who'd snuck into the pasture, the ones who'd caused Elsie to become the bull's target so they could escape—how would they survive their guilt? And what about Peter? Would this cause him to completely give up?

When school was in session again, her scholars would need more help than she knew how to give. A tremor ran through her. The weeks ahead felt darker and colder than a winter's night.

And Grey… Would he ever feel warmth within his soul again?

Oh how she wished she could undo yesterday.

Before leaving the bedroom, she checked herself in the mirror, making sure she'd pinned everything correctly in place. She was descending the stairs when someone knocked on the back door. Nicky barked, running ahead of her. Lena told her to hush, and she obeyed. Since they'd had guests staying with them last night, Lena had lit a few kerosene nightlights, which illuminated the entryway. She told Nicky to stay. When she opened the door, Aaron Blank had his hand ready to knock again.

They both seemed too caught by surprise to speak.

Nicky barked.

"Hush," Lena scolded.

A faint aroma of alcohol surrounded him. He didn't have a jacket, and his short-sleeve shirt and pants flapped in the brisk winds. She hadn't even begun to consider his guilt.

"Kumm out of the cold."

But he didn't budge. Even in the dim glow of kerosene night-lights, his dark, bloodshot eyes held such remorse that Lena couldn't hold his gaze.

He removed his straw hat. "I…I…only did a half job fixing the fence…and now…"

Lena's heart twisted, and she tugged on his arm. "You made a mistake. Kumm. Get warm."

Aaron pulled her in a hug, and she felt him trembling. "My sister. I killed my own sister."

No words came to her. Only pain at what Aaron would carry for the rest of his life. She embraced him warmly. "Kumm." She took him by the arm, and he eased inside.

Nicky growled, and Lena snapped her fingers. "Go lay down."

With her tail tucked, Nicky went to her bed in the kitchen. Lena followed her, guiding Aaron as he staggered. She helped him to a chair. Dirt and stains covered his clothes, and she wondered where he'd left his coat.

"I…I need a bathroom."

"Sure." She pointed to the closest one. He'd been in it a few times in the past when church was held here, but she didn't imagine he could think clearly enough to remember.

He stood and stumbled his way into the half bath.

She added wood to the potbelly stove and set a pot of coffee on to brew. Kneeling in front of Nicky, she gave her a few doggy treats and then patted her head. "You do your job and get fussed at about it." Lena cuddled her nose in the palms of her hands. "Welcome to the real world, I suppose."

Nicky laid her head on the raised edge of her doggy bed, satisfied that Lena had doted on her. Aaron walked back into the room, looking a little better. He seemed to have washed his face and somehow scrubbed a bit of his drunkenness away.

"I…I shouldn't have come like this, Lena. You…you deserve better."

She ached for him. He wanted to be a good guy; she'd never doubted that. But so far he didn't have it in him to follow through. "So do you, Aaron. Kumm, sit. Coffee will be ready in a few minutes. Then we can talk."

He did as she'd requested. He took her hand in his and several times started to say something. But instead they sat in silence.

Days had passed. Grey knew they had, but he hardly remembered any conversations he'd had with people. Tuning out the murmuring of the many voices within his home, he moved from one room to another. He couldn't hear when someone spoke to him, even when he tried, and he couldn't find the strength to try.

Everyone thought him to be a good husband who'd lost his wife. They didn't know the truth. No one but Ephraim knew the strain inside Grey's marriage, and Grey would never tell. He shouldn't have talked to Ephraim either. Elsie had a right to privacy. She had a right to a lot of things he hadn't given her.

He pulled a chair from the kitchen table, walked into the living room, and sat in front of his wife's open casket. Wearing the customary white apron and prayer Kapp that she'd worn on their wedding, she looked so much like she had six years ago.

What happened to us, Elsie?

That tormenting question never ceased pounding inside his heart. He blamed himself. Each tick of the clock had felt suffocating since the moment she'd died. He hadn't realized that even when he and Elsie were the most miserable, hope—constant, threadbare hope—kept him. Tomorrow a service would be held in his home and another one at the grave site. Then it'd be time to close the casket, lower her into the ground, and cover his future with dirt.

"I'm sorry, Elsie."

His Mamm placed her hand on his shoulder. "You need to come eat."

Even with the cooler temperatures of October, his house radiated with heat from all the baking the women had done. Someone with good sense had opened a few windows a couple of inches. But he didn't want food, or fresh air, or conversation. He wanted time alone. "Can you do me a favor, Mamm? After everyone's eaten, can you get them to go home? Take Ivan with you."

"You don't need to be alone, Son."

"Ya, I do. Can you do that for me?"

People had been here day and night. They'd filled his home even before he arrived from the hospital. He understood the Amish tradition, but he needed tonight by himself.

"Please, Mamm."

She nodded. "If you're sure."

"I am."

"Will you come say good-bye?"

"No," he whispered. "I'll see them all tomorrow before and after...the services, and I'll do as I need to then." He choked back his tears. His Mamm patted his shoulder.

After the meal and cleanup, his house grew quieter and quieter as people left. The sun slid behind the horizon. As darkness grew, Grey rose and lit the kerosene lamp. Elsie liked for him to go through their home each evening and light the gas pole lamps and kerosene lanterns.

Through all their silences had he noticed or appreciated the rhythm to their marriage? He returned to his chair. His guilt grew worse with each passing day, and he knew it'd just begun.

His only chance to make it right had ended, taking most of him with it.

Sing for me, Grey.

Her voice ran through him as clearly as the day they married. She'd asked that of him every day until Ivan was born. Tears filled his eyes. If he'd knelt before her and sung to her, without being asked, would she have told him sooner what separated them?

Sing for me, Grey.

He swallowed and straightened the collar of her dress. "Amazing Grace..." He began the song softly and sang louder with each verse, trying to drown out the condemnation in his own heart. Wind whipped through the room, billowing the curtains and threatening to damage the nearby houseplants. He shut the windows. Clouds moved quickly across the dark skies, bringing a sense that only darkness lurked beyond the gray.

Eighteen

Samantha drew a huge circle on the chalkboard. She pointed inside the circle. "This is where everything and everyone you love belongs. Can you begin telling me things to write inside this circle? Don't raise your hand. Just say it aloud."

Children began volunteering answers, slowly at first, but then the responses grew faster and louder, as did their laughter.

Nine days had passed since the incident, and Lena's heart pounded as she watched Samantha interact with her class. Her friend had read about Elsie's death in the local newspaper and stopped by Lena's place to check on her. After Samantha talked to her about posttraumatic stress disorder and other related issues, Lena asked if she'd come talk to her class.

Lena's own feelings were so jumbled she didn't know where to begin trying to sort them out. Hearing Grey sing to Elsie the night before he buried her made Lena teary-eyed every time she thought about it. She'd been in her brother's yard and as Grey's voice carried on the wind, she grew still and listened. She couldn't help Grey with his grief, but with Samantha's knowledge, Lena could make a difference for her scholars. Even Peter was responding well to Samantha.

The school days were long and filled with tears and confusion, but now Lena felt as if they'd do more than mark time off the calendar. She desperately wanted healing to take place.

Wrapped inside a winter coat and a woolen scarf, Deborah stayed warm. The stars shone brightly across the November sky as she slid another mini–pumpkin pie onto a customer's paper plate. The bite-sized pies were rather time-consuming to make but well worth the effort. Customers could purchase five different kinds and sample each flavor. Or they could buy a regular-sized pie to take home with them. After eating the mini-pies, guests often bought whole pies. The success of the last four weeks might not show up in an abundance of money. That remained to be seen. But she and Ada had learned so much about running this type of home business. If they could do this kind of production with so little time to prepare for it, she felt fairly confident they could run an even better pumpkin patch next year.

People armed with high-powered flashlights called to each other from inside the corn maze, and their laughter flowed. Cara stood in the tower, keeping watch and giving humor-filled verbal directions to those inside the maze as they moved from one stamp station to another. She honestly didn't know who had the most fun—Cara or the ones inside the cornfield.

A few feet away Ephraim ran the cash register. Lena came around the side of the house, bringing Deborah a stack of boxed pies. All the baked goodies were ones customers had ordered and paid for in Ada's kitchen. They'd pick them up at this cubicle since it was the last stop at the pumpkin patch before the guests headed home. People could also order and pay for baked goods from this station.

Lena grabbed an order off the counter and began to fill it.

Jonathan's voice carried softly through the air as he sang while driving the hay wagon toward its stop. His breath turned to vapor as it left his mouth. The riders were giggling and singing the little German ditty he taught each time. He brought the rig to a stop, hopped off, and chatted comfortably with kids and adults alike as he helped them down and pointed them in her direction. This was his last ride for the night. This group had been through the maze, gone on a hayride, and spent time with Ada in her kitchen, eating roasted pumpkin seeds and decorating cookies before eating them. In October the children decorated cookies to look like pumpkins and jack-o'-lanterns. Since November had begun, Ada had the customers decorate what she called turkey cookies, which sounded rather distasteful to Deborah, but the kids loved making a cookie look like a turkey.

When she and Ada had enough apples, they ran an apple press, where the children could squeeze out a tiny cup of their own cider. Ada used the pulp to make four-ounce jars of apple butter, which sold much better than they'd expected.

While counting out change to the person in front of him, Ephraim glanced up at Cara, who stood in the tower. He passed a written order for desserts to Deborah.

"I didn't expect her to love this type of work." Deborah read the slip of paper.

"Ich hab." Ephraim spoke the words *I did* quietly. He pulled out a large brown paper bag from under the counter and passed it to her. "It gives her a chance to connect with Englischers on stuff I know almost nothing about—music, television shows, sports."

Deborah opened the bag, ready to fill it with baked goods. "She's crazy about you."

Concern reflected in Ephraim's eyes as he studied Cara for a moment before returning to his register. "I know." He looked at the next customer. "What can I get for you today?"

Folks who'd gotten off the last hayride were now picking out sugar pumpkins for making pies. Then they'd buy some baked goods and head for home. The group currently in the maze had already been on a hayride. Ada's House and Pumpkin Patch would close in less than thirty minutes. She finished filling the order and passed it to the woman. "Denki," Deborah said.

The woman put her nose at the edge of the boxed pies and breathed deeply. "Oh, this will be perfect for our ladies group tomorrow."

As Deborah said good-bye, she noticed Jonathan beside his horse, patting and talking to her. His eyes met Deborah's. He cocked his head, mouthing the words *Surprise for Lena*. He pointed at the barn. Deborah nodded. She hadn't forgotten. Lena would turn twenty-four tomorrow. Since tomorrow was Saturday, Lena would come help at Ada's House for a while, but then she'd spend tomorrow night with her family. So Deborah and Jonathan were giving her a surprise party—with the emphasis on the word *surprise*.

If all went well, they'd celebrate Lena's big day as soon as the last customer left. It'd be a mixture of gag gifts disguised as real presents. But what made this plan more fun was that the trick goods were ones Lena had purchased. With help from Jonathan, Deborah had confiscated the items from Lena's hidden stash.

Jonathan tipped his hat before leading the horse toward the barn. Time to take care of his horse and let her rest until tomorrow afternoon.

Lena nudged Deborah. "Customers at the far side of the pumpkin patch." Lena pointed. "I could go, but I think they need a bit of Deborah advice with the kiddos before the parents have an all-out fight on their hands."

"Oh, ya, sure."

While Lena filled another order, Deborah hurried across the yard and toward the pumpkin patch. Lena had told her that she had a way of working with siblings that kept everyone happy.

She drew a deep breath, taking in the cold air, the array of delicious smells, and the joy of having great friends and family. She'd always cherished them but never more than now. Lena hired a driver and helped Ada in the kitchen on the nights and weekends when she could get here. Ephraim made sure to be here on Friday and Saturday nights. Jonathan had stayed five days straight after Elsie's funeral, helping them make up for lost time. They had designed and cleared paths in the maze and built the tower, and each week he went with her to all the Amish farms, where she bought pumpkins. Cara pitched in as if she'd always been a part of the Amish community. They also baked and sold dozens and dozens of small loaves of Amish Friendship Bread, and she'd be surprised if they had any left to enjoy over a cup of hot chocolate when they closed for the night. But friendship bread to munch on or not, after the crowds were gone, she and her friends would sit in the living room and share events that took place at their stations. And they'd had crowds like this every night for the last four weeks. Clearly the fliers they'd posted in town and the ads they'd taken out in the newspaper were doing their job. She'd expected business to slow to nearly nothing after the Englischer celebration of Halloween passed, but she'd been wrong. If anything, business had picked up.

Her girlfriends she'd been close to most of her life came to help out when they could—Rachel, Linda, Nancy, Lydia, Frieda, and Esther. They had all come on three separate weekends, and it'd been way too much fun to call what they'd done actual work. Unfortunately Anna Mary hadn't come at all. She had a new beau in Lancaster, some ninety minutes away by car. Deborah missed her, but she understood.

"Hello." Deborah waved as she came toward the family. She looked at the girl sitting on the ground, crying. Her brother stood with his arms folded, grumbling about wanting a different pumpkin. "So what is it about that pumpkin that you like so much?" she asked the boy. Either she'd find a pumpkin that suited both of them, or she'd sell them two pumpkins at half price each. Customer service that guaranteed satisfaction seemed to be a main reason they had such great repeat business.

Grey sat in front of a roaring fire. He could feel its heat but still felt gripped by icy remorse, and he wished he knew how to break free. Was this how grief always worked? Did it enclose a person on all sides and never let up, even during sleep? Or was this worse because he'd been such a fool with his time?

Sprawled on the floor between him and the hearth, Ivan quietly played with his wooden toy horses.

"Daed? *Der Gaule kann nimmi schteh.*" Ivan rose and turned to him, telling his father that his horse couldn't stand up anymore. Its hoof had broken off.

Grey held the horse in his hand, wondering if he remembered how to carve little animals. He'd made these for Ivan's second birthday and hadn't carved anything like it since.

Ivan's eyes grew large for a moment, indicating that he'd thought of something. He scurried across the wood floors in his socks toward the back door.

Grey called after him, telling him it was wet outside.

Ivan said nothing as he slung open the back door.

Children. Their resilience astounded him. Ivan missed his Mamm. He crawled into Grey's lap and cried sometimes, but then Grey would read to him, or talk to him of Elsie, or get on the floor with him and play. Soon enough the intensity of Ivan's sadness would ease. Grey's regret hadn't dulled for one moment.

It seemed the most Grey could offer Ephraim at the cabinetry shop was to muddle through his work load. Grey's Mamm kept Ivan, and Grey worked as few hours as he could and still be able to pay bills. Even though Grey had no energy and no clear thoughts to help him accomplish much, Ivan only seemed to need him to be present. So Grey was there. He remembered a man once telling him that regret after a loved one died was like living in hell itself. At the time Grey hadn't understood.

"Daed, kumm."

Grey checked the clock almost wishing it was time to put Ivan down for the night. He had another two hours before Ivan's bedtime. As much as he longed for the ease of free time once Ivan was asleep, he knew that's when another night began, one that seemed to last forever. He rose and went out back.

Pointing to a tree branch, Ivan told his Daed to look. *"Guck."* He wanted a new horse carved from that branch.

Grey told him they couldn't cut that branch. That it would hurt the tree.

Across the yards, his and Allen's, he could see that every room in his friend's home seemed to have at least one kerosene lantern lit. The idea of visiting his friend pulled on him. Allen had come over every day since... Elsie had passed. He'd bring Grey a newspaper, or food from his kitchen, or just a few minutes of talk about the weather. Each time Allen would ask Grey to come for a visit. Since Ivan wanted more from Grey tonight than he could muster, maybe he should go. Ivan needed a distraction, and Allen's home always had children.

"Witt du ans Allen's geh?" Grey asked.

Ivan grabbed his Daed's hand, pulling him toward the steps that led to the yard.

"Whoa." Grey pointed at Ivan's sock-covered feet. They went inside and put on their coats, hats, and boots.

Soon enough they were in the barn, and Grey hitched the horse to its carriage. Grey's home sat at the end of a long lane. No other homes could be seen from here, except Allen's. If Elsie had been so inclined, Grey would have built a bridge across the creek that separated his and Allen's places. But she liked seclusion—cherished it actually.

Maybe if he'd tried harder to understand her.

He couldn't stop the constant rehashing of old topics, so he didn't even try. But he felt as cold and damp on the inside as the weather around him. He hoped his heart would grow used to it so it'd feel normal rather than be this current unbearable pain.

He helped Ivan out of the buggy, and his son ran ahead of him. The boy knocked, and Allen opened the door, welcoming him. He heard the Kauffman clan cheer and clap when Ivan entered.

"Phoebe, Amos, look who's here," Allen called out.

Tears stung Grey's eyes as he led his horse to the lean-to, and he breathed a prayer of thankfulness. It seemed he had little to offer Ivan these days except the steadfastness of quiet love and being with him. But energetic love oozed from others and made up for what Grey could not give. When he stepped inside, everyone spoke a friendly hello just as they always did.

"Kumm." Allen hugged him. "We're just now finishing dinner. Can we fix you a plate?"

Grey shook his head. "We ate at Mamm's a few hours ago."

"You and everybody else had dinner at a reasonable time, I'm sure. We had to wait on Lennie, and she spent today in Hope Crossing at Ada's House and then got to running late."

Lennie stuck her tongue out at Allen. "Watch it, big brother. It's my party, and I'll make you cry if I want to."

Grey helped Ivan out of his coat and then took off his own and hung them on the coatrack. The humor and camaraderie in the Kauffman household caused him to take a deep breath for the first time in a month.

"Kumm," Phoebe said to Ivan before running upstairs. Ivan ran behind her.

While still sitting, Israel pulled the chair out for Grey. "Did what Lena said make sense to anyone?" Israel asked.

Grey took a seat, knowing conversations in Allen's household ran in every direction at once. He always enjoyed the lively banter.

"It's a twist on lyrics to a song," Lennie answered her Daed. "You've heard it when in stores and such. Haven't you? 'It's my party, and I'll cry if...'"

Israel held up his hand. "From your rumschpringe days?"

Allen's wife, Emily, brought a cake to the table.

"Ya." Lennie went to the counter and grabbed a dessert box. "My tenth-grade English teacher had us listen to songs in class and dissect the lyrics. We did that for a few minutes every day as a creative way to understand concise storytelling."

Emily cut a slice of cake and passed it to Grey. He rarely ate a cake he liked, so he passed it to Israel.

Israel took the plate and set it on the table in front of him. "I don't even want to know any of the lyrics. I still wake in a cold sweat when I think of what all you heard and saw while attending public school."

Emily passed Grey another piece of cake. He gave it to Allen.

"Me too." Allen mumbled around the cake. "I worry what the statute of limitations is for any trouble she caused while there."

Lennie set the dessert box in front of Grey, and when Emily tried to pass him another piece of cake, Lennie intercepted it. "No cake for Grey, Emily. Remember?"

"Oh," Emily said, "I always forget about that. Who doesn't like cake?"

"Grey," Allen offered.

Emily laid a hand on her stomach, and Grey realized she was expecting again. She didn't look too far along, but had someone told him, and he'd forgotten?

"With four little ones and one due this spring, I can't even keep straight what *I* like to eat and not eat." Emily giggled.

"I understand." Grey chose to ignore the pang of sadness that smacked him. He'd had such hopes of him and Elsie receiving good test results and finding healing from years of marital stress. Then they'd have had more children.

He put a hand on the box Lennie had set in front of him, but Allen stopped him. "I wouldn't open that if I were you."

Lennie took the container and opened it. "Allen, you're a big scaredy-cat." She passed the box back to Grey before going to the island and getting another dessert box. Grey took a cookie—chocolate chip oatmeal with pecans, his favorite.

He caught her eye, and the look on her face assured him it wasn't a coincidence. "Allen would have brought them by your place tomorrow, but since you're here, please take them with you." She set another dessert box next to Allen. "Just don't touch it, and you'll be safe, big brother."

"What kind is it?"

Lennie shrugged.

He picked it up and smelled it. "Lemon pound cake?"

"Deborah's?" Emily asked. But Lennie didn't respond.

Allen set the box on the table. "Lemon pound cake is my favorite."

Lennie took a bite of the chocolate cake. "I know."

He opened the box and screamed like a girl when four cloth-covered snakes pounced at him. Grey about choked on his cookie.

Lennie put her hand on Grey's shoulder. "*Now* it's a happy birthday."

"Man," Allen complained. "How come you do this to me and not Grey?"

Lennie raised an eyebrow and propped her chin in the palm of her hand. "Because he's not my brother, which means he didn't sow seeds that must be reaped."

Grey cleared his throat. "As a kid, she did warn you regularly that she'd spend the rest of her days getting you back."

"Ya, I did." Lennie waggled her eyebrows. "Besides, I need a favor from Grey."

Grey took another bite of his cookie. "Ah, that explains everything."

"No, not everything." Lennie reached into the box in front of him and stole a cookie. "You don't know the favor."

Conversations came and went as children ran in and out of the room. His grief remained thick and undeniable, but tonight gave him that moment of pardon he so desperately needed. Maybe he'd survive this season yet, at least with enough of him left so he could be a good Daed to

Ivan. That was all he wanted in life now—to be the kind of Daed he needed to be.

When most of the group scattered—the women to clearing the table and washing dishes and Allen to checking on the children upstairs—Grey remained at the table, trying to think clearly enough to hear Israel as he talked. It'd become so easy to stay lost in thought.

"Grossdaadi." Phoebe called for her granddad, and Israel excused himself.

With the table empty of plates and flatware, Lennie walked over and began scrubbing it with a wet cloth. "You doing reasonably okay?"

Grateful at least one person refused to pretend his grief wasn't there, he considered her question. "What's reasonable?"

"Somewhere beyond complete agony and just shy of willing yourself to die, I'd think."

Did that mean how he felt landed in the normal range? He found that thought comforting. "Then I'm doing reasonably okay."

"Gut."

"How are Urie and Tobias?"

She took a seat near him. "Pretty good, I think. At times I have to stop class and just let the scholars talk and cry and draw pictures. Whatever they need."

"And Peter?"

"Withdrawn and sullen. I…I'm still concerned about him. He carries a lot of guilt for being the reason you sent Elsie outside with the other students."

Grey didn't have the strength to talk about this. He carried enough guilt for both him and Peter. If he hadn't been so angry with Peter, he wouldn't have sent the others outside.

Grey shifted. "Elsie's parents said Aaron's taken to holing up in that cabin by himself most of the time."

"Ya, I heard."

"If losing a daughter wasn't enough for Michael and Dora, Aaron's making it worse. I've tried to talk to him, but…I don't know what to say or do."

"Ya, it's hard to figure, but it seems to me all we can focus on is what we can do." She reached down and picked up a wayward trick snake off the floor. "And it's important for you to pull as many stunts on Allen as possible. That may not help *you* much, but it'll do wonders for me." She softly mocked an evil laugh, patted his arm, and headed for the kitchen.

"Lennie."

She paused.

"You didn't tell me the favor."

"I need a donkey for this year's Christmas pageant."

"Real animals?"

"The class voted to do a live crèche."

Her energy for life contrasted with his, and he felt old and even more tired. "I don't own a donkey anymore. Haven't for years."

"Ya, I know. But you have a trailer for hauling creatures, and the Englischer family who bought your donkey will loan him out for a night, right?"

"Ya, probably so, but I'm beginning to think it'd been easier to have a gag pulled on me."

Her lips curved into a smile. "I'll be sure to keep that in mind."

Nineteen

Lena spread a little straw across a section of the schoolroom floor, mentally listing what else she needed to do for tonight's Christmas play. She checked the clock, hoping Grey hadn't forgotten. He'd been at Allen's two weeks ago when she dropped by, and she'd reminded him then about tonight. He'd forgotten all about the play but assured her he'd get the donkey here.

She'd let her scholars off school today so she'd have plenty of time to prepare. Since the Amish didn't take off extra days for Christmas break like the public schools did, she might get a few complaints from parents about her decision but surely not many.

Scholars were supposed to be off school only for Christmas Day and Second Christmas. She loved the Amish tradition of Second Christmas on December 26, which was treated like Christmas itself, only better in her opinion—more relaxed, more visiting time with friends and relatives. She moved to the potbelly stove and stoked the wood.

Someone clomped up the wooden steps. The door opened, and cold air swooshed inside as Grey entered.

"You're here in time."

"That I am." Without looking at her, he moved to the potbelly stove.

He hadn't been to this building since the day Elsie died, and seeing the stress etched across his face, Lena regretted asking this favor. Grey wasn't the same man who'd come to her school nearly eleven weeks ago. His voice was so deep and heavy with grief that it didn't even sound like his anymore. The circles under his eyes and the way he carried himself all spoke of a heartache she couldn't begin to understand.

Loneliness for a future mate swept over her like a nor'easter, but she couldn't imagine what it did to a man who'd lost his mate so very early in life.

He held his hands over the stove. "I put the donkey out back with the other animals." He looked around the place. "Where are all the desks?"

"We lugged them to the lean-to."

Her brothers and Daed had helped her move the desks into the lean-to and cover them with a tarp before they set up church benches and tables. She and her Daed had created the props—a mock stable complete with wooden stalls, a fence, and a cattle gate. The live animals waited outside, tethered to the nearby fence.

"This looks really...different." He took off his hat. "You've gone to a lot of trouble just for a play."

"It's not just a play. It's a reminder of the birth of Christ and all that we hold dear." Lena went to a box of goods sitting on a serving table. "So"—she got out a coffee cup and spoon and moved back to the wood stove—"will Ivan come tonight with his *Grossmammi* and Daadi?"

"Ya. I'm not staying."

Disappointment stung, but she tried to hide it. Lifting the percolator from the wood stove, she asked, "Coffee?"

"Ya."

She filled the cup and passed it to him before returning to the box. As she pulled out items and began to set the table, Grey put his mug on a bench and peeled out of his coat. "What can I help you do?"

His offer caught her off guard.

"The children will start arriving soon to get into their costumes." She passed him a box filled with goodies. "I'd like to have snacks set out for their parents to munch on."

He began unloading the items while she set various empty containers on the table. Without another word Grey opened a bag of chips and one of pretzels.

She tossed him a can of peanuts. "These too, please."

He opened them and dumped some in a couple of containers.

She set a cake box in front of him. "Would you get the cake out and put it down there?" She pointed to the far end of the table.

He looked at the box and pushed it her way. "You open it. I'll put it wherever you want it."

"You too?" She huffed at him and opened the box.

"I apologize, Lennie. I accused you unjustly."

She slid the cake his direction. "Just put it down there. There's a candle inside the box. Stick it in the top of the cake, will you?"

Keeping watch out of the corner of her eye, Lena took a few steps farther away from him. She'd intended to give the cake to Jonathan, and she hoped she didn't regret changing her mind.

As he tried to wedge the candle in place, the top of the cake popped open, and confetti sprang at him. But brightly colored paper wasn't all that landed on him. Icing did too, and she bit her bottom lip to keep from laughing.

He stared at her, frosting spattered across his shirt. The shock on his face struck her as hilarious, and she had to cover her mouth with both hands in order to stifle her laughter.

Watching her reaction, he chuckled. "What'd you do that for? If I don't eat cake, what makes you think I want to wear it?"

She moved in closer and swiped her finger through a dollop of frosting on his shirt before placing it in her mouth. "Who doesn't like cake?" As she feigned innocence, she was poking a little fun at her sister-in-law. The woman never remembered that Grey didn't like cake. Never.

"Lennie. I…I'm tellin'."

"You do that, Grey." She passed him several napkins. "And we'll see who's sorry then."

"Send me out in this cold weather to do you a favor, splatter my shirt with frosting, and then threaten me?"

"What are friends for?"

"Clearly they're to make *you* laugh. How much time did it take you to build that?"

Her Daed walked inside and glanced at Grey. "Man, Grey, I thought you didn't like cake. How'd you end up with it all over you?"

"Tricked by your daughter."

Israel looked at her.

Pretending complete innocence, Lena shrugged. "I have no idea what he's talking about, Daed."

Her Daed poured himself a cup of coffee. "She has no idea what you're talking about, Grey."

"And you believe her?"

"Of course I believe her. If she chooses not to cook, I have to."

Lena choked back laughter, liking the little bit of joy she saw in Grey's eyes. "So who are you going to tell now?"

"You win."

"Wow, you give up easily. I think I like that." Lena took a clean shirt from the huge stack of things she'd brought for tonight. She held it out to him.

He just stood there, looking leery of taking it.

"It'll fit."

"The school's oldest students are eighth-grade boys, so just why do you have an extra shirt with you that will fit me?"

"Because you and Jonathan are very close to the same size, and you happen to be wearing his cake."

A hint of his lopsided smile worked its way into his eyes, and his countenance seemed less heavy.

"Ah." He motioned at the split-rail fence, manger, and hay. "What is all that?"

"The temperature dropped, so the live crèche is taking place inside."

"All those animals are coming in?"

"Sure, why not?"

Grey looked to Lennie's father.

Her Daed shrugged. "You ever tried to change her mind about something?"

Grey shook his head. "Not and been successful. I'll just slip into a clean shirt and take a seat. This I gotta see."

Carrying a shoofly pie, Deborah stepped into Lena's packed classroom. Gas pole lamps were lit and placed in various areas of the room. She shivered, almost aching with cold after her long carriage ride from Hope Crossing. Ada, Cara, and Lori were already here, having arrived in Dry Lake a couple of hours ago via a warm car.

Jonathan had needed to come by carriage so he could return a rented horse to its owner in Dry Lake. Since Deborah's pie hadn't finished baking in time for her to come by car, she rode for an hour in Jonathan's carriage, enduring freezing temperatures. It hadn't snowed in a week, but a foot of the white stuff covered the grounds.

Lena stood at the far end of the room, helping her scholars get into their costumes and practice their lines. She didn't look a bit frazzled as dozens of children asked their teacher questions all at the same time. Actually...she appeared to be having a great time.

Jonathan's hand gently directed Deborah to step forward to allow the people behind them to get inside also.

Grey's parents spoke as they walked in with Ivan. The little boy quietly weaved around people, heading for the bench where his Daed sat. She'd seen Grey last week during the between Sunday when she came to Dry Lake to visit. Seeing Grey was like looking at a used, half-torn dessert box. You could tell he'd once held something good. Tonight he didn't seem as empty or as battered as he talked with people near him, but he kept glancing at the commotion around Lena.

"Little Debbie." Jonathan bent down, drawing closer to her ear as he spoke softly. "Are we waiting by this door for a reason?" His warm breath smelled of peppermint, and when she looked at him to see if he was harassing her or being sincere, she saw someone she didn't recognize. He removed his hat. "What?" His voice held a bit of confusion, but his hazel eyes reflected comfortableness with her.

Her heart turned a flip as the enormity of their friendship seemed to change shape.

"I...I need to set this pie on the table." While thoughts moved through her like loops of warm molasses, she worked her way through the crowd.

For months Jonathan had helped her at Ada's House, receiving small wages compared to the value of his skill and work hours. He'd been diligent and so much fun as they had built a business Deborah was proud of.

He still worked for his Daed, dividing his time between Dry Lake and Hope Crossing. But he'd also begun expanding the blacksmith business to the Amish in Hope Crossing and further east of them—all areas that were nearly impossible for his Daed to get to in a day of travel from Dry Lake. Since all his blacksmith equipment was in his work wagon, and he traveled to people's farms to shoe their horses, he spent the night at Ada's when he worked close by. But the last few months were not her only memories of his being generous with his time. Over the years he'd always offered help whenever she needed it, just as he had for Lena.

Jonathan came up beside her. "You feeling okay? Did you get too cold on the ride here?"

Making space for another dessert on the serving table, she didn't look up at him. Until this moment she'd thought no more of her relationship with him than of the ones she had with Lena, Cara, and Ada. He'd become as close to her as anyone ever had...except Mahlon.

He cupped his hand under her elbow. "Deborah?"

Mahlon's closeness had been a lie. All those years he'd only pretended. Thinking about that confused her more. Who was Jonathan—a good friend or a man who'd stepped up out of loyalty and duty in order to fill the gaping hole Mahlon had left?

She gazed into his eyes, suddenly desperate to understand the relationship between them. "What are we doing, Jon?"

His hazel eyes reminded her of Mahlon, and she could hear what he would've said—*We're attending a Christmas play. Now let's find a seat.* And like the fool she'd been, she'd let him avoid her questions and hide his true self behind her love.

A hint of uncertainty flitted through Jonathan's eyes before a smile crossed his lips. "I'm being a friend and hoping maybe one day you'll want more."

His words startled her, sending concern and shock through her. As a friend, Jonathan was safe. Dependable. And loads of fun. The truth stared at her, and why she hadn't seen it before, she didn't know. Whether as a friend, beau, or husband, he had plenty to offer any woman. Even in her self-absorbed ways, his qualities had been too obvious for her to be completely blind to them. But she realized a horrible thing about herself: outside the realm of friendship, she had nothing but confusion and distrust. Suspicion seeped from the wound Mahlon had left inside her. But how could she distrust Jonathan?

She pulled off her gloves. "Why?"

He blinked, glancing to the table for a moment as if bewildered by her question. "Why?"

The reason for her question seemed very clear to her. What motivated him to want more? Did he feel compelled to stay by her side out of a misplaced sense of honor? He might not even realize what drew him to offer such a thing to her.

Lena spoke loudly. "Please take your seats. If you haven't already enjoyed some refreshments, you can do so after our play. If you have enjoyed refreshments, you may do so again…after our play."

He fidgeted with his hat. "Let's talk about this when the play is over."

Neither of them could do anything else right now but plan to talk later. She spotted Ada sitting in the row in front of Grey. Cara and Ephraim were on one side of her, and a couple of empty seats on the other side were saved for Deborah and Jonathan. She and Jonathan walked toward them.

She moved onto the bench next to Ada. From Ephraim's lap, Lori waved at her. She couldn't help but find the image totally endearing.

When the play began, she casually turned and studied Jonathan, who remained focused on Lena and the makeshift stage. When did Jonathan begin hoping their friendship would become more? Is that what he really wanted? If so, how did she feel about him? She loved being his friend.

"You're staring," Jonathan whispered without taking his eyes off the front of the room.

Voices from the children in the play grew louder, and laughter rose and fell like wind on a blustery day, but she couldn't focus as her heart ran wild with fear. No matter who he was, she'd lose. As a friend, he'd find a girl one day and leave her. Just the thought made her miss him. Did he truly care? After her ordeal with Mahlon, she knew she didn't possess any way of discerning what disloyalties and lies existed in a man's heart.

Jonathan turned to her, his patience clearly evident. "I don't think we should try to figure out where we are or where we're going. It's too soon, and we don't need answers to our questions tonight. Or next month. Enjoy the play."

Boisterous laughter erupted, and they immediately shifted their focus. She didn't know what they'd missed, but mixed in with everyone else's chortles, she could hear Grey's. Dozens of children in costumes, sheep, and Lena's dog all stood inside the now half-fallen fence. She'd missed most of the play while lost in her own thoughts. Lena opened the back door, disappeared for a moment, and returned, pulling the lead to a donkey.

The room cackled as the wind from outside blew out a couple of the gas pole lamps and hay swirled in every direction. If Lena had brought other animals inside earlier, had the lamps gone out then too? Lena tugged, but the creature stopped in the doorway, only half of him inside the building. She moved behind the donkey and pushed. "Did somebody glue her hoofs?" Her voice radiated loudly from just outside.

Her dog barked, and the donkey jolted forward. Lena thudded to the floor. Nicky ran to her and licked her face before she jumped up, straightening her apron. Fresh laughter erupted. Lena picked up Marilyn and set her feet on a wooden crate next to the donkey's head. Lena kept one hand on Marilyn while patting the donkey as the girl recited her lines. When the donkey relieved itself, Marilyn seemed unbothered. "And then the angel said to them…" Marilyn paused. "I smell something."

Everyone broke into laughter.

Marilyn wrinkled her nose and tilted her head one way and then the other, trying to see where that aroma came from.

"Okay, honey, what did the angel say?"

Marilyn spoke loudly. "Then the angel…" She paused again. "You sure they had animals inside where Jesus was bornt?"

"Ya."

Marilyn seemed fully aware that she'd taken over the play, but Lena kept trying to refocus her attention. These plays were always endearing, usually even a little funny, but this time people were cackling without restraint.

The little girl held her nose with her finger and thumb. "Maybe that's why they prayed so much back then."

"I know it's why I'm praying so much right now," Lena added. "Can you say the rest of your lines?"

She nodded. "The angel said to them…" She paused once again. "Teacher Lena, I feel kinda sick."

"Me too." Lena glanced across the room and spotted Marilyn's parents. "Do you not have farm animals at your place, Joe?"

The hilarity rippling through the schoolroom warmed Deborah's heart. Lena had known the community needed this event tonight, even if the weather didn't allow for it to be held outside. And Grey hadn't stopped chuckling. As the play continued, so did the laughter. But by the time Lena drew the evening to a close, she had most people teary-eyed with the depth of what God had begun that night thousands of years ago.

Lena pointed to the back of the room. "We have a lot of refreshments. Please stay for as long as you like and enjoy."

Jonathan continued chuckling as he stood. "Lena is as free spirited as she is an out-and-out mess."

"The floor is a mess," Deborah said. "And now I have to stay and help her clean up."

"Ya, me too."

"I'll stay and pitch in," Grey said. "And I'll see to it Allen stays too."

"We'll be done in time to get some sleep before morning then. Denki." Deborah glanced around the room, noting all the work that needed to be done. "You sure?"

"Ya." Grey adjusted his shirt collar. "Jonathan, fair warning. Don't accept any cake Lennie tries to give you."

Rage burned through Dwayne. How could Lena boldly stand in front of everyone unashamed of the mark God had cursed her with? He'd put a stop to her. In his time. In his own way. He folded his arms, still watching the stupid teacher as she helped the brats out of their costumes.

In spite of the applause she'd received, she disgusted most of the folks here. He fully believed that, but she didn't know it—going about her life like people actually cared for her. It sickened him.

After all his effort, the bull had mauled the wrong woman. It had altered his course, but it hadn't changed his plan.

Twenty

Lena moved closer, reaching for the item in Elsie's hand, but Elsie faded into a new world, taking Lena with her. Valleys. Oceans. Deserts. They moved from place to place, but no matter where they landed, Lena couldn't get close enough to take the item Elsie held out to her.

Lena didn't know what the package contained, but she knew Grey needed it. Determined to reach it, she fought her way through wind, sand, snow, and rainstorms. Weary of fighting while Elsie faded from one world to the next, Lena screamed at her, "If you want me to have it, then give it to me!"

Elsie held out the parcel. A round of knocks vibrated the air around her, and Lena found herself somewhere between awake and asleep. The longing inside her matched nothing she'd ever felt before.

"Lena." Her Daed tapped on the door.

She opened her eyes, realizing it'd all been a dream. Early morning sunlight streamed in through her bedroom windows as she tried to let go of all the emotions the dream had pumped into her.

"Kumm." She sat upright.

"You're not even up. This is a first." Behind his smile, she saw concern. "Should I have left you alone?"

"No." She stretched. "It's Second Christmas. I don't want to miss a minute of it because I socialized too much on Christmas Day. Besides, I'm glad you woke me. I was caught in a frustrating dream."

Maybe the dream meant nothing…or maybe it was her own subconscious reminding her she had yet to give Grey her report about Ivan.

"How long before you're ready to go?"

"Forty minutes, tops."

He started to close the door.

"Daed." Lena pushed back her quilt, feeling a little more like herself again. "Can we go a bit out of our way and stop by Grey's before heading to Ada's?"

"Grey's?"

"I need to take him something."

"It can't wait?"

She slid into her housecoat. "Careful, Daed. Your need to get maximum time out of this rare invite by Ada is showing."

He chuckled. "It is, isn't it?"

"Don't worry. I'll never tell her…as long as you take me by Grey's first."

"Get ready as quick as you can, and we'll go by there."

Lena hurried through a shower and dressing. Once fully ready, she knelt in front of her hope chest, opened the lid, and looked for the report she'd written. After Elsie had passed away, Lena tucked the papers in here, keeping them in the most private place of all. As her fingertips slid over quilts and kitchen utensils, she cringed at the fresh pangs of loneliness.

Twenty-four years old and not even a prospect.

She spotted the edge of the manila envelope and reached for it, but as she did, her tablet of children's names called to her. The contrast between her reality and what she longed for stung. Ignoring the mounting sentiments, she grabbed the report and closed the lid to the chest.

By the time she slid into her coat and went downstairs, her Daed had the carriage hitched. Nicky danced at the front door, clearly hoping to go with her again today. "Can you be good, even around Better Days?"

Nicky sat, as if to assure Lena of her excellent behavior. A shiver of excitement about going, or maybe dread of staying behind, ran through her dog.

"It wouldn't be Christmas without you tagging along, now would it? Kumm."

Nicky ran to the carriage and waited. Lena locked the front door and hurried down the steps. She opened the door to the buggy, and Nicky jumped in first. "Daed, you're in too big of a hurry. I didn't feed Nicky or get a cup of coffee."

"I fed the dog, and"—he reached under the front seat and passed her a thermos—"I'd never let you go without coffee. You get too grumpy."

She giggled. Her faults were plenty—opinionated, stubborn, and too direct at times, to name a few—but getting grumpy wasn't one of them, and he liked teasing her about that. She enjoyed his company, and he'd always been easy to live with. Her mother had adored him, and she wished he'd take a few steps toward finding someone again. "Ever thought of asking Ada out?"

He tapped the reins against the horse's back. "I…I talked to her about it once, a long time ago."

"She didn't want to?"

"It wasn't that…at least I don't think it was. See…Mahlon didn't like the idea of his Mamm remarrying. She thought he needed her to stay single, and she was willing to do that for him, so I didn't pursue her. Besides, I had plenty to keep me busy with a houseful of children."

"Ya, it kept all of us busy." Lena opened the thermos. The aroma stung her nostrils. She put the lid on quickly. "How many scoops of coffee did you use?"

"How many should I have used?"

"Daed." Lena clicked her tongue. "We've talked about this. Two scoops per pot."

"Then you have about three days' worth of scoops in that one jug."

"It's a good thing for you it's the thought that counts."

Her Daed drove down the long lane to Grey's home, and she was glad to see that his horse and rig were still there.

She got out, and Nicky rushed behind her as if afraid she might be left behind. When she stood on the doorstep, she pointed at Nicky. "Sit." Her dog obeyed, and Lena knocked on the door.

Grey opened it, looking surprised to see her. "Lennie, what are you doing here?"

She held up the manila envelope. "I came to give you the results from when I worked with Ivan."

"Oh, I…I…kumm rei." He stepped back. Nicky whined, still sitting where Lena had told her to. Grey motioned. "You too." The dog ran inside, and Grey closed the door, studying her. "Why today?"

"I…I'm actually not sure. I had a dream that reminded me about this, so here I am. I didn't know if I'd catch you."

"Ivan's sleeping in a bit, so I'm letting him rest. Today won't be easy."

"You're spending a good bit of it with Elsie's folks then."

"Ya."

Rumors said the Blanks were in a bad way emotionally. They were bitter and miserable and dragging down anyone around them. She couldn't imagine how hard that would be for Grey and Ivan. "Daed and I are spending most of today at Ada's."

"At Ada's?"

Lena held her index finger over her lips. "I think there might be a little attraction between them."

"Really? Your Daed's been without a wife for a long time now."

"Thirteen years last October. Same as for Ada."

"No one could forget that nightmare."

"Even all these years later I still miss Mamm so badly some days. I can't even imagine what you must be feeling."

"Ya, it's…it's tough." He held up a coffee mug. "Care for some brew?"

"Ya."

He poured her a cup and slid the sugar and cream toward her.

"Denki."

"Would you care to sit for a spell? And I'll ask your Daed to come in."

"I can't stay." She added sweetener and cream and stirred her drink. "And Daed won't come in this time. He wants me to keep it brief. But I can down a cup before leaving. Daed fixed the coffee this morning. I do believe he could live single the rest of his life and never get the hang of fixing anything but water." She took a sip. "Oh, now that's good coffee." She drank a little more before setting the cup down. "Ivan's bright, possibly one of the brightest children I've ever worked with." She passed him the envelope. He opened it and pulled out her report. While he read it, she sipped on her coffee.

"Horse neck, Lennie. I never would've figured this."

"I talked to my friend Samantha about it too. You remember her?"

"Ya, the Englischer girl who used to spend the night with you sometimes and make your Daed nervous that you might get pulled into the world."

"That's her. We're still friends and still get together occasionally. She finished her master's program last year, and this is her first year as a school counselor. I showed her the tests he took, and she agrees with me. It means he's as smart as he is cute, which is never a good combination for the girls' sakes. I imagine he's much like you were at that age, but since I was just a baby then, I can't recall what you looked or acted like."

"I remember the first time I saw you. My Mamm had gone to visit your Mamm. I'd have been nearly five by then. We walked into your Mamm's bedroom, where you'd been born the day before. Your Mamm was still in bed, and you were in her arms. Your Mamm patted the bed, and I climbed up beside her on my knees, getting a good look at you. I remember thinking you looked so little and helpless...and then you let out a scream that about made me wet my pants."

She giggled. "I still have that effect on Allen. Ask him."

He slid the report into its envelope. "I love Ivan the same, no matter whether he's brilliant or slow."

"I never doubted that."

"So you know where I'm coming from when I ask, if he's this bright, why does he seem slow and immature?"

"Maturity will happen. Seems to me his Daed was a short, scrawny kid until...when, eighteen years old?"

"Sixteen, thank you very much." He ran the last words together quickly, with mocked offense.

"Sixteen. And your maturity issues were physical, not emotional, but your son isn't yet six."

"Point taken."

"If you can stand my usual honesty, I think you might be doing too much for him. Your Daed had you doing chores at a young age. My first memory of you had to be when I was five or six. You were in the barn milking cows, tending horses, and cleaning stalls by yourself. I was smitten just watching you."

"Interesting."

"And I remained that way until the old age of seven."

"Clearly you fell in and out of being smitten easily, because I never knew."

He never knew. Not that time or when she was about to enter high school or when she turned eighteen. It'd been a long time since she'd remembered how badly she'd wanted him to have feelings for her like she had for him. But he hadn't, and when Elsie arrived in Dry Lake, he never looked back.

That's just not who they were. With only a minimum of pain and disappointment, she'd accepted that soon after Elsie had arrived.

Lena ran her finger around the rim of the mug. "Remember when Allen stole a pie from Mamm's windowsill? Later that day Mamm questioned him. He lied and said I'd taken it to feed to my dog. You knew the truth, and when you didn't take up for me, I...I hated you...for a while."

"Allen could beat me up. You couldn't. But that story explains a lot about your obsession to get back at people, using desserts."

She couldn't resist smiling as she saw hints of the man he'd been before Elsie died. That awful day removed all rays of light from his eyes like when the sun dropped past the horizon in winter. "My point is that I think you should give him more responsibilities in line with a five-year-old. Does he dress himself?"

"No. How can he?"

"He'll figure it out. He'll be missing that arm the rest of his life. He won't grow out of that. Let him struggle until he's learned ways to compensate. And when he goes to the shop with you, give him some small projects of his own, like organizing the hardware or sweeping up and such. Let him figure out how to do things with one arm."

Grey studied her, looking like he agreed with her bold statements.

She took another sip of coffee. "We all have a handicap. And every one of us had to figure out how to get work done."

"What's your handicap?"

Her face felt warm as thoughts of her birthmark embarrassed her. Had he become so used to the sight of her that he no longer noticed? She traced the spot with her fingers, wondering how men saw her. "Having to put up with you."

He tugged at her hand, pulling it away from her face. "Surely you don't think…"

She lowered her eyes and took a sip of her coffee.

"Lennie." He sounded so shocked. "You're striking. The day we came to see you, Elsie remarked about how beautiful you are."

Unsure how to change the subject, Lena only knew she'd never felt so uncomfortable around Grey. She was blemished. She accepted it. It seemed he'd accepted it too, a long time ago. Perhaps his reaction meant that he no longer felt sorry for her. She liked that thought, but to mention her looks in the same sentence as *striking* or *beautiful* was just wrong. She finished the last of her coffee. "I need to go. I just wanted to make sure you knew the truth about your son."

"I'm glad you did, especially today. I needed some good news." Grey took the envelope to a small, messy desk beside the back door. He shoved it into the plastic standing divider with a bunch of other mail. Rather than getting the envelope in, a stack of letters fell out and scattered on the floor. He grabbed them up, and then stopped suddenly as he studied a letter. Several moments later he tossed everything else onto the desk, but he continued to stare at the item in his hand.

She set her mug in the sink. "I shouldn't have stayed this long. If the carriage had a horn, I'm sure Daed would be using it by now."

Grey didn't look up. She motioned for Nicky and headed toward the door.

She paused. "Grey…are you okay?"

He slid his fingers over the address—Mr. and Mrs. Benjamin Graber. He slid the letter into his pants pocket. "Kumm, I'll walk you out and speak to your Daed."

Grey stood on his driveway as the Kauffman rig drove out of sight. He reached into his pocket and pulled out the letter. It held the results of the DNA testing he and Elsie had done less than a week before she died. He'd thought about these findings several times, but he hadn't realized they'd come in. According to the postage date, it'd arrived here about eight weeks after Elsie died. His Mamm or Daed or a sibling had been bringing in the mail for him when they came for a visit.

The titles of Mr. and Mrs. stirred tornado-force winds inside him. Studying the envelope, he ambled back into the house. If he opened it, he'd know the truth. Had Elsie been in fear all those years for nothing? Or had she shut him out of her heart and out of their bedroom based on reasons he could live with?

He put his thumb under the seal of the envelope and tore a bit of it before stopping. If she were alive, they'd sit down together and open this. He could imagine the tension in the room, as the tests would have decided much of their future. But now that she was dead, did he really want to know what this envelope held?

She'd been wrong about Ivan. If she had shut out Grey without just cause, he'd wrestle with anger again. If the results said either of them had a genetic issue that caused their offspring to have defects, how would he feel then? When his grief eased, would some part of him feel relieved that her death had freed both of them?

Grey paced as anger rose within him. "God forbid!"

He couldn't change that their life together was over, but he could protect her memory and his heart. Still he ached to know the truth. She'd isolated him based on her fears. Had she been right?

Ivan walked into the kitchen, rubbing his eyes. *"Frehlich Zwedde Grischtdaag."* Ivan wished his Daed a Merry Second Christmas.

Grey tussled his son's hair. "Frehlich Zwedde Grischtdaag, Ivan."

His son kept going, heading for the bathroom.

Grey felt as trapped by this medical report as he'd been by Elsie behaving as if she disliked everything about him. He wouldn't chain himself to regret or resentment. He went to the stove and lit the gas flame. Whether Elsie had been right or wrong about them passing down bad DNA to their offspring, he'd never know. He held the letter over the flame. When it caught on fire, he moved to the kitchen sink and watched it burn. "I choose to be free of all that we didn't handle right."

He dropped it into the sink as the last of the paper turned to black ashes. He closed his eyes, feeling guilt begin to release its grip.

Twenty-One

Cara sat on the corner of her bed as Deborah tried to make her hair look like it should. Second Christmas, and Ada had Amish guests arriving soon. "It's no use trying to get it to stay in place, Deb."

"Well, there's no hiding that all you have is a stubby ponytail instead of a bun under your prayer Kapp. But with enough bobby pins and hair spray, we can make the sides stay in place...sort of. Even Englischers who come here from way outside Amish country take note of your hair. One woman had some sort of zoom lens on her camera and asked if she could take a photo of you while you were in the tower."

"Uh, lady, the sign out front clearly says no taking photos of the workers." Cara grabbed her prayer Kapp off the open Bible on her bed and passed it to Deborah. She read a few verses from the Bible regularly, but understanding most of it took knowing history and principles she wasn't familiar with yet. But she kept at it. "Was yesterday what Christmas was always like for you and Ephraim?"

"There were always presents, too much food, and lots of people we loved. Is that what you mean?"

"I...I guess. It just feels like I've entered a different country sometimes."

Deborah wove the last straight pin through strands of Cara's hair. "Well the fact that we kept forgetting to speak English probably has something to do with that feeling."

Cara stood and straightened her dress and apron while looking in the mirror. "It does fit nice."

"Ya, nicer than my dresses fit you. Ephraim knew what he was doing when he hired Lavina to make new dresses. Christmas present or not, a man paying for dresses to be made for his girl or wife, like Ephraim did, has to be a first."

Cara moved to the dresser, picked up another gift he'd given her, and opened it. She ran her fingers over the well-worn pages of *Sense and Sensibility*. The clothbound edition had been published in 1908, and Ephraim had given it to her yesterday for Christmas. From the moment she'd opened it, she'd sensed an odd stirring in her soul.

Ephraim loved books as much as she did. She'd noticed that the first night she slept in his home. Finding the gift had taken him time, effort, and money, but that was only part of what touched her so deeply. When she opened the book, the first sentences filled her like music used to, and she felt the beat of them thrum inside her. The feelings hadn't faded a bit since yesterday.

She used to love books above all else, but that was before she had to drop out of school in order to survive. After that, reading became a luxury she didn't have time for, and music had filled that void. Everywhere she worked, music came through the speakers or the music channels on television.

"He's said nothing about me not taking Lori's bike away." The texture of the off-white pages felt much like an infant's palm.

"What else did you think he'd do?"

"I...I expected at least a little bullying on the topic." She couldn't remember dealing with a man who hadn't bullied her in one way or another. Her husband had been a gentle man in a thousand ways, and she'd grown to love him deeply, but even he knew the fine art of cornering her—and because of it, she'd married him.

She read a line from Jane Austen's book: *Had he married a more amiable woman, he might have been made still more respectable than he was.* She wanted to be amiable for Ephraim's sake, to make him respected again in the community. To make him happier with her than he would have been with Anna Mary or any other woman.

As she skimmed some of the pages, she knew that everything that drew her to music, or to anything else not allowed by her future husband's people, could be found inside books. And she sensed that she might be able to let go of longing for non-Amish things. "I…I want to be able to commit to the Amish faith by springtime. I do."

Deborah smiled and embraced her. "My Daed always says that wanting to make the needed sacrifices and actually doing it is the main difference between those who have peace later in life and those who die in their regrets."

After she'd opened the book yesterday, she'd been unable to look at Ephraim without tears welling in her eyes. When she'd first thought about joining the faith, she had no idea that giving up music would be so hard. But in ways she hadn't realized, music had comforted her throughout her loneliest years in foster care. At fifteen, when she became a dancer at a bar, it'd been her first taste of having power over her circumstances. Her very pulse seemed to carry the beat of music, and it pulled on her so much more than the addiction she'd had for cigarettes. And yet her future husband had stumbled onto something that eased her craving.

Didn't books carry the many rhythms heard in music? Didn't the words inside a story stir the soul like a song? Books were not forbidden, and Ephraim had given her a way to be herself and yet live inside the boundaries placed around the faith.

He hadn't known what his gift would do for her, but now she wished to give him a gift that touched his heart just as much. She'd given him a few gifts yesterday—two new shirts she'd sewn for him, his favorite meal for Christmas lunch, and a card listing why she loved him. He'd seemed really touched by those gifts, but what else could she give that would do for him what he'd done for her?

Deborah pulled on her boots. "Ephraim will be here soon. If you want to get that special breakfast made, you'd better get moving."

Cara gently closed her book and set it back on the dresser. "Will Jonathan be here for breakfast?"

Lacing her boots, Deborah grimaced. "He's spending today with his family."

"The whole day?"

"Ya."

"Did you two ever talk things out?"

She tied a knot in the shoelaces. "No. I've decided he's right. Why force a talk about who we are and what I want from our relationship if I don't know how I feel or what I want? It's like backing myself into a corner to make a decision when I don't have to do that right now."

"Sounds wise to me."

"Ya, that's sort of what Ephraim did with you, isn't it?"

"Very much, only he had the added pressure of not knowing if I'd ever come to believe in God or be willing to join the Amish faith."

"He knew what he wanted, but he gave you room until you knew what you wanted. I really admired that. Mahlon never did that on any topic. He always encouraged me to believe about him what he wanted me to believe."

"I think that's the first time you've ever admitted a flaw in Mahlon."

"It feels wrong to compare him with anyone."

"But doesn't comparing mean we're thinking? Otherwise aren't we just accepting whatever others want us to believe?"

"So you think I need to assess the differences between Jonathan and Mahlon?"

"It's healthy, Deb. If we're not free to figure out the differences between men, aren't we judging them to all be alike?"

"One thing I've learned this year: men are not all alike."

Cara chuckled. "They are as different as fool's gold and twenty-four-karat gold. That's a valuable lesson to learn *before* you choose someone to marry."

"Mom!" The sounds of Lori stomping up the steps vibrated the antique doorknob.

Cara opened the door. "In here."

"Mom!" Lori hollered, sounding really miffed. Cara moved to the landing.

Lori's hands were on her hips. "Why didn't you tell me?"

"Tell you what?"

"You know what, Mom!" Lori's eyes filled with tears. Whatever Cara had done wrong this time had her daughter really angry.

The sounds of the front door opening caught her attention. Ephraim walked in. He smiled at Cara before glancing at Lori, who stood on the stairway with her back to him. "I shoulda been told!" Lori screamed. "I don't want that stupid old bike if it's not allowed."

"Oh." Cara's heart sank. "Okay."

Lori folded her arms, staring at Cara with huge tears in her eyes.

Ada stood at the bottom of the stairs. "I…I didn't mean to mention anything about bicycles. We were talking about the types of toys other Amish children got for Christmas, and when she asked why no one got a bike, I answered without thinking. I'm really sorry, Cara."

"It's okay, Ada."

"You ruined everything, Mom! Why didn't you tell me?"

"Lori." Ephraim's quiet tone caught Lori's attention. "You'll say your piece with respect or not at all."

Lori burst into tears, ran up the stairs, and slammed her bedroom door.

Trying to hide her embarrassment, Cara rolled her eyes. "I'm a horrible mother, I guess." She shrugged. "Merry Second Christmas, Ephraim."

"Ada. Deborah." He nodded at each one. Looking a little unsure of what he'd walked into, he climbed the steps. "Frehlich Zwedde Grischt-daag, Cara." He moved in closer, and Cara's heart pounded.

Deborah cleared her throat and hurried downstairs.

Ephraim studied Cara. "Hi."

"I guess I really messed up again."

Ephraim's eyes moved over her. "Blue is a good color on you."

"I should have told her about the bike."

He caressed her cheek. "Do you know how much I enjoyed yesterday?"

It'd been the best Christmas that Cara had ever had. It made it perfect to know it'd been memorable for him too. The warmth of his hand didn't compare to what he did to her heart. When he kissed her, she'd never felt so secure or loved.

He rested his forehead on hers. "That's a much better greeting."

She liked that he didn't let Lori's outburst rattle him. "She'll make a better Amish member than I will."

"If that's supposed to be a fair warning, I'll tell you again—I don't care that you're not Amish through and through. Our way of life comes easier for her. My guess is, when she's a teen and in her rumschpringe, she'll never waver in wanting to live Amish."

Propping one hand on her hip, Cara pulled back. "And you think I do?"

Ephraim's gorgeous gray-blue eyes revealed little emotion. "The thought has crossed my mind."

The door to Lori's bedroom creaked.

Cara looked around Ephraim to see her daughter peeking through the crack. "You want to talk?"

Keeping the door open just a little, Lori put her lips on the crack. "You shoulda told me."

"I didn't know, not until after we'd brought home the bike."

She opened the door a little more. "I don't want to fight."

Cara motioned for her. Lori ran to her and wrapped her arms around Cara's waist. "You mad at me?"

"No, Lorabean, I'm not."

"I like my bike, Mom."

Cara knelt. "I know. Me too."

"What are we gonna do?"

"I don't know, kiddo. What do you want to do?"

Lori looked at Ephraim and back to her mom and shrugged. "I guess I want to do the right thing."

Cara held her daughter, enjoying the feel of her little arms wrapped around her neck. "Okay. We will. But for now you go on down and give Ada a hug."

Lori nodded. She went to Ephraim. He picked her up and hugged her.

Lori pointed downstairs. "I made you something on the sewing machine you gave me for Christmas. Mom helped me learn how to work the foot pedal by myself."

He kissed her cheek. "You two can do anything you set your minds to. But you can't keep getting mad at your mom when she's doing her best. You don't want her getting mad at you when you're trying but you don't get it right, do you?"

While still in Ephraim's arms, Lori studied her mom. "Nee."

"Gut. Bischt hungerich?"

"Ya."

"Geh, ess." He set Lori's feet on the floor, and she scurried down the steps.

Cara straightened her dress. She didn't know exactly what they'd said, but it was something about eating. She went into Lori's room and made her bed. Ephraim leaned against the doorframe.

"Four of my siblings got new scooters for Christmas. I bought one for Lori a few weeks ago. If you'd like to give that to her for Second Christmas, you can."

Cara placed Lori's favorite book on the nightstand. *Shoo-Fly Girl.*

She should be grateful Ephraim had bought a scooter to make up for her blunder, but she wasn't. She wanted to be the one to give Lori a really special riding toy. Instead she'd done something out of ignorance and needed her daughter's forgiveness. She'd hoped to make a lasting memory together—and she had, but not at all the one she'd planned.

Ephraim slid one hand into his pants pocket. "Your aunt Emma came by last night after I arrived home. She wanted me to let you know they were saving a place for the three of us at dinner. I got the impression she'd invited us earlier."

Startled, Cara tried to piece together the last conversation she'd had with Emma. "I remember her talking to me one night during Elsie's viewing. We were washing dishes at Grey's. But between her tossing in a few Pennsylvania Dutch words and all the commotion, I didn't catch enough words to know what she was talking about." She started out of the room.

Ephraim stood his ground, blocking the doorway. He studied her. "Does Lori know she has relatives in Dry Lake?"

She clicked her tongue and huffed.

"What?" Ephraim stood up straight.

"Nothing." She whisked past him and started down the stairs.

He put his hand on her arm. "There is too something. I know it. You know it. I just don't know what *it* is."

She didn't like standing two steps below him, so she pulled free of his hand and moved back to the landing. "You're patient and kind, and, God is my witness, I never knew good men like you existed, so I should probably keep my mouth shut and behave like a sweet Amish fiancée."

"Do us both a favor and don't."

"Okay, fine. No matter how much I change, it's never enough. Just this morning I began feeling like I could give up music. There is no way you could ever know how huge that is. And now you want me to care about people as if they're real family."

"They *are* real family, Cara."

"No, they are strangers that I've met—ones who left me stranded as a child in a bus station. It took years to give up believing in the people I kept hoping would show up for me, so don't be surprised if it takes years to learn how to let them into my life. I've told you before that I stopped accepting crumbs from tables long, long ago."

"They aren't offering crumbs."

She bit her tongue to keep curse words from slipping out. "Yes, they are. Their own children are grown, meaning time is easier to come by these days. Then I showed up in their driveway months ago and challenged them concerning their decisions. *Now* they want me to visit and hang out? And you're pushing me for them."

"I just asked if Lori knew she had relatives."

"Ephraim." She elongated his name with deep frustration. "Give me a break. Man alive, you don't bully, but you let your will be known."

"And so do you, Cara." His raised voice rattled through the old homestead. He closed his eyes for a moment. "Look, I understand you—where you're coming from, how and why you feel the way you do—but that doesn't keep me from having opinions of what I think you should do next. If I'm wanting too much to happen too soon, I have no doubt you'll say so." He angled his head, a touch of humor reflecting in his eyes. "And sometimes, like today, you can even tell me without cursing."

Cara shook her head, wondering how she could start an argument with someone she loved so completely. "I haven't told her."

"I figured."

"Yeah, but you just had to ask anyway, didn't you?"

"Okay, so you're right. It was more than just a question, but I'm trying, Cara."

She rested against the wall, wondering if she'd ever be all that he deserved. "Me too."

"I know." He moved in close, placing one hand on the wall beside her.

"Why is it so stinking important that I connect with my so-called family?"

He shrugged. "It's not important."

"Oh, I beg to differ, Ephraim Mast. It's very important to you. I just don't know what *it* is."

His gentle smile warmed her. "You won't like *it*."

"I'll survive. Say it, rich boy."

"Uprooting is in your blood. You began running at fifteen, and sometimes I...I'm concerned you haven't really stopped yet, only paused."

"And you think aunts and uncles that I barely know the names of and cousins I don't know at all have the power to change me?"

"Family has a way of causing roots to grow."

"That can be true, but we also know family can cause a person to put on her running shoes. Look at it that way, and you'll be fine."

He lifted her chin and kissed her. "If you stay, we stay. If you leave, we leave."

Her heart turned a flip. He wasn't talking about whether they'd stay at Ada's today or visit her relatives. He meant her joining the faith...or not.

The confidence in his eyes and mannerisms didn't fade. "Right?"

"I told you that I'll join the faith."

He didn't look convinced, but he nodded and stepped back before motioning for her to go downstairs ahead of him.

His insinuation of doubt had her heart pounding. Was she just having a reasonable amount of trouble adjusting to the Amish ways or was she wavering?

Twenty-Two

Lena wrote the date on the chalkboard, her steady hand drawing long loops out of Monday, January 8. A decade ago, on this same date, Allen had fallen from the barn loft and broken his ankle. The image of looking out the window and seeing Grey fight snowdrifts as he carried her brother to the Kauffman house still remained vivid. He seemed so strong that day.

She shouldn't be thinking of him, not like this. He stirred her, and she dared to wonder if one day, maybe a year or two from now, he might consider her. She'd witnessed a lot of single men in her days, and not one of them compared to Grey's quality. And so handsome. He didn't seem to mind her birthmark, and clearly she had the power to make him smile again. So maybe…

She faced her students in first through fourth grades. "Who can tell me what number could replace the word *January* and means the same thing?"

Elmer held up his hand. Lena pointed to him.

"The number one."

"Good." She began writing the different months of the year on the board in random order. With her peripheral view, she could see Peter studying the board. She'd given the older students a different assignment, but he learned best when simply observing the younger ones. She'd used this method a lot without him having a clue. "If we can use the number one in place of the word *January,* what number would we use for the month of June?"

No one answered, but Peter appeared to be thinking.

"If January is number one…," Lena said.

"June is the sixth month," Peter scoffed.

"Exactly." Lena smiled at him briefly. His mocking tone didn't bother her. He used it as a cover. But his lethargic ways did trouble her. He seemed tired all the time and rarely ate. "Scholars, when you've written the name of the month and its corresponding number beside it, please take it to my desk. Peter, would you sit at my desk and check the papers?"

Without even rolling his eyes, Peter moved to her desk. She went to him. Glad for a moment to talk to him quietly where no one else could hear them, she gave him a red pencil. "Lots of smiley faces. Focus on what they get right, and gently correct what they've gotten wrong."

Peter took the pencil from her. "If I have everyone getting this right by the end of today, can I have five points added to my last math test?"

The young man confused her. On one hand he cared about nothing. On the other a few points added to a test actually mattered. "That's too much unfair pressure for you and them. You're working with first graders also. Some of them have yet to fully grasp the concept of the twelve months of the year. But if you have the second, third, and fourth graders able to accomplish the goal by Friday, I'll absolutely give you those points."

His stone face reflected little, but he nodded.

Lena hesitated. "If you need anything, you can talk to me, or I can contact my friend Samantha for you."

Peter stared at the pencil in his hand. "Not everyone gives smiley faces or cares what a person got right, only what they got wrong."

"We can't live based on naysayers, Peter. We all have value and the right to find as much peace with ourselves and our flaws and weaknesses as possible. Why would forgiveness be so important to God if we didn't need it all the time? He knew we would need it from Him, but also from us for ourselves and for others. When we get peace with our weakest areas, we'll find new ways to build on our strongest areas."

Peter shrugged, but he seemed to like what she'd said.

The day flew by, and soon Lena stood outside the schoolhouse saying good-bye to her students. With freezing temperatures and high winds, she hadn't been a bit surprised when a parent, neighbor, or relative came to pick up every scholar. Once they were gone, she went back into the classroom and began grading papers. On nice days she took the work with her, but on days like today when she had a roaring fire in the potbelly stove, she liked to hang around until she could bank the embers. Not only did that make leaving less of a fire hazard, but it also made the room warmer in the morning and starting a fire much easier.

Through the frosted windows she saw the hazy shape of a buggy, and a man got out. Her heart thumped a few extra beats as hopes of seeing Grey became her first thought. The front door opened, and she stood. Aaron Blank removed his black felt hat, revealing hair the same color. Concern ran through her. He was a disheveled mess. His hands shook. Dark puffy circles ran under his eyes. And even at a distance he smelled of stale alcohol.

"I…I was talking to Dwayne a few weeks ago. He was griping about what Peter had told him, that you'd brought some psychologist woman in to talk to the scholars. Is that true?"

"Ya, I thought the children needed someone who knew a lot more about grief and trauma than I do. She's a counselor at the school I attended during my rumschpringe."

Aaron's dark brown eyes studied her before he tossed his hat on a desk and walked to the blackboard. "What kind of a person uses their running-around years to attend school?"

"Well, those Englischer kids would say a really dorky one."

Aaron turned to face her, a gentle smile on his lips. "It doesn't bother you what others think, does it?"

This unusual visit worried her. He seemed to be looking for answers, and she prayed for the right words. "Sure it bothers me. I just do my best to not let it rule me. It still hurts, every time. In my younger years, it'd sting so much I would cry myself to sleep. I find humor helps a lot and doing things I enjoy, like teaching."

He ran his hands across the dusty chalkboard and then rubbed his thumb over his fingertips. "You studied during your rumschpringe. Wanna guess what I did during mine?"

She didn't have to guess. His rumschpringe hadn't ended yet, because he hadn't joined the faith. Based on his age, he should have. His running-around years began either before or around the time he and his family moved here from Ohio, almost seven years ago. And based on glimpses she'd caught of his life, he'd gone from being an occasional-weekend teen-age drinker to a twenty-four-year-old man who stayed half drunk most of the time.

He moved within inches of her. "I need help, Lena, and I don't know who else to ask."

"You came to the right place. The counselor Dwayne told you about is a school psychologist. She can't help you, but she brought me a list of other counselors in case any of the adults in Dry Lake wanted to talk to someone." Lena sat in her chair and began looking through the drawers in her desk. "There's a place called the Better Path, I think." She found the paper. "Ya, that's the name. It's about forty miles from here. I'm not sure who runs it, but she said there's a Plain Mennonite counselor who's a young man like yourself, and he comes highly recommended in his field."

Aaron sat on her desk. "I've got to stop drinking, but I can't imagine how to do that. Daed and Mamm know I drink, but they don't have any clue how much or how often."

"I wish I knew what to say. All I know is you need to take care of you. It will hurt when they are forced to accept it, but at least you're also offering them hope by looking for help."

"They don't even know I'd been told about that fence or that Elsie's death is my fault. If I'd fixed it right when I had the chance…"

His heaviness wrapped around her, but she couldn't think of anything to say about the bull breaking through. "Aaron, if you can tune out what everyone thinks and feels toward you, can you see your way to finding answers?"

He moved to a window and stared at the back pasture where his sister had died three months ago. "Ya, I…I think I can…with the right help."

"Then for now, do what you need to for you. When you're well, you can make it up to them."

"Well." He let out a slow, heavy breath. "I haven't felt well in a really long time." When he turned to face her, his dark brown eyes were filled with tears. "I'm scared that I'll never get free."

"You can't erase how you've spent your rumschpringe or the day Elsie died. But if you win against this need to drink, you can change your future. I know you can." She wrote down the information about the Better Path and held it out to him.

He took it. "Dwayne said that my Daed came by here this morning before school started. What'd he want?"

She wondered how Dwayne knew about Michael coming here. "He came to let me know that there's a school board meeting next Monday."

"Can you imagine how my Daed will feel when he finds out I'd been warned about that bull?"

"Aaron, you thought you'd fixed the fence."

"Ya, while in some half-drunken state."

"He doesn't need to know that. It won't help anything. Just take care of yourself. I'll deal with the school board. But if I were you, I'd avoid Dwayne."

"Dwayne isn't so bad. He's a better man than I am. He's always in control, even when he drinks. He never overdoes it, never gets clobbered."

She feared his judgment concerning Dwayne would come back to haunt him, but she didn't think she could convince him. "You have a good heart, Aaron. And if you get sober, I'll bet you'll even find it."

He went to the desk where he'd dropped his hat. "Denki, Lena. You…

you've always been nice to me. I appreciate that a lot." Without another word he left.

As Aaron pulled away in his buggy, she hoped he'd do whatever it took to get free of past mistakes.

Lena knocked on Crist and Mollie's door, wondering why the school board had chosen to meet here. They were Peter and Dwayne's parents, and she couldn't shake the feeling that she was entering the lions' den. She doubted Grey would come, but she hated the idea of facing opposition without his voice of reason.

Mollie let her in. "Lena." Mollie managed a short nod and motioned to the kitchen table.

Elsie's Mamm looked pale and almost as sad as the day her daughter was killed. All the school board members and their wives were here, except Grey. Dwayne was here too. She guessed it was futile to hope he might not be at a meeting being held in his own home. Sylvan and Lillian Detweiler were here too, which meant old criticisms were coming her way again.

Lena went to a chair and took a seat.

The Detweilers' complaints against her stemmed from the incident last year, the one that caused the board to put her on probation. It'd been such a foolish mistake on her part, but her alternative was to let four children go hungry.

Michael looked up from the papers in his hand. "Ah, Lena, you've arrived."

She'd arrived ten minutes before it was time for the meeting to begin and had managed to be the last one to get here, so she wondered if they'd had a meeting beforehand too.

He called the gathering to order, and Dwayne took a seat at the table. She was in his home, but she'd hoped he wouldn't stay for this part.

They bowed their heads in silent prayer.

Michael interlaced his fingers and placed his hands on the papers spread out in front of him. "Several parents have a lot of questions, but rather than having everyone come, Mollie and Crist will be their spokesmen. They've been gathering questions from parents, and we'd like you to respond to those questions. Since Grey isn't here to take notes, Jake will. It won't take long. Are you ready?"

"Ya."

Crist placed a piece of notebook paper on the table. Only half of it was filled. That gave Lena a little hope. "The first item the parents would like to know is about Elmer. He was on a swing when the chain broke, and he ended up in a cast. Why weren't you aware that the chains needed to be replaced?"

Michael shook his head. "She's not responsible for playground equipment. That's the board's job."

"I disagree," Crist said. "It's the board's job to replace the items. It's hers to inform you."

Michael shook his head and started to say something.

"I can answer his question," Lena offered.

"Okay, Lena, go ahead," Michael said.

"Those chains were only two years old. Not a one of them should have broken, but Daed and I changed them all out after Elmer's accident and before anyone else used a swing."

"Gut. Denki, Lena." Michael made a note.

Crist read the next item. "You buried one of your scholars' cats while the child begged you not to? Is that true?"

Michael lifted his hand. "Who wrote these questions? Lena deals with a large classroom of children, and we can't second-guess her every decision."

"I'd like to at least know where she found the cat," Crist said.

Lena glanced at Dwayne. "The cat's throat had been slit, and it was left in my chair. We all know that mean pranks are pulled on teachers from time to time. I tried to bury it before the children arrived. I guess I could have hidden it in the lean-to and buried it later, but I didn't."

"And you didn't bother to tell the school board that someone left a dead cat in the room? Shouldn't they have been informed?"

"I mentioned it to Grey within a few days of it happening."

Michael tapped his hand against the table. "That answers plenty. She did her job, and I'm sure Grey would have told us if…if…Elsie hadn't…" The sting of Michael losing his daughter had stolen the words from him.

Crist nodded. "Yes, you're right." He looked at Lena. "Were you aware that the bull had gotten into the pasture near the school before the day… of the incident?"

Lena cringed. "Ya."

Michael shifted. "I won't sit here and let anyone blame Lena. It's my field, and my son's bull. We're responsible. End of it. I've told the board for months there's nothing to talk to Lena about."

She ached for Michael. Like Aaron, he blamed himself.

Crist took a sip of water. "The parents would like to know if the school board approved Lena bringing a counselor, a psychologist of some sort, into the school to talk to the children after the incident."

Michael looked surprised. He angled his head toward her. "You brought in an outsider to talk to the scholars without permission?"

"I…I guess I did."

"You guess?" Dwayne scoffed. "You don't know?"

Lena straightened in her chair. "The children were traumatized, and I have a friend who is a school counselor. She only came in to help them sort through their feelings and to offer advice on dealing with trauma and shock. I never left the room while she talked. We did some exercises she suggested—drawing, talking, acting out how we feel. She said and did nothing against our beliefs. Nothing."

Michael breathed deeply. "That wasn't wise, Lena. An outsider we don't know, a psychologist no less, brought in to talk to our children? You had to know this was unacceptable."

Lena steadied her pounding heart. "The day of the incident I saw the trauma that took place in each child's heart and mind. I know Samantha Rogers from my days of attending public school, and I knew she'd have the expertise to help them."

"Peter is worse, not better," Mollie snapped.

Lena tried to find the right words. "That's not Samantha's fault. She did nothing that would make anyone worse. I...I think he's probably better than he would have been without the insights Samantha had to offer."

"I don't believe you," Mollie said.

Lena cleared her throat, trying to guard her tone. "Okay."

"Okay?" Mollie scoffed. "You think what you've done is okay?"

"I'm sorry it upset you, but I think it's been helpful for all the children."

"You're not even a little sorry." The oldest board member, Jake Fisher, scooted his chair forward, making an awful sound as he did. "We don't want some stranger who may not even be a believer offering the children of Dry Lake hope. Why would you step outside of our ways to do this your way?"

Lena steadied her tone, trying to remain respectful. "We allow firemen to come to the school and share their wisdom. They put on their full gear and teach the children how to respond to a fire. I thought Samantha could help in her own area, like they do."

Jake frowned. "So you didn't ask because we allow firemen to come into the school?"

"A problem came up, and then an opportunity for finding some relief surfaced, so I went for it."

"Went for it?" Dwayne's smug smile made her feel sick. "She talks more like a public school girl than an Amish one."

A wave of nods circled the room.

Michael took notes. "Lena, do not allow any outsider to come into the classroom without permission. Clear?"

"Ya."

He gathered his papers. "We can't decide a discipline tonight. I'm dealing with all I can right now. I might as well let you all know about Aaron. You'll hear about it elsewhere if I don't. He's...entered a rehabilitation center somewhere outside of Owl's Perch. I...I don't know what made him think he needed that kind of help, but he didn't ask my opinion. I can't see us trying to make a fair discipline call on this tonight." He grew still as he studied Lena. "I'm afraid you've crossed a line."

Dwayne scoffed, and all eyes moved to him. "I think you should ask Lena who suggested Aaron leave Dry Lake and see a shrink."

Aaron's mother straightened, looking more alert than she had since Lena arrived. Dora ran her fingers over her cheek. "What did you say to our son that made him leave his family when we needed him most?"

Lena's heart jumped, and she knew her face radiated guilt. "I...I know how this looks, but he came to me, and...I...I gave him some information."

"What *kind* of information?" Dora asked.

She wouldn't tell because Aaron might not want her to. "It was a private conversation. I...I was only trying to help."

Murmuring continued, and several board members asked her questions at the same time.

Michael's hand shook when he raised it to silence everyone. "Whatever conversation took place between Aaron and Lena isn't a school matter. Aaron may have chosen badly when deciding who to talk to, but no part of that can affect our decision concerning Lena as a teacher. And we're all too upset to have any sense of fairness in our decision of what discipline to hand down. I say we table this matter for at least a week. All in favor say aye."

A chorus of dull ayes echoed. "Any nays?"

No one said anything.

With his elbow on the table, Michael held his head in one hand. "You will remain under probation, and you are not to allow any Englischer inside the school without the board's permission. Is that clear?"

"Ya."

"We'll take all this under advisement and either let you know of another meeting or send you a letter with our decision. Your actions between now and then will be carefully scrutinized. I'm very concerned, Lena. Do you understand?" He spoke gently, but she saw hurt and anger in his countenance.

"Ya." Lena said her good-byes, grabbed her coat, and left. Cold wind slapped her in the face when she stepped outside. Her heart ached over the board's view of her, and she fought tears while making her way along the narrow path of cleared snow toward the barn. At least Michael refused to make a decision until he and the others calmed down, but the idea of losing her school stung. Her scholars needed that time with Samantha. But if she lost her school because of overreaching her authority, she'd never get another teaching position at any Amish school.

Twenty-Three

Wonderful smells of baked goods drifted throughout Ada's House, constantly reminding Deborah of all she had to be thankful for. She sat at the kitchen table, counting the money they'd made this week. Ada and Jonathan chatted quietly while Cara and Lori sat at the sewing machine making cloth dolls.

Deborah stacked the cash and checks together. "I just can't believe how well our business continues to do, and it's almost six weeks past Christmas."

Jonathan turned a chair around backward and straddled it. "Most of the snows have been perfect for sleigh rides this year. I think that's helped keep things really hopping around here."

"Ya, everything is just working so much better than I figured. But the truth is, we couldn't have done it without your constant help, Jon."

Cara laughed. "And some nights his big reward is getting to sleep in that awful room above the carriage house."

"Well, the upside is I've had a chance to expand the blacksmith business to places the horse and wagon can't reach from Dry Lake in one day."

Lori stayed focused as Ada and Cara helped her sew another faceless doll. Those sold great too, and Lori loved helping to make them.

Ada glanced up. "I never dreamed we'd stay this busy. We've sold every hope chest, coatrack, and side table that Israel made, and he's making more items for us."

Deborah slid the money into the deposit bag. "I hope I'm not all puffed up to think this, but I'm so pleased with us. We've come up with a theme for every season so far, and people have enjoyed each one."

Cara snipped loose threads off the doll in her hand. "We need to start working on a spring theme, but I'm not planting, hoeing, and harvesting according to the Old Ways. So if anyone mentions farming the Amish way at Ada's House, I'll scream."

"I've been mulling over the spring theme," Jonathan said. "And I think farming like the Amish is a great idea."

Cara screamed softly, making all of them giggle.

"It's just the first of February. We have a few more weeks of Amish Winter Wonderland to get through. We'll figure something out soon enough." Deborah removed her coat and Jonathan's from pegs near the back door. "I'm ready." She tossed Jonathan his jacket.

He caught it and opened the door for her. She grabbed her scarf, gloves, and winter bonnet off the shelf. Almost every Friday night, unless the temps were too cold, they walked to the bank to drop the money into the night depository.

Deborah put on her black bonnet, wrapped the knit scarf around her neck and lower face, and wriggled her hands into the leather gloves.

With his hands jammed inside his coat pockets, Jonathan nudged her with his shoulder. "Warm?"

"You know the answer to that," Deborah mumbled through the knit scarf.

"Did you put on the insulated underwear I brought you?"

"That's not for you to know." She pretended offense. "Where's your sense of respectability, young man?"

His quiet laugh warmed her more than all her layers of clothing. "Well, Little Debbie, I think working in a hot kitchen year round puts you at a disadvantage for dealing with cold weather. I could take the deposit to the bank for you."

"At least I wouldn't have to worry you might eat it before getting there."

"That's true enough."

She treasured his sense of humor, his willingness to exaggerate any fault, real or imagined, and laugh in a way that caused amusement itself to dance within her. He walked with confidence and lightheartedness. On a whim she slid her gloved hand into his coat pocket with his hand.

But he didn't laugh or make a joke as she'd expected. His features grew gentle, and he enveloped her hand in his.

"Ah, I'm much warmer now." Even as she teased him, unease ran through her. He'd been honest about how he felt, and it seemed inappropriate to flirt—to make him hope for things she remained unsure of wanting. But her hand in his felt so right that she couldn't make herself pull away.

They walked through the old town where tall brick buildings lined the sidewalks. Once in front of the bank, she pulled her hand free of Jonathan's and slid the thin bag through the deposit slot. When she turned around to leave, Jonathan stood directly in front of her.

He slowly lowered the knit scarf from around her lips. "I can think of something else that might warm you...us."

The aroma of aftershave clung to his hands, and his warm breath smelled of peppermint. Mesmerized by some invisible power, she couldn't respond. He slowly drew closer, and when his lips met hers, even her toes warmed. She moved her hands to his chest to push against him, but her hands disobeyed her and clutched the lapels of his wool coat. The gentleness of his hands against her face and his lips over hers caught her off guard. Never in her life had she experienced a kiss like this.

The kiss grew with each moment, leaving her breathless. When he eased his lips from hers and studied her, she leaned against the brick building for support.

"It's...awfully...hot out here." Deborah tried to make light of what had just happened, but her breathless, trembling words betrayed her.

She pulled the knit fabric over her lips and tried to catch her breath. He ran the back of his fingers across the scarf and her cheek. "Like summertime in February," he said softly.

Staring into his eyes, she understood that Jonathan had a way of making her feel totally secure and incredibly treasured. As she studied him, an odd and unwelcome sensation grabbed her senses. She closed her eyes, hoping it'd go away. It didn't. She sidestepped him, looking down the block. A man seemed to be looking right at them, and she knew he'd returned.

"Something wrong?"

The man eased into a side alley, disappearing completely.

Her legs shook. Was it really Mahlon or just her imagination, conjured up the moment she kissed another man? "Let's go back."

Jonathan glanced up the block and back to her. "You okay?"

Deborah wrapped her arms around herself and started walking. "Sure."

They walked home without talking. Once inside, the stiltedness between them made her want to tell what she'd seen...or thought she saw.

The wall clock showed that it wasn't yet nine, but Ada, Cara, and Lori apparently had retired to the upstairs. Deborah's eyes met Jonathan's. "I...I'm going on to my room now."

"Sure. Good night, Deb."

He turned to leave, to go to his room above the carriage house, then paused. "You want to talk about what spooked you?"

Her heart cinched into a knot. She'd reacted to his kiss with clear desire, and then she'd shut him out. Her behavior felt similar to the way Mahlon used to treat her. And embarrassment filled her as Jonathan wanted to face it openly. She took a shaky breath. "Just shadows of the past dogging me while I try to move forward."

He looked like he wanted to say more, but he tipped his hat and left. She outted the lanterns and stood in the darkness. Had Mahlon returned? The thought bounced around inside her head, confusing her more with each passing minute. She wouldn't know what she thought or felt until she knew whether it was him or not.

She eased into the foyer, looking up the steps for signs of light coming from under doorways. The only room with light was Cara's. She rarely settled down for sleep before midnight. Grabbing her coat and winter bonnet, Deborah went out the front door, moving quietly so no one heard her. While going down the walkway, she put her coat and hat on, but her insides felt colder than the night. The moon reflected brightly on patches of snow, but living in town didn't compare to the fields of undisturbed white at her Daed's place.

When a man moved out from behind a tree just a few feet away, Deborah gasped.

"Easy, Deb." Mahlon's familiar voice caught her. He'd cut his hair short, ridding himself of the curls he'd always hated. He wore a belt instead of suspenders, and his leather coat stood open as if the cold didn't bother him. He looked healthy and carefree.

"What are you doing here?"

"Checking on the two women I love." He shifted, looking surprisingly confident.

He loved her? "What do you want?"

"You."

She ached to say, *It's too late.* But as he stared at her, the words wouldn't leave her mouth. Something about him tugged at her, just as it always had. She should hate him. But all she could think of was that she had loved him before she'd even been old enough to know what love was. Her heart beat hard against her chest, pounding out the many, many feelings she'd had for him almost her whole life. "What does that mean?"

"I'm sorry I left, especially the way I did. I was so confused. I'm not anymore. And I love you. I always have. I want to come back and make it right."

"Make it right? I caught you sneaking off. When I confronted you, you rode off in a car with a friend, leaving me crying on the side of the road. You were a jerk to me and your Mamm, giving no thought to anyone but yourself."

He tilted his head, his quietness drawing her in as it always had. "A jerk doesn't care. I've never for one minute stopped caring."

"Then tell me why, Mahlon. You asked me to marry you, and then you ran off."

"No excuse." Mahlon lowered his head. "I…I messed up."

"No excuse? So either you still don't know, or you aren't telling."

He shoved his hands into his pants pocket. "You've changed since I left."

"Ya, I have. It's been almost eight months, and I've had to survive what you heaped on me. I doubt if you'll ever really know what you've done. You say you want to come back and make it right, but you're sneaking around in the dark, hiding your presence from everyone but me. Why?"

He stared at the ground before looking her in the eye. "I needed to see you alone. To have a chance to tell the full story. I've changed too, Deb. All for the better. I promise you that, but you'll have to give me an opportunity to prove it. I'm living not far from here. I'd like for us to talk, to cover some ground together, before my presence is known. Can you do that much for me?"

"You keeping secrets just never ends, does it?"

"I'm only asking for a few days. That's all."

She wanted to keep it a secret, but not for him. For her. It'd give her the freedom to figure out what she thought before everyone else started pulling at her to think and feel what they wanted her to. Even with her own reasons for doing this in place, she felt like a fool.

If she acted irrationally and Mahlon left again, Ada would pay. The man in front of her was Ada's only child. For any Amish woman, that alone carried a heartache that couldn't be erased. But if he returned, Ada's life would never feel lacking again. Deborah's presence and loyalty could only ease Ada's loss in a tiny way. Mahlon had the ability to erase Ada's sorrow and carry on her family line. "And if I never want to be in a relationship with you again, will you return anyway and rejoin the faith?"

He stared, his hazel eyes still holding power over her, and she hated herself for it. "Think about giving me a second chance, Deb. When you're ready to talk, leave a message for me with the cook at the Family Restaurant in town. I can tell you what you want to know. Just don't tell anyone else for now. Please."

Feeling a need to get inside before she gave him any more access to her heart again, she nodded. "Okay. For a little while." She started to walk off, but he caught her by the arm.

He gazed into her eyes, but she didn't know who stood in front of her—the man who'd always drawn her or a stranger. Or both. Had she ever known him?

His eyes misted. "Denki."

"I'm sorry, Mahlon, but I'm not doing this for you." She pulled free of his arm and headed for the porch, hoping she hadn't just created an opening for him that she didn't have the power to close. If Jonathan discovered that he'd returned and that she was keeping it a secret, Jonathan would walk away and never look back. As steady as sunrise in every season, Jonathan had no patience for girls who played games. He didn't need or ask for answers she didn't have, but he demanded honesty in a relationship.

She went inside and locked the door.

Why had she agreed to keep a secret for one man—a man who had proved unreliable—when it could ruin a promising relationship with someone worthy of her trust?

Twenty-Four

Lena moved the pot of heartland corn chowder from the stove onto the kitchen table, careful to square it on the hot pad.

Valentine's Day.

She set the flatware in its place and tucked a napkin beside it. In all her years since being old enough to be courted or to date, she'd never spent this holiday with just her Daed. At least one girlfriend and she had spent the evening eating chocolate candy and talking until the wee hours of the morning—that was the norm. One year when everyone else had a date, Jonathan had come over, and they'd played checkers, schemed new pranks to pull on people, and whiled away the hours just being pals. This year all her friends had someone special. She'd yet to find a man who interested her, except Grey. But when the time came, he could have any single woman, and he wouldn't consider her.

The sense of being different wrapped around her, and she seemed unable to shake it. The threat of losing her teaching position had made it easy for loneliness to carve its features all over her heart.

While moving the freshly baked bread onto the table, she heard the back door open, signaling her Daed's prompt arrival for dinner. His furniture shop stood less than twenty feet from their home, but she never had to call him—he came in early or on time. Except lately he'd missed a few dinners while he spent more and more time in Hope Crossing with Ada.

"These came for you." He passed her several envelopes. All but one were an odd size and color. He moved to the kitchen sink to wash up.

She set the other notes on the table and studied the business-sized envelope. Her hands felt clammy and her head swimmy. It didn't have a return address, but the handwriting was Michael's. The return address had been omitted on purpose. It wasn't from any one person. It came from the school board. Her heart pounding, she turned her back to her Daed, who remained at the sink, and quietly slid her finger under the loose seal and broke it. She pulled the neatly folded letter out and opened it.

Dear Lena,

We appreciate your years of service. You've been an excellent teacher, and we're aware that no position ever comes without issues, but it seems that you are having too much trouble submitting to the authority of the board. It is our decision that, starting with the next school year, you will be free to find a teaching position outside of Dry Lake. So that we do not hinder you from finding a new position, we will keep our decision confidential among the school board. You will have little trouble finding a teaching position elsewhere. Perhaps you will not find it so difficult to submit to the leadership of a different school board.

Sincerely,
Michael Blank
Enos Beiler
Jake Fisher

Grey hadn't signed it. Either he didn't agree with the decision, or he didn't know what was going on in his absence. She guessed he didn't know. Michael tried not to add more to a person's life than was absolutely necessary.

Her Daed finished drying his face on a kitchen towel. "From your friends, ya?"

Lena stuffed the letter and envelope into the hidden pocket of her apron, drew a shaky breath, and turned around. "Ya, they've remembered Valentine's Day." The envelopes on the table contained cards from each close friend—Deborah, Anna Mary, Rachel, Linda, Nancy, Lydia, Frieda, and Esther. And every one of them had beaus...again.

"Did you remember to send them cards?"

"Hmm?" Lena sat at the table and put the napkin in her lap. "Oh, ya. I did."

With the towel in hand, he took a seat. Lena choked back tears as they bowed their heads for the silent prayer. She tried to gain control of her emotions, but she wasn't ready for the bowed heads and closed eyes to be over when she heard her Daed's flatware shift. Trembling, she stood and dipped the corn chowder into a bowl for him.

He took it from her. "Smells great."

"Denki." She ladled soup into her bowl before sitting and passing him the bread.

"You're awfully quiet of late, Lena."

She nodded. How had she let this happen? What had she been thinking?

Her Daed's usually jovial features had a downward pull. "I spoke to Michael earlier today. He apologized to me for any unease their decision may be causing you. You can imagine his embarrassment when he realized I didn't know what he was talking about."

Unable to speak or eat, she shrugged.

"Are you in danger of losing your teaching position?"

"There are other places to teach."

"This school board covers three districts. If you aren't hired by them, no other district is close enough to get to by horse and buggy. You'd need to hire a driver or move."

She took a long drink of her water, hoping to get through dinner without falling apart.

Daed tore off a hunk of bread. "I didn't think the complaints against you that caused your probation last spring to be fair. It wasn't near the first time those children had come to school without their lunch. Every time you'd sent notes home, given them your lunch to share, and asked others to sacrifice part of their lunch. You had good reasons to send the oldest after the forgotten lunches—"

Lena raised both hands. "I know you side with me, and I appreciate it, but this has nothing to do with John going the wrong direction in my rig and getting hurt. I crossed a clear Amish line. I didn't view my actions as threatening, but the board does. I guess since going to public school, I don't see certain things as a hazard to our faith but as an opportunity to grow."

"What did you do?"

"Samantha came and talked to the class on a couple of occasions, trying to help the children cope with the trauma of seeing Elsie killed."

"Ach, Lena. You must've done it without going through proper channels. Why?"

"I told you why. I knew she'd be good for the class, and I…I invited her. I never let her be alone with any of the students. Everything she said was good and wise and helpful."

"Grey is the clearest, most balanced thinker on that board. What does he say?"

Lena pushed the full bowl of soup away from her. "He's not been to a meeting since Elsie died."

Her Daed stared at her, disbelief and frustration radiating from him. "That's not good for you, Lena. With him gone, those who are complaining will not be tempered."

"You're telling me things I know, Daed. Can we change the subject?"

"Sure. I've been taking different pieces of woodwork to Ada's place, and she's been selling them like hot cakes. I'm taking another load tomorrow. I'd thought about staying in Hope Crossing for a night or two. I've got friends there, and she needs help setting up some new adventures for springtime activities at Ada's House. But maybe it's not such a great time to be leaving you so much."

"Don't be ridiculous, please. I'm not a child."

"Ya, but—" Soft knocking sounds interrupted him. He went to the front door. Figuring someone had come to talk to him about furniture, Lena stayed put.

Her Daed walked back into the kitchen alone. "Peter Bender is on the porch, and he wants to talk to you. He didn't want to come in."

Lena grabbed her coat and hurried outside. Winds whipped through her clothes and up her dress, giving her chills. "Peter." She closed the front door. "What's going on?"

"I…I want to talk to that woman friend of yours, you know, the one who came to our classroom."

Suspicion filled her. Had Dwayne talked him into this? If she dared to bring Samantha into Peter's life after the board's letter, it would certainly be the end of her career. She'd never be allowed to teach at any school ever again. "Why?"

Peter shrugged, and under the silvery moonlight that reflected off the snow, she saw hostility etched on his face. He cleared his throat and sniffed. "I…I got to tell her some stuff I can't live with. I can't tell you or anyone else."

She had no doubt that Dwayne was setting her up. But Peter wasn't. To avoid the snare meant refusing to help Peter after she'd been the one to make the offer. Her throat closed and tears welled. "Ya. Okay." Her hands shook as she wiped tears off her face, hoping he didn't notice. "I'll try to reach her tomorrow and see if she will come out this way again. Can you talk to her here?"

He rubbed his nose and sniffed again. "Don't matter to me where as long as no one else can hear us."

"I can arrange for that. It might be best if you keep this just between us for now. Your parents need to know later on, but talking with Samantha a few times first is ideal."

"Sure. I won't say nothing to anybody." He looked like he wanted to hug her, and her heart melted.

"Go on home, Peter. It's too dark and too cold to be out like this."

He went down the steps and put his foot into the stirrup before pulling himself into the saddle. "Denki, Lena."

The trap set before her was clearly marked. "You're welcome, Peter."

Deborah stood at the window in the dark living room, watching the street. Mahlon had asked for a few days. It'd been twelve. And he wanted more. She'd spoken to him twice. Each time hadn't been for more than thirty minutes—once when she took out the garbage late one night and once when she was feeding Rosie.

At least now she knew a few more things about him. He drove huge trucks across the States. He sincerely regretted giving in to his confusion and running off. And when not hauling, as he called it, he obviously spent his time watching the house. It unnerved her, and she avoided going out at night.

Since his first appearance, she'd felt every emotion over and over throughout each day—anger, resentment, confusion, compassion, and traces of desire. What she'd like to do is jerk him up by the collar and shout at him until he felt some of what he'd dumped on her.

The stairs creaked, and she jolted. Through the dark silence, Cara studied her. "Waiting for Mahlon to show?"

"I… You know?"

"He startled me one night when I'd gone to the barn for a drop cloth. He thought I was you."

"It's not what you think."

"Oh, I bet it's close enough."

"You can't be mad at me about this. You're the one who said I should compare."

Cara sat on the steps. "Do you have any idea what kind of a game he's pulled you into?"

Game?

She looked out the window. The moon dimly lit the yard, and memories of the hard work and successful nights of Ada's House seemed less of a victory now.

"It's not a game. Not for him or me."

"Can you at least admit what you're doing is dishonest?"

Deborah released the curtain and went to the foot of the steps. "He's a truck driver now. Aside from that, I don't even know what he's been doing since he left. Why did he leave? Why is he coming back? I don't want the answers he can give for Ada's sake or anyone else's. I need to know the truth of it for me."

"All reasonable things you could find out without sneaking around."

"I…I need this, Cara. Without pressure. Ephraim gave you time to figure things out. I just need a little time. Everybody has an opinion about Mahlon. They always did. I just want to think without anyone else's opinion crowding in. Surely you get that."

Cara sighed, and Deborah was confident she'd rolled her eyes too. Odd and infuriating as it was, Deborah still had feelings for him. But she couldn't decide if they were real or if they were a fantasy left over from her days of wanting to be his wife and bear his children. What kind of man joined the faith and then left, only to return? From the moment she saw him again, the questions looped together inside her, repeating endlessly, and occasionally a new one would join in, but she had no answers.

"And…and you know how hard it is to live this life. Maybe he…he just thought he wanted something else and then realized he didn't. You don't know. I don't know. But I *need* to find out."

Cara patted the step beside her, and Deborah sat down.

She put her arm around Deborah's shoulder and pulled her close. "Just do me one favor. Don't confuse rescuing love for the marrying kind of love."

Cara's words unleashed years of memories, all telling Deborah the real story. Sketches of her life with Mahlon since they were children connected inside her, clearing away the fog. She saw herself. She saw Mahlon. And she began to understand.

Tears filled her eyes, and peace eased the tightness in her chest. "I think maybe I do know him after all—at least some things about him."

Cara squeezed her shoulder, saying nothing.

Forgiveness slowly scrubbed the anger and confusion from her. "He needs me."

"Yeah, but what do you need?"

"To see Mahlon and talk, I think."

She just needed to leave a message for him at the Family Restaurant and arrange a meeting.

Twenty-Five

While Grey led his horse into Allen's barn, Ivan ran into the house. Grey took a deep breath. A hint of spring floated on the icy air as the sun began to set. The winter nights weren't as dark or as long or as cold as they had been. Patches of snow still lay on the ground, but spring would officially begin next week.

He'd survived winter. There were times when he could sense hope inside him, growing new roots and telling him he had a future. As he tossed some hay in a trough, he heard a noise as if a bucket had been knocked over.

"Hello?" He studied the dark barn. A shadowy figure darted out the side door. Grey hurried outside. A man, maybe Amish, clutched the mane of his horse, mounted it bareback, and took off. He returned to the barn, lit a kerosene lamp, and looked around. Nothing appeared to be missing, and there were no signs that the man had intended to set a fire. Feeling satisfied the person hadn't caused any harm, he put out the lamp and left.

As he approached Allen's house, Ivan appeared in the doorway, excitedly telling him Lena was here.

He didn't know why Ivan sounded so surprised. With Emily expecting a fifth child, Lennie had been here to help her most Saturday nights since Christmas. Lennie added her own flavor of pleasure to an evening.

He stepped inside. Allen smiled. "Glad you're here. I was going to come by your place in a bit."

Grey removed his coat and hat and hung them next to Ivan's. He'd tell Allen what he just saw when the two of them were alone. Lennie sat at the game table, surrounded by two nieces and two nephews. Allen's wife had a smile on her face, looking more energetic than she had in a while despite her due date being in two or three weeks. Ivan stood next to Lennie, studying small cards that were turned facedown on the table. They were playing the Memory Game.

Grey talked with Allen about the weather, planting spring crops, and business at the cabinetry shop. Ivan chose a card, glanced at it, and then picked up another one. He then passed them both to Lennie.

She giggled and tussled his hair. "You are too good at this."

Lennie glanced at Grey for the first time since he'd arrived. Her eyes held that familiar warmth, but she said nothing. He took a seat in the living room, choosing the chair that faced the children's game table. Allen grabbed the newspaper and sat on the couch.

"I'm planning a hunt. Care to go?" Allen asked.

"When?"

"Thought we'd leave this coming Wednesday and come home Saturday. I contacted Dugger earlier in the week to see if he has an empty cabin we can rent, and he does."

"I'll see if Ivan can stay with Mamm for those few days and let you know."

Rounds of applause came from the children's table. Lennie received several hugs before the children took off for the stairs. She remained there, turning the cards facedown. "You didn't even ask him what you'll be hunting."

Lennie didn't look up, but Grey knew she was speaking to him. "It's bird-hunting season. Does it matter the type?"

Her eyes moved to him, shining like emeralds in the glow of the kerosene lamp. "Don't bring back any quail."

"You don't like them?"

"I love quail."

Allen raised one eyebrow before opening his newspaper, looking determined to stay out of this conversation.

Realizing where this conversation was headed, Grey moved to a chair across from her. "So if you like them so much, we need to shoot 'em and bring 'em home to be cooked, canned, or frozen, right?" With the face of the small cards against the tabletop, he shifted them around until she had no idea what was where. She added the last cards to the table, and they began a fresh game.

She picked up a card and tried to find its match. Then she laid both of them down again. "If you shoot a quail, I'll…" She took another card, only this time she found its match, so she took another turn.

When it was his turn, he flipped over a card and then chose another one. "You'll what? Oh, wait. I've got it. You'll throw cake at me or make me ride for two hours in the freezing temps so I can do a favor for you."

"Have you ever listened to a quail?" She picked two cards, but they didn't match.

"It's hard to avoid hearing them in these parts." He lifted a card.

"They are a beautiful-sounding bird."

"Ya, but they're still just birds. They taste good too." He found its match and set it beside him.

"If you listen to a bobwhite, its melody might take you places without you ever leaving your yard."

"It's a bird, Lennie."

She gave a half shrug while winning several more cards.

"Are you actually serious?" He matched three sets before she took another turn.

"I can't imagine picking up a gun to kill anything, so my opinion isn't worth much to a hunter, but it's how I feel."

"How come I never knew this bothered you?"

She studied him, her eyes reflecting dozens of thoughts. "I began feeding quail a couple of years back, and then I saw one that had been shot but wasn't dead." She shuddered.

"Do you still capture critters that have worked their way into your house and release them outside?"

"Maybe."

He laughed and leaned the chair back on two legs. "Allen, we're going pheasant hunting." He lowered his chair. "Of course this means we need a bird dog. Can we borrow Nicky?"

"She's more of a butterfly dog."

"And you let her engage in that activity?"

She shrugged. "Not when I can stop it."

Allen folded the newspaper and tapped it against his leg. "Dugger has a bird dog we can use." Allen tossed the paper on the couch. "You can't listen to my sister, or we'd all be vegetarians."

Lennie clicked her tongue. "Or we could wait on you to fix a meal and starve to death."

Grey laughed. "So we won't go quail hunting. But, Lennie, you do know this means you have to clean and pluck the pheasants as a trade-off."

She won the last few rounds and tossed the cards onto the table in front of him. "If I was any good at plucking feathers off something, I'd have done it to Allen long ago."

He chuckled. "One minute she's sweet, and the next she's sassy as everything."

She stood. "One minute I was asking a favor, and the next I had what I wanted." She gave an evil laugh, then looked at the stairway. "I promised the young uns a game of indoor freeze tag."

When she was out of hearing range, Grey turned back to Allen. "Is she serious about the quail, or have I just been had—Lennie style?"

"I was only half listening and not watching her at all, so I don't know."

"Has she been feeding quail?"

Allen shrugged. "Not a clue. But if she has, we should find out where. Those will be some nice plump quail." Allen smiled. "Wouldn't she love that?"

"Listen." Grey lowered his voice. "There was a man in your barn when I put my horse up."

"A man? Any idea who?"

"None. He caught a glimpse of me and ran. Had a horse waiting near the barn."

Emily walked into the living room, drying her hands on a kitchen towel. She sat down and put her very swollen feet on the coffee table.

He and Allen dropped their discussion, and the conversation among the three of them ambled onto a dozen different topics as the children ran in and out of the room.

Emily held her hand out in front of her. Allen stood, took her by the hand, and gently helped her up. She whispered something to him before leaving the room, and he smiled.

Allen sat. "I'll keep an eye out, and if I see any signs of someone hanging around, I'll tell Emily. You haven't heard news about any trouble, have you?"

"No."

"The midwife gave Emily a cell phone last week in case she goes into labor."

"And you're planning a hunting trip?"

"She's yet to go into labor before her due date, but since you saw someone lurking around, I'm not going anywhere until I'm certain he's long, long gone."

Dwayne rode the horse hard for nearly a mile before he slowed. He struggled a bit to catch a decent breath. Grey had messed up everything.

Dwayne could've made the whole thing look like an out of control horse did the job. Lena finally had gone somewhere without that stupid dog of hers. He could have got her tonight, but then Grey showed up. Dwayne couldn't catch her in her own barn. When she drove a rig, her Daed hitched it for her in the mornings and brought it around to the front of the house. And he met her in the evenings when she arrived home. She arrived at school alone, but the lean-to stood open toward the road. That could mean witnesses.

Her brother's barn seemed perfect, and finally she didn't have the mutt with her. But Allen had come outside to meet her when she arrived. What was it with these men in her life? They treated her better than most dogs. It didn't make sense. Couldn't they see that God Himself hated her?

And she had no right to steal Peter's loyalty. None. He hated her so much he wanted to kill her now and be done with her.

All he had to do was find the right place and the right time.

Twenty-Six

Grey and Allen had talked for nearly an hour uninterrupted by children, who were upstairs with Lennie and Emily. That tended to be unusual, and Grey wondered if he should go up and see if he needed to rescue either or both of them.

Allen stretched and yawned. "I'm hoping Lennie and Emily come down and we play games soon. If I don't win a few rounds of spoons against Lennie tonight, I have to mow her grass all summer."

"I can't believe you bet against your sister, knowing she rarely loses at spoons. You're not as smart as I thought you were."

"You know, you've made that statement about me throughout most of my life. Seems like I'd hit bottom at some point and you couldn't think of me as any less smart."

"You're right." Grey chuckled. "I won't be caught thinking too highly of you again, no matter how low that is."

Bumps from upstairs rattled the ceiling as the children ran across the wooden floor. Bursts of laughter filtered down the stairway. As bedtime approached, Lennie had to be ready for one less child to be under her care, so he should get Ivan and head home. Normally, the adults took turns looking after the little ones, but for some reason she hadn't come back down.

Grey stood. "I need to go on home."

"No, stay," Allen said. "All you're going to do is tuck Ivan in and sit around by yourself. Let Ivan go to bed here. He can sleep over, and you can go home when we're finished winning against Lennie. I do not want to mow her yard all summer."

When he heard Lennie trying to settle the children down, he moved to the foot of the steps and hollered for Ivan. His son peeped over the railing, and Grey told him they needed to head for home in five minutes. Ivan nodded and then disappeared. Grey knew what would happen next. The boys would go in a bedroom and play very, very quietly in hopes of extending the visit. "Lennie?" Grey called.

"Ya."

"You need a hand?"

She came to the top of the stairs, carrying a suitcase.

"Maybe I should have offered to help sooner. You running away?"

She tossed the bag to him. It didn't have much in it, but it wasn't empty. Emily waddled onto the landing with her hands on the lower part of her back. Lennie helped her ease down the steps. Lurking strangers or not, Allen wouldn't be going hunting next week.

"Oh, Allen," Lennie sang softly once at the foot of the stairs. "Guess where you're going tonight."

Allen studied Emily. She shrugged. "My water broke. I called the midwife. She's got two others in labor, so she can't come here tonight. We're supposed to meet her at the clinic."

Allen stood. "You have yet to go into labor during the day."

"Are you complaining to the woman who's in labor?" Emily rubbed her lower back.

Grey chuckled. "The man's never as smart as he should be, Emily."

Lennie headed for the door. "I'll get the carriage."

"No." Allen hurried ahead of her. "I'll get it. Grey, you'll stay tonight and give Lennie a hand?"

"Ya, no problem."

Lennie looked at him and raised an eyebrow, but just as she opened her mouth to speak, a bump from upstairs vibrated the room. She took off even before the child let out a yelp. "I got it. We're fine. Go have a baby."

Emily chuckled. "Those children went wild with excitement when they saw my suitcase. I might just have an easier night of it than your sister will."

"Good. Serves her right." Allen winked at his wife.

Grey walked out with them and helped Emily get into the buggy. Once they were on their way, he went back inside. Lennie sat on the couch, reading to the children. All of Allen's children were dressed for bed. He assumed she'd done that earlier, unless she had a bit of a magician in her.

Ivan glanced up and then down again, clearly hoping his Daed wouldn't tell him it was time to leave. Grey took a seat and read the newspaper. The sense of belonging and friendship surrounded him, and he realized afresh all that he had to be thankful for.

Nearly an hour later he laid the newspaper in his lap. Lennie's reading had done its job. The children were relaxed and sleepy. Snuggled against Lennie, Phoebe had already fallen asleep. When Lennie closed the book, he moved to the couch and lifted Phoebe. Lennie put her index finger over her mouth, picked up little David, and motioned for the other children to follow her. Grey walked up the stairs behind them, enjoying the hushed serenity that now filled the home. Lennie went into the boys' room, and he walked into the girls' room. A kerosene lantern from inside the playroom gave off enough light so he could navigate around the strewn toys and books. Emily wasn't a fussbudget about tidiness. Her energy went into feeding and caring for her growing brood, not picking up toys. Six-year-old Katie crawled into the regular-sized bed. Grey pushed the covers back and slid Phoebe into the bed next to her sister.

"You'll leave a light on?" Katie mumbled as she rubbed her eyes.

"Ya." Grey went into the adjoining playroom and got the kerosene lantern. He turned the wick to its shortest length, causing the flame to barely give off light. Before leaving the room, he noticed a small circle of red tape on the floor. A doll sat in the center of it, holding a small piece of paper.

He moved to the night-light shelf in the girls' room and set the lamp on it. As he stepped out of their room, Lennie came out of the boys' room. "Ivan put on a pair of pajamas belonging to Amos, and all three boys are asleep."

"Time to relax." Grey motioned for her to go down the stairs ahead of him. The wooden steps creaked, reminding him of the age of this homestead. Grey had built his own place, but Allen had inherited his from a grandparent, who'd inherited it from a grandparent. A lot of family life had taken place here, and he wondered if any of them had dealt with as much marital unhappiness as he and Elsie had.

Another shard of isolation gouged at him. It never seemed to end. He'd once stood on a piece of earth by himself, able to see Elsie across a canyon, but he couldn't reach her. The sense of loneliness felt unbearable, but they could see each other, sometimes catch a few words as they yelled back and forth, and he always kept a smidgen of hope that he could build a bridge and cross over.

Lennie held a steamy cup of hot chocolate out to him. He took the cup, trying to clear his mind.

With a mug in hand, Lennie took a seat at the kitchen table. "You didn't stay tonight because I can't handle four children on my own."

Mulling over what to say, he sat down across from her. "No, but an extra pair of hands isn't such a bad thing, right?"

She raised an eyebrow while stirring her drink. "I'm the girl who helped replant the begonias, remember?"

Hiding a smile, he took a sip from his mug. "I was twelve, and it was a pop fly, bottom of the ninth, last out, and I caught it. Do you know what that means?"

"Ya, it means you ruined part of my mother's flower garden and needed my help. We replanted that section with the same type and color of begonias from Mamm's greenhouse." She tapped the spoon on the rim of her mug before laying the utensil on the table. "You and I have a long and odd relationship, ya? Sometimes I was the tagalong sister. Sometimes the tattletale. Sometimes the confidante. Through it all you and I were friends…with or without Allen. And I'd like to know why you've stayed tonight."

As memories of good times eased his sadness, he realized anew how much fun they'd had. Lennie had always mattered, and once she got past the tattletale age, he'd never regretted letting her in on secrets.

She took a sip and licked the chocolate drink off her lips. "I don't need a big brother. You miss Elsie, and I…miss Jonathan. And even though those relationships don't begin to compare, because Elsie was your other half, and Jonathan…well…he'll be someone else's other half eventually, we both are feeling a little lost."

Jonathan not being around was probably another reason she'd spent so many Saturday nights in the last few months helping her sister-in-law, although she might have always spent Saturday nights with Allen and Emily. He didn't know.

Grey turned the mug around and around, remembering parts of their childhood and adolescent years. "Did you ever tell Allen about our conversation before you decided to go to public school?"

With the cup halfway to her lips, she paused. "You and he are still friends, aren't you?"

Grey chuckled. He'd been nineteen and Lennie just fourteen when they sat on her porch swing and talked for hours as she mulled over the idea of attending public school. No one in her family, or in the district for that matter, liked the idea. He'd sided with her on the topic. Right now, she wanted that kind of honesty and friendship again. "I saw a man in the barn when putting my horse in. He ran away, and it's probably nothing."

"Any idea who?"

"No."

"Why would anybody be hiding out in a barn and then run off?"

"I don't know. Why does anyone hide anywhere?"

"I didn't know people hid."

"Sure we do." He stared at the ripples of chocolate mixture in his cup. "People are good at hiding. Some run off. Some close themselves up in a room inside their own house. Some look right at folks while concealing who they really are." When he looked up, she seemed to be puzzled at the turn of the conversation, but he longed to tell her the truth. "I…I fall into that third category." He wanted to confess more than just his hypocrisy, but he couldn't make himself say anything else.

The serenity radiating from Lennie felt like a warm, inviting kitchen during a snowstorm. "Now that you've worded it that way, I can see where I hide things too. We certainly don't tell other people all that we're think-ing or feeling, do we?"

"No."

"I'm going to say something here because, like it or not, it needs to be said, okay?"

"I'm sure I've said worse things to myself already."

"Ya, me too." She paused. "If Elsie were here and you'd been the one to die, would she be free of guilt?"

Her words smashed against his guilty conscience.

Lennie brushed imaginary crumbs from the table as if unable to look at him while chipping away at who he'd become—a man encased in guilt. He'd been the head of his household, and what took place there could not be blamed on anyone else. Elsie had been at fault too, but it'd been his place to make everything right, and he hadn't.

Lennie raised her eyes to meet his. "Would you want her blaming herself like this?"

It hurt to think of Elsie having to survive her part in their unsuccess-ful marriage. He shook his head. But an unmarried person could never understand the confusing, complex relationship between a husband and wife. Until he lived it year after year, he never knew of the silent unity and the silent hostilities between couples. Vows were made in the presence of loved ones, and although no one warned them, they began a journey of expectations, disappointments, misunderstanding, and in his case…rejection while closeness slowly faded, leaving emptiness in its stead.

Unsure how honest to be, Grey searched for the right words. "You can't understand, and you shouldn't, not yet anyway…maybe not ever."

She angled her head, looking confident in her stand. "If I had done exactly as you have, would you want me pressured with the weight of this responsibility, or would you want me to let myself be free?"

He stared at her, unable to respond. Thinking about Lennie being under his same guilt, he gained some much needed balance.

She placed her hand over his. "If you'd want Elsie set free from her shortcomings and wrongs, then free yourself."

Getting complete freedom from his past wasn't as easy as making a decision. He nodded and cleared his throat, ready to change the subject. "Ephraim's hired a new man from Ohio. He starts next week."

She went to the stove and poured fresh hot chocolate into her mug. "Ya? Why's that?"

"Lots of reasons. Business is good. We never replaced Mahlon. As Ivan's only parent, I'm not willing to travel out of town much or work as many hours as I had been, not for the next couple of years."

"Makes sense. Have you met the man?"

"Ya. His name is Christian Miller. He arrived yesterday. Seems to be a nice guy. Single. He's about your age. Does good work. He'll live with the Benders until he can afford something on his own."

"The Benders? Does he know them?"

"I wondered the same thing, so I asked. Dwayne's Mamm and Christian's Mamm have a mutual friend, but until he arrived here, he'd never met the Benders personally."

He saw an unusual look in Lennie's eyes, and he wondered if she was interested in meeting Christian. Each spring Lennie organized an annual Picnic Basket Auction. Not only did it make extra funds for the school, but single couples throughout many districts had met during these functions. In the past Jonathan or a relative of hers bought Lennie's basket, which meant the two would go on a picnic together alone. With Jonathan seeing Deborah, maybe Grey should nudge Christian to bid on Lennie's basket. The idea didn't sit well—probably because he didn't know Christian and also because he didn't want to lose his and Lennie's free time together. Every time he was with her, she made life's burdens seem less heavy.

He took a drink of his hot chocolate. "You planning another auction this year?"

She shifted, looking uncomfortable. "I…I…ya. It's been in the works since fall, so I'll have it."

"You sound unsure."

She shrugged. "Odd year all the way around, I guess. But the classroom needs some items, like the ceiling-to-floor quality relief map and a battery-operated globe with an inner light that I've had my eye on for a few years now." She went to the game table and picked up the box of checkers. "I'm better at this than I used to be."

"Well I certainly hope so. You were what—fourteen the last time we played?"

"Sixteen, thank you very much." She mocked the words he'd said to her three months back.

"Hey, Lennie, what is that red circle of tape in the playroom?"

"Ah, it's part of the Circle of Peace game."

"What's that?"

She set the box on the table and opened it. "It's a game of truth telling. The person who steps inside it must only do so because they want to. No one can put someone there, but they can ask the person if they're willing.

By stepping inside, you're saying you trust the outcome is worth facing the dark parts of yourself."

"Who would want to play such a game?"

"Children who've lied but wish they were free to tell the truth. It's a safe place, because the one listening has agreed to forgive, keep the incident private, and help the person not need to lie next time."

"No wonder it's in the playroom. Only children would play that."

"You think?" Her brows tightened while she held his gaze. "Surely everyone needs to step inside a circle of peace at some point. I know I do. Even when telling the absolute truth, sometimes I later realize I'd been lying to myself."

She seemed to have no concept of the deceit that could take place between people. He hadn't known of such dishonesty either until he found himself caught in it. But if he'd voluntarily stood inside that circle, Elsie would not have listened. And he couldn't have made her tell the truth, circle or not. Once again he realized he'd taken on too much blame for what had taken place inside his home.

He opened the box of checkers. "Red or black?"

Twenty-Seven

Trying to remember all the right steps again, Cara hitched Rosie to the carriage, glad the old horse was back in good form. Birds flittered among the bare tree branches, singing loudly and exclaiming in their own way that spring had finally arrived.

"Just us, huh, Mom?" Lori stepped from one bale of hay to the next.

She and Lori had their coats buttoned tight and gloves on, but with April arriving in two days, the sunny skies and midforty temps had most folks moving about freely again.

"Yes, sweetie, this trip is just for us."

" 'Cause we're gonna talk. Right?"

"Yes." If Cara had known her daughter would get so excited to travel with just her, she'd have done it sooner.

"And we're gonna surprise 'From."

"I think so."

He might not be fully surprised since it was a Friday afternoon and he had to work late. She'd gone to see him a few times in the past when this happened. But she had packed her and Lori an overnight bag, so that would surprise him. Although she wasn't sure where they'd stay. Maybe his place and he could spend the night at his Daed's.

"I brought my story to show him, the one the teacher gave me an A plus on *and* a smiley face."

Cara chuckled. Teachers had so much power over children, and Cara didn't regret letting Lori leave public school to begin at the local Amish school. "Okay, grab your stuff and hop in."

Lori quickly did so, and they were on their way. Lori loved her Amish school and friends. But after being raised a New Yorker and now living among the Amish, her daughter didn't really fit in anywhere.

Neither did Cara, but she was a big girl and used to never fitting in. After her mother died and she entered foster care, she'd been treated like she had leprosy by a lot of the children at school. Even in foster care most of the kids had siblings they went to school with, and they stuck together. She'd slowly grown to despise those who had someone around with the same DNA. It seemed to be an invisible bond that everyone shared with someone—everyone but her.

Truth was, that's why she'd avoided connecting with her mama's family. They all had each other, and her insecurity kept stirring old resentments and fears. She hadn't known that, not until she read a passage in her mother's Bible this morning. Something about…it is not the natural children who are God's children, but it is the children of the promise who are…

It made her realize that, in a way, she was a promise to her mother's family. Her mother had promised to bring her back so her great-grandmother could raise her. Her mama died before that happened, but Ada had been praying for Cara all these years, and a hidden message inside Cara's mother's journal led her here. That was a promise of sorts, wasn't it? And God's promise to accept all those who came to Him also made her a part of this family—a quirky family to be sure with their strict codes of behavior and dress, but they were her family, and she was theirs.

"Lori, honey, remember when you were drawing in my mother's diary and discovered the name Dry Lake, Pennsylvania, had been written in it invisibly?"

She nodded. "We were at that bus station, and I sketched over a blank spot, and an address showed up."

"Yes, that's right. It led us here, and at first we lived in that barn."

"That's where I got Better Days. He was so small and furry and got milk from his mom. Remember?"

"Yes." The thought of it made her eyes burn with tears. God had been so faithful to lead them out of a stalker's grip and into Ephraim's arms—but it'd been a rough journey. "My mom used to live in Dry Lake."

"She did?"

"Yes, and she had brothers, several of them."

"Ephraim's got sisters, more than several."

"My mom's brothers are my uncles and your great-uncles." Cara began trying to piece things together for Lori. Until recently, as long as Lori had food and her mom, she took life as it came. Maybe that was Cara's fault, always running from a stalker and never able to tell her daughter why they had to uproot in the middle of the night or why she had to constantly change jobs and move to a worse apartment than the one before. Or maybe it was a blessing from God, one that had made Cara's life bearable.

She took the long route to Ephraim's so she could go up his lengthy back driveway. She looked down at her daughter, still too young to understand the complexities of family, but now Lori knew they had some roots. And Cara had been the one to tell her, not anyone else in the community. For all the frustrating rules of the Amish, she loved the heart of her people—most of them, anyway.

Her people.

Once on Ephraim's dirt drive, she brought the rig to a stop. "Do you want to drive the rig to Ephraim's?"

"Ya!"

Cara passed her the reins. The fields on each side of them were brown with a few patches of snow still clinging to the earth. An amber and purple glow covered them like a dome as the sun moved toward the horizon. Crows squawked while digging at dried vegetation. Gratefulness kept filling her until she felt like she might pop.

"Pull the reins back gently and say 'whoa.'"

Lori did as she said, tossed the reins at her the moment the horse stopped, and jumped down. "'From!" Her daughter took off running. "I drove the buggy!"

Ephraim came out of the shop and caught Lori before she plowed into him. He swung her through the air, and she was on his hip, deep in conversation, by the time Cara had hitched the horse to a post and walked to them.

Lori brushed wisps of loose hair from her face. "And I got aunts and uncles, my mom said."

"Ya, you do." Ephraim kissed Lori's cheek and put her down. He moved to Cara and engulfed her in a hug. He didn't soon let go either, and Cara knew he'd been waiting for this. He drew a deep breath. "I love you."

"Well, duh." She took a step back. "We got a few things to get straight, mister."

He laughed. "*You* are going to straighten *me* out on something? This I gotta hear."

She walked into the shop. "What's your favorite tool?"

"Why?"

"Don't ask questions. Just answer."

"It's hard to choose, but I guess the table saw."

"Show me."

He walked over to it.

"It's not a hand-held thing."

"Thus the name table saw. You're not going to try to teach me how to use it, are you?"

"Shut up, 'From, and tell me how it works."

"It runs off an air compressor, which is run by a battery-operated generator."

"If you had to give it up for me, would you?"

"Ya."

"Would you miss it?"

"Ya."

"Would you return to it and lose me in the process?"

"No."

"Would knowing that keep you from missing it?"

"You and leaving your ways is not even comparable."

"Yes it is." She grabbed him by the suspenders. "I'm always going to miss some things about my previous life, but I've made my decision, and you can't keep doubting me because I like talking to Englischers about television or music…or, in words you understand, talking to them about how much I used to enjoy my table saw and what all they're making with their table saws."

"I don't like this parallel at all. If Englischers have and use table saws like they have and use televisions, I'll be run out of business."

She laughed. "I believe this is where God intended me to be. I'm not messing that up for anything *draus in da Welt.*"

"Out in the world." His smile seemed never ending. "Very good, Cara."

" 'From?" She tugged on his suspenders.

"Ya?"

"Stop doubting where I'll land. I've landed. I have a lot more adjustments to make, but I'll make them."

"Yes ma'am."

"Now shut up and kiss me."

"Yes ma'am."

"Eeeew." Lori screeched and covered her eyes.

Wearing the silky pajamas and housecoat Samantha had given her, Lena put the muffin tins in the sink to soak. As much as she loved teaching, she loved Saturdays and the freedom to start the day slowly and ease into it. She'd find a school district that would hire her, and she'd keep right on doing what she did best: teach. She'd made some mistakes. Who hadn't? But the complainers wanted something even they couldn't offer—exactness in all things all the time.

Her Daed stood. "Those were good muffins, Lena. Denki. I'm going out to get started."

She dried her hands and followed him out of the kitchen. He stopped at the coatrack and grabbed his straw hat. "You got plans for this morning?"

Lena slowly climbed the stairway. "Getting dressed, which I'm about to do, and then whiling away the hours like a single working woman should."

"You, dressed soon after dawn on a Saturday? I need to write this down in my journal." He smiled broadly and left the house.

Lena went to her room and slid out of her housecoat. The fleece throw blanket on her hope chest tempted her to wrap up in it and get a second cup of coffee. The wonderful thing about Saturday mornings was they were most often hers to do as she wanted. She grabbed the blanket, her Bible, the auction notebook, and a pen before heading back down the stairs.

She spread the stuff on the table, got another muffin and a cup of coffee, and relaxed against the kitchen chair. Wrapped in the fleece blanket, Lena opened her Bible.

She'd never enjoyed her weekends as much as she had recently. Not only did she have a new, two-week-old niece to adore; she had a good reason for spending a lot of time at Allen's. Helping Emily as much as possible after each birth was part of her life. And she stayed with her sisters and other sisters-in-law after they'd given birth too. But this time it'd become an unexpected pleasure. A fair amount of the evenings, Grey arrived in time for dinner, let Ivan go to sleep with Allen's children, and stayed until after midnight, playing games. Allen and Emily's enjoyment in his company ran deep. She'd been tempted numerous times to talk to him about the board's decision to let her go, but she hadn't. He didn't know about it, or he'd have apologized for their decision. But if Michael didn't want to burden Grey with the matter, she would respect that.

She tried to clear her mind of thoughts of Grey and focus on prayer and the Word. After a little while she nudged the open Bible to the side and grabbed the notebook for the auction. Trying to concentrate on her organizational lists spread out on the table was quite difficult. Grey filled her mind—his voice, eyes, sincerity, and even his rare grin. He was the only man she'd given ample opportunities to consider her, but he never did. When she'd gone to him to talk about attending public school, she'd hoped he would say, *Go, and when you're done, you'll be of a good age, and I'll be here waiting.* But he never showed an ounce of interest, not the romantic kind.

She traced her birthmark, wondering how he really saw her. He was past feeling sorry for her as he did when they were children, wasn't he? And what did he mean when he said he hid things while boldly looking at people? What would he have to hide, except his true thoughts concerning how he perceived people?

The question stung, especially since everything about him drew her. Would he ever see her as more than a friend? To marry a man like Grey would make up for all her years alone and be worth every unkind whisper she'd overheard about her being an old maid. Marriage happened young for Amish women. And courting even younger. If Grey slowly grew to love her, she might be twenty-eight or thirty before they were married. That'd be quite a wait, and she had no doubt that he would be well worth it, but could he ever care for her in that way?

That thought skewered her heart. She grabbed the bottle of her favorite lotion off the middle of the table and put a dollop in her hand. The creamy texture carried a mix of fragrant flowers as she spread it over her bare arms and hands. She drew a deep breath and tried to focus on the upcoming Picnic Basket Auction. She had to get her feelings for Grey in perspective. But it seemed that after all her years of pooling the love in her heart, waiting for a man to give it to, she now had no say over how she felt. He'd unknowingly opened the floodgates.

Elsie's rare quietness, beauty, and poise held Grey captive. When he could get past that loss, he might see that Lena had other things to offer, good and valuable things—like a powerful friendship, lots of laughter, and children. Years ago, before he married, Grey had said he wanted a lot of children. For whatever reason, Elsie only gave birth twice.

Since Lena wasn't graceful or gorgeous like Elsie, and Grey would always love Elsie more than her, maybe God would bless them in different ways, like them having a large and strong family. In her mind's eye, she could see his blue eyes and the joy she could bring to him—if he'd give her a chance.

Twenty-Eight

The new worker at the cabinetry shop, Christian, helped Grey load the buckboard with wood to take to Lennie's. April began tomorrow, and the warmth of spring had melted most of the snow. When Grey's Mamm asked to take Ivan to Lancaster for the day, Grey said yes, and he intended to use this free Saturday to make the window boxes he'd promised Lennie.

"Denki, Christian. I didn't realize you'd be here on a Saturday."

"Ya, me either." Christian's toothy grin came just short of laughter. "But Dwayne wanted to see inside the place, so I brought him over. What project are you working on today?"

"Just keeping a promise to the schoolteacher." Grey glanced toward the cabinetry shop, making sure Dwayne was still milling about inside. "Have you met Lena Kauffman yet?"

"I might have. I've met a lot of people in the two weeks I've been here."

"She's the schoolteacher."

Christian's brows knit. "Don't recall—"

Dwayne barreled out of the shop. "Sure you do," he said as if he'd been eavesdropping. "You saw her at church Sunday before last. The one with the stain on her face."

Christian looked at Grey and shook his head at Dwayne's crassness. "Ya. I talked to her for a spell. She's witty and nice looking."

Dwayne looked as if he'd just swallowed bad milk. "Are you crazy? She's not..." He stopped and then huffed. "Whatever."

"Her name is Lena." Grey slid another board into the wagon. "And as the local schoolteacher, she has a picnic basket auction every year. Single men bid on baskets filled with goods single women have made. Of course married women make baskets too, but only relatives—mostly husbands and children—bid on those."

"You're telling me she's not seeing anyone special?" Christian looked very interested in what he'd just learned.

"No," Grey answered, feeling unease grab his gut. Christian had been working with him and Ephraim for two weeks. Grey liked the man, and he'd thought about mentioning this to him before, but he kept getting a catch in his gut. He just figured he needed to know him better first. Today, as Grey looked forward to seeing Lennie, he'd wanted to ease some of her loneliness for Jonathan, but right now he wished he hadn't opened his mouth.

"So"—Christian closed the tailgate to the buckboard and fastened one side—"I could go to this auction, and if I won the bid on her basket, she and I could go on a date?"

"Ya." Grey fastened his side of the tailgate.

Dwayne crossed his arms. "You picking Christian out for her, or do you go around encouraging all the single guys to give her a chance?"

Grey had started this conversation at a really bad time. *If* he should've started it at all, he shouldn't have done so with Dwayne around. "I'm not picking anyone out. I just thought I'd mention the auction to the local newcomer."

Christian stayed focused on Grey. "She hasn't been to any singings since I've been here, 'cause I looked. So I figured she was taken."

Dwayne spat on the ground. "If you'd asked me, I'd told ya to..." He caught Grey's eye and then shrugged. "Never mind."

Grey didn't know what unkind remark Dwayne was going to say, but he had no more respect for Lennie than Peter did. Grey found it encouraging that Christian wasn't bothered one bit by what Dwayne thought.

Christian shifted, turning his back on Dwayne. "When is this picnic auction?"

With the rig loaded, Grey climbed up and took the reins in hand. Regardless of how he felt about starting this conversation, he couldn't undo what he'd begun. "The third Saturday in April."

Christian nodded. "In three weeks. Denki."

Grey slapped the reins without responding. The sick feeling in his gut didn't ease as he drove toward Lennie's, but he couldn't come up with what bothered him so much. It felt like jealousy, but that made no sense whatsoever. He pulled into her driveway and saw Israel in the side yard, applying stain to a freshly made coatrack. He hopped down and went to him. Lennie's dog came up to him, wagging her tail. He petted her. "Morning, Israel."

"Grey, what brings you out this way?"

"Mamm's got Ivan busy for today, so I'm using this time to keep a promise I made last fall. Lennie did some work for me in exchange for me making and mounting window boxes."

"You know, I remember her asking me to make her some of those a few years back." He chuckled. "I guess she gave up on me and came up with a new plan. She's inside somewhere. Go right on in. If you don't see her, just holler for her."

Grey went to the front door, tapped on it, and walked inside. He heard what sounded like a coffee cup chink against a plate in the kitchen, so he walked that way. When he caught a glimpse of Lennie, he stopped cold. The image engraved itself on his heart. Her long chestnut hair flowed. A fleece blanket had fallen off one shoulder, revealing a thin, bright pink strap and a lot of milky white skin. Clearly she hadn't dressed for the day, which meant she must still be in her sleeping clothes. He'd thought all Amish women wore white nightgowns from neck to ankle, but whatever she'd slept in, it wasn't a gown. Papers were spread out in front of her, and she had a pen in hand, looking every bit as gifted in intelligence as she was in beauty. Breakfast dishes and coffee cups still sat on the table.

Desire grabbed him. Lennie danced through him like she'd turned to vapor and entered his very being. How had he not realized what had been taking place within him since...since Christmas?

She took a deep breath and stretched, looking relaxed and absorbed in her own thoughts.

"Lennie."

She raised her eyes to his, and she seemed to awaken dreams he'd given up—dreams of unity, laughter, and hope with a woman. "Grey." Covering her bare shoulder with the blanket, she sat upright. "I...I didn't know you were coming."

He wrestled with guilt. What had he come here for, anyway—to build window boxes or to talk and laugh with Lennie? Right now, he knew the answer to that, but his wife had died in his arms not yet six months ago.

From her chair at the table, Lennie waved her hand. "Grey?"

He demanded his eyes move from her so that his lips could speak. "Uh, I...your Daed said for me to come in." He motioned toward the front door. "I brought the wood and saws to make window boxes."

"Ach, that's *wunderbaar*."

"Ya, I...I need to take measurements...of the window sashes."

"Sure. I'll get dressed. Have you eaten?"

He nodded.

"You can help yourself to a cup of coffee if you like. I'll just run upstairs."

When she stood, he noticed the long pink satiny pants peeking out from the wide gape in the blanket that ran down the front of her. She tugged at the fleece, trying to cover her immodesty. He lowered his head and stared at the floor as she hurried past him and up the stairs.

Her scent of lavender and roses and violets hung in the air. Trying to clear his head, he went outside and began unloading the wood. He wasn't ready to feel any sort of attraction for a woman. He had nothing left in him to give. Besides that, the feelings pouring into him were not who he and Lennie were. She'd been a constant in his life, but when did she seep past being a friend and sink into the deeper parts of his heart?

Thoughts of Elsie tore, and fear ate away. The idea of marriage terrified him. He never again wanted to give someone the power that came through the bonds of matrimony. But he hadn't known that until today. As hidden thoughts continued to reveal themselves, he understood one thing: he had nothing left to give to a marriage—the ideals of it, the struggles, the walls. He...couldn't.

Before he unloaded the last board, Lennie bounded out the front door—cape dress, black apron, and prayer Kapp in place. But none of that stopped his heart from pounding like crazy.

Nicky ran to her, and she knelt, patting her dog. "You might not know this because I kept it really quiet, but a couple of years back, right before school began, I injured my back and had to wear a plaster cast around my torso." She stood, looking rather serious. "It fit under my dress and wasn't noticeable at all. I had some tough eighth-grade students and wasn't sure how I'd corral them into being good for the year, especially since I couldn't move around too well. On that first day I had the windows and doors open, and a strong breeze kept flapping the ties to my prayer Kapp, so I took the stapler out and stapled the ties to my chest. Oddly enough, I had no trouble with discipline that year."

Grey held her gaze, feeling laughter stir as he watched humor dance in her eyes. "You're lying to me, Lennie Kauffman."

"Ya, but I made you smile." She interlaced her fingers and popped them.

He stared at her, awed at how she made him feel stronger than he was, rather than weaker. Surely she wanted no more from him than he could give—friendship. "You are something else."

"Ya, I am. So where do you want to start measuring first, upper-level windows or ground level?"

"I'm not very practiced at this, so let's start at the top. The extra distance will help hide the goof-ups from those looking at your home."

"Good thinking. Is that why my bedroom is on the top floor?"

He chuckled. The hours melted away too quickly as they worked together. She fixed them a quick lunch of leftovers from the night before, a beef stew and jalapeno cornbread, both of which were so good he asked for the recipe. Israel ate with them, and afterward he pitched in to help make window boxes. Grey wouldn't finish today, but a couple of hours next Saturday should do the trick. By evening they'd built, stained, and mounted six window planters. He still had to build two large ones for the front porch, but those would need extra care, so he'd get to them next week.

Lennie lined each wooden box with a mesh often used for screening porches. Then she passed him the stapler to secure them while she went to the greenhouse to get a bag of soil.

From inside the home at a ground-level window, he stapled the mesh in place.

Lennie came around the corner of the house. "Can you take this and fill them about three-fourths full of dirt?"

The top of her head was two feet below the bottom of the windowsill. He reached through the window, easily able to grab the top of the bag of soil as she held it up as high as she could. While he filled the box with dirt, she remained outside, using the squirt nozzle to pressure clean the screen that needed to go back in the window where he currently stood.

"Okay, these two are done." Grey shot one last staple into the mess. "Do you want us to put the screens back on now or wait until you've put flowers in them after the last frost?"

She gazed up at him, smudges of dirt on her face and stains on her dress and apron. Even with the heart of a woman, her countenance seemed like the carefree girl he'd always known her to be. "What's the prediction for the last frost this year?"

He set the bag of dirt in the windowsill and wiped his hands on his pants. "May fourth." Unable to see her, he leaned out the window. "Hey, where'd you..." His elbow knocked the bag of dirt over. He caught the bottom of it, but all that did was cause its contents to flow right on top of her.

She screamed. "Benjamin Graber, I'm telling!" She shook her head, dumping mounds of soil around her feet. He started laughing while she flapped her apron, ridding it of some dirt. She then used the underside of her apron to wipe off her face.

"Oh, ya, this is just really funny now." She glared at him. "You just wait until I tell." She cupped her hands around her mouth. "Daed!"

Her father came around the side of the house, took one glance at her, and applauded. She picked up the hose, wrapped her hands around the spray nozzle, and rotated it back and forth, pointing at her Daed and Grey.

Surely out of respect she wouldn't squirt her Daed, and Grey stood inside her home, with its polished floors, well-kept furniture, and white sheers, so he felt safe. "Ya? So just what are you going to—" Cold water smacked him in the face. While she continued soaking him, he slammed the window. She shifted and bombarded him from the next window right beside the first one. "Lennie!" Laughing too hard to catch his breath, he closed the next window.

The spray of water had caught potting soil off the top of the window planter and whisked it inside. Now soil and water covered a good bit of the floor, curtains, and cloth furniture. She stood outside with her hands on her hips and a thin layer of dark soil covering most of her. The waning rays of sunlight shone from behind her, making her appear to radiate white light. Those brief moments seemed to capture so many aspects of her nature—mischievous, playful, funny, innocent, and daring. "Never think you can predict a prankster, Grey," she yelled through the closed window.

Her Daed eased the hose from her and turned off the spigot. Grey opened the window.

"She has a motto." Israel studied his daughter, clearly amused. "I don't agree with it, but you see what it's like to try to control her."

"So what's this motto?"

Israel grabbed the screens to the window. "Things can be cleaned and replaced. Great moments cannot afford to be lost."

Lennie pointed at Grey's soaked clothing. "And that was a truly great moment."

Israel headed for his workshop. "I'll just put all the screens away until after she's planted flowers in those boxes."

Torn between who he should be as a recent widower, his raw doubts about marriage, and what he felt for Lennie, Grey knew why he was sorry he'd told Christian anything about her. He didn't want him seeing Lennie. He didn't want anyone having time alone with her.

Not anyone but him. Now how did that make any sense when he'd never have anything more to offer her than the friendship of their childhood?

Twenty-Nine

Deborah drove her rig toward town, passing stores and her bank before arriving at the restaurant. After tethering her horse to a hitching post, she walked across the parking lot. She pushed open the door and was greeted by the rattle of plates and waitresses carrying large trays of food. The smell of bacon and hamburgers added to Deborah's queasiness. She moved to an empty booth and slid to the middle of the seat.

The streetlights shone brightly against the blackness of night. A few people were walking along the sidewalk, cars stopped at the red light, and a couple of folks crossed the street. Town life had its own pace. Much more bustling than the farm she'd grown up on, and yet, compared to what Cara said New York City was like, it moved very slowly.

Slowly. That's how she'd let this mess with Mahlon drag out. He'd asked for a few days. It'd now been nine weeks. Nine weeks!

But she knew why she'd let it go on and on. Selfishness. That, and he'd written to his Mamm. The letter had made Ada so happy, so hopeful he might return, that Deborah couldn't find the strength to say anything to Mahlon that might cause him to leave. And for every week he'd stayed, she'd seen and understood more of who she was, what she wanted from life, and why she'd felt so drawn to him.

The bell on the restaurant jingled, and Mahlon walked in. His hazel eyes lit up as he walked to the booth. "Hi." He slid into his seat and stretched his hands over hers. "Thanks for coming again, Deb."

She stared at their entwined hands, hoping the right words came to her.

A waitress set a glass of ice water in front of her. Deborah freed her hands of his and took a sip, trying to settle her nerves. She hated how distant she'd been to Jonathan since the night he kissed her, but what else could she do? At least he'd been gone a fair amount lately with his blacksmith job. Right now he was staying several nights at a farm some twenty miles from here, shoeing a herd of horses.

Mahlon studied her—probably sizing her up and choosing his words.

As a long-distance truck driver, he hadn't been around all that much either. The absence of both men had given her time to think. When she did meet with Mahlon, he'd poured his heart out to her—promising her everything, including making Ada happy with a houseful of grandchildren.

She dipped her finger in the water and traced patterns with it on the table. Contrary to what she'd thought since Mahlon ran off, she did know him. And he knew her.

He wanted to give up his job as a truck driver and go through the steps to become a member of the Amish community in good standing again. He would return only to be shunned. Knowing that, she understood why he'd wanted time to talk to her before he made everyone else aware of his homecoming.

"I've done as you asked, Mahlon."

She'd listened to every word and taken time to think about them. It all made sense now. He'd felt trapped and overwhelmed. He was having panic attacks, but he couldn't say what he was feeling, in part because he didn't know what he was feeling or why. His Englischer friend had offered a way out, and in a state of depression, he'd jumped at it. Now that he was better, he regretted what he'd done. She'd listened. She'd heard. She'd made her decision.

"I sincerely understand why you left, but—"

"No. Don't say *but*. You…we need more time. It's just—"

"Mahlon!" she whispered loudly, elongating his name. Leaving as he did said so much more about him than he could bear to hear. She wouldn't share too much truth for fear of what it might do to him, but she was finished walking on eggshells for him. "It's time, Mahlon. I've kept your secret. I've listened. I've met with you. I've thought about all you've said until I can't stand to think about it anymore. You're not interested in letting me decide what I think. You want to make me see you exactly the way you've decided I should see you."

He stared at the table, unwilling to look at her. She hated that habit. He studied her intently when trying to read her, but otherwise he didn't look up. Truth was, the more time she spent with him, the more things she disliked about him. But Ada loved him, and because of that and because Deborah hurt for the issues he struggled with, she would remain kind and encouraging.

She took a deep breath, wishing he'd make this easier and knowing he wouldn't. "Now I need you to listen to me. Will you do that?"

"Sure. I'll do anything for you...for us." The positive words left his mouth, but dullness reflected in his eyes.

"You've spent so much of your life longing for what could have been. If only your Daed hadn't died. If only you hadn't seen the Twin Towers fall. If only you hadn't been born Amish. If only you could get free. You got free, Mahlon. And now you're thinking *if only* again. If only you could go back and undo. If only I was yours again. Your return isn't about you being in love with me. It's about who you are. I'm part of your new *if only* dream. I hope you return to the faith, Mahlon. Ada needs her only son in a way I can't fill. But...the truth is, I'm not in love with you, and what has died between us can never be revived, no matter how much time I give you."

Tears filled his eyes, and Deborah enveloped his hand in both of hers. He drew her hands to his lips. "How can you be so sure of yourself? I meant everything to you just a few months ago. We can get that back. I know you don't really trust that right now, but it's true."

According to the calendar, he'd been gone almost eight months before he began showing up here again. But it felt like years, based on what she'd learned. Deborah pulled her hands free of his and took a long drink of water. She'd said everything he needed to hear, but he wasn't listening. "Bye, Mahlon."

"You can't mean that."

"I'm sorry." She stood, and when he rose, she hugged him tightly. "You take care of you. And don't spend years wishing for what could have been if you hadn't left. Find what is and embrace it."

He looked confused and furious, but thankfully he didn't say anything. She started to leave and then remembered one more thing. "I won't keep any secrets for you from now on. If you want to tell your mother you're back before I do, I suggest you go see her tonight." She pulled the money out of her pocket that he'd given her since leaving Dry Lake. Laying it on the table, she felt like a piece of her soul had been given back to her. "Take care of yourself."

She hurried out the door and toward her rig, keeping her eyes on the rugged pothole-filled parking lot. Grief for hurting and disappointing him hovered over her. But she'd been fair. She'd listened and thought and prayed and considered. She hated being unable to help him, but she had no doubts she'd done the right thing for herself.

She glanced up at her buggy.

Jonathan.

He stood under the street lamp directly in front of her rig. He had no smile or warmth. "I got done earlier than expected, and Ada said you'd gone to town." He scoffed. "I wondered what would make you come to town alone after dark, so I came looking. Just wanted to make sure you got home safely."

She cringed at the idea of him seeing them through the plate glass window. "Jonathan, it's—"

He jerked open the buggy door. "Don't talk to me right now. Just get in."

She climbed in the passenger's side. A shudder ran through her when he got in and slammed the door. "I can—"

"How long has he been back?"

"Jonathan, would you please lis—"

"How long?" he interrupted.

She'd never seen him angry. His face held no expression, but the tautness of it seemed as unyielding as iron.

"Two months."

"Our own people think that if you have any interest in me, it's only because you can't have him. They think I'm a fool to be willing to accept whatever part of your heart Mahlon didn't take with him. The guys call it 'Mahlon's leftovers.'"

His insult slapped her, and she gasped. "That's mean, Jonathan."

"I'm telling you how it is for me. And I was willing to ignore everyone because I thought they didn't understand. How many times have you two met?"

"There's more to it than that. Will you listen?"

"Can't. Answer my questions first. How many times, Deborah?"

"Six. But he asked me not to say anything for—"

"Mahlon asked and you gave. That absolutely should not surprise me, and yet—"

"Let me explain!" she interrupted.

"More than angry, I'm disappointed. To see Mahlon secretly for any reason— I don't need to hear your explanations for that. You aren't who I thought you were." He stopped in front of Ada's House. "I'll put your horse and rig away before I leave."

She couldn't believe he'd dismissed her without even listening.

He got out, went around the buggy, and opened her door. He motioned for her to get out.

She didn't. "I know I was wrong."

"Good. Then we agree." He stared at her. "Don't make this any harder than it has to be. Not telling me was the same as lying. I don't need to know any more than that. Will he return? Will you give him another chance? Is he asking you to leave with him? Is he just meeting to be friends?" Jonathan shook his head. "It doesn't matter. The only thing that matters is that you lied. I've played second fiddle to him all my life where you're concerned, only then I knew it. This time you cheated me of the right to decide."

Cheated him?

Getting out of the buggy, she found herself almost toe-to-toe with him. She'd been so sure that what she'd done by seeing Mahlon secretly was keep her word to him while discovering her own thoughts and heart. And she'd done her best to get him to rejoin the faith, regardless of whether she took him back.

"I…I didn't see it as cheating… He asked and…"

"Well, next time he asks, I won't be around to mind whether you do his bidding." He sidestepped her and got into the buggy.

"Jon, I…I told him tonight I wouldn't see him anymore, and I wouldn't keep his secret any longer either."

"Do you actually think that's supposed to make this any better? You deceived me while giving him every chance. And you think that's a consolation? You have to be kidding yourself, Deborah."

She'd thought Mahlon abandoning her without warning was the most heart-wrenching experience she would ever go through. That didn't compare to the ache of losing Jonathan by her own actions.

Lena poured Jonathan a cup of coffee. "Can I tell you what I think?"

He took the mug from her. "No."

She set the pot on the stove and pulled a pan of muffins out of the oven. He'd jolted her out of bed over an hour ago. Even at seven o'clock, she'd been sound asleep. Had he forgotten how much she loved slow moving Saturday mornings? It seemed a reasonable perk to being unwed and childless.

They'd been talking for over an hour, and yet he held firm to his unwillingness to listen to reason. She'd seen him angry a few other times, and when he got this way, he stayed there. He'd peppered her with questions, wanting to know if Deborah had told her about Mahlon's return. Thankfully Deborah hadn't said a word to her, or Jonathan would be angry at her too. Most of his questions were aimed at trying to figure out if he knew Deborah at all.

Lena spread a kitchen towel over the bottom of a large bowl. "Deborah's five years younger than you and three years younger than me. She's cared about and tried to take care of Mahlon most of her life. Maybe she just got caught in a situation she didn't know how to handle."

"Do you think she still loves him?"

She dumped the muffins into the bowl and set them on the table. "I'm sure you could learn the answer to that if you'd talk to her." She held the container of food in front of him and placed her hand on his shoulder. "Eat."

He looked up at her. "In other words, fill my mouth and shut up."

She heard the front door open and her Daed's voice as he talked to Nicky.

"Exactly." She patted his shoulder.

Instead of her Daed entering the kitchen, Grey did. He looked from her to Jonathan.

Her Daed walked in after Grey. "I told you I thought she had company in here." He smiled. "How ya doing, Jonathan?"

"Good, Israel. You?"

Daed stole a muffin. "Better now."

Grey removed his hat. "I came to finish the job I started last Saturday."

Her Daed motioned. "Not before a cup of coffee. Come. Sit."

His silvery blue eyes held an unfamiliar look as he studied her. Was it possible he cared to some small degree and Jonathan being here bothered him, or did her hopes have her imagining nonsense? She'd told him months ago about missing Jonathan, but she had been clear he had never been a boyfriend or anything. Hadn't she? In the morning light, with Grey's presence filling the room, she couldn't recall.

"No, but denki." Grey brushed the inside rim of his hat against his pant leg. "I just wanted to warn Lena I was here. I'll be working outside that window mostly." He pointed to the kitchen window. "It won't take long. I made the boxes already. I didn't have any mesh, but all I need to do is add that and hang them." He said his good-byes and went outside.

He'd come inside with her Daed, not chancing another episode like they'd had last week. And he'd come to warn her he'd be on the porch and easily able to see inside. A gentleman, to be sure.

But as soon as she connected all those thoughts, a sensation inside her heart tugged, as if cautioning her that she didn't really know all there was to know about this man. It was a ridiculous feeling. Lena sat and stirred her coffee while trying to control her impulse to run after him and say things she shouldn't. Jonathan and her Daed talked about the weather and hunting for pheasants. If she went to Grey and said Jonathan was just a friend, would she totally embarrass herself?

Very likely so.

She could at least speak to him for a bit, maybe hint that Jonathan was just a friend. She stood. "I'll be back in a minute."

Her Daed grabbed a pair of work gloves off a shelf near the side door and passed them to her. "He left these last time. And he might think that mesh is in the shed instead of in the greenhouse."

"I'll tell him." With the gloves in hand, Lena hurried out the kitchen door. When she saw the door to the greenhouse open, she went inside. The glow of sunlight through the dome, the metal braces running an arc from one side to the other, the aroma of dirt, and the disarray of bags of soil, pots, and seedlings were a familiar mixture she cherished. She'd been thirteen and he eighteen the last time he'd entered her sanctuary. With scissors in hand, Grey had the bolt of screen spread over a rather messy bench. "I see you found it."

His movements stopped for a moment, but then he nodded without looking up.

"I…I figured you'd return to finish the job before planting time."

He made the last snip, freeing one good-sized piece of mesh from its bolt. "Ya, you'll be ready to plant flowers as soon as the first frost is past."

She held the gloves up. "Daed went with me to Allen's Saturday night. He brought these to give to you, but you never came by."

He put the bolt in the corner where he'd found it. "It's time I stay closer to home than I have been."

"He said there needs to be a bridge, and he'd have walked them over."

Grey flounced the mesh. "I better get done and be on my way."

Lena held the gloves out to him. When he grabbed them, she didn't let go. "I…think I may have left you with the wrong impression. See, Jonathan and I…well…he's just here to talk about his love life. That's what friends do."

"I think it's good you've remained friends."

"He's never been anything else. I know I've mentioned that I missed him before, but only because we've always hung out, and he's been seeing someone. Did I tell you that?"

Relief, if it was relief, flickered through his eyes. Whatever she'd seen, it lasted only a few moments. "It's too soon, Lennie."

"Oh…of…of course…I didn't mean that you felt…anything for me." Her cheeks burned with embarrassment, and she released the gloves.

He moved toward the door. Afraid it might be months before she got another quiet moment alone with him, she couldn't just let him walk out without telling him how she felt. She bolted in front of him, and he stopped abruptly.

"I…I'll…wait." Her heart pounded like crazy as she dared to cross all lines of common sense. "I won't say anything to anyone. Not a hint. And I know it's too soon for you to…really care, but if you think you might… one day…I…I'll wait…if you…want…"

He said nothing, and she couldn't read him. Her pulse raced as she stood before him so very vulnerable, and she felt lightheaded. When he didn't smile or nod, she knew she'd misread him earlier. His feelings did not match hers. Again.

She forced a smile. "Okay." Tears blurred her sight. "I…saw things I wanted to see. I'm sorry. I…guess I had to make a fool of myself over someone sooner or later. I trust you'll keep this between us."

He stared at the dirt floor. "Of course."

Desperate to be alone, Lena turned to go. He caught her by the hand, so gently that at first she thought she'd brushed a plant. Upon glancing down, she realized he held her hand.

He studied her. "I…I'm sorry, Lennie."

She tried to gain composure, but tears fell freely. "It's not your fault. I…I should've known."

She pulled free and hurried outside. Covering her birthmark, she went inside and straight to her room. She'd ruined everything—thrown her dignity down a well, embarrassed Grey, and ended all easygoing friendship between them. What a fool. She caught a glimpse of herself in the mirror. Her birthmark had flushed a shade darker and seemed to creep farther up her cheek, like a stamped reminder of who she really was.

Thirty

Deborah stood inside the walk-in pantry with a goal—to reorganize it. It's not what she should be doing. She needed to tell Ada the truth. Her conscience nudged, but it would hurt Ada so badly to know that her son was close by, or at least had been close by, and he hadn't bothered to come see her. It'd already been a week since Deborah had met Mahlon at the restaurant for the last time.

The spring rains pattered against the roof, windows, and siding. Not one customer had knocked on the door all day. It seemed as if God Himself were arranging time for Deborah to break the news to Ada.

Ada came to the pantry door and motioned to the shelves. "They look much like they did thirty minutes ago." She cupped her hand under Deborah's chin. "And you look much like a woman with a broken heart. Want to talk?"

"I don't want to. If...if I could keep it from you forever, I would."

Ada put her arm around Deborah. "Kumm, we've grown too close to hide truths from each other, no matter how painful they are."

Deborah held out a chair for Ada. "You sit. I'll fix us some tea."

Ada tilted her head, concern filling her eyes. Deborah added fresh water to the kettle, hoping she could hide from Ada many of her thoughts and feelings about Mahlon.

He'd taken up Deborah's time and energy, ruined what she had with Jonathan, and then disappeared, leaving her to pick up the pieces. Served her right, she supposed. Mahlon was who he was, and she'd dared to give him the benefit of the doubt, thinking she could make a difference in his choices. But it had never worked in the past, so why had she thought this time would be any different?

Mahlon's leftovers.

Maybe that had been true at first but no longer. And Jonathan shouldn't have said that to her, but it did help her see how her actions made Jonathan look if she had been seen with Mahlon.

She set two mugs on the table before dipping the tea-ball infusers into the canister of fresh tea leaves. Deborah didn't want Ada to know that Mahlon's selfishness in simply abandoning them had ended up setting Deborah free. Inside his quiet ways there stirred constant doubt and drama. He'd have a few days or weeks of accepting his circumstances with gratefulness, and then his turmoil would begin again. She saw that clearly now, and she thanked God she'd been spared from marrying him.

"The water's on to heat. And the tea balls are prepared. Come sit." Ada pulled out a chair and waited.

Deborah had stalled for as long as she could. "I don't know how to cushion what needs to be said."

"Just say it, child. Jonathan hasn't been here much lately. Are you at odds with my nephew and fear what that will do to our business?"

She missed Jonathan, but she had no concerns about the business. They had the money to hire someone to fill in for him as needed. "Mahlon returned."

Ada grabbed her hands. "Is he well?"

"Ya. I've met with him. He asked me not to say anything, so I didn't. But…I don't know where he is now, if he's living in Hope Crossing or moved on. He…he…said he wanted to rejoin the faith…if I'd have him."

Tears trailed Ada's cheeks. "My son wants to return?"

"I…I'm so sorry, Ada."

Confusion filled her eyes. "Sorry?"

Deborah fought tears. Ada had only heard that her son hoped to

rejoin the faith. "I tried to encourage him to return to the fold or at least..."
How could she tell Ada she'd all but begged him to visit her? "The last I
saw him was a week ago. I...fear he's moved on again."

"You met with him, had planned visits?"

The kettle began to whistle. Deborah went to the stove and turned off
the flame. "I did."

"What did he say?"

Deborah stood near her, pouring hot water in a mug. "He...wanted
things I can't give him, Ada. I...I'm sorry."

Ada covered her face and cried. As a storm of tears rolled over her
friend, Deborah moved back to the kitchen chair, feeling helpless.

"Was I such an awful Mamm he couldn't make himself come see me?"

"It's not you, Ada, just like he didn't leave me because of me."

"But he came back for you, right?"

Deborah nodded. "And he said he'd return to both of us and to the
faith if I'd still marry him."

Ada sobbed. After catching her breath, she smacked the tabletop.
"That boy! He should not have asked such a thing of you."

Deborah choked back tears. "I wish I could have done this for you,
Ada."

"I'd not have let you!" Ada stood and engulfed Deborah in a hug. "I
pray he returns. I do." She sobbed. "But I will not give you up to marry a
man who is so unsure of what he wants. Even you don't have the power to
make him happy. But you have it in you to be content and enjoy life, ya?"

"I don't seem to be very good at it, but I...I think so."

"That's not true, Deborah. You left your home in Dry Lake and
moved in with me because you have a good heart. We've had sadness this
year, but even then you kept working your way toward contentedness.
You're grateful too."

"And wimpy."

"Not wimpy. Gentle. Unkindness breaks your heart, leaving you addled for a while. But it is no surprise Mahlon found the world to be a cold place without you. And he knows the Old Ways are not enough unless you are by his side. I used to fear he'd come to his senses after he'd ruined his chance with you. My fears have come true, but he made his choice. Of course he changed his mind, but now you've made up yours."

"Jonathan saw me with Mahlon, and he's furious with me."

"You care for my nephew then?"

"I…I'm sorry. I know it's—"

"You owe me no apology. I take no offense, Deborah. Do you care for him?"

A glimmer of hurt showed in Ada's eyes, but Deborah trusted that their love would see them through the fresh damage Mahlon had heaped on them. She would turn twenty-two next month, and she finally knew what she wanted out of life: to trust God no matter what, to know herself, and to enjoy every piece of life possible—come floods or drought or anything in between.

And she wanted to earn Jonathan's respect back.

And then his love.

"Ya."

"He's more like Mahlon's Daed than Mahlon. My husband, Gerald, God rest his soul, was a good and faithful man. Patient and kind. And so much fun. He was steady and a blessing." She smiled. "Most of the time, anyway. But when he got mad, ach, there was no reasoning with him."

"Jonathan wouldn't even listen."

Ada sat. "Fix yourself a cup of tea and come sit. I'll tell you how to get him to listen."

Grey stopped his horse at the hitching post beside the cemetery. A white split-rail fence surrounded it. He opened the gate and went inside. Rays of light poured through the thick white clouds. He went to his wife's grave site, removed his hat, and stared at the lush green grass.

The minutes ticked by. Birds sang. The aroma of spring surrounded him. The gift of life stared at him.

He cleared his throat. "I...I can't keep carrying the guilt for both of us. *We* made a mess of our marriage. We had our chance, Elsie. I tried. You know I did. After what we went through, the idea of marriage seemed too much to even think about again, but marriage isn't scary. Walls and lies and deceit are. It doesn't have to be that way, especially if friendship is the biggest part."

He shifted, glad this cemetery was out of view of the road as he spoke to the earth covering his wife's remains. "Maybe I shouldn't be ready to care for any woman, but I do. And I can't find hope for the future while wallowing in the guilt of the past. It wasn't all me. I lost sight of that after you...passed from this life."

What was it about a place that drew loved ones when it held only the remains of a physical body? He'd never come here and talked before today. But he had to get free of the guilt and fear that ate at him night and day.

Worse than those things, because of his sense of loyalty to Elsie and his fear of falling in love, he'd hurt Lennie. She'd shared her heart with him a week ago, and he'd let her believe he didn't care for her.

He closed his eyes. The air itself seemed to carry peace, and he drew a deep breath. Feeling as if he'd finally laid down the weight of both his and Elsie's guilt, he crouched and touched the grass over her burial spot. "I'm glad you're at peace, Elsie."

After a moment he went to his carriage. Rather than going home, he went by Lennie's. But Israel said she was at Allen's for the evening.

He tapped on the door. Allen opened it. "Hey, it's been a while since you were here on a Friday night. I didn't expect you to come by." He motioned. "Kumm."

Lennie stood at the sink, washing dishes. Some of the same notes he'd seen spread out on her kitchen table were now on Allen's table. All the children but the baby were in the living room, playing with a child-sized kitchen and eating ice cream.

Lennie looked up as if making sure he was okay. "Hi."

Taken aback, he barely managed a nod. He didn't know what he'd expected, but her reaction assured him that her heart of friendship overrode any other feelings taking place between them.

Emily waved the spoon in her hand before dipping it into the bowl in front of her. "Evening, Grey."

"Emily." He removed his hat. "I…I came to talk to Lennie."

"Ah, the Picnic Basket Auction is tomorrow." Allen took a seat at the table. "Has she roped you into helping with something on that project too? You might as well get used to being asked and learn how to say no. She's always busy with one project or another because she has no love life."

"Allen, please." Lennie dried her hands before glancing to Grey. "I think we've got everything settled. No need to discuss anything else."

She sounded kind and matter-of-fact.

Allen yawned. "Never even been on a date, that treasure hasn't, and at this rate she never will."

"Oh, she will all right." Emily smacked her husband's shoulder.

Never? Grey couldn't believe that, but he wouldn't ask.

"Allen." Lennie waited until he looked at her. "Shut up."

"I'm not trying to pick on you. I just think you need to try a little harder. After all your prep for running the Picnic Basket Auction tomorrow, did you fix a basket for someone to bid on?"

"It's the rules. If a woman over the age of seventeen walks into the schoolhouse, she must have a basket to auction off."

"Gut." Allen tossed a peanut into his mouth.

Grey fidgeted with his hat. "Lennie, can we talk?"

She picked up several papers and a pencil. "I really have a lot I need to get done for tomorrow."

Emily studied him for a moment. Then she looked at Lennie before standing and tugging on her husband's sleeve.

"What?" Allen mumbled.

"I need some help bathing the little ones. They have ice cream all over themselves."

"I thought Lennie was going to help with that."

"She has enough to do, and I just volunteered you."

He shrugged. "I'll be a while. Make yourself at home, Grey."

Waiting on Emily and Allen to get the children upstairs, Grey studied Lennie. She folded her arms, looking resigned to the discomfort he was causing.

The Amish traditions of courting or dating made it easy for young people to keep who they were seeing a complete secret. Grey had always assumed Lennie handled her private life discreetly. And maybe she did. Maybe Allen just didn't know.

As voices faded, she took a seat at the head of the table. "Look, Grey, I know you're sorry for what happened and that you feel bad about it. I appreciate your kindness, but I really don't need you coming here to explain it all more carefully."

Hoping the right words came to him, he placed his hat on the table in front of him and sat near her. "Lennie…I didn't come here for that reason."

The muffled sounds of water running in a tub and children prattling filled the room. He couldn't manage to say anything more.

She gathered some of the papers. "What then?"

"I…I…" He fidgeted with the rim of his hat. "I think I need a minute inside that circle of peace."

She laid the papers down and really looked at him for the first time. "You…have someone."

"No. What would make you say that?"

"If you're asking for pardon while you tell me a difficult truth, I just assumed…"

He put his hands over hers. "Lennie, could you stop jumping to the wrong conclusion for just a minute? See...I..." He shook his head. "Sorry. I'm really not very good at this."

"I can see that." She slid her hands free of his. "They're words, Grey. You choose them in your mind, and then you share them."

Her straightforwardness made him smile. "You were so open about how you feel toward me and what you were thinking. I wasn't ready to admit how I felt. You...you didn't read me wrong."

Disappointment reflected in her eyes. "Sorry, Grey, but I don't believe you. You're just saying that because you're a really nice guy."

"I know how I feel...how I felt before you came to me in the greenhouse."

Her eyes grew large, but it wasn't with excitement. It was wariness.

"You're not going to believe me?"

"I...I want to...of course."

"Good. Then it's settled." He angled his head, studying her. "Or is it?"

A slow, beautiful smile radiated from her. "I suppose it is, but it'll take months before it sinks in."

"Time we have. Actually we've got a lot of it ahead of us, and I know you said you'd wait, but maybe you should consider seeing other men— just to be sure your feelings...you know... aren't out of pity."

"You think *I* feel sorry for *you*?" She laughed. "Surely you can't believe that at twenty-four years old I don't know the difference between love and sympathy. I've waited a lifetime. And you should trust that I know what I want."

His eyes moved over every inch of her face. "I like the way you argue." He squeezed her hand.

"Are you sure you're sure?"

"You were better at accepting that I didn't care than you are at believing that I do."

Her hand eased to her birthmark, an unconscious move he'd bet. "I…I suppose I am."

He eased her hand away and caressed the mark. He ran his fingers down her neck, following the birthmark. When her eyes met his, he steadied his breathing. Gently guiding her closer, he breathed in the scent of lavender and roses. He kissed her cheek and brushed his lips across her skin until he reached her lips. Everything about her tender movements, including caressing his beard, spoke of being at ease with him. After receiving a kiss he'd never forget, he put some space between them.

Her eyes were closed. *"Duh net schtobbe."*

As she whispered *do not stop,* he wished the journey ahead of them wasn't such a long one. He had to be much more careful than they were being right now. Her reputation could easily be ruined if they didn't walk pure for at least another year. He placed his fingers under her chin, willing her to look at him.

"Lennie, we can't be careless. It doesn't matter how we feel. I'm still required to continue my period of mourning before I can court you or before anyone can know about us."

She shifted, sitting up straighter. "Ya. You're right." She ran her fingers over her lips. "That was amazing."

She was absolutely right about that. "We won't be able to see each other much. I can't come to your place just to visit you, and we can't go anywhere together. We can meet here some, but even that will have to slow down, or after our relationship is public, we'll be accused of using Allen's place in an inappropriate way."

"Your kiss was better than perfect. Did…I do it right?"

She had a way about her that fit him so perfectly. How had he never known that? "Was that your first kiss?"

She nodded. "And well, well worth waiting for."

A bump near the top of the stairs startled both of them. Moving his chair slightly, he straightened and put more distance between them.

She reached under the table and held his hand. "I know the period of mourning and propriety puts restraints on you. I don't mind…too much."

"It'll take being very careful and all of that time to win Allen's approval."

She frowned at him. "Why would he not approve?"

"Lennie?" The thumping sound of Allen coming down the stairs made Lennie jolt.

"Build us a bridge between your place and Allen's. Then you can walk over for a few minutes here and there, or come over while we're outside in the spring. Emily and I could bring over a dish of food. That way your visits don't have to be so formal or visible for others in the community to even notice."

Grey held on to her fingers for a moment longer. "I'll build us a bridge…in every way possible."

She grabbed her notebook and pencil. "What does *every way possible* mean?"

Allen walked into the kitchen and motioned Grey toward the sofa. "She's got work to do, and the living room is much more comfortable."

Grey rose, wishing they had time to really talk but at peace with the commitment between them. How had love for Lennie grown such deep roots in such a short time?

Thirty-One

Deborah stopped the carriage in front of Jonathan's home. She, Ada, and Cara had been at the school helping Lena set up for today, but as the morning wore on, she grew concerned that Jonathan might not come to the auction. Armed with Ada's sage advice, Deborah walked across the gravel drive and into his shop.

Jonathan glanced up, and a soft, hesitant smile drew her before he turned away, concealing his heart from hers. He continued working as if she weren't there. She'd not seen him in his leather apron and rawhide gloves in a long time. The apron was marred and stained, and his face had smudges of black, but those things only added to his rugged, handsome appearance. With a sturdy pair of tongs, he moved the horseshoe from the forge to the anvil. Still clutching the tongs with one hand, he began hammering, molding the metal to his will.

"Jon?"

He studied her for a moment before returning his focus to pounding the metal.

His Daed stepped out from a stall. "Well, hello, Deborah. We don't see you in these parts much anymore. You here for the auction?"

"Ya. I came to see Jonathan for a minute first." She waited, but Jonathan didn't stop pounding on the horseshoe. "I need to say a few things, and I think it's reasonable to ask you to hear me." She spoke above the noise.

He finally nodded. His Daed walked over to him and took the tongs and hammer. Jonathan removed his apron and walked outside with Deborah. She'd hoped they would go for a real walk, but he escorted her to the carriage and opened the door.

Although tempted to tell him he was being ridiculous and stubborn, she held on to Ada's advice. "From your perspective, you have every right to end our relationship. And I was wrong but not as wrong as you think."

"Wrong enough."

"I wanted time to think for myself. I did a selfish thing. I know that. I wanted to form my own opinion. Even more than that, I needed time to try to convince him to treat Ada right whether he returns to our faith or not. I didn't succeed, but I know I tried my best. And now we both know that I wouldn't have Mahlon back under any circumstances."

"So he did return to win you again."

Deborah climbed into the buggy. "He did. He said all the sweet, flowery things he's so capable of saying, including how he would rejoin the faith and how he wanted my help in giving grandchildren to Ada."

"That's some heavy temptation he tossed your way."

"No. It carried no temptation, although I expected it to." She drew a breath. "I would greatly appreciate your keeping what I've told you just between us. If he does decide to return and rejoin the faith, I don't want anyone else knowing what I just shared."

"Then you're still protecting him."

"I'm protecting us from being gossips and displeasing God. No part of me answers to Mahlon, but I do pray he finds his way. Hear me on this, Jon—I whisper thanks to God, even in my sleep, that I'm free of my promise to marry him."

He remained unmoving until a slow, easy smile radiated from him.

She took the reins in hand. "I have a picnic basket chock-full of your favorite foods. It'd be a shame if my Daed were the one to win the bid. It starts in twenty minutes. For years you've bought Lena's basket because she's your friend. If you refuse to forgive me as your girlfriend, I hope you will at least remain my friend."

He looked down at his clothing. "Twenty minutes?"

"Wear what you have on. I'm only picky about what's inside a man's heart. Nothing else matters." She studied the strength in his shoulders and arms and smiled. "Well, nothing else matters more than that." She slapped the reins against the horse's back, hoping that she'd begun regaining his respect and that he'd at least be her friend again.

Grey stood in the back of the schoolroom, watching as Lennie spiced up the bidding with quips and humor and handed baskets to the auctioneer. There were times when she snatched the gavel and the battery-powered microphone from the auctioneer and managed to get twice the bid. Ivan sat next to Allen's oldest son. People came in and out freely, buying homemade lemonade and slices of cake from tables set up outside. All of today's proceeds would go into the teacher's fund.

As he watched Lennie, he could feel her lips against his. Since it'd been a first for her, he would have expected her to be self-conscious and unsure. She had no shyness. He liked that. But she did have insecurity about her looks. If he had the power to do it, he intended to scrub that lie out of her life even if it took years. He wished he were free to court her, free to treat her as she deserved. They'd already ventured past correctness for him as a widower. The only thing they hadn't done was make a public admission of it.

He couldn't cross that line. Lennie's reputation would be stained for a long, long time, because becoming involved with someone during their period of mourning was equal to adultery in the sight of many.

Grey jolted when Michael spoke to him. "I didn't expect to see you here today."

Too distracted to have a response, Grey simply shook his father-in-law's hand.

Michael blinked, as if keeping tears away. "I wouldn't have asked it of you, but it's right for all the members of the school board to be here. As chairman of it, I knew Dora and I needed to be here. Although Lena's…" Michael's voice softened as he said Lena's name, and Grey recognized the serious tone.

"She's what?"

Michael shook his head. "You haven't been coming to the meetings. When you're ready, we need to discuss what's going on."

"Michael Blank," Lennie called, "are you paying attention to the teacher?"

The room tittered with laughter.

Michael turned. "Ya, Teacher Lena, I heard every word you said." Michael winked at Grey.

"Well, now that's good. Did you wish to make the next bid on your wife's basket?"

Michael rubbed the back of his neck, clearly comfortable going along with Lennie's harassment. "Uh, the last bid was…"

"Fifty dollars," Lennie assured him.

"Fifty…" His eyes grew large. "I bid sixty."

"Sold!" Lennie exclaimed.

The room broke into laughter.

The auctioneer hit the gavel against his podium. "The first and last bid on Dora Blank's basket is sixty dollars."

Lennie motioned for him to take his seat.

Michael played along, lowering his head like a young man in trouble as he moved to the front of the room to sit beside his wife.

"Anyone else care to talk while the bidding is going on?" Lennie asked.

"Not me," Michael said. "I'm now penniless and can't afford to say a word."

Grey chuckled. Lennie could charm a snake right out of its skin when in this schoolroom. But the school board meetings never flowed as easily. Her nontraditional ways managed to get someone's hackles up all too often. And she'd stand her ground as if the Old Ways needed amending. He'd like to alter them himself about now and be free to see her at will. He looked around and saw Christian watching Lennie, probably ready to bid on her basket when it became available. Dwayne sat beside him.

Grey didn't like the idea of standing by while Christian won the bid and a date with Lennie. Her Daed or brothers might be willing to bid, but they'd drop out when a single man showed interest. He'd wanted to ask Allen to win the bid, but what excuse could Grey give for asking such a thing?

He looked around the room and saw Peter staring at him. He gave him a reassuring smile. He held no grudges against him. Peter nodded, not looking anything like the surly teen who six months ago stood in this very room and back-talked Lennie.

Several more baskets were bid on and sold. A few young men kept upping the bid when Cara's basket hit the block, making sure Ephraim had to pay dearly to share a picnic lunch with the woman he'd marry.

Lennie held up another basket. "Okay, this basket belongs to the beautiful and single Deborah Mast. Who will start the bidding?"

Deborah jumped to her feet.

Lennie frowned. "You're bidding on your own basket this year?"

Deborah hurried to the front. "I'm taking matters into my own hands, so to speak." She snatched her basket from Lennie.

Lennie picked out another basket.

Deborah motioned to her. "You haven't auctioned my basket."

"You took it and confused me, so I've moved on." Lennie raised an eyebrow and put one hand on her hip. "Anyone else here confused?"

Deborah shook her head. "I'm not a bit confused, haven't been for many months. Begin the bidding."

Lennie pointed the microphone near her mouth. "Okay, who will—"

"Everything in this basket is made from scratch," Deborah interrupted, pulling the microphone toward her as she spoke. "All the ingredients are fresh made, including the butter."

"Can I assume you made this with one person in mind?"

"Definitely."

"Couldn't you have written him a note about all this ahead of time and spared the rest of us?"

"That's not how the auction works."

"And this is?" Lennie asked. "Can we cut to the chase here? Jonathan, our good friend Deborah, who used only the best ingredients and no processed foods or leftovers whatsoever, would dearly love for you to win the bid. I suggest you aim high and end my misery."

Jonathan stood. "Three hundred dollars."

Cheers went up, and Deborah smiled broadly, laughing and blushing at the same time as she walked to Jonathan and delivered her basket.

The crowd in the room thinned out as some of the men paid for their baskets and left with a girlfriend, wife, daughter, or mother. Israel won the bid for Ada's basket, and they left. Soon Allen bought Emily's basket, and they left too. Grey moved to a bench, and his son sat beside him. With the sun shining brightly and today's temperature around seventy degrees, Lennie had the day she'd hoped for, a perfect time for picnics. The auctioneer and Lennie continued to take turns grabbing the baskets and asking for bids. As the event organizer, Lennie was called away to tend to some other business a couple of times. While she was elsewhere, the auctioneer took her basket from its place on the table behind him. There were only a few more baskets to bid on.

"The next basket belongs to our own Lena Kauffman."

Christian made the first offer. The moment Christian bid, Dwayne said something to him. Sammy, one of Lennie's older cousins, placed a bid while Christian and Dwayne seemed caught in an argument. Sammy had already bought and paid for his wife's basket, but with Israel and Allen gone, he seemed to be stepping in for them. Christian got up, bid again, and moved seats. Dwayne followed him.

Lennie hurried back into the room with a handful of twenties. He'd bet she'd had to take ones and fives out to her students who were running the lemonade and baked goods table.

Peter raised his ticket, showing the runner his number. "Fifty dollars."

Christian turned, clearly interested in who his competition was.

Dwayne stood. "No. You can't bid on her basket." He looked to Christian. "Or you either."

"Let's keep it calm, boys," the auctioneer said. "Anyone can bid."

"No!" Dwayne whirled around, looking at various people as if panicked. "She put poison in that food. I know she did. She tried to poison me and Aaron. If he were here, he'd tell you straight out."

Michael went down front. "What do you mean?"

"It's true," Dwayne cried out. "She brought us a cake that was poison. Aaron didn't want to make no fuss about it, so he threw it away quietlike."

"That's ridiculous." Lennie motioned. "Take a seat, Dwayne, or take yourself outside."

"Don't let her do this. Please," he pleaded.

"It's okay, young man." Michael put his hand on Dwayne's shoulder. "Just take a deep breath."

"I didn't want to say nothing out loud like this. I tried telling Christian private-like. You saw me. You got to believe me. So many people feel sorry for her because of that mark that they don't want to believe the truth about her."

Lennie placed her hand over her birthmark for a moment.

Grey's heart pounded like mad. "You're out of line, and I think it's time you leave."

"She's a liar and a deceiver." Dwayne sounded crazy, and Grey wondered if he realized that. But whether he was stable or not, Grey believed he knew Dwayne's purpose for bringing this up at this specific time—to cause Lennie as much trouble and embarrassment as possible.

Michael motioned toward the door. "Let's go outside, and we'll talk."

"No, I have to say this. I have to tell the truth. She's destroying men's lives one by one. Ask Peter. He don't want to admit it, but he knows she's a deceiver. At the last school board meeting, they told her never to bring a psychologist into the school again. So you know what she's doing instead? Bringing that woman from the Englischers' school into her house right after school is out, and Peter's been meeting with her behind Mamm and Daed's backs. I bet other students are too."

Grey couldn't believe that. Lennie was stubborn enough to do something her own way, but she wouldn't have hid it from him, would she?

Michael looked to Lennie. "Is this true?"

She didn't respond.

"Lena, we made our position very clear at the last meeting. Is what Dwayne says true?"

Confusion stirred. Lennie was in trouble with the board and had said nothing to him about it? He dismissed the nonsense. She didn't keep secrets from him.

Grey stood. "This isn't the right place or time."

"He's right," Michael said. "There are only three baskets left. If any of you intended to win the bid on one of the remaining baskets, please pay a reasonable fee, and let's end the auction now. I'd like to wrap up today's event and everyone go on home. We'll have a board meeting Monday night."

Lennie maintained control, smiling politely and thanking the first man who made his way down front to pay for one of the remaining baskets.

"Don't let her keep lying to you," Dwayne screamed before anyone left the room. "She knows exactly where Aaron is. She's the reason he went there. She's even chasing after Grey, almost as if she plotted for Elsie to be in that pasture with that bull while Grey stayed in this very classroom with her and Peter. Now Peter needs psychiatric help. Aaron is under the care of a doctor. What she's done eats them up inside, and if you don't stop her, she'll either run Grey crazy or seduce him." He motioned at Grey. "Grey's not falling for her tricks, though, because he's been asking other men to date her. He asked me and Christian. I think he was just hoping to find someone else for her to prey on so she'd leave him alone."

"Enough!" Grey strode to the front of the classroom.

Lennie stared at him in disbelief. "You...you did that?"

Michael and Dora waited for him to respond. If he assured Lennie of his love now, he'd break Elsie's parents all over again. He'd run Elsie's good name through the mud. And he'd ruin Lennie's reputation as well as his own. People inside the schoolhouse waited on him to respond. People who'd been outside had heard the shouting and come in.

She turned to Christian. "Did Grey ask you...to...date me?"

Christian looked at Grey, clearly unsure what to say.

"Well? Did he or not?"

Christian nodded.

Dwayne turned to his brother. "Peter, tell them it's true. Tell them you've been going to her place to see someone."

She folded her arms, trembling as if she were cold. "It's true." Her eyes met Grey's. She brushed her fingertips across her birthmark. The hurt reflected in her eyes pierced him.

She lifted her shoulders and walked out.

Everything inside him wanted to chase her, to make her hear him and trust his love for her. Surrounded by disapproving stares, he knew anything he did right now would harm her more. Dwayne's accusations against her character would die out—all but the one about her setting up meetings between Peter and the outsider.

Thirty-Two

He felt sorry for me? There was no other explanation for him asking other men to date her. His asking her to wait for him was a lie. He was hoping she'd find someone else. That's why he told her to date others. It had to be.

Tears burned Lena's eyes. She couldn't stay and help clean up. Others would need to remove the benches and load them into the wagon, get the desks out of the lean-to and set them up in the classroom, and restore order. She had to get out of here.

At the edge of the pasture, teen boys held attendant tickets that went with each horse and buggy. People were whispering as she passed them on her way to her rig.

He felt sorry for me.

She should have known that. She *had* known that.

A lonely widower and a marred old maid.

Why hadn't she admitted it for what it was?

Pain came in waves, reminding her of the newsreels she'd seen in public school showing the power of a surf during a category five hurricane. It battered against her, and her knees gave way. She staggered.

One of the teens started for her and stopped. "You okay, Lena?"

Willing her body to obey her, she got her footing. "Fine. Denki." She passed the gaggle of teens who stared and mumbled. They'd been students in past years, and they probably pitied her too. Probably laughed, wondering how she could ever expect a man to love her.

Her mother had been wrong. No man saw beyond her mark. None.

"Can we get your rig, Lena?" one of the teens asked. "Do you have your stub?"

She bit back the tears. "I'll get it myself. Denki."

And her job. She'd gone through a few years of public school just so she could be the best teacher possible, and now she'd lose this job in three weeks and probably couldn't get hired for another position anywhere.

After passing more than two dozen rigs that lined the fence, she un-tethered her Daed's horse. Her own horse had been too antsy to harness again today. Lena climbed into her carriage. She'd told herself not to look up, but she did anyway.

People filled the playground and schoolyard, staring at her, whisper-ing. Grey stood with his hand on Ivan's shoulder, watching her. Fresh tears blurred her vision. Distress filled his features, and she knew he'd never intended to hurt her. Never meant for his loneliness to leave him so vulner-able that he'd make promises he didn't mean. The memory of following him out to the greenhouse burned through her. Clearly he hadn't been interested, but his guilt for hurting her must have convinced him to reach out to her.

And then he suggested she see other men.

She pulled onto the road, encouraging her horse to hurry home.

Grey would feel differently if she didn't have the birthmark. How many men would have asked to take her home from singings over the years if she'd had flawless skin like Elsie?

She lifted her face toward the sky, wishing relief would magically float from white clouds and ease her pain.

Oh, God, it hurts.

A mixed-up, half-remembered phrase from a song mocked her, and she thought of its name—"At Seventeen" by...by...Janis Ian.

Just listening to the ballad and deciphering the lyrics in English class had pained Lena. She had tried to avoid the boys' stares and pretend she didn't care. She hadn't wanted their attention, but something short of pity would have been welcome. When they did hang around, she ignored them, not trusting their intentions.

The melody of the song came to mind. The words were fragments she was surely recalling wrong, but they carried heartache anyway. *Those... with damaged faces...imagining lovers...*

She sobbed, begging the words to go away.

After pulling into the barn, she quickly brought the rig to a stop. She unfettered the horse, put her in a stall, and ran toward her house. Her Daed came around the side of the wraparound porch. "I didn't expect you this early. Forget something? Ada and I are on the porch swing, finishing our picnic lunch." He stopped. "You okay?"

"Fine, Daed. I just need to be alone, okay?" She didn't wait for a response before going inside and closing the heavy wooden door. Her dog jumped with excitement. Nicky's piercing yelps and quick jogs around her broke Lena's resolve. She ran upstairs to her room, closed the door, and melted to the floor. Nicky nudged her, accepting her fully. She imagined herself at eighty with her Daed long gone and some dog that would be Nicky the fourth or fifth keeping her company throughout the days and nights.

She pressed her hand down her flat stomach, closed her eyes, and let the tears flow.

Cara held Ephraim's hand as they walked through the field and toward the road. Carrying the half-empty basket, he opened the cattle gate for her and then jiggled it to make sure the latch caught before they started walking again.

He slid his hand into hers again. "I'm glad you enjoy walking on pretty days."

"Next year I want to picnic inside the hedged area you like so much."

"The hiddy?"

"Yep."

"We could have spread our blanket there today if I'd known you preferred my private side yard to a spot by the creek."

"We're keeping the relationship above suspicion. The fact that other couples were sharing that same creek bank is a good thing. Besides, who did you share a meal with inside that hedged area last year?"

"Hey, you weren't even in Dry Lake last April. And the fact that I moved to New York to look for you thirteen years ago negates your right to harass me on this topic."

"Wow. Now that's a good argument, 'From. I'm impressed…and without a counterargument…for now. But I'll find one."

He mockingly sighed before he nudged her with his shoulder.

"Lori said that *hiddy* isn't a real word—English or Pennsylvania Dutch."

"I probably made it up years ago. It's slang for 'hidden place.'"

She wrapped her free hand around his arm. "I like the idea of us having a hidden place. We'll picnic there for sure next year."

"Even if it rains?"

"That sounds even more romantic."

He rolled his eyes playfully. "Women."

While they walked, a buggy came into sight. As the carriage grew close, Cara recognized the driver as someone from Ephraim's district, but she didn't remember his name. He slowed the rig. "Ephraim. Cara. Nice day for a picnic, huh?"

"Sure is, Sammy. You and the Mrs. not picnicking today?"

"I hung around and bid on Cousin Lena's basket for Israel—you know, just to make sure she had bidders. She had other bidders…for a while. Then it all went haywire. Anyway, I bought my wife's basket, but she's at home. Some of the little ones have a stomach bug."

"Sorry to hear that. Did you say something went wrong at the auction after we left?"

"Ya. When Lena's basket hit the auction block, a student bid on it. I thought that was real nice and all, but then Dwayne Bender stood up and shot all sorts of wild accusations at Lena. Accused her of poisoning a cake she gave to Aaron Blank—"

Cara's heart jolted. "A ruined cake?"

"Ya, and he said she's been chasing after Grey. Even hinted she might've plotted Elsie's death just to have him. Who's the new guy at your shop?"

"Christian," Ephraim offered.

"Ya, he was bidding on her basket too. Then after Dwayne said those things, Lena, Christian, and Grey ended up exchanging words, but the conversation made no sense to me. I think Grey must've encouraged Christian to date her. She was fit to be tied. About yelled at Grey over it. I don't know what all's going on, but I know Dwayne's got some serious problems to behave like that at a public function. Maybe Lena quit dating him and he's trying to get back at her. Seems like—"

"I…hate to interrupt," Cara said, "but I'd like to check on Lena."

"Sure, hop in. I'm going right by her place. It'll give me a chance to make sure her Daed or one of her brothers knows what's going on. They won't like this one bit."

Sammy and Ephraim talked about the upcoming spring planting and who was growing what this year. Her heart thumped like mad. If her prank had hurt Lena, she had to apologize immediately. Sammy stopped on the driveway in front of Lena's home. They wasted no time getting out. Through the screen door, Cara could see Israel pacing, and Ada was with him.

She tugged at Ephraim's arm. "I think the cake Lena gave Aaron is the one Deborah and I gave her as a prank."

"What?"

"Remember the night several months ago when your sister and I stopped by to see you at the shop and Anna Mary was there, making a phone call? We'd come to bring something to Lena."

"Ya."

"We brought her a ruined cake as a gag. She was going to see Aaron right after we left. She must've given it to him not knowing we'd pranked her."

Ephraim chuckled. "So your ability to get into trouble isn't confined to just breaking the Ordnung. That's good news, really."

She huffed. "Ephraim."

He turned away from Lena's house and coughed into his hand, trying to hide his laughter.

"You're awful."

"Hey, I'm not the one poisoning people. That'd be my fiancée...and little sister."

She stood on her tiptoes, kissed his cheek, and hurried up the steps to Lena's. Sammy was already inside, explaining things to Israel.

Israel looked beyond Sammy to Ephraim and Cara. "She came in upset and refused to talk."

"May I try?" Cara asked.

Israel gestured toward the steps.

"Which room?"

"Take a left at the top of the steps. First door on your right."

Cara hurried up the steps and tapped on the door. "Lena, it's Cara. I... I know this seems like a bad time, but I really need to tell you something."

Muffled sounds came through the door, and then Lena unlocked and opened it. Lena's eyes glistened with a hint of extra moisture and her cheeks looked as if she'd dried them moments earlier. Cara went inside and closed the door. "It's my fault about the cake. Deborah messed it up, and I talked her into using it as a prank."

Lena burst into tears. "I don't care about the cake."

"Oh." Cara tried to sift through the other information Sammy had shared.

"Aaron knows I didn't try to poison him. Dwayne's being a jerk."

Lena sat on her bed, wiping her tears. "He tried to pawn me off on other guys. Why?"

"Dwayne?"

"Heavens, no. Do you know why a man would do such a cruel thing?"

Cara didn't know who the man was, let alone why. "No."

"It's because of this." She clasped her hand over her birthmark. "It's always been because of this."

Cara sat next to her. Lena had no idea of her beauty, but Cara knew she couldn't change her opinion, not today anyway. "It won't always be. The younger you are, the more outward appearance matters. Then maturity hits…at least it does for most folks, and how a person looks is one of the last things people care about."

"But I lost him to someone perfect once before, and I accepted it within two weeks of them dating. This time…it's not the same." Lena brushed a stray tear off her face. "I'd like to be left alone, okay?"

Cara nodded. As she descended the stairs, she saw Grey through the screen door, and he was coming up the stairs to the house. Then she understood who Lena had been talking about. Grey knocked. Israel came out of the kitchen and went to the door.

"I'd like to talk to Lena."

Israel didn't budge for several moments. Then he looked to his daughter's room and back to Grey again. "You?"

"I need to talk to her, Israel."

"It's too early for you to be standing on the porch at any woman's house, Grey."

Early? Cara didn't understand.

"Go home," Israel demanded, "before the rumors of today damage Lena's reputation as a teacher and a woman."

Grey's eyes met Cara's. "She's too upset for anything to be accomplished right now."

He nodded and left.

Israel turned to Cara. "Anything I can do?"

Cara shook her head, wondering what it would have been like to have a dad.

While Ivan played in the backyard, Grey paced along the creek bank. With too many pent-up emotions to just sit idle, he'd dug the footers for the bridge. Next week he'd put twenty-six feet of support beams in place from his property to Allen's and add concrete to keep them secure, hoping it'd offer him chances to speak with Lennie. By next Saturday he'd have the structure ready to bear the weight of all who used it. Nothing fancy. Plain. Simple. And it'd felt completely right to build it.

Lennie.

He'd so looked forward to knowing she might walk over, with Emily of course, and bring him a meal. The food wouldn't matter. Having a few minutes with her would. And he would cross it in hopes of seeing her, maybe catching a moment alone with her to sustain both of them during this forced separation.

But the secrets she'd hidden from him about what had taken place at the school board meetings and her connecting Peter with Samantha at her home bothered him. He couldn't bear getting involved with someone else who hid more of herself than she shared.

He knew that hidden things were issues to be worked out between couples, except they weren't a couple. He loved her, but that wasn't enough. It scared him to think of how often love alone wasn't enough to overcome the obstacles between a man and a woman.

It shouldn't be that way. That wasn't how God intended it to be. He said that love never failed, which meant that only Grey failed. Again. And again.

But he had to talk to her. He had to assure her…to let her know that his feelings for her were real. Why did she think the birthmark mattered? But she did. And he had to tell her otherwise.

How? He couldn't go see her after all the accusations Dwayne had fired at them. In those few minutes, in full view of more than half the community, Dwayne had spilled kerosene all around Grey and Lennie. One tiny spark between them, and the community would witness their private lives burst into flames. Lennie had handled her life so carefully while she waited for the right man. If Grey remained cautious, Dwayne's accusations would become less than nothing.

His actions over the next few days and weeks held the power to ruin two women's reputations—his deceased wife's and Lennie's. Did he owe it to Elsie to mourn her properly, letting everyone believe they had a strong marriage? Elsie always needed that from him. Even if he didn't owe it to Elsie, admitting that he now loved Lena would hurt Michael and Dora more than they could bear. Every person had a breaking point. He knew Michael and Dora were very close to theirs.

Lena had ignored the school board's mandate and arranged for Peter to disobey his parents' wishes. According to Michael, she'd given advice to Aaron she knew would cause trouble. If she wanted to look at why more men weren't beating down her door, she needed to skip the mirror and take a hard look at her stubbornness to do things her own way. The Amish community stayed strong through each person yielding their own desires for the sake of the community as a whole. There were other ways to get help for her class, Peter, and Aaron.

But he loved her spirit, her willingness to completely destroy her own standing to help someone. Her motivation was love, and she didn't stop because her standing might take hard hits in the process.

To him, that was worthy of his respect. But if he couldn't convince her of his love, his respect for her wouldn't matter.

Thirty-Three

Lena knew today, the Monday following the auction, would be tough to get through. At least yesterday had been a between Sunday, so she hadn't had to face anyone.

Too broken to sleep last night or to think well today, she did her best to keep the tears at bay and teach her scholars. She'd had to walk to school again today. Her once-spirited horse had crossed the line into flat-out unruly. While walking from her home to here, she'd seen people in buggies or working in their gardens and such. The whispers were endless, and her embarrassment complete. Although some waved, asking how she was doing, most kept their distance.

But she'd get beyond this. She'd read in the Bible one time that her life was hidden with Christ, so what people saw wasn't really her.

Or at least that's what she kept telling herself.

Besides, good teachers always had to set aside personal issues and keep reaching out. But after tonight's board meeting, she probably wouldn't be able to teach anywhere. With only three and a half weeks of school left, they'd let her finish out this year. But with Dwayne making the issues so public, she wouldn't be able to find a district that would hire her for next year. If the school board could only see how the counselor had helped Peter, they might not hold what she'd done against her. Samantha had helped release him from his anger and his thoughts of suicide.

She watched Peter. Between Saturday and today, he'd located that deep-seated anger she'd spent most of the year trying to remove. Whatever happened tonight at the board meeting, she knew she'd gambled and lost. Peter had talked to the counselor at her home twice a week for two months. To keep her Daed out of trouble, she'd timed the meetings to take place while he was away delivering furniture, most often to Ada's house. She'd seen progress in Peter, but it'd been destroyed somehow. Probably from the browbeating he'd taken from his brother and parents once he got home on Saturday.

With dread of tonight's meeting and such grief over playing a fool for Grey, she thought today might never end. Deborah had moved on after Mahlon left, and Lena kept promising her heart that she would too. But Deborah had men lined up wanting to court her. Lena? Well, she might have a chance at finding one good man if she could have the birthmark removed.

The clock struck three, and she dismissed the class for the day. Wishing she could remain at her desk, she went outside and greeted parents, trying to respond to them as if nothing were wrong. She helped the young ones get in buggies, but most of her scholars walked home in this type of weather. Before their excited voices faded in the distance, she saw a buggy carrying three men pull into the school's turnaround. The open carriage held the members of the school board—Michael, Enos, and Jake. All except Grey.

Michael brought the rig to a halt. "Lena, we'd like a word with you."

This couldn't be good news, not if the meeting was supposed to be tonight and they'd all come here now. While they got out of the carriage, she closed the school door. They could say whatever they came here for without her sitting in front of them like a frightened field mouse trapped by a cat.

She walked down the three steps and halfway to the rig and waited.

Michael stared behind the school at the pasture where his daughter had died six months ago. "Because of things we learned Saturday and after talking with folks today, we've canceled the meeting tonight. We think it best to say what needs to be said now. I see no need in having a meeting where Grey will try to defend your actions. He's done that for too many years, and the two of you should be ashamed."

Offense burned through her, and tears clouded her vision. "Do you dare hint that Grey and I had some sort of inappropriate relationship—that he was not faithful to Elsie nor I to God? That isn't true. Not even a flirtatious smile or a wink passed between us. He had no interest in anyone but your daughter. And I have never had an interest in someone God has given to another."

Michael stared at her for several moments. "Your reaction gives me hope."

"And I respectfully have grave concerns over yours."

Michael's face turned red. "You are far too opinionated, Lena Kauffman."

Lena's palms sweated, and her heart palpitated as she dared speak so boldly. "You've let a liar deceive you."

"Dwayne hasn't deceived us concerning your disobedience to the board's instructions. You overstepped your boundary and disobeyed our ruling." He held out an envelope. "You are dismissed from your position starting today."

His words struck her with the force of a roof collapsing, and her legs threatened to give way. "What?" She looked from one man to the next. "But I…I haven't sat before my accusers or been given a chance to speak."

"Mollie Bender will fill in for the rest of this year, and we'll find a new teacher for next year."

They'd chosen Dwayne and Peter's Mamm to fill in for her? The unfairness of it shook her, and she fought against tears. Unwilling to let them see even mist in her eyes, she gritted her teeth and gained control over her tear ducts. "Fine." Her heart pounding until she felt sick, she turned her back to them and began to walk off.

"You did this, Lena," Jake called after her. "In months to come, perhaps years, you will see that this is not our doing but yours."

The gravel under her feet crunched as she spun around and took several steps toward them. "And I'd do it again. Peter asked for help. He's old enough to graduate school in three weeks, old enough to go to work full-time, and old enough to begin the freedoms of his rumschpringe, where he'll dabble in the world's ways, but he's not old enough to know if he needs to talk to someone outside of our faith?"

Michael's face showed confusion as he listened to her reasoning. "That issue aside, you disobeyed us. We are your authority. We decide what's best."

"Or you refuse to hear reason and Dwayne decided for you."

"You dare stand here and mock us?"

"I dare to question you. There should have been a meeting where I could have answered the charges against me and lodged my own against Dwayne."

Michael studied the field, and she thought he might give in to her. The hurt and confusion on his face reminded her of the constant pain that tore at him. "We've made our decision, and it is final."

As she tried to absorb the loss, her mind swam with warm memories of the battles fought and won inside that classroom—just as battles were fought and won on every farm and in every home. Good seed was sown out of love and an abundant harvest prayed for, but even among the Amish the lines of right and wrong were not always clear. Should she have done nothing after Elsie's death and let the seeds of shock, grief, and guilt grow a crop unhindered and unchecked?

She didn't know, and she might not ever know. "I'll empty my desk."

After taking the few remaining gloves and sweaters out of the lost-and-found box, she set the container beside her desk. Word of her dismissal would spread quickly. By nightfall everyone would know she'd been released as the teacher. They'd think her a fool, if they didn't already. A silly, ugly, rebellious fool.

What most people thought was one thing, but knowing how Grey felt about her made it unbearable.

The smell of wood stain and the sounds of sawing and hammering inside the cabinetry shop were the most constant things in Grey's life. Since he'd been a teen, he'd worked here, first for Ephraim's Daed and then for Ephraim. He didn't seem to be much good at creating anything of substance outside of work, but inside these walls he built fine, sturdy items that would serve a purpose long after he'd left this earth.

When most of the young men had been out drinking and carousing, he'd stayed faithful to the Amish ways and honed his skills as a craftsman. He'd never been a girl chaser. It never interested him. So how was he now caught in forbidden circumstances and silently living outside the Old Ways?

He couldn't stop thinking about Lennie. The hurt she was experiencing tormented him. He'd spent most of yesterday writing her a letter. It seemed the only way to reach her without causing trouble. There was a chance it wouldn't get to her, but only a small one. Since her teen years, she was the one who took the mail inside most days. As far as he knew, she still did. Even if her Daed found the letter, Grey believed he'd give it to her. He might not approve, but Israel treated Lennie as a respected adult. He'd always let her make up her own mind, just like allowing her to go to public school.

"Grey," Ephraim called to him.

Michael, Jake, and Enos stood in the doorway of the shop. He went to them. If Cara wasn't in the office visiting Ephraim, he would have taken the men in there for privacy.

"We came to tell you there's not a school board meeting tonight," Jake said. "We decided it's best for everyone if you are not put in a situation where you feel the need to defend Lena."

"Am I being replaced?"

Jake shook his head. "No, but we met with Lena already…and we let her go."

"You what?"

"We voted, and we handled it, Grey," Michael said. "It didn't matter what was said at the meeting. She was on probation before she brought a psychologist into the school after Elsie died. We'd already told her she wouldn't be hired again for next year, and we'd hoped she could finish out the year. We'd—"

"Wait." Grey held up his hand. "You had reasons before this Saturday to let her know you wouldn't hire her again for next year? Why? And why wasn't I told?"

"You know that she was already on probation."

"I know she was the Detweilers' scapegoat, and all of you allowed it. That boy drove a rig back and forth to school half of that year. She let him go midday, and he was surely daydreaming while Lena's horse instinctively headed for her place. That accident caused no more than bumps and bruises. It certainly was not her fault. And what about his Mamm's fault for sending those four children to school time and time again without a lunch?"

"You defend her too heartily and too loudly," Enos said.

Michael straightened his straw hat. "Aside from the issue with the Detweilers, she was allowing more and more things to take place that should not have. The board had not approved the counselor who spoke to the class. And Elmer broke his arm while she was nowhere around. The parents had lost confidence in her, but we were going to let her finish the year. However, sneaking Peter in to see a counselor behind our backs and his parents' was too much. His parents thought he was staying after school to study. We didn't need your vote to have enough to dismiss her. We'd warned her not to allow that counselor into the school again, so she had the woman meet with Peter at her home right after school."

"She had a right to—"

"No," Michael interrupted. "She had a right to obey us, and she didn't. And she showed us no sign of remorse for her actions. I do not regret our decision. Mollie Bender will fill in until school is over."

"Mollie? Lena is let go without a hearing, based on trouble Dwayne stirred, and then you hire his Mamm?"

"Jake, Enos, will you wait for me in the carriage?" Michael asked and then waited until they were out of earshot. "I don't like what I see in you lately," he said softly. "You stand up for her as heartily as she does for you. You need to mind your step."

"I have minded my step. And I grow weary of it, Michael."

Without another word Michael left. Grey began pacing, trying to think what to do and how to do it. He didn't know exactly, but he had to see Lennie. Through the plate glass of the office, he saw Ephraim and Cara chatting.

He crossed the large room, tapped on the door, and went in. "They came to tell me that they've fired Lena. I've got to see her, but that could make everything worse."

Cara frowned. "Why would that make it worse for her?"

"It's like Israel said. It's too soon for me to be standing on the porch at any woman's house."

"You and Lena?" Lines creased Ephraim's face as Grey's words sank in.

"I thought you knew that already," Cara said. "You were there on Saturday when Israel wouldn't let Grey see Lena."

Ephraim studied her for a moment. "Ya, but I just thought Lena was too upset to see anyone because Grey had tried to get other men to date… Oh, now I see what's going on." He studied Grey for a minute. "I hope it works out for you two."

Grey nodded, glad Ephraim had no judgment against him—not that he had expected it.

Cara tapped her fingers on the arms of her chair. "I still don't get why Grey going to see her is a problem."

Ephraim quickly explained the ways of the Amish concerning remarriage.

Cara tucked a wisp of rogue hair under her prayer Kapp. "So it's unacceptable to become involved with someone any sooner than a year. Two years are appreciated?"

"Ya."

"Isn't there a verse somewhere in the New Testament that says once a spouse dies, the one left behind is free to remarry?" Cara asked.

"Free to, yes," Ephraim added. "But it's wisdom to wait, and it's the Amish way to push for that. Waiting honors the life of the person who died. It shows inner character and strength to remain alone, and it gives everyone who is grieving time to adjust to that loss before new people are brought into their lives as a family member."

"Everything is so messed up." Grey began to pace again. "And I don't know that I'm in a position to fix anything. I can't undo what the board has done, but she thinks I don't care. She thinks that birthmark keeps her from being beautiful and that I was pretending to care out of pity. How can she not know she's gorgeous?"

"Very, very easily." Cara cut a piece of electrical tape off its roll and put it across Grey's cheek, above his beard. "Wear that for a few weeks, or better yet let's fill in that space with a Sharpie. If you were a kid, everyone would look at that first and then at you. Half of them would make some sort of remark, make up a nickname, and never once let you forget it's there. And men can get away with such a mark much easier than a woman."

"There's no way that's kept men from courting her."

Cara played with the strings to her prayer Kapp. "Sometimes our heaviest baggage isn't who we are. It's who we think we are. And once we believe it, we unknowingly shape our lives after that belief."

Her words reached inside and yanked at his heart. Grey continued to help Lennie believe that lie by hiding behind the traditions of man. He wanted to protect her, but maybe all he was doing was making it easy for her to hold on to the lies she believed—just like he'd made it easy for Elsie to hold on to her lies. If he'd been willing to let everyone in the community think whatever he or she wanted to about their marriage, he'd have gotten help for them. He hadn't protected Elsie, not really.

His days of hiding and helping others hide were over.

"I've got to go."

His mind ran in a dozen directions as he drove his rig to Lennie's. He hurried up the steps and knocked. Nicky barked, but no one answered the door. She didn't appear to be home. He went to her Daed's shop. No one was there either. It was possible she had gone to Allen's, especially with her being upset. He climbed into his buggy, wondering what fireworks his presence at Allen's would cause.

After pulling into Allen's driveway, Grey hurried to the door and knocked.

Emily opened the door, took him by the hand, and squeezed it. "Grey, kumm."

"Is Lennie here?"

Allen walked into the room and stared at him in disbelief. "I cannot believe you're here."

Even as Grey stood inside Allen's home, memories of Lennie filled him—her voice, her sense of humor, her sincerity, determination, and stubbornness. One look into her eyes redefined love to him.

"I know how this must sound to you. And I understand why you feel like you do, but I'm in love with your sister."

"In love with her?" Allen pointed to the door, inviting Grey to leave. "This conversation is not taking place."

"I don't blame you for believing part of the lies Dwayne told. Too many people are, including Lennie. I didn't try to pawn her off. I knew she felt a little lonely and wasn't seeing anyone, so I mentioned to Christian that he could bid on her picnic basket at the auction."

"Christian moved here less than five weeks ago, so somewhere between then and now, you've fallen madly in love with my sister, and I'm supposed to trust your feelings on that matter. You're not in love with my sister. You're using her to feel less lonely. And I won't stand for it."

"Sometimes," Emily interjected, "when a spouse dies, the loved one left behind feels the connection of marriage for the rest of their life. Some marriages do not have that connection even when both are alive."

"What?" Allen's face twisted with disapproval.

Emily held up her index finger and left the room.

The air itself seemed to condemn Grey as Allen's eyes held complete disappointment. But as unreasonable as Allen could be at times, he respected his wife's opinion. Well, he usually did. Grey hoped this was one of those times.

Emily walked back into the room carrying a cracked and chipped teacup and saucer. "Elsie was my secret sister for sharing gifts one year. It wasn't like her to participate, but she did one time about three years ago. When I opened the gift and it was broken, she apologized and left the room. You can imagine how shaken someone like Elsie was to give a broken gift. I followed her, and through her tears she shared a few fragmented sentences, saying it hadn't been broken when she'd wrapped it, but it matched everything else she touched, including her marriage. She didn't say much else, but I was able to see into her world and Grey's." Emily closed her eyes. "Grey has been grieving the death of his marriage for many years."

Allen became completely still.

Emily placed the cup in her husband's hand. "He's been alone for a long time, husband. I believe he loves your sister—a good, solid love you can trust. Can you not look at those two and know in your heart they are right for each other?"

Allen studied the cup as if trying to see what Emily had seen. "I...I want you to stay away from my sister."

"I intend to do everything I can to let her know I love her. I don't care if everyone else stands against us, but you and I have been close friends our whole lives, and I know you love her like few brothers love a sibling."

"What you're doing is inexcusable. You used my home to get close to her. If what Emily says is true, then what I see is a man who knows how to hide who he really is from everyone, including his closest friend." Allen shook his head. "You were married to someone else yesterday. And today my sister is broken! You did this, and you want to call that love? If you don't leave her alone, our friendship is over!"

Allen's words were no idle threat.

"I'm sorry to hear that." Grey left.

Thirty-Four

Dwayne stood in his parents' home trying not to laugh as he listened to the good news. His heart thudded like a drum in his ears, pounding out the rhythm of hatred. But his genius had again proved itself. Lena was fired.

"They let her go because of me?" Peter asked.

"No, because she's an idiot," Dwayne added.

"Why do you have to hate everybody? What's she ever done to you?" Peter's whine grated on Dwayne's nerves.

"That's enough, boys," Mamm said. "I'll be the teacher for the rest of the year."

"From one idiot teacher to another," Dwayne mumbled.

"What did you say?" Mamm asked.

"If I'd wanted you to hear me, you would have. So where is she now?"

His Mamm shrugged. "Jake said she was at the school, cleaning out her desk."

And Dwayne knew she had walked to school. "I got better things to do than stand around talking about Lena."

He went to his room and eased the Hot-Shot from the top shelf in his closet. He'd need this.

His bedroom door swung open, and Peter's confused, almost blank face stared at him. "You think this is funny, don't you?"

"I think it's sad that you're too stupid to know when you hear good news."

"Why Lena? You've been gunning for her since we got here. Why?"

Dwayne slid the cattle prod back into its place. "Oh, I haven't gunned for her. Doubt if I will. Not a good idea." Dwayne moved to his bed and sat down. "You're taking it too hard. She's cursed. The whole community needs to be rid of her."

Peter grew stock-still. "What do you mean by that?"

Ire flew through Dwayne as he realized Peter no longer sided with him easily. Peter's betrayal wouldn't last long. He'd see to that. "You might like her, little brother, but she's done nothing to make you any brighter."

"Of course not. Nobody but you knows anything, do they?"

Dwayne rushed off his bed and shoved Peter to the floor. "Don't you ever think you can talk to me like that. You're too stupid to see she deserves what she gets. Make that mistake again, and I'll give you a flogging like never before."

Peter fought back, swinging and kicking, but Dwayne had fifty pounds on him. He pinned him facedown and pulled his arm up behind his back. A little more pressure, and it'd snap. "Stupid." Dwayne got off of him. "Get out!"

Lena toted the cardboard box as the road continued to stretch before her. It surprised and disappointed her how few items she had to show for all her years of teaching. The weight of her pain seemed insufferable. She'd never envisioned leaving her beloved job like this.

Although her reality never supported her dreams, she'd always believed she'd end her time at the school due to getting married. Teachers never began a school year if they knew they were getting married during that wedding season. Most knew when school ended in May that they would marry during the next wedding season that fall. That made the end of the school year so joyous for the teachers, a special time Lena had celebrated with a lot of teacher friends at other Amish schools. Being the fool she was, she'd dared to believe it would happen to her one day.

Studying the fields for a distraction, she tried to keep her emotions in check. She'd not fall apart until she got home. She just wouldn't. Dwayne Bender thought he'd accomplished something special, but she knew her people. They had reason to be upset with her, and they were. But if he thought this would cause them to turn on her, he didn't know her community. They'd let the board members deal with the issues, and they'd accept their decision, but they'd also begin to see Dwayne for who he was. Life took patience. This wasn't over yet. It couldn't be.

Still…she couldn't stay here and watch them pity her. Sounds of leaves and twigs crunching made her study the patch of woods beside her. It didn't sound like squirrels or even deer. It seemed too loud and very rhythmic, like a person walking. She saw nothing, so she continued on. The noise seemed to be trailing each step she made. Pretending she heard nothing, she picked up her pace and then spun. A shadow of a man ducked behind a tree. Chills ran over her. She moved to the far side of the road, walking fast and looking for a stick or rock or something.

A little relief eased over her when she heard a horse and buggy approaching from behind. It slowed and eased up beside her. "Lennie."

She jolted, dropping her box. Glass shattered, making her cringe.

Grey stopped the rig and started to get out.

She waved him away. "Don't you dare get down to help me."

He stayed in the buggy. "I need to explain things. Let me give you a lift."

She stooped and gathered as many items as she could. Mostly the box contained gifts her scholars had given her—lots of red pencils with her name, various handmade containers for holding rubber bands and the like, and a now-broken vase.

"No." She refused to look at him.

"We need to talk, Lennie."

Gathering the larger shards of the vase, she remembered the day the class had given it to her. It'd been expensive, and they'd gone in together. She placed the pieces into the box. The sound of another buggy approaching caught her attention. "Go, before you're seen."

"I don't care. Anyone and everyone can think what they want to. I'm done hiding. And I'm finished with following the traditions. This is about us."

She didn't doubt his sincerity. But his motives betrayed him. He felt really bad for her and wanted to make it right. She continued to place most of her treasures into the box, but some had been too scattered to find. "Look, your decision to stop hiding stems from the same reason that motivated you to look for me Saturday night—you feel sorry for me. Just go away."

"Ach, kumm on," he complained. "Everything I said Friday night is true. Can't—"

"Stop," she hissed at him. "I don't believe you. Can you understand that?"

"No, I don't get it. I hear you, but it makes no sense for you to feel that way. None."

"Look, it was easy for me to get the wrong idea. I should've known you were just...being nice."

"We were drawn to each other—"

"Ya," she interrupted him again. "You to me because you were lonely and me to you because I was fool enough to believe you loved me."

"Len—"

The buggy coming toward them slowed.

Tears defied her and sprang to her eyes. "Just go. You hurt for me right now and want to make it all better, but that's not enough for me. Would it be for you? When the time is right, you'll find some flawless-skinned beauty and really fall in love."

"I...want you."

His words had the power to carry her into another world, and if she believed he meant it, she couldn't make herself stay away. Before she could open her mouth to speak, the approaching carriage rattled to a stop.

"Hi, Lena." Christian removed his hat. "Need a hand? I took off early today, hoping to catch you."

"I'd rather walk, but denki."

He glanced to Grey and then studied Lena. "Are you sure there isn't something I could help you with?"

She wrapped her arms around the oversized box. "I need to go."

"I guess it's 'cause I'm new to the district, but I don't understand much of what took place on Saturday, except that Dwayne's a jerk. I've been living at his house since arriving here, and I didn't need to see what happened Saturday to know that. Seems like you could at least go for a ride with me."

Noises came from the woods. She didn't want to go anywhere with either Grey or Christian, but she wasn't about to stay on this long stretch of isolated roadway.

"I could use a ride home."

"That's a good start." Christian opened the door and took the box from her.

She nodded to Grey. "Thanks for checking on me. You don't need to again." For a thousand reasons she could list without even pausing to think, she loved Grey. If he had loved her, they could have been unbelievably happy. She forced a smile. "I really am okay."

"I began a bridge."

She wished he would leave well enough alone. "And maybe one day, just from one neighbor to another, I'll cross it while at Allen's." She got in and closed the door.

Christian seemed quite amiable as he drove her home. But the trip lasted too long. Finally he pulled onto her driveway, got out, opened the buggy door for her, and helped her down.

He grabbed the box off the seat. "It's been a rough few days for you, so I'll leave for now, but maybe another time?"

She didn't want to be rude, but why was he doing this? Did he and Dwayne have some sort of bet going on? "I appreciate it, but no. I'm sorry."

He passed the container to her. "It was worth a try."

She went inside and set the box on an end table. Picking out parts of the broken vase, she was haunted by dozens of memories of being a teacher.

Moments later someone banged on the door. Grey, she suspected. Ignoring it, she continued digging for pieces. The door opened, and Grey eased inside.

"What do you think you're doing?"

"I…I'm not letting you hide or run."

Her face flushed. "Me? You're the one hiding your true self, and I know why you're doing it."

"I say you don't, but explain it to me."

"No. All you want is to pick apart my reasoning. You're a nice guy. Nice guys do too much to keep from hurting someone's feelings, including backing themselves into a relationship."

"Ridiculous! I don't know anyone who's that nice of a guy. Certainly not me."

The back door opened, and Nicky flew into the house, barking angrily at Grey as he raised his voice at Lena. A quick glance said her Daed had come in from the shop. "Something I can help with?"

Grey turned to him. "Your daughter is deaf. And if it's all the same with you, I'm not leaving until she hears me."

"I've heard you! You're the one not listening! Tell him to go home, Daed."

"What are you—five?" Grey asked. "Stand your own ground and talk to me like an adult. They're words, Lennie. Choose them in your mind and share them. Or is that only for students and people you want to mold into being who you think they need to be while you keep yourself in knots for not being perfect?"

Nicky growled at him and barked. Her Daed scolded the dog and pointed outside, but Nicky didn't obey.

Lena snapped her fingers. "Hush." Her dog quieted and sat. "My day has been bad enough without you coming here to argue!"

"Then stop arguing. Besides, do you think you'd be better off if I let you believe lies about how I feel?"

As Grey raised his voice again, Nicky growled at him. Daed looked from Lena to Grey. "I…I'll just be in my shop until one of you can hear the other. It's too loud in here for me."

Lena couldn't believe it. Her Daed had taken up for her all her life. He left, pulling the door securely behind him.

She tossed the broken pieces of vase back into the box. "I know things you don't think I know. Do you have any idea how many times I overheard you tell Allen that you felt sorry for me when I was growing up?"

"I never said that!"

"I know you did! You think I'm lying?"

Confusion lined his face as he studied her. "I don't remember…" He paced the room. "Wait. I do remember. Kumm on, Lennie. I meant I felt sorry for you because you had Allen for a brother. I was giving him a hard time for being such a pain."

"Why are you doing this? You never once felt anything for me until I threw myself at you, and even then you were busy trying to pawn me off on other men. You were hoping I'd find someone and leave you alone. You won't change my mind because I know the truth of it, Grey. Now just drop it and go home."

"You really think I would act interested because I'm nice?"

"Oh, I know better than that. Acting interested only came after you were lonely, and even then I had to chase after you and start crying."

He became still. "You…cared…before?"

"What? If you'd known, would you have altered your life to keep from hurting me?" She went to the front door and opened it.

He stood frozen, staring at her.

"Please, Grey."

Without another word he left.

Thirty-Five

After Grey tucked Ivan in for the night, he walked outside. The cool air vibrated with the sounds of spring. Stars shone brightly in an almost cloudless sky. He walked to the creek, looking at the unfinished bridge. Moonlight filtered through the trees and danced on the moving water.

All he could think about was Lennie. He could hear her voice as if she were picnicking outside with her family or playing in the yard with the children.

He'd never thought of her romantically when they were younger. She'd been fifteen when he was twenty. He thought a lot of her and even remembered thinking whoever married her would be a very blessed man, but he wasn't attracted to her. He'd never once considered that maybe it should be him.

He felt as if he'd been standing in a dark room filled with stuff. He couldn't make out what was in it, but it felt familiar. The journey he and Lennie had taken was like someone had lit a kerosene lamp on the other end of the house and walked toward him. The closer the person came to him, the more he could clearly see. Every shadowy object in the room became a memory or feeling he'd carelessly stored and each one revealed one thing—his complete and undeniable attraction to Lennie. But what he wanted from their relationship was more important to him than any-thing the physical draw could give. He wanted...no, he needed friendship, the kind he could never possess without her.

"God," he picked up a rock and tossed it into the creek. "I'm glad we argued. But she's hurting. It's been an unfair journey for her, unfair to lose her school, unfair for Dwayne to get away with his antics. Help her. Please intervene for her." Following the creek, he walked on. "I've done what I could to make her hear me. I need You to open her eyes and ears to the truth. Search my heart and let her know what's in it, Father. If she sees my love, nothing will ever separate us again."

Deborah surveyed Ada's House from her spot in the large booth on the lawn. It was a Thursday evening in late April, and Springtime at Ada's House was well under way. People were taking tours through the Amish homestead, buying crafts and furniture at will. Others were sitting in rocking chairs that lined the front porch. Many bought desserts and homemade ice cream. It'd been warm last weekend, but another springtime dip in temps made it feel a little nippy to eat ice cream, in Deborah's opinion. At least heavy coats were no longer needed.

Some of the older adults were playing rounds of checkers while visiting with each other. At the top of each hour, Ada and Lori led children in playing old-fashioned yard games. Ada's House was busy, but with the few extra helpers she'd hired, thankfully it wasn't panicky busy like last fall. Just right. She poured hot chocolate into a mug and went to the sidewalk near the road.

Jonathan pulled the hay wagon to a stop and jumped down.

"Hey, Little Debbie."

She passed him the cup and winked at him before moving to the tailgate to help folks get out.

As the last person stepped down, she thought she heard a phone ringing. Not someone's cell but the one in the shanty near Ada's barn. She turned to Jonathan. "Ada's phone?"

"I think so, but it won't be Lena. I'm sure it's someone wanting to know directions or hours. The answering machine we set up will handle it."

"I wish she'd call."

"Lena going to Philly whenever life becomes too painful started more than ten years ago. She's not one to call while she's gone."

"It just makes me sick to know how bad she's hurting."

"Me too. If I know her, she's doing what she needs to do to find some peace. Then she'll be back safe and sound." He pointed. "But it was a good idea to pull Israel into helping while she's gone. It's bound to help distract him."

Israel brought his rig to a halt. Jonathan passed her his mug and moved to the back of the hay wagon and helped people down. Deborah went to get Israel a cup of hot chocolate.

A lot of the visitors were new to Ada's House. But she found it encouraging to see so many regulars who began coming in the fall, like the man who stood at the booth chatting with Lori. She sat on the counter, talking nonstop.

He always wore threadbare clothes but spent a few dollars each time, buying something at the booth. He'd never gone inside, but he seemed to like catching a few words with Cara more than anyone else.

Deborah went behind the counter with Ephraim. While he rang up another sale, she spoke to him in Pennsylvania Dutch, asking if Cara had remembered to get the next batch of miniature pies out of the oven. He said that was what she was doing now. A few moments later Cara arrived.

"Oh, perfect timing. Let's set them on the far side of the register and then move them to the container."

The man tilted his head. "Did you make those?"

Cara wrinkled her nose. "Nope, but I kept them from burning."

He laughed. "How come all the Pennsylvania Dutch chattering stops when they speak to you?"

"Mom don't know it very well," Lori said before Cara could answer. "I'm doing pretty good learning it, though."

"Learning it?"

"We only been here a year. Moved from New York."

Cara placed her hand on Lori's head. "That's enough, Lorabean."

Lori nodded.

Cara pulled several whole lemons out of the hidden pocket of her apron. "We needed more lemon slices for hot tea, but I couldn't find the knife."

Deborah held it up. "Sorry. I snatched it."

"You want to see my dog, mister?" Lori pointed to the front porch where Better Days was tethered, watching folks peacefully and enjoying an occasional pat on the head. "Before I started learning the language, we was living in a barn 'cause we found the address of Dry Lake in a diary, but Mom didn't have no money for food or a house. But I didn't mind 'cause I found a whole litter of puppies."

The man blinked. "In...a barn, Cara?"

Cara studied the man, as if a little offended by him. She lifted her daughter and passed her to Ephraim. He nodded and took Lori inside. Deborah assumed he was going to give her a lecture on not telling strangers everything she knew. She moved each pie into the clear plastic display rack.

"I...I didn't mean to get your little girl in trouble. But..."

Deborah paused. Cara cut him a look, reminding Deborah of a side to her she rarely showed anymore.

"Too many questions," Cara assured the man.

He nodded. "Sorry. It's just odd to see...I mean, a woman your age not knowing the language."

"Whatever." Cara shifted. "You can't believe anything children say."

Jonathan walked up. "Uh, forget something, Little Debbie?"

"Oh, Israel's drink!" She passed it to Jon, who walked it back to Israel. Ada stood near the rig, talking with Israel.

"I don't mean to cause no problems. But...you weren't raised Amish?"

Cara paused, staring at him.

He lowered his eyes, his hands trembling as Deborah had seen them do before. "You're...clearly not happy with me, and it's my fault for being nosy." The man walked off and then turned back. "It's clear you don't want anybody knowing about your life. I...I won't say a word of what I know. Your mother wasn't the only one good at keeping secrets."

"My mother..." Cara didn't budge, and she didn't appear to Deborah to be breathing either.

The man weaved between folks until he arrived at the sidewalk and began hurrying away.

"My mother?" Cara's face twisted, and then shock registered. She went around the counter, skirted people, and stopped on the sidewalk. "Hey!"

Deborah followed her, but the man kept going.

"Mister, wait."

But he didn't. Deborah had no idea what Cara wanted, but Ephraim arrived.

Cara cupped her hands around her mouth. "Trevor Atwater!"

Already halfway down the block, the man stopped cold. He turned, and Cara just stared at him.

He waited, but Cara didn't budge.

Deborah placed her hand on Cara's shoulder. "Who?"

Cara closed her eyes, shaking her head. "We've seen him here half a dozen times since we opened, haven't we?"

"Ya, but who is he?"

Cara's breathing was labored. Ephraim stood beside her, saying nothing. The man started back toward them and then turned and walked away.

"I can't believe this. Is it possible?" Cara muttered.

Ephraim shrugged. "I...I don't know."

Israel moved ahead of Cara, staring after the man until he was out of sight. "The last time I saw him, he worked for your grandfather. It's been nearly thirty years since then, but it's him, Cara. All night I kept thinking I recognized him from somewhere."

"Who?" Deborah asked. No one answered her.

"Great." Cara clicked her tongue. "Another set of hurdles to trip over and land on my face." She rolled her eyes. "If he returns, I bet it won't be for a while. I think I spooked him."

"Ya, I think you did," Ephraim agreed.

Cara looked at Deborah, unwavering steeliness reflecting in her eyes. "That's my dad."

Her dad? The man who had abandoned her in a New York bus station? Tears welled in Deborah's eyes and she felt shaky, but Cara stood straight and calm and dry-eyed.

"It's almost time to close up," Ada said. "Let's wrap up a little early and try to enjoy some fellowship with just us. I think we all need it."

Ephraim angled his head, studying Cara. "You okay?"

"You know what?" Cara finally stopped staring at the place where the man had disappeared. "I'm not bad."

Thirty-Six

Late afternoon sunlight streamed through the open window, showing every flaw in Lena's face as she stared in the mirror. Folded inside her hands were glossy pamphlets she'd picked up in Philly earlier this week. She'd needed to get away by herself for a couple of nights, so she'd hired a driver to take her to a hotel. The sights, sounds, and aromas of the Amish specialties at Reading Terminal Market had helped her get this mess in perspective. She'd talked to a lot of Amish people she didn't know, and walked the endless aisles that were lined with booths, each one housing baked goods, fresh fruits or meats, fascinating Amish-made crafts, or deli-type restaurants—all under one roof.

While in Philly she'd also checked into having her birthmark removed. What she'd learned planted a serious temptation within her. There were treatments that could alter her looks. She opened one pamphlet and reread the info. Laser surgery. It stood a chance of removing or almost removing the birthmark. Most likely, however, since she was in her midtwenties, the procedure would only lighten it. But was this what she really wanted?

It didn't have the power to change anything between Grey and her because she'd always know the truth he couldn't admit. But it might change how she felt about herself and maybe make it easier to accept the rejection.

"Lena?" her Daed's voice came through her door.

She tucked the pamphlets inside her dresser along with the still-unopened letter Grey had sent to her. "Ya?"

He opened the door. "You sure you don't want to go to Ada's with me tomorrow?"

"Denki, Daed. I'm just not ready to mingle yet."

Her Daed moved to her bed and took a seat. "I wish your Mamm were here. She'd know what to say."

"There's nothing to say. I have to adjust."

"If you apologize for ignoring the board's instructions and give your word you won't do anything like that again, I think they might hire you for next year."

"You think I'm wrong."

"Ya. I love you just as much, but I don't think any teacher at any school could get away with doing what you did without being suspended or losing her job."

"But he needed help, and I made sure he got it."

"I know. You have a good heart. Even in this uproar, no one in the community doubts that. But you can't ignore our ways, or what a parent wants, or what the school board wants. You can't decide what's best all on your own. You wouldn't want me to do that. When we disagreed during your teen years, you threw a fit, insisting I get a woman's opinion. And since I was a single parent, I did. And you're right—Michael shouldn't have agreed to dismiss you without a hearing. Can you see how all this works?"

She shrugged. "Ya, I guess so."

He patted the bed, and she sat beside him. "Tell me about this matter with Grey."

Her eyes clouded with tears. It'd been six days since Dwayne had exploded at the auction and stirred rumors and caused her to lose her job. She hadn't stopped reliving the humiliation of it yet. "What have you heard?"

"Rumors are saying Dwayne is full of sour grapes because you caught him with my watch and made him give it back. His folks are offended at the accusation, but best I can tell no one is siding with Dwayne. As far as you and Grey, I don't suspect most know what's going on to have anything to say on the matter."

"Most?"

"I'd think someone knows what's going on. Someone always does." He pulled a letter out of his pocket and gave it to her. "Clearly it's not me."

She ran her fingers over the handwriting on the envelope. Grey had written to her again. "I love him, Daed. And I wish I didn't."

"Why?"

"I…I thought he loved me, but…" She traced the birthmark. "I'm thinking about trying to have it removed."

"Lena, every human has flaws. And all of us have to deal with those flaws in each other. Pride makes us want to be perfect outwardly, but nothing can make us perfect inside. Do you really want people awed by an outward appearance that will fade fast with age?"

"If I'd had any experience with men, I wouldn't have been so foolish or gullible with Grey. And if I were beautiful like Elsie, I would've had experience."

"Being flawless won't make him love you." He placed the letter in her hand. "Surely you know that. And I know that *if* Grey isn't in love with you, it has nothing to do with the birthmark."

"You aren't angry at the mess of tangled emotions going on between us when he's only been a widower for seven months?"

"You've had enough people angry with you this week, my dear girl." He stood. "Whatever you do from here, just remember how you would want to be honored if you were Elsie, okay?"

"But how do I know if he loves me or if he's just being nice because he feels sorry for me?"

"Through the same gift that strengthens every good relationship—time and communication." He strode to the doorway.

"Daed?"

He turned.

"Denki. Mamm couldn't have done any better."

He chuckled. "But she didn't burn everything she cooked."

"Again?"

He nodded. "We have no eggs left in the house, and tomorrow is muffin day."

Somewhere deep within, her sense of humor began to stir again. "Those poor chickens—all that work for nothing."

"Feel free to borrow my horse and go by Allen's to get some eggs. And if your horse doesn't settle down soon, we've got to sell her."

"I'm not ready to sell her. I'll try working with her now that I have more time."

"I need to get back to work. I'm taking a small load of furniture to Ada's tomorrow. Can you get the eggs?"

"I don't want to go anywhere yet. We'll just have oatmeal or something else in the morning."

"Sure thing."

Lena moved to her dresser and pulled out the first letter Grey had written to her. When she passed the mirror, she stopped. When had she started letting this birthmark completely define her worth?

She knew others who had obvious outward flaws. Did they want to change their looks too? Her thoughts drifted to Ivan. She would hurt all over if Ivan let what was missing on his body have final say about how he felt about the rest of his body. He'd have to live with having only half an arm his whole life. He could wear a prosthetic, but he'd still have a visible flaw...just like her. If she had her birthmark removed, what message would that send to him or to other people she loved?

She opened the first letter Grey had sent her.

My beautiful, sweet Lennie,

We've known each other forever, and yet it seems, in some ways, we don't know each other very well at all. That doesn't surprise or disappoint me. I look forward to understanding you better, to knowing more of your secrets and flaws and you knowing more of mine.

You're as deep as those gorgeous eyes, as clever and witty and unpredictable (in a good way) as anyone I've ever known. But I am disappointed in one thing…that I have failed to help you see yourself through my eyes.

Please allow me to remedy that right now by sharing memories, thoughts, and truths of who you are to me.

But first, I don't know why I wasn't drawn to you as a young man, but I know it had nothing to do with outward appearances. We were friends, and you were my closest friend's kid sister. You were fifteen when I was twenty. Thankfully, men don't usually fall for teen girls, but I think the reverse happens more easily. I've always thought you were one of a kind—rare and worthy. When you were seventeen, I remember thinking you'd become a beautiful woman and would be a blessing to any man.

Here's a story from our past—

The big boys needed to find that baby frog before little Lennie ate it… Can you remember that? I dare say no, but if you could, you'd remember I was brave and strong and not the one who laid it in your two-year-old lap as a gift in the first place. Okay, we've got that straight, right?

She laughed, and tears flowed freely. What a pair they made. His words continued until he'd filled three pages. He spoke of warm summer nights and private conversations they'd shared and years of them just being friends. Then he shared his journey of falling in love with her—the closest female friend he'd ever had or ever hoped to have.

Was it possible he really did feel as he kept assuring her he did? With that thought pounding at her, she opened the second letter. He'd filled it with white petals from umpteen daisies.

My beautiful, sweet Lennie,

I found a field of daisies… I know they aren't blooming yet, but it's my story, and you aren't here to set me straight. So I found this field of daisies inside the florist shop and picked you a bouquet. After I paid for them at the cash register, I headed home. Along the way, and it's quite a ways to a store…I mean, a *field* like that, I decided to take one flower and do the "she loves me, she loves me not." Unfortunately, it landed on "she loves me not," so I tried another flower, and another, and another. Do you happen to have any daisies in your greenhouse? I'm in need of more.

Your friend, your confidant, your first kiss and, with all that is good in my life, I hope your last…

Somehow that sentence didn't work out as I'd hoped. I didn't mean your last kiss ever. I trust you know what I mean. And I trust as time gives you perspective, you know what you mean to me.

Grey

Feeling his hope and humor in each word, she closed the letter. Oh how she wanted to believe he meant every word. Feeling a little renewed strength, she decided to get out for a bit. They did need eggs for tomorrow, and she really would like to catch a glimpse of Grey.

After harnessing her Daed's horse to the buggy, she drove to Allen's.

Before going into his house, she walked to the far edge of the backyard.
The bridge.

But it wasn't finished. Grey had set the timbers on the cement foundation and nailed half of the decking in place. The wood for the other half
was neatly stacked on the half-built bridge. A toolbox lay on top of the
stack. She studied it, wondering why he hadn't finished what he'd started.
Across the creek and across Grey's backyard sat the home he'd built for
him and Elsie. A few moments later his screen door popped open, and
Grey stepped outside. He strode across the yard, his shoulders broad and
squared. He had a spring in his step, one she hadn't seen in him in years,
and she wondered when it had faded.

He studied her, as if soaking her in. "Lennie." His voice sent warmth
running through her.

"Hi." She pointed to the bridge. "You didn't finish it."

"I realized that I can't be the one to finish it, so I did my part." He
went to the center of it and opened the toolbox. "The hammer and nails
are in here."

"I can see that."

He shrugged. "Whenever you're ready…if you're ever ready."

"I…I'm not."

"Okay." He closed the toolbox. "I didn't think you would be yet. I
know how this must look to you, and I know what people are going to
think, but we know what is between us. Truth of what exists between
couples is all that matters."

His words pulled her, making her almost powerless to resist. But the
man before her—with his perfect body, blue eyes, and gorgeous voice—
couldn't really love her, could he?

Grey shifted. "So…how are you?"

"I don't really know. Confused, I guess." She shrugged. "And surprised.
I mean we were really yelling at each other. I…I can't even believe it."

"Ya. I don't regret it, though. I left knowing you better."

"That's scary."

"You know me better too."

"That isn't as scary."

"Not for you. It is for me."

"Is this how relationships work?"

"Sometimes...maybe. I don't really care how they're supposed to work, only that ours does. You know?"

She sort of did, and she liked how he viewed relationships. But he knew everything about her, and there was something he wasn't telling her. Was it hidden feelings he didn't want her to know about or something else?

"Lennie!" Allen's craggy voice hollered. He hurried over to her. "I didn't know you were here. Kumm uff rei."

He told her to come in, but he had no greeting for Grey? She glanced from one man to the other.

"Kumm," he said again.

She looked at Grey. He and Allen had never been at odds. Grey must've told him, and Allen obviously didn't approve. He'd jeopardize his friendship with Allen for her?

Unwilling to make anything between Grey and Allen worse but wanting to share a sentiment, she thought of something. "I have daisies blooming in the greenhouse. In a few months I might relinquish them to you."

"I'm ready for them whenever you say they're ready."

"Oh, and you can make those flowers say anything you want them to if you know the trick."

"I know how to get the wrong answer. Will you show me how to get the right one?"

She liked the wordplay between them, and an image formed in her mind—moonlight filtering into a dark bedroom. Grey was on a bed, sitting with his back against several pillows, talking and laughing. She lay across the foot of the bed, chatting openly while snacking on something. The bond between them could not be seen by human eye, but even now she felt its magnitude. "I think maybe...someday."

He nodded. As she and Allen walked back toward the house, Allen turned, watched Grey for a moment, and waved.

Thirty-Seven

Dwayne sat in Michael's living room listening to Grey reason with the school board. Dwayne's hands shook with anger as he glared at Peter, and he fought to keep his mouth shut. He'd sown enough seeds of scandal against Lena that everyone ought to hold her suspect. When he prodded people a bit, they said they wanted to leave the matter in the school board's hands, insisting that everyone needed forgiveness over something they'd done in recent months. Bunch of idiots! Not a one took the bait about Lena planning Elsie's demise or chasing after Grey. Not a one! What really had him furious was that Michael had called a board meeting because Grey had insisted. And Grey had talked Peter into answering a few questions.

Grey sat in front of Peter, talking all serenelike. It made Dwayne sick. But Lena had better luck than he'd figured on. Some brother or friend or even her Daed always stepped between him and her, just like when he was tracking her in the woods the other day.

Peter finished explaining what Samantha did and said that week Lena had brought her into the school.

"Denki, Peter," Grey said. "Does anyone want to ask a question or make a comment about this aspect before I move on to another?"

One of the board member's wives spoke up. "Sounds to me like that woman offered a lot of clever ideas and wisdom for helping the children, but I heard nothing any of us would disagree with."

Grey chuckled. "Well said. Anyone else?"

The board members murmured among themselves and their wives, all nodding like hollow little bobbleheads.

Dwayne's Mamm put her hands on her hips. "That don't change that Lena took matters into her own hands. She had no right to decide on her own to bring in an outsider. It doesn't matter if that outsider was giving out gold."

"Yes, Mollie, we realize that," Michael added. "We're not talking about reinstating her right now. We're simply assessing the damage. You seem to think Samantha hypnotized your son, but he keeps saying she didn't."

Dwayne's mother glanced at him, but she didn't tell the board who'd told her that.

"Peter." Grey placed his elbow on one leg. "Samantha only came to the school a few times right after Elsie died. Why did you see her more than that?"

"Lena asked if I needed to talk to somebody. Lena…she's got an eye for what's really happening inside her students. I told her no, but later on, after I kept waking with nightmares and got to where I couldn't stand eating, Dwayne told me I should tell Lena I needed to talk to Samantha again. It helped." Peter looked at his Mamm. "I…I'm sorry, but when I started thinking about killing myself, I just wanted to talk to that woman again."

"Peter!" Mamm screamed. "What are you saying? That's…a…sin!"

"Let's not get into a debate on what is and isn't a sin." Grey put his hand on Peter's leg. "Nothing is a sin because one feels drawn to it. It was a temptation that he sought help to avoid. If being tempted is a sin, then where does that leave Jesus?"

Dwayne's Mamm plunked into a chair. "Ya…ya…I hadn't thought about it… That woman…she helped you?"

"A lot, Mamm. I never saw her do or say nothing that might pull someone from the faith. She only wanted to teach us some things she's learned about dealing with shocking and violent deaths, and she likes learning things I can teach her."

Leeriness crossed Mamm's face. "What did she need to know from a boy?"

"Well, she wanted to know how to measure a horse by hands and the difference between a pony's, donkey's, and horse's personality and what she should look for to know if a horse is a good one. She's been thinking about buying one for her children."

Dwayne couldn't stand Peter's disloyalty, and he refused to hear another word from any of them. Lena had cast a spell on all of them, and the only way to break it was to kill her. He slammed the door as he left, mounted his horse, and rode home. He stormed into the tool shed and found the goods he'd been hiding there.

After he placed the thick part of the baseball bat in the vise, he tightened the clamps. He grabbed the steel horseshoe and lined it up against the wooden bat. He tried it upside down, right side up, and sideways. Sideways was the ticket. It had taken a bit of effort and patience to find a heavy steel horseshoe like this one. But it would be worth all the hassle. He opened a package of screws and began anchoring the shoe to the bat.

Tomorrow would be her last day. He hoped she didn't enjoy it. And he'd just be so very sad to learn her rogue horse had stomped her to death.

Lena set the pressing iron facedown on the heating plate. Her home smelled of freshly made bread. She'd opened the windows at daybreak, and even as it neared noontime, the cool May air kept the room comfortable as she baked and ironed.

Her Daed wouldn't be back from Ada's until nearly dark, and when he did get home, he would have already eaten dinner. But she wanted to take a loaf of bread to each member of the school board and apologize for overstepping her bounds. She still believed the scholars did nothing but benefit from Samantha's visits, but Lena had been stubborn and rebellious to refuse to submit to anyone else's opinions and concerns but her own. She would apologize for her lack of submission.

Other than her family, she'd seen very few people. Five days ago she'd stood in Allen's yard talking with Grey across the creek with the half-finished bridge between them. She longed to finish her half, but that awful feeling of *something* kept tugging at her. If she could get a peace about that one thing, she'd be ready to complete her half of the bridge.

She understood now what he'd meant when he'd said, *I'll build us a bridge…in every way possible.*

The structure symbolized her part in meeting him at a place where they could understand each other, but she just couldn't do that, couldn't promise to be his again until she knew what this catch in her spirit was about.

Her horse neighed loud and long. She went to the front door, but before she stepped outside, unease warred inside her. Nicky jumped up and followed her. "Not this time, ol' girl. She's spooked enough without you getting near her." Ignoring her reluctance, Lena went outside and closed the front door so Nicky wouldn't push the screen door open and follow her.

She hurried down the steps, but that odd feeling caught in her gut again. She stopped and studied the barn. Nothing looked out of the ordinary, and she commanded her imagination to quit being silly. Even as she chided herself, she stopped walking. Nicky's angry bark blasted through the air.

She went back toward her home. As she climbed the steps, a shadow fell, and boards creaked as Dwayne came around the corner of the wrap-around porch.

He tapped a baseball bat on the porch floor. "Going somewhere?" He smiled and held up the bat, showing her the attached horseshoe. "I think you've got horse problems, ma'am." He laughed. "Almost as if somebody has been taking a cattle prod to her. Of course, you make that real easy because you like her kept in the stall. Now that bull wasn't as easy to use the cattle prod on. I had to be on a fast horse that knew how to take direction. And poor Aaron thinks he didn't repair the fence good when I'm the one who undid his handiwork. But the end result was not aimed at anyone but you."

Lena couldn't catch her breath or make her body move. She just stood there trying to think of what to do. Scratching on the solid door, Nicky barked and growled, but she couldn't get out.

Dwayne flinched when Nicky lunged at an open window, knocking over a side table and kerosene lantern. "Just look at how this has turned out. That bull gored the wrong person, but this new plan means Grey can lose two women in the same way. He'll never get over the odds of that. It'll drive him nuts. Who knows, I've come to hate him so much, I just might be around to make it happen a third time."

She had to get past Dwayne and inside her home. If she couldn't get in, just getting the door open would free Nicky. That'd give her time to... to...what? Lena needed a plan.

He gestured toward the barn. "This way, Teacher Lena."

She suddenly remembered a self-defense move she'd learned while in public school. Unsure if she could do it, she felt woozy. He planned on killing her, but she didn't have to make it easy for him.

When she didn't do his bidding, he grabbed her by the arm, jerking her along as he went down the steps. She resisted his pull. "A fighter, eh? I figured on that. It'll make the marks I leave on you look more like a horse stomped you to death."

He moved to the same step she was on and towered over her like Peter had at the beginning of the school year. As he peered down at her, she arched her free hand back, jutting out the ball of it, and jammed it into his nose as hard as she could. Blood gushed, and he stumbled backward; landing on his backside on the steps, he screamed and cursed.

The dog barked and growled while lunging at the screened window. She hurried up the steps, across the porch, and clutched the doorknob. Before she could turn it, his hand caught her by the ankle and pulled her feet out from under her.

Thirty-Eight

With a clipboard in hand, Grey cataloged the shop's inventory. During his next break he'd write to Lennie. He wished he knew the words that would reach inside her heart and allow her to trust him. There were a lot of things about women he didn't understand, but Lennie's belief that men cared more about some physical feature than they did anything else baffled him.

"Grey," Ephraim said.

"Ya?"

He pointed outside. Peter stood beside his horse at the hitching post. "He's started this way half a dozen times. I asked him if I could help, and he muttered your name."

"Thanks." Grey strode outside. "Peter," he spoke softly, but Peter jolted.

"Dwayne..." Peter gasped. "He...he says I'm too stupid to know... and maybe he's right...but..."

"Peter, take a few breaths and slow down."

Peter sucked in air as if he'd been held under water. "It's my fault about Elsie. I should've come to you a long time ago. I...I'm so sorry."

"You didn't cause Elsie's death, Peter. And whatever you did do wrong, I've forgiven you."

Specks of sweat beaded across Peter's pale face. "You won't believe me, and he'll find a way to make me look like a liar."

"I...I don't understand."

"This morning I saw Dwayne with a horseshoe attached to a baseball bat. It's a weapon. I knew it the moment I saw it."

Grey's whole body jolted as if he'd been shot.

Peter wiped his eyes. "I made up an excuse and got Mamm to let me leave school early. As I came through the back field, I saw him leaving with it. Maybe he's right. Maybe I'm just too stupid to add two and two, but I got a bad feeling about this, and he hates Lena."

"You did the right thing." Knowing his own horse was way out in the pasture, Grey grabbed the reins to Peter's horse. "I'd like to get there quick-like. May I borrow your horse?"

"Sure."

"There's nothing stupid about what you've done here," Grey said as he mounted, and then he spurred the animal hard. Dwayne had a mean streak, but surely he was all talk and no action.

No matter how much he tried to convince himself of Lennie's safety, fear tightened around his throat. Thoughts of her being hurt tormented him. And when his greatest fear—losing her—danced a vision before him, he prayed for mercy.

A half mile before he came to the four-way stop, he pulled on the right rein, guiding the horse off the road and through a back pasture. Going this way would take half a mile off the trip. Images around him seemed to magnify as he flew across the field. The sky stood out as a brilliant blue. The hayfield went on for acres and acres, all filled with rich green blades of hay about two feet tall. Finally Lennie's place came into view. Nicky's angry bark echoed off the hills as Grey approached. He brought the horse to a halt, jumped off, and ran toward the house. Nicky leaped at the screen of the window, barking unlike he'd ever heard her before. The dog yapped and growled. The horse whinnied loudly. Lennie screamed. Grey ran as hard and fast toward the barn as he could.

Inside the shadows of the barn, Lennie fell back against the wooden slats of a half wall. Dwayne raised the bat. Grey bolted into the barn, coming between Dwayne and Lennie. Dwayne's bat hit Grey's ribcage, causing Dwayne to stumble backward. Searing pain shot down Grey's left side, knocking the breath out of him.

Several seconds passed before he managed to jerk air into his lungs. He glanced to Lennie. Her eyes were closed, and she hadn't budged. Alarm ran through him. Dwayne regained his footing but not before Grey took hold of a nearby bucket. He met the next blow of the bat with the bucket. The power of Dwayne's swings caused fresh pain to keep pounding through Grey's chest, and he grew weaker. "Put the bat down."

"Make me."

Holding on to the bucket, Grey deflected blow after blow, while backing Dwayne away from Lennie. The horse kicked and whinnied harder with each thudding sound. Grey saw a cattle prod in the horse's stall. And Dwayne's plan began to make sense—the bat with a horseshoe attached, the cattle prod, Dwayne fighting with Lena in the barn. "It's over, Dwayne. No one is going to believe both of us were stomped to death by her horse. Put the bat down."

Dwayne swung again and again, each time aiming for a different part of Grey. He warded off the blows with the bucket, but exhaustion and pain slowed him. Dwayne came at him again, and Grey went to his knees. Holding the bucket above his head, he withstood another hit. Something black lunged at Dwayne, hitting him square in the chest and knocking his upper body into the horse's open stall. Nicky jumped back, barking like mad. The horse kicked and stomped as Dwayne tried to get out of the stall. Grey got to his feet and reached for Dwayne to pull him out. The horse kicked again, its back hoof catching Dwayne in the temple, and he fell over. Grey grabbed Dwayne by the feet and dragged him out of the stall.

He lay unmoving on the ground.

Grey ran to the half wall where Lena lay motionless. "Lennie."

Nicky nudged her, licked her face, and whined. While going to his knees in front of Lennie, Grey patted the dog, unsure how she got out but thankful she had. "Sit." Grey pointed, not wanting the dog's excitement to jar Lennie. Nicky did, studying her owner.

Lennie rubbed her head, moaning. One arm lay lifeless, and she cradled it while slowly prying her eyes open. Fear owned him as memories of losing Elsie beat against him.

"Grey." She gasped in pain before reaching for him. "You okay?"

"Ya." He drew her fingers to his lips and kissed them. "I need to go get help. Just stay still, okay?"

"I'm not hurt bad. I promise." Tears filled her eyes. "He only managed to hit my arm, and then I hit the back of my head on that wall when he pushed me."

Grey kissed her forehead and her cheeks, breathing in the beauty of life. "I was so worried." His lips moved over hers. He cradled her face. "I need to get us some help. You've got to be seen."

"Dwayne?"

Grey turned to look at Dwayne's still body. "I think he's dead."

The sound of hoofs grew louder until Ephraim came into sight, riding bareback. He brought his horse to a halt just outside the barn. "Peter said…" He studied the scene for a moment. "Do you need help?"

"Ya. I want Lennie seen, but we need a driver to take us."

Ephraim took off for his place to make a call.

Lennie tried to stand. "I want out of here."

Grey stood and helped her up. She moaned in pain. "My ankle's hurt too. I don't think I can put any weight on it." She cradled her lifeless arm.

He gently steadied her, concerned about possible hidden injuries. After a glance at Dwayne, she buried her face against Grey's chest.

"Kumm." He wanted to carry her but feared he might make her injuries worse. Leaning on him, she slowly walked across the driveway and yard and to the steps of the front porch. The screen on one of the open windows was ripped. Nicky had jumped through it to get to them.

Lennie sat on a step. "If I'd followed my gut, I would've never stepped outside."

Grey sat beside her, and she rested her head against his shoulder. "And if you hadn't followed your instincts to have faith in Peter, he wouldn't have come and told on his brother."

Nicky put her head on Lennie's lap.

Grey ran his hands over hers, feeling the softness of her skin, so grateful she was safe. "You know I love you, don't you?"

"I want to believe that, but from the beginning I've had this catch inside me that makes me feel like you're hiding something."

She'd picked up on the lie he carried. But his life before her, the one between him and Elsie, would never be open for another woman to know about. His marriage deserved that much from him, didn't it? He drew her fingers to his lips and kissed them. "Some things are best left alone, Lennie. I'm not one of your students for you to mold. Do you trust me?"

She said nothing for several long minutes.

"Grey?"

He kissed her forehead. "Ya?"

"If you'll bring me a pot of daisies from the greenhouse while we wait for a driver, I'll show you how to land on 'she loves me.'"

He held her hand that wasn't hurt and gently squeezed it. "I'd like that."

"Lena." Her Daed tapped on her bedroom door, waking her.

She moaned in pain while trying to sit up, realizing she still had Aaron's letter in her hand. The pages of the lined paper crinkled as she shifted. "Ya?"

Midmorning sun streamed through her bedroom window. Nicky lay on the bed beside her. The dog had not let her get out of sight since she'd come home from her surgery at the hospital two weeks ago. Lena had a plate in her arm, a sprained ankle, a mild concussion, and a lot of bruises— all of which were diagnosed through the proper tests and addressed without a night's stay at the hospital.

Her Daed eased the door open. "I wouldn't wake you, except Peter's here. He's downstairs, hoping you'll see him. Are you up to it?"

Two weeks of bed rest and she'd yet to have an easy day of recuperation. But she'd begun to need less pain medication and to feel a little stronger each day this week. The doctor had said the type of sprain she had meant she couldn't put much weight on her leg. He gave her a medical boot to wear, but since she couldn't use crutches because of the injury to her arm, she'd had to wait for her ankle to heal enough so she could walk using only the boot. She'd been able to get up and move around for short periods the last few days.

"Okay, I need a housecoat. Deborah and Cara washed clothes and put them away last night, so I'd look for it in the closet."

While her Daed rummaged through her closet, she tucked Aaron's letter under the covers, unwilling for anyone to catch a glance at its contents. He was doing well but knew he had a long way to go yet. He hadn't chanced returning to Dry Lake for Dwayne's funeral for fear of what it might do to him. It'd been hard for him to admit how blinded the alcohol had kept him. He'd thought Dwayne to be a better man than himself. The news that Dwayne had dismantled a part of the fence, purposefully making it easy for the bull to get into the wrong pasture, and had angered the bull with a cattle prod had only shifted Aaron's sense of guilt, not removed it. The encouraging news was that Aaron continued on, not drinking since arriving at the Better Path.

Her Daed passed her a housecoat and eased pillows behind her back. With her arm in a cast and a lot of bruises, shifting didn't come easy. After a little help from her Daed, she slid her good arm into her housecoat and hung the other side of the terry cloth cover-up around her shoulder.

"You getting hungry?"

Lena wrinkled her nose. "You doing the cooking?"

He laughed. "Ada's here."

"Again? And on a Saturday this time. That means she's missing her busiest day at Ada's House."

Her Daed's cheeks flushed. "With so many folks stopping by, she's coming whenever she can to help fix desserts and coffee."

"Well, I'm glad my suffering is working out so well for you."

"Ya, me too."

She laughed and then yelped with pain.

He placed her prayer Kapp on her head and kissed her through it. His hand rested on top of her head, and his eyes appeared to be misting.

Grey had saved her life and sustained three broken ribs from the hit he took for her. If Dwayne had hit her full force in the head, as he'd aimed to do with that one blow, she'd have died. The memories of that day were endless, rarely fading from her thoughts.

During that awful time she'd had the wisdom to stall Dwayne by getting him to talk. He'd been itching for years to brag about his genius in stealing from homes in her area, killing pets, and setting her up as his best victory yet. He saw her as no more valuable than a barn cat—to be done away with at will. She shuddered. Neither his viciousness nor his wanton desire to kill her could ever be fully explained.

He'd left a lot of bruises on her, but when he'd started swinging that bat, she dodged it, deflected it with boards, a saddle, and her now-injured arm. When he'd slung her against that wooden wall, knocking her unconscious and unable to defend herself, Grey arrived and took the blow for her.

"I'm safe, Daed."

He cleared his throat. "You keep it that way." He picked up a pitcher of water and poured her a glass before he opened a bottle of pain medicine. "Half a dozen girlfriends are also downstairs, hoping for another visit."

"Don't any of them have a Saturday job?"

He held out the glass of water and a pill. "I'm not asking that. You're the one on enough pain meds to be so candid. You do it."

She suppressed laughter. "I'd like to see Grey."

"I know, and I'm sure he'd like to see you. Discretion says to wait."

When she and Grey had returned from the hospital the day of the incident, her Daed had asked him not to stay and not to visit. While in the waiting room of the hospital during her surgery, Grey had to answer a lot of questions for the police and for the church leaders. According to her Daed, it didn't take long for the church leaders to realize Grey cared for her. When they asked Grey, he didn't deny it, and the church leaders began discussing what to do. A few hours later a preacher confided to her Daed that because Grey and Lena had been through so much together this past year, they were considering freeing him of the usual time restraints and protocol on a widower. But the preacher cautioned her Daed that Grey needed to keep his distance until a decision was reached.

Grey told Lena he was willing to stay, that the whole community could think of him what they wanted. But Lena asked him to go home. She didn't want to be the cause of trouble for Grey, so now they waited.

"Any news from the church leaders?"

"Not yet. These things take time."

She rubbed her head. With all the medications, she could barely think. "How long since Dwayne's funeral?"

"Eleven days."

"How does Peter look?"

"Rough, but better than I'd have expected."

"Send him on up."

She lay back and closed her eyes, thinking of Grey and the life they had ahead of them.

Grey was right. He wasn't a student to be molded. If he chose not to share whatever caused that catch inside her, she'd respect that. She didn't have to figure out every angle of what was wrong in someone's life and insist they become all she thought they should be. Be willing to help? Yes. Track down the source of the problem and refuse to let go until she saw the wanted improvement? No.

That was God's job, not hers.

Peter eased the door open, looking pale and shaky.

"Hi. Kumm." She motioned to one of several chairs her Daed had set up in her room for visitors.

He sat in the chair farthest from her. "Mamm and Daed said they won't be coming, but I know they're sorry. They didn't know him like I did. Christian saw it too. But we only thought he was mean. I didn't know he was...there's a word our new counselor uses...oh, ya, psychologically disturbed."

"All is forgiven, Peter. You tell them that for me, okay?"

He nodded. "I...I'm sorry I called you ugly and stupid. You're not."

"Forgiven."

Silence fell between them. She wanted to thank him, but should she? His actions had saved her, but his brother had died. "I...I'm proud of you, Peter."

He shifted. "I've been thinking...a lot, and...well...I was so busy pointing out your flaws, I couldn't see my own."

"It works like that for all of us at some point, especially teens. You aren't the first to point out my birthmark, nor will you be the last. I've considered trying to have it removed, although it doesn't sound like they can do much more than make it fade."

"No. You...you shouldn't do that. If you can make yourself perfect on the outside, where does that leave me and others like me who have marks stamped on our insides? I can't have what Dwayne's done removed by some doctor. I gotta live with it. I gotta carry that stain the rest of my life, hoping a few people can see beyond it to love me anyway."

"That's good insight, Peter. Really good. Have you and Grey talked any?"

"We had a good long visit last night. You and him got something going on?" He lowered his head. "I shouldn't ask that. But if you don't, you should. I think he likes you."

"Ya, I think so too."

Peter stood. "I need to go. Mamm and Daed get worried right quick-like these days."

"Denki for coming by."

He closed the door as he left. Last night Deborah and Cara had washed Lena's hair for her and helped her bathe. With some assistance she could manage to get dressed, visit with her friends for a little bit before sending them on their way, and maybe even bake some cookies to take to Grey. It was midmorning. Surely she could do that small list by midafternoon.

She moved ever so slowly through the next four hours, but with Ada's help, Lena went to the porch with her hair neatly done, a clean dress on, and a box of fresh chocolate chip oatmeal cookies in hand. Well, the dress was mostly on. Ada had to cut it, add material, and resew it, but the patch-work dress looked normal as long as she kept her good arm through one sleeve of her sweater and had the other side pinned in place. The top part of the boot was hidden under her dress.

She and Grey hadn't spoken of their future, but she knew he loved her. They fit. And he didn't want flawless. While drifting in and out of a drug-induced state, she had finally understood the core of who Grey was. He wanted friendship most of all—the kind only a man and woman in love could have.

Her Daed led his horse and smooth-riding carriage to her. "You sure you don't want me to drive you there?" He opened the door, and Nicky hopped in.

She passed Daed the box of cookies and slowly climbed into the buggy. "I need to see Grey. Your horse takes no effort to direct. You know that. Go have coffee with Ada. Surely she's not here just to help me and be a hostess for my guests."

Her Daed glanced through the screen door of the house. "I hope not."

"Maybe it's time you found out. I won't stay long, and I won't go again until the church leaders and community approve. But no one will frown at me going to his place to give him a proper thank-you."

Her Daed passed the box to her. "Ada and your siblings were trying to keep it a secret so you wouldn't do any of the work, but they've planned a huge dinner."

She took the reins in hand. "Sounds wonderful. I'll be home in plenty of time for that."

He closed the door to the carriage. Her Daed's horse clipped along at a nice speed. Her own horse was in the pasture. Lena planned to work with her to rebuild trust, but she didn't know if the now high-strung mare would ever be useful again.

The warmth of May soaked into her healing body. After nearly a mile she drove up Grey's long gravel driveway, parked the rig, and got out. Ivan ran outside and greeted her, saying they'd been fishing earlier. He and his Daed had cleaned the fish, and now his Daed was in the shower.

When she awkwardly climbed out of the buggy, he pointed at the cast on her arm and her medical boot, asking what had happened. She made up a story about tripping over her shadow. He laughed, and when Nicky bounded out of the buggy, ready to play, Ivan was totally and happily distracted. After they talked and played with Nicky for a bit, she passed him the box of goodies and told him to let his Daed know she was here.

She meandered to the creek and watched the pristine water flow downstream. Life, like the water drifting by, never stopped moving. She longed to embrace every moment without regard to flaws—hers or others—and to end each day knowing if it was her last, she'd loved freely.

"Lennie," Grey called as he strode toward her. His movements weren't stiff, but she imagined his ribs still caused him a good bit of discomfort. Unlike her arm, there wasn't anything that could be done for ribs except pain relievers while he healed. He came within feet of her, and his body language spoke of wanting to embrace her. "Should you be out and about like this?"

"Ya. My strength is starting to return." She looked at the stockpile of planks still sitting on the bridge. "I want to build my side."

"Now?"

She nodded.

"Lennie, with your injuries, you can't possibly be up to it."

"If I help about as much as a preschooler and you do the rest, I'm up to it. The question is whether you'll accept that as me building my half."

"You're here and doing what you can. I'll never want more."

He couldn't have given a more perfect answer, and with it he'd stolen even more of her heart. "Are you able to do that kind of work?"

"There's plenty I can't do yet, but this will be pretty easy. We'll move slowly and secure the boards with a minimum of nails for today. The job can be finished right in a week or so when we're both feeling stronger."

Grey brought a few planks at a time and laid them on the bridge next to her. She slid each one into place. With his help she hammered nails part of the way in, and he finished securing them for her. A warm breeze made the bushes along the creek rustle. The pristine water gurgled softly while glistening in the sun. His silvery voice washed over her as they worked. With most of the bridge already done, it didn't take more than thirty minutes to complete.

She stood in the middle, and he joined her. He took her by the hand

and intertwined his fingers with hers. The catch in her gut concerning him hadn't let go, but she had peace about it.

"I have some good news." Grey drew a breath. "The church leaders came to see me while I was cleaning fish. We have permission to see each other and marry next wedding season."

Without warning, tears brimmed. She put her one arm around his waist and leaned her face against his chest. "That's what I've been hoping for—freedom to choose." After the embrace she gazed up at him. "But I think we should only see each other quietly at Allen's or my Daed's until October—not out of hypocrisy or sneaky hiding, but out of respect for how hard it will be on others, like Elsie's family, if they see us together too soon. They need time, and us waiting for a year after her death to be seen out together is not asking too much."

"I think most people have figured out how we feel, Lennie."

"Ya. But people knowing and having to observe it are two very different kinds of pain. And when we go public in October, they'll be pleased we tempered our actions out of respect for the Old Ways. Besides, I think *we* need quiet visits inside Allen's or Daed's home with no stares and lots of calm, easygoing time to really get to know each other."

"Are you doing this for me—to keep folks from thinking less of me? Because if you are, I don't mind what anyone thinks. Not anymore, Lennie."

"I…I've waited so long, Grey." A tear escaped and ran down her cheek as she laid the truth of her heart open to him. "I'm sure you can't imagine how lonely it got. And now I have you. I want to enjoy being courted without feeling people's frowns or knowing I'm hurting someone."

He wiped the tear off her face before kissing her cheek. "I…need to tell you something…at least a sentence or two, just so you know." He stroked her cheek and down her neck, tracing the path of her birthmark with the back of his fingers—as if assuring her he cherished who she was.

She waited, but he said nothing. Whatever he needed to say battled with him to stay hidden. "I'll hear it as if you were inside the circle of peace."

He drew a deep breath. "My marriage was…was…" The pain in his voice said so much more than his words. "Difficult. Troubled, really. We had no bridges. No way to cross over. We'd just taken a few steps toward a second chance when she died."

What? She didn't say the word, but she wanted to. His confession didn't fit with who she'd thought him to be. He had known years of loneliness too. His words, as few as they were, changed her. The news didn't make her feel superior or more secure. Grey himself had freed her of insecurity without a word about his marriage. But what he'd confessed gave her understanding of many things about her future husband.

He rubbed the center of his chest, exhaling freely. "I so needed to say that. I needed *you* to know."

"Ya, you did." She looked up at him, desperately wanting a kiss.

He cradled her face before he placed his lips over hers. Her heart went wild as dreams of being married to him and having children warmed her. "Will you marry me before next year's wedding season is over?"

"Ya. How about February?"

"February." Grey rolled the word around as if thinking about the pros and cons. She'd chosen the end of the wedding season, giving them four months of openly courting before they wed. He slowly kissed one side of her face and then the other. "It's a good plan. In the meantime I intend to steal a kiss or two when no one is looking."

She tugged on his shirt collar, pulling him close. "Like this?" She gently pressed her lips against his.

Ada's House Series

Main Characters

Lena Kauffman—twenty-three-year-old Amish schoolteacher in Dry Lake.

Israel Kauffman—a forty-five-year-old Amish widower. Lena's father. He's been quietly interested in Ada Stoltzfus for a long time.

Allen Kauffman—twenty-nine-year-old brother of Lena. Close friend of Grey's. Married to Emily, and they have four children.

Benjamin "Grey" Graber—twenty-eight-year-old Amish man married to Elsie.

Elsie Blank Graber—twenty-seven years old. Married to Grey Graber.

Ivan Graber—five-year-old son of Grey and Elsie Graber.

Cara Atwater Moore—twenty-eight-year-old waitress from New York City who lost her mother as a child, was abandoned by her father, and grew up in foster care. Cara has been stalked for years by Mike Snell. She and her daughter, Lori, found their way to Dry Lake in *The Hope of Refuge,* and Cara is now engaged to Ephraim Mast.

Lori Moore—Cara's seven-year-old daughter. Lori's father, Johnny, died before she turned two years old, leaving Cara a widow.

Ephraim Mast—thirty-two-year-old, single Amish man who works as a cabinetmaker and helps manage his ailing father's business and care for their large family. He and Cara became friends during her visit to Dry Lake when she was a child.

Deborah Mast—twenty-one-year-old Amish woman who was engaged to Mahlon Stoltzfus in *The Hope of Refuge.* She's Ephraim's sister, but she lives with Ada in Hope Crossing.

Mahlon Stoltzfus—twenty-three-year-old Amish man who was engaged to Deborah in *The Hope of Refuge*. He ran off without explanation, leaving his widowed mother and Deborah to cope with life and bills on their own.

Jonathan Stoltzfus—twenty-six-year-old Amish man who is good friends with Lena Kauffman.

Ada Stoltzfus—forty-three-year-old widow whose only child is Mahlon. She's a friend and mentor to Deborah Mast. She took Cara under her wing in *The Hope of Refuge*.

Aaron Blank—twenty-four years old. He was raised Amish but hasn't joined the faith. His sister is Elsie. He runs his parents' dairy farm.

Michael Blank—Elsie and Aaron's father and the chairman of the school board for the local Amish school.

Dora Blank—Michael's wife and Elsie and Aaron's mother.

Anna Mary Lantz—Ephraim's ex-girlfriend and one of Deborah's good friends.

Emma and Levi Riehl—an aunt and uncle of Cara's who inadvertently contributed to her being abandoned as a child and consequently being raised in foster care.

Robbie—an Englischer who is a co-worker and driver for Ephraim's cabinetry business. He is a driver for several Old Order Amish families.

Nicky—a mixed-breed dog whose personality and size resemble the author's dog, Jersey.

Acknowledgments

To my family, co-workers, and friends—If life tempts me to doubt God's faithfulness, I remember you.

Our teen broke a toe in the spring of 2010, and because of that, my husband and son came in contact with a wonderful physician—John A. Alsobrook, MD, Northeast Georgia Physicians Group, Sports Medicine, Buford, Georgia. As an author writing a trauma scene, I couldn't let such a great resource go untapped. I'm very grateful to say that the doctor was willing to return a call from someone looking for help with fictional characters in trauma. Each time I needed advice, Dr. Alsobrook was truly informative, focused, and fun to work with, which means he will be called upon again ☺.

To my Old Order Amish friends, who provide insight and direction before I begin to write each story, correction on any inaccuracies in the manuscript once it's complete, and our own hiddy where we can chat, as well as good food, fun fellowship, and a cozy bed to sleep in—Thank you!

To my expert in the Pennsylvania Dutch language, who wishes to remain anonymous—Your input is invaluable. It may not feel like it to you, but authenticity gives great pleasure to readers.

To those who work so diligently on every aspect of making each book a success, my team, WaterBrook Multnomah Publishing Group—It'd take a nonfiction book to express how honored I am to know and work with each of you! From marketing to sales to production to the editorial department, you are so much more to me than time allows me to express. From the president to the newest savvy person added to the house, you're all making a difference in the lives of authors and readers.

To Shannon Marchese, my editor—I believe that if I were to write for you until I'm a hundred years old, I'd still be soaking up your knowledge and learning how to craft a better and stronger story.

To Carol Bartley, my line editor—I always look forward to the amazing polishing job you do. Your expertise, open-mindedness, gentleness, and humor strengthen so much more than the story. I trust you, and I take pleasure in working with you.

To Steve Laube, my agent—My time and creativity would be buried under the work load of business if it weren't for you. I shove things onto your plate and return to what I love doing, writing. Thank you for being so knowledgeable, trustworthy, and understanding of an author's dream—to *write*!

To Marci Burke, my good friend and critique partner—In our seven years of working together, you have yet to let me down even once.

To my sons—When I'm in isolation mode during writing, it is your taps on my office door, early-morning phone calls, and spur-of-the-moment visits to whisk me away for a meal or a game that remind me I'm loved. And to my two daughters-in-law—You are help when I need it, laughter when I don't expect it, and strength when I have none of my own.

And lastly, to my husband—Every year and decade we celebrate together, I understand more that it'll never be enough. I'm content with many things but never when it comes to having time with you.

The
HARVEST
of
GRACE

AN ADA'S HOUSE NOVEL

CINDY
WOODSMALL

To Linda Wertz,
a dear woman who values God's creatures
and labors to exhaustion to make a difference.
You touch lives without realizing it.
You offer a different lens to view life through
to all who are blessed to come in contact with you.
And to your husband, Rick,
who believes in you as much as he believes in the One who created you.

And to every farmer,
who understands all too well
the mountain of troubles that you face,
the lack of support from those who need you most,
and the constant effort you put into finding solutions.

One

From her perch on the milking stool, Sylvia patted the cow's side and cooed to her, enjoying the warm softness of the cow's hide. "You're feeling better now, *ya?*" Puffs of white vapor left her mouth when she spoke, and her fingers ached from the cold.

The cow mooed gently as if answering her.

Sylvia removed the claw milker from the cow's udder and sprayed Udder Care to prevent chaffing and to ward off mastitis. She set the stool and bucket out of the way, moved to the far end of the stalls, and pulled the lever that opened the tie rails, releasing the last round of cows from their milking stalls.

Daed lifted two buckets of milk and headed for the milk house. "What are you humming this morning?"

"Oh. Uh…" She hadn't realized she was humming, so she had to pause for a moment and think. "Moon River."

"Sure does sound nice. This place don't seem the same when you're off. No one else I know hums while working a herd." He disappeared into the milk house to dump the fresh liquid into the milk tank.

Unlike a lot of Daeds, Sylvia's hadn't minded when she bought an iPod during the early years of her *rumschpringe*. The *Englischer* who picked up their milk three times a week had always recharged it for her. But then, five years ago, it fell under a cow during a milking and was trampled to death. Since she still hadn't joined the faith, she could've bought another iPod, but Lilly was seven by then and hanging around the barn more. It would have hurt Lilly to realize that her older sister didn't always keep the Old Ways, so she never replaced it. But she missed some of her favorite songs, like "Moon River." The lyrics about the dream maker always made her think of Elam.

Her pulse quickened as she envisioned Elam next to her in the barn. His good looks seemed more suited to modeling in Englischer ads than managing a dairy herd, and she found his physical presence frustratingly compelling. He frequently mentioned marriage lately, and she could imagine their future together, always being close to him, waking alongside him in the mornings. But she had reservations too. Didn't she want more from true love than heart-pounding attraction? Maybe she just needed to spend more time talking with him about their "rainbow's end," and all her reservations would melt into nothingness.

She patted a few cows on the rump, gently moving them along. The herd desperately wanted in the barn at milking time, each cow hurrying to a stall in the milking parlor, but they weren't eager to leave the building afterward. Their contented lowing and the ease with which they lumbered outdoors toward the bunk feeder and water trough made her smile. The large creatures were the same today as they'd always been—peaceful and productive.

In a side stall a new calf nursed from its mother. Ginger slid her head across the wooden gate, and Sylvia rubbed her long forehead. Sylvia had been up half the night making sure Ginger didn't have any trouble bringing the calf into the world. Fortunately, Sylvia hadn't needed to pull the calf or call a vet. Both were victories she was proud of.

Two years ago after she'd cried over the death of both a cow and her calf, her Daed did the unthinkable. He gave her the right to tend to the breeding of the herd as she saw fit. Her ways took more effort than his, but she'd not lost a cow or a calf yet. Milk production was up, and the overall health of the herd had improved. She had her grandpa's teachings to thank for that.

Her Daed returned from the milk house. "I bet you're thinking about *Daadi* Fisher."

"Ya, I think of him every time a healthy calf is born." As a child she'd been her grandfather's shadow while he tended to the cows, and she'd been young when he began training her in the value of careful breeding and vigilance during every labor and birth. In spite of her being a girl in a patriarchal society, he believed in her. When he'd passed away a couple of years ago, she thought her heart might break.

Daed headed toward the remaining buckets of milk.

Sylvia pushed the wheeled cart that carried all her milking supplies toward the mud sink. "I need the two heaviest of those buckets, Daed."

"Two?" His eyes met hers, reflecting interest. "You making more yogurt already?"

"I am."

"Are we eating that much, or are you selling that much?" He poured the white, frothy liquid into a sterilized milk can for her and securely tamped down the lid.

"The answer to both is yes."

It was rare to see a smile on Daed's face before breakfast, but he grinned broadly. "*Sell iss gut,* ya?"

"Ya, it's a good thing." She pushed the supply cart into the milk house section of the barn and then returned to the parlor. "Daed, do you mind if I go to the house early? A bad dream woke Ruth up last night. I promised her that this morning I'd prove it was just a dream."

He tossed a pitchfork into a wheelbarrow and went into the first stall. "Sure, go on."

Sylvia abandoned her usual routine and climbed the haymow. After finding the mama cat's new hiding place for her kittens, she gently placed

Ruth's favorite tabby into the inside pocket of her coat and then went back down the ladder.

"Hey, Daed."

He turned, and she pulled out the kitten, once again hinting at her ultimate goal: for Ruth to be allowed to keep this one inside the house when the little fur ball was a week or so older.

A lopsided grin caused one side of his face to wrinkle, and she wondered what had him so jovial this morning. "Just don't get me in trouble over it. And make sure Ruthie knows it can't stay inside. Barn cats tend to become mean once they get a little age on them."

Sylvia put the milk cans into a wooden handcart. "They wouldn't if—"

"Go already." He shooed her toward the barn door. "I don't want to hear any more of your newfangled ideas about how I could run this farm differently. They always cost me money and energy."

His tone was playful, but she'd be wise to accept that he meant his words…for now. He'd come a long way in accepting her ideas concerning the farm. She often wondered if he'd give her any say if he had a son. She'd never know, because he had nine daughters, of which she was the eldest and the only one with a heart for farming.

His other daughters were more typical and girlish in every possible way, preferring housework over farm work. The three teenagers—Beckie, Lizzie, and Naomi—hated farming, always had. Lilly, who'd just turned twelve, would never complain about anything, but the smells and hard work made her queasy. The four youngest—Ruth, Barbie Ann, Salome, and Martha—were a hazard in the barn, causing Daed to shoo them away if they set foot inside the milking parlor.

Pushing the milk cart, Sylvia hurried from the barn to the house. Last week's snow glistened under the early morning sunlight. She toted the heavy milk cans inside one by one, being careful not to lean the containers against her body and squish the kitten.

The warmth of the entryway made her cold fingers scream in pain. Delicious aromas of sausage, biscuits, and coffee made her mouth water and her tummy rumble, keen reminders of how long and cold her night had been.

Her *Mamm* was adding wood to the stove, and Lizzie stood at the sink, washing dishes. There was never a shortage of dirty glasses and plates in a house with eleven people.

Sylvia removed her wader boots. "Morning."

Lizzie yawned. "That it is, and it arrives way too early in this house."

"Why, there you are." Mamm closed the door to the stove, smiling and motioning for her. "*Kumm.* Warm yourself. How's that mama cow?"

"Ginger and her newborn are doing great."

"I'm glad, but a girl shouldn't have to work like you do."

"I love it. You know that."

Mamm put her arm around Sylvia's shoulders and squeezed. "Still, we need a solution, and your Daed's found one that is right around the corner."

Sylvia would never get used to Daed making plans about the farm without telling her. "What does that mean?"

Naomi came through the back door, carrying an armload of firewood. She held the door open while Beckie entered with a lighter bundle of wood.

Beckie's blond hair peeked out from under one of Daed's black felt hats, and her blue eyes shone with spunk. "Good grief it's cold out there. Isn't it time for warmer weather?"

Mamm pulled several mugs out of the cabinet. "Your Daed said they're calling for a long winter and a late spring this year."

Clearly her mother had no intention of answering Sylvia's question. She'd find out whenever her Daed was ready for her to know.

Naomi dumped her load of wood into the bin and quickly straightened it. After she finished, Beckie tossed hers in and began warming her hands over the stove. Naomi straightened the mess, piece by piece. Getting the morning firewood used to be Beckie's job, but she wasn't good at doing chores by herself. Not making beds, washing dishes, or getting firewood. She would come back with only a couple of pieces of wood, and later, when Mamm wanted to add fuel to the stove, the bin would be empty. Sylvia and her sisters used to fuss about doing their jobs and then having to help Beckie with hers, but arguing only made everyone's days miserable. In the end, someone still had to help Beckie in order for all the chores to get done.

On washdays when it was time for Beckie to gather the dirty clothes, she seemed half-blind, always forgetting a few hampers, including the diaper pails. Since Naomi, a brown-haired beauty, was as meticulous as they came, she and Beckie were assigned to work together. Beckie was sweet and plenty smart. She just needed to mature, and Sylvia trusted she'd do that one day. But at eighteen, she had a ways to go.

Beckie dusted her gloved hands over the woodbin. "These temps wouldn't be so bad if someone in this room"—Beckie stared at Sylvia, amusement dancing in her eyes—"wouldn't abandon her side of our bed to tend to cows. I woke up lonely and with my toes freezing."

"You could've bedded down beside Ginger. Then you wouldn't have been lonesome or cold."

Beckie peeled out of her gloves. "Ew, gross. I will never be *that* frosty or alone, thank you very much. It's unfair that we ended the day just right, and the next thing I know, I'm in a cold bed all by myself."

Sylvia couldn't help but smile. Beckie and she had slept in the same bed since Beckie was old enough to leave her crib. And as far back as Sylvia could remember, they'd ended most days in the same way, sharing things only sisters did and then whispering, *"Im Gott sei Lieb"*—in God's love—over each other, putting their joys and sorrows in His hands before they fell asleep.

The kitten mewed, and Mamm stopped pouring coffee into a mug.

Beckie gazed into Sylvia's eyes, doing her best to suppress a laugh. Lizzie glanced her way and seemed to purposefully drop a plate onto the countertop in an effort to distract their mother. Thankfully it wasn't breakable.

"Meow." Beckie mimicked the kitten and did a good job of it. "Meow."

Mamm sighed. "Beckie, stop that. I thought I heard a real cat."

"Me too." Lizzie mocked scolding Beckie as she picked up the plate.

Mamm didn't like or trust cats. Rational or not, she worried that they'd scratch one of her daughters' faces and leave scars.

"I can't find my homework." Ruth's whiny voice was a clear indication of how poorly she'd slept last night.

"Coming." Mamm wiped her hands on a dishtowel. "She's so miserable this morning that I don't know if she can go to school."

"I'll see to her." Sylvia hurried toward the doorway of the kitchen. "And she'll be in the mood to go within the hour. I'm sure of it."

"I hope so," Mamm said. "She loves school like you love farming."

"Ah, but she'll grow out of liking school," Sylvia teased before getting to the steps.

"Wait," Mamm said.

Sylvia stopped and turned.

Mamm propped her hands on her small hips. "You need to eat."

"Oh, she's fine," Beckie said. "I'll fix her some coffee and take it to her."

"You girls." Mamm sighed. "Something's going on. I know that much."

"We're just pitching in to help each other like you taught us," Lizzie said.

"Ya, uh-huh." Mamm slung the dishcloth onto her shoulder, a move she repeated dozens of times every day. "You all stick together like peanut butter and jam." She motioned for Sylvia to go. "Well, do whatever you're going to do. But I want food in you within the hour. You were out most of the night, and you also need to get some sleep."

♦

Mamm's correcting tone grated on Sylvia a bit. It never seemed to dawn on her Mamm that by Sylvia's age, she was married and had been running her own home for more than four years. She had one child and another on the way by twenty-two. But as long as Sylvia was unmarried, it seemed she'd be treated like a child.

When Sylvia stepped into Ruthie's bedroom, her little sister was sitting on her bed, crying. The sight of it tugged on Sylvia's heart. She covered her lips with her index finger and closed the bedroom door. "Shh. Don't squeal. But look what I have for you." Sylvia eased the kitten from her pocket.

Ruthie's eyes lit up, in much the same way Sylvia imagined her own did whenever Elam came to the house. "Whiskers." Ruth held out her hands. "She is alive."

"I told you it was just a bad dream." Sylvia placed her hand on Ruth's forehead, checking for a fever. She didn't seem to be coming down with a bug.

"How'd you get Whiskers past Mamm?"

"The little fur ball likes to snuggle in warm places."

Sylvia laid Whiskers in Ruth's lap. She'd no more than gotten Ruth and Whiskers settled and content when Martha started crying, demanding someone get her out of her crib, which woke Salome and Barbie Ann.

The day became a blur of tending to little ones, doing laundry, preparing meals, taking the school-age children to school and picking them up, and helping Beckie make herself another new dress. Sylvia didn't know why Beckie felt she needed one by that evening when she wasn't going anywhere, but they got it done before supper. Sylvia also managed to squeeze in a nap before returning to the barn for the second milking.

The good part was that the busyness made the day hurry by. Sylvia looked at the clock for the umpteenth time. Elam should be here any minute.

Daed had gone to the bank a few hours ago, and he had instructed Lizzie and Lilly to help with the evening milking. When her sisters filled in for Daed, the process always took longer. Darkness fell long before they left the barn for the night, and the stars twinkled brightly.

As they crossed from the barn to her home, she spotted Elam's rig in the carriage house. Her heart went wild. Why hadn't he stepped into the barn to say hello?

She and her sisters went inside the house and peeled out of their coats, scarves, and boots. Kerosene lamps were lit throughout, giving off a warm glow.

Elam's voice filled her soul as it softly rumbled through the house. She followed the sound of it until she found him with her Daed, sitting in the office, looking over papers. With his head bent over a calendar, she was able to study his handsome features unobserved.

Have they been talking business? To her knowledge they'd never done so before. She knew about milking cows and breeding and delivering calves, but she understood almost nothing about the other parts of farming—the finances, the land, growing crops, and what it took to keep the silos filled.

Elam jotted something down. "I think if the weather cooperates and we plant the alfalfa earlier this spring than you have in past years, we could rotate the crop and gain sufficient growing time to have enough silage to increase the herd numbers."

We? Something about his use of the word bothered her. But she knew better than to speak up. If her Daed wanted her input, he would have asked her to join the meeting. Still, it seemed they at least could have invited her to listen to the conversation.

Elam set his notes aside and lifted a stack of papers. "I think this'll work. It might take a few—" He spotted Sylvia standing in the doorway.

Daed glanced up and then returned to studying the documents in front of him. "You were saying?"

Elam rose to his feet. "I have no idea." He closed the gap between them, and a desire to be his thudded inside her chest. "Hi."

"Hello." She longed to kiss him. It'd been so long since their first kiss. She'd never forget it and that quiet evening as the horse and carriage ambled along under the harvest moon. "What are you two up to?"

"Nothing much." His eyes bore into hers with such intensity it was all she could do not to blush. She felt beautiful—wanted—and not at all like an odd duck.

"Elam," Beckie called. "Kumm. Surely it's time you returned to our game."

Elam's smile warmed Sylvia's insides as he winked before peering around her. "Later, pipsqueak."

"You'd better watch out calling her that," Sylvia whispered before Beckie came into the room. At eighteen, Beckie did not like being treated the same as the rest of the brood.

Elam held his hand a few feet off the floor. "It's not my fault she's about this big." He glanced at Beckie while smiling at Sylvia.

Beckie's cheeks flushed pink, and Sylvia wished he wouldn't pick on her. She tended to be dramatic about her petite size and anything else she was teased about.

Elam enfolded Sylvia's hand in his, and her knees felt weak.

Daed moved around them. "Kumm, Beckie. It's their time to be alone."

He pulled the door closed, which was against the house rules he'd made. When a beau visited, he had to earn the right to see his intended in a room by themselves, but even then the door was to remain ajar.

"Alone at last." Elam peered down at her before kissing her forehead.

Oh, how she longed to tilt back her head and let him kiss her lips. The desire overwhelmed her, and she felt like a fallen autumn leaf caught in a windstorm. Her Mamm said that there was nothing wrong with feeling so attracted to Elam, that it was as natural as getting hungry and needing sleep—as long as her feelings didn't turn to actions. But Sylvia wished it'd ease up so she could think with a clear head.

Elam slid his arms around her. "Your Daed has hopes for us, and we've agreed to start working the fields together this spring. But my dreams have nothing to do with farm work. They're haunted by a certain raven-haired beauty." He lowered his lips until they brushed her ear. "I love you. Marry me, Sylvia."

His whisper and his words drew her, but they also jarred her like rock shattering against pavement. Part of her had hoped for this moment since he'd stolen that first kiss last fall. That part nudged her to embrace him and say yes. But she remained still, knowing her whole heart wasn't committed.

She wondered where she fit inside his and her Daed's plans.

She had reservations when it came to the traditional idea of marriage, and she'd told Elam so. An Amish man's life barely changed when he married. His wife looked after him as his mother had—making clothes, cooking three times a day, and doing laundry. He kept doing the same job he always had, whatever it was. But a woman had to be ready to take on the responsibility of running a home and giving birth to baby after baby, sometimes into her forties, as her mother had.

As much as she thrilled at being with Elam, Sylvia wasn't sure she was ready to begin that journey. Something else nagged at her too, and she wished she knew what.

Easing away from him, she tried to gather her thoughts. The papers on the table sat in the light of the kerosene lantern on Daed's desk. She flipped through them, realizing the two of them were revamping the day-to-day running of the farm. "I didn't know you were this interested in our farm."

"I am now. My Daed would have to make room for another son to join him in his timber framing business. But your Daed really needs me."

The farm needed manpower, and Elam had plenty of it. That didn't bother her at all. What bothered her was her ignorance concerning his plans. He hadn't even thought to discuss them with her.

"It seems like you'd talk to me about all this before talking to Daed."

"I speak to him about business matters and to you of marriage. Would you prefer I turn the two around?" He chuckled at his joke.

Sylvia joined his laughter. "Definitely not, and I'm sure Daed appreciates that."

"Ya, me too."

She lifted an official-looking paper that had both men's signatures on it.

"Hey." Elam spoke softly while cupping his hand under her chin. "I just proposed. You did hear me, right?"

She placed her hand over the center of her chest. "I carry you in my heart, Elam, and in my head…all the time. You know that. But at the risk of angering you, I have to ask again. Doesn't it seem out of place that you're making plans for the future, our future, without even talking to me?"

"I was aiming to surprise you, which you don't seem to appreciate. Your grandfather left you his house, and it makes sense for us to live and work here. Doesn't it?"

"Ya. Sure it does."

"Look, Sylvia, I know you have funny ideas about how things should be sometimes. And you have some wild thoughts about what a marriage needs to look like. But I didn't expect this response—or, rather, lack thereof—and I *can* tell you I'm not thrilled about it."

"I'm sorry." She set the paper on the table and eased her hand into his, once again pulled in by his mysterious allure. "I…I was just caught off guard. I'm too surprised to have an answer right away."

"What's there to think about? You want to be with me… I know you do."

"Nothing, really, and I do want to be with you. But I can't say yes this moment. I need a little time to absorb it all."

He stood there, so tall and unbelievably handsome, and she should be melting in his arms. She wanted that, so what was wrong with her?

"You said it yourself, Elam. I'm weird sometimes. The fact is, I don't react to much of anything the way most people do. There's no reasoning it out. Just give me a couple of weeks. I'll be able to explain what's going on inside me then, okay?"

"Ya, okay. There's time, since we don't need to make any plans until spring. But I want to get married this fall, Sylvia."

"This fall?"

He pulled away from her, his features growing hard. "You don't have to say it like it's a disgusting idea."

Sylvia was surprised by his sudden irritation. "I didn't mean it that way. I'm sorry it sounded so rude."

"I'm going now. But you should sort through whatever's holding you back—and as soon as possible."

Her heart fell as he walked out, heading straight for the back door. Despite her conflicting feelings, she hadn't wanted him to leave, especially not while he was upset with her.

"Elam?" Daed rose from his spot across from Beckie, upsetting the checkerboard as he did. "Leaving so soon?" He glanced at Sylvia, silently asking her half a dozen questions.

"I need to go. We'll talk later." Elam paused at the hatrack and grabbed his coat.

Beckie went to him. "But we haven't had supper yet or played a game."

"Another time, Beckie." He put on his black felt hat while his eyes stayed glued to Sylvia. "We'll talk again when I'm not so angry."

Sylvia nodded, wishing he hadn't announced to her whole family that she'd upset him.

Beckie moved to her side. "What's going on?"

Sylvia didn't answer. Some things were too private to share, even with Beckie. But no matter how much Sylvia wanted to keep her silence about this, she doubted she could. She never had been much for keeping truths to herself.

Without another glance her way, Elam walked out the door. Surely after he cooled off a bit, he'd see that her request was reasonable. A little time to think, and she'd be ready to give him the answer he wanted.

The two horses struggled to pull the loaded wagon. Sylvia slapped the reins against the team's back, urging them out of the feed store parking lot and onto the main road. Heavy gray clouds hung low, and a cold wind from the west had begun to blow.

She'd taken her homemade yogurts by Eash's Market, bought groceries, and picked up what seemed sufficient cow feed to get them through the rest of this unusually long winter. That was everything… she hoped.

Sylvia tapped the reins again, urging the horses to hurry. Her thoughts remained on Elam. It'd been three weeks since he'd come to the house. How much longer would he wait before talking to her?

When she'd seen him at the church meeting, he'd seemed unable to take his eyes off her. That had to be a good sign.

She loved him. That she knew for sure. But were they ready to marry? And how could he make plans with her Daed to change the operations of the farm and never once consider asking her opinion?

She didn't expect her Daed to understand her. He lived in a man's world and made do with daughters to help him. But Elam was supposed to know and love the real her, oddities and all.

Now that she understood what had bothered her so much, she was ready to talk to him about it. If he could see her side of it, and if she could see his side, they could work this out.

The house came into sight, and a bitter wind chilled her as she pulled into the driveway.

Elam. Her heart raced as if it'd been tapped by the reins. He and her father were hurrying into the barn. Surely this meant Elam was over being angry at her. It could mean that he'd decided to start working with her Daed in spite of her, but why would he wait until a Friday night?

Gusts of wind nipped her face as she brought the rig to a stop near the back door. She hopped down and ran two bags of groceries inside. "Hello?"

Her Mamm hurried toward her.

"Elam's here," Sylvia said. "Will you get the others to finish unloading the wagon?" She spun on her heels, ready to shout Elam's name and run for the barn the moment she was outside, but her Mamm caught her arm.

"Beckie wants to see you."

"Can't she wait?"

"No. It's best if you go on and talk to your sister. She's in the wash house."

Sylvia stared at her mother, waiting for an explanation, but Mamm simply nodded toward the washroom. Sylvia unbuttoned her coat and went through the narrow hallway that connected the wash house to the main house. Maybe now she'd find out what her sister and their parents had been whispering about for more than a week. Other than a few hints of being excited about something, Beckie had been unreadable, which had never happened before. Her sister had remained silent whenever Sylvia had asked her about it. Whatever it was, her Mamm seemed quite displeased.

"Beckie?"

The moment Sylvia saw her sister, she noticed several things. She wasn't happy, she didn't have on her prayer *Kapp,* and she wasn't making eye contact. Beckie stoked the fire in the small potbelly stove, closed the door to the stove, and set the face of a pressing iron on it.

Since learning what Sylvia had told Elam the night he left, Beckie had been distant and quiet, not offering any words of comfort. And she'd been going out every evening.

Sylvia pulled off her gloves. "You're ironing on a Friday afternoon? What'd you do wrong while I was out?"

Beckie turned to her. "Nothing. I washed my prayer Kapp, and I want it to look just right for tonight."

"Ah, you must be going out again."

Beckie nodded, but Sylvia could read no emotion in her face.

"Mamm said you wanted to see me."

"Ya." Beckie fidgeted with a few loose strands of hair, tucking them carefully back into place.

"And…"

Beckie had obviously done something she shouldn't have—borrowed a dress and stained it or ruined another of Sylvia's prayer Kapps or borrowed money from Sylvia's stash. "Whatever is on your mind, dear sister, can we speed this conversation along? I forgive you. There. It's done. Elam is here, and I want to go see him."

Beckie licked her lips. "He's not here to see you."

"He said that?"

She nodded.

"I guess he's still mad at me after all. Is he here to help Daed?"

"No. Well, maybe a little. But Elam's not upset that you turned him down. Not anymore."

Tightness moved into Sylvia's chest. "I didn't turn him down. You know that. I only said I needed a little time. You reminded him of that, right?"

Beckie shrugged. "I'm sorry, but it's for the best, Sylvia."

Panic began to race through her. What had happened? "Beckie, it's not for the best to let Elam think I don't want to marry him. It's just that twenty-two feels young."

"Nonsense. Most brides marry much younger than that…Amish ones anyway. I don't think you really love him."

"That's ridiculous. What would you know about it?" Sylvia's world tilted. Why was she having this conversation with Beckie? None of it made sense.

Beckie placed a clean towel on the ironing board and gently laid her prayer Kapp on it. "He's…he's here for me."

"Oh, honey." Trying to think of the most gentle way to correct her sister, Sylvia stepped closer. "You must have something mixed up. I—"

Beckie's face turned red, and she shook a finger at Sylvia. "Of course you'd think that! No way could he be interested in a pipsqueak like me, right? Well, he's asked me to marry him, and I wasn't stupid enough to tell him to wait!"

"Elam did what? No!" Her sister's betrayal burned through her, charring everything she held dear.

Beckie's face softened. "I shouldn't have blurted it out. I'm sorry."

"You…you've been seeing Elam?"

"Ya."

Hurt and confusion churned within her, and Sylvia couldn't catch her breath. "I have to talk to him. This is all wrong. He loves me. Wants me."

"Sylvia, no." Beckie moved in front of her, an unfamiliar steeliness in her eyes. "Don't make this harder than it has to be."

Sylvia stepped around her sister, ran out of the wash house, and headed for the barn. Rolling clouds moved quickly across the sky, shrouding the land in winter's gray.

Surely Elam wouldn't… Beckie had to be wrong. The idea of her sister being disloyal hurt too much to bear. And Elam's betrayal? Impossible.

Sylvia hurried into the barn and stopped short. Neither man noticed her.

"Elam."

When his eyes met hers, she was no longer confident that Beckie was mistaken.

"It's not true, is it?" Tears threatened, and she swallowed hard. "Tell me you didn't ask Beckie to marry you."

Her Daed studied her for a moment before he lowered his head and went to the milk house, giving them privacy. Her Daed's reaction made her head spin, and she longed to wake from this nightmare.

Elam walked over to her but fixed his eyes on the floor. "I told you I'm ready to marry this next wedding season."

Part of her felt numb, and part of her burned as if someone had dumped scalding water on her. "You sound as if you don't care who you marry. I thought you loved me."

"I wasn't the one who sounded sick at the idea of getting married this fall." He lifted his eyes, and she could see his contempt. "And the truth is, I don't think you're ever going to be ready."

"That's not true." How had the feelings between them soured so quickly?

"Do you love me?"

"If I said yes, what difference would that make now? You've betrayed me with my sister."

"Let's assume the answer is yes. That means you turned me down in spite of how you feel. Why? That's all I want you to answer—for yourself, Sylvia. Why?"

Dozens of thoughts ran through her, and she didn't know which to voice first. "She's my sister, Elam. How could you do this?"

"If I wait, will you marry me?"

Was he setting her up so he could make more points in his argument, or was he proposing again? Her head pounded. "Are you...asking?"

"I—"

"Stop it," Beckie hissed, interrupting his response. She moved between them, facing Sylvia.

Elam seemed perfectly content to hide behind her sister. Who was this man? Obviously a disloyal liar. As if piecing together a quilt, she began to see a new pattern forming.

On the weekends, after she and Elam finished milking the herd, he'd go into the living room while she showered and put on fresh clothes. How many of those nights had she come downstairs and found him and Beckie cackling over some line in a book or a game of some sort? Often he'd sit between the two of them as they took turns reading aloud. She never once had challenged Beckie about it.

What a fool she'd been. And she feared that her sister was being one also.

Beckie moved closer. "Sylvia, please, open your eyes. I love him so much more than you ever did. Since you turned him down, I see no reason for you to stand in our way."

Sylvia fought to remain standing when all she wanted to do was sink to her knees and sob. "How could you do this to me? You're my sister, and you know how I feel about Elam!"

"I know how *he* feels. He loves *me,* Sylvia. And it's clear that I love him more than you do."

Sylvia looked past her sister, wondering how Elam had managed to steal both of their hearts. Had he kissed Beckie too? Was Sylvia blinded by attraction? "How can you be so sure? I'm no longer sure he has any clue who he loves." She hoped Beckie would hear that truth.

Elam slid his hand into Beckie's, and Sylvia thought she might die from the pain of it. "I asked her, and she said yes. It's done."

The undeniable fact that they'd been seeing each other behind her back scattered the words inside her until she could find none to try to reason with her sister.

The door to the milk house creaked as it opened, and her Daed came toward her.

Sylvia motioned at the twosome. "How can you agree to this?"

Her Daed gestured for Elam and Beckie to leave. "We'll finish up." He waited until they were gone.

Tears ran down Sylvia's face. "How could you be a part of this?"

"I'm not a part of it any more than you are. I've talked to Beckie until I have no more words."

"Do you not have enough loyalty to me to refuse her?"

"Sylvia." Daed pulled out his handkerchief and passed it to her. "I couldn't have stopped what happened." He motioned for her to walk with him as he went to a horse's stall on the far side of the barn and grabbed a bridle. "I can dictate certain things over her, but no parent can predict or prevent something like this. No matter who Elam ended up with, the damage was done before either of us knew what was happening. You have it in you to forgive and let go. Beckie doesn't." He bridled the horse. "You can help your Mamm forgive too. She's fit to be tied, as your sisters will be when they find out."

Sylvia stared at her father, unable to believe his casual attitude toward Elam and Beckie's traitorous behavior. "I can't stay here and watch them marry."

"It'll be tough. I know it will." He put a saddle on the horse and began tightening the girth. "But before Daadi Fisher died, he did something that's never been done before. He left a fourth of the family farm to a granddaughter—you. He bypassed every son and grandson to do it. You were grieving too deeply to know what all was happening, but for a while I thought there was going to be a feud over it. And I wasn't sure the church leaders would allow it, but in the end they did. Don't tell me you'd give up your inheritance over a man. I won't believe it. Besides, if you don't keep giving the dairy farm all you've got, you'll own a fourth of nothing but bills."

"You're not hearing me." She nearly shrieked at him. "I can't stay here."

"You've always said that the old place Daadi Fisher left you is too far from the herd for your taste. Let Elam and Beckie live there. It'll give you some distance, as if they're neighbors. You and I will run the herd and milk production. He and I will produce and harvest crops, keep the silos filled, and deal with the waste management. It's a huge place, and if we handle things right, you won't have to see him often. It's far from ideal, but it's the best I can offer."

She'd never considered living in the two-bedroom house Daadi Fisher had left her, but the idea of Elam and Beckie moving there made her sick.

"Daed, I don't care where they live. I have to get out. Why can't you understand that?"

Hints of anger shadowed her Daed's face before he drew a deep breath. "This is home, and no unmarried daughter of mine is moving away. It's not respectable, and I won't have it. You can find the strength, Sylvia. I know you can."

"Is Elam doing this because of those papers you two signed?"

"No. But if I'd known then how this would turn out, I wouldn't have taken him on as a partner. I'm sorry, Sylvia. Really sorry." He held the leads out to her, giving her permission to go riding until she felt better. "I'll see to it that you can get away for long weekends as much as possible. You can stay with cousins and aunts from other states for weeks at a time during our slow season. But this is home. I can't imagine living here without you, and running away isn't acceptable."

She stared at him, too broken to feel any hope for her future. It was beyond her how either Beckie or Elam could do this, but for both to betray her was more than she could bear.

Daed sighed. "Trust me. It'll all turn out for the best. I know it will."

She took the reins from him, desperate to steal away for a few hours and get as far from the happy couple as she could.

As she rode the horse out of the barn, she didn't bother drying her tears. Her vision blurred so much she could barely tell where she was going, and she knew it'd remain that way for a long time.

Two

Three years later

Faint sounds of someone moving in the next room ended Sylvia's few hours of sleep. It had to be Elam.

The darkness of early morn surrounded her, and she wished she could hide in it forever. She pushed the warm quilts away and sat upright.

Light from a kerosene lantern stretched under the closed bedroom door, flickering softly. The silhouette of two cribs, both holding sleeping little ones, reminded her of where she was—trapped somewhere between love and duty.

It'd taken a while to bury her feelings for Elam after he and Beckie married, but she'd managed it. She'd helped Beckie a lot during her pregnancy and after the twins were born, but it'd been reasonably easy for Sylvia to juggle her schedule and keep a comfortable distance from Elam.

Then, six weeks ago, whooping cough had disrupted their routine. Sylvia had considered that illness extinct. She discovered the hard way that she was wrong. The doctor called it an easily communicable disease, and it'd spread through her family like scattered seed on a freshly plowed field. Sylvia had been vaccinated as a child when a health-care worker came to the house. Elam had been vaccinated as a child too. The doctor believed that was why the two of them remained virus free.

Beckie and their parents were among the first to be hit, and Beckie remained as weak as a newborn kitten, so Sylvia and Elam had no choice but to tend to the farm and family around the clock like a married couple.

His footsteps quietly echoed against the stillness, and feelings she hated burned through her.

Her niece cried out, coughing and whining. Sylvia moved to Rhoda's bed and ran her hand across the mattress until she located the pacifier. She placed it in Rhoda's mouth and patted her back, hoping the infant would go back to sleep before waking her twin brother.

When Rhoda fell asleep, Sylvia went to Raymond's crib and placed the back of her hand against his little cheek. If he still had fever, it wasn't much. She drew a relaxing breath. The symptoms of whooping cough wouldn't last much longer.

The sound of Elam's muffled footsteps made their way through the door. Sylvia grabbed her housecoat and pulled it into a ball against her chest. Thoughts of their long night together, sitting in this quiet room, echoed through her. They'd given the twins a breathing treatment, then talked for hours while rocking the little ones. When he passed Raymond to her, their hands brushed, and desire ignited—the kind that should happen only between him and Beckie.

Her skin tingled. She hoped he wasn't about to enter the room, and yet a part of her wished he would.

A shadow glided under the crack of the doorway and stopped. Her heart pounded. A moment later the shadow disappeared. The familiar screech of the back door opening and then shutting said he'd gone to the barn. She had to join him. He had no other help, not with her Daed, Mamm, and most of her siblings down with whooping cough.

Years of avoiding him, of working opposite milking shifts, had come to an abrupt halt with this illness.

She went to the dresser, lit a kerosene lantern, and pulled out a newspaper ad she'd clipped a month ago. The ad was for help on a dairy farm belonging to an Amish man named Michael Blank, who lived in Dry Lake, a couple of hours southeast of here. Far enough away that she'd never have to see Elam unless she came home for a visit.

She'd shown the ad to her Daed, hoping to convince him to let her go. But he'd bristled at the idea and said he didn't want to hear anything else about it.

He'd never let an unmarried daughter move away from home, and she'd dropped it. But now she clung to the idea of leaving as if it were her only chance of escaping temptation. And maybe it was.

Daed had kept his word, and over the past three years, she'd visited relatives whenever time allowed. She'd gone to singings and dated men from across four states, and not one of them interested her. What was her problem?

Whatever it was, she had to get out of here.

After this time with Elam, living in the main house with her parents would no longer be a sufficient barrier between them. Living a few miles away with a relative wasn't good enough either. She'd still see Elam at church meetings, community functions, and family gatherings.

She peeled out of her nightgown, convincing herself that in spite of whatever had stirred between them last night, today was just another day of farm work and babies. She dressed for morning chores, then quietly opened the bedroom door, went to the mud room, and put on her boots, coat, and hat before heading for the barn.

Cold winter air filled her lungs. The sky's dark majesty sparkled with dots of white light, as if trying to assure her that its vastness covered more than her problems.

As she drew closer to the barn, she heard the faint sounds of Elam moving through the morning routine. Bracing herself, she went inside.

"*Guder Marye,* Sylvia."

She nodded in response to his softly spoken *good morning,* refusing to get pulled into a conversation. If talking could milk cows, he'd never need anyone's help.

She moved toward the wheelbarrow of silage, feeling his eyes on her.

Don't look. Just don't.

Her eyes moved to his, and she felt caught.

He's forbidden. She didn't need the reminder, but the phrase ran circles in her mind.

After filling the troughs with feed, he opened the gate, and the cows nearly stampeded into the milking stalls. As soon as the cows put their heads through the stanchions, she began locking the panels. He grabbed the nozzle of the hose that hung overhead through an elaborate scheme of cables and pulleys and squirted the cows' udders.

"Hey, Sylvia."

She finished locking the devices and grabbed the milking stool. A diesel engine in the milk house ran the refrigerator for the bulk tank and powered the air compressor for the portable milkers, but she had to start the milk flowing from each cow before the machinery could do its job.

"You okay?" Elam asked.

"I'm not getting sick, but I can't say I'm okay."

"Ya, I know. Me either. Just don't be mad."

She wasn't angry. Terrified, maybe. Definitely overloaded with guilt. But too confused about herself to be angry with him.

After she cleaned and primed the first cow, Elam moved next to her with the claw milker and its attached bucket. She tried to get up, grab the stool, and move out of the way before he got too close, but instead she managed to trip into him.

He steadied her, his eyes never leaving hers.

With confusion and desire churning inside her, she went to the next cow. She hated Elam, but she still felt as though he were a magnet, drawing her closer. She longed to feel his lips against hers.

Think, Sylvia, and stop feeling.

"Did you get any sleep after I left last night?"

How she slept was none of his business. "Rhoda's breathing easier." She patted the cow as she stood to move to another one.

Elam's hesitant smile drew her. "I never doubted you'd get the twins through this ordeal safe and sound. You have strength…determination that the rest of us don't." He moved closer.

Every part of her begged to slip into his arms. She passed him the milking stool and took the nozzle, keeping a safe distance.

She had to get out of Path Valley, but she doubted Michael Blank would hire her. She didn't know of one man, Englischer or Amish, who'd hire a female farmhand—not unless she was part of a package deal that included a husband.

Even if Michael Blank would give her a chance, how could she convince her Daed to let her go? He couldn't make her stay, but he could cut off her contact with him, Mamm, and her sisters.

While her mind searched for solutions, she and Elam continued milking the herd. By the time all eighty-two cows were milked, the sun shone brightly through the slats and the dirt-streaked windows. Once the stalls were empty again, she sterilized the milkers and buckets while Elam scraped the grates and cleaned the stalls. After scrubbing the bulk tank, she started spreading white lime sand onto the concrete floor. As soon as Elam joined her, she set the shovel aside and went to the mud sink. He could finish by himself.

When she turned to leave the wash area, Elam stood directly in her path. He searched her eyes the way he had when they were dating.

If she had the guts, she'd ask him what was going on between them. But it'd take so little to dismantle her will. She tried to step around him, but he moved in the same direction.

"Sorry," she mumbled.

He touched her cheek, sending both surprise and warmth through her.

She commanded her body to turn and walk away, demanded herself to break free of his spell, but she couldn't budge. No matter what Bible verse she tried to grab, she wanted what stood before her. "I…I need to…go."

As if the two of them were floating dust particles, they continued hanging in midair and yet moving toward each other. How many times had she dreamed of kissing him again? His lips met hers, and suddenly nothing existed but the feelings that ran between them.

She pushed him away, tears stinging her eyes. Her skin burned with embarrassment. "Get away from me, Elam."

"I don't want to," he whispered. "What are we going to do?"

She knew how he felt. "You have to help me get out of here. Daed doesn't want to let me go, but he'll listen to you."

He brushed a tear off her face, looking weary and sorry and trapped. "Okay."

The door to the barn creaked open. "Sylvia? Elam?" Her sister's hoarse voice sent alarm through her. Beckie's brows furrowed as she looked from Sylvia to Elam. "What's going on?"

Sylvia's heart shattered into a hundred pieces. "I…I tripped, and he caught me." It was a believable lie. Beckie often teased that, when Sylvia was tired, she had all the grace of a newborn calf. Guilt ate at her, and she no longer recognized any part of herself.

Coughing, Beckie grabbed a nearby wall for support.

Elam hurried to her, placed his arm around her, and guided her back toward the house.

Desperate for a moment alone, Sylvia went to the tack room and closed the door. She covered her face with her hands and sobbed, her whole body shaking.

Three

June

Shoving a thick packet of money into his pocket, Aaron left the small bank. He'd emptied his account of ten years' worth of hard work and diligent saving. Even in his worst years, he'd never touched his savings account, and now he had something to show for all that time spent doing what he hated—dairy farming.

He crossed the parking lot to the hitching post, removed the leather reins, and mounted his horse. With the click of his tongue, he was on his way.

Hope tried to spring up inside him, but heavier realities overrode it. A feeling of griminess had taken up residence inside him long ago. His thoughts, emotions, and even the blood that pumped through his veins felt as layered in black soot as the rooftops and porches of homes near industrial smokestacks. He didn't suppose he'd ever be free of it. But he had a plan that would bring as much joy as someone like him could expect.

He stopped in front of the appliance store where he worked, tethered his horse at the post, and went inside.

Aaron walked the narrow aisle, enjoying the business ideas pulsing through him. The cash in his pants pocket gave him a sense of power over his future. A smile tugged at his face. The idea of owning and operating this store fit who he was, and in spite of the weight of his past that he carried, he could see a good life ahead of him.

A middle-aged Old Order Amish couple stood at the sales counter. The man plunked cash into Leo's hand while his wife wrote their address on the invoice so they could have the new wringer washer delivered.

A dusting of eagerness lifted his spirits. He couldn't recall the last time he'd been excited about anything. Owning this business felt more right than anything he'd ever done.

If he signed the papers and put down earnest money today, he could own the shop in about two and a half months. Well, he and the bank. Leo would still hold the note, but he'd retire come September, leaving Aaron as the proprietor. Aaron had to be ready to take over by then.

As he walked through the display area, the wooden floor creaked. Only natural light illuminated the room, and open windows were the sole source of ventilation. Leo wasn't Plain, but he handled his business in a way that made the Plain folk feel right at home. There were living quarters above the store, large enough to house Aaron and his parents comfortably until he could afford better.

Thoughts of his parents dampened his mood. An Amish couple well past their prime with only one surviving child—who'd ever heard of such a thing? If his older sister hadn't died last fall, and if his parents' six other babies had survived, they would have other children to rely on. Aaron didn't doubt he'd still be the black sheep of the family, but at least they'd have white sheep to help them. Instead they had only him.

And he wouldn't let them down. Not again.

Shaking off the negative thoughts, he studied the many types of wringer washers, cookstoves, hot water heaters, and stoves for warming a home. Not one appliance in this store needed electricity. Depending on which sect of Amish or Mennonite the buyers were, they might use solar energy, coal, wood, battery, various types of gas, or diesel fuel. The store had some of those items in stock, and others could be ordered through a catalog.

Though Aaron had been working here for four months, he didn't know much about running a store or about appliances. But he'd grown up on a dairy farm, and he knew how to work hard. Besides, he'd always been a quick study when his heart was in it. And his heart was definitely in this.

Leo shook hands with the customers, promised a delivery time, and told them good-bye. The bells on the door jangled as the couple left.

Aaron stepped up to the counter. "I have the earnest money, and I'm ready to sign the papers."

While putting money into the register, Leo's eyes lit up. He and Aaron had been talking about the possibility of this for at least eight weeks. "A man with a plan and money to back it up—I can't argue with that. However, there's one thing we haven't talked about. My lawyer friend brought it up last night while he was drawing up the papers. A cosigner."

Aaron found it hard to catch his next breath. "But…" He had no one who would cosign with him. "I've brought you more than the agreed-upon down payment, and once I take over, I'll pay you each month from the money I make until I own the store outright. Isn't that enough?"

"Well, it's just prudent to have someone with good credit back you in case of default. You're going home. Get your dad to sign it in front of a notary public, and we'll be all set."

A sick feeling crept into Aaron's stomach. Money he could come up with. His Daed's signature was another matter.

Leo came out from behind the counter. "Let's go to my office and sign the papers between us, and I'll give you the ones you need a cosigner on."

After signing the papers, Aaron mounted his horse and began the ride back to the Better Path. Country stores lined the main street of the small community. The idea of town living sat well with him. He prayed that after he moved here, he'd never live on a farm again.

But first he had to convince his parents to sell and move with him.

Until he left home in January, they had no idea that he was addicted to alcohol and that he'd made a mess of his life along the way. He didn't know how much they knew even now, except that he'd entered rehab five months ago. After being sober for a couple of months, he hadn't returned home. Instead, he'd started working at the appliance store and leading groups at the rehab center where he'd been living since arriving in Owl's Perch.

But he'd realized that he could never truly move on until he acted like a responsible only son by making amends. He figured—no, he knew— that the best way to make up for the past and for his unwillingness to be a farmhand was to get his parents out of that money pit they called a dairy farm.

As his horse ambled toward the Better Path, the sun hung almost directly overhead. Fields were thick with tall, green hay that needed to be cut, dried, and baled for the first time this season. A second and probably a third time were sure to follow.

Farm work. It never ended. And no matter how hard farmers tried, they never got caught up.

Trying not to dread what lay ahead, he put his horse to pasture and went into the rehab housing unit.

He shoved clothes into his canvas bag. He liked the idea of leaving rehab. He was ready.

Well, maybe he was.

He'd certainly learned a good bit about his addiction and how to manage it.

Alcoholic. It had taken him months of rehab and counseling to accept that label. Adding the word *recovering* in front of it did nothing to lessen his embarrassment. But he had to face his past, even if his only goal now was to extract himself from it.

Someone tapped on his door.

"Kumm."

Paul Waddell stepped inside the small room. "Hannah sent you these." He held up a tin. "It has some of the leftover cookies from last night's going-away tribute."

"That's really nice. Thanks." Aaron set the canister on the bed before opening his nightstand and taking out the small stack of letters he'd received from Lena.

Lena—probably the only friend he had left or maybe ever had to begin with. She'd been the one who told him about this rehab facility. He hated the choices he'd made that caused him to come here, but checking himself in was the best decision he'd ever made.

Paul closed the door and sat in the reading chair beside the bed. "Today's the day."

"Ya."

He'd never met a man like Paul—a straight shooter, untraditional, and so very patient. In fact, sometimes the breadth of Paul's tolerance grated on Aaron's nerves. His wife, Hannah, was still in nursing school, but she kept close tabs on everyone who went through the rehab program and even joined the meetings whenever it was family group session day, which took place once every three to four weeks.

There'd been six family sessions during Aaron's time here. He'd invited his parents to every one, but they hadn't come. When they didn't answer a single letter he'd sent them, Paul sent formal invitations on the Better Path stationery, but he didn't get a response either.

"How are you faring?" Paul asked.

"Good and bad, I guess." Aaron moved to the dresser. "The good part is I just signed the papers and put down money on the appliance store."

"You made a plan and followed through. I've seen that strong suit numerous times since you arrived here."

"Unfortunately, I'm losing valuable training time in order to return to Dry Lake, a place I'm definitely not wanted. I'm aiming to be back mid-August, but as long as I'm in Owl's Perch and ready to take over the shop by September first, I have nothing to worry about. That gives me at least eight weeks to do what I should be able to accomplish in four."

"It could be tougher than you expect."

Daed had always claimed the farm was his dream, but surely he'd had his fill of it by now. Despite how Aaron's parents felt about him, he was confident they'd jump at selling the old place and join him in becoming merchants in Owl's Perch. They just needed to warm up to the idea. It would certainly be easier to make a living here.

Aaron put the last of his things into the backpack. He slung the strap over his shoulder and picked up the tin. "I could use a ride to the bus station."

Wiping sweat from her brow and loosening the top buttons on her shirt, Sylvia moved to the open hayloft doors, hoping to feel even a smidgen of breeze on the hot June day. The Blank farm stretched out before her on all sides, and although fence lines divided one pasture from another, no one else's property was in sight.

Another two hours of work in this sauna known as a hayloft and she'd have accomplished her goal. Since breakfast she'd tossed, dragged, and toted bales of hay to one side and straw to the other—all in hopes of making it easier to get at whichever one she needed.

What would possess someone to intermix the two so carelessly?

She leaned against the doorframe, studying the beautiful wild flowers and rolling fields where a contented herd grazed.

Her cows. She didn't own them, of course, but Michael Blank had hired her to tend to them. He trusted her, and she hadn't let him down. When she arrived here four months ago, the herd was in dire need of diligent care. The overall health of the cows matched their milk production—poor. But after working endlessly, she had good reasons to bask in her accomplishments.

She wished it were possible to feel joy again, but she didn't believe she deserved to be happy. Even contentment was beyond reach. She hadn't been able to resist Elam, and the weight of her sin lay heavily upon her. Finding peace was impossible, even with her new start. She alone was responsible for her actions. She knew it. God knew it.

She shoved her hands into her pockets. Elam's life went on as it always had, but she'd had to give up everything.

When her Daed realized he couldn't talk her out of leaving home, he warned her she'd be giving up her portion of the farm and all the money he'd put back as a salary for her over the years. He even said she couldn't write to her sisters, nor would he allow them to write her.

She had left anyway. No one but Elam would ever know why.

Thoughts of home flooded her. She missed her sisters most of all. Any sense of accomplishment disappeared as heaviness tightened its grip. If she thought it would do any good, she'd pray for relief.

Unfortunately, working like an ox came easier than whispering a simple prayer. In the distance the treetops swayed as the humid air stirred, and she wondered if she'd ever pray again. She had called out to God after her adulterous kiss with her sister's husband, but all she could manage was to beg for forgiveness. God's silence bore down on her without relief, and she'd given up praying altogether. She had hope for this farm, but she had no peace inside her, and she missed it.

By the time she milked the cows tonight and tended to the barn, she'd barely be able to lift her feet and walk to her cabin. Freedom to start anew came with a physically exhausting price. If she could sleep at night, it'd help. She would take a long bath before bed tonight, hoping she'd be able to clear her mind and heart.

Soft mews caught her attention, pulling her back to the present. She climbed over several bales of undisturbed straw and shifted a few out of the way before she spotted four young kittens that appeared to be about three weeks old. The mother was nowhere to be seen, but by the look of things, she'd been taking good care of her litter.

Sylvia sat among the bales of hay and pulled the kittens into her lap, stroking each one, hoping to make them more people-friendly than their wild mother. If she had any money, she'd get them fixed and teach them to trust humans. Every barn needed good mice catchers, but a little effort could keep them from being feral hunters.

After several minutes she left the kittens sleeping in the hay and headed for her cabin. It was run-down and small, but each evening as she trudged back to it, the last rays of golden sunlight enveloped it, as if promising that one day the ache inside her would ease.

Until then she found solace in her new home here with Michael and Dora Blank.

Four

Cara studied the Pennsylvania Dutch phrase in the notebook before her, wishing it made sense. The preacher and his wife sat across the kitchen table from her. They'd invited her to come to their home twice a week between now and the end of summer as their gift to help her learn the language. Cara needed to know a little German and a fair amount of Pennsylvania Dutch, and she had serious concerns whether she'd ever get the hang of either of them. But if she didn't, she had no chance of receiving the church leaders' approval to marry Ephraim come fall.

"I don't know." She closed the book and pushed it away. "Male, female, child, adult, singular, plural—nearly every word changes based on who is being spoken to. I can't do this."

Preacher Alvin reopened the book and set it in front of her. He tapped it with his rough hands. "Try again."

His patience and his confidence in her were comforting. She pulled the notebook closer. Studying the phrase again and comparing it with other words, she finally understood. "So *Gott segen dich* is used when the person is talking to only one other person, and *Gott segen eich* is used when the person is talking to at least two people, right?"

"Gut, Cara." Esther's weathered cheeks rose slightly when she smiled. "What do the phrases mean?"

"Both mean 'God bless you.' "

"*Wunderbaar.*" Esther had been teaching German to Amish young people for nearly fifteen years, but this was her first time to teach Pennsyl-vania Dutch. She held up a flashcard. "*Saage es,* Cara."

"You said, 'Say it.'"

"*Gut.*"

Cara stared at the image of an infant on the card. "*Bobbeli.*"

"*Gut.*" Esther held up another hand-drawn card, this time of a horse. Cara tapped her pencil on the table. "*Langsam?*"

Esther smiled. "*Letz.*"

Wrong. Cara definitely knew the meaning and pronunciation of that word.

"*Langsam* means 'slow.' It could be a slow one of these, I suppose."

"Horse... Oh, *Gaule.*"

"*Gut.*" Esther put the cards on the table. "Our time's up for today. You're doing fine."

"*Denki,* Esther." Cara closed her notebook. "But I know how I'm doing, and *fine* isn't the word for it."

"You're doing your best. That's all God asks, and He'll take care of the rest. Just you wait and see."

One could not be fully accepted into a culture if she or he couldn't speak and understand a reasonable amount of the language. As with most things Amish, she could see the reasoning behind that belief, but that didn't make learning the words any easier.

The preacher bowed his head in silent prayer, and she followed his lead.

Peace eased through her. Nearly everything that had happened over the last year had defied logic. Maybe developing the necessary skill in the languages would too. When she came to Dry Lake from the Bronx a year ago, she wanted only one thing—to protect her then seven-year-old daugh-ter from a maniac stalker. But she got so much more. She found Ephraim, a man who'd been willing to do whatever it took to help her. He'd been shunned because of his unrelenting support for her. And in the process, she found God…or He found her. A more mature believer would know which.

Whoever found who, she never would have believed it possible to shake free of her stalker, get out of poverty, and start fresh. The Old Order Amish ways were far from being like a fairy tale, but the love and hope she'd found inside this community had done much to make up for all the years of brokenness.

"Cara?" The preacher's voice interrupted her thoughts, and she opened her eyes.

Alvin rubbed his hand across his mouth, clearly trying to hide his smile. "I said *amen*…twice."

Cara headed for the door. "Well, maybe you cut the prayer time too short." She sounded sassy as she teased, but she knew Alvin and Esther didn't mind.

"Who'd have ever thought extended silent prayer time would bring such a smile to your face?" Alvin grabbed his straw hat and followed her.

Once outside, Cara saw Ephraim in his buggy, waiting for her. He'd gone through Amish instruction and joined the faith nine years ago. Understanding Ephraim was a little like trying to understand God. There was no logic. It made no sense. But his power to change everything for her was undeniable. How Ephraim had stayed single in a society that put so much stock in marriage also defied her understanding.

His strawberry blond hair peeped out from under his straw hat. His broad shoulders and lean body always caught her eye. One glimpse of him and she found it impossible to keep the pleasure of it off her face.

She paused on the front porch. "I wasn't praying as much as thinking of all the things I'm grateful for," she told Alvin.

He put on his hat, making sure it fit snugly. "Feeling gratitude is much like a prayer all on its own. If you thank Him for those things, it becomes a prayer."

"You think so?"

"Ya, I do. You're doing a good job with the language classes. And you did pretty well with the first instruction class too."

Instruction classes. She had eight more sessions to go, and each would take place on a church Sunday between now and fall. The lessons covered the principles of the Christian faith and living Amish.

She heard hesitation in Alvin's voice, as if he wanted to add a *but*. Hoping to avoid that conversation, she thanked him for his time and hurried down the steps and into the buggy. Whatever he saw in her attitude or mind-set that needed to be adjusted would show itself soon enough without her digging around for it.

Ephraim and Alvin exchanged a few pleasant words. After Ephraim said his good-byes, he clicked his tongue, and the horse started plodding along.

Cara moved a little closer to him, keeping the expected respectable distance.

He moved the reins to one hand and placed his arm on the seat back behind her. "This is the rig we used to get you back and forth when you first landed in Dry Lake and hated me."

"I never *hated* you. I just didn't trust you. And I didn't like how much power you held over my situation. And your viewpoint concerning my minor thievery really irked me. And…okay, fine, I did dislike you a little, but only for a short while. You didn't care for me either."

"That's not true." He slowed the rig. "I liked you from the time we met as children."

He was twelve and she was eight when her mother brought her to Dry Lake for a visit. Neither their age nor gender difference kept them from having fun. "That was a great week, wasn't it?"

"Ya. Afterward I kept returning to *our* tree, waiting for your mom to bring you back like she said." He released a long breath. "That was my first heartbreak."

Jealousy crept up her spine It seemed that he'd spent his years as a bachelor dating nearly every single Amish woman in Dry Lake and the surrounding communities. "Yeah, the first of several."

His hand moved to her back and caressed her. "Ya, just the first." He pulled into a driveway and stopped. "Stay put." He hopped out, went around the rig, and held out his hand. "The second time I had my heart broken was when I went to New York some eight years later to search for you and never found you."

She stared at him from the rig. He had no reservations about telling her how he felt, and she reveled in hearing it, but loving words didn't roll off her tongue. She adored him, but saying so directly seemed impossible.

Shooing his hand away, she climbed down on her own. "You're too good at these verbal games we play. Fine, you win. Maybe you did care."

His smile assured her she hadn't offended him by being sarcastic or rejecting his offer of help.

She peered around him. "What are we doing at Lena's?"

He laughed. "Been paying attention much?"

"Shut up and answer the question."

He placed one hand on the rig on each side of her, capturing her body and her full attention. "I can either shut up, or I can answer your question. I cannot do both." His eyes caught hers and stayed there. "The third and last time I had my heart broken, I was thirty-two years old. You'd waltzed into Dry Lake, stolen my hopes again, and then made plans to leave."

"I didn't *waltz* anywhere." She'd fled in terror from a stalker and stumbled into Dry Lake in utter confusion, with only shards of memories from her childhood. She hadn't remembered Ephraim, not really. When they talked about it later, they figured the lapse was due to the trauma of her mom being killed soon after they returned to New York.

His hands moved to her face. "I love you, Cara."

Her heart constricted, making her wish she could share her feelings as easily. "Of course you do. We're engaged. Remember?"

"I never forget it for a moment. You and the preacher seem to be getting along nicely. That's a good sign."

"He's really not so bad."

"I'm sure he appreciates you thinking so."

Ephraim's closeness reminded her once again that he wasn't like any other man she'd ever known. He was amazing…and she was ordinary. She clicked her tongue and huffed. "Do you intend to kiss me or just keep driving me crazy?"

A throat cleared, and they turned to see Lena's dad with a handsaw gripped in his fist, looking at them. Ephraim released her and eased back, as if an Amish man showing affection in public were normal.

Israel looked amused. "Is there a reason, Ephraim Mast, why you're on my property—and about to kiss your girl?"

"Yeah, there's a reason," Cara piped up, ready to harass Israel. "Ada sent us over to give you a few lessons on how to get a kiss and make it count."

Israel dropped his saw and seemed unable to move. Ephraim flashed Cara a look that said she'd gone too far. She didn't think so. *Good grief!* Israel and Ada had both lost their spouses something like fourteen years ago. From what she'd seen when they were together, they were clearly attracted to each other, but nothing had come of their friendship yet.

Israel cleared his throat and picked up his saw. "I'd like to say, 'Well, then, carry on. I'm paying attention.' But that seems too brash."

Cara burst into laughter. "You just said it, didn't you?"

"Who, me?" Israel feigned innocence.

If she'd had a father growing up, she'd have wanted him to be like Israel. "So where's Lena?"

"On the other side of the house, near the road. She's weeding the flower beds and adding fresh mulch."

Cara brushed a string of her prayer Kapp away from her face and over her shoulder. "How is she managing that with her arm in a cast and a medical boot on her sprained ankle?"

"She moves slower than usual and makes sure to wear at least one work glove."

"How's she really doing, Israel?" Ephraim asked.

"Pretty well, considering a maniac tried to kill her less than six weeks ago. I've not seen any signs of nervousness or bad dreams. Cara, you're welcome to interrupt her for a visit."

"Okay, thanks." Cara headed in that direction and then turned to Ephraim, silently asking him why they'd stopped here.

Ephraim adjusted his suspenders. "Israel, we'd like to pick up Lena if you don't mind."

Ah, now Cara knew why they'd come. Ephraim was helping to arrange a meeting between Lena and his friend Grey. The two couldn't court openly or be seen together very often for several months yet. Cara couldn't really explain the reasons—something about Amish ways and Grey's expected period of mourning. Maybe.

"She'll be glad you've come by to get her. What's the plan?"

"We're going to the shop to do a bit of cleaning, maybe play a game or two."

Cara knew they'd do exactly as Ephraim said—clean and then play games. He wouldn't lie.

"Sounds good." Israel nodded once, giving his stamp of approval. "I imagine Grey is already there and will be glad she came to *help*." Israel smirked and winked at Cara.

Yep, if Cara could have had Israel as a dad, she wouldn't have spent her whole childhood feeling unloved. "Do you happen to need another daughter? I've been thinking of adopting a dad."

Israel moved toward her. "I'd be honored. I take it things didn't go well with your father the other night."

Cara's insides flinched. "I...I... You talked to Trevor?"

"He came to talk to you too, right?" Israel asked.

She shook her head. She hadn't seen the man but once since he'd abandoned her at New York's Port Authority Bus Terminal when she was eight. In April he'd shown up during one of their tourist events at Ada's House. Something he said gave away his identity, and she called to him, but he walked off. She hadn't seen him since. Then she discovered he'd been hanging around for months during several of the outdoor events at Ada's House.

"Oh." Israel looked sorry for bringing up the topic. "I went to the lumberyard in Hope Crossing for supplies a few days ago and bumped into him. We went to the Family Restaurant to eat, and he said he was going to see you that very night. We talked about it for quite a while."

Her good mood drained away like water poured onto desert sand. Resentment unseated her sense of thankfulness. "You bought him food, didn't you?"

"Well, sure."

"Did you give him money too?"

Israel looked sheepish. "Ya, a little."

"So, in essence, you paid him to say what you wanted to hear. That's how it works, Israel." She'd seen plenty of no-account people in her life, and she could almost promise what someone like Trevor would do. "If you see him again, ignore him. Then you're guaranteed to hear all sorts of things you don't want to hear, but at least it'll be honest."

"I think he's changed, Cara."

Fuzzy caterpillars change. Snakes don't. But someone like Israel wouldn't understand the kind of man Trevor was. People like him didn't change, not for the better anyway.

Cara drew a deep breath, determined to keep her thoughts to herself. The church leaders were backing her with their time and patience so she could succeed at the language, instruction classes, and whatever else was necessary for her to join the faith this fall. They were doing their part and more.

And she would do hers. All she had to do was keep control of her actions and her tongue, even where her so-called father, Trevor, was concerned.

Five

The dull hum of the bus had droned relentlessly until Aaron got off in Shippensburg and walked the six miles to Dry Lake. The full moon played hide-and-seek as feathery silver clouds rolled across the sky.

An odd rhythm beat inside his chest as he came closer to his parents' home.

He left the main road and cut through the back pasture near the Amish schoolhouse. Images of his sister being mangled by his bull in this field haunted him. He could see her body flailing into the air and thudding to earth again. The bull stomped her over and over again. As the memory taunted him, his legs almost buckled.

His sister's voice echoed inside his head: *You're their only son. Be a man, get your life straight, and do whatever it takes to help them. They need you.*

He couldn't count the number of times Elsie had said that to him. She'd understood what rheumatoid arthritis had done to their Daed much better than he had. Aaron's drinking had blinded him to everything. But now he'd returned to make things right. Knowing Elsie would be pleased lessened his guilt somewhat.

He crawled over the back fence and kept walking until the homestead came into sight. The old two-story brick farmhouse looked the same as it had when they'd moved here nearly eight years ago.

It seemed awfully early to be in bed, but he didn't see any light coming from his home.

His folks never locked a door, so he went inside. The lingering aroma of his Mamm's cooking filled the air. How many meals had his mother fixed for him that he'd never thanked her for, never showed up for, never cared about?

He set his canvas bag on the kitchen table and lit the metal kerosene lantern. "Mamm? Daed?" He grabbed the lantern by the handle and worked his way through each room. "Hello?"

No one answered.

He looked out the kitchen window toward the barn. It stood dark too, but the cows weren't bellowing to be fed and milked, so they'd been looked after.

A figure cutting across the back field caught his eye. He watched for a moment and realized the person was heading for the cabin. The small building couldn't be seen from here, and at the time he left for rehab, his parents seemed to have forgotten the run-down place existed on their property. But his drinking buddies knew about it.

He hurried outside and took the shortcut through the woods. When he came into a clearing, he nearly ran into a woman.

"Frani?"

Her thin, blond hair fell a few inches below her shoulders, and thankfully she'd put on some weight, but her posture said she carried even less hope than she had the last time he saw her five months ago. She'd always talked about getting sober, but those words had faded over the years— maybe in some ways because of him. She'd been a decent friend, and he'd never once encouraged her to stop drinking. Instead, he'd invited her and the others to bring booze to the cabin night after night.

"Aaron, you're finally back. I had a feeling you'd be here tonight." She held up a six-pack of beer, and he wanted it. All of it. "I brought you a welcome-home gift."

He didn't need to touch a six-pack to feel its magnetism. It woke him during the night and plagued him throughout the day.

He glanced toward the thick row of trees that surrounded the cabin.

He couldn't really see it, but he thought he saw a kerosene light shining from a window. "Are there others inside?"

"Nope." She dug a cell phone out of the back pocket of her jeans, flipped it open, and pushed buttons. "But I'm giving them a call."

The clumsiness of her moves and the slur in her words indicated that she was more than a little intoxicated.

Aaron took the phone from her and ended the call before passing it back to her. "There won't be any more drinking at the cabin, Frani. Not tonight or any night."

"Why not?"

"Because I said so." Trying to explain his new goals was a waste of time in her present condition. He looked toward the hidden parking area but didn't see any vehicles. "Where's your car?"

"Where it's supposed to be. Don't worry. Your folks won't see it."

"Kumm." He headed toward the thicket where his old friends used to park.

"Wait." She stumbled. "Me and some of the gang have been by the cabin lots of times in the last five months. It's neat and tidy every time, but you were never there."

Neat and tidy?

She pushed strands of dirty hair out of her face. "We've missed you."

Before rehab, he might have believed they actually cared, and the power of that would have dragged him wherever they wanted. But now he saw a big enough sliver of truth that he understood. He hadn't been missed—only the right to use the abandoned shack on his property.

He took her by the arm and started walking. "I'll drive you home."

When he got back here tonight, he'd board up the cabin. That should put an end to his old drinking buddies coming around.

When they reached her car, Frani passed him the keys. Before sliding into the passenger seat, she pulled a pack of cigarettes out of her jeans pocket. She groped through the trash on the dashboard until she found a lighter, lit up, and stared out the window while filling her lungs with smoke.

Aaron ran his hand over the steering wheel and started the engine. He'd learned how to drive in this car, cruising dirt roads late at night, drunk with his friends. All of that was over now. He hadn't joined the faith yet, but he intended to as soon as he and his family were living in Owl's Perch.

While Aaron drove, Frani finished her cigarette without saying a word.

He wrestled with what to say to her. He wanted to bury the past. Everything he needed to accomplish—winning his parents' approval, starting fresh, earning a little respect within the Amish community, avoiding having beer waved in his face—would be easier if he didn't have to see her again.

But she deserved to have someone help her do what she'd always dreamed of—getting sober. Maybe she'd forgotten about that hope, but he bet that somewhere inside her that dream still existed. His sister might still be alive today if he'd had the clear thinking of a sober man. He had no way of knowing how the past might have played out if he hadn't been a drunk, but he did know that if Frani stayed on this course, the possible disasters ahead were endless. And she deserved better.

As he pulled into a parking space in front of Frani's trailer, a young woman with a fussy baby on her hip came outside. "Well!" the girl yelled.

"Home sweet home." Frani sighed. "Thanks a lot, Aaron. Now that my sister knows I'm here, I'm stuck." She held out her hand for the keys.

"I'm not walking home for the second time tonight. I'll park your car in the usual spot and put the keys under the mat."

"I'll have to walk that far to get my car back?"

"That's right. You need help getting inside?"

"No thanks."

"Get some sleep, Frani. We'll talk after you're sober."

She got out, taking her beer with her.

He left, determined to board up that cabin tonight. Since his parents were out for the evening, it was a perfect time to kick out anyone in it and to nail the shutters closed.

Once back at the house, he went to the pegs that lined the wall beside the back door. His tool belt still hung there, just as it had before he went away. Had his parents held on to it for him, hoping he'd return? Or had they simply not bothered to move his stuff?

He grabbed the lantern, lit it, and headed toward the path that led to the cabin. The trail was much clearer than when he'd left five months ago. Even if his parents remembered this cabin was here, they had no need to go back and forth from the cabin to their house or the barn. Either vagabonds or old drinking buddies were using it. Whatever the case, they had to go.

He climbed the two wooden steps to the cabin's front door and turned the knob. Locked. The place was dark, so he set the lantern on the porch floor, withdrew his hammer from his tool belt, and tapped on a windowpane in the door. The ancient glass shattered. He reached inside, twisted the deadbolt, and opened the door, taking the lantern in with him.

Frani was right. The place showed no signs of the mess he'd left. No empty beer bottles or pizza boxes scattered about. Instead, three brown cardboard boxes sat in a neat row on the floor along the edge of the wall. He pushed one with his foot. It had contents. Other than the boxes, the rooms were as bare as ever. Except for the trash being picked up, nothing seemed different…until he noticed the table beside the front door.

Flowers? Tiny blossoms, scrunched together and lying on a table. They reminded him of the ones his sister used to pick as a young girl and give to their mother. The depth of Mamm's loss hit him again, and he drew a deep breath.

An aroma of gardenias surrounded him, but the smell hadn't come from the scrawny, uprooted plants. Faint sounds of water dripping echoed against the quietness. He followed the noise, expecting to find a leaky faucet or broken water pipe.

As he drew closer to the bathroom, he noticed reflections on the hallway floor, apparently from candlelight flickering in the next room. The door to the bathroom stood ajar about two inches. He eased it open. A tendril of black smoke looped from an almost used-up candle. Bubbles, mounds of them, wavered in the tub as if someone had been there moments earlier.

He swung the lantern to cast light into the hallway behind him, making sure he wasn't about to get clobbered by a stranger. He saw no one.

Water swooshed, jerking his attention back to the bathroom. A woman's head and shoulders slowly came out of the water. She leaned back against the tub, wringing water from her long, black hair.

It seemed that she hadn't heard the glass shattering or him coming inside. He took a step back, aiming to get out of the cabin before he startled her or before her husband showed up. As he slowly took another step backward, the floorboard creaked.

She screamed. Not a dainty, feminine scream or even a frightened one. She was mad.

He hurried through the living room. Almost at the front door, he tripped over something. His kerosene lantern went one way and his hammer the other. His palms landed in broken glass, sending pain through him. He jumped to his feet, grabbed a couch cushion, and used it to douse the burning wick from the broken lantern.

The woman bounded out of the bathroom, holding the puny candle and wearing a housecoat...*his* housecoat. The one his mother had made for him as a Christmas present a few years back. She stood about five and a half feet tall and looked quite thin under that oversized housecoat.

She picked up his hammer and threatened to throw it at him. "I've told all of you before. Get out of my house!"

"Don't throw that. And this is not *your* house, lady."

She winged the hammer at him full force, and he jumped out of the way, but the tool still smacked him in the knee. "Ouch!" He rubbed his leg. "You're the one who's trespassing!"

"Why don't you idiots try coming up with a new line? I'm tired of that one."

"This *is* my place."

"Yours? Really." Her candle sputtered out. In the darkness she grabbed what sounded like a box of matches and struck one. She held it up toward him and gave him an unfriendly once-over. "That makes you Aaron Blank, I suppose."

"Ya." He wiped his slightly bleeding palm down a pant leg and then held out his hand. She didn't take it.

"Your Daed said you wouldn't be back."

"Nonetheless, here I am."

She tilted the match closer to him as if he might be a vision. "Great. This is just great." She yelped and slung the match from her. Within a few seconds, she'd lit another one. She moved to a gas pole lamp mounted on wheels that stood in the corner. After lighting it, she glared back at him. "Of all the deadbeats I've had to deal with—people removing the screens and crawling through the windows or poking screwdrivers through the screen door and letting themselves in even while I'm standing in plain sight—none of them did this kind of damage." She picked up the couch cushion and sniffed it. "Kerosene," she mumbled and tossed it back onto the floor.

Aaron glanced at the mess he'd made. It wasn't that bad. "Why did you say this is your home?"

Ignoring him, she went into the other room. When she returned, she had on shoes. She grabbed the kerosene-soaked couch cushion, and glass crunched under her soles as she walked to the front door and tossed the cushion outside. "Obviously, you haven't spoken to your parents about the transformation of this place from hangout to homestead."

"They know I used this place as a hangout?"

"Sure. And a lot more. Your Daed caught some of your *friends* here one night soon after you left, and they filled him in on everything."

Aaron shuddered to think of all she must have heard about him.

The wheels on the gas pole lamp clattered as she moved the light closer to study him. She didn't say it, but he clearly heard her: *Drunken louse!*

"And you have their permission to live here?"

"This is a dairy farm. It's not unusual to offer a place to live in exchange for help." She went back into the kitchen.

He picked up the remains of his lantern. "I should be going. You can tell your husband I'll have the glass in the door replaced."

She returned with a broom. The image seemed fitting. All she needed to do was climb aboard and ride it.

"If I were a man, would you assume I had a wife?"

"Well…no. But you said…." He tried to think of exactly what she'd said that made him think she was married. "I guess I thought… I mean, Daed would not hire just a woman to help with the farm work."

"Why? Because *just a woman* would do a worse job than you did?"

"You don't have to get ugly about it. I know I'm no dairy farmer." Aaron raised his hands. "I realize I got your dander up, intruding on you like I did. And rightly so. But can we call a truce?" He moved to the table and lifted the flowers toward her. "Please?"

She gave a disgusted sigh mixed with a faint laugh. "You're going to offer me wilted weeds that I picked myself?"

He shrugged.

"Fine." She took the pitiful-looking things. "Since you're not a dairy farmer, we shouldn't cross paths while I'm doing my job."

"You'd have to take up that request with my Daed. The prodigal son isn't supposed to come home unwilling to work for his meals and a place to sleep."

"Michael and I have an agreement. No one comes into the barn during milking times unless I've invited them."

"Then we don't have a problem." He went to the door. "I'll get the glass fixed tomorrow. Wait. Tomorrow's Sunday. I'll get it fixed Monday."

"No need. But thank you anyway."

"I really think I should." He put a bloody hand on his aching leg. "Mostly as a way to ward off any would-be trespassers. It'll protect them."

He was fairly sure he saw a smile underneath her obvious frustration.

"Any chance you know where my parents are?"

"They said they were going to Abner Mast's for the evening. Some kind of fellowship dinner's taking place there tonight."

"Okay. Denki. Good night."

"Good night."

He wondered if she milked the herd by herself, but he didn't dare ask. If all his father had for help was a girl, talking his folks into selling the farm would be easier than he'd imagined.

Six

Aaron jolted awake and jumped off the couch. Sunlight filled the room, as did the sounds of his mother making breakfast. A familiar ache moved inside him. He'd tried to wait up for them last night. Before nodding off, he'd left a note on his Mamm's pillow, telling them he was home and asking them to wake him when they got back.

They hadn't, so he prayed for the right words and walked into the kitchen. Only Mamm was in the room.

She turned to see him, but no smile crossed her face, and she didn't open her arms to hug him.

"I'm sorry, Mamm."

She pulled three plates out of the cabinet and set them on the table. "You should be." She backed away from him. "How could you just disappear like that? Your sister…died. And we needed you."

He pulled out a chair and sat. "I know. But I couldn't help anybody."

"I didn't even know you had a drinking problem until—"

"I'm better now." Aaron wondered if either of his parents had even opened the letters he'd sent them while in rehab.

His Daed came downstairs, wearing his Sunday best. He walked stiffly past Aaron without more than a glance at him and took his place at the head of the table. Mamm set a cup of coffee in front of him.

"Am I supposed to be honored you've returned?" his Daed asked.

"No. But I'd be honored if you'd hear me out."

His Daed looked at him directly for the first time. "Not on the Lord's Day."

"Tomorrow, then?"

Daed shrugged. "You will ask for forgiveness, and I will have no choice but to give it. But I can't imagine that you have anything else to say that I'll find useful."

His mother set a cup of coffee in front of Aaron and trailed her hand across his shoulders before taking her seat. It wasn't much in the way of affection, but it was better than her reaction a few minutes ago.

They bowed for the silent prayer. Not a word was spoken while they ate, not even an invitation for Aaron to join them for church. Did they not want the community to know he'd returned?

After eating very little, Daed rose. "I'll get the rig."

Mamm put the dishes in the sink and wiped off the table. That's all the cleaning the kitchen would get on a Sunday. "There's leftovers in the refrigerator for your lunch. It's not much."

"It'll be plenty."

A weak smile crossed her lips. "If you were to put on Sunday clothes and get in the buggy, he wouldn't throw you out."

"Denki, Mamm. But it'd be best if I wait until next time." Aaron wasn't ready to face everyone just yet.

She left the house, and Aaron sat back in his chair. The sounds of the horse and buggy going down the long driveway slowly faded.

"Home sweet home." He mumbled the words sarcastically, but he'd known coming back would be tough. He'd embarrassed his parents deeply and hurt them twice as much.

He intertwined his fingers, trying to find words to pray for them and himself, but he only heard the echo of his parents' silence.

A clanging sound came from the barn, drawing him to the window. His knee ached where that woman had hit him with his hammer.

About half the herd stood outside the milking parlor, banging their heads on the metal gate, wanting in. Surely his dad and the girl had milked the cows before church. Was that a person's shadow in the barn? He hustled out the door, trying to ignore the twinge in his knee.

Once inside the barn, he noticed the line of cows in the milking stalls. The woman from last night stood beside a cow, humming. Who hummed while milking?

Her black hair was loosely braided and hanging down one shoulder, but she wore a prayer Kapp. She couldn't be Amish. No way. She had on men's pants, a shirt, and suspenders—all of it looked like his clothes from when he was a scrawny teen. The pant legs stopped an inch or two above her ankles. He guessed she was his age. He had a hundred questions for her, and he intended to ask every one of them before leaving the barn.

She spotted him and nodded. "Aaron." Her smooth tone held a degree of politeness.

"I heard a racket."

"It's just me and the cows."

"And you are?"

She paused. "Oh. I assumed Michael had told you." She wiped her hand down a pant leg. "I'm Sylvia."

He shook her hand, caught off balance by her effort to be nice.

"You agreed last night not to trespass in the barn when I'm working, remember?"

"Of course I remember. I wasn't drunk."

Her eyebrows rose. "If you say so."

"I say so." He took the hose and rinsed the next cow's udder.

She tucked loose hair behind her ear. "I was hoping you and I wouldn't have to argue anymore." Her calm manner made her seem like a different person from the one he'd argued with last night.

"I know how you feel. You made that clear." But he wanted answers.

The best approach was probably to avoid being too personal too quickly, so he'd start out talking to her about the obvious thing—milking cows by herself on a Sunday morning. "Daed went to church this morning, so I guess Sundays are your day to milk alone."

She got the milk flowing with little effort. After dipping the cow's teats in the iodine solution and wiping them off, she attached the milkers. "*Alone* is the key word."

He'd worked by himself on Sundays a hundred times in order to avoid attending church, and he wondered if that was her reason too. "Nope. *Sunday* is the key word."

She rubbed her forehead, probably trying to figure out how to get rid of him.

He adjusted the pressure on the nozzle. "Daed was strong enough today to help milk cows. The two of you could have been done in plenty of time for church, but instead you're here, and he's gone."

The taut lines in her face told him a couple of things. One, he was right about *Sunday* being the key word. Two, she was a fairly easy read. He wasn't particularly good at reading people, at least he didn't think so, but this woman spoke loudly without saying a word.

"Look, I know every evasion tactic when it comes to avoiding church. You don't want to go? No one gets that more than I do. But I'm not leaving you with this herd to milk by yourself. No one has to know I helped. When we're done, you can go have an uninterrupted bubble bath."

She shook her head. "Can't you just respect my wishes?"

"Not today." He went down the line, preparing each cow. When his father's arthritis kicked up, Aaron had been expected to run the farm without anyone's help. His Daed shouldn't ask that of someone outside the family, and Aaron wouldn't allow it.

He pointed at her outfit. "Are you Amish? Or did you borrow that prayer Kapp like you borrowed my old clothes?"

"I was raised Amish, just like you. Much to my parents' disappointment, I haven't joined the faith."

"I get that. So, Sylvia, since we've established that you're Amish and that you avoid attending church, how many visits have you received from the local church leaders?"

"A few."

"Only a few?"

"Preacher Alvin told me about a woman named Cara that the church leaders have been dealing with. They feel they handled her situation too strictly and were unfair to her, so I'm reaping the benefits."

They worked side by side for a good fifteen minutes in complete silence. She refilled the troughs with feed, getting ready for the next group. "Isn't there somewhere else you'd rather be?"

He'd go see Frani later today and talk to her about trying to get clean. He figured he'd need to repeat that conversation numerous times before she began to hear him. But even if she was up, she'd have a monstrous hangover.

"Nope."

"Why come back now?"

He paused, unsure what to say. He couldn't discuss his plan until he'd revealed it to his parents, and they weren't ready to hear it yet. He shrugged. "It's home."

She stopped and stared at him. "You're here to stay?"

"It's complicated. I just... Actually, I'm not sure it concerns you."

"You're right. It was rude of me to ask."

He couldn't figure her out. The agitation between them was like two male cats squaring off, yet she spoke softly and seemed determined to be nice.

"Tell me about yourself. I've never heard of a woman running part of a farm on her own."

"Me either."

"But…" He elongated the word.

"Your Daed needed help, and I needed the work."

"I see."

"If you insist on staying in the barn against my wishes, I'd appreciate it if we could work without talking."

"Oh, come on. I'm not asking about your love life."

She bristled. He'd obviously hit a nerve. His conscience kicked him. He shouldn't be prying into her personal life. But goading people into disliking him came easy. He'd used it for years to keep up his defenses.

"Just explain to me why a young, single woman is handling a dairy herd."

Her hand moved gently down the cow's side. "Amish wives and daughters help run farms all the time. Is it that much of a stretch for me to work on one that doesn't belong to my parents or husband?"

"An Amish feminist. I bet that goes over well with the menfolk."

Her brows furrowed, and he saw innocence reflected in her eyes. "An Amish what?"

"Never mind. So where's your family?"

"Path Valley."

"Where's that?"

"Two hours northwest of here by carriage."

"That's quite a ways."

"I…I think it's far enough."

Was that fear in her voice? The girl he met last night didn't seem prone to being afraid. "So what's his name?"

After a sigh she picked up one of the buckets and headed for the milk house.

Instead of badgering her with questions, he should've been emptying those heavy buckets. He moved toward her, reaching for the sealed bucket.

"I'm fine."

"Please."

She stopped and let the bucket thud onto the ground.

Aaron tried to suppress his smile.

Her face flushed. "Please just get out. What is wrong with men your age? Is it impossible to respect the wishes of a female?"

"Maybe your wishes lack good sense."

She closed her eyes for several long seconds. When she opened them, she picked up a half-empty bucket and its claw milker, went to the next cow, and began humming.

He knew he was acting like a jerk, and he couldn't explain why he was putting so much effort into irritating her. This wasn't who he was. Not really, and certainly not when sober. That question circled his mind as he took two full buckets into the milk house, removed the lids, and dumped the contents into the bulk tank.

With empty buckets in hand, he reentered the milking parlor. Although he didn't spot her immediately, he followed the sound of her humming and found her on a milking stool in the tenth stall.

He started to apologize several times, but he wasn't able to say the words. He sighed and picked up another full bucket to take to the milk house.

"It's obvious that you don't want to be here." She glanced up at him from her milking stool. "Perhaps next time you can follow that instinct and avoid coming into my barn."

Her barn?

He paused, thinking of what he knew about her and had seen in her eyes and actions since the moment he'd found her in the cabin. Last night he'd thought his father had hired only a girl when this place needed a team. There was just one of her, but she had fearless grit and determination, both of which would make his task harder.

But he'd succeed. He had no choice.

No single individual had enough strength to make this place profitable. She'd grow weary of trying or fall in love at some point, marry, and move off. It was inevitable. But he didn't have time to wait for either of those scenarios.

He needed his parents to open their eyes about the farm's condition—and the changes to his character. And his best chance of getting them to agree to his plan was to get Sylvia to quit and go back home.

But how?

Sylvia walked to the creek behind her cabin. Loneliness weighed heavier on Sundays. Only work that was absolutely necessary was allowed on a Sabbath, which meant she could milk the herd and nothing else. All those unoccupied hours gave her time to really miss her sisters, especially Ruth.

Sunlight sparkled off the murky water. The cows were probably upstream, wading in the creek to cool off. The temperature had to be nearing the nineties, and it was only early June. The almanac said this summer would be unusually hot and dry, which would take a hard toll on livestock and crops.

She needed to be working—cutting hay, scrubbing the milk house and parlor for inspection, and tending to the cows' hoofs and udders, for starters. Michael said the farm had a lot of debt, but if she kept her nose to the grindstone, this place was bound to become profitable soon. He hadn't shared the financials with her, but it couldn't be that bad.

Hearing the sound of crunching gravel, she walked to a clearing to catch a glimpse of its source.

Aaron Blank was finally leaving the house.

She'd like to know why he'd come home. Michael had told her that Aaron cared nothing for dairy farming, so he hadn't come back to work.

With him gone for a while, she could visit with Michael and Dora and enjoy the kind of Sundays she'd had since arriving here. She went to the old homestead and knocked lightly as she stepped inside. No one greeted her.

That wasn't normal. She went into the living room. Michael sat on the couch, staring out a window. Dora was in her rocker, holding a book, but she wasn't reading.

"Hello?" Sylvia whispered.

Michael turned to her with a forced smile. "I've been wondering where you were."

He didn't sound like himself.

"*Kumm rei,* Sylvia. We could use a bit of cheering up." Dora lifted her book. "I can't get enough light to be able to see."

"And you can't find your glasses, right?" Sylvia looked around, trying to spot them. She snatched them off the top shelf of a bookcase and passed them to Dora. "Now, who do you think put them way up there?" She eyed Michael.

He smiled again, this time a real smile. "I look better to her when she can't find those things."

Dora put on her glasses and began reading.

Sylvia hadn't seen the Blanks look this sad in months. When she'd arrived, neither Dora nor Michael had any words left in them. They'd been blessed with only two children. Their daughter, Elsie, had died eight months earlier in a terrible accident, and their son, Aaron, had left without a word three months later and entered rehab.

Sylvia, Michael, and Dora had spent their evenings together during the cold winter months after she arrived. She and Michael played games and read. She and Dora baked and sewed. After a while Michael and Dora slowly began to open up. Dora had said that talking to an outsider helped them. And it had helped Sylvia feel as if she mattered. After leaving her parents and sisters, she needed someone to treat her like family.

"What was the sermon about today?" Not that she wanted to know. But talking about religious things always lifted Michael's and Dora's spirits.

Within an hour they were relaxed and appeared to be feeling better, just as Sylvia expected. She took the Old Maid cards out of the drawer, and Michael joined her at the table for a game.

Dora took off her glasses and adjusted the frames. "Michael, did you use my glasses for reading last night?"

"Hush now, Dora." Michael grinned. "You're going to give Sylvia the idea we're a cranky old couple."

"Nothing worse than someone thinking that." Sylvia shuffled the deck.

"We are not a cranky old *couple*," Dora retorted. "He's the only crank."

Sylvia burst into laughter and dealt the cards.

Michael picked up his hand. "Aaron's back."

Afraid he might read her displeasure if she looked at him, Sylvia kept her focus on rearranging her cards. "We met when he came by the cabin last night."

She wouldn't mention his being in the milking barn that morning. Fresh grief had settled over Michael and Dora for reasons she didn't understand, and she wouldn't add to their sadness by insisting Michael keep Aaron out of the barn. Either she'd convince Aaron herself, or she'd have to accept that he did what he wanted.

Michael laid down his pairs. "I talked to Clay Severs last week. I think we can get a good price for our hay if it is an early cut. If we wait, he's likely to buy it elsewhere."

She spread her cards on the table facedown. "I'm ready to start cutting hay tomorrow right after we do the morning milking."

"I wanted to talk to you about that." Michael chose one of her cards and added it to his hand. "While Aaron's here, he needs to work. I'll still help with the milking, but it'll make your day easier if he and I do the hay. After all, you have an inspection to get ready for."

Her pulse quickened. She liked the idea of not having to bale hay but wasn't thrilled about Aaron being the one to help. She could see two possible scenarios. Since he'd left the farm in ill shape, he might unintentionally damage her and Michael's efforts. Or maybe he'd returned to prove that he could be a valuable worker after all. Then he might take over everything important to her...just as Elam had.

Seven

Lena sat under a huge shade tree in her brother's yard, enjoying a lazy Sunday afternoon despite the fact that her arm inside the cast itched like crazy in the heat. Her Daed and all her siblings, their spouses, and their children were here at Allen's. Adults and children sipped lemonade, ate cookies, and played badminton, horseshoes, and games of tag.

Wishing Grey were here, she kept glancing at the bridge that connected his property to her brother's. She held her two-and-a-half-month-old niece, who was fidgeting and fussy, and her Daed sat in a lawn chair next to her. She and her Daed had always been close but even more so after her mother had passed away.

Lena cuddled and jiggled baby Elizabeth. "Your mama will come feed you soon." After a bit of cooing to her, Lena drew a toothless smile from the baby. The warmth of holding a little one brought her such joy and hope that she wondered how it would be possible to love a child of her own even more.

She peered through a gap in the lilac bushes, looking for Grey.

Daed leaned closer. "You can't miss him already. You were together just last night."

"Ya. But we were interrupted, and I want to really *see* him. And to be together without the concern of hurting the Blanks."

She and Grey had enjoyed two hours together at the shop, cleaning it and then playing cards with Cara and Ephraim. But then Ephraim's Daed walked in with Michael and Dora, wanting to show them a cabinetry project. Their pained expressions when they saw their former son-in-law laughing and at ease were too much to bear.

She didn't like sneaking around to catch a few minutes with Grey. She loved him enough to put all of herself into his hands—her soul, her body, her future. And she believed God's goodness had brought them together. But to court openly right now would wound Michael and Dora, and she couldn't do that.

"You're the one who convinced Grey to keep your relationship a secret from the community," her Daed said.

After Grey had saved her life a few weeks ago, then refused to leave her side at the hospital, some folks became suspicious about their relationship, including the church leaders. It felt wrong to hide their romance, as they'd been friends since childhood and hadn't begun falling in love until several months after his wife had died. But Grey and Lena had chosen to protect Michael and Dora's feelings by giving them a year to grieve the loss of their only daughter before Grey and Lena started courting.

Very few people knew about their plan to start courting in the fall: Grey's coworker and friend, Ephraim Mast, and his fiancée, Cara; Lena's brother Allen, who was Grey's closest friend and her closest sibling, along with his wife, Emily; and, of course, her Daed.

"I stand by my decision, Daed, but I ache to go for long rides or walks and talk for hours. When we made our choice, I didn't realize how long spring and summer would last."

"You chose to honor others over yourself. Don't regret that just because it's difficult."

His words worked their way into the deepest parts of her. If anyone knew about being patient for the sake of someone else's feelings, her Daed did. He'd been a widower for fourteen years, and he'd tried to court Ada, without success, for the past five, maybe longer. At least they were occasionally seeing each other now.

She leaned over and looped her arm through his. "I have the best Daed there is."

He squared his shoulders. "I know."

Lena chuckled.

A rig of Amish folks from within the community arrived. They climbed out of the wagon and filled the yard, ready to play games and enjoy a Sunday afternoon.

Her Daed nodded toward the bridge.

Grey's five-year-old son, Ivan, raced over it. Lena looked through the shrubbery that ran along the creek bank to see if Grey was crossing the yard.

Because Grey was a widower and Lena's face was marred with a noticeable birthmark, many would think he was marrying her merely because he needed a wife for himself and a mother for his son. At first, despite how much she loved him, she'd had her own doubts about how Grey really felt and why, but he and God helped her see the truth. Grey had told her, "I know what people are going to think, but we know what is between us. Truth of what exists between couples is all that matters."

When he'd said that, she saw into him, and she knew their love was everything she'd hoped for. And at twenty-four, she'd had lots of time to build her hopes.

She caught a glimpse of him as he stepped into the clearing, and joy coursed through her. When he crossed the bridge they'd built, it was all she could do not to run into his arms.

Grey spoke to her siblings, in-laws, and friends as he'd always done at gatherings, but she knew he was trying to appear nonchalant as he came toward her.

Her Daed stood. "Grey."

Grey walked over to him and shook his hand. "Hello, Israel. Beautiful out here, ya?"

Her Daed glanced at Lena, not the least bit fooled by Grey. "Ya, it is. Sit, please. I'm going to the side yard to check on my grandchildren."

Her Daed had given them a minute to talk.

With his back to everyone but her, Grey approached the chair. His eyes connected with hers, and she felt his love all the way to her toes. "Hi, Lennie." He took Daed's seat and leaned in to adjust the baby's prayer Kapp. As he did, he placed his hand over Lena's for a moment. "I was beginning to think Ivan would never wake up so we could walk over here."

"Ah, so that was the holdup."

He sat back. "He doesn't usually take long naps, so I figured he really needed it."

"Sounds like a reasonable assumption. I dreamed about him the other night. You know, cooking meals for him and reading to him."

Grey interlaced his fingers, looking thoughtful, but he'd barely uttered a syllable when Lena's sister-in-law Emily interrupted them.

"You must be ready for a break."

Lena studied the beauty of her niece. "Never."

"Still." Emily lifted her fussy daughter from Lena's arms.

Grey stood, offering his chair to Emily. "I should probably go play a game of horseshoes."

Lena nodded. If he stayed with her too long, it'd draw attention.

While chatting with her sister-in-law, Lena saw movement on the road. A man. He looked familiar.

Aaron.

She stood and began hobbling toward him. When she reached Grey, she tugged on his arm. "Look. It's Aaron." Her friend had quite a stride, and she needed to hurry before he was gone again. "Aaron!"

Grey put a supportive hand under her good arm as they continued toward the road. "Easy, Lennie."

Aaron turned, and the moment he saw her, he grinned and began closing the gap between them. He engulfed her in a gentle hug.

"Look at you." Lena put space between them.

"I sure have missed you." His eyes moved to her cast and the medical boot on her foot. "I didn't realize you'd been this injured. Your letter only said you were bruised all over."

"I'm mending just fine."

Aaron and Grey looked unsure how to greet each other. They'd been brothers-in-law for nearly six years, but Lena had no idea what their relationship had been like. Strained, she'd guess, with Aaron's drinking.

Aaron held out his hand. Grey took it and pulled him into a hug. "I'm proud of you for going for help like you did, and I'm glad you're home."

Aaron backed away, staring blankly. "I…I appreciate that." After several long moments he turned to Lena. "Are you really okay?"

"I promise. So when did you get back?"

"Last night after dark."

"Tell me how you're doing."

He looked at all the people in the yard. "Not here. Can we go for a walk?"

"I'm barely off my crutches, so I can't do much walking. But we can pull a set of chairs into a more private spot in the yard."

He nodded toward the guests. Several people were glancing his way and whispering.

"Or we can go for a ride in Daed's rig, and you can tell me everything," Lena said. "But first you should say hello to everyone."

"Nobody except you wants to see me." He looked at Grey. "Sorry, but I know it's true."

Grey put his hand on Aaron's shoulder. "That's not true of me. I hold nothing against you. But you and Lennie should go for that ride. If you ever care to come by the house, I'd like that."

"And I'll help break the ice with everyone here." Lena slipped her hand into his and squeezed it. "There won't be a better time than now."

Aaron hesitated, studying the crowd.

Grey squeezed his shoulder. "I'll hitch the horse to the rig for you and Lennie while you shake folks' hands."

Aaron nodded. "All right. Let's do this."

She turned to everyone. "Look who's here." Smiling with confidence, Lena silently dared any of them to give Aaron a lukewarm reception.

Cara had never been a fan of Mondays, but having to study the handwritten pages in front of her made this one worse. She put her elbows on Ada's kitchen table. *"Begreiflich."* She had no doubt she'd butchered the pronunciation, but she should know the meaning by now. Sighing, she turned the paper over to find the answer.

Begreiflich meant "easy."

Yeah, right.

Ada set a cup of coffee and a slice of pie in front of her. "I heard that sigh. Maybe this will help."

Through the kitchen window, Cara saw Deborah hanging laundry on the line. Cara's eight-year-old daughter, Lori, chased her dog, Better Days, with a hose, and he in turn chased her. Cara removed her prayer Kapp and the rubber band holding back her rather short ponytail. She ran her fingers through her hair. "How am I ever going to learn this?"

Ada took a seat. "Well, the good news is the church leaders want you to pass. So they're not going to do any nitpicking."

"But I'm tired of sitting through services that make no sense, though

I do like Ephraim explaining it all later in the day. Why is learning Pennsylvania Dutch so hard?"

"You've only been here a little more than a year, Cara. And look at all you've learned. You've been focusing on the heart of matters. Ya?"

"It's hard to believe I'm the same person I used to be. But if I'm honest with myself about all the garbage I still carry, I can't believe how far I have to go."

"You'll get there, dear, because you're in love."

"So much so it's almost sickening." Cara chuckled. "But for some reason I can't manage to tell Ephraim how I really feel. I beat around the bush and make wisecracks."

"I think he knows. Loving and gentle words don't come easy for you. They don't come easy for me either."

"You say lots of loving things to Deborah and me."

Ada sipped her coffee. "Ya, but you two are like daughters to me. You're each a gift from God, for which I'll always be grateful. Still, I would like to be able to voice how I feel to a man."

Cara leaned back, enjoying Ada's openness. The woman was like a mom one moment, a best friend another, and always a trusted confidante. Truth was, Cara had never been around a mother and her adult children. Was this what it was like? "Just any man or one in particular?"

Ada's eyes flashed with surprise at Cara's question, but before Cara could coax a response, someone knocked on the door.

Ada stood. "I think I've been saved by the bell...or rather a knock. You study, and stop thinking about Ephraim."

"That's impossible," Cara called after her.

As she looked over her notes, she heard Ada talking and then her footsteps coming closer. "Cara."

When she looked up, she saw that Ada's face had lost all its color. "There's a man at the door. It's...Trevor Atwater."

Cara trembled. "Are you sure?"

"I looked at his ID."

Images flooded Cara's mind. Her mother hiding her in the attic to keep her out of his sight. Standing at her mother's casket. Her dad taking her to the bus station. Him demanding that she, an eight-year-old girl, stay put as he turned his back on her and walked off. Horrible emotions pounded her like claps of thunder.

"I'll take care of it," she said. "Thanks."

The hallway between the kitchen and the foyer had never seemed so long.

He stood in the entryway. It turned her stomach to see him in Ada's home. She motioned for them to go onto the front porch, and they went outside. Sarcastic, bitter words came to mind. "Can I help you?"

"Carabean, it's me...Dad."

Only her mother had called her that and only at really tender moments. Cara called her daughter "Lorabean" at such times. But this man had no right.

"Cara," she corrected. Actually she'd prefer "Mrs. Moore." Or better yet, for him never to say her name at all.

He nodded respectfully, looking unsure of himself. "I've been thinking about what your little girl said..."

"You had no right to approach my daughter and ask her leading questions."

He wouldn't have had the chance to talk to Lori if Ada's House, with its outdoor booths and activities, weren't a place for tourists. He'd hung around the booth where Cara sold desserts and drinks, and he'd bought items and talked to Lori and her for weeks before he said something that made her suspect who he was.

"I was trying to figure things out." His eyes reflected bewilderment. "But I understand less now than ever. Your daughter said something about the two of you living in a barn and your not having been here very long. I don't understand, and I need to."

You need? What did she care what he needed?

Sarcasm begged to be unleashed, but thoughts of Ephraim and the need to protect her standing in the community caused her to keep control. "It's a long, personal story, one I'm not interested in sharing with you."

He didn't flinch or show anger. He seemed resigned to her dislike of him. "You have plenty of reasons for being angry with me. But I want to make things right."

She laughed. "Is this some type of reality show? Are there cameras somewhere that I can't see? Surely that's the only thing that would make you say something so..." Ephraim surfaced in her mind again, and Cara shut up. She cleared her throat. "I don't need you to do anything except leave me alone."

"But I have to know, Carabea— Cara. Lori said you don't know the language, but you must have learned some of it while growing up in Dry Lake with Emma and Levi."

As a child, Cara was supposed to have been passed off to Levi, her mom's brother, and his wife, Emma. They were going to raise her, but...

"No comment."

"But I'm your dad."

"My father was a drunk. And Mom hid me from you as much as she could until she died. I was told a car struck her. Is that true? Or did you kill her while I was tucked away in that tiny wall space?"

His expression became defensive. "Of course not. Your mom meant everything to me. She was walking to work, and a car ran a red light, hitting several pedestrians. She was the only one who died."

He rattled off the horror like a well-rehearsed performance, but her body shook the way it had the day she learned her mom was dead. Her mother had loved her and had tried hard to protect her. What had this man done?

She wrapped her arms around herself to keep from striking him. "I needed a lot of things from you growing up, and I got none of them." The words came out hoarse and shaky. "For the first time since Mom died, I have a chance to choose who and what I want and to be happy. But my chance is fragile." She hated being so vulnerable with him. "So can you please just leave me alone?"

"But Emma and Levi were supposed to—"

"You stupid, drunken idiot! Don't you dare talk to me about what Emma and Levi were supposed to do. You left me at a bus station! No one showed up for me but the authorities. I was hauled off to foster care. And here's the kicker: those were some of the best years of my stinking life!"

The man clutched the porch railing. "No. You're wrong. I made sure you were with Emma before I left."

"You dreamed that up so you could live with yourself. With the help of Mom's diary, I found my way here a year ago. A year ago!" She pointed her finger in his face. "Go drown yourself in drink, and leave me alone!"

"Cara." Ada's arm slipped around her. "Kumm."

Nothing felt real, not Ada's tenderness or standing on the porch or finally facing her dad. She could be caught in a dream for all she knew. In spite of Ada's prompting, she couldn't stop venting her fury on the man before her.

"All you had to do was pass me off like some stupid baton in a relay race, and you couldn't even do that. Mom would hate you for that."

"Kumm, Cara." Ada tugged at her. "Now."

She pulled Cara inside and closed the door.

Shaking as if she were having a seizure, Cara paced the floors, ranting. "Idiot. He has no clue. None." When she looked up, Ada wasn't there, but Lori was.

"Mama, what's wrong?" Tears filled Lori's eyes. She ran to her mother and wrapped her arms around her waist. "You're scaring me."

Cara breathed deeply, trying to calm herself, but she felt terrified and powerless. The old, uncontrollable anger had taken over, just as it had when she ran away from foster care, fueling her ability to survive. *Oh, God, help me.* She didn't know anything else to pray.

Cara patted Lori's back. "I'm fine, and so are you. Dry your tears." She pulled Lori free of her. "There's nothing to cry about."

"Cara?" Deborah spoke softly as she entered the room. "Is there anything I can do?"

Cara looked at her daughter. "You stay with Deborah for a little while. I need to go for a walk, okay?"

Lori wiped her eyes. "I want to go with you."

Deborah corralled Lori. "Let's make double-fudge cookies. Big fat ones. When your mom gets back, they'll make her feel better."

A tentative smile eased across Lori's lips. "Okay."

As the two of them headed toward the kitchen, Cara went to the window. Ada stood on the sidewalk, talking to *him.*

She hated him. It didn't matter that she wasn't supposed to. There was no way to get free of what he'd done to her life, just as there was no way to escape her hate.

When she'd seen him a few weeks ago, she'd thought she could cope. She'd known his presence would be a difficult obstacle, but now she knew she couldn't tolerate him. If the church leaders discovered her weakness, they'd tell her she needed at least another year of growing spiritually and learning before she could join the faith.

Ada stepped inside, closed the front door, and leaned against it. "He's gone."

"Forever?" Cara's voice sounded small and vulnerable. She didn't want to feel anything for her dad, not anger or compassion or anything.

"I don't know." Ada drew a shaky breath. "You were merciless, Cara."

"He lived exactly as he wanted, and I'm supposed to walk on eggshells so he doesn't feel too bad about it?"

Ada closed her eyes. "I'm not saying you weren't justified in your reaction to him. I'm sure you didn't come close to unleashing all the pent-up anger you've stored over the years. But if you want to be free of him, you have to extend what he doesn't deserve—mercy and grace."

"I have no clue what that means." Cara flew out the front door and slammed it behind her.

Eight

Aaron stood in the equipment shop, dripping with sweat as he continued to fight with the blades on the hay mower. His fourth day back home, and he'd accomplished nothing. Not clearing the air, mending relationships, taking any stress off his parents, or making headway toward returning to Owl's Perch. He tried to loosen the bolts that would free the blades of the hay mower.

If you'd cleaned it properly last year...

He'd spent yesterday cleaning last year's dried mud and hay off the mower. As soon as he finished removing the blades, he'd sharpen them and put the rig back together, and then, joy of all joys, he'd be ready to start mowing the hayfield.

Disgusted and irritable, he set another blade next to the grinding wheel.

His Mamm was warming up to him some, but his father had little to say. Daed had listened while Aaron asked for forgiveness yesterday, but he'd walked out of the room when Aaron tried to explain about his past behavior and addiction.

He was used to the silence between them. It'd been that way for nearly ten years, except now there was clearly unspoken anger in the silence.

He'd earned their anger and lack of respect, but if they could see their way clear to forgive him, they'd realize that he was trying to do the right thing by them. Farm work was no picnic, but the real problem was the unspoken resentment between him and his father.

However, his folks certainly liked Sylvia. When she walked into the house for meals, Daed became someone Aaron didn't even recognize. He was kind and witty. Aaron didn't blame Sylvia. It wasn't her fault. But she believed that with enough effort the farm could be profitable. Only a fool thought the *Titanic* could be patched with a little elbow grease and kept afloat.

The dinner bell rang.

Despite being hungry, he preferred not to go inside for another round of tactful coldness. But he would. He wiped his hands on a greasy cloth and tossed it onto the workbench.

When he entered the house, he saw his mother at the stove but no sign of his Daed or Sylvia. "Smells delicious in here, Mamm."

She smiled without making eye contact. "It'll be ready by the time you wash up."

Walking up the stairs to his room, he removed his suspenders, unbuttoned his shirt, and peeled out of it and his T-shirt. A two-minute shower would help.

He opened the door to his room and found Sylvia asleep on his bed. She had on a dress, but her prayer Kapp and black apron were lying on the chair.

"Aaron, honey?" his Mamm whispered loudly as she topped the stairs.

He pulled the door closed. "Let me guess. You forgot to tell me she takes naps in my room."

Mamm wiped her hands on a dishtowel. "It's the quietest and coolest room during the day. She was out all night dealing with a calving. You can wash up in our room. I imagine she'll sleep awhile today. She never made it to her own bed last night."

He curbed his desire to remark that she still hadn't managed to make it to her own bed. Was everything that had once been his now hers? "Not a problem."

"There's a basket of clean towels and clothes on my bed."

After a quick shower he went downstairs.

Daed walked in, carrying the mail. "Are you going to be able to get that hay mower in working order or not?" Daed hadn't glanced up to acknowledge Aaron's presence or mumbled one *hello* since Aaron had arrived home, but he wanted updates on his work. Daed sat at the table and began opening the bills.

Aaron moved to his chair. "It'll work—not great, but it'll do its job. The blades still need sharpening. If I can get them to hold an edge, we'll be okay. It's a really thick crop of hay this year."

"Sylvia fertilized the fields with chicken manure a couple of times so we could get a bumper crop."

"Of course she did," Aaron mumbled.

"What's that supposed to mean?"

"She's...different."

"Ya, she is." His Daed didn't seem to mind her strangeness even though his parents were as traditional as they came. Maybe their need for her had stretched their capacity to tolerate differences in people.

"We even managed to get the dent corn planted in the west field." Daed opened a business-sized white envelope. "It'll take time to get us out of the hole we're in, but Sylvia and I are making progress." He stared at the DairyAll bill he'd pulled out.

DairyAll provided equipment for farmers and carried loans for the purchases. His folks had owed them money since the day Daed had bought this place. Daed laid the bill on the table, and Aaron caught a glimpse of it.

"Horse neck." He picked it up and studied it. "We owe that much?"

"We?" His Daed took it from him, folded it, and slid it back into the envelope.

Mamm passed Aaron a glass of icy lemonade. "A cooling tank went out, along with sterilizing equipment and half the milkers. It all had to be replaced last winter."

He set the drink down. "That payment is three months overdue. And it mentions putting a lien on the place in four weeks if a payment isn't made."

"I know all that," Daed snapped. "What do you think, Son, that I'm too stupid to understand what the statement says?"

Aaron bit his tongue and willed himself to speak quietly. "No, of course not. It shocked me, and I was thinking out loud."

"Do me a favor and don't use that super-nice, you're-an-idiot tone with me."

Aaron nodded. Even his effort to sound respectful had managed to annoy his father.

Daed put the bill beside his plate. "If we get that hay in and sold, we can make at least one full payment, maybe one and a half. That will keep the threat of the lien at bay for a while. If the weather cooperates, we might get three harvests this year."

Aaron groaned inwardly. "And you'll face something similar again next year and the next. There are easier ways to make a living, ones that aren't filled with *ifs*." He took a breath. "You could sell the farm."

"That's ridiculous, although I'm not surprised you are suggesting it. I'm a farmer. I farm."

"Daed…could you bear with me and listen for just a few minutes, please?"

"You won't stop at a few minutes."

"Please."

Daed pulled out his pocket watch, opened it, and laid it on the table. He folded his arms. "You have two minutes."

"This place is too much for you. Maybe if your rheumatoid arthritis didn't keep you from working some of the time, it wouldn't be. But it is.

I'm not the same man who left here five months ago. I'm clean. I'm here to help you get out from under this place. There are other jobs you'd enjoy and could do."

"Like what?"

"Well…what about selling appliances to Amish folks?"

"Appliances?" Similar looks of displeasure appeared on his parents' faces.

"I've put money down on Plain People's Appliances. It's a store in Owl's Perch."

"Our family has farmed for as far back as the records show, and you want us to move to town and sell machines?"

"I know it sounds strange to you right now, but it's work we can do together as a family. It'll be much easier on your joints. We'll be closer to doctors and pharmacies and—"

"Sylvia, honey," Mamm interrupted him. "Kumm."

Sylvia stood in the doorway, apron on and prayer Kapp in place, looking at him as if he were a monster.

"Did we wake you?" Daed closed his watch and put it back into his pocket.

"No."

"Gut. I saw that new calf and her mama. They both look strong and healthy. You're doing great."

"Denki."

Aaron was sure she would continue doing great, until Daed wore her out. Then again, Daed acted different with Sylvia. Kinder. Gentler. Was it just an act?

Mamm set the casserole on the table. Sylvia stared at Aaron, shaking her head as if she couldn't believe the kind of man he was. Guilt tried to climb into the pit of his stomach and steal his appetite, but he had nothing to feel bad about. His parents were his responsibility. She was merely the hired help, and he didn't owe her anything.

Sylvia went to the cabinet and grabbed a serving bowl, then dumped peas from the stovetop into it. After a flurry of activity, with the two women getting items from the fridge, oven, and stovetop to the table, all four of them bowed their heads for silent prayer.

His Daed shifted, letting everyone know prayer time had ended. Then he sliced the meatloaf and passed the platter to Sylvia. She took a serving and passed the plate to Aaron. Bowls of vegetables were swapped back and forth until everyone had a full plate.

Sylvia put a napkin in her lap. "We have ten heifers on track for calving between now and September. With any luck we won't lose a heifer or a calf in the process. Then we can get the mamas back in with the milking population and have a few bull calves we can sell."

Aaron had put a new venture on the table for his Daed to consider, and now this girl was casually filling his head with false hope, talking about the herd as if they were turning milk into gold. She'd done a remarkable job on the farm. He wouldn't argue that. But it wasn't enough. When it came to the Blank dairy farm, it'd never be enough.

He downed his drink, wishing she wasn't there so he and his Daed could really talk.

"With that kind of progress, I'm sure we won't need to sell," his Daed said.

Aaron set his glass on the table. "Daed, we should talk about that privately."

"Sylvia's worked here from before sunup to after sundown for four months, and although milk production still has a long way to go, she's helped turn things around. She loves this farm the way I'd always hoped you would and the way I still hope my grandson will one day. It's worth hanging on to for Ivan."

"Ivan, Daed. Really?" Aaron tried to keep the disrespect from his tone. Ivan hadn't even begun school yet, and when he graduated, years from now, Aaron was confident he wouldn't be interested in farming.

Grey hadn't been. Over the years Grey had pitched in if they were in a bind, but he'd never considered quitting his work at the cabinetry shop to make his living on this farm. And Aaron's sister had never asked him to. Their son was like Grey. Even with his disability, he loved woodwork and carving. Aaron believed Ivan would follow in his father's footsteps. Besides, with the financial mess the farm was in, his parents couldn't afford to hold on to it until Ivan was old enough to be of real help.

The hurt in Daed's eyes lasted only a moment. "I won't talk of selling, especially behind Sylvia's back."

Aaron propped his forearms on the table, staring at her. "She's a hired hand, not someone who should've worked her way into your hearts and loyalties."

"Don't you talk to me about loyalty, Son."

"Daed, I'm—"

"We're not discussing this."

"No, of course not."

Daed passed the DairyAll bill to Sylvia. "Aaron saw this, and he thinks we should sell. I don't agree, but it's time you knew the truth of what we're facing."

Aaron figured his Daed was telling her now because if he didn't, Aaron might.

Concern lined her features as she studied the bill. "What's a lien?"

Daed shrugged and pushed his plate away. "Nothing to worry about with the progress we're making."

Aaron wondered if she recognized how absurd it was for his Daed to show her the statement and then skirt around explaining it.

Sylvia turned to his mother. "Dora?"

Mamm's eyes filled with tears, and she shook her head. This was so typical of his parents, shrugging off their problems even when directly asked about them. Aaron didn't consider himself any better when it came to coping skills, though. His tendency had been to drown himself in beer so he didn't have to face his issues.

"We're in default on a loan," Aaron said. "Because of that, DairyAll has the legal right to put a lien on the property. It means they get their money first when the farm is sold."

"We're not selling, so what difference does that make?"

"If they put a lien on the place, Daed will owe more money than the farm is worth. A place can't be sold for more than it's worth."

"But if he's not interested in selling," Sylvia insisted, "it doesn't matter, right?"

"He also can't borrow more money if—no, *when* something else goes wrong," Aaron said. "If equipment goes out and he can't afford to fix it, you'll be milking by hand, and production will drop. And he'll have to buy feed rather than grow it. If he can't sell enough milk to pay the mortgage, he'll lose the farm, and his credit will be worthless. He'll have nowhere to—"

"Okay," Daed bellowed. "She's got the idea."

Sylvia stared at the DairyAll statement. "This is bad news, certainly. But I don't see how it changes anything. Our plan all along was to get the bills paid." She tilted her head, making Daed look at her. "Right?"

"Ya." His Daed sounded weary. "But the pressure is on. It's almost mid-June already, and we haven't made our first cut. We've got to get that hay cut and out of the field. If we have enough help to accomplish that before it rains again, we can get top dollar for it. Can we depend on you?" Daed kept his eyes on his plate, but everyone knew the question was directed at Aaron.

"I'm here to help," Aaron said, "but I think you have to be realistic. The debt outweighs our resources. After the hay is harvested and sold, you and Mamm need to go with me to Owl's Perch and look at the shop."

"No thanks."

"In exchange for your coming to see it and really hearing me out, I'll give this farm my all for the next ten weeks." Aaron figured he had nothing to lose by that deal. He was stuck here regardless.

"Ten weeks?" Mamm asked.

"That's when I need to be back in Owl's Perch." He had nearly two more weeks after that date before he *had* to be there to take over the shop, but there was no sense in telling them. He was going to be in Owl's Perch as close to mid-August as possible. He needed the training time before Leo retired.

His father raised his eyes, studying his son. "There's no way to know if you're telling the truth about helping out through the summer. You lied to us for years, never doing half of what you were supposed to do."

"That's a warped perspective. You were laid up in bed most of the time, unable to work. I really tried, but you got up just long enough to see what I hadn't accomplished, never once mentioning what I had done."

Daed stood, his chest puffed in challenge. "You've always had your own slant, your half-truths and lies. I bought this place for you, and you ran out on us!"

Aaron rose to his feet, daring to meet his Daed's challenge eye to eye. "For me? Really, Daed? You're going to call *me* a liar and then make a statement like that? Did I ask for a farm?"

Daed put an arthritic finger in Aaron's face. "I'm supposed to sell the farm, move elsewhere, and trust you won't up and leave us? I don't trust you into next week, let alone next year."

"I've changed! Maybe if you'd talk to me instead of avoiding me, you could see that. I'm clean now. And I've come back here because it's the right thing to do. I'm the only family you have left."

"You've come back here because you need something from me. I don't know what it is yet, but there's a reason."

Aaron wished he could say no, wished Leo hadn't required him to get his Daed to cosign. Instead he tried to keep a blank face while sidestepping his Daed's question. It'd be best to keep the request for the signature to himself for now.

"Michael." Mamm moved to stand between them. "We need his help, and he's offered us two and a half months in exchange for one day of our attention."

Daed turned to Sylvia. "He'll run off or do shoddy work. You need to know that."

She reached across the table and picked up the pile of bills. "Until then, he'll help us. We need him."

Aaron loved being treated like a pack mule, especially by a young woman who stood to gain too much by his efforts. Then again, he needed her help to keep DairyAll from putting a lien on the farm.

Daed sighed. "Okay. You work through the summer, and your Mamm and I will go see this store."

"And listen while I explain the ins and outs of that kind of business."

"Ya."

"Then it's a deal."

"You two sit." Mamm went to the refrigerator. "It's time for dessert." They took their seats.

She pulled out a plate and set it in front of Aaron. "I fixed your favorite."

"Peanut butter pie. It looks fabulous." Aaron lifted his fork. "Denki, Mamm."

"So this shop is in Owl's Perch?" Mamm gave Daed a piece of pie. "Where's that?"

"It's in Perry County."

Daed looked a little surprised.

"Ya, that's right," Aaron said. "It's in the valley below that lookout area you've always loved."

Aaron hoped a seed of desire to escape this farm had been effectively planted in his parents' hearts. Now it just needed watering.

Mamm started to pass a slice of pie to Sylvia, but she stood. "I need to check on the calf."

As Aaron watched her walk out, his heart pounded with feelings that made no sense. Maybe this was how it felt to undermine someone's dreams. What he really needed was a way to make her want to go home or to another farm.

Nine

The warm, sudsy water slid over Cara's hands while she scrubbed the pots and pans as if they'd offended her. The worst of the heat was gone for the day as the sun began to set, but she couldn't find any solace in the pink hues outside the kitchen window or the clip-clop of rigs passing by.

Thoughts of the way she'd exploded at Trevor plagued her. If the church leaders caught wind of how she'd treated him—and they could if Trevor chose to go see Emma and Levi and ask why they hadn't picked Cara up at the bus station all those years ago—her plans to marry Ephraim could be jeopardized.

But she doubted Trevor could follow through on anything, so she didn't need to worry about him telling community members about her outburst. And she'd confirmed that Ada and Deborah wouldn't tell. So why couldn't she just forget about the incident? The man certainly had no problems forgetting about her...until recently.

Squeals and giggles from outside drew Cara to the back screen door. The fenced yard was a wonderland to her daughter, who'd been raised in some of the poorest sections of New York City.

Lori tugged on one end of a towel while Better Days pulled on the other. "Look, Mom. I'm winning."

Cara stepped outside, noticing that several items had been jerked off the clotheslines. "Lori Moore! Stop right this instant! What are you thinking?"

Lori froze in place.

Cara clenched her fists, trying to calm herself. This wasn't like her. She wasn't a yeller. They were the mom-and-daughter team that fought against the odds, not with each other. But fury assaulted her just as it had yesterday when Trevor showed up. She swallowed, trying to gain perspective. "Clothes on the line are not toys for you and that dog to rip up."

Her daughter nodded, and Cara wondered what she must sound and look like from Lori's perspective. She hadn't meant for her tone to be so rough, but she burned with offense.

She'd always loved her daughter's silly ways; even the careless or thoughtless ones were a beautiful reminder of childhood innocence. Had Cara let Trevor steal that part of her too? She'd groused her way through last night and all of today, and her anger continued to grow.

She picked up the towel that Lori and Better Days had been playing tug of war with. It was an old one that Cara had given them weeks ago. Deborah had washed it, and Lori had removed it from the line. Cara picked up the other pieces, realizing those belonged to Better Days too.

She turned to her daughter. "Why didn't you tell me?"

Lori broke into tears and ran into the house.

Cara eased into a nearby lawn chair. *God, help me. I'm so angry I can't stand myself or enjoy my daughter or think clearly.*

A few minutes later Deborah eased out the back door and sat in a lawn chair next to Cara. She put her hand gently over Cara's, reminding Cara of the months she'd spent comforting Deborah after her fiancé dumped her and ran off. Deborah had struggled for a long time, but in the end she was glad to be free of him and had slowly fallen in love again—this time with a man worthy of her.

"What am I going to do?" Cara asked.

"Maybe you need to talk to your dad."

"His name is Trevor. Please don't refer to him as anything else."

Ada stepped outside, holding Lori's hand. "It's time for all little girls to get a bath, but I think she needs to see you first."

Cara opened her arms. Lori ran to her, climbed into her lap, and snuggled.

After brushing wisps of hair off her daughter's forehead, Cara kissed it. "I'm sorry, Lori."

"What's wrong, Mama?"

"I think I ate Oscar the Grouch."

Lori's brown eyes stared up at her, but she didn't smile. "I can't remember you ever yelling before. You wag your finger sometimes or count to five, but you don't yell."

Cara had never seen any benefit to yelling. Besides, Lori wasn't the kind of child who required a raised voice in order to listen. But after facing off with Trevor, Cara couldn't imagine taming the beast she'd freed from its cage. Even as she held her daughter, she felt enough pent-up hostility to rip something apart.

She pulled Lori close. "I love you, Lorabean. And moms yell sometimes, just like you get sassy once in a while. It doesn't mean you don't love me, does it?"

"No way!"

Squeezing Lori tight, Cara kissed all over her face and neck until her daughter giggled wildly. "Go on inside with Ada. I need to talk to Deborah."

Lori hugged Deborah good night and skipped up the back steps with Better Days ahead of her. "Ada, you gonna tuck me in and read to me tonight?"

"I'd like that. What are we reading?"

"You mean you don't know?"

Their voices faded as they went deeper into the house.

Cara searched for a way to explain to Deborah the depth of her rage

but came up empty. "No one's supposed to join the faith harboring obvious unforgiveness. And this isn't going to fade away."

Deborah played with one string of her prayer Kapp. "I thought you
were ready to deal with seeing him."

"Yeah, I thought so too. Until he showed up. Why should we have to
forgive people for doing wrong if they'd do the same thing again if given
the chance? If the church leaders learn about our situation and believe I
should treat Trevor with respect and forgiveness, it'll cause nothing but
trouble for me and Ephraim. It'll look like I'm the problem, but I'm the
one trying, and I wasn't doing bad until Trevor stepped in."

"I know you're trying, and so do they."

"God revealed Himself to me when I didn't believe in Him at all. If
He saved me in this condition, why can't I stay the way I am?"

"Is that what you want—to stay like you are right now?"

Cara moaned. "Oh, dear God, no." She rose from her chair and
stared into the evening sky. Was He listening to her right now? "You don't
understand."

"You're right. I don't, and I won't pretend to. But you do."

Cara turned. "What does that mean?"

"You understand the emotions stirred in you and whether you want to
embrace them as gifts from God or refuse them because they're not something you want."

"I don't get that choice, Deb. Can't you see? They're already inside
me—days and weeks and months and years and decades of anger and
heartbreak! And I was able to box that up and tuck it away until the source
showed up on the front porch."

"But he's here now. And the box has been taken out of its hiding
place."

"Your patience and insight are really annoying, you know."

Deborah smiled. "I'm trying my best not to be. Does that count?"

Cara plunked down in her chair, sighing. More than anything she longed to be perfect for Ephraim, but so many obstacles stood in her way. "Can you imagine what he'll think?"

"Who?"

"Your brother. He's such an upstanding member in the church, and he's engaged to me, a holy terror."

Deborah chuckled. "And if you hadn't returned, he'd be single his whole life, dating different women, searching for his one true mate who never showed up."

Cara squeezed her eyes shut, a storm of anxiety raging through her. Forgiving Trevor wasn't possible. But letting Ephraim know of her weakness and anger was.

"Think he's still in his shop?"

"Probably. If not, with all the windows open, he can hear the office phone ring from inside his house."

Cara stood. "You know, for an annoyingly patient person, you can be pretty helpful."

"I'm just glad you didn't get mad at *me*." Deborah raised an eyebrow, teasing her.

Cara took a deep breath. It was just Tuesday, and Ephraim usually visited only on the weekends, but she longed to see him. Maybe he'd hire Robbie to bring him to Hope Crossing tonight.

Ten

Darkness surrounded Sylvia as she slid into a pair of pants and a shirt. She breathed in the early morning air, trying to ignore the concern that weighed on her. The possibility of Michael losing or selling the farm felt like another personal failure.

After putting on her shoes and prayer Kapp, she left the cabin and walked the narrow path toward the main driveway. Only a few stars peeked through the summer haze, and the waning moon gave very little light. A few cows were moseying toward the barn and mooing softly. Before she had the milking parlor ready, the herd would be bellowing at her, ready to be let in, fed, and milked.

When the barn and farmhouse came into sight, tears pricked her eyes. The buildings stood firm against the dark morning, looking like a dream—one she longed to protect.

The Amish who'd come to America hundreds of years ago wanted two things—religious freedom and land to farm. She felt a kinship with her ancestors but understood that farming was a continuous battle that would never be truly won. Was Michael so weary of the fight that Aaron could talk him into selling?

She went into the barn and lit several kerosene lanterns before climbing into the haymow. She counted out ten bales of straw and began tossing them to the ground. Michael would arrive in a few minutes, bringing her a cup of coffee and a kind word before he helped milk the herd.

She dropped another bale to the ground.

"Whoa!" a male voice hollered.

She looked through the hay chute. "Michael?"

A man stepped into view through the rectangular hole. In the dim light she saw Aaron dusting straw off himself.

She grabbed the strings to another bale. "Why would anyone stand under a hay chute while someone is lobbing bales?"

"I wasn't *under* it. I was getting close enough for you to hear me. The bale broke in midair and scattered." He held up a travel mug. "Truce?" He glanced down. "I'm afraid the lid has straw and dust particles all over it now."

"Please step back so I can finish this task."

He did so without argument, which surprised her. She tossed the last few bales, then climbed down the ladder.

Her cup of coffee sat on a ledge. Aaron was using a pitchfork to spread the straw in the stalls. Apparently he hadn't taken seriously her command to stay out of the barn.

"Daed hurt his back last night," he said.

"Ach, no!"

Aaron shrugged as if there were nothing else to say on the topic. He'd explained his presence with a brief sentence, without even making eye contact. She liked that. But she was worried about Michael.

"Is he in a lot of pain?"

Aaron paused. "I didn't ask."

"How badly did he hurt it?"

He went back to spreading straw. "Hard to tell, and I doubt he's got the money to see a doctor."

"What caused it this time?"

"Just bending over to take off his socks."

She cleaned straw off the lid of the mug and took a swig of her coffee. "I can milk the herd by myself."

"Ya, I know. But I can't cut the fields without someone following the mower to keep it free of buildup. If I have to get off the mower every ten minutes to clean it myself, the crops will ruin in the field before I'm finished mowing it."

"So you figured you'd help me in exchange for me helping you?"

"Trust me, I tried to work something else out."

She giggled. "I bet you did."

"Then let's get to work." He forked a mound of straw and tossed it into a stall, then spread it around.

She'd never seen anyone move as quickly as he did. But they both knew if the hay wasn't cut, dried, baled, and put away before rain moved in, they wouldn't get a good price for it.

."You're sure now is the best time to start cutting?" she asked. "I mean, you checked the forecast?"

"Ya. They're predicting seven days of hot, dry weather."

He seemed as determined as she was to get full price for those acres of hay. But he wanted it for a different reason—so his parents could pay off their debts and sell the farm.

She grabbed a pitchfork. "Once we get out from under some of these bills, we'll be fine. You can go run your appliance store, and we'll handle the farm."

Aaron moved from one stall to the next. "You are definitely underestimating the issues here. My Daed has health problems, and the two of you cannot make this farm profitable." He paused, looking sorry about something. "Why is it so important to you?"

"Lots of reasons."

"Like?"

She considered whether to answer or not, but he understood making mistakes, didn't he? "My Daadi Fisher planted the desire in me to be a good dairy farmer. If he were alive, he'd be disappointed in how I handled his farm—slowly giving up and letting someone less qualified take it over.

He'd be even more disappointed in how I handled some decisions. The Blank farm is my second chance."

"Well, maybe the answer is in looking elsewhere for a third chance."

"This is your Daed's dream. And I seem to be *his* second chance."

"Daed has to find a dream that fits his limited mobility. And you can find another farm to work."

"No. You could. I can only go where my Daed allows. He's not thrilled I'm here, and he's made that really clear, but if I went somewhere without his permission, I'd have to be willing to walk away from my whole family and never see them again." She began dumping feed into the line of troughs. "The biggest reason we're not doing better is because all I know is the herd, breeding, and milk production. I've never planted or harvested crops or dealt with bills or filled silos or handled dozens of other things that are part of running a farm."

"Sylvia, come on. The problems here couldn't be fixed even if you had superpowers in all those areas."

"But, given time, I can make this farm earn a profit."

He moved to a straw bale, jerked the strings off, and jabbed another load with the pitchfork. "No, you can't. I'm sorry you're caught in this. But you and Daed have to face reality."

Grey had come to work early, hoping to talk to Ephraim. But it was almost lunchtime, and Ephraim had yet to arrive. Grey had worked at this cabinetry shop for more than ten years, and he'd never seen a day when Ephraim wasn't here before anyone else—except during his rumschpringe when he moved to New York, and then when he was shunned and not allowed to work at all.

It had been the worst shunning Grey had ever heard of, and Ephraim had kept Cara unaware of it for quite some time. Normally, a man was allowed to keep his job, but the leaders wanted Ephraim to understand what it'd be like to lose everything. Ephraim never budged about helping Cara. And in time the church leaders came to see Ephraim's point of view.

Hearing a horse's hoofs against the gravel driveway, Grey glanced out the shop's office window. Ephraim had finally arrived.

Every time Ephraim did something out of character, Cara was at the root of the reason—whether she knew it or not. Grey never would have guessed Ephraim to be the kind of man to turn his life upside down for any woman. But Grey knew one true thing: no one could predict what love would do to the heart, mind, and soul of a man. It might register as mildly and pleasantly distracting. Or it might level a man, like a blazing fire destroying everything in its path.

He figured both Ephraim and Cara fit into the latter category, although he didn't know Cara well. He certainly hoped she felt as strongly about Ephraim as Ephraim did about her.

That was what Lennie had done to Grey—leveled him. But seeing her holding that baby on Sunday had really rattled him. With her having umpteen nieces and nephews, he'd seen her with babies plenty of times. But this was different, and he hadn't slept decently in the three nights since.

Ephraim walked into the office, yawning. "Everything going smoothly?"

"Ya. We're on schedule. I received two calls from people wanting us to come do measurements and talk to them about wood types and estimates."

Ephraim took a seat and yawned again. "I should've called you from Ada's."

"Not a problem. Is everything okay?"

Ephraim massaged his shoulders. "I don't know. Cara called me last night, and we were up most of the night talking." He suppressed another yawn. "I stopped by the house before coming here. Daed said you opened the shop really early this morning."

"Ya. And it's been a smooth day." Unwilling to put more burdens on Ephraim, Grey turned back to his desk and finished filling out the paperwork for the calls he'd taken earlier.

"Good." Ephraim opened and shut a few desk drawers, then stopped suddenly. "Why'd you come in early?"

Grey swiveled his office chair to face him. "It can wait."

"But it doesn't have to, so tell me now."

Grey stared at the floor, battling with himself. "I…I told you that Elsie and I spent years in separate bedrooms."

"Ya."

"Well,"—Grey slouched in the chair—"I eventually found out why. Because of Ivan's missing arm and our stillborn child, she thought we had bad genes, and she didn't want to chance our having more babies."

Ephraim's face wrinkled.

"Ya." Grey sat upright. "She was wrong not to tell me sooner, and it destroyed years of our marriage. After I finally learned what the problem was, I insisted we have tests run. The results didn't come back until after she died, so I burned them. I didn't want to know."

"Why?"

"If I discovered Elsie had been wrong all those years, I'd have wrestled with anger, maybe even bitterness."

"So by burning the test results, you were protecting your feelings toward Elsie."

"Ya. But I never thought I would remarry. I couldn't imagine being willing to." He broke into a smile whenever he thought of Lennie. "Then Lena happened. But when I saw her holding Elizabeth a few days ago, I realized what I've always known—babies mean everything to her. I knew then that I had to tell her. But how?" Grey shook his head. "And what will happen to us when I do?"

Ephraim leaned forward. "Last night I learned that Cara is struggling with some issues that could keep us from being able to marry this fall. Even though I hate the idea of having to wait a year or two—because it may take that long before she can stand in front of the church leaders and honestly say she has no malice against anyone—I'd still choose going through this now, before we're married. What she's dealing with is disappointing and frustrating, but it's also real and honest. I'm not sure I even realized that myself until now."

"Well, it's nice that all my gabbing while on the clock is of some benefit to you too. Thanks, Ephraim. I needed to talk."

"Anytime. I'm glad all those years of you keeping everything bottled up are over. They are over, aren't they?"

"They are."

He just had to find a way to be alone with Lennie so they could talk.

Eleven

The sun bore down on Aaron's aching neck and shoulders as he kept an eye on Sylvia. If she lost her balance and fell forward or if her clothing got caught in the blades, she'd be the victim of a bad accident.

He stood in the mower cart, almost as harnessed as the horses. Sylvia followed behind with a pitchfork in hand.

The ground mower snagged on something, making it jump and jerk. "Watch out!"

Until he yelled, she hadn't noticed what was happening. She took a step back just as the blades jumped upward.

"For Pete's sake, Sylvia! Pay attention!"

She gestured that she was fine and he should keep moving. They'd covered maybe two hundred feet when she yelled for him to stop.

Not again! He ground his teeth and tried to pull the team to a halt, but the horses refused to obey him. He kept a firm but gentle tug on them until they yielded. Then he looked at the wad of hay caught in the mower.

He waited while Sylvia jabbed the pitchfork between the blades and dug out the fresh hay, dislodging the clump. Left in the blades of the ground mower, the mounds of hay would damage the machine, and it would merely run over the hay rather than cut it.

"You know," he said, "we wouldn't be having this much trouble if you hadn't put so much fertilizer on the field."

She peered at him from under his Daed's straw hat, but she didn't respond. He shouldn't have said that. She was doing him a huge favor by helping like this, but exhaustion was getting the best of him.

As she resumed her work, he remembered how she'd started the morning: wearing a dress and apron with a straw hat. They'd begun cutting near the main road, where carriages passed, and she hadn't wanted to stir up controversy if it could be avoided. She was like him in that respect. When they'd moved away from the main road, she'd returned to her cabin and changed into his old work clothes. She had looked awfully cute in a man's straw hat and a dress.

He was miserably hot, tired, and hungry. Who in their right mind would want to own a farm?

She motioned for him to get moving again, and he slapped the reins against the horses' backs. As always, they didn't want to start up. That he understood.

Sylvia moved to the front of the rig, grabbed the harness, and tugged. She patted the lead horse, cooing to it in Pennsylvania Dutch. "Kumm." The two-thousand-pound creature took a step.

They'd barely finished that row when his mother came into sight, carrying a basket.

"Mamm's here," he bellowed, gesturing toward the road.

Sylvia nodded, jabbed her pitchfork into the ground, and headed for her. The moment his mother spotted Sylvia, she smiled and waved. If he could get past his own surliness, he'd admit what a comfort and asset Sylvia had been to his parents in his absence.

While he unhitched the team, Mamm and Sylvia spread a blanket under a shade tree and unloaded the basket. Aaron led the horses to the two five-gallon buckets of water he'd set up for them. After tying them to ground brush, he walked over to the blanket.

The women had bowls of food spread out on the blanket. Plates. Two cups of icy water. Flatware. Bread. Butter. Cloth napkins. Steaming vegetables. And green-bean-and-ham casserole—one of his favorites. In Mamm's eyes anyone working a farm needed the noon meal to be the largest of the day, whether they could make it to the table or not.

"This looks wunderbaar, Mamm. Denki."

Sylvia patted the blanket. "Dora, why don't you stay and eat with us?"

Mamm finished loading a plate of food and passed it to Aaron. "I told Michael I'd take the horses back to the barn and bring a fresh pair while you two ate."

Sylvia rubbed Mamm's shoulder. "How's he feeling?"

Embarrassment and guilt churned inside Aaron. She really did care about his parents. No wonder his Daed had reinvented himself. It was easy to respond positively because Sylvia was gracious to them.

"I can't tell which is worse, the pain or his anger over the injury."

"Well, he'd better rest up," Sylvia said with a grin. "If he thinks I'm letting him win the checker championship just because of a little back pain, he's wrong."

Mamm smiled. "I'll tell him."

After Mamm left, Aaron and Sylvia ate in silence, and the edginess he'd felt while working faded.

"I shouldn't have yelled at you about the amount of hay to cut or paying attention," he said. "I…I'm sorry."

She blinked, her brown eyes showing amusement as she cupped her hand behind one ear. "You're what?"

"Have hearing issues, do you?" He stifled his laugh but not his smile.

"No, not at all." She took a sip of her water. "It's just that those words from a man's mouth are like a foreign language."

"I apologize, and you turn it into an insult of all men?"

·"One must make the most of every opportunity on that topic."

He chuckled, and her lips formed a charming smile. She was probably easy to get along with when someone wasn't trying to goad her all the time.

Once again he wondered what had happened to make her leave her farm and come here.

"It's so miserably hot." She wiped her forehead with the back of her wrist. "Enough days of this could make a person black out. Have you ever passed out?"

"You mean while sober?" he scoffed.

She didn't frown or laugh at his wisecrack but just dug into the basket and pulled out two bowls covered with plastic wrap. "Banana pudding." She removed the plastic from one.

He leaned against the tree. "You know, I've been thinking about our conversations since we met, and it seems to me that you have a problem with guys. So tell me, Sylvia, what makes you dislike the male gender?"

"Are you going to pick a fight with me at every meal or just when I say something that's a little personal—like asking about your health?"

"You didn't say anything that bothered me." That was a lie. He didn't like her acting as if they were friends.

She took a few bites of her pudding before setting it aside, then removed her hat, lay down on the blanket with her back to him, and propped her arm under her head. Within two minutes her shoulders moved up and down in a slow, rhythmic pattern.

Who are you, Sylvia Fisher?

Twelve

Sylvia hobbled into the barn, her muscles screaming. The dark morning sky held no charm for her today. She found the kerosene lanterns lit, the bales of straw down from the loft, and Aaron spreading it on the stalls.

He looked up for a moment, then returned to his work. "Coffee's on the ledge."

She tried to walk normally as she went to the mug. Gingerly she picked it up with her aching, blistered hands and took a drink. "Denki."

"You should thank Daed. He won't let me leave the house without it."

She wasn't the only one who was sore. Aaron grimaced as he moved at half the speed he had yesterday. She dreaded the work ahead, but they had at least two days of stirring the cut hay and letting it dry before it could be baled.

"We have four teens coming to do the evening milking until we get the hay out of the field," Aaron said, "and Daed's able to supervise them, so we can keep mowing while they tend to the cows."

"There's no money for that."

"I promised to pay them when we sell the hay."

"But we need that money."

"I know that. But it'll take us another week if we have to do the milking as well. We'll be too tired to keep up the needed pace in the field, and the rains might move in before we're done."

She set her coffee on the ledge. "You're right. As I've said, I don't know much about baling hay."

"Well, this is an awful way to learn."

"Agreed." She grabbed a pitchfork. "My head feels woozy from working in the heat all day, my hands are blistered, and my feet ache all over."

"And it'll be worse before nightfall."

Just what she wanted to hear.

They moved through the milking as if they'd worked side by side for years. While he harnessed a set of horses to take to the field, she went into the house and rustled up snacks and drinks.

Dora should be the one keeping them fed throughout their workday—snacks, drinks, and meals included. She moved better these days than when Sylvia first arrived, but grief over losing her daughter kept Dora from being able to hold to a schedule. She got things done whenever she could manage it.

Sylvia carried the basket of food and a blanket to where they'd begin cutting. They had finished mowing near the road. Today's path wouldn't allow anyone to see her, so she didn't change out of her pants. Last night when she got into the bath, she noticed her legs were covered with scratches, though not nearly as many as there would have been if she'd stayed in her dress all day.

To her surprise Aaron wasn't strapped into the cart. She put the blanket, drinks, and food under a tree before pulling fingerless gloves out of her pants pockets. Even with gloves, she'd earned several blisters yesterday.

"Kumm." Aaron motioned for her. "You're in the cart today."

"Why?"

"If we're going to survive the next two days, we have to swap jobs. Each position works different muscles."

"My sisters and I used to do that with our vegetable garden."

He helped her get the team's rigging around her shoulders and firmly placed in each hand. "How many sisters do you have?" he asked as he adjusted the straps.

"Eight."

"Any brothers?"

"No."

"Do all your sisters have the same rule about who can enter the barn during milkings?"

"I don't want to talk about my family."

"Of course you don't." He tugged on the straps around her. "Does that feel okay?"

"It's fine."

"The horses don't like stopping, but if you pull back too hard, you'll split their mouths."

"Horses I know."

"Okay, let's get this glorious day under way." He sounded sarcastic, and she ignored him.

Time seemed to drag as the sun moved across the sky, and the heat was more suffocating than the day before. Her body ached as if she'd been beaten.

They changed the worn-out horses for mules midmorning, and Sylvia passed Aaron a hunk of coffeecake. The mules proved so stubborn and frustrating to work with that Aaron traded them for a set of horses they'd used yesterday. They shared a lunch and then worked through the hottest hours of the day. By the time the sun flirted with the tree line, Sylvia's legs shook with exhaustion, and her peripheral vision burned with brown spots.

"Whoa!" Aaron yelled. He wiped sweat from his brow and freed the blades of thick hay. He held his back as he slowly stood up straight. "It's time to call it quits."

"There's at least forty more minutes of daylight."

"We're done for today. End of discussion!" He threw the pitchfork to the ground.

Part of her wanted to cheer, not just because he had insisted they quit, but also because he wasn't afraid to say when enough was enough.

He loosened the horses and passed the reins of one to her. "I shouldn't have yelled."

"Forget about it."

"You still like farming?" he asked as he stepped into the lead position.

"The only thing I don't like about farming is working with mules."

His laughter echoed off the hills.

She trudged through the thick, uncut hay to get the canteens, lunch containers, and blanket. Just before reaching them, she tripped and fell, seeing snatches of images on her way to the ground—the trees, the ocean of ripe hay, a ladybug on a strand of dry grass, and finally the ground. Everything turned brown for a moment, and she fought to inhale, but she couldn't catch her breath.

"Sylvia!" Aaron ran to the last place he'd seen her just before she seemed to disappear into the ground.

He found her lying facedown in the grass, and she didn't appear to be breathing.

He gently sprawled his hands along her back. She moved, and relief made his knees go weak. "Sylvi." It felt right to refer to her as Sylvi, to call this odd woman by a name that no one else used.

She tried to roll over, but he had to help her. The movement caused her to jerk air into her lungs. Apparently, the breath had been knocked out of her.

"You okay?"

Seconds ticked by as she lay there blinking, as if trying to focus her vision.

"What happened?" he asked.

"I…I don't know."

"Don't try to get up." He ran to the picnic basket and returned as fast as he could with a canteen of water.

He sat beside her and lifted her head to help her get a sip. "You really scared me. One moment I saw you marching across the field, and the next you were gone. I thought maybe you fell into an abandoned well, like you sometimes find on old farms. You know, the kind that farmers dug long ago and then boarded up when they went dry. The thought of them makes me shudder."

She took another sip, then mumbled, "No more."

He gulped down a drink, closed the canteen, and set it next to her.

Relieved that she seemed to be all right, he put a piece of hay in his mouth, trying to look relaxed and unperturbed. "I can't do this stupid, overfertilized field by myself, you know."

She stared at the evening sky with its streaks of pink and gold. "I really don't like you."

He chuckled. "Ya, back at you." But he didn't really feel that way. He wished she was more unlikable, but how could he not enjoy someone as sincere and focused as Sylvi, even with her oddities? "But you're a good worker. Never seen better."

She slowly raised herself to a sitting position. When she tried to stand, he got up and helped her. She wavered a bit, no doubt feeling the effects of a day of manual labor in soaring temps.

"Maybe you should stay put for a little longer."

She rubbed her temples. "Not here. I'm bug food in this grass." She teetered, and he grabbed her arm.

"Kumm." He steadied her as they slowly walked back to the blanket. He helped her sit and passed her the water. "Did you really think you and Daed could have done all this alone?"

"I thought we could hire some help. He didn't tell me how much debt there is. I knew money was tight, but it is for most farmers."

He nudged the canteen, encouraging her to drink. "Was it tight on your farm?"

"Some years were really tough, but my grandfather's father owned the farm outright. It's been passed down and divided up for generations, but there hasn't been a penny borrowed for decades. When milk prices drop and equipment prices go up, money is tighter, and we hire fewer workers, so the days are longer. During good years equipment is bought or repaired, we grow the herd, and we save up."

"Your folks have the ideal situation."

"You couldn't convince my Daed that having nine daughters and no sons is ideal for a farmer."

He doubted that losing six babies, having their only daughter die, and raising a son who'd been nothing but a disappointment was any better. He opened a container of fruit and offered it to her. "This'll help."

The sounds of evening grew as they ate a few grapes and waited for her strength to return. He didn't feel antsy or annoyed sitting with her. Truth be told, he liked having an excuse to talk to her and almost regretted that he needed her to leave the farm.

He nudged the grapes toward her again. "How did you land here?"

"Your Daed put an ad in the paper, and I responded. Our fathers spoke on the phone a few times, and then the three of us met halfway between the two places. The men talked until my Daed felt sure I'd be safe, and I came home with Michael. But I paid a high price."

"You mentioned that earlier. How?"

"In many ways my Daed feels the same about me coming to work this farm as your Daed does about you leaving home when you did."

"Parents always think we're the problem, which in my case is only true about ninety-eight percent of the time."

She laughed. "Michael said you guys moved here from a farm in Ohio about eight years ago."

"That we did." He let his mind wander back over the years. "I was seventeen. Daed assured me time and again that this would be our promised land. Before we moved, night after night he talked about this place and had me totally sold on the idea."

"Why'd they leave a farm in Ohio to move to Dry Lake?"

"If they didn't tell you, I won't."

"Seriously?"

Irritation stirred within him. "You think that because they've told you every embarrassing thing about me, I'll share their problems?"

"We all have embarrassing things. Your folks needed to talk, and I listened. Much of the time they reminisced about Elsie. And about how you hate this farm and how they found out that you drink—I mean, drank."

"They'll talk about it, but they refuse to say the word *addict*, let alone admit I am one."

"Is that important?"

"I'd like them to understand at least one or two things about me. Real forgiveness would be nice too. Not that forced 'I forgive you' that Daed gave me while meaning the exact opposite. Isn't that what family is about? Forgiving unconditionally?"

Sylvia's forehead wrinkled, and she stared into the distance. He wondered what had happened in her family to cause her to leave home and attach herself so strongly to someone else's parents.

When she turned back toward him, he saw tears in her eyes.

"You sure you're feeling okay?"

"Ya." She swiped at her cheeks with the back of her hand. "I miss my family, that's all. But part of the reason I'm here is that I don't want to see...some of them, especially one sister."

"That must've been some fight."

"No one in my family even knows how to get here, so I accomplished my goal. I guess that means you and I are both a twisted array of faults."

"I guess so, but unfortunately I still win by a long shot."

She gave him a slight grin. "You know, you're almost tolerable right now."

"*Almost* being the key word."

"Will I have to hurt myself again to see a repeat performance?"

Heat flushed his cheeks. "No."

"I'm glad to hear it."

"Ya, if you get hurt again, I won't be the least bit tolerable."

She broke into laughter. "That was mean, Aaron Blank."

"You wouldn't want me to be too nice. You might go into shock or something."

They had ten weeks of working together ahead of them, and it would make it easier if he could enjoy her company. But the issue that was most important to him—getting his parents to sell the farm—sat between them like an immovable boulder.

He picked up another piece of hay and chewed on it for a while before tossing it aside. "Do your sisters like farming too?"

"No, none of them. Beckie is married, so Daed now has a son-in-law working beside him."

"Is she the one you argued with?"

Sylvia's features melted into a pool of sadness. "Aaron, I know I started this conversation, but I don't want to talk about that. Ever."

"Sure. Okay."

But they didn't need to talk about it again. He now knew what to do. He'd write to her sister Beckie, sending a detailed map and inviting her to visit. Once Sylvia talked things out with her sister, she'd want to go home. Maybe not right away, but at least she'd be willing to help him get this place ready to sell. After she left, his Daed and Mamm would see the wisdom in moving and owning a shop with him. It was best for all of them. Even Sylvia.

All he needed was to find her home address in that mess of papers on his Daed's desk.

Thirteen

When Grey stepped out of the shower, he heard voices in his kitchen. He wrapped a towel around his waist and opened his bedroom door a crack. "Mamm? Is that you?"

"Ya. We brought supper. Hope you don't mind."

"Ya, actually I do. So we must destroy the evidence as quickly as possible."

His Daed laughed. "I agree."

"*Dabber,* Daed," Grey's five-year-old son pleaded. *"Ich bin hungerich!"* Ivan urged his Daed to hurry, but cheerfulness was evident in his voice.

Grey had left work a little early that afternoon and taken Ivan fishing, which he did sometimes on Fridays. They'd had fun, but by the time he'd cleaned the fish, bathed Ivan, and then taken a quick shower, they'd both grown quite hungry. Besides, whatever his Mamm had prepared would be better than anything he could fix, including freshly caught fish. He was glad his parents had come over. The house was too quiet most weekend nights.

"Ich kumm glei naus." Grey assured his son he'd be out soon. He'd been teaching Ivan more English, as Lennie had suggested. Ivan was catching on well, but Pennsylvania Dutch was still much more comfortable for him.

After Grey dressed, he walked over to his nightstand and slid the letter he'd been writing to Lennie into a drawer under his T-shirts. He'd finish that later. He didn't mind his parents knowing, and when they did find out, they'd be happy for him. But in the fall, when he and Lennie began courting, he didn't want his parents put on the spot if someone asked when the relationship had begun. As for himself, he didn't care who thought what. He'd been faithful to his wife in every nuance of the word even years after she'd shut him out of her life.

Walking into the kitchen, he rubbed his hands together. "Edible food. There's nothing quite like it." He took plates from the cabinet and began setting the table.

His Mamm laughed. "Ivan says you cook pretty good."

"I'm not bad but nothing like you, Mamm."

They were halfway through the meal when someone knocked on the front door.

"Kumm."

Ephraim stepped inside and bid everyone a warm hello.

Mamm fetched a plate. "Kumm. Eat with us. There's more than enough."

"I can't stay. Cara's expecting me at Ada's House." He shifted, looking a little uncomfortable. "I didn't mean to interrupt your dinner."

"It's no problem," Grey said. "What's up?"

Ephraim handed him a paper that showed the layout of a room. "Israel needs some measurements taken for a set of cabinets he wants built in his shop. I was hoping we could get the information logged this weekend and begin work next week, but I can't get to it. I was busy doing the books for the shop and lost track of time. I should've been in Hope Crossing an hour ago."

Grey looked over the diagram. "There's no description of the type of wood."

"Israel said to check with Lena. He's wanted this done for a while, and the two of them can't agree on exactly what's needed."

Ephraim had brought Grey exactly what he needed: a legitimate reason to be at Lennie's—one that would hold up no matter who dropped by unannounced.

Mamm scowled. "I have a question."

Grey's Mamm always had questions, lots of them.

She put her elbows on the table and folded her hands. "Israel makes furniture for a living. Why would he hire you to build a set of cabinets?"

"Probably because we can build it faster and better," Grey said. "That is our skilled area, Mamm, just like Israel could build a kitchen table and chairs faster and better than we could."

"Okay. That makes sense. So, Ephraim, have you and Cara set a wedding date yet?"

He shook his head, maintaining a casual posture. "We're hoping for fall, but the languages are giving her some trouble."

"I 'spect so," Grey's Daed said. "If I'd had to learn our languages from scratch as an adult, it would've made me think twice about even trying to join."

"Ya. She's pretty frustrated right now. And I'd better be going before she's frustrated with more than just the language."

Grey's parents laughed.

Grey walked out with Ephraim. Robbie sat in his truck, waiting. "I appreciate this, Ephraim."

"I think she stayed home tonight, although that could've changed if one of her friends dropped by."

Lennie had a lot of energy and even more friends, so it was very possible he'd arrive and she'd be elsewhere. Grey went back inside. He saw his parents nearly every weeknight, and he enjoyed their company, but right now he wished they'd head home so he could go see Lennie. The minutes dragged into two hours before his parents left with Ivan.

Grey hitched his horse to a rig. Pitch black painted itself across the summer sky, and he thought he heard thunder rumble in the distance as he drove toward Lennie's. When he arrived, he couldn't see any light coming from her home or her Daed's furniture shop. Disappointment bit.

He pulled farther onto the driveway. The greenhouse glowed dimly, reminding him of a full moon against a field of damp, ripe hay. After tethering the reins to a hitching post, he strode toward one of Lennie's favorite havens. It tended to be muggy inside the greenhouse in summer, but she'd put in screened doors and windows so she could enjoy working in it at night, free of the day's overbearing sun and the night's pesky mosquitoes.

He went to the door and started to knock, thinking that'd be less startling than just barging in. When he heard a man's voice, he went inside, expecting to find Lennie and her Daed.

Instead, Aaron sat on one of the long workbenches, talking seriously. Lennie stood at another workbench, her back to Grey and her side to Aaron. An oversized pot sat in front of her, and Nicky lay on the dirt floor nearby, watching and wagging her tail.

It felt right to see Elsie's brother like this. Grey knew firsthand the struggles the young man had been through, and right now he looked better than Grey had ever seen him—healthy, sober, as if he'd found an inner compass. But a twinge of concern pricked him.

"Grey." Aaron nodded casually.

Lennie wheeled around, a beautiful smile greeting him. Her gloved hands were covered in potting soil, although he couldn't imagine what needed to be potted in mid-June. Her eyes moved to his and stayed. "Grey." Pulling off her gloves, she walked to him. "What brings you here tonight?"

When she moved in close, he couldn't find his voice. He pulled the work order from his pocket.

Pleasure danced in her gorgeous bluish green eyes as she took the paperwork from him. "Oh, for Daed's shop?"

"Ya." He pointed at the schematic. "But he's asking for an abundance of storage space for the amount of room we have to build in."

"We've talked about it before, but it's been a while. Give me a minute, and I'll walk over with you." She went to her workbench. "Are these cabinets going to be open faced?"

"It's my understanding that he's leaving that up to you."

"That's because he's playing chicken." She opened a tube of glue, spread it on the edge of a broken pot, and squeezed two pieces together before passing it to Aaron. "Hold it just like that. If you do, I'll come by your place tomorrow and invite Sylvia to an outing tomorrow night or Sunday."

Aaron mocked frustration. "But you already agreed to do that."

"Ya, and now I've added a price tag. Stay put. I've wanted that pot glued for quite a while. Now that you've volunteered to hold it just so for the next several hundred minutes…"

"Lena." Aaron elongated her name, fussing and laughing. Then he shifted his attention. "Grey, any chance you'd be willing to help milk the cows once in a while?"

"I'm willing. I helped your Daed whenever I could right after you left. But then he hired a young woman…"

"Sylvia Fisher."

"Ya, that's her name."

"And I bet she asked you not to come anymore."

"She was nice about it, but ya."

"See, Lena, I told you. Sylvi is weird. Who turns down good help in exchange for the grand prize of working seven days straight, week after week?"

"Sylvia, I suppose."

Grey listened to the banter, and the concern tugged at him again. "Lena."

She looked surprised, but he didn't know why. She pointed at Aaron. "You stay."

"Yes, ma'am."

When she opened the door, Nicky bolted ahead of them. Lena left the greenhouse, carrying a lantern. Grey followed her, and she gave him the light.

"You called me Lena," she whispered as they walked across the dark yard toward the small shop behind the house.

"So?"

Laughing softly, she dug a skeleton key out of her pocket and shoved it into the lock on the shop's door. "I don't know that I've ever heard my real name come from your lips."

"What are you doing?" His muted voice fell against the humid air.

Jiggling the key, she looked up at him. "Currently I'm fighting this door. In a moment I'm hoping to be kissed."

He took over the key but couldn't make it open the lock. "I don't think you realize how much Aaron likes you. He's home and sober, and maybe he's looking for a girl."

"He's doing no such thing. Not by coming here, anyway."

The door jarred as he finally unlocked it. "You've been his only connection within this community for months. He wrote to you at least once a week. And you answered, right?"

"Sure. But this is Aaron. I know him, and he'd never think like that toward me." She set the lantern on a workbench. "We're friends."

"Just be a little more…distant in your responses to him." He slid his hand into hers. "For his sake."

"Okay." She tilted her head back. "I miss you. It was so much easier to get quality time at Allen's back when we were just friends."

"I even let you win at checkers." Her scent of lavender mixed with roses and violets drifted into his soul.

She smiled up at him. "Evenings and mornings and weekends will be ours soon enough."

He squeezed her hand and lowered his lips to hers. The soft sweetness of her called to him.

The screen door to the greenhouse banged shut, and he knew Aaron was heading their way. "Aaron," he whispered, brushing her cheek with a kiss.

She caressed his hand before putting several feet between them and then motioned toward the empty wall. "How deep does Daed want the cabinet?"

"Hey, Lena," Aaron called as his footsteps echoed off the small wooden porch of the shop.

"Ya?"

He opened the door and walked in. "I think the pot is secure enough to hold together while it finishes drying, and I need to head out. It's been thundering, and I have to get back so I can promise Sylvia it won't rain."

"You can't promise that."

Concern flashed through his eyes. "Well, I can't make it come true, but I can and will promise it."

"Why?"

"Because she knows the hay we've cut will lose at least half its value if it rains before we get it baled and out of the field."

It sat well with Grey that Aaron seemed to care how the farm was doing. He'd never seen that in him before.

"Grey, would you give him a lift home?" Lena asked. "After cutting hay all day, he walked here."

Grey folded the papers and shoved them back into his pocket. He knew that underneath Lennie's request to give Aaron a ride was her desire for Grey to spend a little time with his son's grandparents. After the way Michael, as head of the school board, had refused to stand up for her last year, he found it illogical that she cared so much about him and Dora. But he appreciated that she did.

"Sure."

Fourteen

From the dessert booth in Ada's front yard, Cara kept an eye on the road, looking for Ephraim. When the sun finally went down, the temperatures dropped, but humidity clung to the air as thunder rumbled. The street-lights illuminated the area surrounding Ada's House, and shots of light-ning blazed across the distant sky. The storm seemed to be skirting them.

After a day of helping Deborah and Ada bake in a hot kitchen, she soaked in the cool reprieve. Deborah ran the register, and Cara boxed up the orders as they sold one dessert after another. Customers buzzed everywhere.

She noticed an unfamiliar rig come to a halt about halfway down the block. Amish friends in carriages didn't park down the block. They used the hitching post or the barn behind the house.

The bishop got out, and a strongbox of heaviness seemed to open inside her. Maybe Sol had stopped by to get a fresh view of Ada's thriving business. Or maybe he'd come because Trevor had tattled on her.

Ephraim had said not to worry about the fallout. If it became an issue, they'd deal with it one step at a time. Was it any wonder she loved him so? Deciding not to give Trevor another thought, she placed two boxes with shoofly pies on the counter.

"Deb." Cara taped the order on top of the boxes and grabbed another ticket to fill. "I want to do something really nice for Ephraim."

"Ya, like what?"

"You're his sister. I was hoping you'd know."

"Not a clue. Before moving to Hope Crossing with Ada, I cooked a few meals, did his laundry, washed dishes, and cleaned his house when I wanted to do something nice for him. Those are things guys appreciate."

"We agreed I wouldn't go in his house for more than a minute or two when I'm in Dry Lake, not until after we're married." She watched the bishop slowly wind his way toward her. "No sense inviting trouble, especially since I'm a magnet for it."

"I could go with you."

Cara shook her head. "Cleaning or cooking for him isn't the kind of gift I'm looking for."

"What are you looking for?"

Ada hurried out to meet the bishop and redirected his steps.

"I don't know. Something…" She gazed up at the evening sky. By nightfall a new moon would be somewhere, invisible to the naked eye. How long had it been since she and Ephraim had enjoyed the night sky through his telescope? He had set it up in his hiddy, which was off-limits to her for now because of its secluded nature. "Oh, I've got it!"

Deborah jumped, dropping some of the customer's change on the counter. Laughing, she picked it up and handed it to the man. After thanking him for his purchase, she turned to Cara. "What's your idea?"

"Let's have a picnic tomorrow night. All of us—Ada, Israel, Lena, you, Jonathan, Ephraim, Lori, and me. We'll go up to the mountain, spread out blankets, eat lots of food, play some games, and stargaze."

"He'll love that…I think. Won't he?"

"Are you saying I know your brother better than you?"

"You know him better than anyone."

Cara elbowed her gently. "Good answer, Deb. And, yes, he will totally enjoy an evening like that." She slid half a dozen cookies into a bag. "There isn't a problem with us doing all that on a Sunday, right?"

"No. It'd be a fellowship for singles, not much different from people having a singing at their home. And we'll have the necessary chaperones because Ada and Israel will be there."

"How will we get everything up that mountain?"

"I'll get Jonathan to bring us a cart."

"Perfect."

Cara kept watching for Ephraim. She'd made supper for him, and it waited in a warm oven. When he arrived, they'd take the food to one of the picnic tables set up for customers under the large oak in the side yard, and she'd sit with him while he ate. But the desire to do something really nice for him had been on her mind since he'd left on Wednesday morning, physically and mentally exhausted. In the three days since, they'd only been able to chat for a few minutes here and there on the phone. At least his cabinetry shop and Ada's barn had phones.

"Cara, sweetheart," Ada called.

She looked around and spotted Ada standing beside the bishop near his carriage, motioning to her. Her chest tingled. The conversation must require privacy, and seclusion was hard to come by at Ada's House on a Friday or Saturday.

Whatever was going on, she wasn't going to let Trevor Atwater do any more damage than he already had.

"Wish me luck," Cara mumbled.

"Luck?"

"Yeah, like, 'Break a leg, Cara.'"

Deborah's face scrunched into confusion. "What?"

"You people really need to watch more television."

Deborah grinned, realizing what Cara was talking about. "Oh, ya? Why don't you tell the bishop that?"

Cara headed for Ada, wishing she knew some trade secrets about acting.

"Hey, Cara," Deb called.

Cara turned.

"Break a sweat." Deborah suppressed a smile, feigning innocence. They hadn't stopped sweating night and day for weeks.

"Thanks."

Before Cara got halfway to the rig, Ada met her. "He'd like to talk with you, alone." Ada straightened Cara's apron, looking her straight in the eyes. "Mind your manners, and think before you speak." She said the words lightly, but the motherly look in her eyes conveyed much more. Ada hugged her, then excused herself. Cara walked to bishop's rig.

"You've been good for her," he said.

"She's been good for me too."

"When Mahlon left the way he did, I wasn't sure how we could help her or Deborah survive it. You pulled off a marvel. And I want you to know I've seen a good heart in you, as good as any Amish person I'm responsible for."

"Did you know Ada prayed for me from the moment she heard my mom was pregnant? I think her prayers are the only reason I found my way to Dry Lake."

"Very possible. I know they were part of God's plan to get you here." He straightened his suit jacket. "I also think God had more in mind than changing just your life when He brought you here. We've all been changed for the better...all except your Daed."

Trevor had told on her. But to whom?

"What do you mean?" She had a good idea, but she didn't want to assume anything and end up volunteering information.

"I understand Trevor Atwater came by here earlier this week and learned news that was very upsetting."

"It's old news, and the fact that he discovered it twenty years after the event shows how careless he has been with following up."

"Perhaps we should all meet together and talk."

"Why? It's settled. He wanted to know what happened, and I told him."

"Did you forgive him?"

"He didn't come to be forgiven."

"True. But when he discovered the truth—that you had been abandoned—I'm sure it was difficult for him."

For him? She was the one who'd had to survive her childhood. All he had to do was hear about it.

"He needs your forgiveness, Cara, and it's the godly thing to do. You understand that, right?"

The idea sickened her, but how long would it take to say the words— a few minutes, an hour at the most? She could do that with her worst enemy.

"Are you ready to forgive him?" Sol asked.

No. A thousand times no. But she couldn't tell him that. If she had a choice to say anything other than yes, she would. Her mouth went dry. "Yes. I am."

"Good."

Ephraim got out of Robbie's car, and her heart turned a flip. He'd be relieved that she'd agreed to face her father and meet the bishop's expectations.

"Perhaps it'd be good for you to spend a little time with him," the bishop said.

What? No way! The words begged to leave her mouth, but she didn't let them.

"He is your Daed, and you've been separated from him for twenty years."

Ephraim came up to them, and Sol shook his hand.

"How's everything going?" Ephraim asked.

"Good, I think. Cara?"

"Yeah. Good." Her chest tightened again. Lying didn't come as easily as it used to.

"Cara and Trevor are going to spend two or three evenings together over the next few weeks."

Ephraim's eyes widened, and disbelief was written across his face.

Cara's hand moved to her hip, and she kept telling herself to lower it. She clutched at the only straw she could think of. "Don't you people have some sort of regulation against an Englischer spending too much time in an Amish home?"

"He's hurting, and you've added to it, Cara. You need to do what is necessary to send him on his way in peace. And then peace will come to you and your home."

"Why would you want me spending time with an alcoholic?"

"He said he hasn't touched a drink in more than ten years."

"And you believe him?" she spat. "Forgive me. I'm just not sure he's capable of being honest. If he thinks I'm as naive as my mom was, he's mistaken."

Sol ran his hand down his beard. "What Trevor says may or may not be true. But the other night when he showed up at Emma Riehl's, Preacher Alvin witnessed a man broken by the words of one of our own, and we must make things right."

"Oh, come on." She put both hands on her hips. "He's upset that Emma and Levi never came for me like they agreed." She pointed a finger at him. "No one is laying Trevor's remorse and so-called brokenness on me."

Sol glanced at Ephraim and took a deep breath. "It's not just for Trevor but for you too. It's also for Emma and Levi. They've struggled with guilt since you found your way here. Can you imagine what it was like for them to realize that the confusing conversation they had with your dad twenty years ago was a serious request to come pick you up at the bus station?

After agreeing to come, they discounted the conversation, thinking he was drunk, and chose not to follow through. If you can't forgive your father, you're saying you haven't forgiven them. And all three of them *need* your forgiveness."

Cara did feel bad for Emma and Levi. But the bulk of the misunderstanding was Trevor's fault, not theirs. She huffed. "Fine. I'll sit with him for a couple of evenings, but I won't mollycoddle him."

He smiled. "That's not at all the attitude I was hoping for."

"I'm trying." A lump in her throat made it hard to talk.

"Keep fighting the good fight, Cara, and you'll win. So I'll bring your Daed here tomorrow?"

"No!" She jolted at her tone. "I...I'm not ready."

"Monday, then?"

He had no idea what he was asking. She couldn't stand the idea of looking Trevor Atwater in the eyes and apologizing. Not yet. She needed time to brace herself...or at least learn how to be a decent actor.

She nodded. "On Monday."

Fifteen

In the steamy bathroom Aaron applied shaving cream to his face. He ran his razor under the hot water before swiping it down his cheeks.

He and Sylvi had finished cutting the hayfield yesterday, and tomorrow he'd begin the rounds of stirring it until it was dry enough to bale, but today had been a peaceful between Sunday. Nonchurch Sundays always had an extra restfulness about them, but he'd be ready to attend next week's meeting.

He'd asked Lena to invite Sylvia to a gathering of some sort so she could make some friends and have an evening away from this blasted farm. When Lena had come by last night, he'd taken her to the cabin to introduce her to Sylvi, and Lena had invited her to come to Ada's House today for a group picnic on the mountain. Aaron hadn't expected Lena to invite both of them to such a nice event.

When Sylvi balked at going, Aaron told her that he'd asked Grey to help Michael with the milking today so they could have this Sabbath day off. He wasn't surprised that she was frustrated by his changing the milking roster without asking her, but he had thought she'd be more open to the idea of getting away for a night.

Instead, she seemed uninterested and distant. She was polite, but she carried an unusual coolness about her.

Sylvi hadn't come to the house for breakfast this morning, and he'd gone to Frani's just before lunchtime. He wanted to be a friend to Frani as he should've been years ago when she first started talking about getting sober. She couldn't do it on her own any more than he could have.

Aaron checked the clock. It was almost three, so Lena and her Daed would arrive soon. Since hiring drivers wasn't allowed on Sundays, they'd travel by carriage to Hope Crossing. He finished shaving and put on his Sunday pants and shirt. When he stepped outside, he saw Sylvi walking into the barn. She probably wanted to speak to Grey about the evening milking.

Aaron hurried across the triple-wide driveway that separated the house from the barn. "Hey, Sylvi." He stepped out of the heat and into the milking parlor. She turned. "You're going tonight, right?"

She backed away, looking at the horizon as if trying to block him out. "No, but denki."

The sound of gravel under the wheels of a carriage let him know Lena and her Daed were approaching.

"You need to get away for a few hours."

She glanced at him, but rather than frustration he thought he saw fear or concern. "I'd rather stay here and help with the evening milking."

He'd had an easier time reading her that first morning in the milking barn than he was having now. What was going on?

Israel brought the open carriage to a halt near them. "Afternoon."

Aaron turned. "Hi, Israel, Lena. We need a few moments."

"Gut." Israel climbed down. "I want to speak to your Daed, and Lena brought your Mamm flowers." He went around and helped Lena out of the carriage since her medical boot and the cast on her arm made the process awkward.

"Daed, this is Sylvia." Lena shifted the pot of flowers she held. "Sylvia, this is my Daed, Israel."

A few niceties passed between them before Lena walked to the house and Israel went into the barn.

"You need a break," Aaron said. "We worked hard last week and have another tough one coming up."

"Why do you care what I do? Can't I spend the day however I like?"

"There's a real person inside you, not just a farmhand. I think you do your best to keep her locked up under a constant work load. Am I wrong?"

"I don't—"

"I know. You don't want to talk about it."

From the corner of his eye, he saw Lena and his Mamm come out of the house and cross the driveway.

"You've isolated yourself long enough. Someone should have insisted you meet a few people before now. You're letting Daed use you for his benefit, and I'm using you to get this farm sale-ready, and it all starts again tomorrow. Now, please, get in the rig."

"You can't insist I go."

"Then can I bribe you?"

She looked at him as if his behavior disappointed her. "No."

"It's a simple evening out. Why does it have to be a big deal?"

Grey, Daed, and Israel came out of the barn, talking. Lena and his Mamm drew near and waited.

"We're ready," Aaron said loudly and motioned for her to go to the rig. Sylvi didn't budge.

"Aaron." Daed moved forward. "Is there a problem?"

"We shouldn't ask so much of her. And she shouldn't give it. Seven days a week is too much."

"Actually, Dora and I were talking about this last night. We have asked too much." Daed winked at Sylvia. "I hear that Ada's House is never dull."

While his Daed spoke softly to her, she glanced at Aaron, those beautiful brown eyes expressing hundreds of thoughts he'd like to be privy to.

What he'd really like to know is why he cared what she thought or felt. In spite of a few pleasant conversations here and there, they weren't friends. They weren't exactly enemies, but they were close to it—in a civilized, respectful sort of way. Her patience and gentleness caused him to drop his normal obnoxious shield.

Sylvia turned to Lena. "I didn't mean to be rude, and it really is a nice invitation."

"You know," Grey said, "I can come every Sunday evening to help Michael."

"And I could come by every Sunday morning," Israel said.

Daed shrugged. "I don't know. That's an awful lot to ask of—"

"We'll take the help." Aaron shook Israel's hand and then Grey's. "Sylvi will be off every Sunday. Daed and I will rotate Sundays. Denki. Now that it's settled, it's time to go."

Anger flitted through Sylvia's eyes. He'd stepped far over the bounds of dealing with what she considered *her* herd. But he didn't care. She needed one day of rest a week, and now she had it.

He opened the door to the carriage. "Sylvi, get in, please, or I'll tie you to one of the horses."

She got in, but her tight mouth and stiff movements indicated she was not at peace, nor was she eagerly anticipating the evening.

Sylvia felt like an overstretched rubber band—taut and at the breaking point. Frustration with Aaron banged around inside her, but he was right. She had kept herself buried under a heavy work load. She had since Beckie and Elam had betrayed her. Before that, work was enjoyable but just one aspect of who she was. Now work was everything. She hadn't expected anyone to figure that out, least of all Aaron Blank.

When they finally arrived at Ada's House, Aaron helped Lena out of the rig. Before he could turn to help Sylvia, she jumped down. He was so pushy.

The white clapboard house looked huge and homey and inviting. A hand-painted wooden sign out front read "Ada's House, Baked Goods and Seasonal Activities."

A woman in her late thirties or early forties opened the front door. "Welcome. Welcome. I'm Ada. Since yours is the only face I don't recognize, I'm going to say you're Sylvia."

Sylvia nodded, unsure whether to offer her hand or not.

Before she could decide, Ada hugged her. "I'm so glad you came." She turned to Aaron with obvious pleasure. "Look at you. You are a sight for sore eyes, young man." She engulfed him in a hug too. "I bet your parents are glowing."

"Not so much."

"Don't worry. They'll come around."

Ada's eyes moved to Israel. "Good evening."

He removed his hat. "Ada. It's always nice to get another invite."

"And you're always welcome, but tonight is Cara's doing. She and Deborah and Lori are taking a load of items up the mountain. She'll be back shortly."

"Ada," Lena said, "how about giving Aaron and Sylvia a tour?"

"Sure. Kumm."

They went through the house and walked the grounds. Five days a week—Tuesday through Saturday—Ada, Deborah, and Cara made desserts, and five nights a week they sold them, along with Amish-made items like jellies, canned goods, wall hangings, dolls, and furniture Israel made. People paid for tours, hayrides, and various events that changed with the season—like going through a corn maze in the fall and cutting fresh ears of corn off the stalk, shucking them, and cooking them in an outdoor kettle.

Sylvia couldn't imagine wanting to see so many strangers every day, but Aaron had lots of questions and seemed quite taken with the idea.

When they went into the kitchen, a young woman came in the back door. "Ada, did you—" She stopped short. "Oh, we have guests."

"Cara, this is Aaron Blank," Ada said.

"Blank?" Cara repeated, clearly trying to place him. "Oh, Lena's friend."

Aaron laughed. "There are so many descriptions you could have used just then, and you happened to choose my favorite."

Ada put her hand on Cara's shoulder. "This is Sylvia. She's new to Dry Lake."

"Ah, someone newer than me. Good."

"You live in Dry Lake?" Sylvia asked.

"No, but I stayed there for a few months. My fiancé and his family live there, so it'll be home for me…one day. Ada and Deborah are from there. Of course, everyone is related or connected somehow. It drives me nuts trying to figure it all out. Do you know everyone already?"

"Not at all. Aaron and his parents mostly."

"Mom!" A little girl jerked open the screen door and ran inside. "Can Better Days go with us when we go up on the mountain?"

"I don't think so, honey. We'll have picnic foods spread out on the ground, and you know how uncontrollable he gets."

"Please?"

"I'll think about it."

"Hello?" a man's voice called out.

Cara's eyes lit up, and she and Lori headed for the front door.

Ada laughed. "That'd be the fiancé."

Sylvia met Ephraim, his sister Deborah, and Deborah's beau, Jonathan. Everyone grabbed something—a game, a snack food, or a drink—to take up the mountain. Sylvia carried a blanket. She hadn't seen this much bustle of activity since leaving home. As she thought of her sisters, she longed to see them again.

Ephraim put Better Days on a leash and passed it to Lori. Lena sat on the back of the cart with her feet dangling toward the ground. They began the trek up the hill.

Ephraim and Cara walked to the far left of the group, talking quietly together. Deborah and Jonathan went ahead of the cart, walking hand in hand. Israel led the horse, and Ada walked beside him, leaving only Lori and Sylvia behind the cart.

Aaron walked up beside her. "Are you talking to me yet?"

"Only if you make me or embarrass me in front of a group of people, which you seem to insist on doing."

His shoulders slumped slightly. He walked to the cart and jumped onto the back beside Lena.

Sylvia determined to look in any direction except his, but she could feel his eyes on her. In a moment of weakness, she looked at him, and he held her gaze.

She wasn't sure what his relationship was with Lena. When he'd brought her to the cabin last night to invite Sylvia to come today, she'd been confident they were seeing each other, though Michael and Dora had said nothing about a girlfriend. It was part of the reason she didn't like his invitation to come tonight. She had no interest in being a third wheel. Besides, he didn't act like he had a girlfriend, and that bothered her. A man should talk about his girl. Be clear about his feelings for her.

But this evening Aaron and Lena seemed more like friends. However, Sylvia wasn't good at reading signals between men and women. She'd had no clue Elam cared for Beckie, yet he loved her enough to carelessly and quickly throw Sylvia aside. It became obvious that while Elam and Sylvia courted, he and Beckie had been having *moments* together—the kind that looked innocent but entered the soul and drew one human to another.

She turned her attention to Lori and Better Days. Lori slid her hand into Sylvia's and smiled up at her. The simple gesture warmed Sylvia's heart.

"'From and Mama are getting married, and I can't wait."

"That's nice."

"I don't remember my daddy. Mom says he died when I was two. I think 'From needs us. He lives all by himself."

"I live by myself too."

"I think that's sad. I like living with lots of people in the house, especially my mom. When I'm old like you, I'm gonna have lots of friends live with me." Lori splayed her hand. "And five dogs."

Sylvia chuckled.

The more they talked, the more Sylvia longed to see her sisters. Lizzie would turn twenty soon. Naomi had just begun her rumschpringe. Next year Lilly would be sixteen and of age to attend singings. Would her youngest sisters begin to forget her?

Aaron got off the back of the cart and moved somewhere ahead of it and out of sight. Several minutes later he returned with a handful of wildflowers and held them out to her. "I know I was out of line, and I'm sorry I embarrassed you. Truce?"

She took the flowers, feeling as confused about who this man was as she had the night he'd broken into her cabin.

When they reached the picnic spot, she spread out her blanket and helped Ada lay three others side by side. They all ate together, and the food was delicious and the conversations entertaining. Lori moved from adult to adult, clearly welcome in every heart.

Each woman came over and sat with Sylvia at some point, welcoming her warmly and chatting or inviting her to play games. Sylvia joined the group for badminton and volleyball.

Aaron partnered with various people at those same games, including her. Until tonight she'd had no idea he had such a deep, wonderful laugh.

The sun slid below the horizon, painting the sky with streaks of purple and pink. The men built a small fire, and the women roasted marshmallows. Ephraim set up his telescope, but Sylvia lay on her back, watching the stars. The dark sky looked like a beautiful, dazzling ceiling when in reality it was openness that went on forever. A longing to talk to God washed over her, but she didn't know what she could say that He'd be willing to hear.

Aaron sat beside her and lay back. He was silent for so long that she wondered if he'd fallen asleep. When she turned her head to look, his eyes were open, staring into space.

If anyone could handle how she felt about church without totally disrespecting her, Aaron could. Connecting with God through prayer and songs used to be fun—seven days a week, but especially on church Sundays. Gathering with loved ones and focusing on the creator of all things had made her soul sing. But how long had it been since then? Since she betrayed God, or since He let Elam betray her?

"You've freed up my Sundays, but I can't go to church," she said.

Aaron rolled on his side, facing her, quietly thoughtful for several long moments. "Why?"

She shook her head. "I…I used to love going before…"

"Yeah, I figure anyone who can tolerate milking cows twice a day, seven days a week, wouldn't feel the services are too long or boring."

"You didn't go last week either."

"I was embarrassed to see people when I first returned. Lots of reasons to feel that way—all of them my own fault. We haven't talked about this, but I know you've been told that I'm partially responsible for my sister's death. Everyone knows it, but no one says a word to me."

"I don't think anyone blames you, certainly not your Mamm or Daed."

His brows furrowed. "Sure they do."

"No they don't. Michael blames himself."

"But he never said…and I thought…" His voice sounded hoarse.

Before Aaron had returned, Michael had said a lot of things about him. Things she wouldn't tell. It wasn't her place. But it sickened her to know how much Michael cared and how little he showed that to Aaron.

"Talking with parents doesn't come easy," she said, "for them or for us."

He cleared his throat. "Some are better at it than others. Watch Lena and her Daed."

Sylvia wondered if Lena's close relationship with her father was one of the things Aaron liked about her. A wave of envy rippled through her, catching her by surprise. Did she really care what he admired about Lena?

Shaking off the unwanted thoughts, she said, "Speaking of Lena, she told me a few minutes ago that my invitation to this event was your doing."

"I figured it was about time you had a little fun."

"It was nice of you."

"That happens every once in a while. Catches me off guard every time."

She laughed. "I can't remember when I've had a better time. Everybody's been friendly and fun. Authentic…which is nice."

"Well, everyone here has their own troubles. Lena's been in hot water with the school board this past year. Ephraim was shunned. Ada's son was once engaged to Deborah, but he left without a word to anyone. Church leaders asked Cara to leave Dry Lake. I don't know about Jonathan or Israel, but since they're human, I'm sure they've received and given hurts and have embarrassments they can't erase."

"From what little your parents told me about you, I didn't expect you to come back."

"Me either. But the more time I spent in prayer, the more I knew I had to do two things—come home to face everyone and be a decent son to my parents."

"Prayer?"

"Hard to believe, isn't it? Before I hit bottom, the only words I said to God aren't repeatable. My parents have their faults and all." He paused. "But they deserve better than what I've dished out to them."

Cara sat down on the other side of Sylvia and lay back on the blanket. "It's time to stretch out and enjoy the sky with the naked eye."

Ephraim lay beside her, and soon a long line of folks were lying on the blankets, staring at the sky.

Lori squeezed between Cara and Sylvia. "Let's sing. Sylvia, do you know any good songs?"

"I bet I know one you're familiar with. 'Miss Mary Mack, Mack, Mack.'"

Lori bolted upright and sat with her legs crossed. She held up her little hands. "You know the clapping game?"

Sylvia sat up. "I most certainly do."

"Think you can keep the pace?" Lori bobbed her head, exuding confidence. "Mom says I'm the best!"

They sang the song and changed up the clapping game as they went along.

"Your mom's right," Sylvia said. "You can move at this. But can you sing it in Pennsylvania Dutch?"

"I don't know enough of those words yet."

Sylvia sang the Pennsylvania Dutch lyrics, and they clapped hands to the rhythm.

Cara moved closer. "Say that first line again—'all dressed in black'— in Pennsylvania Dutch."

Sylvia repeated it, and Cara followed suit. Then Sylvia taught her the pronunciation of the next line.

Within a few minutes Cara had the song down pat. *"All is all. And dressed is gegleed. And black is schwarz."* She reached behind her, patting

Ephraim on the arm. "Songs. That's our answer to my learning the language!"

He sat up, clearly interested.

"Sylvia, do you know any English songs?" Cara asked.

"A few. Mostly Elvis songs."

Everyone broke into laughter.

Aaron had a strange look on his face, an expression somewhere between amusement and confusion. "Elvis?"

"I owned a used iPod in my rumschpringe, so I listened to whatever songs were already on there when I bought it—until it fell to the ground during a milking and a cow stepped on it."

"Stupid cow," Lori said with a giggle.

"How'd you keep it charged without a computer?" Cara asked.

"The Englischer guy who picked up our milk recharged it for me."

"Do you know any Elvis songs?" Ephraim asked Cara.

"Oh, yeah. 'Heartbreak Hotel,' 'Don't Be Cruel,' 'It's Now or Never,' 'Jailhouse Rock.' And you'll love this: 'You ain't nothin' but a hound dog cryin' all the time.'"

He laughed. "I think I've heard that one somewhere."

"Think you could teach me some more Pennsylvania Dutch words for songs I know?" Cara asked Sylvia.

"Sure. Why?"

"I have to learn the language, and I need help."

"Oh. I'm glad to try, but when?"

"I go to Dry Lake on church Sundays for instruction class, and I meet with Esther and Alvin on Tuesday and Thursday afternoons to study Pennsylvania Dutch and German. I can easily come to your place on any of those days and other ones too, I'm sure."

"The hay will still be drying Tuesday, so that'll work this week. After that we'll figure out our days week by week."

"Ever milked a cow?" Aaron asked Cara, chuckling.

"I'm certainly willing to learn."

"Speaking of cows...," Aaron said. "Four o'clock in the morning comes awfully early."

"Just one more game," Deborah said. "It won't take more than twenty minutes, and everybody can remain right where they are. Think about the person you walked up the mountain next to tonight, and tell the first thing you remember that person saying when you met."

"I'll go first," Lena said. After a short silence she said, "I'm done, because I didn't *walk* up the mountain with anyone."

The laughter made Sylvia feel lighter than she had in many months. Well, that and Cara needing her. And having a pleasant conversation with Aaron. And having an evening with new friends.

"Ephraim, you're next," Deborah said.

"I was twelve and Cara was eight when we met. The first thing I remember saying to her is 'Are you a boy or a girl?'"

Cara cackled. "That was closely followed by 'Do you fish?'"

"Hey, she had on jeans and had really short hair. I was confused."

The laughter didn't stop.

"Cara, what's the first thing you remember saying to Ephraim?" Deborah asked.

"Oh, man, we're going back twenty years, but I think it was 'You got a name?'"

"And the next time you saw each other?"

Ephraim chuckled. "Fast-forward twenty years, and I didn't recognize her while trying to get her out of Levina's old barn and off my property. I remember asking her if she was from around here. I was trying to be polite before insisting she move along. To which my lovely wife-to-be replied..." He gestured toward her with his palm upward.

"'Is that the Amish version of "Haven't we met before?"' You should have seen his face turn red with embarrassment and anger."

Amid the chortles Sylvia longed to know more of their unusual story.

Deborah proceeded to ask each couple. Jonathan told of Deborah's early days in school and some of the stunts he pulled on her. Deborah talked of the first time she began to be drawn to him.

"Aaron, what's the first thing you said to Sylvia?"

"I don't think that's such a good thing to talk about."

Sylvia scoffed. "He's a chicken because he's afraid to mention that the first time we saw each other, one of us wasn't dressed."

"Not dressed?" an echo of voices said.

"I can't believe you just shared that," Aaron said.

Among the hoots and claps, Sylvia stood and gestured for them to quiet down. "I was in a tub with mounds of bubbles the first time he saw me. When he went into the other room, I put on a housecoat, so I was fully covered by something at all times."

Deborah smiled. "And what's the first thing you said to Aaron?"

"Get out of my house!"

The group howled and clapped.

"To which Aaron said, 'Lady, don't throw that.' To the best of my memory, the next thing he said was 'Ouch!'"

"She threw a hammer at me!" Aaron's eyes stayed on hers. "My poor knee hasn't recovered yet." He stood, mocking a fresh limp.

The roars of laughter filled Sylvia with a joy she thought had died long ago.

"You all can stay," Aaron said, "but we have to head home. Sylvia's usually out cold hours before now. Can we borrow a horse and rig from someone?"

Israel stood. "Not necessary. We need to call it a night too. You can ride back with us."

Sylvia gathered the blanket, thinking that Aaron made little sense. He pushed her and insulted her—like when he complained about her putting too much fertilizer on the hayfield—but then made sure she was invited tonight, caring very much that she got a night off. And he talked about God as if he'd shared a cup of coffee with Him or something. No condemnation or gnashing of teeth, just trust and faith in Him. How did someone who'd been where he had freely talk to God? And why did Aaron care that she be a part of tonight?

Sixteen

Aaron rubbed an oversized cotton handkerchief across his face, wiping away the sweat. The horse pulled the hay rake up and down the field. Stirring the hay wasn't anything like cutting or baling it. He'd been in the field less than three hours, and he'd almost completed the job. He'd stir it again tomorrow. Praying the rains would stay away was a daily thing, much like asking for the strength to stay sober.

Desire for a drink pounded him. Unbridled. Unmatched. Unwanted.

Most days he could ignore wanting a drink. It was like his own shadow. It never went away, but as long as he didn't try to outrun it or give up because it was always there, he knew he could win the battle.

Today the shadow taunted him, and he didn't know how to free himself of it. Not one ounce of faith seemed to stir as he petitioned God for help.

"Aaron," Sylvi called to him, yelling above the creaking and groaning of the hay rake, the swooshing of loose alfalfa, and the racket of the horses pulling the contraption.

She stood at the edge of the field with a picnic basket in hand. He brought the horses to a stop. Until this moment he'd barely caught a glimpse of her today. His Daed had helped her milk the cows this morning, and stirring hay required only one person.

By the time he unhitched the horse and walked to her, she had a blanket spread out and was unloading the basket.

"Your Mamm brought this out to me and asked if I'd find you. Your Daed's asleep, and she doesn't want us waking him. She's on her way into town to get supplies." She put a piece of oven-fried chicken on a plate. "I gave my word, so tie the horse to some shrub and come eat."

He did as she said.

She met him with a bowl of water, soap, and a towel. He washed up, dumped the water, and followed her back to the blanket.

She paused, watching him. "You okay?"

"Just one of those days."

"What's that mean?"

"You wouldn't understand. It goes with the territory of once being addicted to something."

"I might understand more than you think."

His interest was piqued. "Do you have a poison?"

Innocence radiated in her eyes. She had no clue what he meant.

He couldn't help but smile. "Never mind."

He ate while she stared at her plate.

She set the dish on the blanket. "I'm not an addict, but I've struggled in other ways—unable to think of anything else night or day. It drives and molds you until you slowly become someone else, someone you don't like. But it doesn't matter because you don't care. In your mind you know it makes no sense to want it, but that does nothing to ease your craving."

"Ya, exactly." Maybe she did understand. But he wouldn't ask her twice what tempted her.

She pinched bits of bread off her roll and ate them. "We can get top dollar for this hay, and we should be able to get three, maybe four cuttings without reseeding, right?"

"Ya, that's right. If the weather is good all summer, not too dry or too wet."

"Then wouldn't we make enough money to end the threat of a lien?"

"That'd get Daed caught up on every bill with some money left over. But we can't sell everything we plant. We have to store some hay for the winter. The acres of corn in the west field could become a cash crop too, but we have to use it to fill the silos."

"Isn't there any way for us to get ahead, even just once?"

Aaron wished she hadn't asked, wished she'd make his life easier and accept defeat. She wouldn't abandon the farm with the work that needed to be done to sell the place. He knew that. But if she could let go of hoping for the impossible, he'd feel much better about the situation. "There might be a way. But help just once would not be nearly enough."

"It might be. What did you have in mind?"

"If Daed asked for enough hay, straw, and silage from other farmers to get him through to next spring, and if the farmers had enough to share, and if we managed to get three harvests of hay to sell—the combination of those things could give you the boost you desire."

She pursed her lips and sighed. "That's a lot of *ifs*."

"*Ifs* and farming are looped together like strands of fiber in a hand-woven basket." The disappointment in her eyes bothered him. "I don't want you to get hurt in this, Sylvi. You can help get the farm in proper shape to sell and stay until it sells, but you need to plan to move on when that happens."

She stared out over the land as if willing it to meet her needs. "I know you're telling me like it is."

"No reason not to."

"I don't think anyone's ever done that for me before. My Daed and… other men I've known seem to think they need to keep certain things cloaked when it comes to the big picture."

Her openness unnerved him, making his defenses rise. "Don't get the wrong idea. I'm not your answer to anything. And I'm not interested in helping you find answers."

"I know that." She said it matter-of-factly. "But you seem to be transparent with me. And I want us to be that way for each other."

If she wanted transparency, he could pull her to her feet and lecture her on getting real about the farm. But just then he noticed someone near the edge of the woods. He stood, watching an Englischer woman with an infant on her hip draw closer.

Frani.

When he glanced at Sylvi, her doe eyes reflected a genteel spirit of absolute resolve. She had strength, no doubt, but she couldn't handle what was real for him.

"I need to go. Thanks for lunch."

He turned his back on Sylvi and headed for Frani.

Cara stood in her bedroom, staring into a mirror, assuring herself she could do this.

Who was she kidding? She couldn't express regret and pardon to the man who'd abandoned her. Been a mean drunk. Made her mother's life miserable. Been a no-account father. Shown up here on false pretenses. Then run to Emma and Levi and tattled about her outburst at him. Why was *she* the one who had to apologize?

Her relationship with Ephraim was not the reason she had to meet with Trevor. She'd planned to join the faith back when she mistakenly thought Ephraim loved Anna Mary. So she'd be in this fix whether Ephraim was in the picture or not.

This war raging in her had to be dealt with, but how?

She moved to the side of her bed and knelt. "Dear God, I know it's wrong, but I *hate* him. And I can't act my way out of it."

Memories flew across her mind like stones from a slingshot, one after another, hurting her as if they had just happened. Trevor had been worse than useless when her mother was alive and completely useless once Cara entered foster care. Biting coldness moved inside her. That frozenness used to define her. It didn't now, but she wasn't free of it.

"Cara." Ada tapped on the door before opening it. "They're here. Ephraim too."

Cara remained on her knees, unable to move. A tingling sensation ran through her fingers and toes. "I'll be down in a minute."

Ada closed the door.

Cara's mind went numb too, but at least the memories had stopped. She remained on her knees, a silent lump of screaming pain. She closed her eyes and rested her forehead on the edge of the bed. No tears fell as emptiness overshadowed her other emotions. Emptiness and rage were strange bedfellows, but the two went together—at least they did for her as far back as she could remember.

She thought she heard someone knock on the door again, but she wasn't sure. Too drained to respond, she ignored it and kept her face buried. She didn't know how much time had passed since Ada had come to her room, but she kept waiting for the strength to apologize to Trevor. Her jaws ached, but she hadn't yet whispered a prayer.

The door clicked open. Just like when she was a little girl in the homes of strangers, she couldn't make herself look. She used to keep her eyes shut tight, unwilling to stare into the eyes of people paid to keep her, and tell them good night. She'd lie there, trying to remember what her mother had looked like and hoping to see her in her dreams when she fell asleep.

A warm, strong arm slid around her shoulders.

Ephraim.

She kept her eyes closed, unable to look at the love or understanding or expectation or disappointment in his eyes. He placed his hand over her folded ones.

"I can't do it. You weren't there. You don't know how he ruined my life."

He didn't say anything, but the warmth of his embrace began to ease the ache inside her. She folded her arms on the bed, placed her forehead on her wrists, and wept. His gentle, silent love touched her deeply, and his presence seemed to reach into the wounds of her childhood. He couldn't touch her past, of course, but he offered her a future filled with love and respect. Suddenly love was tangible, as if she could hold it in her hands, as if it could be shaped and molded at will. And the monstrous ache and hatred of the past could be absorbed into the love he gave her today.

The battle of dealing with anger and resentment at her dad wasn't over. It had probably just begun. But she felt equipped to fight…and for the first time had hope of eventually winning.

Her tears stopped, and she wiped her wet cheeks. "Thank you." She rose, opening her eyes.

Shock pierced her, and she gasped.

No one was in the room with her.

Seventeen

Sylvia walked into the Blank home, knowing she was late for supper. Michael sat at the dinner table, hidden behind a newspaper. Dora stood at the sink, shoulders slumped while she stared at dirty pots and pans. Aaron leaned against the edge of the counter. He seemed irritated, but he offered her a half smile.

Dora pulled a plate of food out of the oven and set it on the table. "Here you go, dear."

Sylvia moved to the table and took a seat. Michael jerked the newspaper away from his face and folded it. She bowed her head in silence.

After she took a few bites, Sylvia turned to Michael. "Daisy's gone to the briars in the east pasture. Unless it's a false alarm, I'm sure she'll deliver by morning. I'll sleep in the hayloft tonight. That's the best place to hear her if she starts bellowing."

"See?" Michael gestured toward her as he glared at Aaron. "That's how it's to be done."

Sylvia glanced from one to the other, sickened that Michael was using her in his attack on Aaron. Michael had been cold and difficult with his son since he'd arrived home. She'd started out treating Aaron much the same way, but Michael's hot and cold temper grated on her nerves.

"Daed,"—Aaron took a mug from the cabinet—"this conversation has nothing to do with my farming skills."

Sylvia looked down and examined the plate before her, wondering what she had interrupted.

"If you'd given heed to what needed to be done over the last eight years and spent less time indulging your whims, we wouldn't be in this mess."

Aaron poured himself a cup of coffee before sitting at the table. "You've said that over and over in the last few hours. Can we change the subject?"

"I should've known you had someone in Dry Lake." Michael smacked a palm against the folded newspaper. "Now I understand why you've come back. Well, that girlfriend of yours and her child can't live on this farm. I won't have it."

Sylvia felt as if a cow had kicked her. *Girlfriend?*

"She's not my girlfriend," Aaron said. "She's a friend who's lost her job, and if she can't find another one right away, she'll lose her trailer in the next couple of weeks. If that plays out, she and AJ will have nowhere to go. I won't let that happen. She can help out around here. I'll pay her expenses. And we have an extra bedroom."

"Where are her own folks?" Dora asked.

"They're not willing to help her right now."

"Go figure!" Michael barked.

"Maybe they're justified, but I won't let her and AJ go without a home to live in."

"Is he...yours?" Dora's hands shook while she held a napkin over her mouth, as if trying to take back the words she'd spoken.

The question rang alarms inside Sylvia. An uncomfortable dusting of jealousy settled over her, but the emotions made no sense. Beyond her own confusing feelings, she knew conceiving a child with an outsider was an unforgivable sin in the sight of many in their community. The mistake couldn't be hidden or managed. Or even solved by marriage—unless he left the faith altogether.

"Are you more likely to let her stay here if I say yes?" Aaron asked.

"Answer your mother."

"No. She's not my girlfriend. Not now. Not before," Aaron said quietly through gritted teeth. "I have been visiting her since I returned but just as a friend. She needs someone who understands to talk to her."

Michael's fists pounded the table. "If you'd been the man you should've been, you wouldn't be friends with that kind of trouble."

"Keep saying it, Daed, and maybe your yelling will turn back the hands of time, and I can do everything right the second time around."

Sylvia ached for all Michael couldn't see. In his blind anger he didn't trust anything Aaron said. She saw integrity and faults in each man, but what could she possibly say to make a difference between them? Should she remain quiet, as Dora did?

"Look," Aaron said, "I'm sorry you disagree with me, but Frani needs help. I'm only asking for a little time to try to convince her to go to rehab."

"Why you?"

The lines on Aaron's face grew taut. "Because we're friends. Is that so hard to absorb?" He sighed. "I think she'll listen to me, so maybe I can make a difference. And, honestly, I feel a little responsible for ignoring her when she used to say she wanted to get sober."

Sylvia studied Aaron, wondering if he'd always had a good heart in this type of situation or if he'd grown one because of his own journey.

Michael looked at Sylvia and motioned to Aaron. "My son thinks I'm going to fall for his lies all over again just because he's been here helping for a few days." He jabbed his finger at the tabletop as he spoke. "I can't prove what you're really doing when you *visit* Frani, but I've played the fool for you once, Aaron, believing your excuses and lies about where you were and what you were doing. I'm not falling for it twice."

Aaron slumped, seeming resigned to both his Daed's anger and his Mamm's indifference. But if Sylvia knew him at all, his patience was wearing thin, and his ability to curb his typical sharp retorts wouldn't last much longer. And she didn't blame him.

"Michael, I know you missed Aaron when he was gone, and yet now that he's back, you're angry with him all the time." Sylvia swallowed hard. "You have me on a pedestal and him in a ditch. Neither image is accurate."

Michael paused, and for a moment he appeared to waver in his anger. "I've talked to your Daed, Sylvia. I know you'd never pull an ounce of what he's pulled over the years."

Sylvia drew a breath. "When I was a young teen, I made a decision to handle myself carefully. The preachers spoke at every service about pure living, and my soul latched on to their words when I was very young." Her insides turned cold, and her hands began to shake. "I didn't drink or lie or do anything I needed to hide from my parents. I even decided I'd never kiss a man unless I was willing to marry him." She took a sip of lemonade, hoping to stop her voice from quivering.

Michael nodded. "That's as it should be. Respectful of your parents."

"I agree, only that's not the end of the story. I fell in love, and the young man asked me to marry him. But…he changed his mind, and we never married."

Her head pounded, and tears threatened. The words felt trapped inside her chest, but she wanted to free them, to give Aaron some relief— and herself. "Unfortunately, the last time I kissed him"—she closed her eyes, wishing there was a way to erase what she'd done—"he was married to someone else."

She drew a ragged breath, lacking the courage to confess the whole ugly mess of how she'd betrayed her sister. "When I imagine God…I think of Him shaking His fist at me, angry and unforgiving. But I can't undo what I've done." She cleared her throat, determined not to burst into tears. She stood. "If you'll excuse me…"

She dashed out of the house, ran across the driveway, and was well into the pasture before she slowed, gasping for air. After walking through the field and across a footbridge to the creek, she came to Daisy's hiding spot. The cow stood very still, panting. Labor had begun. Sylvia left her alone and walked along the muddy, winding creek.

If Michael shared her revelation with her Daed, the explosive reaction to her sin would ricochet around her forever. But that wouldn't be the worst part. Beckie learning the truth would be far worse, more than Sylvia could bear to imagine.

Trembling, she returned to the footbridge and sat, watching the creek amble through Blank land and keep right on going. Had she helped Michael see that she was no better than Aaron? Or had she just sealed her own fate? She drew her knees to her chest and wrapped her arms around her legs, wishing she could erase her image of God as one who was as angry and unforgiving as Michael. She longed to see God the way Aaron saw Him.

Eighteen

Lena hurried around the kitchen, finishing preparations for supper. She'd had another doctor's appointment. This time they'd replaced her arm cast with a shorter one. Afterward, she'd pursued a new job prospect and gotten so distracted that she'd lost all track of time. Excitement pumped through her.

When the school board had let her go, everything she'd worked so hard to achieve had been taken from her. Now that her name had been cleared, they'd hire her again. But women teachers weren't to begin a school year if they knew they'd marry during it, so even though her relationship with Grey was a secret for now, she would not reapply for her old position. She could teach and make a difference without being in a classroom.

A rig pulled into the driveway and headed for the barn. Her Daed was home. She couldn't wait to tell him about her job interview. She wished she and Grey could talk, but she'd write him later tonight.

"Lena?"

Nicky bolted from her bed in the corner of the kitchen, wagging her tail as she went to greet Daed.

"In the kitchen."

She put a thick towel over her cast and grabbed a hot pad with her other hand, then opened the oven door. She pulled out the casserole dish and, by balancing it on her towel-covered arm, moved it to the top of the stove. "Daed, where have you been?" She dumped a loaf of freshly baked bread out of its pan.

The familiar screech of Daed's turning on water in the mud sink near the back door echoed through their home. She wondered how long she'd live in Grey's home before it carried any of the wonderful sentiments that this one did.

"I had an errand to run," Daed answered.

"Well, I have good news, and you weren't here to share it with." She spoke loudly while setting the chicken spaghetti on a hot plate on the table. "You won't believe this." After grabbing two goblets containing his favorite gelatin salad out of the refrigerator, she turned.

"Try me." Grey's voice caused joy to skitter through her.

She broke into laughter. "Benjamin Graber! What are you doing here?"

"Your Daed came and got me. Seems he intends for me to do the work I didn't get done last Friday."

Her Daed entered the room, grinning. "It is perfectly respectable for me to be seen bringing him here to do some work. We can't get away with it often, mind you."

She wrapped her uninjured arm around her Daed's neck. "You're the best."

He didn't make a retort of any kind, which wasn't normal. When she pulled away, he looked sad in spite of his smile. "I don't know why I encourage this relationship. I can't imagine what it will be like once you've moved out." Behind his jesting, there was a flicker of raw pain she hadn't seen since her mother had passed away.

She hugged him again, but words failed her.

A little unsure whether to embrace Grey in front of her Daed, she motioned for him to take a seat.

Grey removed his hat. "You have a new cast."

"I do." She held it up. "It's called a short cast, and it's definitely more comfortable than the last one." She wiggled her fingers. "But my hand tingles."

"What'd the doctor say?" Grey asked.

"It's normal, and he gave me instructions for new exercises that will strengthen my shoulder. He'd like me to start walking without the medical boot for a few minutes each day and work up to a couple of hours, but never if it causes pain."

"Everything is healing as it should?" Her Daed studied her, as if trying to be sure she was telling them the whole truth.

"Ya. I have to keep going back for routine checkups, but he thinks I'll be out of my cast and boot by the end of the summer."

"I know you're tired of seeing the doc so often, but it makes the two of us feel better." Grey winked and moved toward the stove. "Can I help?"

"Slice the bread for me, would you?" She poured them each a glass of icy water.

After everything was on the table, she and her Daed put their hands on the table. Grey seemed unaware they were waiting on him to do the same.

"We hold hands during prayer," Lena said. "That is, unless Daed has frustrated me to the point that I won't hold his hand."

"A word to the wise," Daed said with mock sincerity. "Don't come home for dinner when she gets that way."

Grey chuckled and enfolded her hand in his, and she didn't want the silent prayer to end. Little in this world seemed as perfect as praying with Grey, but it lasted only a minute before Daed shifted, ending the prayer time.

"What's your good news?" Daed scooped chicken spaghetti onto his plate.

"I have a new job."

Mild alarm took over Daed's expression. "Without talking to Grey?"

"As you know, it's extremely difficult to talk to him."

"Ya, but, Lena, you could have written to him and waited for an answer. I know you've been raised without a mother most of your life, but not even to communicate with him about it is unheard of."

She studied Grey. "Do you mind?"

"Not at all. I trust your judgment."

Her Daed got up from the table and looked for something in the refrigerator. "Still, Lena, right is right."

"Israel." Grey held up the bowl of freshly grated Parmesan.

Her Daed returned to the table and took it from Grey's hand.

Grey wiped his mouth on a napkin. "You seem concerned that Lennie was raised with just a father. Maybe you're afraid she's too independent and more set in her ways than your other daughters were because she's several years older than they were when they married. I like her the way she is, Israel. She won't be a perfect wife. And I won't be a perfect husband. I don't want perfect."

Lena knew what he did want: friendship—the deep, mysterious kind that only happened between a man and woman who loved enough to marry.

Daed cleared his throat. "I guess I was out of line. I suppose that means I'm not perfect either."

"You're close enough for me," Lena said. "And Ada too, I think."

One corner of her Daed's mouth lifted, revealing his pleasure in what she'd said. "So tell us about this new job of yours."

"I found an ad in the newspaper from an Englischer woman who teaches her children at home. I went to see her. She's expecting her seventh child this fall and would like help with both teaching her children and running her house. We'll take turns. One of us will teach while the other tends to the littler ones and meals."

"You like this idea?" Daed asked.

"It's perfect for me. I can teach and hold babies, and my hours will be really flexible. She will pay me almost as well as my position at our Amish school did. And I can continue helping her throughout this year even *if* I were to marry." She didn't like using *if,* but any talk of marriage with someone other than Grey was improper at this point.

"It sounds like a good fit for you." Grey said the supportive words, but was that concern she saw in his eyes?

They discussed the weather and how business was going at the cabinetry shop. When the sunlight waned, Lena lit a kerosene lantern.

Grey got up and began clearing the table. "We need to talk, Lennie."

Her Daed stood. "I'll leave you two to chat." He clicked his tongue, and Nicky hurried toward the door. "I'll be in the shop whenever you're ready to discuss the cabinets I need built." Her father's footsteps faded, and soon the screen door slammed shut behind him.

"He's struggling with the idea of letting you go."

"I know. It's weird. One can never tell how a person will feel when faced with new circumstances."

"Speaking of facing new situations, I...we..."

She waited, but he didn't continue. Instead, he set a pile of dishes in the sink. She'd seen him this way a few times since they'd fallen in love but never before that. They'd been friends forever, but when it came to the intimate side of sharing, he struggled to talk to her.

"What's the topic?" she asked.

"Us."

"That's my favorite subject."

He folded his arms and leaned against the sink, facing her. "It won't be tonight."

"I doubt that. So what's up?"

He stared at the floor, and she could feel the war going on inside him.

"Grey," she whispered as she moved directly in front of him. Hope for their future danced inside her. She placed her hands on his face, drew him close, and kissed him. "Tell me what's bothering you." She caressed his beard. "Whatever it is, I care about you more than *it*."

His silvery blue eyes bore into hers as if looking for the strength to tell her. He took her hands into his. "Remember when I told you last month that my marriage was troubled and that Elsie and I had taken a few steps toward a second chance right before she died?"

She nodded.

"One of those steps involved medical tests. See, it's possible that…" He stopped again.

When she realized how burdened he was, she led him out the back door and sat on the steps. This had been their place to talk years ago. "When I was a young teen, we talked for hours. You were my confidant. I was so smitten with you I couldn't stand it."

He sat beside her and propped his forearms on his legs. "Lennie."

She looped her uninjured arm through his and laid her head on his shoulder. "Whatever it is, we'll deal with it. Now, take a deep breath and spit it out."

He jerked air into his lungs. "There might be something wrong with my DNA. It may not be possible for me to have healthy children."

Fear jolted her body, but she held on to his arm and didn't lift her head. The desire for children had always been a part of who she was. Her need to nurture children was why she had become a teacher. She had a list of children's names in her hope chest. Silently she cried out to God.

He'd told her that his marriage had been difficult. He hadn't wanted to betray Elsie by telling others about their struggles, but he also didn't want any secrets to come between Lennie and him. Apparently he'd held on to this one.

"I had tests run last fall, ones that would confirm if there are certain hereditary issues."

"What did the results show?"

"I don't know. I burned them."

She fought to keep her voice from faltering. "Why?"

"It doesn't matter."

"So we don't know *if* there's a problem." Tears threatened, not just for herself, but for the heaviness Grey had been carrying. This gentle, loving man lived inside a prison. "But the doctor will have a copy of the results. After you contact him and learn the truth, we can go from there."

"It sounds easy enough, doesn't it?"

The grief in his voice pressed in on her until she finally understood. Learning the truth had a finality to it that he didn't want to embrace. He'd ignored and repressed his concerns until he no longer had the strength to do so.

"Grey, we can work through anything. Where is your faith?"

He removed his arm from hers and interlaced his fingers. Staring into the distance, he said nothing for several minutes. "You don't understand. You're young and full of ideals about what marriage will be. But I can tell you, the inability to have children has the power to destroy us."

"No it doesn't. I'll never, ever regret falling in love with you."

"You're starry-eyed and in love." His shoulders slumped. "But time could change that. You were lugging around baby dolls before you could walk—and every year after that until you turned thirteen and started baby-sitting. It's a part of your makeup."

Sitting up straight, she gazed into his eyes. "You can't honestly believe that if the tests come back with disappointing results, it's the beginning of the end of us."

"I didn't know that's what all my reservations boiled down to until this moment. Either I lose you now or years from now."

She knelt on the step below him. "How can you talk to me as if we're doomed because we may have serious problems to face? Life dishes out what only God can get us through." As the words poured forth, she knew it was more than just her speaking. She felt His Spirit moving in her. "About two months ago we were standing on opposite sides of the creek where the bridge is now. We hadn't talked for weeks because I wasn't sure you really loved me. Remember?"

He traced the birthmark across her cheek and down her neck. "I'd been bearing my soul through letters, and finally you came to look me in the eyes."

"While we talked, I saw an image in my mind's eye. I believe God Himself was showing me how you really felt, encouraging me to accept as truth what you'd said and written to me. To finally believe that you loved me."

The gentleness in his eyes warmed her. "What did you see in that vision?"

"Us. Married and in your bedroom. Moonlight painted the room with a silvery glow. You were leaning against pillows, and I was lying across the foot of the bed while we talked. We were so happy, and in that snapshot I felt what could never be seen with the human eye or understood by logic—the magnitude of our friendship. It was rich and deep and beautiful." Even now she could feel the power she'd experienced when she saw that image. "Only you or I have the power to take that from us, Grey."

He held her hand, stroking it but saying nothing. The summer evening sounds of crickets, June bugs, and frogs surrounded them.

She hurt for all he'd been through and his worry over their future. "I will grieve for a season if we can't have children. But my dreams will break for all time if I can't have you."

"It's not that we can't have children. It's that we mustn't. If the DNA tests confirm there's a problem, we could conceive child after child with severe handicaps."

Heat prickled her skin at the image, and she thought of Ivan, who'd been born missing part of one arm. Ivan was quiet like his Mamm had been, but having tested him last year as a forerunner to starting school this fall, she knew he was brighter and more of a problem solver than most.

"Earlier tonight you said you didn't want us to be perfect. But you want perfect children?" she asked.

"Not perfect, but at least with a fighting chance to be whole."

"Special children are a blessing, and I trust God with those things. Always have. And once we're married, you'll be by my side too, protecting, strengthening."

"Lennie, full-term babies die with the kind of issues we're talking about. I can't protect you from the brokenness that will take place."

She remembered his and Elsie's grief-stricken faces when they buried their stillborn son. "Grey, you've been through so much in the last six years. Has it caused you to forget how to trust God?"

He lifted her hand to his lips and kissed it. "I should have seen this before, but it's clear now that it's not God's ways or this fallen planet that I'm afraid of." He caressed her hand. "It's losing you."

"Think about who I am. Is that really possible?"

An unsure smile slowly grew more confident. "Are you saying it's not?"

"I am."

"You're not taking this the way I thought you would."

"I don't like your news, but I love you. That won't change. You've been letting worry talk, and you've been listening."

"Ya, I guess so."

"And there are ways to prevent getting pregnant. I learned about them in public school."

"The bishop would never allow that."

"Are you going to ask him?"

Grey blinked. "I thought… Never mind." He cleared his throat. "Personally, I believe the union between husband and wife stands before God on its own. If you agree, then whatever decisions we come to on this will be between Him and us."

"I trust God, and I trust you to hear Him."

A smile tugged at one side of his mouth. "Pray with me. Then whatever we think our next move should be, we'll do it in agreement."

With their heads bowed, she cried to God. The idea of burying their babies hurt deeply. But with Grey holding on to her hands, she already felt strength pass between them.

Nineteen

With a rolling pin in hand, Cara flattened a double portion of piecrust against the countertop. Lori sat on the floor beside her, lightly prancing her homemade cloth dolls over Better Days's ribcage as he lay still, wagging his tail.

When she'd come downstairs Monday night to meet with Trevor, the bishop, and Ephraim, she didn't have any anger left in her to lash out with, which was a welcome improvement. But she didn't apologize either, not really.

Her memory of coming down the stairs and into the room where the men were seated was fuzzy. The God event that had taken place before-hand seemed to have displaced her, as if only part of her were there.

She clearly remembered talking to Trevor. "I'd intended to pretend my way through this," she'd told him, "but I can't. And I won't lie. So if I've said things you didn't deserve or treated you worse than I should have, I'm sorry. Personally, I don't see how my honesty comes close to comparing to what you did to me, but apparently you think so. And the church leaders seem to agree with you."

Feeling woozy, she had taken several deep breaths. But as she'd stood there, she'd felt empowered to speak her heart. "I actually do hope I can forgive you one day, for my sake more than yours. That's all I can offer you right now, and it's a ton more than I want to give. But I'm willing to aim for some type of bearable reconciliation."

He'd stepped forward, shaking the way old alcoholics tend to do. "Thank you." His eyes had misted, a half-starved man gratefully accepting the meager scraps being offered.

Hatred had melted from her, leaving a strong residue of dislike in its place. She should have been more specific about how often he could visit, but it hadn't dawned on her at the time. He'd rented a room in someone's house not too far away, which made dropping by easy for him.

The front screen door closed with the familiar rhythm of two thuds, one thump, and numerous taps. Someone had either come in or gone out. Footsteps echoed against the wooden floor. Heavy ones.

He had entered the house. He'd come Monday and yesterday. Would he visit *every* day until she put a stop to it?

She had no idea what to call the man who was technically her father. Before the mandated visits, she'd called him Trevor a few times. But now even that seemed too personal, and just thinking the word *Dad* made her physically nauseous.

Answering the door when he showed up and having to let him in without really welcoming him was awkward—as if her pride kept her from being able to perform that simple task. So she'd told him not to knock.

Now that seemed like a mistake. This was the only real home she'd had since her mother died, and she'd allowed him to come in at will. Not only did she not know what to call him; she didn't know how to deal with him.

He opened the swinging door to the kitchen. "Morning."

She returned his nod. "Hello."

He knelt beside Better Days and smiled at Lori. "How are you this morning?"

"Okay," Lori whimpered before getting up, moving to Cara, and wrapping her arms tightly around her mom.

Her behavior reminded Cara of the trauma her daughter had experienced after she'd witnessed the police handcuff Cara and threaten to haul Lori off to foster care. Ephraim had arrived and intervened, despite his reservations. Later that evening, in an effort to soothe Lori's panic, he'd brought her favorite puppy from the litter in the barn. Lori had taken to Ephraim immediately, but she didn't like her own grandfather. Cara had no doubts that Lori was picking up on her mother's feelings toward Trevor.

She kissed the top of Lori's head and gently unlocked the girl's arms from her waist. "Why don't you take Better Days outside for a while?"

Lori picked up her dolls, skirted as far around Trevor as possible, and went outdoors with Better Days.

"Would you like some coffee?" Cara asked.

He shook his head. "I thought maybe we could go for a walk, all three of us."

"I have lots of work to do."

He didn't respond, and she refused to look at him. She cut out miniature piecrusts, wishing Deborah and Ada would get back soon from making deliveries to bakeries and picking up supplies. Someone running interference would be very helpful.

He leaned against the sink and folded his arms. "What are you making?"

She leveled a look at him before focusing on the dough in front of her. It was obvious she was making piecrusts. Thoughts of her mother scurrying up the stairs with her and hiding her in a cubbyhole behind the wall of the attic screamed at her.

Two days. That was all that had passed since her odd encounter while kneeling beside her bed. It was God who'd held her, wasn't it? It seemed impossible that He cared that much for someone like her. At times she found it easier to believe the whole thing had been her imagination. But, in spite of herself, she knew it had happened.

She tried to apply those feelings of love and acceptance to the man in the room with her, but it wasn't working. Not yet. Maybe never. God's intervention had touched her mind and heart deeply, but it hadn't done much to free her of bitterness and rage.

"Look, Cara, I know this is hard for you," Trevor said. "From the things you said Monday evening, it's obvious you think I ran to Emma and Levi to complain about your outburst. I didn't, but I have no words to describe what your news did to me. It's my own fault. I know that. But all these years I've believed you were happy and safe here with them. I had to know what happened, to separate facts from fiction. I'm sorry that the bishop got involved and that now we're both stuck going through the motions."

"If you don't want to be here, then why not make our lives easier and just go away?"

"For me, I want to be here. For you, I'd leave if I could. But we both need to prove to the church leaders that you're ready to join the faith this fall. If I walk away now, it'll make your efforts to become Amish harder, won't it?"

She hadn't thought about that, but he was right. Now that the bishop knew about her outburst and her bitterness toward Trevor, if he left without their coming to some sort of peace, she'd not be allowed to join the faith—a faith that believed in gentleness toward those who'd wronged them and forgiveness at all costs.

"I guess it's best you're here…for practical reasons."

"I'm glad we understand each other about this." He watched her cut another miniature piecrust. "Can I help?"

"I guess."

He went to the sink and scrubbed his hands.

When he returned to the work station, she passed him a disposable pan. "Lay it upside down on the dough, and slice around it. Getting them up in one piece takes practice, and I don't have time for mistakes."

He pressed the pan onto the dough, following her instructions carefully. His eyes rose to meet hers, and she realized they shared the same eye color—golden bronze. Why would he act so humble and willing to follow her directions? What did he hope to gain?

The rolling pin hit the floor with a thud, breaking in to her thoughts. She picked it up, scrubbed it, and dried it. When she turned around, her father had set a row of pie tins along the countertop, brushed each one with oil, and begun putting piecrusts in them. Moving from cutout to cutout, he efficiently fixed each one, including the decorative edge.

"Where'd you learn to do that?"

"Your mom."

Cara wished she hadn't asked.

"Don't you remember any of our Sundays together?"

She shook her head. "I can barely remember what she looked like."

He pulled his billfold out of his back pocket and passed a small picture to her. "It's awfully faded."

The photo showed all three of them in what looked like a park. Trevor was holding her, and she had her arms wrapped around his neck, giggling by the looks of it. Her mom's smile radiated back at her.

But the image in her hand washed out and was replaced by a more familiar one. "Cara," Mama whispered, touching her lips with her index finger. "Don't make any noise." She turned on the flashlight and put it in Cara's hand. "You sleep here unless I come back for you." Cara clutched her doll in one hand and the flashlight in the other.

"Melinda!" Her father's footsteps echoed like a monster invading their home. Her mother closed the small door to the attic wall.

Cara passed the snapshot back to him.

"You don't remember?"

"I recall plenty. Do yourself a favor and don't ask me about it."

"It wasn't all bad, Cara."

She swallowed and managed a nod.

"You know," he said as he washed his hands again, "there are perks to my being around. I have a car. It's beat-up, but I could make it easier for you to get back and forth to Dry Lake."

"Don't you want to get a job?" Since it was obvious he'd be around for a while, she liked the idea of his doing something that would keep him out of her hair.

"I had one as a school janitor until recently. I get the shakes so bad at times I can hardly stand up, and they let me go."

"Years of drinking can do that to a person."

"You have your mama's sense of honesty."

"I know of a couple of people who need a farmhand. Aaron Blank and Sylvia something."

"Friends of yours?"

"I just met both of them Sunday evening. She's going to help teach me the Amish language starting tomorrow."

"Another obstacle to joining?"

He acted so interested and caring. If she told him he was a fake, he'd look hurt and argue. Maybe she should test him a little, let him see his own insincerity.

"Yeah, but I can't let her do that for no cost, and money is always tight for me. If you want to make up for the past so badly, how about paying for the lessons? That's what dads do, isn't it?" She talked to Better Days in this same tone when he misbehaved.

A sweet-looking smile crossed his face. "I'll speak to Aaron Blank about that job opening."

He wouldn't last long doing farm work, especially in this heat. But it'd keep him from having so much free time on his hands.

Aaron climbed the ladder to the haymow, looking for Sylvi. He'd gone to the cabin and the pond behind it as well as to the milking parlor but hadn't found her. The old wood moaned under the weight of his body.

Five days had passed since she'd told him and his parents about having kissed a married man. She had revealed her wrongdoing for his sake, to try to make his father understand that people make mistakes but can change. And other than a brief "thanks," Aaron hadn't mentioned a word about it to her. They'd worked from sunup to sundown Wednesday through Saturday, but they'd only spoken when necessary and avoided any mention of that topic.

He'd kept to himself more this week, thinking silence would build a thick partition between them. Instead, an invisible connection had formed—at least for him. No matter how much he tried to deny, ignore, or sabotage the bond, it only grew stronger. He had no idea what she thought or felt other than determination to hold on to this abomination she called a farm.

A quick glance into the haymow said she wasn't there either. He climbed into the loft, hoping to spot her in one of the pastures. Instead, he found her sound asleep on a blanket against a mound of loose hay. Four kittens were bunched up in her lap, sleeping.

He sat, leaning against the frame of the barn, and watched her.

He was drawn to her, fascinated by her, and thirsty for more time with her. He'd never before been pulled like this by anything—except alcohol. The realization scared him senseless. He'd already proven he lacked good judgment about what attracted him.

So why was he here?

On Friday, with Trevor Atwater's help, he and Sylvi had finished baling the hay, and yesterday they'd loaded it onto several wagons. It now sat inside the barn, waiting to be sold. His excuse for searching for her was that he had a buyer, a person that he had begun talking to a couple of days ago. The man had come by earlier today, but since it was Sunday, Aaron was limited to agreeing to sell it to him tomorrow. And the man had agreed to a top-dollar price. She'd like that.

After all their work getting the hay in before the rain came, they should've celebrated last night—had a feast with special desserts or something. Instead they did what they always did when work or mealtime was over—they went their separate ways. Then again, how could they celebrate together when they saw the completed task as accomplishing opposite goals?

She stretched and drew a deep, relaxing breath. When she saw him watching her, she frowned and rubbed her eyes. "Hi."

"You're not an easy woman to find." It struck him how true his words were. Anytime he thought he saw her—figuratively speaking—she shifted and revealed something different. Like a mirage, she appeared, only to disappear.

She sat up, rearranging the kittens. "What do you want?"

"I have good news. A man has offered top dollar for the hay."

"Clay Severs?"

"No, a different man. Clay's idea of a fair price was way too low."

"You shook hands on it with this other man?"

"Ya. He's picking it up and paying for it tomorrow."

"That's great." She closed her eyes tight before blinking a few times. "What time is it?"

"Five."

Her eyes grew large. "I knew I was tired. It was all I could do to stay awake during church this morning. I think Cara pinched me three times."

"You should've stayed home and slept instead."

She huffed. "Very funny."

He'd knocked on her cabin door an hour before time to leave for church, then returned in a rig to pick her up. She wasn't pleased. To convince her to go, he agreed to do one favor of any sort for her if she'd get in the rig. Without another word, she got in.

"So have you decided what favor I owe you?"

"You shouldn't ask that when you're sitting near an open hayloft door three stories above ground."

He laughed. "I wouldn't recommend tossing me out until we get the next field cut and sold."

She moaned. "Next field? Oh, Aaron, don't use such mean words. I can't stand the thought of more hayfield work right now."

"Sorry. I didn't mean to ruin your Sunday afternoon."

A tabby kitten climbed up Sylvi's chest and snuggled against her neck.

"There's something else I'm really sorry about. I shrugged off what you did to try to help Daed and me get along better. Time will tell, but I think your story has given him a new perspective. It took guts to share your past, and I should have thanked you properlike."

Her brows wrinkled a bit, and he wondered if she found him as difficult to understand as he found her. "Why didn't you?"

He gathered a small handful of hay off the floor and tossed it out the doorway. "I don't know. Maybe because I know I haven't earned your kindness. And we have opposing visions. It's like we're enemies, and yet we're not."

She put the three sleeping kittens on the blanket. Keeping the other one in her hands, she moved to the hayloft door next to him. "I can see that." She sat, dangling her feet toward the ground. "There's always been plenty unsaid between my Daed and me too. It's the way he is with all his daughters. Good man. Diligent and faithful to God, family, and community, but…"

"You wanted more."

"I longed for him to understand me. I had that kind of relationship with my grandfather. And Daed seemed fine with my voicing an opinion or questions—in small amounts. Based on what I'd said, he even changed certain aspects of how we farmed. But I kept my mouth shut as much as I could stand. I didn't want to ruin what we did have."

"I hate how tough it is to build a good relationship and how easy it is to ruin it."

"You and Michael could win an award for what's left unsaid between you two."

He cleared his throat. "When I was a kid and even well into my teen years, we talked about everything. But after we moved here, he and Mamm changed. They'd been through hell in Ohio, and every hope they had was centered on this farm in Dry Lake. Within weeks of moving, Daed started feeling exhausted and weak, and the knuckles of his thumbs hurt. Within a couple of months, all his joints ached, and shortly after that he was diagnosed with rheumatoid arthritis. He made it worse because he stopped trying to use his hands. He'd spend weeks in bed, and when he got up, he'd start in on me about everything I hadn't done. The farm was going to seed…and it was my fault."

"Is that when you started to hate farming?"

"Probably. The next few years I worked like crazy trying to live up to what he wanted." He ran his fingers over the dust on the rough-hewn planks. "It never happened. I was so miserable that I'd do anything for a break from the weight of it. From that first beer, the experience was…an escape. So I started partying with anyone who wanted to come to the cabin and bring drinks. I couldn't get enough. It's not Mamm's or Daed's fault, but they made it easy. Never checked on me. All those times I didn't come home at night, they thought I was sleeping in the barn."

"Maybe if you really opened up with Michael as humbly and unaccusing as you just—"

He put his index finger to his lips. "Don't, please." He stared at the rolling hills dotted with grazing cows. The sight might look beautiful to her, but it made him feel like a slave to a bunch of completely stupid creatures. "Can we change the subject?"

She nodded. "How's Frani?"

"She's a mess. More pigheaded than I am. But there's hope that she'll decide to get help."

"When your Daed hired me, he said I could share the cabin with anyone I wanted...as long as it wasn't a man, of course. I think he had my sisters in mind. But if it comes to that, she can stay with me for a while."

"Thanks. That's really generous of you." Aaron chewed on a piece of straw, mulling over whether to ask her a question or two. "What happened between you and the man you..."

"Elam." She stared at the horizon. "We fell in love, but when he asked me to marry him, I wasn't ready. I wanted another year, maybe two. Three weeks later he asked...someone else. A few years after they married, the emotions between us resurfaced. That's why I came here."

The depth of grief in her brown eyes made a twinge of physical pain run through him. Maybe he shouldn't have written that letter. He hadn't known this was her reason for leaving Path Valley. He'd thought she was here because of a feud with her sister. That was what she'd said, wasn't it?

The upside was that she had no idea Beckie had ignored his letter. So far.

"Hey." She tossed a little hay at him. "Just because I don't want to talk about that doesn't mean you can't talk at all."

He wrestled with the idea of asking her to go for a buggy ride. At almost twenty-six, he'd never asked a girl to go anywhere. It'd be nice if he had some experience to rely on. He wondered how Elam had asked her out the first time and what she might expect from a beau.

Idiot! What am I thinking? They couldn't get all cozy. He intended to sell this place and leave. She was bent on convincing him not to sell and probably wished he'd just leave. The key word in either scenario was *leave*.

Sylvia moved closer and dusted off the hay that she'd thrown on him, quickly brushing her hands over his shoulder before picking a stray piece out of his hair. "There, now you look all perfect and handsome again."

Did she think him handsome? He liked that idea, although he knew he shouldn't. He took the lone piece of hay from her and quietly placed it on her head. They laughed before she plucked it off and dropped it out the window.

"Oh, I almost forgot." She passed him the kitten and rubbed behind its ears. "During the after-service meal, a couple of the single girls invited me to a singing tonight."

"And you said yes? That's unexpected." His eyes locked on hers.

"Not that much. I've been to singings all around Pennsylvania, some in Ohio too."

"Really?"

"I used to get away from the farm for weeks at a time, staying with cousins. We went to singings and outings."

"That's a side of you I wouldn't have banked on."

"It was fun. I never found another guy I liked, but I met lots of interesting people. A girl named Mary is coming to get me. Do you want to go with us?"

His heart beat a little faster at the idea, but he wasn't the kind of person to attend the overly chaperoned event, boys on one side and girls on the other. A fair number of the parents seemed to want a spotless attitude to shine from every youth, and he wasn't a mask-wearing type of guy. "Spare me."

She laughed. "That's a definite no." Then she hustled down the ladder.

Seeing the top of her head vanish, disappointment settled over him. He could have talked with her the whole evening and enjoyed it more than doing anything else. It was apparent she didn't feel the same way.

Twenty

·In the upstairs bathroom Cara held a washcloth under cool water, hoping to find some relief from this awful heat wave. She wrung it out and wiped it over her face and neck. The old mirror hanging in front of her matched the banister, moldings, doorknobs, and other fixtures in Ada's House—worn, but classic.

This house had character and stamina. It gave shelter from the elements, provided a place to be a family and meet each other's needs, and even offered a way to make a living. In a metaphorical way, she wanted to be like that too—protective, hospitable, and a unique asset.

But she couldn't stop rehashing the hurt and misery her dad's choices had caused her. She wanted to be free, not just so she could settle the issue with the church leaders, but so she could focus on healthier things.

He'd lived as he wanted to, making poor choices all along the way and not caring one iota about her. Who she was today—the ugly, awful past Ephraim helped her shoulder—wasn't her fault. If Trevor had stopped indulging himself in liquor long enough to make sure his daughter was in safe hands, she would've grown up being the kind of woman Ephraim deserved.

"Cara?" Deborah tapped on the bathroom door.

"Come on in."

Deborah opened the door, moved to the sink, and picked up her toothbrush. "Jonathan found this neat little ice cream parlor about two miles from here. It opened earlier this summer, but he just discovered it a few days ago. Since we're closed this evening, we thought we'd put our night off to good use. Would you and Lori like to go with us?"

Deborah and Ephraim didn't favor each other as much as some siblings, but they'd both stolen her heart. "You sure Jonathan wouldn't mind? Maybe he'd like a little time alone with you." Jonathan helped around Ada's House nearly every night and worked as a traveling blacksmith to Amish farms during the day.

A beautiful dusting of pink shaded Deborah's face as she loaded toothpaste onto her brush. "He's the one who said to ask."

"Really? I knew I liked that young man of yours." Cara stepped aside to let Deborah brush her teeth. After Cara removed her prayer Kapp, she pulled the bobby pins out of her half-fallen hair and brushed it in an effort to recapture all the loose strands.

Deborah had been seeing Jonathan for quite a while, and their relationship had been tested. Mahlon, her ex-fiancé, had come back for her and promised to do whatever it took to win her back. But instead his visit had convinced Deborah that the kind of man she really wanted was the opposite of Mahlon—a man who embraced life and people, who gave because he enjoyed it, who didn't need her to keep him in line or to make sure he had enough reasons to want to live.

And Deborah had all that in Jonathan.

Deborah rinsed her toothbrush. "Here, let me." She ran a brush through Cara's hair. "Since Amish women don't cut their hair, I didn't realize it grew in again so slowly. You've been growing it out for more than a year, and it's not even to your shoulders yet."

"That's partly because it started out shorter than most men's hair. And maybe my hair grows really slowly."

"Why'd you keep it so short?"

"It was convenient and cute, in my estimation. When I saw all the

Amish women with their hair pulled back, I thought that was silly. If you're going to keep it hidden, why not cut it short?"

"I can see thinking that way." Deborah looped a covered rubber band around Cara's hair and pinned it in a bun. "So are you going with us to the ice cream parlor?"

Cara put on her prayer Kapp again. "Sure." She went to Lori's room, where her daughter sat on her bed, reading aloud to Better Days. "We've been invited to go with Deb and Jonathan for ice cream. Care to—"

"Yes!" Lori hopped up and gave Cara and Deborah a hug before bounding down the steps, Better Days running ahead of her.

"The dog stays, Lori."

"Aw, Mom."

"He'll eat your ice cream, mine, Deborah's, and Jonathan's."

"Well," Israel said.

Cara spun around.

"Good thing he's not eating my ice cream."

"Israel." She wanted to hug Lena's dad, but that suggested a closeness she didn't really have with him. "I didn't know you were here."

"I wasn't. Now I am. What's all this talk about Better Days eating ice cream?"

Lori hurried over to him and took his hand. "You seen Ada yet?"

"I most certainly have." He pointed up the stairs.

Ada stood behind the banister, peering over it. She wore a clean dress and apron and a beautiful smile. She looked more youthful than ever as she slowly made her way down the stairs.

"So where's Jonathan?" Cara asked.

The sound of footsteps on the wooden porch made them turn toward the screen door.

He stood there.

Israel glanced at Cara, waiting to take a cue from her. But she stood in a pool of hurt, unsure how to cope with *his* presence. It was as if each time she saw him, she dealt with the same raw, unbound pain she'd grown up with.

"Trevor." Israel motioned for him to enter. "Good to see you."

When Trevor stepped inside, Lori took a step back, withdrawing her hand from Israel's. She moved beside her mother and wrapped her arms around Cara's waist.

Jonathan came in the front door. "I've connected the hayride wagon, minus the hay. Now we have room for everyone." When he spotted Trevor, he looked at Cara as if checking on her.

She wanted to shake her head, but something stopped her. Maybe she should feel sorry for Trevor. He looked out of place, standing in the middle of a group obviously bent on going elsewhere.

In the eleven days since he'd begun working at the Blank farm, he hadn't been around much. And she'd enjoyed every moment of his absence. Nothing like dairy farming to keep a person constantly busy.

"I'll just be going." Trevor looked at Cara. "Have fun. I'll see you later."

When he walked out, everyone stood there awkwardly, looking anywhere but at her.

"Okay, fine. I hear you." She stepped onto the porch. Her father's shoulders were slumped as he went down the sidewalk.

An image of herself at sixteen, scantily dressed and dancing at a bar, flashed before her. Circumstances had trapped her into making choices she wasn't proud of. Had they trapped him too?

"Wait." Cara hurried toward him.

He turned.

"You could go with us."

"That's okay, Carab—" The hurt reflecting from him tugged at her. She closed her eyes. "I want you to come with us."

"No you don't."

"So you're giving up?"

He barely shrugged. "I'm not much of an arguer."

"Was Mom?"

He shook his head. "She had a strong will, but like most of her people, she wore it quietly and politely."

Cara's eyes misted. "I still miss her."

He nodded. "So do I. Every day, all day long."

His words stunned her. He used to say that to her before bedtime on a good evening. They'd had good times? The realization made her shudder. "You…read to me on the couch while Mama sat in her chair mending clothes."

A faint smile eased some of the sorrow from his eyes. "Yeah, that's right."

She remembered that when it was time for her to go to bed, she'd say, "I love you," and he'd say, "I love you more. Every day, all day long."

She'd gag on those phrases if she tried to speak them now. "You should come with us."

"You really want me to?" The disbelief in his voice rattled her.

She nodded.

"Lori won't like it."

"I'll let Better Days go with us, and you can give the dog a lick of your ice cream. She'll like that."

He scrunched his face. "Do I have to eat the rest of the cone afterward?"

She stood speechless for a moment until she realized he was teasing her. She chuckled. "Is it okay if I call you by your first name?"

"Of course."

"How about a horse-and-wagon ride to the ice cream parlor, Trevor?"

"I'd like that."

She turned toward the house. "Deb, you guys ready?"

While everyone piled into the wagon, Cara stepped inside the house. "Come on, Better Days." The dog bounded out the door, to the wagon, and onto Lori's lap. Cara climbed into the wagon, and Lori beamed at her mom.

Israel drove with Ada beside him. Trevor shifted, his thin frame looking uncomfortable on the wooden slats. "Where's Ephraim?"

"He doesn't usually come to Ada's House during the week."

"Why not?"

"He logs a lot of hours at his cabinetry shop in Dry Lake."

"He seems like a good man."

"He is." She bit her bottom lip to keep a goofy grin off her face. "I first met him when I was eight. As an adult he came to New York, looking for me."

They spent the ride in stilted, uncomfortable conversation. But at least she was able to talk civilly to him.

The ice cream parlor had walk-up windows and picnic tables under huge shade trees. Everyone except Trevor picked out a favorite flavor, then moved to a table. Trevor stayed in the wagon with Better Days.

Cara ordered three cones and sent Lori back to the wagon with Trevor's. After gathering some napkins, Cara handed Lori her ice cream, and she hurried to Deborah and Jonathan's table.

Cara moved back to the wagon and sat on the tailgate. "If cameras were allowed here, I'd fill a photo album a month with pictures."

Trevor licked his ice cream while trying to keep forty-pound Better Days at bay. "You could probably snap some privately of those closest to you and keep them tucked away."

"Yeah, maybe. But I'm already on the bishop's most wanted list, though I've managed to stay off the deacon's list. I'd like to keep it that way."

"The deacon coming to see someone is a bad thing?"

"He visits when a person is in violation of an Amish rule. From what

I've seen, the bishop tries to intervene in situations and steer folks the right way. If the deacon is called in, he drops the gavel—no debate allowed."

"Guess it'd be best for you not to be caught with a camera."

"I wish they'd at least allow one family picture every four or five years. Nothing fancy but something like the shot you have of Mom and me."

"I look at it every day."

"I don't have a single photo of Lori's dad to show her."

"Why not?"

"I needed to get out of New York fast, so I took Lori and left everything behind except the clothes on our backs…and her book bag."

"Maybe you could return to New York to get your things."

"Oh, I can just see the Plain folks finding out I'm running over to New York for a couple of eight by tens."

"I guess not. Those pictures meant a lot to you, though, didn't they?"

"Certainly not more than our safety. But they would mean a great deal to Lori. She doesn't have any memories of her dad, and he loved her so much—both of us, really. I think she'd cherish having photos of them together. Even more so when she gets older. I realized that when I saw the picture of you and Mom."

"Where in New York did you live?"

When she told him the name of the apartment building, his eyes lit up. "I know right where you're talking about. I used to work as a handyman at the apartments across the street."

"Really?"

"The manager of your apartment building would've had cleaners get rid of anything left behind."

She shrugged. "Yeah. Probably."

"Anyone who might've salvaged your stuff?"

Her heart glimmered with a touch of hope. "Lori's baby-sitter lived next door. It's possible she grabbed a few things and is holding on to them."

"You should write to her."

The hint of excitement faded. "I can't. It's best if my whereabouts remain a secret."

"Creditors?"

"Worse. I'd rather not talk about it."

Better Days lunged forward, taking a swipe at Trevor's ice cream. The sudden movement made him drop the cone, and Better Days lapped it up.

"And Lori wasn't even here to see my great sacrifice," he said.

His humor caught her off guard, making her realize she saw him as less than human, which he wasn't. Maybe building some semblance of a relationship with him was possible after all.

Twenty-One

Grey rinsed off the last of the flatware, but his mind remained on Lennie and their future. She loved so deeply and had enough resilience to cope with disappointments and grief without turning against him. No one would ever understand what that meant to him, but he was still unsure what his next step should be. He placed the handful of utensils into the dish drainer.

It had been two weeks since they'd talked. Except for the one church Sunday, he'd not even caught a glimpse of her. He still wasn't sure what he should do about the test results. Grey released the water from the sink and began to dry the dishes.

This decision wasn't about what he wanted. Lennie trusted him to hear God in the matter, so he kept setting aside his personal feelings while praying.

His son came inside with a small, hand-carved horse in his hand. After telling Grey that Israel was coming, Ivan asked for two things: a cup of cold water and permission to go across the bridge to Allen's house.

Grey glanced out the window and saw Israel cross the backyard. He'd used the bridge, which might mean Lennie was at her brother's this afternoon. Since today was the Fourth of July and all of Israel's family loved watching fireworks, they might be having a midweek gathering. It would be nice to see her, even if they'd be among a large group and would have to keep their distance.

Grey poured Ivan a drink and gave him permission to go to Allen's. He opened the screen door. "Hello, Israel. Kumm rei. What brings you here?"

Israel walked in. "I have a proposition for you to think on."

Grey took a glass out of the cabinet and filled it with icy water. He passed it to Israel. "Have a seat and tell me about it."

Israel pulled out a chair and sat. "I haven't talked to anybody but Ada about this, and I'm not ready for others to know just yet."

"Now I'm curious."

Israel grinned. "I asked Ada to marry me, and she said yes."

"Congratulations. That's great news."

Israel grinned while staring at the table. "I didn't know a man with grown children could feel like this. It's taken a long time for things between Ada and me to work themselves out. To say we're really happy about it doesn't begin to tell the tale."

"Lennie may be just as excited as you two when she learns of it."

"I suspect so." Israel took a drink. "We'll tell everyone soon enough, but one of Lena's first questions will be where we'll live, which is why I'm here." Israel smeared the condensation on his glass, fidgeting for no apparent reason.

Grey waited.

"I don't mean for my idea to interfere with your plans or hopes for your and Lena's future. You'll be the head of your household, so I'm coming to you with my idea. If you don't like it, I won't mention it to Lena. It's just an offer, one you can turn down, and I won't take it personal."

"Okay."

"You built this house, and maybe you and Lena want to move in here, but I'd like for you to think about moving yourselves and Ivan into my house when the time comes."

Israel had one of the nicest and prettiest places in all of Dry Lake. "Your place? Why?"

"Lena loves that old home, and I can build furniture anywhere. But Ada can't run her business here in Dry Lake. We don't get enough tourist traffic, and she loves operating Ada's House. So what I propose is a sort of house swap. You get my place, which has several rooms for a growing family, acreage, barns, and Lena's beloved greenhouse, and I get your place to put up for sale. Eventually that money will go to my other children to divide equally."

That was a really generous offer. Maybe too generous.

Israel slid his glass one way and then the other. "I'd do just about anything for Lena. I guess you've figured that out by now. And it's hard on a woman to enter another woman's home and build a life with someone, especially if she's never been married before." Israel sighed. "Am I butting in where I oughta stay out?"

"No. I agree with what you're saying. But how would the rest of your family take it? It's more their homestead than it is mine."

"If anyone minds, they'll get over it within a few days. Lena's been running that home since her mother passed, and it's hers. No one will deny that. Ada thinks if you two will be living there, it will make planning the wedding even more special for Lena."

"Ada knows about Lennie and me?"

"Ya. I had to talk to someone about giving up Lena. I know I'm not supposed to feel that way. Lena's nearly six years older than her sisters were when they married, but the idea of letting her go isn't coming easy."

"I'll take good care of her."

"Oh, heavens, I know that. And she'll do the same for you." Israel took a long drink. "Just think on my idea and let me know. This plan does have one stipulation."

"What's that?"

"The whole family is to gather there at least once a month in cold weather. We've always done that, and it's the only place that has room for all the children, spouses, and grandkids. Allen's place works in the summertime because we can overflow to the outside."

"You're right about Lennie and her home, and I'm sure the idea of moving into this one would give her some trouble." Grey had built this home, but it held a lot of memories. He really liked the idea of Lena and him getting a fresh start elsewhere, but he'd never entertained the idea because it wasn't affordable. "It's quite a gift."

"I'd appreciate your taking me up on my offer."

"Lennie would love it." Grey could imagine the excitement mirrored in her bluish green eyes. They might not be able to fill the rooms with children, but living there would always give her joy. "Of course I accept, Israel. Denki."

"Gut. Ya, that's gut." Israel finished his drink. "We'll talk to her about it as soon as Ada and I are ready to announce our news. I think Ada's right. Lena likes to know what's ahead when she can. It gives her time to get her feet under her."

A quiet calmness fell over Grey, hushing all the confusion and uncertainty inside him. He knew what he needed to do now. He'd get the test results. Whatever they learned, it would give Lennie and him time to get their feet under them.

Lennie had never failed to find contentment with any situation. It might take her a little while sometimes, but she put her will to work when it came to being happy. He'd seen her do it dozens of times, like when the school board removed her as a teacher even though that was all she'd ever wanted to be. Now, less than three months later, she'd found something else to joyfully fill her days this next school year—helping a homeschooling mom.

"Hey." Israel stood and set his glass in the sink. "We're having a spread of cold cuts and fruit at Allen's tonight. After supper we're going to load up in a few wagons and go watch fireworks in Shippensburg. I think you should join us."

Grey wouldn't go with them on the outing. That was for family members. But he could visit for a while before they left.

And he'd find a private moment to tell Lennie that he intended to find out the test results.

Twenty-Two

The aroma of dinner filled the air, and Sylvia's stomach growled. She stood in the driveway, waiting to see how many pounds of milk the cows had produced since the buyer's last visit two days ago.

The Englischer pulled a receipt off his ledger. "I think you'll like what you see."

She glanced at the numbers. "Oh I do. And I won't be the only one."

Milk production had increased consistently over the last several pickups, and Aaron had gotten top dollar for the hay. Both were very encouraging pieces of news.

"I'll see you day after tomorrow," the man said.

"The milk will be here. Bye." She folded the receipt and headed for the farmhouse. Since Aaron's apology in the hayloft more than two weeks ago, they'd managed the farm together without too many disagreements, although he didn't like her letting expectant cows find their own birthing spots. He preferred putting them in a large, clean stall.

She stepped inside the farmhouse but stopped cold when she saw Aaron walking around the table, setting it for dinner.

"Oh, good, you're here," Dora said, stirring a pot on the stove.

Aaron looked up. "You're late."

"Indeed I am." She laid the receipt on the counter before washing up to her elbows in the mud sink. "So...you're placing the flatware? What universe have I been transported to?"

"Can't a man pitch in without you making a big deal out of it?"

She dried her hands and arms. "Do you know how many men it takes to replace a roll of toilet paper?"

He shook his head.

"No one does. It's never been tried."

He laughed. "Do you know how many women it takes to make a man sorry he attempted to pitch in?"

She shook her head.

"One." He pointed at her. His demeanor was light and playful.

She stuck her tongue out at him. "Where's Michael?"

"Fetching the mail." Dora put the large pot in the center of the table.

Aaron poured a glass of water and handed it to Sylvia. "I wish he wouldn't wait until suppertime to do that. He opens it on the walk back, and the contents never make for good mealtime conversation."

Michael walked in, sorting through a handful of mail. He passed Aaron a letter. "This one's for you."

Aaron opened the envelope, read the letter, and laid it to the side.

Dora sliced huge chunks of homemade bread and placed one on each plate. She glanced at the envelope. "That looks like another letter from the place where you stayed."

"The Better Path," Aaron said. "Did you ever open any of the ones they sent to you?"

"I did once," his father said. "That was enough." He held up another envelope, showing it to Dora. It was from the Better Path and addressed to her and Michael.

Dora picked it up.

"If you're going to read it," Aaron said, "I'd suggest doing so later."

Ignoring her son's advice, Dora tore into it. "It's an invitation." She passed it to Michael. "Is that place like Alcoholics Anonymous?"

"I've never been to an AA meeting, but it's probably similar. It's designed by a Plain Mennonite, and it's for people in the Plain community."

Michael shook his head. "It's sad that Plain people need that kind of facility."

Aaron's anger flashed in his eyes. "It's even sadder when people know they can't cope well, yet they refuse to get help."

Embarrassment clouded Michael's features. "I handle things just fine. And I'm not getting into an argument tonight."

Sylvia loved the Blanks, but Michael's anger and Dora's submissiveness to him when it came to Aaron continued to disappoint her.

Dora poured a ladle of stew over the bread on each plate. "Why would we get an invitation to visit the Better Path since you're no longer there?"

"I'm supposed to attend the meetings at least twice a month, but I haven't gone since I came back here four weeks ago. This weekend is a group meeting, where everyone who's part of the program can have family or friends come. Since you never responded to my letters, I've never had anyone attend the group meetings for me."

Michael tossed the envelope toward the trash bin. "I'm not going this time either."

The disappointment on Aaron's face was minimal. No doubt he'd known what his Daed's reaction would be and had braced himself.

Dora finished pouring the stew and sat down. They bowed their heads for the silent prayer. Michael followed with an "amen."

Sylvia pulled the cloth napkin into her lap. "When is the meeting, Aaron?"

"This Saturday."

"Are you going?"

"I need to."

She turned to Michael. "I can handle a day of milking while you go with Aaron."

"Let it go, Sylvi," Aaron said.

She studied him, disappointed in the apathy she heard in his tone and saw reflected in his eyes. If every person who attended that day would have at least one family member or friend there, Aaron should too.

The clinks of flatware against plates resounded in the quiet room. When the meal was over, Aaron excused himself and left the house.

Sylvia turned to Michael. "I think you should go to the Better Path on Saturday."

"It's bad enough he's going. I won't embarrass myself by stepping into that place."

There were so many arguments on Aaron's behalf that she wanted to voice. But it wasn't her place. Michael was her father's age, and even though the feelings between Michael and her were often like that of a parent and an adult child, she was just a hired worker. She looked to Dora, silently begging her to speak up.

Dora rubbed her forehead as if it hurt. "Michael." She spoke softly and waited for him to look at her. "You won't stop reminding Aaron of his past mistakes. You won't help him when he tries to make up for previous wrongs. And you won't attend a meeting that might help him with his future. What exactly are you willing to do for our only son?"

Sylvia longed to grasp Dora's hand and shout "denki!" Instead she remained still and silent.

Michael's face reddened. "Why should I do anything for him when he'll just up and leave again? And when he does, there'll be no note. No warning. He'll be here one day and gone the next."

Now that she knew Aaron better, Sylvia couldn't imagine him doing such a thing. He'd left home to get straightened out and had returned a hard-working, focused man.

Dora lowered her head. "If he'd asked your permission to go to this place and get help, would you have let him?"

Sylvia waited, but Michael didn't say anything. "Is this how you feel about me now too?"

He closed his eyes and put his head in his hands. "I've thought on your story about you and that married man, and you were wrong to do what you did, but that's different from what Aaron did. Your incident happened once, and you fled the temptation. Aaron wallowed in his sin and hid it from us for years. It's not my fault he needed such a place."

With Michael having that kind of stubborn attitude, Sylvia didn't understand how Aaron could remain so loyal to his parents. She'd given Elam the best of her heart, and he hadn't been loyal to her. He hadn't been loyal to Beckie, either. Yet Aaron had been good to his folks in spite of the way they treated him.

"I've been working with Aaron for a month now. He's not perfect." She reached across the table and put her hand over Michael's. "But he deserves someone who believes in him."

Dora ran her fingertips along the edge of the table, keeping her eyes lowered. "Does he know you began looking for someone you could hire to help him months before he left here?"

Michael shook his head. "He wouldn't believe me, and if he did, he'd say it was too little too late."

"It might let him know that we care. Would it be so horrible to admit we were wrong too?" Dora asked. "To let him see that we need him as our son, not just as a laborer?"

"I...I can't."

Sylvia was suddenly drained of all energy. She knew Michael felt deeply. During the months before Aaron returned home, she'd spent long evenings in the living room with Michael and Dora and had come to understand how much Michael loved his son. He needed Aaron far more than he needed a farmhand, but things she didn't understand, maybe pride and hurt, kept the two of them at odds. She couldn't help but wonder if Michael would open his heart before it was too late.

Dora moved to a chair closer to her husband. "If we went, we could go see that appliance store too. You promised we would."

Michael stood, looking frustrated and unsure of what was taking place. He sighed. "Okay, fine. We'll go." He looked at Sylvia. "All three of us. Grey won't mind stepping in to help on Saturday."

"But…" Sylvia saw no reason for all of them to attend.

"We're all going. But no one tells Aaron in case something happens that keeps us from making the trip."

She wished she could convince Michael to let her skip the outing. She had no problem supporting Aaron at the Better Path, but she didn't want to witness Michael and Dora walking through the appliance store. What if they liked it and the idea of moving began to grow on them?

Twenty-Three

Cara sat at the treadle sewing machine, making another cloth doll. Lori had gone with Ada and Deborah to deliver special order cakes to two shops. In a few hours customers would fill Ada's House, but at ten in the morning, it was quiet and peaceful.

Better Days went to the door, wagging his tail.

"Hey there, little pup." Trevor's raspy voice flowed through the empty home. He tapped on the door and then walked inside, carrying a brown bag about the size of a tissue box. He saw Cara working near a window in an open area off the foyer.

"He's not a puppy," she said. "Had his first birthday in April."

"Don't kid yourself, Cara. This dog is quite the puppy. Not an ounce of him is a watchdog, though, unless you count watching people walk right in your front door."

"He's a good fit for Ada's House. Can you imagine having a territorial dog with all the customers who come in during a week?" Cara snipped threads. "You're not working at the farm today?"

"Morning milking is done, and the barns are cleaned out, so I'm on break for a few hours." He pulled a treat out of his pocket and fed it to Better Days.

Trevor didn't seem to mind running back and forth regularly between Hope Crossing and Dry Lake. As dilapidated as his car was, it never gave him a lick of trouble, and he acted as though he enjoyed carting her around. That made it easy for her to go to Sylvia's to study…and to drop by the cabinetry shop to see Ephraim for a few minutes on the way. Cara liked Sylvia and appreciated the lessons, but her favorite part of going to Dry Lake was seeing her fiancé. Having Trevor around actually made her life easier, but taking his help was almost too effortless, and she chafed over it.

Trevor stopped petting the dog. "I wanted to come by and let you know I'm going away for a few days."

In spite of how far they'd come, she felt a burst of hope at the idea of his being gone, even briefly. "When?"

"This weekend."

Cara couldn't decide if she wanted to know where and why. "Looks like I'm going to be without a free ride this week." She sounded as if she were just using him, and part of her balked at being so distant toward him while allowing him to be of service to her.

"I'll probably be back before Tuesday."

Probably? She stopped messing with the material in her hand and stared at him, wondering if he might not come back at all. She couldn't deny that he had begun to matter a little, and that bothered her.

"I brought you something."

She took the package from his hand and peered inside. A used book. *The Hiding Place* by Corrie ten Boom. It seemed odd that she and Deborah had used the phrase *hiding place* when talking about Cara's anger with Trevor, and now he'd brought her a book with that title.

She read the back cover. He'd bought her a biography of a Holocaust survivor. She loved reading, but she hadn't read a biography since dropping out of high school.

"I bought it at a used bookstore a couple of miles from here. I gave your mom a copy for Christmas one year, and it became her favorite book. I'm not sure what happened to her copy."

"Did she love to read?"

"There isn't a word to describe how much she enjoyed it."

She opened the book. "Ephraim, Lori, and I love reading." Inside the front cover was a handwritten sentence. "Did you write this?"

"No. I didn't even see it there."

She ran her fingers over the cursive writing. *Never be afraid to trust an unknown future to a known God.*

Emotions rolled over her. "It's a saying of some sort." She passed him the book.

"That's a quote by Corrie ten Boom."

Never be afraid to trust an unknown future to a known God. "I like it."

"Good."

She skimmed through the book, catching just enough to know what she'd be doing tonight after everyone else went to bed. "Thank you."

He didn't answer, and she glanced up.

"Hello?" Jonathan called as he came in the front door. His almost white-blond hair looked like sunlight beaming under his hat, and his hazel eyes carried a gentle confidence. Deborah could look forever and not find a man better suited to her.

"Hey, Jon." Cara gestured from one man to the other. "Trevor, you remember Jonathan Stoltzfus. He and Deborah are courting."

"Yeah, he's been here several times while I was here," Trevor said. "Good to see you again."

Cara knew they'd met, but so many people came in and out of Ada's House that she didn't want to assume Trevor had everyone's names straight yet. "What are you doing here?" she asked Jonathan.

He peered into the other room. "Is it just us?"

"Yeah. Sorry. Deborah's making deliveries with Ada and Lori."

"Gut."

"Good?" She laughed. "That's a surprising answer. What's up?"

"I thought I had timed it right to miss her. I want you to come with me so I can show you something. I need your expertise."

"Mine? I know nothing about everything."

Jonathan chuckled. "Now that's just not true. You have great hunches and a good grasp of the big picture. Besides, you have Deborah pegged better than anyone else I know."

Cara found his opinion of her too lofty, but she lowered the needle into the cloth and released the presser foot. During one of her many sewing lessons, Ada had said that was the position to leave the machine in— the needle in a piece of cloth and the presser foot resting on it. "I'm game." She glanced at Trevor. "You?"

His eyes widened. "You're asking me to go too?"

She stood. "I am."

Trevor turned to Jonathan, wordlessly asking for his response.

"Ya, sure. I bet you know a thing or two about older homes."

Trevor pulled out his keys and dangled them. "Need a ride?"

Jonathan shook his head. "It's a stone's throw from here."

It surprised Cara how excited she was for Deborah. She hadn't realized it until now, but in some ways Deborah resided in her heart much as she imagined a sister would. "A house?"

He nodded. "I'm only checking into it right now. And I'd like to keep it a secret until I'm sure that it's the right house and that I qualify to buy it."

"Oh, Deborah's going to like the sound of that."

"Not a word, Cara. I know how you two stay up and talk half the night sometimes."

Cara made a zipping motion across her lips. A dreamlike feeling surrounded her. Before she landed in Dry Lake, she'd had only shards and fragments of relationships. But today with her *dad* beside her and her future brother-in-law inviting her to share in his excitement, she sensed a wholeness she'd never known before.

Aaron carried a fifty-pound bag of milk replacer into the calf barn and plunked it onto the ground. Trevor had already begun to muck out the stalls. Whatever the man was like at one time, he was now a hard worker. Aaron pulled at the nylon thread to break the bag's seal, but the cord broke instead.

"Here." Trevor hurried to him, reaching into his pocket. He pulled out a knife, whipped the blade open, and slit the bag.

"I need to get one of those."

Trevor smiled. "My beat-up old car and this knife are the only things I own that are of any use. It's a folding Buck with a lockback design." Trevor closed it with one move of his thumb. "Take a look."

Aaron held it. "It's got a nice weight to it."

"A man of means like you wouldn't have any trouble buying one of these."

Aaron passed it back. "I'll think about it."

It'd be rude to say he had less cash than Trevor. The man owned almost nothing, and the Blanks owned hundreds of acres, but they were up to their eyeballs in debt. However, people who lacked didn't want to be told how tight money was for a landowner with cattle, horses, crops, several carriages, and two houses.

"I could use a ride to Owl's Perch this weekend," Aaron said. "If I paid you, could you take me?"

"Actually, I was gonna ask for this weekend off."

"Oh, okay. I can get a ride elsewhere." Aaron had no idea if that was true, but it was the polite thing to say.

"Where's Owl's Perch?"

"Perry County, not far from Duncannon."

"I'm heading to New York on Saturday. I'd have to pass close to Owl's Perch. What time do you need to be there?"

"About two."

"Your dad and Sylvia doing the milking by themselves?"

"Ya. It was just the two of them for several months. They'll be okay."

"I can drop you off. But you'll have to figure out another way home." Trevor slid his knife into his pocket.

"So what's going on in New York?"

"Were you here when Cara arrived in Dry Lake?"

Aaron hated being reminded of all he didn't remember. "Technically, I'm sure I was."

Trevor filled the ten-ounce measuring cup with powdered milk and dumped it into a sterilized calving bottle. "Technically?"

Aaron turned on the warm water at the mud sink. "When you came here to ask for work, you said you're a recovered alcoholic."

"Yeah. Been sober nearly twelve years." He pointed at the bottle in Aaron's hand. "Uh, I wouldn't do that if I were you."

"I'm just preparing the bottles for the calves."

"Sylvia will want to feed them herself. I just get the bottles ready with powder and set them on the shelf." Trevor fixed a second bottle and put it on a shelf near the sink.

"Not today she won't. Mamm roped her into helping can corn and green beans." Aaron added two quarts of water to each bottle before turning off the water.

Trevor had been down the same rough road as Aaron and had been sober much longer. Aaron wanted any words of wisdom the man might have.

"I've been sober about six months."

Trevor moved to a fresh bale of hay and forked a hunk of it. "So you were here when Cara arrived more than a year ago…and yet you weren't."

Aaron put the nipples and rings on the bottles and shook them. "Pretty much. I don't remember her coming to the community, but at some point I heard Ephraim had been shunned concerning her."

"What'd he and Cara do that caused Ephraim to get shunned?"

Aaron moved to the calves' pens and stuck the first bottle through the gates. A calf latched on hungrily. "I heard she and Lori were living in a barn, social services came for them, and Ephraim stepped in and took them to his home. He was sleeping in his shop, but when the elders confronted him and told him to get her out of his house, he refused."

Trevor spread hay in the stall while the calves were occupied and out of the way. "I can see why Cara and Lori trust him so much."

"That's all I know, just stuff I heard. I have years that are a jumbled, fuzzy mess inside my head."

"Cara told me that when she moved away from New York, she left everything behind. I'm going to see if the apartment manager or a neighbor might've held on to anything of theirs. I'm hoping somebody kept photos and maybe some special knickknacks."

"Sounds like a nice gesture. Does she know?"

"I want to keep it a surprise. So how are you doing with your sobriety?"

"Still sober. Still tempted not to be."

"Trust me on this one thing, Aaron. It's a battle worth fighting every day and every night."

A calf nudged the bottle, trying to get more milk to flow, and Aaron almost lost his grip on it. "Cara must've been, what, sixteen or seventeen by the time you sobered up?"

"I lost contact with her when she was eight, but, yeah, I was sober before her seventeenth birthday."

"You lose a lot, don't you? Booze lures…and then destroys."

Trevor climbed out of the last stall. "It does that. But it ruins far more than just *your* life."

Aaron's heart thudded against his chest. He knew the truth of Trevor's words. "The possibility of taking up the drink again scares me."

"Good. Fear keeps us from sticking our hands into a fire, walking through briars barefoot, and all sorts of stupid stuff. When being afraid of it goes away, you'll likely think you can handle a drink or two or a night or two out drinking. Don't believe it. People like you and me can't ever afford to believe that." Trevor put the pitchfork away and began cleaning the mud sink. "Both of my parents drank, and I started young. My mom once said she put a tablespoon of whiskey in my baby bottle every night so I'd sleep. But I thought I'd gotten free of it by the time I turned eighteen. That's when I met Cara's mom."

Trevor's confession rolled over Aaron like a threshing machine.

The calves had drunk all the milk, and Aaron tossed the bottles into the sink.

Trevor turned on the water and began disassembling the milk jugs. "I drank most of Cara's childhood away, and she's got the scars to prove it. If you ever have a child, you'll know that the word *love* doesn't begin to cover how you feel about that little being." Trevor dipped his head. "Not that Cara would ever believe that, and who can blame her? There's not one shred of evidence that I ever cared. To rebuild a relationship, there's gotta be something you can point at and say, 'Remember when I helped you build this or helped you make a good grade on that or taught you to swim?' Something…anything."

Aaron's skin felt clammy. Trevor spoke of honest, giving, caring love—the kind that couldn't be his if he ever started drinking again.

Trevor turned off the water and set the bottles upside down in a rack to dry. "When Cara came along, her mom and I thought we'd hit the jackpot." Trevor pursed his lips and released a heavy breath. "Yes, sir, we thought our ship had come in, you know? She was just that precious to us."

"Can I ask what happened that started you drinking again?"

"We had some issues. Melinda's heart was still broken over another man when we married, and I wasn't sure if she loved me or was just a loyal woman. But I kept trying, and so did she. Bills were never ending, and I lost a couple of jobs. Between all those things and how I grew up, I carried the constant feeling of being worthless. But there were some great times in spite of the pressures. I finally got a job that really suited me—as a handyman at an apartment complex. It came with free rent and enough money so Melinda could stay home with Cara."

Trevor grabbed the bag of milk replacer and put it inside a huge wooden barrel. He put the lid on it and tapped it down, ensuring no mice could get to it. He seemed to be buying time so he could gather the strength to finish the story.

"One day while I was fixing a light fixture in another family's apartment, a toddler wandered into the room. He grabbed hold of my ladder, smiling up at me, and I didn't think nothing about it." Trevor wiped tears from his eyes. "Next thing I knew, my metal toolbox fell off the top rung of the ladder and hit that little boy on the head. He died almost immediately."

"And you couldn't cope with the guilt."

Trevor shook his head. "It destroyed me. I always knew I was of no account as a drunk. But when I saw that I was of no account when sober and doing my best, I lost all will to fight. Poor Melinda did everything to reach me and give me strength."

Tears ran down Trevor's face. He put his hand on Aaron's shoulder and cleared his throat. "Whatever you do, stay sober. All those years of drinking made everything a thousand times worse, and the people I loved paid the highest price." Trevor let go of him and walked out the back of the barn into the pasture.

Aaron whispered a prayer, asking God for the ability to hold on to Trevor's words. Surely the tragedy of Trevor's story would strengthen his own resolve to remain sober. Addiction didn't bow to logic. It didn't yield to a man's dreams. It never surrendered to anything easily, including the will. For him, it took a combination of tools: determination, patience, and, most of all, the ability to surrender to God while fighting his own instincts.

What Trevor had just given him, the viewpoint from the bottom, and what the Better Path gave him, the truth of his condition and a community of support, were about all an addict could hope for. And he was grateful for every bit of help.

Twenty-Four

Sylvia looked out the side window of Robbie's car and then at the invitation in her hand. Michael sat up front, talking to Robbie. Dora and she had said little since the ride began more than an hour ago.

According to the time specified for family and friends to arrive, they were a little late. Trevor had picked up Aaron about four hours ago. But she'd had to find a missing cow and her calf while Michael milked the herd, and then she had to shower and get ready.

"This is the Better Path?" Michael asked.

Robbie pointed to a shingle hanging from one side of the porch.

"It's a house," Dora said.

"Appears so."

Three horses with carriages were tied to nearby hitching posts. Sylvia was sure the sight of Old Order Amish buggies made Michael regret his decision to come. He didn't want other Plain folk to see him going into a place like the Better Path.

"I have to go into Harrisburg and run some errands for Ephraim," Robbie said. "I should be back about the time you're ready to leave here and go to the appliance store."

"We appreciate your driving us," Michael said.

"Ephraim's needed me to get to Harrisburg for nearly a month. It's working out just fine."

Sylvia got out of the car and climbed the wooden steps to the porch, trusting that the reluctant Michael and Dora Blank would follow her. The house looked historic, but it wasn't in need of paint or fixing up. The sign on the glass part of the door invited folks to enter, so she did.

She walked into a large room with wooden floors, a huge staircase, and lots of doors off to the sides. The room was filled with people holding small paper plates of food and clear plastic cups filled with ice water or soft drinks. The air-conditioned room felt marvelous. Nothing like a swelter-ing summer to make one appreciate places with electricity.

She held the door open for Michael and Dora as they trailed in.

She noticed photos of Mennonites hanging on the wall, and she could tell with one glance which sect each person belonged to. Outsiders often thought all Plain people dressed alike, but every Amish and Mennonite group had its own style of dress and head covering.

A young Mennonite woman walked toward them. "Hi." She smiled, welcoming them as if she was glad to see them regardless of who they were or why they'd come. "May I help you?"

"We're looking for Aaron Blank," Sylvia said.

"Well, you're in the right place." She motioned to a room off to the right. "I was just chatting with him. I'm Hannah Waddell."

"I'm Sylvia Fisher, and these are Aaron's parents, Michael and Dora."

"It's a pleasure to meet you." Hannah shook hands with each of them, then raised a finger, took a step back, and said, "Paul?"

She'd not said it loudly, but a man several feet away immediately looked at her. She smiled at him. He excused himself from the person he was talking with and headed straight for her.

"Paul, these are Aaron's parents, Michael and Dora, and a friend, Syl-via Fisher."

Paul shook Michael's hand, then Dora's, welcoming them. When he came to Sylvia, she said, "I don't think he'd say I'm a friend."

Michael frowned. "I thought you two were getting along."

Sylvia didn't know what to say to that. Aaron didn't snipe at her as much as at first, but they were in a tug of war over the farm's future. It was possible that Michael didn't realize he was the rope.

Paul glanced at Hannah, a warm smile passing between them before he returned his attention to the newcomers. "We're really glad you're here. Let's find Aaron and let him know. Then maybe we can all chat for a bit."

"I didn't come to talk," Michael said.

"What did bring you here?" Paul asked.

"Sylvia, mostly."

Paul shifted. "Aaron's quite a man, but the more support he has, the better he'll be at fighting the good fight."

A baffled look covered Michael's face, but he said nothing. Sylvia let Michael and Dora follow directly behind Paul, then fell into step after them. They walked into a room where there were twelve chairs arranged in a circle. Aaron was one of a half-dozen men sitting and talking.

"This is our group counseling room," Paul said. "Men and women come here to share their experiences—temptations, failures, and victories. Right now they're just visiting." Paul moved toward Aaron, with Michael and Dora right behind him. He touched Aaron on the shoulder.

The initial shock on Aaron's face soon turned into a smile. He stood. "I didn't think you were coming."

Dora hugged him, whispering something Sylvia couldn't hear.

Michael backed away, clearly indicating that he didn't want to be embraced. He nodded at Sylvia. "This was her idea."

Aaron's eyes met hers. "Why?"

She glanced at his parents before shrugging.

"Why don't you help yourself to some food and look around?" Paul said. "Then we'll all go someplace where we can talk more privately."

Hannah directed Michael and Dora to a table spread with snacks, but Sylvia hung back. Paul was talking to Aaron, and when he turned to face her, she smiled briefly and went to the far end of the room. She looked out the window. This was someone's farm at one time, and the rolling hills and pastures were gorgeous.

"I don't understand you," Aaron said, startling her. "If fences are mended between my parents and me, that will make it easier to convince them to move."

"Some things are bigger than you and me and that farm."

"Why, Sylvia Fisher, I do believe you've committed blasphemy." Standing there grinning, he—with his broad, powerful shoulders—demanded her attention. "Would you like a tour?"

She didn't regret coming or pushing Dora and Michael to do so, but she felt confused by the emotions Aaron unearthed. "No, thanks. I'm fine right here."

He took her by the hand. "Kumm."

The warmth and power and gentleness of his grip confused her even more. When they were outside, she pulled her hand free. They walked the grounds, and he showed her what he called the dorm rooms. Then they toured the stables before taking a seat at a picnic table.

"If it won't bother you," Aaron said, "I'd like to ask Mamm and Daed to go by the appliance store while they're this close."

"That was Michael's plan from the start."

"He said as much?"

"Ya, but I wouldn't put too much stock in it. We're in the area, so it makes sense."

"I take it that going there wasn't your idea."

"I bet it smells of rubber and grease and diesel fuel." She wrinkled her nose. "I'll feel sick at my stomach before we're through."

"This from a girl who drinks her coffee while milking cows."

"It's true. I'll feel closed in, like I can't breathe."

"Good grief. There are windows."

He seemed to think she was kidding. But being in a store often gave her a headache. Maybe it was the dyes or fumes that emanated from the items. "I'm not saying my reaction isn't weird, but I always feel that way in a store. Nauseated and suffocated."

He laughed. "You're serious, aren't you?"

"Very."

Michael and Dora came outside, each with a plate and drink in hand. Michael sat next to Aaron. "This place isn't at all what I thought it would be. I expected something like a hospital but a lot dirtier."

"I wrote about the Better Path in my letters, describing it. It's a clinic that does its best to meet the needs of the Plain community—mental and physical."

"And the problem you deal with—is it mental or physical?"

"It's sort of both. Alcohol is habit-forming both physically and psychologically. I'm sure Paul can explain it better."

"But you knew it was wrong when you began."

"I didn't get into it or out of it because it was *wrong*. Black-and-white reasoning may work for you, but it doesn't for me. Drinking brought relief, but I had to get out because the escape turned into a nightmare."

"So what happens when you want relief again?"

"I'll take a vacation."

Michael set his sandwich on his plate. "Be serious, Aaron."

"I hit bottom, Daed. And while I was there, I found God. There's power between Him and me, and I rely on that. Even so, I can't promise I'll never mess up. I can assure you that if I do, I won't waste any time getting help."

"I'm supposed to trust that's enough?"

"No. I can't live up to your expectations. But you're supposed to trust that God is enough. That no matter what else happens, He's sufficient to forgive and strengthen."

"I guess when we go to talk to Paul, I'll be blamed for lots of stuff."

"That's not what we do here." Aaron grabbed a potato chip from his mother's plate and munched on it. "Not long after I began rehab, I saw myself through God's eyes, or at least a little of how He sees me, and the power of His love compared with the ugliness of who I'd become changed me. Then I saw what I'd done to you and Mamm through your eyes, and I came home to try to make amends. That's what Paul will do—help you see me from a different perspective than your usual disappointment and anger."

"I don't—" Michael's growl was interrupted when Paul came to the table.

"Would you rather meet out here or in my office?" Paul asked. "It won't be long—maybe fifteen, thirty minutes."

Everyone looked to Michael for an answer, but he said nothing.

Sylvia stood. "Either way, this chat needs to be between Aaron and his parents."

"She's right." Michael stood. "In your office."

Sylvia glanced at Aaron, who gave her a slight smile before the four of them left.

Michael was talking about what had brought Aaron here. That was good. She wanted to be glad only for Aaron's sake, but somehow whatever mattered to him mattered to her too.

Her interest didn't stop at the normal kindness extended from one human to another. She cared for him. She liked who he was and who he'd chosen to be.

And it had her rattled.

Twenty-Five

Cara sat on the couch reading *The Hiding Place*. It had been her constant companion for days, and whenever she had a few minutes, she read more of it. She'd never loved a book this much. She read and prayed and then read some more. This Corrie ten Boom had a handle on how to walk in forgiveness, and Cara had benefitted from reading her story.

"Hey, Mom." Lori ran into the living room and held out the familiar gray blue hardback of *Shoo-Fly Girl*. "Time for you to read to me! We're almost to the end of the book."

"Yeah, for the umpteenth time this summer."

"Please finish it for me again."

Cara set her book to the side and tapped her own cheek. Lori kissed her several times before Cara engulfed her daughter in a hug. "Love you, Lorabean."

"Love you too, Mom."

Lori snuggled against her. The heat didn't matter. Cara had her daughter in her arms, and she'd never mind that, no matter how high the mid-July temperatures soared. Per her daughter's request, they had on matching dresses. Better Days lay on the wood floor, panting.

Later in the day customers would begin arriving at Ada's House, but for now dinner, which for the Amish was the largest meal of the day, regardless of when it was served, was done. The kitchen was clean, and all sorts of baked goods and handmade items were ready to be sold. Since

Trevor wasn't here to take her to see Sylvia, she'd studied the languages on her own that day. At the thought of how well she was learning of late, joy bubbled up inside her.

She opened the book Ada had given Lori and continued reading *Shoo-Fly Girl* aloud. At the end of the last chapter, she bent her head to kiss her daughter's forehead and discovered that Lori had twisted the strings of their prayer Kapps together.

Cara looked up and was surprised to see Ephraim standing there, quietly watching them. Better Days stood next to him, nudging his hand for attention. Cara gently bumped Lori's shoulder, getting her to look up.

"'From!" Lori tried to run to him, but their intertwined prayer Kapp strings stopped her.

"Ow!" Cara yelped and quickly unraveled them.

The moment Lori was loose, she ran to Ephraim. He picked her up and hugged her.

Cara rubbed her scalp where the head covering had been attached to strands of her hair with a straight pin. Those pins kept the Kapp on no matter the work or the weather, but *ouch*.

Lori clasped her arms tight around Ephraim's neck and kissed his cheek before hopping down.

Ephraim embraced Cara and took in a deep breath. "My favorite part of the week."

"Tuesdays?" Lori asked.

"No." He touched her on the nose. "Anytime I'm with my two favorite people."

"What are you doing here in the middle of the week?" Cara asked.

"My sister called me at the shop about an hour ago. Said she had news she wanted to tell both of us and asked if I'd come. So I dropped everything and had Robbie drive me."

Cara slid her hand into his. "Would you like some lemonade while we wait for Deborah?"

"Anything cool in this heat would be great."

Cara led him through the hallway.

Ephraim held Lori's hand too. "You don't seem very surprised that Deborah has news for us."

Cara shrugged. "Nope."

"Is it what I think it is?"

"You can't ask me that."

"Sure I can. Listen carefully. Is it what I think it is?"

She chuckled, opening the swinging door to the kitchen without answering his question.

Ada stood at an ironing board, carefully easing a flat iron over a prayer Kapp. "Hi, Ephraim. This is a nice surprise."

"I need to show up unexpectedly more often," he said, smiling.

"You do that." Cara grabbed a glass for him from a cabinet. "Of course, you know that after a couple of times it won't be unexpected anymore." She poured a glass of lemonade and gave it to him.

"Hello?" Deborah called from the front door.

Ada put the iron facedown on the stove. "In the kitchen."

Deborah and Jonathan entered, hand in hand and glowing. "We have news to share." Deborah stared at Jonathan, radiating love. "Jonathan has asked me to marry him."

"And she said yes," Jonathan added.

Chatter filled the room as hugs were exchanged. Then Deborah paused in front of her brother.

"Ya," Ephraim whispered. "Totally, one hundred percent."

Deborah hugged him.

Cara would have to learn the history behind that conversation later.

"But that's not all," Deborah said to the room at large. "Ada, I know you wanted us to move in here, but he's buying us a house."

"As long as you're happy, Deborah."

Cara knew Ada's words were true, but she also had to be disappointed.

Cara would move to Dry Lake once she and Ephraim married, and now Deborah was moving. But Ada adapted to the changes as a mother would, even though neither Cara nor Deborah was her daughter. Whatever aches Ada felt didn't match the joy of seeing her "children" happy.

"Do you want to see it?" Deborah asked.

Ada moved the iron to the cooling shelf on the back of the stove. "Absolutely. Is there time to get there and back before we open for business tonight?"

Jonathan rubbed his chin. "Hmm. I'm not sure. I say we give it a try and see."

Ada moved directly in front of her nephew. "What's this smirk on your face?"

"We're buying the house next door."

Ada's eyes grew large. "What?"

He leaned against the countertop. "You two are in business together here, so it made sense. But if you prefer, I suppose I could buy a place in Dry Lake."

Ada pushed his shoulder. "Don't you dare." She hugged him. "Which one is it?"

Deborah took Ada by the hand and headed for the front door with the rest of the group following.

Cara couldn't help but think about what God had given Ada through the love between her and Deborah. Ada had lost her husband more than a decade ago, and her only child had left last year, cutting her off from him. When Deborah and Jonathan had children, Ada would be able to live out her days as if she were their grandmother.

The beauty of it awed her. Heartache stomped its way into everyone's life, but it seemed that love never stopped planting seeds or harvesting crops.

And forgiveness. The thought came to her as if it wasn't her own. But it made sense that forgiveness had to be planted in the midst of hurt. Since Trevor had given her *The Hiding Place,* she'd been praying almost constantly about forgiving him. If Corrie ten Boom could forgive the Nazi soldiers and prison guards who had so severely mistreated her and her sister during the Holocaust, surely Cara could manage to forgive Trevor.

"Look!" Deborah pointed to the house across the empty lot to the right.

Ada's eyes grew large. "You wouldn't tease an old woman."

"I just might," Jonathan said, "if I saw one."

"It gets better." Deborah tugged at Ada's hand, and they all headed down the sidewalk toward the house. "It seems my husband-to-be has bought half of the land we've been renting for the corn maze, picnic tables, and hayrides."

"I had no idea you were rich," Ada teased.

Jonathan laughed. "Far from it. But I've been pinching pennies ever since I finished school and started working full time. With the money I had, I made a down payment and signed a contract for a small mortgage. And it was all worth it when I saw the look on Deborah's face."

Deborah held open the door, motioning for everyone to walk through. The conversations echoing through the house felt warm and rich to Cara's mind and soul. She held Ephraim's hand as they made the tour, soaking in being part of a family. Lori ran up and down the steps half a dozen times.

The property even had an outbuilding that Jonathan could convert into a smithy shop. A day or two a week he'd still put all his blacksmith equipment in his work wagon and travel to Amish farms to shoe horses, but he'd work out of this shop the rest of the time.

After walking through the house, talking about possibilities, hopes of babies, and an extension of space to Ada's House, they started the trek back.

While going up the front walk at Ada's, Cara spotted Trevor sitting on the porch steps. A small box sat beside him. The sight of him didn't bring up hurtful images and stored resentment nearly as much as it had a few weeks earlier.

"Lori," Cara whispered, "go tell Trevor about Deborah's good news."

Lori stared up at her mom before looking to Ephraim.

"I think that's a good idea," he said.

Lori shrugged. "If you say so." She ran ahead. "Hey, Trevor, guess what?"

A rare but warm smile crossed his face. "Hmm... It's cold in Antarctica?"

"No, silly. Deborah's gonna marry Jonathan and live right there." She pointed.

The smile on Trevor's face broadened. Lori had talked to him the way she did to everyone else. He looked at the newly engaged couple. "Congratulations."

Ada, Deborah, and Jonathan chatted with him briefly before going inside. Lori went in with Deborah, prattling the whole time about having a sleepover at Deborah's house one day.

"Trevor,"—Cara motioned toward the house—"care for some lemonade?"

"Not right now. I brought you something."

"You don't need to keep doing that. Besides, I haven't finished the book you already brought me. It's really good, though."

He picked up the open corrugated box and held it out to her.

Ephraim leaned in. "Looks interesting."

Cara took the box from Trevor, walked inside, and set it on a side table. Familiar frames filled with family photos startled her. "Where did you get these?"

"I went to your old apartment building and talked to the manager. He looked up which place had been yours, and he knew who'd rummaged through your stuff before he threw it out."

She studied the images, glad to have them again in her hands, but at what cost? "You shouldn't have."

"It's not that big a deal," Trevor assured her. "New York's less than five hours from here."

She couldn't believe he'd done this for her, but fear threatened to seep out from under locked doors. She looked at more of the pictures. "Who had these?"

"A woman named Agatha Brown. She said she used to baby-sit Lori sometimes."

"Yes, she did." Cara pulled out the last frame, which held a picture of Johnny, Cara, and Lori as a toddler. She showed it to Ephraim, and when his eyes met hers, she wished he could see through them and into her mind to understand the concern building inside her.

He took the picture. "Trevor, did anyone ask you about where Cara is living now?"

"Mrs. Brown did. She wanted to hear all about Cara and Lori."

"She's the only one?" Ephraim asked.

"Yeah, why?"

"A man from Cara's days in foster care used to stalk and threaten her. That's why she left New York with nothing and lived in my barn for a while."

"I…I'm sorry." Deep hurt mirrored in Trevor's face. "But, Cara, honey, it's one of the largest cities in the world, and I was in your building for only a couple of hours. No one but the manager and Mrs. Brown knew I was there. Besides, surely that fella has lost track of you by now and probably lost interest."

Trevor made sense, and her fear retreated. "You're right." She looked at the back of a frame. "I need a screwdriver or butter knife."

Trevor pulled a knife out of his pocket and popped open the blade before she could blink. "I can use the blunt side of this to push those clasps out of the way. But why do you want to?"

"I never had enough frames, so I stashed older pictures behind newer ones. I put duplicates there too."

He took the back off the frame and pulled out two hidden photos.

Cara held up two pictures with Johnny in them—one when Lori was a newborn and one when she was almost two.

"You're pleased?" Trevor studied her.

"I am. Look." She moved closer to Ephraim, pointing out a stuffed puppy in Lori's hand that looked very similar to Better Days.

Her stalker, Mike, had done so much damage that it was natural to feel overwhelmed at just the thought of him, but Trevor was right. She had nothing to fear, and he'd done something for her no one else could—driven to New York on his own, found her old apartment building, and brought Lori pictures of her father.

She should hug him and really thank him, but she couldn't make herself go that far.

"Come on." She motioned to Trevor. "Let's show these to Lori."

Twenty-Six

Aaron closed the pliers over the loose strand of barbed wire and twisted the metal around and around, tightening it. More than a thousand feet of fence ran behind and ahead of him. It had taken him two days, but he'd almost finished repairing the half mile of fence line. A horse stood nearby, hitched to a work wagon loaded with topsoil. Sweat trickled down his face and neck as he used all his strength to tighten the eight feet of thick wire from one fence post to the next. His arms shook with weariness, and his legs felt weak.

He jerked the post back and forth to test it. It held tight, so it didn't need fresh dirt packed around it. He withdrew a pad of paper and a stubby pencil from his pants pocket and jotted a note.

Farming wasn't as miserable when he knew other people were on the property, helping him keep up. He stood straight, working the kinks out of his back.

Seeing Sylvi cross the field toward him caused his insides to do a little jig. It was a beautiful sight to behold—a dark-haired woman in a purple dress walking across green pastures. She held two half-gallon thermoses in her hands, but as thirsty as he was physically, he was thirstier for a conversation with her.

Aaron moved to the next fence post.

Sylvia had done more than dismantle the walls he'd tried to build between them; he found himself wishing she'd go with them when this place sold. Not that his Daed had agreed to sell yet, but he was moving in the right direction. Ten days had passed since Sylvia and his parents had gone to the Better Path and then to the appliance store. Aaron couldn't control how he felt about Sylvia any more than he'd been able to control his desire for alcohol. Terrifying situation, really.

"Hey, Sylvi." He clamped the pliers onto the wire. "Mamm too tired to walk this field again?"

She came to a halt near him. "No."

He exerted muscle power to twist the wire, which was what Sylvia did to his insides with no effort at all. Her presence had him curious, though. She usually didn't bring him drinks or food unless Mamm couldn't do so.

Sylvi set one thermos on the ground and opened the spout on the other. She held the jug out to him.

He shoved the pliers into his tool belt, removed his work gloves, and took the thermos. The icy water tasted wonderful as it cooled his whole body. He wiped his mouth with the back of his hand. "What's up?"

She got the large tin bowl out of the wagon. "Remember the favor you said you'd do for me if I'd go to church without arguing?"

"Is it finally time for it?"

"Ya." She filled the bowl with water from the other thermos.

"So what can I do for you?"

She walked to the horse and set the bowl of water in front of it. "There's a farming issue."

"There are hundreds of farming issues. You only earned one favor."

Technically he owed her far more than that, but he'd rather not admit it openly.

The lines of tension in her face didn't fade even a little as he teased her. She walked over to the back of the wagon and sat on the tailgate. "Men never want to talk to a girl about farming."

The embarrassment on her face bothered him. She was smart enough to understand whatever the issue was, even though no one had taught her the financial ins and outs of farming. It angered him that someone had treated her as if her opinion didn't matter.

"What's the problem?" He removed his tool belt, put it on the tailgate, and sat beside her.

"Some men from the EPA showed up about twenty minutes ago."

What little energy he had left drained from him. He'd heard stories of government agencies stopping by farms to enforce new regulations. "Someone from the Environmental Protection Agency is here?"

"Something about the fence lines along the creek banks being in the wrong place."

The thought of moving all the fencing along the waterway made him want to crawl into a hole. "Where are these men?"

"They're driving along the fence line in their truck. I asked Michael to have them start in the east field so I'd have time to talk to you."

He liked having her respect, though he longed to rail against the futile pursuit of farming. "So what's the favor, Sylvi?"

Her brows knit and her eyes searched his, looking as if she thought her request had been clear. "To listen as if you have my heart for the farm and then help me understand what the problem is and how it can be fixed."

He heard the fear in her voice. If she had no understanding of the problem, she had no chance of finding a solution. And he realized afresh how much she loved this place.

Sylvia kept searching the horizon. "There are the men from the EPA." She pointed to a knoll a couple hundred feet away.

He looked across the field and saw a truck headed their way. He dreaded the two possibilities that could come out of this conversation— the work it would cause him or the standoff it would bring between him and this branch of government.

"I'll go see if your Mamm needs anything." She took the jug from him. "Will you come to the house to talk to me after they're gone?"

"No." He pulled a handkerchief out of his pocket.

"Why?"

He removed his hat and wiped sweat from his forehead and the rim of his hat. "You're not going to the house. You're staying right here."

Her eyes met his, and a smile lifted her face.

The truck came to a stop, and two men got out.

Aaron put on his hat and looked at Sylvia. "If you have a question, ask it."

They hopped off the tailgate.

"Aaron Blank?" one man said.

"Ya?"

The men stepped over clods of uneven ground. "I'm Dusty Randall." Aaron shook his hand. "This is Brian Clayton. We're with the Environmental Protection Agency. We understand you run this farm."

"About half of it, actually. This is Sylvia Fisher. She runs the other half."

Randall blinked. "Oh. I owe you an apology then." He held out his hand to Sylvia. "I didn't realize… Mr. Blank said I needed to talk to his son."

Sylvia didn't say a word as she shook his hand.

"What's the problem?" Aaron asked.

"You're in violation of federal regulations. Someone from the EPA came through here years ago and explained to all the farmers the regulations concerning fence lines and fresh waterways. According to my records this farm wasn't in operation at the time. The sale of it to your father and his reestablishing it as a working dairy farm flew under our radar. We're not sure how that happened, but we're here to work with you to fix the problem."

Randall began explaining about the Clean Water Act and the laws that governed where fences could and couldn't be put and where animals could and couldn't trod or graze. He pulled out a stack of papers stapled together. "There's more information in here, but the bottom line is, we need to get these fences moved as quickly as possible. You can keep the old fences up for property-line purposes, but the new fence has to keep the cows a hundred feet from the creek."

"A hundred feet." Aaron mentally calculated how many hours of work it would take, how many miles of fence line would have to be moved, and how many acres of grazing land he'd lose. "What about the pasture on the other side of the creek? How are the cows supposed to get to that land to graze on it?"

"A culvert will need to be built, and the fence will attach to the railings so the cattle can't get to the water."

Aaron moaned. Did these men have any idea the amount of work and money it would take to build a cattle crossing of that type? "Then we have to find a new way for the cows to get water."

"We'll help you as much as we can."

"How?" Sylvia asked.

"When the paperwork's all filled out, you should qualify for a grant."

Sylvia stepped forward. "What's a grant?"

"It's money given by the federal government for a specific purpose. It's not a loan. If you qualify, the money must be used for its intended purpose, but you won't have to pay it back. Our help is part of the package deal. We'll bring in the manpower and the machines to dig the postholes, place the concrete or metal culvert, and run some or all of the line. You can get your own supplies with the grant money, or we can provide them. You can be here directing or leave it all up to us. If you don't feel you can accept a government grant to help offset the costs, you don't have to. You have the right to do it however you want. If you do it on your own, you'll have ninety days to comply. If you want our help, it'll have to be done in thirty days. We have other projects on the schedule after that." Randall passed Aaron the stapled papers.

Aaron looked at the fat stack. "What's this?"

"Details outlining regulations and offering solutions. This farm is clearly struggling with outdated equipment. A modern system that helps handle waste management would make your days much easier and protect the environment too." He turned to the other man. "Would you get him an information packet?"

Clayton grabbed a thick manila envelope out of the truck and handed it to Aaron.

"Everything you need to know is in there," Randall said.

"Excuse me," Sylvia said. "Will moving the fence fix all the problems?"

Randall drew a deep breath. "There could be penalties for the years of violation. Either you or your father might need to go before a board and explain why you weren't compliant to the laws."

"How stiff a penalty?" Sylvia asked.

"Hard to say. The regulations take into account the number of cows and each day you've been in violation."

Her face went ashen. "A penalty for each day, and it's been years?"

If she'd seen farming through rose-colored glasses before coming to the Blank farm, those glasses were being ripped off her face. That wasn't a bad thing, but Aaron wished the men would leave and give her a chance to absorb the news.

"We'll need time to read this information and think about what we're going to do," he said.

"Sure." Randall pulled a phone out of his pocket. "Today's July 24. Allowing time for all the work you do, it'll probably take you close to a week to read through everything and fill out the necessary forms, so I'll be back out July 30. But, like I said, if you want our help, we only have thirty

days from today to resolve this issue. And the sooner you show coopera-
tion, the better the penalty assessment will go."

"I understand."

The men climbed into their truck and drove off.

Sylvia eased onto the tailgate. "How could we farm all this time and
not know about this regulation?"

"I'm sure the answer to that is in here." Aaron tapped the stack of
papers.

"Has anything like this happened before?"

"No. Usually there's no grant money to help out. This could be easier
to deal with than most of the problems that come up on a farm."

"If we qualify, will Michael accept money from the government?"

"I don't know. Taking government money isn't a comfortable position
to be in. I'm not even sure how I feel about it. Are you?"

She shook her head. "No."

"Whatever is decided about the grant money, the fences have to be
moved. This place can't be sold as a working farm if it's not in line with
federal regulations. To get around that issue, we'd have to sell the herd,
and I'd have to drop the price so low we couldn't pay off the mortgage."

He expected her to tell him she needed the fence moved in order to
keep the feds from shutting down their operation, but she said nothing as
she walked to the spot where she'd left the thermoses, gathered them, and
put them in the wagon.

"I'm heading back," she said.

Watching her strength evaporate was more than he could stand. She
took the horse's water bowl and dumped the remaining contents on the
ground. Tears welled in her eyes. He didn't know what to say. She'd taken
a hard hit. Why did he feel as if he'd been the one to issue the blow?

"How about I give you a lift back to your place or the barn?"

Passing him the bowl, she offered a tender smile. "I'll walk. Denki."

He fought the temptation to offer comfort or put his hand on her shoulder. The lesson had to be learned, and softening it for her would be a lie. She slowly made her way across the field. Why did this godforsaken money pit matter to her so much anyway?

Seeing her now was like watching someone drown, and he could do nothing about it.

Could he?

Twenty-Seven

Lena stood at the counter of the doctor's office, paying her bill. Dr. Stone had removed her cast and kept her medical boot. Her arm tingled a bit, especially her fingertips, but mostly it just felt weird not to be wearing a cast. The doctor had said she was doing really well but that the damage to her arm had been extensive. He'd lined up months of physical therapy.

She'd hoped her hand and arm would be completely healed by now. But considering that Dwayne's goal had been to kill her, she was beyond grateful.

Just as she reached the exit, a man opened the door for her from the outside. When she looked up to thank him, she saw Grey wearing a knowing smile.

"I spotted your horse and rig when I pulled in and wondered if I'd catch you. I see the cast is off."

Lena held up her hand and wiggled her fingers. "Ya."

He gestured toward her carriage.

She went to the hitching post and untied her horse. "Today's the day you find out what the test results were?"

"It is. Dr. Stone agreed to examine the genetic specialist's reports and interpret them for me."

A nervous shiver ran through her as she stood at the hitching post, playing with the leather strip she'd used to tether the horse. "Good. I'm glad. This has bothered you long enough."

"It could bother me even more before it's all over. I didn't sleep well last night."

"It's a weighty thing." She wouldn't tell him she'd lost sleep over it too. "Do you know how much I'm looking forward to our years together? Whatever you find out in there does not change that." She opened and closed her hand, trying to rid it of the tingly feeling.

"Do your fingers feel funny?"

"Ya. Dr. Stone said the stinging and numbness should go away over the next few weeks. I begin physical therapy tomorrow. But I can't wait to get my gloveless hand in potting soil."

"I think you simply like to play in the dirt, Lennie."

"Remember when we booby-trapped the door to my greenhouse?"

Grey laughed at the reminder of the time they'd placed a bucket of soil on top of the doorjamb. "The look on your Daed's face when all that dirt landed on him was priceless."

"And as soon as Daed was gone, we reset the trap, remember? But my brother still didn't come through the door. However, the very expectant preacher's wife did."

Grey rubbed his chest, a gesture she'd come to understand in the last few months that meant a heaviness was lifting from him. "She didn't appreciate your joke one bit."

"Oh, *my* joke, was it? May I remind you I was only nine, and you were a savvy fourteen-year-old?"

"Ya, that's it. I was savvy." His laughter slowed, and he studied her, his eyes radiating affection. "And the community wonders why all your girl-friends started pulling stunts on each other. I knew why the first time I heard about one of those tricks."

"You never told on me." She went to her carriage and got in. "We'll be fine no matter what the results are. Although I do have concerns for the rest of the community."

"You're something else."

She winked at him. "Don't you forget it, or you'll find yourself on my hit list."

"I won't forget." He held up his hand as if taking an oath. "Is there any way we can talk once I'm done in there?"

"Jonathan asked me to meet him at Ada's after my appointment here. Since you're so close to Hope Crossing, why not go there when you're done? So many Amish come in and out that no one will think anything of your dropping by."

"We might not have much privacy, but I'll come by when I'm done here."

Lena pulled onto the main road, praying for God's mercy over their future.

Cara put the photo of Lori's dad, Lori, and her into a frame she'd bought at a consignment shop downtown. Her daughter had carried the picture around for weeks with no signs of losing interest, so Cara had no other option. If she didn't frame it, Lori was going to ruin it.

She ran her fingertips across the cool, metal frame. It was hard to imagine ever having been the woman in that photo.

The stairs moaned softly as someone walked up them.

Ada stopped at Lori's bedroom door and then came and sat beside Cara. "He looks like a good man."

"When I met him, he gave me something I'd spent years looking for: protection from Mike. Did you know that's what brought us together?"

"No. You've never talked with me about it."

"I was a waitress in the diner he managed, and when he caught wind of what Mike was doing, Johnny had no qualms about killing the man, if necessary, to protect me." Cara set the frame on Lori's nightstand. "When I think about all that God has done to protect me rather than about the hardships, I see everything differently. Even my landing here is because Mike was relentless."

"God used that man's evil intent for good."

"Does He do that?"

"Ya. The first mention of it is in Genesis, when Joseph's brothers sold him into slavery. Keep your eye out for it in the New Testament. Over and over again, evil men heaped unspeakable torment on good people, and God brought good out of it. All those men who hung Jesus on the cross meant it for evil too."

"Deborah?" came a voice from outside the room.

"That's Lena." Ada went to the door and called, "She's not here at the moment. I'll be right down."

The pitter-patter of Lori's feet echoed through the old house as she ran from the kitchen to the foyer to welcome Lena. Ada dusted off her apron and ran her fingers roughly over her cheeks to give them color.

Cara straightened Lori's bed. "Why do I get the idea you're hopeful that Lena's handsome Daed is with her?"

Ada grinned. "I have no idea."

"You really like Israel, don't you?"

Ada grew serious. "Tell me one thing not to like about him."

"Well, if he's not here, you won't like that about him."

"True enough."

They both walked down the steps to greet Lena. Ada stepped into the foyer first. "Deborah's out with Jonathan, having a bit of lunch."

"Guess I'll wait," Lena said. "I'm supposed to meet him here."

"Is your Daed with you?" Cara asked.

"Not today. I came here from Dr. Stone's." Lena held up her cast-free hand.

Ada gasped. "Well, look at you. I didn't even notice."

"Her mind was elsewhere," Cara teased.

"Shush now, Cara, or I'll put you to work."

"And that's different how?"

Ada laughed. "It's not, but it sounds tough. Lena, how about some lemonade?"

Lena sat on the steps of Ada's front porch, waiting for Jonathan. Lori sat beside her and peppered her with questions about the Amish school in Dry Lake. Cara and Ada were in one of the porch swings. But the picturesque image of good friends gathered on a peaceful summer's day drinking homemade lemonade didn't line up with the concern beating out a strong rhythm inside her chest.

Grey's tests had been bothering her more than she'd expected, and right now her mouth remained dry no matter how many sips she took of her drink.

"Lena Kauffman." Jonathan appeared from nowhere. His grin made her jump to her feet and scurry toward him. He met her halfway up the sidewalk and embraced her. "My goodness, I don't see enough of you anymore."

She squeezed him tight. "Well, that happens when a girl's best guy friend gets a girlfriend."

He backed away. "Look at you! No cast. No medical boot. And no limp."

She held out her hands and turned around. Jonathan applauded as she finished her full circle.

Deborah stepped in front of Jonathan and gave Lena a hug. "You look healthy and perfect."

"Well, the healthy part I'll believe. Where have you two been?"

"We found a little place to have lunch," Jonathan said. "I want to show it to you."

"Now? You can't be hungry again."

"Kumm." Jonathan bent his arm at the elbow and held it out to her. She looped her hand around his arm, and they began walking.

Lena paused. "Deborah, aren't you coming?"

"You two go. He wanted to visit with you alone for a bit, and if I go, I'll talk the whole time."

They hadn't walked more than thirty steps when he stopped. "We're at our destination. What do you think?" He waved toward the house.

A well-kept Victorian home stared back at her. "Oh no, you did not."

"Oh yes I did." Jonathan took her on a tour of the house. "It was built in the mid-eighteen hundreds, and it needs work on the inside, but Deborah and I love it." He told her of their plans and how he'd proposed. She adored seeing him completely happy.

He'd been in love with Deborah for years. He'd courted other women while Deborah planned to marry Mahlon, but tears welled in Lena's eyes when she thought of how patient and hopeful he'd remained. Even in the face of apparent defeat, he'd waited without complaint to see if God would give him a chance with Deborah.

"Hey," Jonathan scolded her. "There are no tears allowed over this."

Years of memories of their friendship and his loneliness for Deborah melted her, and a sob escaped.

"Okay then," he growled. "Cry like a girl." He hugged her. "I knew no one would understand what this means to me like you would. Now all we have to do is find the right person for you."

She wiped her face and touched her lips with her index finger. "I do have someone."

"Who?"

She heard Deborah's voice and went to a window. Deborah and Grey were walking toward the house. "It's Grey."

Jonathan grinned. "I should have known. You two will be good for each other. How long will you wait to court openly?"

"October, probably the middle of the month. I...I need a few minutes to talk to him if you could help manage it."

"You got it."

Deborah walked inside. "I gave you twice the amount of time you asked for. Was it enough?"

Grey followed her in.

"Perfect timing," Lena said.

Jonathan pulled out his pocket watch. "Deborah, did you finish making that batch of cookies you promised Ada?"

"No, but she won't mind."

Jonathan slid his watch back into his pocket. "And when Lori notices you didn't keep your word, what will you tell her?"

Deborah made a face and gave Lena another hug. "I gotta go. You two finish showing Grey the house."

"Lena, I want to go with Deborah." Jonathan pulled out a key and passed it to her. "Lock up when you leave."

"Not a problem."

Deborah and Jonathan walked hand in hand out the door and down the sidewalk.

Grey removed his hat and hung it on the newel post of the banister. Lena waited, hoping for good news, but unwilling to ask. The empty old house was too quiet. Not even a clock ticked.

He looked deep into her eyes. "The subject of chromosomal issues is a complicated one, and I'm sure I won't use all the right jargon, but according to Dr. Stone, the test results indicate I don't have any of the issues he was concerned about. The specialist only tested for certain hereditary issues, but he saw nothing that would cause deformities of any kind."

Unable to speak, Lena straightened his already straight collar. He drew her hand to his lips and kissed it.

"You're finally free." She wrapped her arms around him and laid her head on his chest. Relief and expectation over their future wrapped around her as they stood in this unfamiliar home that she knew they'd visit for decades to come.

Twenty-Eight

Aaron sat at the kitchen table reading the documents the EPA men had left. He'd begun right after lunchtime. Now supper was over. The cows were milked—no thanks to him. And Sylvi and Trevor were probably done bottle-feeding the calves. Yet the pages about government regulations, grants, and teamwork between farmers and the EPA went on and on.

He'd thought some of those self-help books that were required reading at the Better Path were dry. This stuff was so parched it could make a person die of thirst while sitting in a pool of spring water. But as he read, he realized there might be ways to get the much-needed help for this farm, the one-time boost that Sylvia had asked him about. The thought made him queasy, yet he intended to share the idea with her, not just because it was the right thing to do, but also because he wanted to quiet her fears. To see her excited.

When he heard a car pull up to the house, he headed for the door, glad for the interruption. As Frani got out of her car, he walked down the steps to her.

"You know how I kept telling you my folks weren't willing to help me?" Frani asked.

"Ya."

She leaned against the car. "You've made your bed, now you can lie in it," she mimicked, wagging her finger.

He laughed. "Sounds familiar."

"Well, they made a deal with me."

"What kind of deal?"

She rolled her eyes and sighed. "Said they'd help me in all sorts of ways if I agreed to go to rehab. Even offered to keep AJ while I'm there."

"And?" He waited.

"I'm going."

"Frani, that's great." He hugged her. "You won't regret it."

She grabbed his shirt and held him tight. "I can't believe how scared I am. What if I mess this up like I have everything else?"

He backed away, wishing he knew the right thing to say. "Make sure you don't. You have to fight for yourself and for AJ. Where are you going?"

"Some place in Baltimore that Mom knows about and trusts. My parents said if I come home clean, I can move back in. Like I'm looking forward to that. But if you can stand it, I can. I might even go back to school." Her cell phone rang. She pulled it out of her pocket and looked at it. "It's Mom. I told her I'd just be a minute." She hit a button that made it stop ringing and shoved it into her pocket. "I gotta go. I don't suppose you got a number where I can reach you?"

"No. But you won't be allowed to call anybody for a while anyway. You can write me."

She tilted her head. "Where? Aren't you selling this place and moving?"

"Well, yeah, but not for at least a couple of weeks, maybe four." It struck him that his time was running out. But more than that, he wasn't in a hurry to get off this land and move to Owl's Perch. "Write to me here. And then I'll send you my new address."

"I don't want to lose touch."

"Then don't. The farthest I'm going is no distance by car."

"I don't understand, Aaron. Why did you try so hard to get me to go for help?"

He shrugged. "I should've heard you years ago when you drank the night away but kept talking about getting sober. You wanted it long before I did. And this has sort of been like reaching into that part of my life and grabbing hold of one redeemable thing."

"Aw." She hugged him. "That was really sweet."

He patted her back and stepped away. Hugging her was like embracing a cousin. A small scrunch was plenty.

She smiled. "I won't ever forget what you've done for me over the last couple of months—yakking at me about God and my future. It took someone who's been right here, someone who knew the real me and still believed I had a fighting chance, to get me this far."

"It's not near far enough."

"I know. But it's a start." She tugged on his shirt before hopping into her car. "See ya."

He waved as she drove off, glad she'd chosen to follow the once-buried hope of getting and staying sober. They might write a few letters here and there. Maybe they'd see each other a couple of times a year, but other than the days they'd spent drinking, they had little in common.

Longing for time with a woman he did connect with, he wondered if Sylvi might go with him to Shippensburg to get an ice cream. It was a long shot, and he couldn't say it was a particularly wise idea for them to spend more time together, but he didn't care. He was going to ask anyway, right after he showered and shaved.

But whether she agreed to go or not, he'd tell her some of the new farming ideas that were forming in his head.

Annoyed and irritable, Sylvia soaked her aching body in the bubble bath. She'd scrubbed the milking parlor and tank room for hours, getting ready for tomorrow's inspection. For what? To give the place a little more value when it came time to sell it?

Her usual way of ridding herself of frustrations wasn't working, so she got out of the tub, dried off, and dressed. It was time to own up to the facts. Aaron had come home with a plan, and he was slowly accomplishing it. Michael's defenses and anger continued to fade. Not that he'd admit it openly, but she saw subtle changes in him—the look of pleasure on his face instead of resentment whenever Aaron came to the table.

What really had her in a foul mood was seeing Aaron all cozy with Frani out in the driveway. And Sylvia had volunteered to let the woman live with her! She was such an idiot. He clearly wanted a different kind of life—one that didn't involve a woman who sometimes smelled of Holsteins. She seemed to care only for men who wanted something or *someone* else. Did all men have to connect with women on an intimate level behind other women's backs?

Maybe some food would make her feel less grumpy. She wandered into the kitchen and looked through her mostly barren cupboards.

Someone tapped on her screen door, and she turned to see Aaron. He held a large manila envelope in his hand, and his smile stirred fresh irritation. She had no interest in hearing about other ways to make the farm more valuable when he put it up for sale.

"Sylvi, I have something to show you."

She pulled a jar of peanut butter out of the cabinet. "Great."

He stepped inside. "Is something wrong? I mean, other than the bad news we got about the fence?"

"No." It was a lie, but how could she tell him the truth?

Aaron set the envelope on the small kitchen island and sat on a barstool. "I think I understood you better when you threw that hammer at me."

She opened the jar of peanut butter and grabbed a knife. "So, does Frani need to move in here?"

He leaned his forearms against the island. "Actually, she doesn't."

She faced the counter, her back to him, determined not to let him see any sign of the swell of relief moving through her. "Good. I'm sure having her own place will make your relationship with her easier."

He sighed. "I've already explained my connection to Frani." He tapped the manila envelope. "Look, I brought you some information that may be useful in your quest to keep this farm. I thought maybe we could talk about it. But I guess you're not in the mood."

He stood and headed for the door, and it thudded behind him.

Until she saw him with Frani, she'd thought he was totally honest with her. So why did their hug make her think otherwise? Her stomach turned. *Jealousy.* Unwarranted and unfair to him.

"Aaron, wait." She hurried out the door and tried to catch him as he strode up the lane, but her bare feet slowed her. "Aaron, please."

He turned, and she gingerly made her way to him on the gravel.

When she looked into his eyes, she knew a simple apology wasn't enough. "I saw you and Frani smiling and hugging, and I…" She shook her head. "You still frustrate me, with your defenses and contradictions. But…"

His anger faded, and he sighed. "It's not like that between Frani and me. Sylvi, think about it. Have I done anything that says I'm in a relationship with Frani?"

She crossed her arms and held herself tight. It was time to come clean with him. "When Elam asked me to marry him and then asked someone else so soon afterward, I realized he must've shared moments with her while courting me. I had no idea, and I felt like a fool not to have known."

"Moments?"

"I'm sure you feel it when we have a moment—when we share a laugh or talk about something meaningful, and our friendship grows stronger." Her face flushed.

"I like our moments."

"I do too. But I won't be so foolish again, having them with someone I shouldn't." She scooted dirt around with her bare toe. "I've been on the other side of that fence too. I was close to the woman Elam married, and because of the moments he and I shouldn't have shared, I ended up betraying her."

Aaron brushed strands of loose hair out of her face. "And yourself."

Tears filled her eyes.

"You know forgiveness from God is there for the asking."

"I did ask. Over and over until I gave up."

"If you asked, He forgave you. Walking it out until you feel that forgiveness inside you—that's often a different issue. But you have to accept that He forgave you. It's a done deal."

Her tears refused to stay at bay. She wanted so much to believe that.

"You seem to be carrying enough guilt for you and Elam both. Some of this belongs to him, you know. I mean, you didn't chase him down and hogtie him, did you?"

She couldn't help but chuckle. His kindness and humor warmed her.

"Frani came to say good-bye because she's going into rehab at some place in Baltimore. The night I returned home, I saw her headed for this cabin, and I figured God had put her in my path for a reason. I now see that I needed her too. As I talked to her, I got fresh perspectives on all the reasons sobriety is so important. When her rebellion reared its head, I understood more of my own. And as it turned out, it was sort of like getting to reach into the past and salvage someone else's life." He gently brushed a strand of wet hair from her face, looking at her as if he truly cared. "She and I both needed that. But she's nothing else to me."

"I shouldn't have gotten upset with you. It's just—I can't figure out how I feel about you."

He gazed down at her. "I'm confused about how I feel too. Seems all we really know is how we feel about this homestead."

She laughed. "It's a stressful mess on the Blank farm, isn't it?"

"Uh, ya."

She swiped at her wet cheeks. "So you brought me hopeful news, and I dumped my baggage on you."

He flexed his biceps, which looked rock solid under his short-sleeved shirt. "I can carry it." He lowered his arm. "You were carrying most of my load before I ever showed up."

Looking him in the eyes, she saw a true friend standing in front of her. She knew that much. "You're doing that *almost tolerable* thing again."

He shrugged. "Blanks aren't tolerable. We're difficult. You don't have that figured out yet?"

"Well, you're all rather confusing. I've got that much clear. I mean, you care about your parents, and they love you, but no one can admit that. You stormed back here, fuming about dumping the farm and trying to corner *and* bribe your parents to go with you, but you haven't sat down and told them why it's so important to you."

"You want me to confess that I think they're not capable of knowing what's best for them or of accomplishing anything even if they did know?" His half smile and tone signaled his dry sense of humor at play.

"I want you to admit the truth to yourself and them—that you feel deeply and you rarely know what to do with it. Your parents are the same way, Aaron. And each of you is hiding behind the walls you've built."

"I hate to disappoint you, but you're seeing this all wrong. They care deeply about *you,* and I'm glad for you and them, but that's where their affections end, Sylvi."

He wasn't convinced that they were invested in him, but he was on the farm to do the right thing, and she admired that loyalty in him. It was past time that someone told him they cared, but she had little proof to back up her statements.

"Michael put the want ad for farm help in the paper last September," she said.

Disbelief registered on his face. "In September?" He mulled that over. "That was even before Elsie died."

His forehead remained tight as he stared at her, processing what she'd said. That meant Michael had known Aaron was struggling with the work and had tried to find a solution. It was a tiny peek inside the usually locked door of Michael's heart.

Aaron rubbed the back of his neck. "Are you sure?"

"Positive. My dream of coming here began then, but my Daed wouldn't hear of it."

"You have scary dreams, Sylvi."

She laughed. "You never once considered the freedom to farm this land and work with this herd a worthy goal?"

"Ya, actually I did, but that was a long time ago. A better question is, why didn't Daed tell me he was trying to get help? Why keep that a secret?"

She shrugged. "Remember your first Sunday home when you refused to leave the barn? You were angry that your Daed would let me work on the Sabbath by myself, but you couldn't see that Michael was purposefully giving me the freedom I'd asked for. Later you insisted I have Sundays off, as a break, and even did your part in helping me make friends. That's not your Daed's way. If I want to be left alone, that's what he's going to give. It doesn't mean he's heartless. For him, it means the opposite. You're all each other has, and I can't understand why you let your thoughts and feelings push you away from each other rather than drawing you closer."

A shadow passed over Aaron's face, and she wondered if she'd said too much.

She gestured toward the porch. "Care to sit?"

He nodded, and they sat on the steps.

Sylvia drew a deep breath. "Maybe I'm out of line to tell you this, but I've been holding my piece, giving your parents and you time to open up on your own."

"Not so sure the earth will last that long."

She couldn't help but chuckle when Aaron turned on his parched humor; it wasn't always what he said but the way he said it that made her laugh. "You may be right about that. But Jesus said, 'Blessed are the poor in spirit: for theirs is the kingdom of heaven.' And clearly there's a lot of inner poverty between you and your folks. Dirt-poor, honestly."

"Ya, I guess so. I always thought we fit the part in the Sermon on the Mount about those who mourn and hoped we'd find comfort, but that hasn't worked out so well either."

"Mourning? Because your sister died?"

He sighed, gazing down the narrow footpath that led from the cabin. "Throughout their marriage my parents lost six newborns, which is why they had only two children...and now just one. Instead of the losses drawing our family closer, each one scattered us to the wind, emotionally."

Sylvia studied his handsome face, realizing anew how deep his thoughts ran and seeing the magnitude of the mismanaged feelings that had pulled him toward drinking. "Michael and Dora are very tender-hearted people, even with thick walls guarding that tenderness. They're sensitive, much like you. Maybe Elsie was too. I don't know, but it seems that for gentle people such losses here on earth are even harder to bear."

His eyes searched hers. "You think we have a gentle spirit?" He sounded skeptical.

"I see your heart, Aaron. It is tender. You build up your walls with drinking or with biting comments, and now you're trying to pull them down. Perhaps Michael is so critical of you because he recognizes he's still hiding behind his walls. I've known a few men in my life who didn't have that tenderness of heart, who lacked sensitivity. No good comes of it. But after watching your family, it seems to me that when people feel deeply and try to bottle it up, it makes a mess of every relationship."

"I agree that our lack of communication has created chaos." He turned to her. "But here's something that is true. More than coming by to talk about the farm, I wanted to see if you'd care to go for a buggy ride into Shippensburg for some ice cream."

It was a bold request. He was making himself vulnerable. As she sat on the steps under the canopy of trees in the cool of the evening, she couldn't conjure up one scenario where it would hurt to spend a little personal time with him. If he sold the farm, she'd have a few good memories to take with her to the next place. If he set up a business in Owl's Perch and left her here with his parents, she'd have spent an evening building a bond with the owner's son.

She had to admit that beyond her logical reasons to go with him, her heart weighed in heavily. Spending time with Aaron satisfied some part of her she couldn't understand.

Despite his feelings about the farm, she wanted a chance to enjoy a romantic relationship with him. She admired his steely determination, his humility in admitting when he was wrong, and his desire to change for the better. His tenderness in understanding her pain and truly caring. His loyalty in returning for his parents and his unwavering faithfulness to them.

Not to mention his newly found strength of character. It had been seven months since he'd chosen to free himself of alcohol, and regardless of all the problems that had reared their ugly heads, he kept walking that path. She knew his journey wasn't over, but she felt confident that he would remain honest about the struggle.

Was she finally seeing him for who he really was? How would she know if she didn't give herself at least one evening out with him?

She stood. "I can't think of anything else I'd rather do."

Twenty-Nine

Cara pulled a sheet of cookies out of the commercial gas oven. She set the pan to the side to cool and slid another one into the stove. Worry kept pricking her conscience, but Cara attempted to wrestle it into silence. So far her emotions listened to her about as well as Better Days did.

For several nights she'd dreamed about not being allowed to join the faith for years. Now thoughts of not qualifying hounded her. Instruction classes got harder each session, and in spite of Sylvia doing a great job of teaching her the language, Cara had a long way to go.

Trevor jerked open the back door. "Need a hand?"

"Uh…" She looked around for something he could help with. "How about squeezing some lemons?"

"Sure." He went to the refrigerator and took out a basketful.

He used the glass hand juicer to squeeze several lemons while she sliced whole ones into thin strips and dropped the pieces into a vat. Sweat trickled down her chest. She was finally able to respond to her father with patience and compassion—not a ton of it, but enough that they could struggle through the awkwardness.

Trevor poured the pulp-filled juice into the large vat. "You've been quiet the last few days."

"Just thinking. I do that sometimes."

"I see."

She rinsed a rag in cool water and wiped the back of her neck. July temperatures and constant baking in a home without electricity made for a hot kitchen even with the sun dipping below the horizon. But living and working here was one of the best things to have happened to her.

Voices of children playing outside and of adults browsing in the gift shop down the hall surrounded her. God had brought her back to Ephraim through the oddest of circumstances. Surely she could pass instruction classes and learn enough of the languages to join the faith and marry him *before* he gave up or they were too old to have children.

Trevor dumped the lemon rinds into a tin bucket. She and Lori would dry them in the sun along with rinds from oranges and limes, then add them to a mixture of homemade potpourri.

She moved back to her work station and stirred sugar into a large container of lemonade before putting some of it in a glass pitcher.

"Your mom used to make lemonade with slices of lemon. Don't know that it helped the flavor, but it sure makes it look tasty." Trevor wrung out a washrag and wiped the work station where they'd made the lemonade. "I…I got a letter today."

She set a mixing bowl on the counter and measured out butter and sugar, wondering who would've written to him here.

He held out an envelope. "The lady from your apartment building sent you a letter."

Cara snatched it, studying the postmark. Trevor had been back little more than a week. The envelope was postmarked a few days after he'd left New York. She ripped it open and pulled out a letter and a newspaper clipping.

"What does it say?" Trevor asked.

Scanning the letter, her eyes caught the name Mike Snell, and a wave of dizziness made her sit. Agatha's words seemed to move about the page.

"Cara?"

"It...it's about...my stalker. Agatha didn't want to say anything to you, but..."

Mike had moved into her apartment the night she left. He'd stayed there until the rent was due, waiting for her to return.

Her hands trembled as she skimmed the newspaper page, trying to figure out what piece of information Agatha wanted her to see. Then she saw it: an obituary for Mike Snell. It listed his date of birth, parents' full names, and the borough where they lived. It was definitely the same Mike Snell who'd stalked her for more than a decade.

But she felt no relief, only nausea.

She returned to reading the letter. Agatha wrote that she wasn't sure if the letter would reach her, but she hoped it found her safe and happy.

She laid the letter, news clipping, and envelope on the table, then rose and went to the refrigerator. She pulled out eggs, cracked several on the edge of the bowl, and added them to the butter and sugar before throwing the shells into the sink.

"May I?" Trevor held up the letter and news clipping.

"Yeah."

She shoved the blades of the rotary mixer into the batter and turned the handle, round and round, faster and faster. Her knees were wobbly. She'd see Ephraim tomorrow after another language lesson, and she wondered if the news would have any effect on him.

"You're upset." Trevor set the papers to the side. "I don't understand."

"Yeah, me either." She took the hand mixer out of the bowl and slammed it down on the counter, spattering cookie dough. "I spent so many years wishing he was dead...wishing I could kill him. And now I...I feel like I can't breathe. A man's life is over."

"Did you expect to rejoice?"

"The old me would have...I think." Since she was young, she'd known the finality of death. Nothing was as changeless or hopeless as life leaving a body and never returning. After it happened to her mother, nothing was ever the same again. But why did she find the finality of Mike's death so disturbing? She stared at the letter and newspaper, wondering what he'd died of.

Relationships were often complicated, disappointing, or even a source of pain, but until someone died, there was always a possibility for change. Whatever condition Mike's relationships were in when he died, they would remain that way forever—including whether he ever came to know God.

The bond with her dad wasn't what either of them had wanted, but they were here and working on improving it.

Where was Mike?

It was absurd to compare the two. They were nothing alike. Yes, Mike should have been in jail where he couldn't wreak havoc. But dead?

She'd been worried and melancholy over whether she'd join the faith this year or next or the following year, but she had hope—both in this life and the next one. What did Mike have?

She'd never once thought of praying for him. If Ada hadn't spent a lifetime praying for her, where would she be?

She blinked, realizing her dad had gotten the cookies out of the oven and had finished mixing the batch she'd begun. "Trevor," she whispered.

He stopped stirring the dough. "Yeah?"

She wanted to say that she forgave him. That she was enjoying getting to know him and looked forward to his being around so they could continue making progress. Instead she shrugged. "I'm glad you went to New York and brought back pictures for Lori." She couldn't even manage to tell him "thank you"?

He put a dollop of cookie dough on a pan. "Anything like that you need, I'm here to do it, Carabean."

Tears pricked her eyes. She cleared her throat. "So, are we still on for you taking me to Sylvia's tomorrow?"

Thirty

Tired of trying to grasp the complicated solutions, Sylvia folded the papers on farming that Aaron had brought to the cabin. She tucked them under the edge of the quilt on the ground beneath her and lay back, staring at the billowing gray clouds. Two kittens were curled up in her lap asleep, and two played beside her. She'd carried them in her picnic basket along with a jar of water, a sandwich, the blanket, and farming information to study. Bringing the cute balls of fur to this private spot had been her best effort to make this nonchurch Sunday as pleasant as possible.

But the day stretched out like warm taffy, looping round and round and seemingly growing longer with each spin. As a child she'd once seen taffy being made in a candy shop. She hadn't liked the smell of it, and when the candy maker cut off a piece for her, she didn't like the taste of it either. She had to laugh at the fact that working in a barn didn't bother her, but the aroma of artificial flavoring and mass amounts of sugar did.

That appliance store of Aaron's had made her feel much worse. It smelled like fumes from an old bus, and that always made her headachy and nauseous.

She believed a lot of things about her were odd, but she'd never minded it until Elam chose her sister over her. Beckie was beautiful and dainty and, she guessed, all the things men looked for. Truth was, Beckie could have had her choice of men.

Trying not to think about it, she focused on the sky. The clouds moved across it, hinting at a possibility of rain. She'd been desperate for the weather to stay dry while she and Aaron baled hay, but now, seven weeks later, she felt as much angst wishing it would rain.

They hadn't gotten a second cutting of alfalfa yet. They would soon, but it'd grown slowly because of the lack of rain, and she doubted they'd get a third cutting before fall. The field corn she and Michael had planted days before Aaron returned had suffered too. They needed a good yield from it to help fill the silos for the winter, but it looked rather scraggly from a distance, and she couldn't make herself walk into the field to see it up close.

The good news was that, being part of the silage, the kernels themselves needed very little moisture in them. Surely this current weather pattern would help in that department…maybe. She didn't really know. All she knew was that Michael's resolve to keep the farm seemed to be evaporating along with the ponds and the creek bed. Not that he'd actually said those words. But she'd walked into the Blank home a few days ago and had seen him reading a newspaper ad for nonelectric appliances. They didn't need a new appliance of any kind, so he was probably entertaining the idea of a lifestyle change.

"Sylvi." Aaron's voice echoed around her.

She sat upright. This little spot, nestled in a patch of trees between an unused field and a pond, was supposed to be too secluded for anyone to notice her.

Aaron crossed the field, carrying something in each hand. Her heart beat a little faster at the sight of him. Something about his ways made her want to know his thoughts and opinions, even if they were his frustrations about the farm or his parents.

He stopped at the edge of the quilt, holding a thermos in one hand and a plate covered with aluminum foil in the other. The fact that he'd gone out of his way to locate her gave her some much-needed assurance that he was worthy of her growing fondness for him.

She hid her smile, not wanting to give her thoughts away. "How did you find me?"

"I think I know all your favorite resting places now." He held out both items.

She wanted to respond, but suddenly she felt shy in light of his efforts toward her. On mornings when Michael didn't come to the barn before milking, Aaron always brought her a cup of coffee. But Michael had insisted on that. Three days ago he'd brought her helpful information about farming. She hadn't had time to figure out what all the gibberish meant; still, it showed his willingness to share the burden of the farm with her.

"It's not a marriage proposal, for Pete's sake."

His sarcastic humor relaxed her, and she moved the kittens to her other side and patted the quilt before taking the items from him. "Denki."

"Not a problem."

He bent his knees and put his forearms on them, reminding her of the one thing she kept trying to overlook—that he was, above all else, a man. One who seemed different from any other she'd ever known. And the relaxedness of between Sundays looked good on him. Actually, his appeal was just as strong the other days of the week. Her trying to stay too busy to notice hadn't worked. But it wasn't, by any means, just his appearance that made him look good. What attracted her came from deep within him and radiated through his eyes and showed in the determined way he carried himself.

She opened the thermos and poured icy water into the lid. She brought the drink to her lips and enjoyed the coolness as the liquid filled her mouth and slid down her throat. After setting the cup on top of her picnic basket, she peered under the aluminum foil. "Bread pudding! I love this stuff."

"Mamm said you did."

"You even brought me a fork." She dug into the gooey confection.

"Mmm." The sweet, soft, cinnamon-flavored bread melted in her mouth. "Delicious. And still warm. Care for a bite?" She held a forkful up to him.

"Not me, thanks. Never been a fan of bread pudding."

"Your mom has a new recipe. You ought to give it a try."

He didn't look convinced, but he opened his mouth, and she eased it past his lips. "Oh, wow." He chewed and swallowed. "That's actually quite good."

"Isn't it?" She took another bite. "Dora made a batch for me with her old recipe last winter." Sylvia mocked a cough and shuddered. "I had to tell her the truth, and I passed on to her a much better recipe, one that belonged to my great-grandmother." After taking another bite, she held a second one out to him.

Aaron leaned back on his elbows. "This spot is sort of nice."

"Close your eyes."

His chestnut eyes held a spark of challenge, but he closed them.

"Now feel, hear, and breathe in everything around you."

He lay back and propped his hands under his head. He took a deep breath, and a trace of pleasure showed on his face.

Sylvia remained sitting upright, but she closed her eyes too, hearing a crow caw, a fish in the pond jump, and wind rustle through the trees. "Everything you sense, Aaron, has been here long before this country began, yet every bit of it is new, right here today, for you." Her eyes refused to stay shut, and she watched a smile caress his face.

"You do have a way of making a person value a day." He opened his eyes and looked at her. "But the joys of nature can't make a small dairy operation like ours less of an uphill battle."

"I wasn't trying to change your mind, only open it to the world around you."

"Is that what you like about dairy farming, the romantic view of it?"

"Oh, please. No real farmer can keep a romantic image of the job. Besides, I never said I was in love with cows."

He sat upright. "Yes, you have."

"When?"

"Well, not in words. But your actions have said it."

"My great-grandparents were dairy farmers, as were my grandparents, and now my Daed. And they made a decent living doing it."

"I don't know your family's operation, Sylvi, but times have changed. You have to have substantial growth to compete these days, and this place isn't set up to sustain that kind of expansion."

"Your Daed has barns, cows, and milking equipment—everything a farm needs for a healthy dairy business."

"The profit margin isn't equal to the work load, especially considering what we'd need in order to grow. If they were equal, I wouldn't feel like it's such a waste of time."

Unsure what to say, she took another bite of the bread pudding and then gave him a bite. She took a deep breath. "Between Sundays are actually sort of nice."

Aaron took the fork and plate from her. "Your turn to close your eyes."

She stared at him.

"Go on. I did it for you."

She closed her eyes.

"Feel the ground under you and the breeze on your skin," he said. "Pay attention to all the sounds—the birds and the wind. Smell the aroma of hayfields, flowers, and distant rain."

She relaxed and relished the nature surrounding her.

"God is everywhere, Sylvi." Aaron's whisper sent chills over her body. "You can't avoid Him by refusing to attend meetings. You only avoid acknowledging Him." He brushed his fingers across her back. "You don't have to go to church to find Him, but you can't hide from Him by avoiding it. I learned that the hard way. I show up in my rig at your place every other Sunday because I want you to find peace with your mistake, with yourself. It seems you need to face the church folk during Sunday meetings." His hand rested on the center of her back. "The answer you need won't be found in running any more than mine was found in drinking."

Sylvia wished going to church would magically erase her shame, but it magnified it. Ready to put some emotional distance between them, she shifted away and huffed. "I think you're in cahoots with the church leaders."

"When I began running from God, I wish someone had been willing to make me angry if that would have kept me from doing things my own way. Caring people aren't the enemy, Sylvi. Apathy is."

Aaron didn't seem to have an apathetic bone in his body. She didn't know why that was so important to her, but she truly valued it. And whether he liked it or not, he'd just confessed that he cared about her.

"I need to mention a few recent changes I've worked out. You want to hear them now or later?"

"Now, of course."

"We're not planting or harvesting any more crops," he said. "I've rented the fields to Mennonite farmers who own tractors and modern equipment. It's the right thing to do for both our sakes."

"What about the field of corn that's almost ready to harvest?"

"I've worked that out too. They'll harvest it for a percentage of the crop. We won't make as much money, but we won't work ourselves to exhaustion either."

Michael had given the running of fields over to Aaron, and she wouldn't argue. If they weren't in such a tight fix for money, she'd be thrilled with the idea.

He dug something out of his pocket. "I brought you more than a dessert."

The white envelope was thicker than if it held a letter. "What is it?"

He shrugged. "Hopefully not the cause of a fresh argument."

She licked her lips before taking the envelope and opening it. "Money?"

"Did you forget what it looks like?"

She closed the envelope and held it out to him. "Michael and I have an agreement. I receive pay after the overdue debts are paid."

"Ya, I heard, and I've already gone a couple of rounds with him on this. Here's the deal, Sylvi. If you work on the Blank farm, you get paid. End of discussion."

"Where did you get this?"

"It took some juggling, I'll admit. But the bills are paid, and nothing's been borrowed."

"The overdue bills are caught up?"

"No. I'm not a miracle worker. But we've paid enough that the threat of immediate liens and repossession of equipment is over…for now. Take the money, Sylvi."

A lump formed in her throat as if the bread pudding had stuck there. He was settling up debts. Did that mean he'd found a buyer for the farm without having to put it up for sale? "Have you accepted a down payment from someone?"

"No. We wouldn't do that without telling you."

We? "So your Mamm and Daed have sided with you about selling?"

He leaned back on his elbows. "Take a breath, Sylvi. I brought your favorite dessert and a long-overdue payday. That's all."

She turned the envelope over, saddened by its contents. He had four weeks before he had to take over at the appliance store, and he was doing all within his power to get there by then.

With the issues on the farm—the drought, Michael's arthritis giving him fits, and being in violation of EPA laws—Aaron only needed to wait a few more weeks, and his parents would be more than ready to sell and move to Owl's Perch with him.

The farm wouldn't be sold by the time he took over the appliance store, but it would be on the market.

Sadness pressed in. He'd told her all along that this was the way things would work out, but mourning the loss of another farm was going to take its toll. She'd believed she could make a success of this place. And she realized for the first time that somewhere inside her had been a faint hope that her coming here had been some kind of fate. As if there was a slim possibility that God would give her a second chance.

Thirty-One

Aaron poured a cup of coffee and added cream and sugar, hoping he had the right amount of both. Cup in hand, he walked down the driveway toward the path to the cabin. Every morning about this time, Sylvi returned from milking, washed up and changed out of her barn clothes, and came to the house for a midmorning break. Warm winds stirred the summer air, and thunder rumbled across the cloudy sky. The first of August would arrive the day after tomorrow. His time here was dwindling rather than dragging.

Sylvi came out the cabin door, looking scrubbed, with a few loose strands of damp hair hugging the nape of her neck. She walked his way without looking up. His heart beat like crazy as her presence caused an avalanche of emotions.

She was about ten feet away when she finally noticed him. "Well, hi there." Her energetic, willful smile mesmerized him.

He paused under a canopy of rustling trees and held out the coffee.

"Denki." She took it from his hands. "To what do I owe this treat?"

"I wanted to talk to you for a minute, and we can't talk easily with Mamm and Daed around."

She brought the mug to her lips. "Mmm. That's delicious. Did you make it?"

"Ya."

Closing her eyes, she took several more sips.

"I altered it from the way Daed does it. I've noticed that you like desserts with cream, so I added extra."

"I expect this same concoction again, you know. It's a good thing I work hard enough to burn off all these calories." She stretched a bit, as if working a few kinks out of her shoulders, then let her free arm fall to her side. When the back of her hand brushed his, he stroked her soft skin and dared to slide his fingers between hers. Her eyes bored into his, and she took a step back before wrapping both hands around the mug. "What did you need to talk about?"

He shrugged, unable to think of anything except kissing her. It'd be a dangerous move, altering everything between them. But it could be worth it. Stepping closer, he leaned in, pausing mere inches from her. She smelled delicious. "Let's forget the farm for a minute, Sylvi. Be here with me, just us and nothing else."

She didn't argue or turn away. That had to be a good sign. But he waited, hoping for some indication that he was welcome.

"Convince me," she whispered.

He placed his mouth on hers. The delicate softness of her skin was beyond what he'd imagined. But she didn't return the kiss. She held firm to the cup of coffee between them.

He kissed her again, and this time she responded.

A good ten seconds later, she tucked her head. He kissed her forehead while catching his breath. He'd never dreamed that a kiss could mean so much.

He straightened and put a bit of space between them.

She drew a deep breath and ran her fingers along her lips. "I've never... wow."

Never and *wow* had to be good, right? Aaron laughed. "My thoughts exactly."

Her cheeks flushed, and she headed toward the main driveway. He fell into step with her. He knew he shouldn't stare, but he did anyway.

She sipped her coffee. "This confuses things."

"Ya, I know." His voice was husky. "But I'd do it again."

"Me too. But in light of our differing goals, it seems rather short-sighted."

For the first time he wondered if maybe they had the wrong goals. "What did you want to talk to me about?" she asked again.

"The grant money. I spoke to Daed, and he believes we have no other choice than to accept it. The fence line has to be moved, and we don't have the money to do it ourselves."

"Are you okay with taking grant money?"

"I want to verify with Dusty Randall that it doesn't come with strings, but otherwise, ya, I am. What do you think?"

"I can't say the idea of taking government money is easy to accept. But I'm not sure we have a choice. The government is demanding something we can't do on our own."

They stepped onto the main driveway and turned toward the house.

"Was there anything else you needed to talk to me about?"

"There is one thing I've been wanting to ask." He shoved his hands into his pockets, and they walked in silence. The minutes dragged by as he fought to ask a question he wasn't sure he wanted answered. "Do you still love him?"

"Who? Elam?" She rolled her eyes, looking disgusted. "No. A woman can't remain in love with a man she doesn't respect." She took a sip of her coffee. "Old feelings and unfulfilled dreams tugged at us. But even then I knew what I felt for him wasn't love or respect or anything else worth having."

"It sounds as though you really spent some effort trying to under-stand your feelings. Until I went into rehab, I'd always tried to bury my emotions instead of examining them." He didn't know if he was mak-ing sense, but it was part of the reason he'd started drinking. It wasn't that his parents had been unfair or that he hated being a farmer. He drank to bury emotions that needed to be felt, dealt with, and released or expressed.

She grabbed him by the suspenders, and they both stopped walking. "Be that as it may, you are a good man." He smiled down at her, loving the way she thought. And the way she expressed her heart to him. "I like who we are together."

Something unfamiliar to him flickered through her eyes before she released his suspenders and stepped around him.

He fell in step beside her. "I know we've muddied the waters. But let's take a little time to think, and then we'll talk."

Dust billowed on the driveway toward the main road. A vehicle was heading their way. Their time alone for the day was coming to an end too quickly.

He'd made no promises, and she'd asked for none. But he was connected to her more than he'd known was possible.

"Aaron," Dusty Randall called while pulling his truck to a stop beside them, "you ready to discuss moving fence lines?"

"You want to go with us?" Aaron asked Sylvia.

"No. You need to head up the fence-line project. I'll take care of the rest of the chores."

With a nod to Brian Clayton in the front passenger seat, Aaron opened the door behind Randall and climbed into the cab of the truck.

He couldn't stay on this farm. That much he knew. If he asked, and if he gave Sylvi time for the idea to grow on her, would she be willing to leave with him?

Thirty-Two

The rain pounded on the roof as Cara wrote "Happy Birthday, Sylvia" in yellow icing across the cake's chocolate frosting. Ada walked out of the room, carrying a load of freshly folded towels.

Ephraim dipped his finger in the bowl of frosting. "So I finally make it here again midweek and on a perfect night, since Ada's House has no business on rainy days, and you're leaving. What's with that?"

Cara passed him a spoon with remnants of the gooey chocolate. "Poor planning on your part?"

He took the spoon from her, gazing into her eyes. "It's your loss, you know."

"Hey, no being mean to me. It's bad enough I'll miss out on enjoying a rare night off with you. Between your workweek and the weekend busyness at Ada's House, I feel deprived enough already. Of course, you could go with us."

"To an all-girl event? No thanks. Besides, there's only one of you I wanted to spend time with tonight." He pulled her close. His lips had almost touched hers when Lori ran into the kitchen.

"Ew!" she screamed.

"Cut it out, you two." Ada's laughter-filled voice came from the other room.

Ephraim backed away and passed the spoon of frosting to Lori. Her eyes grew large, and she ran to show Ada. Ephraim focused on Cara, moving his eyebrows up and down. "Now where were we?"

Cara closed the gap between them. "About here…" She held his face, but just before she kissed him, Deborah walked into the kitchen.

"Oh, sorry." She went to the refrigerator. "I forgot to mix up a pitcher of lemonade for tonight's gathering."

Cara released him and shrugged. "Who'd have thought a simple kiss was too difficult a task to accomplish—in private, no less!"

Ephraim shrugged. "Eventually there will be only one interrupter in our house—Lori."

Deborah set the lemons and hand juicer on the island. "But not for long." She sang the words.

Ephraim grinned, and although he'd not said much on this topic, Cara knew that he really looked forward to having children. She did too. Still, it was strange being around men who looked at marriage as an honor and a multitude of children as a gift. Unlike newly married Englischer couples, Amish ones hoped to conceive as soon as possible—just another way that the ideology still felt foreign to her.

When Cara had found out she was pregnant with Lori, she feared her husband would be angry with her. He wasn't, but he hadn't wanted children until that moment. And after Lori was born, he didn't intend for them to have a repeat performance. She understood and had embraced that line of thinking herself, but here, where family wove itself together like a huge safety net, her view on conceiving was completely different.

Deborah cut a lemon in half and nudged it and the juicer in front of her brother. "If you want me out of here, get busy helping."

Ephraim made quick work of his job, and soon the two-gallon jar of sweetened lemonade was ready. Deborah left it on the counter and headed for the swinging door.

Trevor walked in as Deborah walked out, and Cara's eyes met Ephraim's. Maybe they'd have to move the refrigerator to block the door.

"Nice work, Cara." Trevor pointed at the cake. "I left the Blank farm about fifteen minutes ago. Everything is calm and quiet. The cows and calves are tended to and the barn scrubbed, and Sylvia went to her cabin for the night rather than working on a puzzle or playing a game with Michael."

Cara put the cake into a dessert box. "Good. She'll be surprised when we show up."

Ephraim and Cara walked onto the porch with their hands full. The cloud-covered daylight had little power behind it, but it wouldn't be dark for another two hours. Ephraim held a large umbrella over Cara, and streams of water ran off it as they huddled by Trevor's trunk, loading the birthday items.

Cara caressed Ephraim's face. "I feel sort of bad about messing up your plans."

"Don't. I like what you're doing."

"But you had a driver bring you and made arrangements for him to pick you up four hours from now."

"I'll cancel with Robbie. He'll be more than glad not to come get me. And Trevor can drop me off on his way to taking you and Deborah to Sylvia's."

"We're going by Lena's to get her too."

"You're enjoying yourself with your girlfriends. How could I possibly mind that?"

She leaned in and stole a kiss. "I like you, Ephraim Mast."

"I was hoping for more than *liking* me."

She rested her head on his chest, wanting to tell him how she really felt, but saying the words *I love you* seemed impossible. Not all that long ago, she'd recalled as a child telling her dad that she loved him. Maybe that was her hang-up—she and her dad had openly said they loved each other, and then he'd abandoned her. In truth, she didn't know what her real problem was, but unless she was talking to Lori, those words turned to ash inside her throat. Telling Lori she loved her was easy. That was what moms did, and she had told Lori the first time she held her. But that was different. Cara wasn't vulnerable in that relationship. In other relationships she always skirted actually saying those words.

Always.

Even when she and Ephraim first spoke of marriage, she didn't tell him that she loved him. When he said it to her, she said things like "Well, duh" or "Of course you do." He knew she loved him, but she'd like to be able to say it.

The front door to Ada's House slammed, causing them both to glance that way. Trevor and Deborah stood on the porch, wrestling with an umbrella. Her dad wasn't anything like she'd expected. He seemed to have an understanding of commitment and love.

Cara walked Ephraim to the front passenger side door and then took the umbrella. "I'll be right back."

After going inside and giving Lori a hug and extracting a pledge that she'd be good for Ada, Cara piled into the car with the others, and they headed out. Ephraim was dropped off first. Then Trevor stopped at Lena's house.

Lena hopped into the front seat where Ephraim had been minutes earlier. "I'm so glad you thought of this, Cara. Is it an all-girls night, or will Aaron be there too?"

"He might drop by. I see him for a few minutes fairly regularly when Sylvia's teaching me songs in your language. But he won't stay long. He never does."

"Is there anything between him and Sylvia?" Deborah raised her eyebrows quickly several times, obviously hopeful of Cara's answer.

"Sometimes I think there is," Cara said. "Other times I don't."

One thing Cara had learned about riding in a car with the Amish was that they seemed to forget the driver was listening.

Trevor glanced at her in the rearview mirror and smiled before focusing on the road. He looked at her and treated her differently than any other man she'd ever known. Then it dawned on her. He responded to her like a dad.

His daughter. The words churned inside her brain. It wasn't such a horrid thing to think of him as Dad, was it?

He stopped a couple of hundred feet from Sylvia's cabin and turned off his lights. The rain had quit, and Cara got out of the car quickly. They took the items out of the trunk as quietly as they could and sloshed along the muddy path. Before they reached the porch steps, Cara unboxed the cake, and Deborah lit the candles. They stood at the bottom of the porch like Christmas carolers, singing "Happy Birthday."

Sylvia walked outside, took one look, and broke into a huge grin. "Cara Moore, what have you done?" She hurried down the steps.

"Make a wish."

Sylvia closed her eyes before blowing out all the candles. "You're the best student I've ever had." She hugged Cara.

"Uh, yeah, I'm the *only* student you've ever had."

Sylvia hugged Deborah and Lena. "Is she always this sassy?"

"No," Deborah said. "Sometimes she sleeps."

Her friends chortled, and Cara stuck out her tongue.

The idea of Trevor driving off without even a "thanks" from her bore down heavy. They were making progress, and she should show her gratitude.

"You guys go on inside." Cara passed Deborah the cake. "I'll get the lemonade and join you in a minute."

The three women went up the porch steps, chatting feverishly as they peeled out of their muddy shoes. She couldn't hear all of what was said amid the laughter, but she caught bits about cutting huge slices of cake.

By the time Cara returned to the car, Trevor had already lifted the jug out of the trunk. "Here you go. I'll pick you up around nine?"

"Perfect. Sylvia turns in early."

"You would too if you got up at four. Ephraim would probably still be up then. You want to stop by and see him?"

"Yeah, uh…thanks." There, she said it.

"Be here then." He climbed into his car.

He treated her like a beloved daughter, and she treated him like a servant. What was she, fourteen? Yet she still hated the idea of really thanking him.

He started to pull away.

"Trevor."

He stopped the car and got out. "Did you need something else out of the trunk?"

He had the track record of a drunk and the heart of a father. What did he really want? If she fully forgave and embraced him, would his work be done and he'd leave?

No longer able to justify withholding love, she set the jug of lemonade on the hood of his car. "I forgive you." As the words left her mouth, her chest felt weird and prickly. "Do you think maybe you could forgive me too?"

"You're my Carabean. I'll always forgive you."

"You scare me." Her voice cracked, a lifetime of longing trying to force its way free from where she'd locked it up years ago.

"You're the only good thing I've ever done."

For a moment she saw an image of what had to be his life—a barren wasteland, miles and miles of parched, dried earth. Then she saw herself, not as an oasis, but as this man's one lost pearl.

Words failed her, but she put her arms around him. He held her.

She backed away. "You'll pick us up at nine?"

"I'll be here, Carabean. Whenever you need me, for as long as I'm able, I'll be here."

She swallowed hard. "Thanks, Dad."

Thirty-Three

With the morning and early afternoon chores done, Sylvia made her way to the cabin. Birds sang, and the wind rustled the thick canopy overhead. After the heavy machinery the EPA had brought in had droned on and on for two weeks, they'd finished earlier today and were finally gone. Now only gentle sounds echoed in her ears.

While the laborers ran various types of equipment, she'd put up with the noise and odors of modern-day progress, though it had taxed her nerves until she barely recognized herself. But now that the work was done, she hoped to feel more like herself within a day or two.

The job had taken much longer than expected, mostly because the list of necessary improvements kept growing as the men worked. New fences were built on each side of the creek, a huge open drainpipe that ran from one side of the creek to the other was set in place, and concrete had been poured to secure the pipe. The rains forced the men to run double rows of silt fences on both sides of the creek as well. When the fields dried and the freshly seeded earth yielded grass, the cows would use the newly constructed concrete-and-earthen bridge to get from one part of the pasture to the other. For now a temporary barrier was in place to keep the cows off the fresh seeding.

She went inside the cabin and spotted a sink full of dishes. She never could figure out how that happened when she ate most of her meals in the Blanks' kitchen. It'd be nice if Cara came by for another language lesson.

Sylvia needed the distraction and the friendship. But no one—not Cara, Aaron, or Michael and Dora—could fill the void that missing her sisters left inside her. Some days she felt their absence more acutely than others, and she was having that kind of day.

She shuddered and bit back tears. Busyness was the answer, so she went into the wash house at the far end of the cabin. Since it had been raining so much, she had mounds of laundry that needed to be washed and hung out to dry.

While sorting clothes, she heard the familiar sound of a rig—either going up the Blanks' driveway toward their farmhouse or coming down the much smaller path to the cabin. For a brief moment she imagined it was Aaron coming for a visit, but she knew better. He didn't drive a rig to her place except on church Sundays and sometimes on a weekend night when asking her to go for a ride. Besides that, she'd not seen much of him in the last couple of weeks. He'd been spending long days with the EPA workers.

It could be Cara.

A pounding on her front door made her stop sorting laundry and leave the wash house. She entered her kitchen, craning her neck to see who stood at her screen door.

Beckie!

Sylvia's heart stopped, and she was rooted to the floor. Her sister's face was somber. Did she know what had happened with Elam?

Beckie spotted her and broke into a smile. "Sylvia." She flung open the door and ran to her. "Oh, I did find the right place, and I made it all on my own. Can you believe it?" Beckie swamped her in a hug.

Sylvia breathed in the aroma of her little sister, wanting to wrap her arms around her, but her body wouldn't budge. "How..."

"I'm fine." Beckie took a step back. "Let's look at you." She brushed a few stray hairs from Sylvia's face. "Still the same, aren't you? Your hair always needs a fresh combing and pinning midway through your workday, but do you ever redo it?"

Sylvia pulled away from her. "Would you care for something to drink? A glass of water?"

"What's going on? You don't seem the least bit happy to see me."

Sylvia put her hands on her sister's shoulders, trying to look pleased. "I…I'm just surprised."

"You should be. I mean, *me* taking on something like this by myself? You always told me I could do whatever I set my mind to. I never believed you until today."

Sylvia managed an encouraging smile, but hypocrisy stuck in her throat. "How about that drink now?"

"Ach, ya. Denki. It's so hot today."

They went into the kitchen. Sylvia grabbed a glass and moved to the refrigerator.

"Looks like you've had lots of rain of late," Beckie said.

"Ya." Sylvia handed her the cold water.

"Kumm." Beckie took her hand and led her to the living room. "Tell me about this place and what's so great about it that caused you to leave your sisters."

Sylvia's palms sweated. "It was time for me to go."

"Well, I'm sure we wore you out. Everyone down with whooping cough except you and Elam." Beckie took several long sips of her drink. "But surely you're ready to come home by now."

Plagued with guilt, Sylvia rose. "You had a long drive. I should water and feed your horse." She headed for the door.

"Oh, Shady can wait." Beckie followed her outside.

The horse frothed, and sweat soaked his body. "Oh, Beckie. Look at him. He's been in this August heat on black pavement for hours."

Beckie growled. "You drive me nuts, always thinking of the animals first."

Sylvia chafed. If Beckie had any good sense, she'd have waited a month for cooler weather or made arrangements to get a fresh horse at a midway point. There were Amish folks along the way who'd have gladly met that need. "Beckie, I'll just be a few minutes taking care of Shady. I'm sure you need a little time to freshen up and rest."

"I guess…but I made this trip to visit with you."

Sylvia could barely think. How was she supposed to have a conversation with her sister? She envisioned her guilt being tattooed across her face. "What about?"

Beckie frowned, looking confused and amused. "Have you been here so long that you've forgotten we need no subject to talk on? We just get started, and it stops when one of us falls asleep. But I do want to talk about your coming back home."

"Falls asleep? Are you…staying?"

"Of course, silly. I brought my overnight bag. Remember when we used to pack our bags to spend the night in a homemade tent in the kitchen?"

Overnight bag? Sylvia jerked open the door to the carriage.

"Are you just going to stare at it?" Beckie giggled.

As if Sylvia's world had slowed to the pace of cold molasses, she removed the bag from the carriage and passed it to Beckie. Her sister had a set of very active twins at home, and she intended to spend the night away? Sylvia looked at the bulging sides of the bag, wondering how long Beckie intended to stay.

Her eyes flashed with excitement. "I'm so proud of myself for making it here. I kept asking Elam to bring me, but you know what he's like. When he wants something, there's no stopping him, and when he's not interested, there's no motivating him. He simply tuned me out. When I said I'd go by myself, he kept coming up with reasons I shouldn't make the trip. But here I am."

A dozen memories of Beckie as a little blond-haired, blue-eyed girl all excited about birthdays or having tea with their dolls ran through Sylvia's mind. No one lit up a room like Beckie.

Sweat spattered when Sylvia patted Shady. "The barn is a little ways from here, so I'll be a few minutes. The rest room is in the hallway to your right, and there's stuff for sandwiches in the pantry and refrigerator."

Beckie smoothed her hands down the front of her dress, revealing a bulge. She smiled radiantly. "I might doze off. The little one and I have had quite an amazing day."

Without another word Sylvia took the horse by the reins and began walking. She wished Aaron was there to talk soothingly to her and to keep her company until she felt her strength return, just as he had that day she fell in the field. But he was somewhere along the fence line, double-checking things, taking notes, and looking for any scraps of barbed wire.

Beckie waved. "Hurry back. We have so much to talk about."

Sylvia wanted to beg God to help her keep the awful secret. Beckie was a long way from home and expecting. Sylvia had to make the visit pleasant. Her inability to lie, even through silence, was poor and part of the reason she'd fled the Fisher farm as quickly as she could after the incident with Elam.

Her mind racing, she led the horse into the equine section of the calving barn. Hoping she'd catch a glimpse of Aaron, she watched for him while removing the rigging, walking Shady some more, and wiping him down. But what could Aaron say other than she had to get through the visit?

The horse's rib cage continued to expand and contract in quick succession. Sylvia feared she might walk into the barn tomorrow and find the poor creature dead from heart failure. After giving him small portions of feed and water, she promised she'd return to give him more within the hour. She had no choice but to go back to the cabin.

Walking down the main driveway, she saw Trevor driving toward the farmhouse. He must have come early for the afternoon feeding. They exchanged waves.

The lane back to the cabin had never been so short. When she walked inside, Beckie was stretched out on the couch. She moved her arm from resting over her eyes. "This cabin sits off all by itself, surrounded by a patch of woods. I could never get any sleep in a place like this. Do you share it with someone?" Her sister sounded relaxed, as if maybe she'd dozed off.

"No."

Beckie sat upright.

Sylvia tried to steady her nerves. Maybe she needed to stay busy. She went to the kitchen sink.

Beckie followed her and leaned against the counter mere inches away. "Are you okay? You don't seem like yourself."

Sylvia poured dish detergent into the sink and turned on the faucet, wishing she could drown out her guilt. "I'm fine."

"Elam said I shouldn't come." Beckie reached over and turned off the water. "I was so mad at you when you left. I know you came to help a man hold on to his farm, but how could you leave us like we didn't matter? And why didn't you write? I don't care if Daed was angry that you left and forbade you to write the girls. I have my own mailbox. He would have never known."

Beckie was always keenly aware of what she felt and wanted, but she seemed unable to imagine what others might feel or need. Hadn't Sylvia remained by her side as a faithful sister while Beckie and Elam married and had babies? But Sylvia's difficulties because of that situation never seemed to bother Beckie at all.

Sylvia turned on the water again. "I've been busy. When I left home, this farm was struggling, and my only help was a man with health issues." If she couldn't get Beckie out of here soon, that would be the first of a hundred white lies she'd tell before this visit was over.

Beckie put her hands on Sylvia's shoulders and faced her squarely. "But there's more help here now, right? Aaron Blank?"

Some of Sylvia's ability to think returned to her. Who'd given Beckie directions to the farm? Their Daed had come only halfway, so he couldn't have written directions for her.

And who told Beckie about Aaron's return? Had Michael given up on keeping the farm and contacted her sister in hopes of encouraging Sylvia to return home?

Sylvia gently pulled away from her sister's grip, turned off the faucet, and plunged her hands into the soapy water. "If you intend to spend your visit trying to convince me to come home, I'll go fetch a driver for you now. We have one on site, and I'll pay the fee myself."

Beckie looked stung by the sharp words. "Why would you rather live like this than on our farm, surrounded by a family who loves you? Daed does, you know. He's angry that you chose to go elsewhere to work, but he loves you."

He wouldn't love her if he knew what she'd done. None of them would.

"I need you to let this go, Beckie." Sylvia jerked her dripping hands out of the sink, dried them on her black apron, and went into the wash house. She attached a hose to the mud sink and laid it in the wringer washer. Nothing was as noisy in an Amish home as the diesel-powered air compressor that ran the wringer washer. She flipped the switch, bringing the machine to a roar.

Beckie came to the door. "Sylvia!"

"I'm not coming home."

"And what will you do when these people don't need you anymore?" Beckie shouted above the racket.

"I'll find another farm that does."

"You think Daed's going to allow that?"

Sylvia tossed dirty dresses and aprons into the tub, and it jerked them in tiny movements one way and then the other—much like her insides felt.

Right now she didn't care what her Daed would allow. She was twenty-six years old and not a member of the Amish church. The only power he had over her was whatever she chose to give him.

Beckie skirted around Sylvia and turned off the machine. Immediate silence fell.

"For months since you left, Daed has hinted that I asked too much of you. That I relied on you constantly. I didn't want to believe him, so I tried getting by without anyone's help. All I managed to do was prove him right." She exhaled, deflating like a balloon. "It got so bad that Elam called his sister. She's living with us now, and it's awful. If I promise to do better and let you have a life of your own, will you come back? Please?"

Brackish water sat in the machine full of still-dirty clothes. "No." Sylvia turned off the hose and withdrew it from the washer. "For once, Beckie, respect my answer and drop it."

"I have to know why! Do you hate me that much?" Beckie stomped her foot, and tears fell from her eyes.

Anger swept through Sylvia and caught her in its rushing current. "Because I refuse to be stuck in a barn alone with your husband ever again! Is that a good enough reason for you?"

Sylvia's own words didn't register until she saw the horror on her sister's face. Beckie took a few steps back, stumbling over a pile of clothing. Sylvia grabbed her to keep her from falling.

When Beckie regained her footing, she jerked free. "What are you saying?"

Tears burned Sylvia's eyes, and she couldn't mutter one word. What had she done?

Beckie shook her. "Tell me what happened!"

"I'm sorry, Beckie. We never meant..." She wiped her tears and drew a breath. "We kissed."

"You kissed my husband?"

Sylvia lowered her head, unable to admit it a second time.

"Wh what? No! When did this happen? I trusted you!"

"No you didn't. You *needed* me."

Beckie gasped for air, tears streaming down her face. She ran out of the room and toward the front door, gaining speed as she went.

"Beckie, wait. Please." Sylvia ran after her. She caught up to her at the bottom of the porch steps and grabbed her arm. "I didn't mean to blame you. It's my fault. I know that, and it's why I left. I'm so sorry. That kiss meant nothing to Elam, I promise you."

"We both know better than that," Beckie screeched. "I hate you for this."

Sylvia wiped her tears. "What can I do? I ran away from him—from all of you—as soon as I could."

Beckie held her stomach protectively while taking in a sharp breath. "All this time I've missed you, and Elam kept ignoring my pleas to visit, saying that he had no time and that you needed a life of your own. You both make me sick."

"We made a terrible mistake, Beckie. We didn't tell you because we didn't want to hurt you. He loves you."

"I want to go home."

Sylvia hesitated. Now that the truth was out, she wanted Beckie to stay and talk to her, to find a bit of peace. She knew her desire to fix the situation was unfair but couldn't help longing for it.

"Now!" Beckie's scream flew through the air. "I want to leave now!"

"Okay. Just sit on the porch steps for a minute and breathe. I'll get Trevor to drive you home." She'd have to figure out how to get the horse and rig to her later.

Tears blurred Sylvia's vision as she ran to the barn. She spotted Cara's father in the calf barn, scrubbing bottles. "Trevor, I need a favor."

He looked at her with narrowed eyes. "You okay?"

"Will you take my sister home?"

"Sure. I'll be done here in—"

"She doesn't want to wait."

Trevor set the bottles in the mud sink and dried his hands on his pants. "Okay." He pulled keys out of his pocket. "You want me to pick her up at the cabin?"

"Please. I'll ride with you."

They went to his car, which sat under a shade tree, its windows open.

When the cabin came into view, Sylvia saw her sister, overnight bag in hand, sitting on the top step.

"You going too?" Trevor asked.

"No. Wait here."

"Not a problem."

Beckie rose, looking pale and shaky.

Sylvia took the bag for her. "He'll need directions."

Beckie lifted her apron, revealing the pocket underneath, and pulled out two items: an envelope and a folded piece of paper. She opened the paper. "And to think I was so proud of following these directions to get here."

"I'm sorry." Sylvia kept repeating the phrase, but it held no power, no source of relief for her or Beckie. The handwriting on the envelope looked like Aaron's, and her guilt began to mold into suspicion and anger. She pointed at it. "Who wrote to you?"

Beckie handed the directions to Trevor, then threw the envelope on the ground and hurried to the car. Sylvia put her bag in the backseat.

As Trevor drove out of sight, Sylvia's dam broke, and she fell to her knees and sobbed.

When she could breathe again, she picked up the envelope from the mud. The return address told her what she'd hoped wasn't true. Aaron had written to Beckie.

Thirty-Four

From inside Ada's fenced backyard, Cara dipped an oversized wand with dozens of holes into a vat of homemade bubble mixture. She held it at arm's length and slowly made a circle. Hundreds of bubbles floated through the air, making Better Days bark with excitement while Lori danced through them.

"Watch me, Mom!" Lori stretched high and gently caressed a bubble in her hands without it bursting. She blew into it, making it larger.

"That's beautiful."

"This is the best bubble recipe ever, huh, Mom?"

"The best, Lorabean."

"Look!" Lori hollered and started running.

Cara turned to see Ephraim coming out of Ada's house. Lori leaped into his arms, and he lifted her into the air before settling her near his waist.

Cara crossed the yard. "When we're married, I'm going to jump into your arms whenever you arrive."

Ephraim grinned and reached for her with his free arm. "Do I have to lift you over my head?"

"Maybe." She hugged him and Lori at the same time. "We won't be busy tonight, and I'm not going anywhere, so is this my second chance at a midweek date?"

He set Lori's feet on the ground. "Show me how well that bubble stuff works."

Lori hurried to the vat of mixture.

"The bishop and deacon are on their way," he said quietly. "They're not more than a minute or two behind me. As far as I know, it's just a routine visit to see how you're doing now that you've had time to work through some of your issues with Trevor."

"I'm not in trouble for using secular music to learn the language?"

"How would they know that?"

"Preacher Alvin and Esther noticed a huge, sudden improvement in my comprehension and speaking skills. When they asked, I told them the truth."

Deborah stepped outside. "The ministers are here. They're waiting in the living room."

Cara went ahead of Ephraim, straightening and smoothing her clothes. Being in a test period was no fun, and she looked forward to the day when all this was behind her.

The two men stood in the living room, talking and chuckling.

"Cara." Sol held out his hand. "I hope we're not coming at a bad time for you."

"No. This is fine."

"Gut." He motioned to a chair at one end of the room. "Have a seat." She sat facing the couch and chairs. "Mostly we just want to ask you some questions and keep up with your progress."

Mostly?

The men, including Ephraim, took seats facing her.

They bowed their heads. Ephraim winked at her before closing his eyes. A minute later he cleared his throat, and she opened her eyes to see the others waiting for her to finish her prayers.

"Cara," the bishop began, "are you getting along with your dad?"

She was in a sticky situation here. It was her nature to want to tell these men to mind their own business. "What you really want to know is if I've forgiven him and how well I'm working that out."

"Ya, that's right."

Saying the words to her dad had been hard enough, and she didn't do it because these men said she had to. She'd told Ephraim, but only because she wanted the man she loved to share in the joy of reconciliation with her.

Ephraim got up and moved to the chair beside Cara. If anyone understood how difficult she found this kind of meeting, Ephraim did. He took her hand into his. "I think you should just talk about what the last two months with your dad have been like."

She took a deep breath. "Well, I started seeing Trevor as a man who struggles with his weaknesses, his longing to undo the impossible, and the loss he's sustained by his own hand. I've begun to feel compassion and understanding. It wasn't because of any one thing, and I have to be honest that his kindness has made forgiving him much easier. If he was as sharp-tongued with me as I've been with him at times, I'd still resent him. So I haven't done anything worthy of accolades. I'd like to get to where I can do what I'm supposed to without the other person having to meet me halfway, but I'm not there yet. I'm sorry if that's not good enough, but it's where I am."

The bishop looked at the deacon and received a nod. "Cara, you still have to complete the instruction classes and be able to converse reasonably well in German and Pennsylvania Dutch. As the leader for the instruction sessions, I can say that everything looks good for you to successfully complete them within the next few weeks. I talked to Alvin, and he assures me you're doing remarkably well with the languages."

"What?" She wanted to look to Ephraim for confirmation, but she was afraid he'd fade into nothingness and she'd wake to find herself in bed.

The bishop leaned forward. "Cara, what we've come here to say is that we expect you and Ephraim to be able to marry this coming wedding season."

Her heart leaped, and she jumped up. "Really? I'm doing that well?"

"You are."

She wanted to dance, but instead she balled her hands into fists. "Yes!"

Ephraim got up and hugged her like a long-lost friend. After several minutes of celebration, she wondered why they were telling her this now.

She and Ephraim separated, still holding hands. "I haven't completed everything or been baptized yet."

"True," the bishop said. "But Ada brought it to my attention that you and Ephraim have made no plans for a wedding this coming season. Since that is no easy feat to pull off, we feel you should be free to begin making plans."

She knew next to nothing about Amish weddings. What she'd heard about the feasts and the daylong ceremony made little sense to her. She'd never even seen one. "I don't suppose we could elope?"

"No," the ministers said in unison, then chuckled at their response.

"Sorry to pounce," the bishop said, "but no one elopes. If special arrangements need to be made, we do a small wedding in a quick manner."

"I like the sound of that," Cara said.

Ephraim leaned in and whispered, "He means if a couple comes up expecting before they're married."

"Oh. How many people will we need to invite?"

"Hundreds of people in this community have been looking forward to the day when Ephraim marries," the bishop said. "They will feel cheated if they don't get to attend the wedding."

Cara's mouth went dry, and she glanced at Ephraim. "Hundreds?"

"If we're careful with the invitation list," Ephraim said, "I imagine we could keep it down to six hundred guests."

Cara laughed. "Six hundred? And we're to feed them two meals, cakes, drinks, and whatever else the day calls for? I hope God still multiplies fishes and loaves." She knew she had loved ones who'd enjoy sharing the work load. She wasn't sure how she'd foot the bill, but after all it'd taken to get to this point, coming up with the money was nothing. She gestured toward the kitchen door. "This calls for a celebration. May I fix you a plate of our best desserts and something to drink?"

Aaron walked the silt fence line with a mallet in one hand and the horse's reins in the other, making sure the stakes were driven deeply enough to hold against the torrents of rain predicted for tomorrow afternoon.

He had hours of double-checking ahead of him, but if he could get done today, he could help Sylvi with the routine farm work tomorrow. Then maybe they'd both have enough energy to go out that night.

An odd sensation skittered over him, causing him to stop and scan the field. Finally he spotted Sylvi marching toward him. The intensity of her steps caused him to mount his horse and ride to her.

"Hello there."

She shook something at him. "Explain this to me."

He slid off his horse, and she thrust an envelope at him. One glance and he knew what it was. "Did she mail it back?"

"No. She came here." Sylvi's eyes swam with tears. "How could you do something behind my back like this? I trusted you."

Her body and voice trembled as she spoke. He'd known she and Beckie would probably have a rough meeting at first, but she was beyond upset. Something had gone very wrong. "I shouldn't have sent it without your permission."

Sylvia balled her hands into fists, crunching the paper into nothing. "She didn't know!" Sylvia sobbed. "Not until today."

"Didn't know what?"

She bent slightly, looking as if she might collapse. "She's Elam's wife!"

A jolt thundered through him, and then the scope of the situation became clear. This was why Sylvi struggled deeply to forgive herself. "I didn't know."

"But you knew enough. You knew I'd come here willing to end all communication with my family." She walked off.

He ran after her. "I thought it was because of a spat of some kind."

"You thought you could get rid of me by bringing Beckie here. It'd be all you needed to get Michael and Dora to sell this place, wouldn't it?" She hurried away.

"Sylvi, please."

She turned. "Say it, Aaron. Look me in the eyes, and tell me the real reason you did this."

The betrayal reflected in her eyes made him sick, and he couldn't defend his actions.

She tightened her fists and screamed toward the sky—a painful, broken cry. Then she folded her arms and slowly gained control of her tears. "You wanted me gone, and you didn't care what it took to accomplish it."

"Maybe when I sent the letter," he admitted. "But not now."

"I thought you were honest with me. You never once mentioned having written my sister. Every moment between us was a lie!" She stormed off. "Stay away from me!"

Aaron watched her slowly disappear past the dip of the rolling fields. Questions ran wild inside him, and he couldn't find one solid answer he could trust.

He made his way to the barn. His thoughts jabbed him mercilessly as he readied the stalls. Was she right? Had he lied to her this whole time? Initially, he hoped Beckie would visit, the two would make up, and Sylvi would want to go home. But what had he been hoping for since falling in love with her? And did it matter? She wanted nothing else to do with him.

Half of the cows were milked before Trevor showed up.

"I took Sylvia's sister home."

"I figured as much."

"They both seemed really upset." Trevor released a set of milkers from a cow and grabbed the bucket. "Is there anything I can do?"

Aaron shook his head. He had no idea what he could do himself. He thought of Trevor on the ladder inside that apartment building and the toolbox falling on that little boy's head. The toolbox had just fallen on Aaron. Or maybe he'd shoved it onto Sylvia. Either way, there was no undoing what had been done.

Thirty-Five

Aaron lay on his bed, staring at the ceiling. Darkness and heat clung to the early morning. Hours from now Sylvi would walk through the blackness to the milking parlor, and he'd meet her there, hoping she'd forgive him.

He'd spent the night lying here, trying to sort through his motivations. Sure, at the time he'd wanted Sylvi to go away. He'd come home with a goal, and she stood in his way. He had expected her and her sister to argue, but he'd banked on Sylvi's more gentle nature taking over and enabling the two to settle their differences. She'd then pack her bags and be on her merry way, leaving him free to convince his parents to sell the farm.

He'd never once thought the letter might rip their lives apart.

He sat up, putting his feet on the floor and his head in his hands. The image of Sylvi's brokenness brought another round of fresh pain.

He caught a glimpse of an insight and latched onto it.

He'd broken an unspoken rule—one person did not reach into another person's life and make decisions for her...or him. It seemed this was a lesson he should have learned long ago.

As his thoughts followed that trail, he understood something else. It wasn't his place to pry his parents' grip free of this farm. He wasn't wrong in showing them options for a different life or in sacrificing his time to help them. But his way was overzealous.

He was doing for them what he wished they'd done for him—see the problem and get involved. But they were mature adults with the right to hang on to this black hole until they or the bank said otherwise.

He'd offered them a good, sound plan to move to Owl's Perch. It made sense for him and his parents to stay together since he was their only surviving child. Since Daed wasn't easy to get along with, asking both parents to move into the living quarters above the appliance store and his Daed to help run the shop was a huge sacrifice. But…

He'd learned in rehab that a spouse, friend, or parent can't make someone want to get clean. And he couldn't make his parents want to leave this place. He'd banked on having more influence over his parents than he really had. It was now mid-August, and his Daed trusted him a little more but not enough. He hadn't expected his Daed to be grateful for what he was trying to do, but he'd thought his Daed would cooperate more by now.

After moving to his desk, Aaron lit a kerosene lantern and looked through the informational documents the EPA worker had left. He found the page titled "The Struggle to Make Small Farms Profitable." Unfortunately, it all hinged on one thing—getting that boost Sylvi kept looking for. He took out a notebook and began writing down information.

By the time he heard his parents moving around downstairs, he'd come up with a couple of plans that might work. After putting each idea for a specific section of the farm into its own folder, he gathered his work, tucked his small notebook and pencil into his pants pocket, and went downstairs.

A sense of nostalgia tugged at him as he gazed at his parents in the kitchen, dimly lit by a kerosene lamp. His Daed stood at the counter with the percolator in front of him, making coffee. His mother kneaded a bowl of dough, probably preparing a batch of cinnamon buns. They had legitimate reasons to struggle with coping. Mamm had carried eight children to term, and only two had survived past the first few hours or days of life. They left Ohio under duress, and then they lost his sister in a horrific accident. But his sympathy for those terrible events and for Daed's battle with arthritis didn't offer any solutions. Answers for the future were what mattered, not heartbreak for the past.

He put his plans on the kitchen table. "We need to talk."

His Daed lit the eye on the gas stove and set the percolator on it. "What's that?"

"A new set of plans that I believe represent your best chance for making this farm both manageable and profitable."

"Is it something we can do and afford?"

"You'll need money and some restructuring to get it started. I should be able to get out some of the cash I put down on the appliance store—it was more than what was needed anyway. I'll get back as much of it as I can."

His mother moved toward him, eyes wide with hope. "Are you staying?"

"No."

Sylvi didn't want him here, and he'd done what he came to do—face his parents and give them his best until it was time for him to take over the store. Surely they would cosign the loan papers, even if they didn't go with him, so that his agreement with Leo would be satisfied.

Anger shrouded his Daed's face.

"Daed, you can't do to Sylvi what you did to me. If you want to keep this farm, you have to be willing to do your share or hire full-time help for her."

"You do more bellyaching than a girl."

"This isn't about me. I'm here on Sylvi's behalf. You drew her in on promises, much as you did me when you wanted to move here from Ohio. You bought this place because you had a dream, but then you gave up and blamed me for every failure. You can't do that to her."

Daed grabbed a newspaper off the counter and threw it across the room. "How dare you—a strong, healthy man in your twenties—judge me! I've been through hard times you know nothing about."

"I'm sure that's true. But you need to decide whether you're capable of pitching in to achieve your dream—or if you even want to. If you can't or won't, then free Sylvi before all this hard work breaks her."

"You always think I'm not fair. Life isn't fair. I'd think you'd know that by now."

"You need to be honest with Sylvi. If you don't want this place enough to pull your weight or hire the needed help, say so."

"I do want this place! But I don't have the money to hire help, and a man with back problems can't work that milking barn twice a day every day."

"The barn can be redesigned with a ramp for the cows so you don't have to bend so much. And once the overdue bills are paid, you can start setting aside money to buy supplies."

Daed wagged his finger. "I may not handle as much around here as you think I should, but I've never run out on this family. You abandoned us. After your sister died, milk prices plummeted, the cost of feed and veterinarian bills skyrocketed, and you left!"

"So did you. You crawled into your bed and became just as unavailable as I was when I went to rehab."

"We moved here for you."

"Hogwash."

Daed had left Ohio because his own father had divided up his farm based on the number of grandchildren in each of his children's households. Daed's brothers ended up with hundreds of acres. Daed was left with only forty acres and the right to use the dairy barn.

For years his parents had carried the grief over their six lost babies. When Daadi Blank divided the land based on living grandchildren, it was as if he'd cursed them in front of all their relatives and friends. It was too much for them to handle, so they found this farm in Dry Lake and moved.

His Daed picked up the folders and flung them. "Why don't you keep your money and your plans and just go? We don't need your help. Sylvia and I were managing just fine without you."

"No, Michael, you weren't. Besides, he's our only child." Mamm turned to Aaron. "He grieved for you constantly, and I prayed day and night that you'd come home again. Please don't leave now."

"Don't beg him. He made up his mind years ago." Daed jerked a chair away from the kitchen table and sat, but his harsh words and movements didn't hide the pain in his eyes. "You want to go, go."

Aaron took the seat beside his father. "Daed, I know you have hurts, really deep ones. But you shouldn't have dumped your agony and garbage on me. We've become just like you and your dad—only worse. Well, I'm tired of making excuses for you, and I'm finished trying to fix your problems."

His Daed stared at him, eyes filling with tears. "Then leave."

Spiteful words coursed through Aaron until he thought they'd explode from him. He marched out the back door, slamming it behind him.

Black skies hovered, and the cows mooed, ready to be let into the barn and milked. He stomped across the wet fields. He'd always believed his Daed loved him, but now he wasn't so sure. Pain throbbed inside his chest. He'd taxed his parents for years, lied to them, and embarrassed them in front of the community. But Daed's hardness wasn't rooted in Aaron's behavior. His father didn't like him, plain and simple.

He wished he could talk to Sylvi, but she wanted nothing to do with him right now and for good reason.

Even with the hostility between his Daed and him, he didn't regret coming home. He'd do it all again a hundred times over for the chance to get to know Sylvi. And to let his Mamm know he loved her and was sorry for bailing on them the way he had.

Hurt swirled around inside him, picking up other hurts as it went. At least now he understood a little better why he'd felt the need to escape. And he wanted that escape right now. A six-pack would take the edge off. Two would do a better job. What else could he do? There were no answers, not to his and Sylvi's relationship, not to his and his parents'. He walked the fence line, using the moonlight to avoid the huge tractor ruts wherever he could.

Everybody used something to escape, right? His Daed crawled into bed for weeks at a time. Sylvi left home and worked herself into exhaustion. What was so wrong with his way?

The mud and earth shifted under him. A cracking noise rumbled, and suddenly the lower half of his body dangled in a hole. He tried to dig his fingers into the ground, but the mud came loose. He grabbed onto wet grass, trying to find something that would keep the rest of his body from being pulled into the hole.

He slid farther. "No. God, hear me, please!"

The grass yanked out by its roots, and Aaron plummeted. Everything around him went pitch black.

Sylvia woke with her eyes burning, her body aching, and the same pressing question that had kept her up most of the night—what should she do now? Darkness filled the room, and she wished she could hide in it forever. It didn't matter that she'd cried herself to sleep. Nothing had changed. She owed God and her sister a price she could never pay.

Thoughts of Aaron crowded her mind, confusing her even more. She pushed herself upright, determined not to think about him. She didn't know who'd handled the milking last night, but she needed to get to the barn this morning. Heaviness pressed down, as if she were trying to carry a newborn calf on her shoulders.

Without putting a match to a lantern, she slid into her clothes and made her way along the shadowy path. Light shone from inside the barn. If Aaron was there, she'd leave.

She stepped inside. The stalls were already bedded, feed sat in the troughs, and the doors were open to let the cows enter.

Trevor looked up. "Morning."

"Is it just you today?"

"Yeah. Aaron had me come in early."

Good. At least she wouldn't have to see him.

Tears welled again, and she turned away to grab the spray bottle, paper towels, and stool. How many times would she believe in a man only to be made a fool of? She sat beside the nearest cow, cleaned her udder, and prepped her for milking.

Trevor paused near her. "I don't know what's going on, but whatever it is, please don't run from it. Face it, Sylvia. I give you my word it's the only way. New cities can be built on top of old ruins. Did you know that?"

Maybe she shouldn't bare her soul, but she had to talk to somebody, and Trevor didn't seem like the kind who would judge her unfairly. "But I knew right from wrong. I walked right into the middle of lust and stayed there."

"God forgave Paul, who called himself the chief sinner. From what I understand, he tortured, imprisoned, and killed people in God's name. What makes you think you're better than he was?"

"Better? I don't think that."

"Sure you do. God forgave the worst sinner. The Bible says so. Only thing I can guess is that either you think you're too good to take the same grace Paul took, or you think God is too weak to supply it."

Tears spilled onto her cheeks. She didn't want to agree with him, but his bluntness held wisdom. Needing fresh air, she walked outside and looked into the dark sky. Was it really possible to make things right between God and her?

"God, please…I can't undo what I've done. If I could relive it, I'd never let myself or anyone else get me in that same situation, but I did let it happen, and I'm sorry. What can I do now? Please, I need Your guidance and strength."

As her muted whispers pierced the quiet around her, energy and hope trickled into her. And she knew what had to be done. She had to go see her sister.

She returned to the barn. "Trevor, I need a ride to Beckie's. I don't know how long I'll stay or if my Daed will let me come back. But I have to talk to Michael and then go."

Thirty-Six

Sylvia's stomach clenched and her fingertips throbbed with an odd numbness as Trevor drove down the narrow road toward her home. The trip to the Blank farm had taken Beckie more than two hours by horse and carriage, but it had taken Trevor less than thirty minutes to drive here.

It was well past lunchtime. Since she didn't know what she'd face when she arrived home, she had spent the morning talking to Michael and Dora, doing laundry, and packing all her clothes.

She hadn't seen Aaron. He was probably still working the fence line, which was just as well since she didn't know what to say to him.

One battle was all she could handle today.

Trevor passed her brick homestead. The red milking barn still needed a new coat of paint. The herd stood grazing in the lush fields. A little farther down the road, he pulled into the driveway in front of the eighteenth-century gray stone house where Beckie and Elam lived.

In spite of looking like her home, it didn't feel like it. It had lost its homeyness the day she learned that Elam intended to marry Beckie. With a little time, she could have adjusted to that disappointment easily enough if not for two things—Elam's backstabbing sneakiness at dumping her for someone so close to her, and her inability to get away from him. The real shame was that the mess had given a mediocre man too much power over her emotions.

Trevor put the vehicle in Park. "I think the best way for you to reach me when...if you're ready to come home is to call Ephraim's cabinetry shop. Either I'll get the message from him, or he'll bring it to the farm." He passed her a piece of paper with Ephraim's name and phone number scrawled on it. "How far to the nearest phone?"

"Unless the bishop has approved one for someone closer, it's two to three miles away." She opened the car door, her head swimming. "I can get to it easily enough when I'm ready. Thanks for the ride."

"Glad to do it."

The tires crunched against the gravel driveway as Trevor left.

Movement near the pasture, some two hundred feet away, caught her eye.

Elam.

As he walked toward her, her legs felt more like flimsy rubber bands than muscle, sinew, and bone. But the reaction came from dread of facing her family with her sin exposed, not from any feelings for Elam. Nothing about him interested her anymore.

Still, memories of their best courting days ran through her mind. Whatever she'd found so special about him eluded her now. He'd been charming, to be sure, and everyone flocked to him as if his boyish good looks and handsome smile inflated his value. Aaron was far more attractive to her, and he thought nothing of his looks. But Elam relied on his appearance and hid his disloyalty behind it. He'd been slowly maturing for years, so maybe he'd changed, but the person she knew was self-absorbed, conceited, and manipulative. She'd seen those flaws when they were courting and had foolishly been willing to overlook them.

Elam stopped within five feet of her, looking drained and subdued. There wasn't a hint of the bold-faced, overconfident man who had married her sister.

She cleared her throat. "I didn't intend to tell her."

"I'm glad it's out."

His words gave her some much-needed hope.

He studied his home, sadness radiating from deep within. "I wanted to tell her so many times, but I couldn't make myself. It seemed unreasonably selfish—even for me—to lighten my load by dumping it on her."

She needed to make sure every speck of unfinished business and all secrets between them were attended to. "You were right when you said I was never going to marry you. It never would've happened."

"Why?"

"You don't want to hear it."

"I need to know."

Elam waited, and thoughts of Aaron tugged at her. "You had no sense of loyalty. No ability to care about what I needed over what you wanted."

Within a week of knowing her, Aaron had more respect for her position on *his* farm than Elam ever had of Sylvia's place on a farm she partly owned. Aaron understood her better than she had herself—her avoidance of church and her drive to overwork. He put effort into planning breaks for her. The man in front of her had no understanding of being someone's equal partner, and she wondered if he had the capacity to really love someone. Aaron did. She'd seen it in the way he treated his parents and Frani.

And her.

A new ache for her sister banged around inside her.

Sylvia turned to face the house Elam and Beckie called home. "My regret is deep, and I need to tell Beckie that. But I don't know if she'll hear me."

"Maybe she will. Even if not, I think you're right to try. I knew when she got home yesterday that she'd found out. She took to bed immediately, made me swear I wouldn't tell her parents or sisters what was going on, and kicked me out of the bedroom until further notice."

It surprised her that Beckie hadn't told their parents or sisters. Beckie held the power to make them all hate her while gaining sympathy for herself for years to come. Wasn't she going to use it?

Sylvia started up the brick walkway.

"Sylvia."

She turned back to Elam.

"I'm sorry for the way I broke up with you, for the way I took over your responsibilities of running the farm, for taking advantage of your loneliness when you were just trying to do the right thing by Beckie and your family."

Her heaviness lifted a bit. But she'd thought it had been her idea to give up her farm duties piece by piece to avoid coming into contact with him. It sounded as if he'd planned that.

Aaron would never have done that to anyone, least of all her. Even when he had no feelings for her, he'd made sure she understood his plan. No manipulation. But plenty of stubborn concern—that she worked too hard, kept herself from making friends, and had turned away from God. And he worried where she'd land when he sold the farm.

Her anger had blinded her. If he'd thought contacting Beckie would have been truly bad for her, he wouldn't have done it.

She tried to free her thoughts of Aaron. "I've asked forgiveness from God, and I'll give it to you." She hoped God liked her a lot more than she liked Elam. "I'm going to see Beckie."

As Sylvia walked toward Beckie's home, Lilly rounded the side of the house with a bowl in her hands.

"Sylvia!" Her face lit up. She hurried to the steps and set down the bowl before running to Sylvia and engulfing her in a hug. "Oh, you're home." She squeezed her tight. "For good?"

Sylvia returned the warm embrace. Concern that her father would refuse to let her leave again—and that he'd insist on gaining control of her once he learned of her sin—lifted. She wasn't staying. "No, just for a few days."

Lilly took a step back. "Don't you dare leave again without giving me your address. If I have it, I might be able to talk him into letting all us girls write. If not, I'll wait until I'm in my rumschpringe. He won't even try to stop me then." She glanced back at the house. "Beckie came home yesterday so sick she went straight to bed. We figured the heat was too much on her, driving that distance and being pregnant. I was bringing her some of Mamm's famous chicken noodle soup."

"I'll take it to her. Where are her little ones?"

"We're keeping them at our house until she feels better."

"Tell Mamm and Daed I'll be up to see them later, but I need to see Beckie first."

Lilly's eyes shone bright. "I'll make your favorite dinner. Will you be ready to eat in a few hours?"

She doubted it, but she squeezed Lilly close. "Absolutely. Denki, Lilly."

Sylvia took the bowl of soup into the house with her, grabbed a spoon from a drawer, and went to Beckie's bedroom door. She tapped and heard movement, but Beckie didn't respond. Sylvia eased the door open. Beckie lay curled in a ball, staring at the wall.

"Beckie, honey?" Her sister stirred a bit. "Are you hungry? Mamm made you some soup."

Beckie slowly worked her way to a sitting position. She still wore the clothes from yesterday as well as her prayer Kapp. But it was a good sign that she hadn't screamed at Sylvia or thrown anything—yet.

"What are *you* doing here?"

Sylvia set the bowl on the table. "I came to beg forgiveness."

Beckie scowled. "Get out."

"I'm not leaving. If you need to drag me in front of the whole family and humiliate me so your anger will subside, then do so. But I won't leave until I've eased your pain…and forgiveness would be really nice too."

Beckie stared at her. "I have no words to begin to tell you what you've done to me."

Sylvia knelt beside the bed. "I can't begin to explain the depth of my sorrow."

Beckie looked the other way, clenched her fists, and crossed her arms tightly. The minutes ticked by, and Sylvia remained on her knees.

"Im Gott sei Lieb," Sylvia whispered. *In God's love.* It was their phrase, the one they used to say in bed after talking about everything—their joys and hopes and fears and anger.

Beckie jumped as if Sylvia had startled her. Tears welled in Beckie's eyes, but she said nothing.

Every night, no matter what was happening around them, they had put it all in His hands and had fallen asleep believing every good thing came from His hand and every bad thing that happened or that they did could be engulfed by His love. They weren't little girls anymore, and their ability to sin seemed to have grown along with their bodies, but had God's love gotten any smaller?

Beckie patted the side of the bed. "Get off your knees, Sister."

Sylvia moved to the edge of the mattress. Beckie struggled to speak. Her hair was a mess, which was unlike her. Sylvia went into the bathroom, retrieved a hairbrush, and sat on the edge of the bed next to her. Her sister shifted, allowing Sylvia room to get behind her. Sylvia removed the straight pins that held the Kapp in place, then took out the various hairpins, slowly unwinding her golden locks.

Sylvia brushed her sister's hair. "It'd be nice if we could untangle life the way we can untangle the knots in our hair."

Tears fell from Beckie's eyes. "I started something with Elam because I wanted to steal him from you."

Sylvia's heart jerked wildly, but she continued to brush her sister's long locks.

Beckie wiped her nose on the wadded mess of tissue in her hands. "My plan worked out well, don't you think?"

Sylvia kissed the back of her sister's head. "He loves you, Beckie."

Silence hung between them while Sylvia pinned her sister's hair into a bun. Then Sylvia picked up the bowl and spooned up some broth.

After Beckie took a bite, she wiped her mouth with the back of her hand. "I don't hate you like I said. I know I carry some of the blame too."

Her sister's graciousness caught Sylvia off guard, but it explained why Beckie hadn't told their parents and sisters.

She swallowed another spoonful of soup. "I need you. Now more than ever."

"I can't stay. We both know that. Besides, you're a grown woman well capable of taking care of yourself and your family." Sylvia continued to spoon-feed her sister.

"It's true what Daed said, isn't it? I relied too heavily on you."

Needing a moment to adjust her thinking, Sylvia set the bowl to the side. "Ya, and I let you."

Beckie smoothed the sheet across her lap. "Can you and me and Elam work this out somehow...enough so you could come home?"

"This isn't my farm anymore, and I don't want it to be. Besides, I don't belong here. I started out with a dream." Understanding began to trickle in, and she longed for it to pour like last week's gullywashers. "Actually, I started out with what I thought was a dream. I wanted to be a strong, capable woman unlike any other Amish woman I knew. But what I really wanted was to find someone who respected my thoughts and skills. Someone who wanted an equal partner, not a farmhand." She took Beckie's face into her hands. "I'm so, so sorry."

Beckie passed her a tissue. "I knew better than to try to take Elam from you. What kind of a sister does that? I'll tell you—one who's spoiled and selfish and jealous and a host of other things it's taken me years to figure out."

"And love was mixed in with those reasons too, ya?"

"I'm not convinced it was." Beckie's eyes moved to the bedroom doorway and stayed there. "For either of us."

Sylvia turned toward the door to see Elam standing there.

"Sylvia,"—he removed his hat and entered the room—"I need to talk with Beckie alone, please."

Sylvia rose and quietly slipped out of the house.

Thirty-Seven

Cara tapped the reins against the horse's back as she headed for Ephraim's. He wanted them to come to the shop around lunchtime today, so she and Lori had spent the night at Lena's. With her dad working extra while Sylvia was gone, it was easier to stay in Dry Lake than to try to get back and forth.

"You're getting better at handling a rig, Mom."

"Denki."

Cara had spent the travel time finally admitting that Trevor wasn't just a man the church leaders wanted her to be nice to. She also explained to Lori who each person in Ephraim's family would become to her after the wedding. Since arriving in Dry Lake and learning she had relatives here, Cara had continually balked at telling Lori about family relationships, in part because it was painful to explain and in part because it was so confusing. Most of all, Cara never trusted how long these people would remain in their lives. Why tell Lori about Trevor if he might up and disappear, hurting her in the process? But now Cara knew that as long as illness or some other unforeseen issue didn't interfere, Trevor would always be near, and she was actually thankful for that.

Lori wiped sweat from her little nose. "I didn't have any grandpas, and once you and 'From get married, I'm gonna have two."

Cara mulled over the Pennsylvania Dutch language until she came up with the right words for *You have one Amish grandfather and one Englischer grandfather.* "*Du hab eens Daadi un eens Grandpa. Ya?*"

Lori's eyes grew large, and she giggled. "Wunderbaar, Mom! 'From will be proud of you." Lori brushed a fly away from her face. "I don't think I'll always call him 'From. After you marry him, he'll be my Daed."

Her daughter sounded so mature. Cara couldn't help but enjoy the idea of having babies.

After pulling into the driveway, she brought the carriage to a halt. Lori jumped down and ran into the shop. In a few months her daughter would be as comfortable with Ephraim's family as if she'd been born into it. For that, Cara would be eternally grateful.

Grey stepped outside. "Hi, Cara. Ephraim's finishing up a business call." He took the horse by the reins. "I'll tend to her."

"Thanks." She stepped close to him so she could speak softly. "How's Lena?"

His grin gave him away. "As beautiful and amazing as ever, even from a distance. I expect I'll have a letter from her in my mailbox when I arrive home this evening."

"I'm glad you and Lena at least have the mail to make your relationship a little easier. How much longer before you two can court?"

"Seven weeks. Maybe a little more if Lennie feels Michael and Dora need it." He didn't sound the least bit perturbed at having to wait for his former in-laws to be ready.

"And you don't mind her calling the shots on the timing?"

He smiled. "Lennie has insight and instincts that I'd be a fool to discount. Besides, she'll trust me without question in other areas over the years." He pointed toward the shop where Ephraim was talking to Lori. "He's off the phone."

"Thanks, Grey."

Ephraim walked toward her, holding Lori's hand. "How about if the three of us have a late lunch in the hiddy?"

"I didn't bring any food."

Lori covered her mouth, snickering.

A conspiratorial look passed between Ephraim and Lori. He lifted his straw hat for a moment and wiped his brow. "I knew I was forgetting something." He replaced his hat and held out his hand. "Kumm."

Cara refused to take his hand. "What's going on, 'From?"

He looked at his empty palm and then to her. "I never would've taken you for a stick-in-the-mud."

She slid her hand into his. They crossed the wide berth between his shop and his home. Once on the far side of his house, they went toward his hiddy. It stood surrounded by hedges on three sides and open to a pasture on the fourth. A porch swing hung from the branch of a huge tree. He used this hidden place to relax and stargaze, and she looked forward to the day when they could come here at will, without concern for how it might look to others.

Lori ran through the man-made opening in the hedges. She gasped and clapped her hands. "Yes!"

Cara eyed Ephraim. He'd done something. He shrugged and motioned for Cara to enter ahead of him.

She stepped through the opening and spotted a blanket spread on the ground with two picnic baskets on it.

"Look, Mom. It's a surprise."

Cara turned to Ephraim.

He smiled. "Surprise."

"Uh, yeah, but why?"

"My stepmom made it for us. It's filled with traditional foods served at weddings."

Ada had been explaining Amish wedding dishes to Cara. "This was really thoughtful."

Ephraim sat on the blanket beside Lori. Cara joined him.

They tasted all the different foods, and Ephraim explained what they were. The roasted chicken and mashed potatoes seemed usual enough, but she'd never tasted cooked celery. It was sweet and had the consistency of a relish, only she couldn't imagine eating a relish as a side dish. There were several types of salads along with cheeses, cold cuts, breads, and lots of desserts. She could see why these foods were served at weddings.

The meal was simple and delicious. They talked and ate. This would be home in a few months.

Ephraim winked at her. "We did it, Cara."

Cara loved him enough to last a dozen lifetimes. "Yeah, and all it took was a shunning, a reconciliation, a salvation, learning two languages, forgiving Dad, and a partridge in a pear tree."

"And a God who knew how to weave it all together."

She inched her fingers across the blanket until they found his. "I love you."

His eyes searched hers, telling her he knew her well. "I know," he whispered hoarsely.

She intertwined her fingers with his. "Even though the words may never come easy, loving you does. And I'm determined to find other ways to let you know how much I love you every day for the rest of my life."

The cabinetry shop echoed with the taps of hammers and the rasping of hand sanders. There was no hint of finishing early today, even though it was Friday.

Grey opened the leather pouch that held his set of carving tools. He picked out a 35 mm bent gouge and began making a design on a cabinet door. One of the many things he appreciated about this job was that it made good use of his artistic skills.

He hovered over the walnut panel, carving an intricate pattern reminiscent of something from the eighteen hundreds—per the customer's request. Wood shavings curled as he carved, and he brushed them to the floor.

"Grey," Ephraim called to him.

"Ya," he answered without lifting his head. He finished sculpting the tiny section he'd begun and then looked up.

Ephraim stood in the double-wide doorway, talking with Michael Blank. If Michael had come to the shop specifically to see Grey, the topic must be important. Grey wiped off the tool with a clean cloth and slid it back into the leather pouch, then walked toward them.

The last time Michael had come to speak with him, he was displeased with Grey for not agreeing with him and the rest of the school board about letting Lena go. Michael had been Grey's father-in-law for six years, and Grey knew he easily recognized when others were wrong but rarely saw his own part in an issue. They had politely butted heads on more than one occasion.

Before Grey closed the gap between them, Ephraim said his good-byes and returned to sanding an oak cabinet.

"Michael." Grey extended his hand.

Michael took Grey's hand and pulled him close. "Have you seen Aaron?" he whispered.

"Not today. Is there a problem?"

Michael stepped back, holding his forehead while staring at the floor. "We…argued." He cleared his throat. "But that was before daylight, and I haven't seen him since."

It was almost time for the shop to close for the day, so Aaron had been gone at least twelve hours. "He's not been here. If he needed to talk, you might try Lena's place."

"I've already gone there. She hasn't talked to him. I spoke with Trevor too. He didn't take him anywhere."

"What does Sylvia think?"

Michael glanced behind him, clearly checking to see if anyone had moved within hearing distance.

"Kumm." Grey motioned toward the office. They went inside, and he closed the door. Michael still looked uncomfortable. Grey closed the blinds on the windows between the office and the shop.

Michael's hands trembled as he removed his hat. "Sylvia is devoted to the farm, but she left early this morning, saying she needed to visit her folks. She wouldn't explain why. She's not even sure if she'll be able to return. I don't understand."

Grey motioned to a chair.

Michael shook his head and paced the small room. "Aaron said him and me are just like me and my Daed, only worse." His eyes revealed pain and confusion. "Is it true? Am I just like my father?"

"I've only seen him a couple of times." The man had come to Grey and Elsie's wedding and returned for her funeral. Elsie never said much about anything, including the family they'd left in Ohio.

Michael dropped into a chair and stared at the ground, his shoulders stooped. "My Daed made decisions, and you could agree or get out. Is that how Aaron secs me?"

"Maybe he just needs time to cool off." Grey knew Michael feared that Aaron had left for good or that he'd started drinking again—or both.

Michael shook his head. "This morning Aaron said he was going to get money out of the appliance store and give it to me, to help the farm run better. Now I can't find him."

"Let's call the appliance store and the Better Path. Maybe he got there another way." Grey picked up the receiver and dialed information. Once he had the phone numbers, he placed the calls and pressed the button for the speakerphone so Michael could hear the conversations.

Neither Leo nor Paul had seen Aaron in a month. Grey thanked the men and said good-bye.

Michael took short, choppy breaths. "What have I done?"

"You've been the best father you could be. Paul just said you even went with Aaron to talk to his counselor and to see the shop he wanted to buy. Those are good things."

Michael rubbed his eyes with the palms of his hands. "Dora pushed me to go. And I knew if I didn't, Sylvia would never have the same respect for me. I wouldn't have gone otherwise."

Grey didn't know what to say, so he kept silent.

"Aaron used to love farming. Did you know that?"

"No." Grey took a seat, knowing that Michael needed to talk.

"When I started looking to move here from Ohio, he was just a teen, but he was already an amazing farm manager and worker. I was impressed, and I wanted to give him something he could be proud of—a farm with enough land to expand the herd as he saw fit." Michael closed his eyes. "But he hates it now." He rose and walked to the far corner, his back to Grey. "I have to stop lying to myself. It's true. I'm as exacting and difficult as my Daed, maybe worse." He turned, tears welling in his eyes. "You know when I began to see it?"

Grey shook his head, silently praying for Michael.

"When I saw myself through Sylvia's eyes."

"Sylvia's?"

"Before Aaron came home, she respected me. But when she saw how I was with my son, my anger and nagging, she began to look at me differently. I kept telling myself she just didn't understand, but I'm the one who's been blind." He blinked as if he'd just realized something. "I told Aaron he had no right to talk to me the way he did this morning or like he's done in the past. But the truth is, he was trying to get me to understand him. And I couldn't—or wouldn't." He slumped into the chair and put his head in his hands.

Elsie had been similar to her father—they both felt deeply and shared little. Because of that, Grey had some insight that might help...if Michael would hear him. "No one in a household can decide what's right for everyone else—not a husband, a wife, or a parent of grown children. But if everyone's willing to listen, they can talk things out and find a compromise."

Michael sighed. "I'm afraid we've never lived like that. After burying six babies, Dora and I were a solid block of grief by the time we moved here. All I wanted was to give Aaron a farm he could develop. When he got fed up trying to turn a profit, my grief turned to anger. Nearly every word my son spoke added to my hurt and rage." Tears spilled down Michael's face. "I asked myself countless times why he abandoned us to go to Owl's Perch. The real question is, why did he care enough to return with an offer for us to move back there with him?"

"You'll never know unless you ask."

Michael drew a deep breath and stood. "I have to find him."

"Want me to come with you?"

"No, not yet. I need to do this on my own." Michael opened the office door and paused. "There is one thing you can do."

"Anything."

"Pray."

"Absolutely."

Thirty-Eight

Aaron stared at the hole twelve feet above his head. The blue sky above him faded, turning to a charcoal gray. Soon it would be as black as it had been when he'd fallen into this pit before daylight. The thought of facing a full night underground seemed intolerable, but for the first time in his life, he had no alternatives.

He sighed, too exhausted to hold another raging vigil. He'd screamed in anger throughout the day—yelling at Daed, life, and most of all this stupid abandoned well. Now he sat in silence, staring upward, wondering if he'd die down here.

His hands trembled, and his body felt heavier than it should—the toll of not having any food or water since last night's dinner.

Sylvi was the only one who might come looking for him. His Mamm might go to the porch and scan the farm, but she'd never think to wander a field in search of him. His Daed might consider it, but he'd never do it. He'd assume what was easiest to believe—that Aaron had run off.

He wasn't physically hurt, other than a few bruises and aching joints from landing so hard. But the pain in his heart was severe.

He hated what it would do to Mamm if no one found him. She'd spend her life praying for him to return.

Sylvia would blame herself, thinking that she'd run him off or that she'd caused him to take up drinking again. If she kept working the farm, she'd find him one day—or his bones. Then she'd know the truth...and blame herself more.

Without water, he'd die in a matter of days.

A crow cawed as it crossed the sky above him.

Aaron's mind kept running down various trails of thought, scattering like a handful of hay dropped from a high loft. He had no reason to reel in his imagination, so he let it meander.

His father's problems were bad. He needed room to grieve the loss of six cases of infant death and the death of his twenty-seven-year-old daughter, Elsie, as well as his disappointment in Aaron. And he needed to find ways to cope with his arthritis. But Daed's bottom-line problem was that he was never grateful for what he did have. When each new loss hit, Daed took on more pain without ever having freed himself from the previous hurts. Aaron understood how it happened but vowed that he would cope differently.

He closed his eyes, listening to the wind move across the summer grass. He breathed in the aroma of the rich soil and remembered the conversation he'd had with Sylvi about seeing God in the nature around her.

"Okay, God, I hear You."

As clearly as if he were talking with Sylvi, he could hear God inside him, chastising him for all his years of feeling sorry for himself. Being truly thankful would give him power over his desire to escape. It was the ultimate freedom from the day-to-day heartache and grind of living.

He leaned his head back against the cool, craggy earth and began telling God everything he was thankful for, beginning with the walls around him and the ground under him. As the hours passed, his faith grew.

He began to see the farm the way Sylvi saw it—beautiful and strong. A heritage that their forefathers sacrificed for, regardless of the cost. They understood the toil it would take and yet were grateful for the chance to work the fields.

While it made no sense, trapped as he was, he'd never been more content.

"God, please get me out of this pit. I want…I need a second chance with Sylvi."

Aaron said that prayer countless times in between his lists of things to be thankful for.

"Aaron!"

Chills ran over his body, and he stood up. Was he imagining things? The voice sounded like…his Daed's.

"Down here! Daed, can you hear me? I'm down here!"

His Daed continued calling to him, and Aaron kept screaming. Daed called. Aaron answered. And nothing happened.

How many times had they been this close and yet unable to see or hear each other?

"Daed!" Aaron screamed with all his might.

His father's voice faded into nothingness, leaving only the sound of the wind crossing the fields above him. Aaron closed his eyes, trying to hold on to hope. Wanting to believe he'd get out of this prison. In his mind's eye he saw the farm—the green pastures, growing crops, and meandering herd. Sylvi's cabin. The main house.

They looked different from down here.

Digging a fingernail into the packed dirt, he breathed in the smell of rich soil, and he could feel this place inside him now. Sylvi felt it so deeply, and he wanted a chance to give it back to her.

"Aaron?" His Daed's voice returned, sounding hoarse. Aaron couldn't believe he hadn't given up. Maybe he didn't know his Daed as well as he'd thought.

"Daed! I'm down here, in a hole in the ground! Can you hear me?"

Silence. Aaron prayed. He cupped his hands around his mouth. "Daed!"

"I hear you. But where…"

"A hole. Look for a hole." He could hear noises, scrambling of some sort. Dirt from above fell on his head.

"Aaron?" His Daed set a kerosene lamp near the edge of the hole.

"I'm here. You found me." Relief and excitement ran like a stampede through him. He'd been given a second chance—or maybe it was his third or fifteenth. How would a former drunk know? How did anyone know?

Daed's face poked over the top of the hole as he reached as far into the well as he could. "Are you hurt?"

Aaron reached for him but couldn't come closer than two feet from his fingertips. Still, he found peace in the near connection. "No. I just need a way to get out."

"I'm so sorry, Son." His Daed sobbed.

"It's okay."

"No, it's not. You told the truth, and I knew it when I heard it. We'll get you out of there and really talk. I love you, Son. Hang on, and I'll be back as quick as I can with a ladder."

Aaron sank to a sitting position again and began making a fresh list of all he was grateful for.

Lena sat on her bed, writing to Grey. Months of his letters surrounded her. Most nights she opened and read every one of them, but she hadn't seen him, except at a distance, in nearly a month. Nicky lay on the cool floor, panting.

Michael had come by yesterday, looking for Aaron. Thankfully, Aaron dropped by earlier this morning to assure her he was safe. He didn't stay long enough to tell her much of anything, only that he wasn't missing and that a driver was waiting to take him to Owl's Perch.

"Lena?" her Daed called as he tapped on her door.

"Kumm."

He opened the door, but he didn't enter. "I came to tell you that there'll be a family meeting downstairs within the hour. Your siblings and their families will start arriving in about forty minutes."

Excitement scuttled through her. "A meeting on a Saturday night? This must be really important. What's up?"

A grin made creases around his eyes. "You don't want me taking time to answer your questions when I brought someone to see you." He moved to the side.

Grey stepped into her room, and happiness flooded her.

"Grey!" She flew into his arms.

Daed laughed and closed the door behind him.

Grey caressed her cheek, and the warmth of his hand strengthened her. "Hi."

He pulled her into a hug and held her for several long moments before he raised her chin and kissed her.

She gave a final squeeze before going to her reading chair, removing a few articles of clothing hanging over it, and gesturing for him to sit.

She sat on the edge of her bed. "Do you know what this family meeting is about?"

He nodded. "I won't stay for it. It's for family, and your Daed assures me most of your siblings still don't know about us."

"True. Are you sworn to silence about the meeting?"

"No. Actually, your Daed and Ada think you should know before hearing it with everyone else."

"Daed and Ada?" She resisted the desire to let out a holler of excitement. "He must've asked her to marry him."

"He did, and she said yes."

"This is fantastic!"

"It is." He grinned. "But there's more. Israel wants to give you this house."

Lena's heart leaped. Marrying Grey, raising a family with him, *and* living here would be the fulfillment of every dream she'd ever had. "How do you feel about that?"

"We have so many great memories here—a lifetime, really. I can't think of anywhere I'd rather live."

She crossed the room and knelt in front of him. "You're not just saying that because you know it would thrill me?"

He trailed his index finger along her jaw line. "If my only reason for doing it was for you, that'd be more than enough reason."

She soaked in his assurances, knowing he loved her just as her mother had promised her before she passed away: *When the time is right, you'll be drawn to the right man. And he'll be drawn to you. And he'll love you deeper and higher than most men are capable of. I promise you that.*

Thirty-Nine

Sylvia sat on the porch with her parents and Lilly, rocking the glider back and forth. Thoughts of Aaron swam through her day and night, even in her sleep. She'd been so angry with him before she left, and she longed to find him and talk it all out.

The sun hung low in the sky as Sunday drew to a close. This was the kind of Sunday she'd missed so badly her first few weeks on the Blank farm. But now her family surrounded her, and she'd never been so lonely.

She'd been here since Friday afternoon. Whenever the family shared a meal, Sylvia had to answer dozens of questions about living on the Blank farm. She kept pointing out to Daed how safe and happy she was there, but he still wanted her to stay home.

Beckie didn't want Mamm or Daed or any of their sisters to know what had happened between Elam and Sylvia. Sylvia didn't ask why, but she hoped that the reason had more to do with keeping peace among the family than personal embarrassment on Beckie's part. Maybe her little sister was finally maturing.

Sylvia had spent two days thinking about her future and Aaron. She knew without a doubt what she wanted. "Daed."

He propped his arm on the back of the porch swing he and Mamm shared. "What's on your mind?"

"I'm going home in a few days."

"This is home."

"It's the home I grew up in. And I'll keep it in my heart every day. But it's not *my* home. Remember when I was little, you'd always say, 'Someday you'll have a home of your own'?"

"I want you here. We can make this work."

"No, Daed." As she spoke, she could feel the impact Aaron had had on her. "Just because you want something from me, that doesn't mean it's reasonable to expect it."

Lilly squeezed her hand. "Hmm, I think those words must be from the book of Aaron."

She and Lilly had stayed up late last night talking, and Sylvia had told her all about Aaron.

"You shouldn't have insisted I stay here after Elam married Beckie," Sylvia said. "I *needed* to go."

Daed glanced at Mamm before nodding. "I've had time to think while you've been gone. I was trying to keep my family together and all my daughters safe." He shrugged, looking pained that he'd lost the battle. "But now I can see that sometimes home isn't the best place for a daughter to be." He sighed. "So is the Blank farm home from now on?"

"No."

"What?" He frowned. "Then where are you going?"

"Wherever Aaron goes. If he'll have me."

Lilly squealed. "I thought you must be in love with him."

Sylvia knew she might have quite a road ahead of her to win him over. It might take a good bit of patience, but Aaron was worth it. "We'll most likely live above an appliance store, at least for a while."

"You hate stores," Mamm said. "You're barely willing to go in a store to sell yogurt or pick up an item or two. You've never bought fabric because it takes too long to pick it out, and you feel sick by the time we're through."

"I'll use my will to get over it or ask a doctor for an allergy pill or something. It has to be something like fumes or dyes that bother me, right?"

Daed smiled that gentle, knowing smile that defined him so well. "You're determined. I see it in your eyes. You go, Sylvia. Wherever you land, we'll come visit you when we can."

Forty

Sylvia had called Ephraim's shop early Monday morning and left a message for Trevor to pick her up today, Tuesday, as soon as his morning chores were done. That would put her back on the farm in time to have lunch at the Blanks' table. If Aaron was still on the farm, she imagined they'd set aside farm work for the afternoon, take a long walk, and talk until time to milk the cows that evening. If he'd already moved to Owl's Perch, she'd go there.

Either way, she intended to talk to him today, to apologize and pledge to help him make a success out of the appliance store—if he'd have her. She didn't have any skills to offer him that would be useful off the farm, but she'd do her best to learn.

Mamm sat in the rocker next to her, shelling peas. Her Mamm found shelling peas as relaxing as Sylvia did taking baths. All her sisters were nearby, on the porch or in the yard, waiting to tell her good-bye. Beckie and Elam sat on the steps, holding hands while watching their twins play. The three of them hadn't handled a lot of things right, but healing had begun—thanks to Aaron.

She couldn't wait to tell him.

Daed came out of the house with a glass of water. He motioned for Lilly to get up. When she did, he took her place next to Sylvia.

Daed put his arm on the back of the swing and laid his fingers on her shoulder. "Girls," he said, and all her sisters immediately turned to look at him. "Go play or something. I want to talk to Sylvia."

They quickly dispersed. Beckie and Elam went for a stroll toward Mamm's vegetable garden, each one holding a twin's hand.

Her Daed reached into his pocket and pulled out two folded checks. "I shouldn't have kept your wages this long. You know it's typical for parents to keep the largest portion of earnings throughout their child's teen years. I had no right to keep holding the money from you this long, but I was afraid you'd take it and move off. Since you're determined to leave either way..." He passed her one check.

Sylvia unfolded it and about jumped out of her skin. "Thirty-five thousand dollars?"

"It only amounts to a little over two hundred dollars a month for all those years you worked this place seven days a week, from the time you graduated from the eighth grade until six months ago."

"Ya, but during that time you gave me some spending money each month."

"I'm glad you're pleased."

Her Daed didn't like to talk finances with a woman, so she'd wait and ask Aaron if she owed taxes on it.

Daed passed her the second folded check. "It's also time Elam and Beckie paid a little rent on that house you inherited. Not much, mind you, but say a hundred and fifty dollars a month?"

"That sounds great." She opened the check. It was signed by Elam and was for...five thousand dollars. She almost choked. "Back rent?"

"Ya."

"Wow. I should've come home sooner."

Her Mamm stopped shelling peas. "I wish you had. He held his ground, not allowing us to write or visit you so you'd miss us and want to come home, and all the while he's been a grizzly bear to live with."

"Susie Mae, do you have to tell everything you know?" Daed asked Mamm.

"It's true," she said.

"I didn't say it wasn't." Daed rubbed the back of Sylvia's neck, silently letting her know that he loved her. "Later on we'll figure out something about your portion of the farm. Rent it from you. Pay dividends. Buy it. Something."

Too excited to contain herself, Sylvia wrapped her arms around him. "Denki."

Her father held her. She knew he didn't want to let her choose her own path, yet he'd given her the funds to do just that. She rose and embraced her Mamm before returning to the porch swing. She rubbed the checks between her fingers. This money would keep Aaron from owing so much on the appliance store. Then he'd have an easier time meeting the monthly bills. That always made life more pleasant.

Or he might want to use it to pay off the extra loans on his parents' farm so it'd be easier to sell.

She couldn't wait to see him, but she had so much she needed to tell him that she wasn't sure what to say first or how to say it.

Gratefulness and relief filled her. Aaron had been right—she'd asked God to forgive her, and He had.

Today, as she reaped a harvest of grace, she felt forgiven. While sitting on the porch swing, gently swaying back and forth with her Daed beside her, waiting to return to Aaron and make things right, her heart cried *thank you* to God time and again. She was forgiven.

Trevor pulled into the driveway.

"My ride's here," Sylvia called out.

A stampede of young women and fast-growing girls hurried to the front yard.

Trevor jumped out and took her overnight bag. "Morning." He barely glanced at her before putting her suitcase in the trunk.

The next few minutes were a blur of hugs, farewells, and promises to write and visit. Her Daed held her for nearly a minute before opening the car door and saying good-bye.

She waved out the window to her family until she could no longer see them. Then she turned toward Trevor. "So what's going on at the farm?"

He grimaced and fidgeted with the steering wheel.

"What's wrong? Did we lose Charlotte or her calf?"

He shook his head. "Mom and calf are fine. It took me awhile to finish the milking and feed the calves, that's all."

"You did all that by yourself?"

"Yeah. Michael hurt his back, and…Aaron wasn't available."

A nervous chill ran through her. "What does *not available* mean?"

"Can't say exactly." Trevor shook his head.

Disquiet ruffled her insides. "Trevor, don't do this. Is something wrong?"

"I'm under orders to keep my mouth shut, but Michael will tell you everything you need to know."

Nausea rolled through her. She'd been unfair to Aaron and then walked off. Had he left the farm for good and Michael didn't want Trevor telling her? Was it possible Aaron had started drinking again? There'd certainly been enough stress on him lately to tempt him. They rode in silence, but Trevor seemed anxious. He pulled into the driveway.

"Go on up to the main house," she said.

"Let's drop your stuff off first." He turned onto the small lane that went to her cabin. She waited in the car while he stopped, got out her suitcase, and set it on the porch.

A stranger came around the corner of her house, spotted her, and retreated. She got out of the car and called to him. "Excuse me."

The man didn't return, but she heard a noise inside her cabin. She hurried up the steps and ran in. There were muddy shoe prints everywhere.

"Hello?" She followed the sound of dripping water and walked to her bathroom. New tile. New cabinets. New sink. Same beautiful old tub.

She ran her hand along the teal and beige tile. "Trevor?" She turned toward the hallway. "Tre—"

She gasped. Aaron stood there, so tall and strong.

"Aaron!" She ran to him and wrapped her arms around his neck. "I'm so, so sorry."

He held her. "Me too."

"I was so scared. Trevor wouldn't tell me anything."

"I wanted to surprise you. Do you like it?"

"Yes, of course." She took a deep breath before letting him go. "I have something for you." She pulled the folded checks out of her hidden apron pocket and placed them in the palm of his hand. "This is to go toward your purchase of the appliance store."

He opened them. "Where… But…"

"It's back pay and back rent. My Daed wanted me to stay, but I told him I had to go home, and that home is wherever you are."

Aaron's eyes grew large. "I…I wasn't expecting…" He put his arms around her. "I got my money back from Leo, all but a thousand dollars, and he's put the store up for sale again."

"What? Why?"

"Because I realized that this farm means too much to me to give it up and walk away. It's home."

"But…"

"So much happened while you were gone. Daed saved my life."

"He did? How?"

"It's quite a story. I'll tell you all about it later. But after he rescued me, we talked. He opened up and apologized, and I could feel how deep his sorrow ran. Like mine did after I got sober."

"I'm so glad." Tears stung her eyes. "But it doesn't mean we have to stay here. I don't care where we live, as long as we're together."

"You really missed me." He cradled her face, looking a little baffled by that realization.

"I did."

"Daed was afraid that once you got to Path Valley, you'd have to stay there. I told him you'd be back, that nobody could keep you from this farm."

"Nothing and nobody could keep me from *you*."

His hands were warm on the sides of her neck as his thumbs caressed her face. "I want to stay here. Even before your money, we had enough to revamp and start fresh. If you want to add yours, we can—"

She placed her fingers over his lips, stopping him from saying anything else. "Forget the farm, Aaron. Be here with me, just us and nothing else."

He drew her close. "Sylvi, will you marry me?"

She leaned in, her lips inches from his. "You know I will."

Epilogue

At the edge of the yard, Cara paused under a canopy of golden leaves, soaking in the remnants of her wedding. Her day had begun at sunrise. Now stars twinkled. The cool October air smelled delicious and earthy. Conversations and laughter carried on the breeze as the last of the wedding guests departed in their horse-drawn carriages, leaving only family and the closest of friends.

Nine hours ago, under crystal blue skies, Ephraim had walked her down the aisle between rows of borrowed chairs set up in his Daed's backyard. Before the bishop they vowed their lives to each other. Ephraim said it was the first outdoor Amish wedding he'd ever heard of, but the church leaders allowed it, and it couldn't have been a more gorgeous day.

During the feast afterward, they sat at the corner of the bride-and-groom table with the singles of the community. By tradition she and Ephraim couldn't share a table with just their closest friends, but they had plans for tonight that would make up for that.

She prayed a silent thank-you for the blessing of friends who had become so important to her and Lori. In many ways they had saved her as much as Ephraim had. It was becoming apparent to her that the strength to live Plain came from God, a supportive family, and dedicated ministers. Some things were worth every sacrifice it took to have them—and for her, this life was one of them.

She and Ephraim would carry memories of this day into their future together. There were many Amish wedding traditions, revelations to her, that she'd always hold dear—like the groom walking the bride down the aisle and loved ones sharing a day of feasting and singing with them.

There were also Amish traditions she'd never get fully used to, like the bride and groom cleaning up after their own wedding. As the festivities wound down, Ephraim helped the men move furniture back in place and load a wagon with benches. She worked with a group of women, helping to wash and dry dishes. But Cara loved having and being part of a safety net. She had people who'd always be there, no matter what. And they had her.

Ephraim's parents would head for bed as soon as their brood was asleep for the night. In a few minutes the newlyweds would go to Ephraim's house with their friends for a more intimate time of playing games, singing, and eating. When she'd learned that Ephraim and she couldn't have their closest friends at the wedding table, he came up with the idea of having a get-together after everyone else went home. He said that he'd braced himself for the possibility of not being able to marry her for another year or two. He had no qualms postponing their alone time for a few hours with good friends.

· Ephraim came out the front door of his Daed's home, smiling. "There you are."

She'd seen him go in and out of that house many times in the last week. There'd been so much to do to prepare for their wedding that Lori and she had moved from Hope Crossing into Ephraim's place a week ago, and he'd been staying in the Mast home. His parents had welcomed her and treated Lori as if she had always been one of their grandchildren.

"Daed," Lori hollered.

Ephraim turned. Their daughter stood in the doorway of the Mast home, wearing her nightgown. Ephraim's stepmother, Becca, who'd been trying to get her children and Lori settled for the night, stood behind her.

He clapped his hands and opened his arms. That was all the encouragement Lori needed. She ran barefoot across the lawn.

Lori would spend the night with Ephraim's parents. Tomorrow, after they finished cleaning up from today's ceremony, she'd return with Deborah and Ada to Hope Crossing. Lori was enjoying being a niece to all of Ephraim's sisters, even the ones younger than she was.

She jumped into his arms. "Daed." Lori hugged him. "My Daed."

Cara suppressed laughter. Since the wedding ceremony that morning, her daughter had peppered nearly every sentence to Ephraim with *Daed*. Having spent most of her life without a father, Lori used the name as if she were applying salve to her heart.

"Will you tuck me in, Daed?"

"I will. But then you have to stay in bed and go to sleep. It's very late for little girls." He touched the end of her nose.

While still in Ephraim's arms, Lori reached out and hugged her mom. "Good night."

"Good night, Lorabean." Cara kissed her soft cheek. "You be good for *Mammi* Becca."

"Okay, Mom. Me and Daed's sisters are gonna play dolls tomorrow!"

Ephraim chuckled as he kissed Cara on the cheek. "I'll be back soon. Don't move."

"Would you bring my sweater when you come? I left it near the wood stove."

"Absolutely." He hurried toward the house, making Lori giggle with delight.

Cara waved at a carriage of folks leaving Mast property and heading home. Most of those who'd stayed this late had helped set up, cook, serve, and clean. When any of them had a family member marry, she and Ephraim would return the favor. The Amish cycle of service and gratitude had begun for her.

Her dad came across the yard toward her. He'd been extremely helpful this week, doing whatever Ephraim or she needed to prepare for today. "Hey, girl, you look cold."

"Ephraim's bringing me a sweater as soon as he tucks Lori in."

"I'm taking the last few Hope Crossing guests home. If you don't need anything else, I'm going to stay there this time."

"You've made enough trips back and forth today." She hugged him. "Thanks for everything, Dad."

"You're more welcome than you can imagine." He squeezed her tight. "I'm proud of you."

"Today wouldn't have been the same without you."

"Thanks, Carabean."

She had never asked him why her mother felt the need to hide her whenever he was drunk. Was he mean, or had her mother wanted to keep her from seeing her father intoxicated? She didn't know. It didn't matter. He wasn't that man anymore, and she wasn't willing to embarrass or hurt him in any way.

"I'll see you at the cabinetry shop at ten, day after tomorrow," Trevor said, "to take you to that hotel you picked out."

"I sure am looking forward to spending a few honeymoon days at the beach."

As her dad left, Ephraim strode toward her, carrying her sweater. While walking, he waved to the people in the last buggy headed for home.

She wondered where their friends were. They had served two meals, plus rounds of snacks, for six hundred guests, so tomorrow she and her girlfriends had mounds of laundry to do. The men had to return heavy borrowed items, like serving tables and stacks of dishes, but now it was time to set all thoughts of work aside and go to Ephraim's.

He held up the sweater. "Here you go." His smile warmed her so much she almost didn't need a wrap.

She slipped her arms through the sleeves. The thick black sweater set off the dark purple of her wedding dress. She'd chosen to wear the color of royalty, for she truly felt like a daughter of the King.

The style of her dress was the same as everyday Amish clothes—plain and simple. For the first time in her life, she could have afforded a fashionable wedding dress with delicate fabrics and had a fancy hairstyle, but whether she was Amish or not, those things would never interest her. She was more of a no-frills woman, so that fit in well with her new lifestyle.

Ephraim kissed her forehead. "I can't believe we're finally husband and wife."

She snuggled into his embrace. "It was the best day ever, wasn't it?"

"I've never seen such a celebration." He ran his hand up and down her back. "And we're married," he whispered.

She could feel the intensity of his joy as he held her.

Cara tilted her head back, and Ephraim took her hint. When his lips met hers, he didn't hold back. As her mind rushed with thoughts of all she had to be thankful for, her heart swelled at the magnitude of her blessings.

Applause grabbed her attention. She pushed back from Ephraim and saw Lena, Grey, Sylvia, Aaron, Deborah, Jonathan, Ada, and Israel—all grinning.

Israel clapped the loudest. "Hmm. I guess I *am* ready for those lessons on how to give a kiss and make it count."

Ada gently elbowed him before easing her back against his chest. He wrapped his arms around her and kissed her cheek, then stepped forward. "We really appreciate the invitation to join you tonight," he said, "but if it's okay, we'll go visit Michael and Dora for a bit before calling it a night. Ada will stay with them tonight and be back tomorrow to help you."

"You sure?" Cara asked.

"Ya. It's Grey and Lena's first date night, and she doesn't need her Daed there. You know?"

"If that's what you want, we understand." Ephraim shook his hand, and Cara hugged him and Ada. They walked toward the barn to hitch their rig.

Cara slid her hand into Ephraim's and shifted her attention. "Where have you girls been?"

Lena glanced up at Grey, who stood directly behind her with his hands on her shoulders. "Oh, we had a little...rearranging to do."

Sylvia hid her face behind Aaron's shoulder, but she couldn't conceal her grin.

What had her friends been up to? She narrowed her eyes at Lena. Had the queen of pranks struck again?

Cara looped her arm through Ephraim's and headed for the house. The other three couples—Lena and Grey, Deborah and Jonathan, and Sylvia and Aaron—walked with them. Cara noticed that all their friends looked as if they were hiding something.

"Okay, spill it. What have you done?" Cara asked.

"Who...us?" Lena asked, feigning innocence.

Once in Ephraim's yard, Lena glanced up. Cara stopped short, following her eyes and studying the darkened shadows of the tree above her.

When she saw what they'd done, she burst into laughter. "How am I supposed to get all that laundry done now?"

"What's up?" Ephraim asked.

She pointed. "Our wringer washer!"

Grey nodded at Lena. "She did it."

"Uh, yeah. Like she could do that all by herself," Cara said. "And no excuse by you, Mr. Graber, is going to stop me from getting back at both of you at your wedding."

Grey chuckled. "By all means do your worst."

Aaron's laughter blended beautifully with Sylvia's giggle. "We want in on that action."

Cara knew that Aaron and Sylvia would have time to help her devise a plan. His creative ideas for transforming their farm, added to Sylvia's knowledge of milk production, had transformed an uphill battle into an enjoyable living. They'd reduced the size of their herd by half, rebuilt the milking stalls, rented the fields, and used the milk they produced to make A&S Yogurts, a product that would be fully organic within the year. They already had three health-food stores stocking the product.

Both of them would go through instruction classes next summer and join the faith before they could marry next fall. But they didn't mind the wait. They intended to enjoy the long engagement period by really getting to know each other.

Deborah and Jonathan would marry in January. Ada and Israel were going to marry a couple of weeks before Lena and Grey's ceremony in mid-February. But Lena and Grey wouldn't announce their plans to marry until after the first of the year.

Every couple was different. The things that had drawn each man and woman together were as varied as the colors of nature. All the couples had been through their own sets of trials and mishaps. But the ability to grow closer while navigating those heartaches had caused their love to become stronger. Love was so odd. It could fight the fiercest battle and cradle the most delicate creatures. It never failed to beckon or give hope to the hopeless, and she knew love would continue to do so, no matter what good or difficult things lay ahead. With Ephraim beside her, Cara opened her arms to embrace their future.

They all stood there, looking up at the dangling wringer washer, chuckling. One by one, under God's twinkling night sky, each man took his loved one in his arms and for a brief moment tuned out the world.

Ada's House Series

Main Characters in *The Harvest of Grace*

Sylvia Fisher—A young Amish woman who is the oldest of nine daughters. She loves the family dairy farm.

Beckie Fisher—Sylvia's closest sister.

Elam Smoker—A young Amish man interested in Sylvia.

Aaron Blank—Son of Michael and Dora. After his sister died, he went into rehab for alcoholism.

Michael Blank—Aaron's father.

Dora Blank—Michael's wife and Aaron's mother. Her daughter, Elsie, who was married to Grey Graber, died in a terrible accident.

Frani—Former drinking buddy of Aaron's.

Cara Atwater Moore—Englischer from the Bronx who lost her mother as a child, was abandoned by her father, and grew up in foster care. She married and had a daughter, Lori, but Cara's husband died when Lori was two. While fleeing a stalker, she discovered clues to her past in her mother's diary. That, combined with vague memories from her childhood, brought her to Dry Lake. She is now engaged to Ephraim.

Trevor Atwater—Cara's father, a widower. He was an alcoholic for most of Cara's childhood.

Ephraim Mast—Amish man who works as a cabinetmaker in Dry Lake with Grey Graber. He is Deborah's brother and is engaged to Cara.

Lori Moore—Cara's daughter. She calls Ephraim "'From" and has a dog named Better Days.

Deborah Mast—Amish woman who is Ephraim's sister. She lives at Ada's House in Hope Crossing and was engaged to Ada's son, Mahlon, before he left his family, his home, and the faith. She is now in love with Jonathan.

Jonathan Stoltzfus—Amish blacksmith. He is in love with Deborah.

Lena Kauffman—Amish woman. She has a bluish purple birthmark on the right side of her cheek and going down her neck. She lost her teaching job in Dry Lake when she disobeyed unfair rulings made by the school board, and Michael Blank, head of the board, refused to stand up for her. She is in love with Grey.

Grey Graber—Amish widower. He's a skilled craftsman who loves his work at the cabinetry shop owned by Ephraim Mast. He was married to Elsie Blank for almost six years. Their son, Ivan, was born with a missing arm, and they had a stillborn son a year later. After Elsie's death, Grey fell in love with Lena.

Ada Stoltzfus--Amish widow in her forties. She is a friend and mentor to Deborah and Cara, who help her run Ada's House, a bakery and gift shop in Hope Crossing that allows tourists to participate in some traditional Amish events.

Acknowledgments

To my Old Order Amish friends who helped me so faithfully as I wrote about delicate events—My heart is yours.

To the Old Order Amish farmers who spent long hours helping me understand all the ins and outs and challenges of running your dairy farms without electricity while meeting government regulations—I admire the tenacity in you and your families. Thank you for sharing your stories about how the stream-bank fencing program affected your farms—the fair and unfair, the ultimatums, and the generous help the government provided.

To my expert in the Pennsylvania Dutch language—I struggle with the languages as Cara does in this novel, and you are even more patient than her teachers. Your expertise and your patience are both appreciated.

To WaterBrook Multnomah Publishing Group, from marketing to sales to production to editorial—With each book we produce, I'm even more honored to be one of your authors.

To Shannon Marchese, my editor—Only the two of us and God will ever know all the obstacles that kept falling across our path as I wrote this book. Because of how you faced every challenge, I respect you even more.

To Jessica Barnes, my editor on this project while Shannon was on leave—Oh my! You entered my life during the roughest of times and remained calm, helpful, and hard working. Without you this book would not be in readers' hands, and my nerves would be frazzled rather than healed. At the time I may not have let you know how truly and deeply grateful I am.

To Carol Bartley, my line editor—You do your job excellently, but more than that, you helped me believe in myself. In my most difficult times of writing, I reflect on that. Thank you.

To Kathy Ide—You are ever faithful when I need you. Thank you.

To Steve Laube, my agent, and Marci Burke, my good friend and critique partner—Both of you make me a better person and author. Thank you.

To my husband, sons, and daughters-in-law—Time with you makes life a beautiful patchwork quilt. I love and respect each of you with all my heart.

And to the newest member of our household, my brother Leston, who moved in with us when my dad passed—You are a challenge and a gift, as is every good thing on this earth. I love to laugh with you. I look forward to reading with you at night. I can't help but cry when you do—so stop that! ☺ I'm grateful to be your little sister. May your happiest days be ahead of you.

Glossary

ach—oh

all—all

Alt Maedel—old maid

as—that

ausenannermache—separate

awwer—but

begreiflich—easy

Bobbeli—infant

da—the

Daadi—grandfather

Daadi Haus—grandfather's house. Generally this refers to a house that is attached to or is near the main house and belongs to a grandparent. Many times the main house belonged to the grandparents when they were raising their family. The main house is usually passed down to a son, who takes over the responsibilities his parents once had. The grandparents then move into the smaller place and usually have fewer responsibilities.

Daed—dad or father

dei—your

denki—thank you

die—the

draus—out

duhne—do

Englischer—a non-Amish person. Mennonite sects whose women wear the prayer Kapps are not considered Englischers and are often referred to as Plain Mennonites.

es—it

fescht—firm

Frehlich Zwedde Grischtdaag—Merry Second Christmas

Gaule—horse

gegleed—dressed

gern gschehne—you're welcome

geziemt—suitable or becoming

Grossdaadi—grandfather

Grossmammi—grandmother

guck—look

gut—good

Heemet—home

Helf—help

Hund—dog

immer—always

iss—is

Kapp—a prayer covering or cap

kumm—come (singular)

kummet—come (plural)

kumm rei—come in

langsam—slow

letz—wrong

liewi—dear

losmache—loosen

loss uns—let's

Mamm—mom or mother

Mammi—grandmother

meh—more

nee—no

nie net—never

nix—no

Ordnung—The written and unwritten rules of the Amish. The regulations are passed down from generation to generation. Any new rules are agreed upon by the church leaders and endorsed by the members during special meetings. Most Amish know all the rules by heart.

Pennsylvania Dutch—Pennsylvania German. *Dutch* in this phrase has nothing to do with the Netherlands. The original word was *Deutsch*, which means "German." The Amish speak some High German (used in church services) and Pennsylvania German (Pennsylvania Dutch), and after a certain age, they are taught English.

Plain—refers to the Amish and certain sects of Mennonites.

Plain Mennonite—any Mennonites whose women wear the prayer Kapp and caped dresses and the men have a dress code.

raus—out

rumschpringe—running around. The true purpose of the rumschpringe is threefold: give freedom for an Amish young person to find an Amish mate; to give extra freedoms during the young adult years so each person can decide whether to join the faith; to provide a bridge between childhood and adulthood.

Sache—things

schtehne—stand

schtobbe—stop

schwarz—black

schwetze—talk

sich—themselves

uns—us

verhuddelt—confused

waahr—true

was—what

Welt—world

wunderbaar—wonderful

ya—yes

zammebinne—bind

zerick—back

Pennsylvania Dutch phrases used
in *Hope Crossing*

Bischt hungerich?—Are you hungry?

Der Gaule kann nimmi schteh.—The horse cannot stand.

*Die Sache, as uns zammebinne, duhne sich nie net losmache, awwer die
Sache as uns ausenannermache schtehne immer fescht.*—The things
that bind us will never loosen, but the things that separate us will
always stand firm.

draus in da Welt—out in the world

Du bischt daheem.—You're home.

Du hab eens Daadi un eens Grandpa.—You have one Amish grandfather
and one Englischer grandfather.

Duh net schtobbe.—Do not stop.

Frehlich Zwedde Grischtdaag—Merry Second Christmas

Geh, ess.—Go, eat.

Gern gschehne.—You're welcome.

Gott segen dich.—God bless you. [singular]

Gott segen eich.—God bless you. [plural]

Guder Marye.—Good morning.

Gut is was ich bescht duh.—Good is what I do best.

Haldscht Schul fer die Handikap?—Do you teach at a school for the
handicapped?

Heem geh?—Go home?

Ich bin hungerich.—I'm hungry.

Ich bin kumme bsuche.—I have come back.

Ich geh in die Handikap Schul.—I'm going to the handicap school.

Ich hab.—I did.

Ich hab aa die Cara mitgebrocht.—I have brought Cara with me.

Ich kumm glei naus.—I'll come out soon.

Im Gott sei Lieb—in God's love

In dei Heemet?—In your home?

Kummet rei.—Come in.

Kumm mol, loss uns geh.—Come on, let's go.

Kumm raus. Loss uns schwetze.—Come out. Let's talk.

Kumm uff.—Come on.

Kumm uff rei.—Come on in.

Loss uns fische geh.—Let's go fishing.

Loss uns Heemet geh.—Let's go home.

Mir esse un no gehne mir.—We'll eat and then we'll go.

Net im Haus. Is sell so hatt zu verschteh?—Not in the house. Is that so
    hard to understand?

Saage es.—Say it.

Sell iss gut.—That is good.

Was iss es?—What is it?

Wie bischt du Heit?—How are you today?

Witt du ans Allen's geh?—Do you want to go to Allen's?

Witt fische geh?—You want to go fishing?

Ya, en verhuddelder Hund.—Yes, a confused dog.

Ya, in paar Minudde.—Yes, in a minute.

---

* Glossary taken from Eugene S. Stine, *Pennsylvania German Dictionary* (Birdsboro, PA:
   Pennsylvania German Society, 1996), and the usage confirmed by an instructor of the
   Pennsylvania Dutch language.

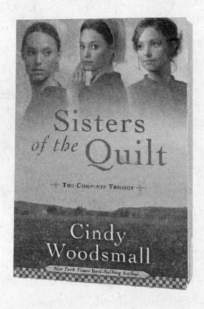

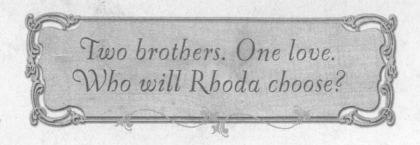

Their love could ruin lives.
But will God reveal a path
that would allow them to walk
through life together?

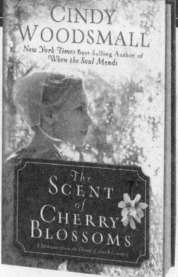

As spring moves into Pennsylvania and Annie spends time amongst the cherry trees with the handsome Aden Zook, she wishes she could forget how deeply the lines between the Old Order Amish and Old Order Mennonite are drawn.

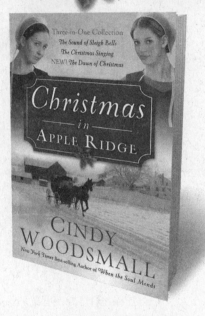